LOST MAN'S
RIVER

Peter Matthiessen

LOST MAN'S RIVER

THE HARVILL PRESS
LONDON

First published in 1997 by
Random House, New York

This edition first published in 1998 by
The Harvill Press
84 Thornhill Road
London N1 1RD

www.harvill-press.com

1 3 5 7 9 8 6 4 2

Copyright © Peter Matthiessen, 1997

The map on pp.VII–IX copyright © A. Karl / J. Kemp, 1990

Peter Matthiessen asserts the moral right to be
identified as the author of this work

A CIP catalogue record for this book
is available from the British Library

ISBN 1 86046 424 6

Printed and bound in Great Britain by Butler & Tanner Ltd
at Selwood Printing, Burgess Hill

For dear Maria with
much love and gratitude
for her generous forbearance
and great good sense throughout
the long course of this work

Author's Note
and Acknowledgments

A man still known in his community as E. J. Watson has been reimagined from the few hard "facts"—census and marriage records, dates on gravestones, and the like. All the rest of the popular record is a mix of rumor, gossip, tale, and legend that has evolved over eight decades into myth.

This book reflects my own instincts and intuitions about Watson. It is fiction, and the great majority of the episodes and accounts are my own creation. The book is in no way "historical," since almost nothing here is history. On the other hand, there is nothing that could *not* have happened—nothing inconsistent, that is, with the very little that is actually on record. It is my hope and strong belief that this reimagined life contains much more of the *truth* of Mr. Watson than the lurid and popularly accepted "facts" of the Watson legend.

—from the Author's Note for *Killing Mister Watson* (1990)

Lost Man's River is the second volume of a trilogy and, like the first, is entirely a work of fiction. Certain historical names are used for the sake of continuity with the first volume (including the name of the narrator/protagonist Lucius Watson and his family members), and certain situations and anecdotes have been inspired in part by real-life incidents, but no character is based on or intended to depict an actual person, and all episodes and dialogues between the characters are products of the author's imagination.

Once again, I am grateful for the kind assistance of the pioneer families of southwest Florida, who cheerfully supplied much local information, both historical and anecdotal. None of these friends and informants are responsible for the author's use of that material, or for his fictional renditions of the life and times of these families and others.

—Peter Matthiessen

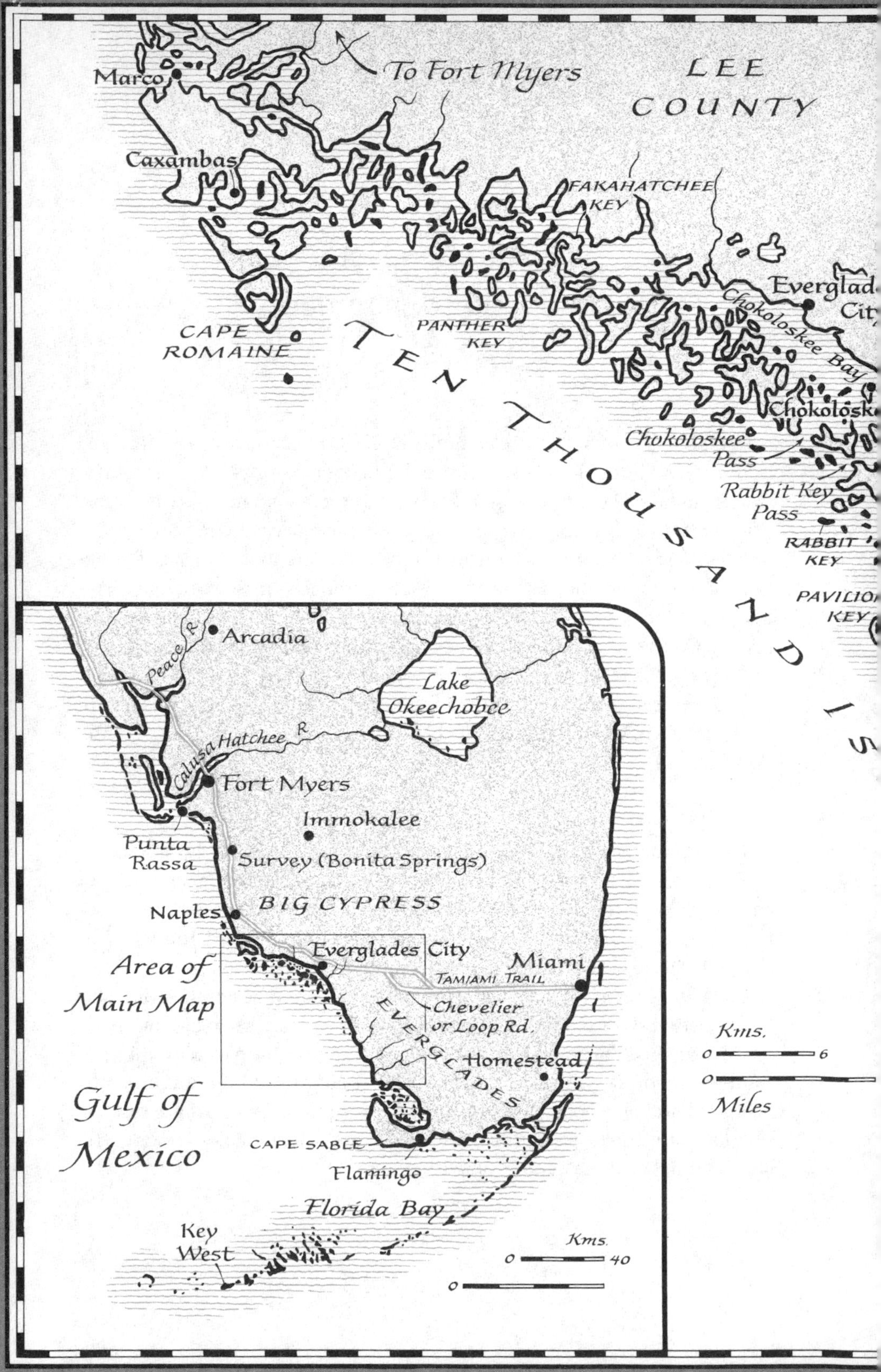
Marco
To Fort Myers
LEE
COUNTY
Caxambas
FAKAHATCHEE
KEY
Everglad
City
Chokoloskee Bay
CAPE
ROMAINE
PANTHER
KEY
TEN THOUSAND IS
Chokolosk
Chokoloskee
Pass
Rabbit Key
Pass
RABBIT
KEY
PAVILIO
KEY
Kms.
0
6
0
Miles
Arcadia
Peace R
Lake
Okeechobee
Calusa Hatchee R
Fort Myers
Immokalee
Punta
Rassa
Survey (Bonita Springs)
BIG CYPRESS
Naples
Everglades City
Miami
Area of
Main Map
TAMIAMI TRAIL
Chevelier
or Loop Rd.
EVERGLADES
Homestead
Gulf of
Mexico
CAPE SABLE
Flamingo
Florida Bay
Key
West
Kms.
0
40
0

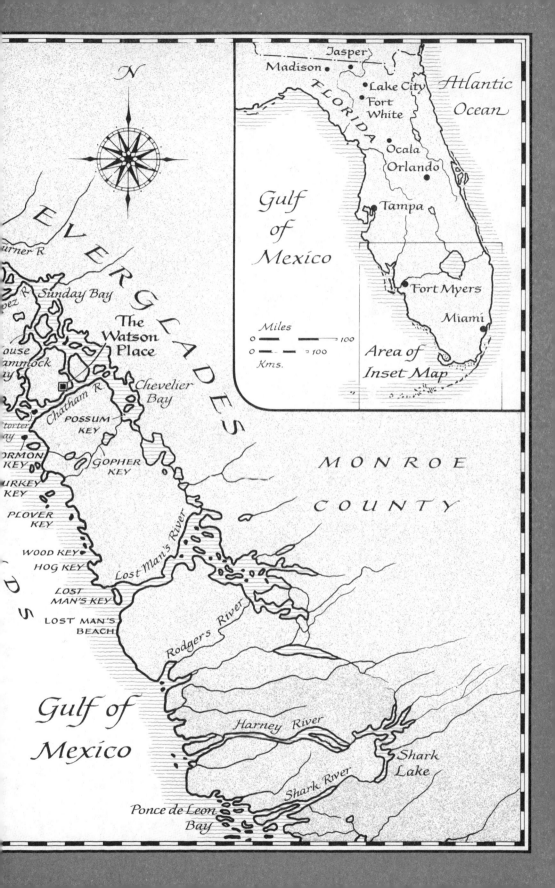

". . . the dread of something after death,/ the undiscovered country, from whose bourn no traveller returns . . ./ makes us rather bear those ills we have,/ than fly to others that we know not of"

—*Hamlet*, Act III. i

E. J. Watson

His paternal grandparents:
   Artemas Watson (1800–1841) and Mary Lucretia (Daniel) Watson
   (1807–?)

His parents:
   Elijah Daniel Watson ("Ring-Eye Lige")
       b. Clouds Creek, S.C., 1834
       d. Columbia, S.C., 1895
   Ellen Catherine (Addison) Watson
       b. Edgefield Court House, S.C., 1832
       d. Fort White, Fla., 1910

Edgar Artemas* Watson
   b. Clouds Creek, S.C., November 7, 1855
   d. Chokoloskee, Fla., October 24, 1910
1st Wife (1878): Ann Mary "Charlie" (Collins) Watson, 1862–1879
       Robert Briggs "Rob" Watson, b. Fort White, Fla., 1879–
2nd Wife (1884): Jane S. "Mandy" (Dyal) Watson, ca. 1864–1901
       Carrie Watson Langford, b. Fort White, Fla., 1885–
       Edward Elijah "Eddie" Watson, b. Fort White, Fla., 1887–
       Lucius Hampton Watson, b. Oklahoma Territory, 1889–
3rd Wife (1904): Edna "Kate" (Bethea) Watson, 1889–
       Ruth Ellen Watson/Burdett,[†] b. Fort White, Fla., 1905–
       Addison Watson/Burdett,[†] b. Fort White, Fla., 1907–
       Amy Watson/Burdett,[†] b. Key West, Fla., 1910–
Common-law Wife: Henrietta "Netta" Daniels, b. ca. 1875–?
       Minnie Daniels, b. ca. 1895–?

*Apparently he changed his second initial to J in later life, dating roughly from his return
from Oklahoma, ca. 1893.
   [†]Not real name.

Common-law Wife: Mary Josephine "Josie" Jenkins, b. ca. 1879–?
  Pearl Watson, b. ca. 1900–
  Infant male, name unknown, born May 1910. Perished in hurricane,
  October 1910.

EJW's sister: Mary Lucretia "Minnie" Watson, b. Clouds Creek, S.C., 1857
  Married William "Billy" Collins of Fort White, Fla., ca. 1880
  Billy Collins died in 1907, Minnie in 1912 (both at Fort White).
  The Collins children:
  Julian Edgar, 1880–1938
  William Henry "Willie," b. ca. 1890–
  Maria Antoinett "May," b. ca. 1892–
  Julian and Willie's "descendants":
  Ellen Collins[†]
  Hettie (Hawkins) Collins[†]
  April Collins[†]

ALSO: EJW's Great-Aunt Tabitha (Wyches) Watson, 3rd wife and widow of
  Artemas Watson's brother Michael; instrumental in marriage
  of Elijah D. Watson and Ellen Addison. Born 1813, S.C. Died at Fort
  White in 1905.
  Her daughter Laura, childhood friend of Ellen Addison.
  Married William Myers ca. 1867 (Myers died at Fort White in 1869).
  Married Samuel Tolen ca. 1890. Died at Fort White in 1894.

†Not real name.

LOST MAN'S
RIVER

Prologue

DEPOSITION OF BILL W. HOUSE
October 27, 1910

My name is William Warlick House, residing at Chokoloskee Island, in Lee County, Florida.

On October 16, this was a Sunday, some fishermen came to Chokoloskee and told how a Negro had showed up at the clam shacks on Pavilion Key and reported three murders at the Watson Place and advised the men that Mr. E. J. Watson ordered his foreman to commit these killings. This foreman was a stranger in our country name of Leslie Cox. When Watson's friends and kinfolk in the crowd got hard with him, the Negro changed his story, saying Cox done it on his own, but the men concluded Watson was behind it.

Ed Watson was at Chokoloskee when the story came in there about the murders, so Watson said he would fetch the Sheriff from Fort Myers. He swore that Cox had done him wrong, and not only him but them three people he had murdered. This was the eve of the Great Hurricane of October 17. He left in storm before the men got set to stop him, and we thought for sure we'd seen the last of him.

Three days after the storm, Watson showed up again at Chokoloskee. The men advised he better stay right there until the Sheriff came, and Watson advised he didn't need no Sheriff, said he knew his business and aimed to take care of it his own way. He bought some shotgun shells in the Smallwood store, where my sister Mrs. Mamie H. Smallwood advised him how them shells was still wet from the hurri-

cane, and Watson advised, "Never you mind, ma'am, them shells will kill a rattlesnake just fine." He aimed to go home to Chatham River "and straighten Cox out before he got away"—them were his very words. To show he meant business, he promised to return with Cox's head.

Watson was red-eyed in his appearance, very wild, and nobody didn't care to interfere with him. So Watson headed south down Chokoloskee Bay. We stood on the landing at Smallwood's store and watched him go, we reckoned he'd keep right on going for Key West, we figured we'd seen the last of him for sure. But four days after that, October 24—last Monday evening—he came back. We heard his motor a long way off to south'ard, and a crowd of men went down to the landing to arrest him. E. J. Watson seen them armed men waiting but he come on anyway, he was that kind.

The hurricane had tore the dock away, weren't nothing left of her but pilings, so he run his launch aground west of the boat way and jumped ashore real quick and bold almost before that launch came to a stop. He had got himself set before one word was spoken, holding his shotgun down along his leg.

Watson waited until all of us calmed down somewhat and got our breath. Then he told the men he had killed Cox as promised but the body had fell off his dock into the river and was lost. He showed us Cox's hat, showed us the bullet hole from his revolver. He put his middle finger through the hole and spun the hat on it and laughed. He was laughing at us so nobody laughed with him.

My dad, Mr. D. D. House, was not the ringleader, never mind what some has said, but because no other man stepped forward, it was D. D. House who done the talking. I and my next two brothers, Dan Junior and Lloyd House, was in the crowd. I don't rightly recollect no other names. Mr. D. D. House reminded Watson that a head was promised and a hat weren't good enough. He said the men would have to go down there, look for the body. And he notified Watson that until Cox was found, or the Sheriff showed up, it might be best to hand over his weapons. An argument sprung up over that, then Watson swung his shotgun up to shoot D. D. House and would have done it only them wet shells misfired. The men opened up on him all in a roar, the bullets spun him all the way around, and some of 'em claim they seen the buckshot roll right out them double barrels as he fell.

Watson's neighbors that had straggled in from the Lost Man's River country after the hurricane, them men stayed out of it, they stayed back up there by the store and watched. There wasn't a one of them raised a hand to stop it. Them fellers from Lost Man's never raised no sand about their friend Ed Watson till after he was dead, which was kind of late to start a argument.

Some has been trying to point fingers, claiming us Chokoloskee men was laying for Watson, fixing to shoot him down no matter what. Or some has give hints that so-and-so panicked and fired the first shot, and that this man was the only one responsible. I don't rightly know who fired first, and they don't neither. I will only say *that Mr. Watson was not lynched nor murdered. We took his life in self-defense, and the whole bunch was in on it from start to finish.*

Ain't none of us was proud about what happened. We was shocked to see our neighbor laying there, face down in his mortal blood, with his young wife and little children not fifty yards away in the Smallwood store.

Nobody having much to say, we went on home. Next morning we took the body out to Rabbit Key and buried it. By the time we got back to Chokoloskee, Sheriff Tippins had showed up lookin for Watson and was waiting on us there at Smallwood's landing. We was took in custody and brought north here to Fort Myers to give testimony.

Transcribed and attested: ✘ *William W. House [his mark]*

Witness: (signed) E. E. Watson, Dep. Ct. Clerk
Lee County Courthouse, Fort Myers, Florida
October 27, 1910

The Bill House deposition had arrived in the mail unaccompanied by note or return address (the postmark was Ochopee, Florida) in response to Lucius Watson's ad in the Fort Myers *News-Press* and also in the Lake City *Advertiser* in Columbia County, where his Collins cousins were still living.

> Historian seeks reliable information for a biography of the late sugarcane planter E. J. Watson, 1855–1910

What had startled Lucius most about the deposition was his brother Eddie's signature as the deputy court clerk who had witnessed and transcribed Bill House's testimony. He had forgotten that. But as a researcher concerned with the substance of the document—he was preparing a biography of his late father—he had found no significant new information beyond what could be inferred between its lines. On the other hand (as he noted in his journal, doing his best to maintain an objective tone), the document was critical as the one firsthand account of E. J. Watson's death that had come to light:

The Bill House testimony makes clear that the Chokoloskee men killed E. J. Watson despite the testimony of the unidentified "Negro" that the brutal slayings two weeks previously at Chatham Bend had been committed not by Watson but by his foreman, Leslie Cox, a convicted murderer and fugitive from justice who had turned up a few months earlier at the Watson Place.

According to this deposition, his neighbors shot E. J. Watson down in self-defense. Though this claim has been made for more than a half century by the participants, others in the community assert to the present day that at least some of those involved had planned the killing, justifying the lynching with the claim that otherwise Watson might evade justice, "as he had so often in the past." Combinations of these theories have also been suggested—for example, that the crowd was at the breaking point of fear and exhaustion in the wake of the murders at Chatham Bend, then the Great Hurricane, and that even if Watson had not meant to harm them, he had made a desperate bluff with shotgun or revolver which was met by the nervous crowd with a barrage.

The document leaves open another urgent question—did one man execute him with the first shot, and the others fire reflexively in the confusion? Though House denies this, the evident need to deny it—and a certain defensive tone—suggests some missing circumstance behind the rumor. If there is truth in it, then who was this man who fired first? Whom was Bill House trying to protect?

The most critical question is whether or not Cox killed those people under the influence or direction of Mr. Watson, as "the Negro" first stated but subsequently denied. Another much debated question is whether or not Watson executed Cox (as he would claim) when he returned to Chatham Bend after the hurricane. If so, did he act in a spirit of justice or in retribution? Or did he do it—as some continue to maintain—to eliminate the only man who might testify against him, knowing that if he came to trial, the black man would be discounted as a witness?

In the climate of fear in the community, almost no one believed that Leslie Cox had been killed by E. J. Watson. For many years afterward, a dread persisted that Cox was still alive back in the rivers, ready to strike again. But if Watson did not kill Cox, then what became of him? With the passage of years it seems less and less likely that we shall learn the fate of that cold-blooded killer who appeared so suddenly and wreaked such havoc, then vanished into the backcountry of America. Somewhere in the hinterland, a man known in other days as Leslie Cox may still squint in the sun, and spit, and revile his fate.

Chapter 1

Caxambas

In his old cabin lighter up Caxambas Creek, Lucius Watson sat straight up in the shard of moonlight, ransacking torn dreams for the hard noise that had awakened him—that rattling *bang* of an old car or truck striking a pothole in the sandy track through the slash pine wood north of the salt creek. No one else lived out here on the salt marsh, nor was there a mailbox on the county road, a half mile away, which might betray the existence of his habitation.

A dry mouth and stiff brain punished him for last night's whiskey. He licked his lips and squinched his nose to bring life back to his numb skin, then rose and peered out of the window, certain that some vehicle had come in from the paved road and eased to a stop inside the wood edge where the track emerged onto the marsh—the point from where the black hulk of the lighter, hard aground in the shining mud of the ebbed tide, could first be seen by whoever had come down along the creek on midnight business. And still he heard nothing, only small cries of the earth, forming on the surface of the great night silence. Tree frogs shrilled from the freshwater slough on the far side of the road, in counterpoint to the relentless nightsong—*chuck-will's-widow! chuck-will's-widow! chuck-will's-widow!*—which came from the whiskery wide gape of a mothlike bird hidden in lichens on some dead limb at the swamp edge, still and cryptic as a dead thing decomposing.

The Gulf moon carved the pale track and black trees. Having come in stealth, the intruder would make the last part of his approach on foot, and—

Lucius's heart leapt—*there!* A blur against the wall of the moonlit wood detached itself from the tree shadows and moved out onto the track.

An Indian, he thought at once, though how he knew this he could not have said. The figure paused a moment, looking and listening. Then he came on again, following the sand track's mane of grass, at pains to leave no sign. Caught by the moon, the object that he carried on one arm was glinting.

Lucius moved quickly to drag pants and shirt onto his bony frame. He lifted the shotgun from its rack and cracked the cabin door, cursing himself yet again for isolating himself way out here without a telephone—or plumbing or electricity, for that matter. Yet the simplicity of this houseboat life contented him. It was simplicity he needed, as another might need salt. A cracked cistern and a leaning outhouse which had served a long-gone fish shack at the bog edge, a Primus stove and a storm lantern with asbestos filament—these took care of his domestic needs. Perhaps once in a fortnight, he retrieved his negligible mail at Goodland Post Office and bought his stores, and had a meal and a few whiskeys at the roadhouse.

Above the mangrove on the creek edge rose high wind dunes—highest point on Marco Island, where in the old centuries the Calusa Indians had taken refuge from seasonal hurricanes. Eventually the Spanish had come, and the fishing settlement, and the clam-canning factory. Now developers of creekside land had burned the old factory and the last of the old fish shacks and cleared the sabal and the gumbo-limbo to make way for hard artificial lawns for northern buyers.

Near the sheds, the Indian's silhouette turned in a slow half circle, sifting the night sounds like an owl before passing behind the leaning outhouse and Lucius's old auto and some rusted oil drums and the hulk of his old boat and pausing again at the foot of the spindly low dock over the salt grass. He was big and short-legged and round-shouldered, with a small flat butt. In the cold shine of the moon, he glided out over the bog, slat by split slat, and the dock creaked and swayed a little as he came.

Breaking the gun, Lucius Watson dropped two buckshot shells into the chambers and snapped it to. At the click of steel, the Indian stopped short, his free hand rising in slow supplication. He stared at the black crack of the opened door. Very slow, he bent his knees and set some sort of canister down on the dock with a certain ceremony, as if the thing were dangerous or sacred. Slowly he straightened, hands spread-fingered, arms out to the side. His big swart pocked face was expressionless. He tried a smile. "Rural free delivery," he said.

Widening the door crack with the shotgun barrels, Lucius stepped outside. Under the moon, the glinting canister appeared to pulse. "Get that damned thing back over to the road," he told the Indian.

"It ain't a bomb or nothin," the man murmured. The Indian's raven hair was dressed in red wind band and long braid, and he wore a candy-striped Seminole blouse and black leather vest, blue jeans and sneakers, with a beaded belt tight on a junk-food belly. He raised his eyebrows, awaiting some change of heart, but when the white man only motioned with the gun, he shrugged and bent and retrieved his offering in one easy motion and returned over the centipedal walkway to the land.

On his hunkers on the road, arms loose across his knees, the Indian awaited him, watching the gun. Lucius pointed the barrels down along his leg. Back in the night shadow of the trees, he could just make out the hulk of an ancient pickup.

Asked if he had come alone, the Indian nodded. Asked who he was, he identified himself as a spiritual leader of the traditional Mikasuki out on the Trail.

Lucius said, "You came halfway across Florida in that old junker to deliver this—"

"Burial urn. The old man sent it." With a generous wave, the Indian invited him to admire the urn. "He seen your ad in the paper about Bloody Watson."

"Mr. E. J. Watson? Planter Watson? That what you meant to say?"

The big Indian sighed. "Our old-time Indin people down around Shark River, they always thought a lot of Mr. Watson, cause he give 'em coffee, somethin warm to eat, whenever they come up along the rivers. Had good moonshine, too. Folks say he killed some white people and black ones but he never killed no red ones, not so's you'd notice."

Lucius Watson had to laugh. This hurt his head. "*What* old man?" he scowled.

"Call him Chicken-Wing."

"Chicken-Wing. So Chicken-Wing said, 'See that Mr. Lucius Watson gets this burial urn on the stroke of midnight.' Am I right so far?"

The Indian nodded. "Stroke of midnight," he assented slyly. "Them were his very words."

"Christ." Lucius tried to focus on the urn, which was a cheap one, ornamented with crude brassy angels. "And you don't know his real name."

The Indian shrugged. "Used the name Collins when I first come acrost him, some years back. Course that don't mean nothin. Them people out where he is livin at don't hold so much with rightful names. Call him Chicken on account of he's so scrawny—"

Lucius hoisted the gun, and the sudden motion hurt his temples, making him curse. "Come on, dammit! You come sneaking in here after dark—!"

"Just brung that urn, is all. The way I told you." His black eyes remained fastened on the gun. "Guess I'll be gettin along," he said, easing to his feet.

Lucius broke the gun and ejected the shells and stuffed them into his pocket, feeling ridiculous. "You better come on back over to the boat, have some coffee before heading back. Who's that in the urn? Let's start from the beginning. If this old Collins wants to see me, why didn't he come here himself?"

"He don't feel so good." The Indian eased his nerves with a low belch. "Other day, one them frog hunters lives back out there come by my camp and let me know Old Man Chicken wanted to see me. Told me Chicken been rottin in his bedroll goin on three days, hardly a twitch, so them men figured he was close to finished. Soon as I got there, Chicken says, 'For fifty years I been standin in the way of my own death.' I weren't so sure what he meant by that, but it sounded like he had about enough.

"Next thing, he told me where you was livin at. Said, Take this here urn to that man Lucius Watson, he's my rightful hair. Tell him he better come see me, cause I got me a whole ar-chive here on his old man—whole carton of documents and such. And if *that* don't do it, you just tell him that them bones in that urn used to be his brother."

"That's *Rob* in there?" Lucius laid the shotgun on the grass and sank to his knees in the white sand beside the urn. He lifted and turned it carefully in both hands in a tumult of emotions. Rob Watson! To clear his head, he took deep breaths of the night air, filling his lungs with the heavy bog smell of low tide. He set the urn down again and stared at it.

Using a bird bone taken from his shirt, the Indian drew a sort of spiral in the sand. "He reckons you owe him a visit. He's the one sent you them old papers where some man tells how them Chokoloskee fellers killed your daddy."

"My God." Lucius sighed. "Tell him I'm coming." Whoever he was, this old Collins knew what had become of Robert Watson, having somehow come by his remains before Rob's own siblings even knew that he was dead.

Pressing huge smooth hands to his knees, Billie Jimmie rose as slow as smoke, to such a height that Lucius Watson, a tall man himself, had to step backwards. "Gator Hook," the Indian said. He set off down the white moon road without a wave. At the wood edge, he half-turned to look back, then disappeared into the dark wall of the forest, leaving Lucius alone with the strange urn, under the moon.

Gator Hook

The day after the Indian appeared out of the forest, Lucius Watson drove eastward on the Tamiami Trail through the Big Cypress, which opened out into wet saw grass savanna. A century ago, in the Seminole Wars, the Indians still crossed their Grassy Waters, *Pa-hay-okee*, to the high hardwood hammocks where palm-thatch villages and gardens lay concealed from the white soldiers. Since then, the bright waters had been girded tight by the concrete of progress, and a wilderness people, like the native bear and panther, could scarcely be imagined anymore. Of the half-hidden dangers which in the nineteenth century had sapped the spirit of the U.S. Army and led at last to its defeat, what remained were the tall scythes of toothed saw grass and the poison tree called manchineel, the treacherous muck pools and jagged solution holes in the skeletal limestone, the insect swarms which could drive lost greenhorns to insanity, the biting insects and thick water moccasins, opening their cotton mouths like deadly blossoms, and the coral snakes and diamondbacks on the high ground.

Beyond the tiny hamlet at Ochopee, Lucius crossed the small bridge over the shady headwaters of Turner River, which flowed south through shining grasslands and the brackish mangrove coast to the backwaters of Chokoloskee Bay. In the fiery sunshine which arose from the Atlantic horizon, the stately pace of his antiquated auto, putt-putting and rumbling like an old boat, permitted a calm appreciation of the morning. Strings of white ibis crossed pink sky, and egrets hunched like still white growths on the green walls of subtropical forest that had taken hold on the higher ground along the Trail. Over the savanna flew a swallow-tailed kite which, in recent days, had descended from the towering Gulf skies, at the end of its northward migration from the Amazon.

Delighted, Lucius stopped the car and climbed onto its dented roof to follow the bird's hawking course over the Glades. Before him, the bright expanse spread away forever, seeping south and east over the infinitesimal incline of the ancient seafloor which formed the flat peninsula of southern Florida. In the distance, like a green armada sailing north against the sky, rose isolated hardwood hammocks, tear-shaped islands in the slow sparkling sheet of grassy river. The hammocks were rounded at the northern end and pointed at the south from long ages of parting the broad water that the Indians knew as River Long or *Hatchee Chok-ti*, transcribed by the early white men as "Shark River"—"the Undiscovered Country," Lucius's father had called it, evoking not only the remoteness of that labyrinthal wilderness but its mystery. "From whose bourn no man returns," Papa intoned. In those days, there was no sign of man, only fine cracks in the floating vegetation made by narrow cypress dugouts, which left scarcely more trace than the passage of great birds in the Glades skies.

Placing one hand on the hot metal, Lucius made the jump down to the road. Though the road jarred him, he was grateful he could still do this without undue creaking. He straightened and stretched and gazed at the silent savanna all around. How terrible and beautiful it was! At one time, Mikasuki water trails had traversed the Glades from the east coast to the west, and permitted a passage of one hundred miles from great Lake Okeechobee south to Florida Bay and the Gulf of Mexico. In recent years, with the advent of the Park, the Indians had been banished from *Hatchee Chok-ti,* and the last of the wild Mikasuki—Billie Jimmie's people, who refused to join the acculturated Indians on the reservations—lived in small camps along the Trail canal, guarding their old ways as best they could behind vine-shrouded stockades which hid all but the roofs of the thatched *chekes.*

At Monroe Station, the old aid and rescue post for early motorists, Lucius turned south on the narrow spur which joined the Trail to the old Chevelier Road. Known these days as the Loop Road, the track had been reduced by decades of disuse to a narrow passage pocked and broken by white limestone potholes and marl pools. In places it was all but lost in the coarse crowding undergrowth of the subtropics, and brush and thorn raked and screeched at the car's doors as it lurched along. Farther on, the road lay submerged beneath risen water of the spring rains, and frogs and crayfish and quicksilver sprinklings of sun-tipped minnows moved freely back and forth between the warm gold of the marshes to the south and the soft silvers of the pond cypress to the northward.

But now the sky had clouded over, casting a pall of gloom over the swamp, and his sunrise mood of early morning evaporated with the dew, giving way to restlessness, disquiet. All his life, Lucius's moods had been prey to shifts of light, and now a dread and melancholy dragged at his spirits, as heavy as the graybeard lichen which shrouded the black corridors between the trees. In forcing his way into this road, he seemed to push at a mighty spring which, at the first faltering of his resolve, would hurl him outwards.

*

Gator Hook was a shack community on a large piney-woods hammock south of the Trail. The hammock lay on the old road named for the Chevelier Corporation, which was named in turn for an irascible old Frenchman—an ornithologist and plume hunter—who had once attempted a citizen's arrest of Lucius's father. In the intoxicated days of the Florida Boom, back in the twenties, the Chevelier people had pioneered a track due west from the Dade County line through the cypress swamps and coarse savanna drained by the upper creeks of Lost Man's River. Its destination was Chevelier Bay in the Ten Thousand Islands, a wilderness region advertised as "the Gulf Coast Miami." The developers were confident the authorities would approve their road as the middle section of the cross-Florida highway, but at Forty-Mile Bend, the engineers had turned "the Tamiami Trail" toward the northwest, into another county. The Chevelier Road was still ten miles short of its destination when the Hurricane of 1926, followed three years later by the Wall Street Crash, put an end to the last development schemes ever to be attempted in the Ten Thousand Islands. By the time the Trail was finished, in 1928, the Chevelier Road had been all but abandoned.

In the Depression, the sagging sheds and dwellings of the Trail construction crews at Gator Hook became infested by fugitives and gator hunters, hobos, drunkards, and retired whores, in a raffish community with a reputation for being drunk on its own moonshine by midmorning. This lawless place, eight miles due west across the cypress from the Forty-Mile Bend on the Trail, was cut off from the rest of Monroe County by hundreds of square miles of southern Everglades, which, together with the Ten Thousand Islands, formed the largest roadless area in the United States. In the forties, the old road was decreed a northern boundary of the new Everglades Park, but Gator Hook remained beyond administration, to judge from the fact that the Monroe County Sheriff had never once made the long journey around the eastern region of the Park to this isolated and unregenerate outpost of his jurisdiction.

For a number of years there had been rumors of an old drifter out at the Hook who talked incessantly of E. J. Watson, and it had occurred to Watson's son that this drifter might be the killer Leslie Cox, yet this seemed so unlikely—was that his honest reason?—that he had never bothered to come out here to find out. Most local people still believed that Cox had escaped (perhaps with Watson's help) and made his way to the wild Mikasuki still living down around Shark River. Since the Seminole Wars, those undomesticated Indians had sheltered outlaws and other fugitives from white men just as, in the old century, they had sheltered runaway slaves. Under a half-breed identity (and Lucius could remember the man's Indian black hair and heavy skin), Cox had laid low for years back in the hammocks. Avoiding west coast settlements where he might be spotted, so it was said, he would sometimes accompany Indian trading parties to the east coast at the Miami River, where he traded otter pelts and gator hides for coffee and flour, moonshine, axes and steel traps, rifles, ammunition. With the advent of the cross-Florida highway Cox had drifted to the shack community at Gator Hook, hiding his identity from the inhabitants.

Among old-timers in the bars and on the docks along the coast, the legends of Cox and Watson never died. Lucius could not take all these stories seriously, but because Gator Hook with its anonymous inhabitants was so remote and little-visited, this particular rumor had troubled him long before the visit from Billie Jimmie. And now there was a real old man who claimed to have information about Watson. Was it possible that Leslie Cox had changed his name to Collins?

*

The sun, ascending, drew soft mist out of the cypress. From the sharp corner where the spur met the dead end, he headed east again, and in time the land rose slightly and the bright water withdrew beneath a ridge of pine. Blurred trails wandered aimlessly into the thornbush and palmetto, and here and there, half-hidden, the rusty red of a tin roof showed through the greens. In the roadside ditch bald tires languished among bedsprings, beer cans, rain-rotted packaging, unnatural objects of bad plastic colors, strewn through the catclaw and liana at the wood edge.

At a makeshift car dump in a corner of the road, four old men were playing cards on a sawhorse table. The stiff figures turned toward him as he passed, but no hand rose to return the stranger's wave. None of the four reminded him of Cox, though it was unlikely that he would have recognized the man, not having laid eyes on him since mid-September of 1910, on the same day he last saw his father. He had only a dim memory of that husky, sullen, and unshaven figure, hands in pockets, slouching apart from the small knot of people who were waving good-bye to Lucius from the riverbank at Chatham Bend. Yet seen up close, even an aging Cox would not have lost those small neat ears set tight to his head, as in minks and otters, nor the dim crescent of the mule hoof that had scarred one cheekbone, nor the dull, thudding voice, abrupt and heavy as the grunt of a bull gator.

The Gator Hook Bar was a swaybacked cabin, greenish black, perched on posts as a precaution against high water, and patched with tin and tarpaper against the rains. As the only roadhouse in this remote region, it served the rudimentary social needs of the male inhabitants and their raggy squalling females—lone backwoods crazies of both sexes, he had heard, apt to poke a weapon through a rusty screen and open fire on any unfamiliar auto making its slow way through the potholes, blowing out headlights as it neared or taillights as it fled and sometimes both. According to the legend of the place, the one victim unwise enough to stop and make an inquiry about this custom had been shot through the heart. ("Them boys sure appreciate their privacy," someone had said.)

The roadhouse was entered and departed through a loose screen door at the top of a steep narrow wooden stair, down which its customers were free to tumble at any hour of the day or night. Beside the stair was a pink limousine with mud flaps and bent chrome which had come to rest among three rusty refrigerators, a collection of oil drums, triangular sections of charred plywood, a renegade toilet, and a fire-blackened stove of that marbled blue so ubiquitous on old American frontiers. The limousine's rear axle was hoisted on a jack—high as a dog's leg on a hydrant, Lucius thought, noticing the dog lying beneath it—and the wheel had been missing for some years, to judge from the weeds grown up around the hub.

Through the torn screens came wild hoots, hee-haws, and tremendous oaths rolled into one blaring din by the volume of the country music from the jukebox. As Lucius Watson emerged from his old car, he was greeted by "Orange Blossom Special," which burst forth in fine cacophony and wandered out over the swamp north of the road.

On this morning of late spring, dilapidated pickups and scabbed autos had emerged from the swamp woods well before noon, and an airboat—a sled-shaped tin skiff with a seat raised above the caged airplane engine and propeller in the stern—was nudging the bank of the open marsh across the way. Parked askew was a new black pickup truck on high swamp tires. Passing the cab, Lucius jumped backwards, startled by the thump of a heavy dog, which had not barked, simply hurled itself against the window. The silent dog—a brindle pit bull male—seemed to churn and froth in its need to get at him, stiff nails scratching on the steamy glass.

"Now don't go pesterin ol' Buck!" A scraggy man in red tractor cap and dirty turquoise shirt whacked the screen door wide and reeled onto the stoop. When Lucius said he was looking for a Mr. Collins, the drunk waved him off. "Ain't never heard of him!" The man had long hard-muscled arms, tattoos, machete sideburns, and a small beer belly. Half-blinded by the sun, he cocked his head, trying to focus. "Ain't you a damn Watson?"

"Billie Jimmie around?"

"No Injuns allowed. You're Colonel Watson, ain't you? You sure come to the wrong place." The man jerked his thumb back over his shoulder. In a harsh whisper, he said, "Don't you go no further, Mr. Watson, lest you want some trouble." He nodded his head over and over. "Don't remember me?" He stuck his hand out, grinning. "Name is Mud," he said, just as this name was shouted by a rough voice from inside. Turning, he lost his balance, almost falling. He clutched the rail and sagged down onto the steps, denouncing someone in a pule of oaths and spittle.

Mud's red cap had fallen off, and Lucius picked it from the steps as he ascended. By now he had recognized Mud Braman from Marco Island, gone drink-blotched, and near-bald. Seeing his pallid scalp at eye level, the livid eruptions and scratched chigger bites, the weak hair and ingrained grime—seeing the soiled and scabbed human integument that could barely contain the furious delusions trapped within—Lucius perched the red cap gently on his head. "I knew your dad," he murmured, stepping around the rank cinnamon smell of him and continuing up the stair.

Inside, a man was loudly narrating a story. At the appearance of a silhouette in the torn screen, a silence fell like the sudden hush of peepers in the marsh, stilled by the shadow of a heron, or by a water snake, head raised, winding through the tips of flooded grasses. When the stranger entered, two scraggy men on the point of leaving sank back into their places, and the dancing women in their pastel slacks and helmet hairdos, breasts on the roll in baggy T-shirts, squawked and catcalled.

Lucius was stopped inside the door by a husky barefoot man, suncreased, with old dirt in the creases. From hard green coveralls—his only garment—rose a rank odor of fried foods and sweat, spilled beer and cigarettes, crankcase oil and something else, something rancid, a smear of old mayonnaise, perhaps, or gator blood, or semen. Expressionless in big dark glasses, this figure crowded him without a word, as if intent on bumping chests and backing the stranger out through the screen door. Then that same rough voice which had yelled at Mud now bellowed "Dummy!" and the man stopped and removed his glasses, and dull eyes gazed past Lucius with indifference as he turned away. His dark sun-baked back and neck and shoulders were matted with black hair.

The man who had yelled was Crockett Daniels, who had recognized Lucius Watson, too, and nodded sardonically at Lucius's grimace. Daniels crossed the room to confer with a big one-armed man who leaned on the far wall, then went to the makeshift plywood bar, where he poured two glasses of clear white spirits from a jug. Brusquely he offered one to Lucius, who accepted it with a bare nod. The moonshine was colorless, so purely raw that it numbed Lucius's mouth and sinuses and made his eyes water. The two stood grimly side by side, elbows hitched back on the plywood, faced out across the room, and they sipped moonshine for a while before they spoke.

"Speck" Daniels was a strong short man with a hide as dark and hardgrained as mahogany, and jutting black brows and a hawk beak, and dark grizzle in a fringe around a wry and heavy mouth. Straight raven hair, gone silver at the temples, fell in a heavy lock across his brow, and his green eyes were bright and restless, scanning the room before returning to the big black-bearded man in combat boots and camouflage pants and a black T-shirt with a wrinkled red stump in the right sleeve.

Fixing Lucius with a baleful glare, the one-armed man resumed a story interrupted by Lucius's arrival. "One time down in Harney River country"— and he pointed his good arm toward the south, toward the Park—"I shot me this gator at night, nailed that red eye, and damn if that sucker don't sink straight down into black water, could been nine foot deep! I don't generally miss, but I got this kind of a creepy feelin, and didn't rightly want to go in after him. That big ol' bull might had plenty of fight left, he might been waitin on me! Made sense to leave him where he lay. At night, it ain't the same as what it is in the broad open daylight. When a man gets to feelin uneasy, in the night especially, well, he best mind that feelin, or he got bad trouble."

Saying that, the big man slapped angrily at the stump of his lost arm. Chest heaving, he stared around the room, ready to challenge anybody about anything. The hard high brush of coarse black hair that jutted from his head like a worn broom gave him a look of grievance and surprise. On his good arm was a discolored tattoo—an American flag set about with fasces and an eagle rampant, talons fastened on a skull and crossbones. The red and white of the stars and stripes were dirtied and the blue purpled, all one ugly bruise.

"That war vet you're lookin at is Crockett Junior Daniels," Speck said in a speculative voice, not sounding pleased about it.

"Yessir, folks," Crockett Junior roared, "that big ol' sucker might could chomp your leg off! Might be holed up way deep in his cave, and you proddin down in there tryin to find him with your gator hook, nudge him up under the chin, try to ease him slow, slow, slow up to the surface where you got a shot, and him gettin more uproared all the time. First thing you know, he has got past the hook some way, he's a-comin up the pole, he's just a-*clamberin*! And there you are, up to your fool neck in muddy water and no hope at all to make it to the bank—if there *is* a bank, which mostly there ain't, out in that country!" He looked around the room. "Them kind of times, all you can do is stand dead still, hope that scaly sonofabitch gets by you in the rush!

"Now, that ain't a experience you are likely to forget, I'm here to tell you! You go to huntin gators in the backcountry, you gone to earn ever' red cent you make! And that's all right, that's our way of life and always has been, takin the rough nights with the smooth. But since the Park come in, you go out there"—he was pointing south again—"and go to doin what your daddy done, and grandpap, too, and next thing you know, you find yourself flat up against some feller in a green frog outfit that the federal fuckin gov'ment got sneakin around back in our swamps! Know what he wants? Hell, *you* know what he wants! Wants to steal your hard-earned money! Put your pore ol' cracker ass in jail!"

The big man pointed a thick finger at Lucius Watson. "Or maybe he ain't in a green suit! Maybe he just come walkin through that door there, tryin to look like ever'body else!"

Speck said calmly, "Folks here at the Hook ain't got no use for invaders, notice that?" He turned to Lucius. "Mind tellin us what you're doin out here, Colonel?" He grinned at Lucius in unabashed dislike. "That's what your friends call you, ain't it? Colonel?"

"You my friend now, Speck?" Lucius drank his glass off to the bottom and came up with a gasp and a warm glow in the throat and face. Like bristling dogs, they avoided eye contact, pretending to watch the one-armed man, whose anger was rising.

"Thing of it is," Crockett Junior bawled, "them damn Park greenhorns and their spies will belly right up to that bar, pertend to be your friend; keep a man from supportin his own family! And you out in that dark ol' swamp night after night, way back in some godforsook damn slough you can't even get to in a boat, and half-bled to death by no-see-ums and miskeeters. One night out here is worse than a month in hell! And finally you're staggerin home across the saw grass, cut to slivers and all cold and wet and more'n half dead, and thankin the Lord that you're comin out alive, cause you got two thousand dollars' worth of gator flats humped on your back. And sure enough, one them rangers has you spotted, or maybe he's layin for you near your truck back at the landin."

Here the big man paused in tragic wonderment, and when he resumed speaking, he spoke softly. "Speakin fair now, what's a man to do? If that ranger goes to chasin you, I mean, or tries to stop you? Or tell you you're under arrest, throw you in jail?"

Speck Daniels watched his son without expression. "They heard this same ol' shit in here a thousand times," he said.

"Now I ain't got nothin personal against that ranger," Crockett Junior was saying, choked by strong emotions. "Might could be a real likable young feller, just a-tryin to get by, same as what I'm doin. Might got him a sweet lovin wife and a couple real cute li'l fellers back home waitin on him, or maybe just the sweetest baby girl—same as what *I* got! Ain't no difference between him and me *at all*!" He looked around him wide-eyed to make sure these people understood how astonishing it was that he and this park ranger both had wives and children, and how large-hearted his concern for that ranger's family was. "But if'n that boy tries to take my gators, well, I got my duty to my people, ain't that right? Got my duty to take care of my little girl back home that's waitin on me to put bread on the table! Ain't that only natural?" He looked around the room. "So all I'm sayin—and it would be pathetical, and I am the first one to admit it—all I'm sayin, now, if any such a feller, and I don't care who, tries to keep me from my hard-earned livin?" Shaking his head, he fixed his gaze on Lucius once again. "Well, I'd sure be sorry, folks," he growled, as his voice descended to a hoarse hard whisper, and he pointed southward toward some point of destiny in a far slough. "I surely would be sorry. Cause I reckon I would have to leave him *out* there!"

The hard whisper and the twisted face, the threat, had finally compelled the crowd's attention, and it turned a slack and opaque gaze upon the stranger.

Speck Daniels snickered. "Tragical, ain't it? *Leave him out there!* I reckon that's about the size of it."

"That a warning?" Though Lucius spoke casually, his heart quickened with fear.

"Yessir," Speck said, ambiguous. "Out in this neck of the woods, a stranger got to watch his step. That is a fact." And still he did not look at Lucius but gazed coldly at the huge maimed man holding the floor. "Junior there, he went clean acrost the Pacific Ocean to fight for freedom and democracy, and he killed plenty of 'em over there just like they told him to, and he give his right arm for his country, too, while he was at it. Uncle Sam give him a purty ribbon, but that boy would of had a whole hell of a lot more use out of that arm."

He nodded, somber. "Course they's some of these dumb country boys is proud to give their right arm for their country—least their daddies is proud and Uncle Sam is proud, and the home folks gets to march in a parade. But I reckon I don't feel that way, and Junior, he don't neither, not no more. We know it's our kind that does all the fightin, and our kind that gets tore up and killed, long with the niggers, while the rest of 'em stay home and make the money." He kept nodding. "That big boy there had to learn them things the hard way, and he's still hot as hell. If he don't get a hold on his ragin pretty quick, there is goin to be bad trouble for some poor feller that don't know enough to get out of his way."

Speck licked his teeth. "When he's like this—all this uproarin, I mean—Junior sleeps like he is dead or he don't sleep at all. Won't talk to nobody, only them other vets. Might not say a word to his own daddy for two-three days, then busts right out with the answer to some damn question you forgot you asked him. Either way, he is crazy as all hell, and dangerous, and them other shell-shocked morons he keeps with him might be worse. Mud Braman ain't nothin but a crazy drunk, don't know what he's doin from one minute to the next, and that other one with all the personality"—he pointed at Dummy—"his uncles was in that bunch that killed that lawman at Marco back in Prohibition, so whatever the hell is the matter with that feller, he comes by it natural. Might break loose and shoot everyone in sight and you'd never have no idea why he went and done it."

Speck Daniels sighed. "Some days I think ol' Junior might be better off if I was to take him out into that swamp back there and shoot him. Before he shoots somebody else, out of his natural-borned suspicion. Maybe some stranger who just wandered in here off that road."

Daniels contemplated Lucius, sucking at his teeth as if tasting something bad. "You plannin to tell me what you're huntin for out this way, Colonel? Ain't me, I hope."

Lucius shook his head. "You live here now?"

"Nosir, I sure don't. When I ain't livin on my boat, I got me a huntin camp back in the Cypress, got a surplus tent and a good Army stove and a genuine plastic commode, also a nice Guatemala girl that come by mail order. But these days," he whispered—and he cocked his head to see how Lucius would receive this information—"I'm campin in your daddy's house, down Chatham River."

Lucius maintained his flat expression, not wishing to show how much he resented the idea of this man living on the Bend. Since his father's death, the remote house on its wild river had been looted and hard-used across decades by hunters, moonshiners, and smugglers, but now the Watson Place was deep inside the Park. To reveal to a man he knew disliked him that he was flouting federal law by camping in the old Watson Place seemed strangely out of character, unless Speck meant this as some sort of provocation.

"Parks is talkin about burnin down your house." Speck grinned a little, meanly. "Claim she's so banged up by hurricanes that she's a hazard to Parks visitors!" His grin shifted to a snarl. "Stupid lyin bastards! In all the years since Parks took over, they never had one visitor at Chatham Bend! Not even one!"

Lucius Watson nodded. From offshore, no stranger to that empty coast could find the channel in the broken mangrove estuary where Chatham River worked its way through to the Gulf—one reason that Papa had liked that river in the first place—and even the few tourists who could read a chart might ream out their boat bottom on the oyster bars. Because of the huge drainage canals in the Glades headwaters, the rivers ran shallow, with big snags and shifting sandbars, and there were no channel markers because moonshiners such as Crockett Daniels rigged lines to them and dragged them out.

Speck considered him a moment. "Yep, they're set to burn your daddy's good old house right to the ground."

"Why do you care? It's not your house."

Speck Daniels cocked an ugly eye. "Don't the Bend belong to all of us home people?" His voice had risen in a spurt of anger, and Crockett Junior turned their way. "Same as the whole Thousand Islands, the whole *Everglades*? Why, Godamighty, they's been Danielses out here for a hundred years! I lived and hunted in this country my whole life! You tellin me them greenhorns got more right to this backcountry than I do?" He spat hard at the floor. "Anyways, what the hell kind of a tourist would beat his way three-four miles back up a mangrove river to take a picture of some raggedy ol' lonesome place walleyed with busted windows, and the doors all choked by thorn and vines? Not to mention bats and snakes, wasp nests and spiders and raccoon shit—smell like a kennel! That house ain't had a nail or a lick of paint in years! Screen porch is rickety, might put your foot through, and the jungle is invadin the ground floor. That blow last year hit one hundred fifty at Flamingo. Them winds tore out the last of your daddy's windows, tattered the roof, just lashed and blasted that strong house till she looked gray and peaked as a corpse!"

Despite his vehemence, Speck Daniels's green eyes kept moving, as if much of his fury was feigned and the rest exaggerated, and when he spoke again, his voice was calm. "Well, you know somethin? That storm never done her no real harm at all. Tore up the outside, which is all them green-horns look at. Inside, she's as solid as she ever was, cause your daddy used bald cypress and Dade County pine. She'll be standin up there on her mound for another century!" What had saved the place to date, he said, was its lo-cation far across the Glades from the Park headquarters at Homestead. Alone and unvisited, way back in a forgotten river, and long hard miles by land or sea from the nearest road, the abandoned house did not justify the cost of its own destruction, and anyway, all the bureaucratic details—the burning permits, the requisition chits for fuel, not to speak of the fire crew, boat crew, and boat—had never been assembled in the same place at the same time.

"Hell, there ain't nothin to burnin down a house, you know that good as I do!" Daniels banged his glass down on the bar. "Any Injun nor nigger, woman nor child could turn a pine house to hellfire in four minutes flat! Toss a coffee can of boat gas through the winder, flick your cigarette in after it, and go on home! I mean, Christamighty! But they ain't done that, and you know why? Cause they'd rather blow up a paper storm, waste our tax money in some big-ass federal operation, make some bureaucrat look like he done somethin important!"

"You paying taxes these days?" Lucius inquired. The moonshine was spreading through his body, which glowed with a deadly calm.

"Why hell, yes, Colonel! First man to step up to the window ever' year!"

They grinned together briefly, without pleasure.

*

A couple of months before, Daniels confided, he'd been contacted by a lawyer in Miami who was seeking a court injunction against the burning and was trying to reach the Watson heirs. He wanted someone on the place to make sure the house did not burn "by accident" before the case could get to court, and also to learn if the Park would force the issue by seeking to evict his caretaker. He wanted to gauge the strength of the government's legal position as well as its resolve.

"Parks ain't tested it so far, and they know I'm on there." Speck cocked his head with another sly smile. "Course I was on there anyway, takin care of my own business, so ever'thin worked out purty nice."

The Miami lawyer had a big reputation, big connections. He was a crony of politicians and a "fixer." Lucius must know him, Daniels said, because he'd been born on Chatham Bend, Ed Watson's namesake.

Affecting indifference, Lucius shrugged, but he resented this, as Daniels knew he would. Why would Watson Dyer pay a moonshiner and gator poacher to protect that house before getting in touch with the Watson family? To hell with that, he thought, I'll go myself. I'm going home. They can't burn down the Watson house with a Watson standing in the door!

"First time he called, it seemed to me I knew the voice, but some way I couldn't place it," Speck was saying. "The man was complainin how he never could catch up with the Watson boys. I told him, Well, the oldest boy ain't never been heard from since the turn of the century, and the next one, Eddie, don't want nothin to do with that old place. Course Colonel might be interested, I says, but you'll have trouble comin up with Colonel, cause he moves real quiet and makes hisself real scarce and always did." Speck Daniels laughed, but his green eyes weren't laughing. "Ain't goin to tell me what you're lookin for out here?"

The more Lucius thought about going home, the more excited he became, though he tried not to show it. "So what does Dyer want? With Chatham Bend, I mean."

"Might want a ronday-voo for his pet politicians, wouldn't surprise me—booze-and-girlie club, y'know. I been thinkin I might join up to be a member." But there was no mirth in Daniels's wink, and he got right back to business. "All I know is what I picked up on the phone. But he must be up to somethin big. Went to a lot of trouble to find out that Crockett Senior Daniels knew the Watson Place and might be just the feller he was lookin for."

Asked what he had been doing on the Bend before he took up caretaking, Daniels lit a cigarette and squinted through the smoke. "That ain't your business." He winked to show he was only joking, which he wasn't. "Maybe I been studyin up to get me a good job as a Park Ranger, on account of I done more rangin in their Park than all them stupid greenhorns put together."

Sipping the white lightning, Lucius said "You make this stuff at Chatham Bend? When you're not out caretaking, I mean?"

Daniels measured him. "You ain't obliged to drink it, Colonel. You ain't obliged to drink with me at all."

Asked about the airboat and the new black truck, Speck remained silent, but Lucius persisted. "Run this stuff up here at night by airboat? Lost Man's Slough? Broad River? Gator hides, too?"

"That airboat's his'n, and the truck." Daniels jerked his chin toward Crockett Junior. Asked next if he owned the Gator Hook Bar and if this place was an outlet for his product, Speck gave up trying to be genial. "Still askin them stupid questions, ain't you, Colonel? You ain't changed much, boy, and I ain't neither, as you are goin to find out if you keep tryin me. It's like your daddy said that day, 'I ain't huntin for no trouble, boys, but if trouble comes a-huntin me, I will take care of it.' "

"He never said anything that stupid in his life!"

Daniels grinned at him. "Is that a fact?" He reached to refill Lucius's cup, to smooth things over. "Course I weren't nothin but a boy, but I knew your dad, y'know, to say hello to."

"Knew him to say good-bye to, might be more like it. One of the last to see Watson alive, one of the first to see him dead—whichever."

In a gravelly voice, Speck Daniels growled, "I asked you real polite what you was up to, out this way." He rapped his glass down. "Asked you twice."

Lucius set his own glass on the bar, pushed it away from him, trying hard to focus. He was sick of talking. "I'm out here looking for a man named Collins."

"No you ain't." Speck shook his head. He looked over the crowd, then announced loudly, "You are a damn liar." They watched Crockett Junior push himself clear of the wall and move toward them. "I ain't seen you in maybe twenty years and all of a sudden, you show up out here, way to hell and gone off of your territory. You think I'm some kind of a fuckin idjit?" Still watching his son, Speck persisted in a low flat tone, "Think I don't know why you're snoopin around where you don't belong?"

"Easy now. Hold on a minute—"

"You been snoopin and skulkin all your life, you sonofabitch! Nobody never knowin where you was at, let alone what you was up to. Maybe you don't know it, boy, but you come pretty close to gettin yourself killed, back in the old days!"

"By you?"

"Could be."

"You threatening me, Speck?"

The one-armed man moved in behind him, and the man called Dummy had drawn closer, too. The room went silent. The crowd waited beady-eyed for some stray scrap of event, like hungry crows. Lucius said, "The man I'm looking for calls himself Collins. Old Man Chicken, Billie Jimmie calls him."

"Chicken-Wing?" a woman yelled. "He ain't but about four damn feet from where your elbow's at! Under the bar!"

*

Despite the heavy humid heat, the man who lay beneath the bar on a soft litter of swept-up cigarette butts was covered right up to his closed eyes in dirty Army blankets poxed with black-edged burns. "He's comin off a drunk," Speck Daniels snarled. He toed the body with a hard-creased boot, and the body emitted an ugly hacking cough, then a gasping rattle that might have been some sort of deathbed curse. "When Chicken-Wing washed up here years ago, we made him barkeeper, ain't that right, Chicken? Paid him off in trade. All he could put away and then some, and he's still hard at it! Come to drinkin, he don't *never* quit! Don't know the *meanin* of the word!"

"Crockett Senior Daniels!" the voice said bitterly from beneath the blankets. "Damn redneck know-nothing!"

Speck grinned. "I know my ass from a hole in the ground, which you ain't known in years!" In good humor now, he winked at Lucius and kicked the body harder. "Come on, Chicken! Say how-do to Colonel, boy, because he's just leavin!"

Hair like greasy wet tufts of a duck emerged from the olive blankets, followed by a soiled, unshaven head, a sad reek of booze and urine. The old man lifted the singed blanket to his mouth before turning toward Lucius, so that only the eyes showed, peering out through hair and beard like a wild man peering through a bush. Lucius thought he glimpsed something familiar, but he saw at once that this man was not Cox. A scrawny claw crept forth to grasp the tin cup of mixed spirits and tobacco juice which Dummy, at a sign from Speck, had ladled from a slops bucket under the bar. The old man grasped it avidly, knocking it back with one great cough and shudder.

At the sight of Lucius, the eyes came blearily into focus, then misted over before closing tight. The head withdrew. From beneath the blanket came dire curses and more coughing. "Don't a dying man get no privacy?" he yelled.

Lucius went down on one knee beside the pile of blankets. "Mr. Collins? You wanted to see me?"

"Go on back where you come from, boy!"

"We have to talk," Lucius said urgently. "You can stay at my place till you're better."

With his good arm, Crockett Junior Daniels lifted Lucius off the floor, turned him away. The drunk yelled after him, "Don't mess with 'em, boy! I'll see you down the road!"

At the door, Mud Braman tried to block his way. "You're Mister Colonel, right? Mister Colonel Watson!" At a sign from the one-armed man, Dummy thrust his palm against Mud's face so that the nose and bulging eyes stuck out between his fingers, then shoved hard with one thrust like a punch, sending Mud back through the screen door. Striking the rail, he spun into his fall, making a half turn in the air before he dropped from view. A scaring *bang* rose from the bottom of the steps.

Lucius jumped after him down the stairs as Speck Daniels observed them. "Poor ol' Mud has flew down them steps so many times you'd think he'd get the hang of it, but he just don't," Speck said.

Mud Braman, on hands and knees, was red-eyed with pain and disillusionment. "See how they done? I tried and I tried to be in friendship with these peckerheads, done my best to help out where I could! It ain't no use!" Yet when Lucius tried to help him up, Mud cursed him. Wiping the blood from his gashed brow with the back of a grimy hand, he tottered through the dirt and weeds to the pink limousine and dragged himself into the backseat like a sick cat, pulling the door shut with loud creaks because the hinges were all bent and rusted and the rank growth of weeds kept it from closing. "Anybody thinks that Mud R. Braman is goin to take any more shit off these skunks better think again!" came the voice from within.

Speck Daniels yelled at the pink auto, "You ain't hurt none, boy! You can thank the Lord you got skunks for friends, cause otherwise you wouldn't have none at all!" Seeing Lucius headed for his car, Speck raised his voice to a hoarse shout. "*Lucius* Watson! Lucius Watson ain't nowhere near the man his daddy was, ain't that right, Lucius?"

Grinning, Speck stood rocking on his heels on the top step, hands in hip pockets. "Lucius? You don't aim to say good-bye? And here you ain't even told me yet how that ol' list of yours is comin along!" Getting no answer, he yelled louder. "How come Henry Short ain't on your list? Ain't never died off yet that I ever heard about. Or don't a nigger count, the way you look at it?"

Lucius backed his old car around, the tires spitting mud. He idled in neutral in the ruts as he cranked his window down, the better to contemplate the furious man on the top step. Behind Daniels's head, over the roof peak, a turkey vulture made trackless circles through the sky, the red skin of its bare head glinting like a blood spot on the sun.

Speck licked his lips. "You and me is very different, Lucius, I am proud to say. If I believed a certain man helped to kill *my* daddy, Lucius, I sure wouldn't go to drinkin with that feller, Lucius, like you done just now. And I sure wouldn't need no damn ol' list to tell me what to do about it, neither. That man would of come up missin a long time ago."

"Crockett Senior Daniels." Lucius pronounced the name slowly, as if to lock it in his memory. "I do believe that is the last name on the list." Wobbling the old clutch into gear, he exulted at the flicker in Speck's grin, and drove off chortling, yet he knew he had pushed his luck, and his heart was pounding. A man as ruthless and wary as Speck Daniels would hear those last words as a threat, and a threatened man, as Papa used to say, was not a man to turn your back on in the Glades country.

The List

In December of 1908, E. J. Watson had been acquitted in a murder trial in north Florida, a notorious event that had required Gov. Napoleon Broward's intercession to prevent a lynching. Eddie Watson and their sister's husband, Walter Langford, had testified for the defense, yet upon their return to Fort Myers, these two refused to discuss the trial with the younger brother, asserting that stern silence in this matter was "a family decision" made with their Collins cousins in Columbia County. The silence deepened two years later when "the head of the family"—Eddie's snide way of referring to his father—was killed by the Island men on Chokoloskee.

Taken in custody by Sheriff Frank B. Tippins and brought north to Fort Myers, the Islanders had been deputized as "the Watson posse," although their quarry was already dead and buried. This stratagem, which avoided worsening the scandal with a public trial, was approved by Banker Langford and by Eddie Watson, who soon thereafter left his employ as deputy court clerk in order to take a job in Langford's bank. Eddie refused to discuss the hearing with his brother or reveal to Lucius the identities of those who had participated in their father's death, lest Lucius attempt to seek revenge or otherwise "act crazy."

From the start, Lucius Watson had lashed out at the whole business as hypocritical disloyalty to Papa. For a time, he had an ally in his sister, Carrie Langford, who had also loved their warm and jolly father and would not believe that Papa had been guilty of the alleged crimes. (Carrie was especially tormented because in recent years—since the murder trial in Columbia County—she had turned her father from her door, to protect her husband's business reputation.) Sharing grief and bewilderment as well as the hope that somehow dear Papa would be vindicated, the two were stoic in their stifled rage at the street whisperings, the stares in church, the seething gossip which attended the reburial of the blood-blackened, half-rotted corpse exhumed from Rabbit Key and reburied almost furtively in Fort Myers Cemetery. Only the Langfords' prominence and wealth had protected the family from public disgrace. But eventually Carrie, too, would adopt the code of silence, telling Lucius that she could not bear any further talk about dear Papa. Walter and Eddie were right, she had decided. For the sake of her poor children, Carrie wept, she must cut Papa from her life and mind as best she could. When she begged Lucius not to mention him again, he turned and left her house without a word, completing his estrangement from the family.

Clearly, his upright siblings in Fort Myers had no wish to learn "the truth" about their father, perhaps because they lived in dread of what such ancestry might signify if even one of the terrible tales proved to be true. And despite his loyalty, Lucius himself was uncomfortably aware of shrouded memories, half-hidden, half-forgotten—specters of the half-light, dimly seen, which drew near the surface of certain dreams and threatened to burst forth into the waking day. If Papa had deserved his reputation, then what did it mean to be the get of such a man, the biological consequence, the blood inheritor?

"You're drunk! You're talking crazy!" Eddie had shouted when Lucius asked these dire questions at a Thanksgiving celebration at the Langfords, scarcely a month after the death. And all reminded him of the clan decision never to speak of their ancestor again.

Lucius cried, "Well, maybe I *am* crazy! Who knows? If Papa was who you think he was, I might wake up one day and just start killing people! And you might, too! That doesn't scare you?"

*

That winter of 1911, estranged from his family and unable to rest, he had set off in search of his beloved oldest brother, who had not been heard from since he'd fled from Chatham Bend ten years before. Lucius took the train north to Fort White, in Columbia County, in the hope that Rob might have been in touch with Granny Ellen Watson or their Collins cousins.

Granny Ellen, he discovered, had died a few months before her son, and Aunt Minnie Collins had no idea who Lucius might be, far less what he might want of her. Aunt Minnie, who would die within the year, had been sheltered from the scandal (and indeed from her own life) by morphine addiction and premature senescence. Like one rudely awakened, on the point of tears, she would not speak with this interloper in her household, who only added to her confusion and distress.

As for her children, they scarcely remembered the young cousin who had stayed with them briefly sixteen years before. Sympathetic at first, his relatives became uncomfortable and then impatient with his questions, reminding him of the code of silence which the Collins clan had scrupu-lously observed. Shamed in their rural community by their uncle Edgar, they were not grieved by his death, and when Lucius finally understood this, he burst out, "He was acquitted! He was found innocent!"

The Collins brothers did their best to mend things. They had loved their uncle, they acknowledged, but they would never agree that he was inno-cent. When Lucius departed, Cousin Willie called from the train platform, "Y'all come back and see us, Cousin Lucius!" This was meant kindly, yet they were content with his departure and could not hide it.

While in Fort White, Lucius had learned the whereabouts of his father's widow, who had fled Chokoloskee and gone to live near her sister Lola in northwest Florida. Edna Watson was close to Lucius's age, they had been dear friends, and he felt sure he would be cheered by a good visit with his lit-tle half sisters Ruth Ellen and Amy and their roly-poly brother, christened Addison after Granny Ellen's family. But Ruth Ellen was still terrified by the din and violence of the shooting, which Little Ad had witnessed, and even Amy, only five months old on that dark October day, struck Lucius as sub-dued and melancholy, rather timid.

His young stepmother was kind to him, and nervous. He had dragged un-welcome memories to her door. Though Edna was too shy to say so, her sis-ter, pressing him to leave, warned him gently that "Mr. Watson is a closed chapter in that poor girl's life." At the railroad station, Lola informed him that Edna would soon marry her childhood sweetheart from Fort White, who had offered to give his name to her three young ones.

*

In Fort Myers, Lucius worked awhile as a fishing and hunting guide for Wal-ter Langford's business associates. After his years at Chatham River, he was a skilled boatman and fisherman and a dead shot. He was also a loner, pre-ferring books to loud camaraderie, and indeed so quiet as he went about his work that his brother-in-law received indirect complaints, not about Lu-cius's guiding, which was expert, but about his "unfriendly" attitude, his si-lence. Try as he would to be "one of the boys," he was hobbled by introspection, guilt, and melancholy. At heart he was a merry person who saw something amusing wherever he turned, but in his darker times, Lu-cius's humor turned cryptic and laconic. His one close friend—and eventu-ally his lover—was a young girl named Lucy Dyer whose parents had worked at Chatham Bend in the first years of the century and who retained fond childhood memories of "Mr. Watson."

In the dull white summer of 1912, Lucius sought refuge in the Merchant Marine, taking along a duffel full of books. Upon his return, he was prevailed upon by Carrie to attend the University of Florida at Gainesville. There he passed three years in quest of a degree in American history, proposing for his thesis a life of the Everglades pioneer and sugarcane planter Edgar Watson—an objective biography which (he proposed) might replace the legend with the facts, and testify to E. J. Watson's intelligence and generous nature as well as his remarkable accomplishments. But his outline was rejected as too speculative—"too subjective" was what was meant, since the candidate was Watson's son. However, the faculty was much impressed by his deep knowledge of remote southwestern Florida, even to its Indian people and its wildlife, and urged him to prepare instead an account of pioneer settlement on the Everglades frontier.

At first, he had resented his professors for having dismissed his parent as a subject unfit for biography. (At the same time, Lucius understood that, in light of what had been written about Papa in the magazines and newspapers, unanswered by any protest from the Watson family, they could scarcely have concluded anything else.) Dispirited, he turned instead to the proposed history of southwest Florida, which progressed rapidly. It was nearing completion when he lost heart and abandoned it, and a few weeks later, he dropped out of graduate school without a word. For the first though not the last time in his life, Lucius Watson embarked on a prolonged alcoholic odyssey which only ended when he awoke in jail.

Returning eventually to Fort Myers, he went straight to the Langford house and stood before the family, ready to endure their recriminations. Poor Carrie gasped at his appearance. "Oh, it's such a *waste!*" she mourned. Inevitably Eddie reminded him of his profound debt to the generous man who had paid for his tuition—here Eddie bent a meaningful look upon his own employer, Walter Langford, who frowned, judicious, from his armchair, rapping out his pipe. Whether Walter frowned over the waste of Lucius's efforts or the waste of money—or perhaps in simple deference to the onset of his evening haze, brought on by whiskey—Lucius felt ashamed that he had accepted Langford's money in the first place.

It was Lucius's "morbid fear of life," Eddie declared, which had caused him to flee the university before completing his thesis and receiving his degree, and which also kept him from settling down and getting married. ("That poor, dear little Lucy Dyer!" Carrie had grieved, when Eddie condemned his brother's unmarried status.) A churchman and sober citizen who shared most and possibly all of Walter's opinions, Eddie was already married, with two daughters. Sprawled in an armchair, one leg over the arm, he sighed in his most world-weary way, shaking his head over his brother's ingratitude and chronic folly.

Next day, without notifying Lucy, Lucius enlisted in the U.S. Navy. He

went overseas with a vague ambition to die for his country but came back
having failed in this as in all else. Still brooding about his murdered father,
still fantasizing about Southern honor (and even honorable revenge upon
the ringleader—or perhaps the first man to fire—since it seemed impractical
to wipe out the whole posse), he had convinced himself that to salvage his
own life, he must return to the Ten Thousand Islands, not only to confront
the executioners but to learn just why Edgar Watson had met that grotesque
end on October 24th of 1910, at Chokoloskee.

*

Before departing for the Islands, Lucius spent one broken evening at the
Langford house—their new brick house on First Street, at the foot of the Edison Bridge over the river. On this occasion, Eddie declared that Lucius's "un-
healthy obsession" with his father's death was merely a way of lending false
significance to his own immature and feckless life. And when Lucius was
silent, he went on to warn him that returning to the Islands could only end
in violence, since the local men, in their guilt and anger, would inevitably
feel threatened by E. J. Watson's son. This dire prediction evoked an outburst
of dismay from Carrie and unusually deep frowns from her husband, who
stepped at once into the pantry to fortify himself with a noble whiskey, in
which Lucius joined him. And whiskey fired the final argument over Lucius's declared intention to find out precisely what had happened on that
fatal day nine years before—find out just who had shot at Papa, and what
evidence there was, if any, that E. J. Watson had ever killed a single soul.

"Oh Lord! You *are* crazy!" Eddie hollered.

"Name one person," Lucius shouted back on his way toward the door,
"who ever claimed that he saw Papa shoot at *anybody!*"

"Precious Lucius" thought himself superior, Eddie was yelling, for refusing to honor the family agreement never to discuss their father. And Carrie
chimed in—"You *did* promise, you know!"

"You people promised! I never promised a damned thing!"

Carrie was reprimanding Eddie as the door closed—"He is *not* feckless! He
is simply romantic and impractical!"—but she did not disagree with Eddie,
not entirely. When Lucius had gone overseas without advising Lucy Dyer
that he was going, the desperate girl had confessed her love for him to Carrie, and recently Carrie had learned that he had not called on Lucy since his
return. The next day, too ashamed to make amends—he had some idea that
he must first prove himself worthy—he departed for the Ten Thousand Islands.

*

At Chatham Bend he found a boat tied at the dock, and the family of Willie Brown camped in the house. Though old friends of his father, the Browns seemed uneasy, unable to imagine why a Watson son would ever come back to the Islands. Willie Brown assured him that they would move out whenever Lucius was ready, by which he meant "ready to live alone." Fearing that loneliness, he told them they were welcome to stay on in the main house while he patched up the old Dyer cabin down the bank. A few days later, when he returned from Everglade with a boatload of supplies, the Browns were gone.

Lucius wandered the overgrown plantation in the river twilight. In the old fields, cane shoots struggled toward the light through the thorn and vine. Fetching his whiskey from the boat, he sat in the empty house all that long evening, until finally he was so drunk and despairing that he crawled outside and fell off the porch steps, howling in solitude. Next day he headed south to Lost Man's River, where Lee Harden and his Sadie, who were close to his own age, had always been his friends and made him welcome. On impulse, he offered them the place on Chatham Bend. They were disturbed by his haggard appearance and did not believe that he was serious, and Lee Harden had lived on the Bend as a small child and had no wish to return there, having already filed a claim on Lost Man's Beach. He thanked Lucius politely, reminding him that the Hardens were fishermen. There was no sense in letting a forty-acre plantation go to waste. Anyway, they informed him gently, the Chevelier Development Corporation had somehow acquired rights to Chatham Bend.

Having no heart or temperament for a legal battle, Lucius abandoned the Bend and built a cabin near the Hardens at South Lost Man's, where he resumed his former life as a commercial fisherman. Though he did his best to be friendly with everyone, he refused to ignore his father's death. He wished to identify every man who had been present in that October dusk on Smallwood's landing, and to look him so squarely in the eye that he could not doubt that Watson's son knew all about his participation. In this way, he hoped he might be free of that bitterness and atavistic shame which had crippled his spirit for so many years.

The first man Lucius sought out for advice was Henry Thompson, who had worked for E. J. Watson back in the nineties and later became captain of his schooner. Henry had always been his father's friend and had denounced the killing. Yet it seemed that Henry was avoiding him, perhaps because he himself avoided Chokoloskee, where the Thompsons lived. When they finally met one day on the dock at Everglade, and he asked Thompson who had been involved, it appeared that Henry had forgotten. Though he put both sets of knuckles to his temples and racked his brain extra hard, he could not recall a single name from that crowd of men. When Lucius expressed astonishment, Thompson turned cranky, as if held responsible unjustly. He all but suggested that Watson's son had no business returning to the Islands in the first place. "All that Watson business" was over and done with, he told Lucius, and the less said about any of it the better. He did not add "if you know what's good for you," not in so many words, but very clearly that was what he meant. Better let sleeping dogs lie, Henry advised him as they parted, and anyway—this was shouted back over his shoulder—Mr. E. J. Watson still owed Thompsons money! After that day the Thompson family, which had always been so friendly, turned cold and avoided him, like the Willie Browns.

But Lucius persisted in his quiet inquiry, speaking with anyone willing to discuss his father's life and death. The men of Everglade and Chokoloskee had liked "Ed Watson's boy" back in the old days, and when he had first returned, and appeared friendly, some of the men put their uneasiness aside and answered questions about Mr. Watson's years on Chatham Bend, his crops and economics, boats and marksmanship, his moonshine and plume-hunting days, even his wild rioting in Tampa and Key West—anything and everything but the dark events which finished in that October dusk at Smallwood's landing.

They called him Colonel. The nickname had not been affectionate, not in those early days, but only certified his separation from the Island people due to his courtly educated tones and "city manners." The more amiable he became, the less they trusted him, in their stubborn suspicion that his friendliness was intended to disarm them while some course of bloody retribution was being plotted. As posse leaders, the men of the House family had most reason for concern. The patriarch, Daniel David House, had died two years before, but the three House boys who had taken part were very leery of him, especially the eldest son, Bill House.

Rumors drifted like low swamp mist through the Islands that "Colonel" Watson was asking the wrong questions. The local men became more taciturn each time he approached. Braving cold-eyed silences everywhere he went, Lucius did his best to avoid blame or rancor, but the Islanders grew ever more uneasy—indeed, those families which had decried the killing were at least as reticent as those which had participated, or approved it. Some were wary, some were scared, backing inside and shutting the door when they saw Watson's son coming. He could knock for ten minutes without response, knowing that if he touched the latch, somebody hidden behind that door might blow his head off. That this quiet and soft-spoken man would risk this—that despite the hostility of the community, he kept coming back—was only more proof that "Watson's boy," who could "drop a curlew

bound downwind with a bullet through the eye," was "every bit as dangerous as his daddy."

Yet one by one, by various means—cryptic allusions and sly woman talk,
drunk boastful blurtings—he learned the names of "the men who killed Ed
Watson," and from early on, he kept a list, with commentary. Every gleaned
scrap of information gave him his excuse to brood over the names, eliminate
one, write down another, or simply refine, make more precise, the annota-
tions which kept the list scrupulous and up-to-date. Coming alive, always
evolving, the list seemed a justification of his return to the Ten Thousand Islands, reassuring him that what he was doing was research for that abandoned biography which might redeem his father's name. At the very least, it
eased the pain of a lost decade of inaction and self-loathing in which he had
forgiven neither his father's killers (as he still perceived them) nor the Watson sons—Lucius Watson in particular—for failing to find an honorable resolution.

Fed mostly now by stray allusions, random gossip, the list of names with
its revisions and deletions, footnotes, comments, and qualifications, grew
ever more intricate and complex, as what had begun as a kind of game became obsession. For a few years, he went nowhere without it. The folded
packet of lined yellow paper, damp from the subtropical sea air, had gone
transparent at the creases from sweat and coffee spills and cooking grease
and fish oil, and so specked by rust from tools and hooks and flecked with
sundry bread crumbs and tobacco, that Lucius could scarcely decipher the
small script and had to write out a fresh copy—a renewal ceremony and a
source of secret satisfaction. So long as he kept perfecting it, making certain
it was accurate down to the last detail, he would never have to give it up. It
filled some void and longing in his life—he knew that. Yet he could not admit
this to himself for fear of removing its peculiar healing power, and the order
it brought to his wandering mind.

He dreaded finishing the list, not wishing to deal with his inability to act
upon it. He did not believe he could take a human life, even in the name of
family honor. And though he could accept this, his romantic side would always be disappointed, knowing that the hickory breed of old-time Watsons
would have acted forcefully in retribution, never mind the morality or consequences. He longed to talk with his brother Rob, whom he remembered as
hotheaded and outspoken—hardly a man to accept family dishonor.

By the end of his first year in the Islands, there were threats. Although
afraid, Lucius perceived his potential martyrdom as a resolution of his life,
somehow less terrifying than cowardice or weakness. One night he dreamed
of the huge crocodile which had lived in Chatham River throughout his boyhood, hauling out on the far bank as if to watch the house. One day it

attacked an alligator. When its prey washed up half eaten, Papa said, "That's not much of a gator anymore." He spoke balefully, as a cautionary lesson to the younger children, who were only allowed to splash in the river shallows when that fourteen-foot creature was across the river, laying out there like a drift log, in plain view. In his dream Lucius rowed across the river, and the monster had opened its terrible jaws in a slow warning, then risen suddenly on its short legs and thrashed into the current in a great brown, roiling surge. Because he had challenged his own death, it was there just underneath him, awaiting its moment to capsize the skiff and seize him and drag him down. He awoke in horror.

*

Though he had sense enough to keep his list a secret, the time would come when he was shunned on Chokoloskee Bay. One day on the dock at Everglade, outside Browns' fish house, he received a warning from "your daddy's oldest friend" to "stop this snoopin around, for your own damn good." Kicking dirt hard, Willie Brown said, "I weren't mixed up in it, and I spoke agin it, but I'm giving you fair warnin all the same. Any of these local men who figures E.J.'s son is out to get him might feel obliged to get that feller first, you take my meanin, Lucius?" Willie Brown, who had called his father E.J., was one of the few who still used Lucius's real name.

For once, his brother Eddie had been right. The crude warnings and drunken threats were followed by the hornet whine of a bullet across his bow, the echo of a rifle shot across the water. Then one day his boat was sunk on one of his rare visits to Chokoloskee. Hearing of this, the Harden family—the last friends whom he could trust—prevailed on him to head south around Cape Sable and fish out of Flamingo until things cooled down.

During Lucius's stay in Flamingo, where he lived at the house of his father's friend Gene Roberts, his brother Rob had come looking for him in Fort Myers. During his brief visit, Rob told the Fort Myers family almost nothing about himself except to say that he was always "on the road" and had no address where he might be located. Rob had learned from Carrie that Miss Lucy Dyer might know their brother's whereabouts, but all Lucy could tell him was that Lucius might be living near the Harden family at Lost Man's River. Rob traveled by mail boat, then rowed a skiff for the last twenty miles, from Everglade to Lost Man's, where Lee Harden, suspicious of this intense stranger (Rob had called himself John Tucker), would only reveal that Lucius Watson was away.

*

Returning to Lost Man's, Lucius was determined to dispense with the useless list he had worked on for so many years, always changing and adjusting and revising, always striving to get closer to the fact, the "truth," which might permit him to put the thing behind him, and his father, too. He realized that, short of his own death, there was no end to that list, any more than there could be an end to life itself. Far from putting his heart to rest, its very existence had become a burden and a danger, rebuking him not only for his failure to avenge poor Papa but for the folly of his self-banishment to the Islands, and for the huge part of his life which had been wasted. How much better that time might have been spent in a real life with Lucy Dyer, raising children—that was his fresh new dream.

That year, Lucius received word of Walter Langford's death. He arrived in Fort Myers too late for the funeral. Carrie assured him that she understood, but it was plain that she could not quite forgive him for never having visited or written. "Nobody seriously expected you," Eddie said sourly. With customary spite, from behind his hand, he informed his younger brother that the President of the First National Bank had "died of drink," having failed to provide properly for their sister. As for himself, he was prosperously embarked on his own insurance business.

During his visit, Lucius entrusted Lucy Dyer with a packet for Rob Watson in the vain hope that Rob might turn up again. Since he could not bring himself to destroy it, he enclosed the posse list, to avoid any chance of its discovery by the men listed and to be rid of it once and for all. But a few years later, in the course of changing households, Lucy would misplace the packet, as she confessed to Lucius in a letter which also brought word of her recent marriage to old Mr. Summerlin. So stunned was he by her abandonment (he had somehow assumed that his first love would await him forever) that he scarcely noticed her mention of the list.

In the next years, he made a hard sparse living as a hunting and fishing guide and commercial fisherman, and most of the men accepted him again as talk of his list died down. His only trouble came about through his association with the Hardens, whose side he would take in a dangerous feud with the Bay people which had ended in the murder of two Harden sons.

*

In 1947, when the Ten Thousand Islands were appropriated for the national park, Lucius moved north to Caxambas. There he found a warm welcome from the women and children of the Daniels-Jenkins clan, whom his father had always spoken of as "my backdoor family." A decade later he returned to the University of Florida at Gainesville, where he accepted a teaching post as an assistant professor while completing his *History of Southwest Florida.*

In his class was Sally Brown of Everglade, a lovely young woman with long flaxen hair bound loosely with rawhide at her pretty nape who had recently separated from Lee Harden's son Whidden and returned to college.

Sally made herself wonderfully useful in his work, not only as a researcher but as a source of information on the Island families. Of Everglades pioneer stock on both sides—he had almost forgotten that she was Speck Daniels's daughter—she had repudiated what she perceived as the racism and redneck ignorance in her community which had made life so dangerous for her husband's family. But as she ruefully confessed, her fierce tirades in defense of the Hardens had reawakened a lot of the mean gossip which that family imagined had been put to rest, until finally the Hardens themselves rebuked Whidden for not bringing his wife's tongue under control. For this reason—and others—the marriage had come apart. "My fault," Sally admitted, making no excuses.

Sally Brown was passionate, intemperate, and very angry (he suspected) for more primal reasons than those that she invoked. Though never certain how much he could trust her version of local events, he liked her because she was generous and wry and because her high opinion of "Mister Colonel" Watson, learned from the Hardens, had made her delightfully affectionate right from the start. Indeed, he felt affectionate himself, and had longed to kiss her from the first day she came by his rooms to say hello.

Lucius had been careful not to flirt with Sally, even in an avuncular sort of way. A courtly and old-fashioned man, he thought his need unnatural, considering their discrepancy in age. He also condemned it as immoral, since he was close to the Harden family and had been a sort of uncle to her husband, back in the early days at Lost Man's River. Besides, he was unhappily aware of his emotional limitations, which all his life had made him choose loneliness over commitment, no matter how fearful he might be that his one life on earth would pass him by. One night in a bar, he had confessed to the attraction, denouncing himself as "a dirty and villainous old man." Sally, who had long since known he was attracted, informed him that his whole attitude was ridiculous.

Meanwhile, his *History* had been well received by the university press, which encouraged him to proceed at once with his biography of E. J. Watson. The proposal specified, however, that a pseudonym be used for both books, since the subject had already been cited in the *History* as a notable pioneer in Florida agriculture, and the editors questioned the suitability of extolling the author's father in both volumes, all the more so when this parent—as they not so subtly reminded him—was indelibly associated in the public mind with something else. Thinking it dishonorable to hide behind another name, he withdrew the *History*.

Sally Brown had applauded his intention to mend his father's reputation, all the more so since E. J. Watson had always been a good friend to Whidden's family, and like those Harden boys down at Shark River, had been "murdered in cold blood by those damned rednecks." And it was Sally who finally persuaded him that a pen name was preferable to abandoning his project or damning his father with faint praise. Together they constructed a "family" pseudonym, L. Watson Collins. A year later, when the *History* was published, L. Watson Collins moved back to Caxambas, where he set to work on the biography, and placed the ads requesting information on his subject which would produce the Bill House deposition.

*

One day at the crossroads store where he picked up his mail, Lucius received a formal letter requesting that he get in touch with Watson Dyer, in Miami. Attorney Dyer notified him that his father's house was now officially scheduled for demolition by the National Park Service and offered his own services to help protect it.

In the early years, Dyer explained, the Park had not bothered with the Watson Place, since its first task had been the construction of paved roads and facilities between Homestead and Flamingo that would open the eastern region to the tourists. But now, pursuant to Park policy that "the region be returned to its natural condition as a wilderness," all sign of man was to be eradicated, even the rain cisterns and fruit-bearing trees. The old camps and shacks at Flamingo and Cape Sable, together with those at the river mouths and on the outer islands on the Gulf, had already been destroyed, and the Watson house on Chatham Bend was the only house left standing in the Islands except for the shack of an old loner who had been granted a life tenancy on Possum Key and the Earl Harden cabin at Lost Man's River, which had been taken over as a ranger station.

Although Lucius had heard these rumors from Speck Daniels, the formal notice was an unpleasant surprise, for the first and last house ever built on Chatham River would always be what his heart told him was home. Letter in hand, he strode angrily to the pay telephone outside the store. Over a bad line, after stiff greetings, Lucius demanded, "What do those idiots mean by 'natural condition'? Before Indian settlement or after? Before *which* Indians? Do they hope to wipe out every trace of the Calusa? Those Calusa canals? It would cost millions just to fill them in, in all that backcountry! And how do they propose to level and fill without gouging more scars on a fragile landscape than they were trying to eliminate in the first place? If the Park wants the Watson Place back the way it was, it will have to bulldoze all forty acres of Chatham Bend into the river, because the Bend is nothing but shell mound, don't they realize that? One huge Indian midden, built by human hands!"

Like an unseen presence in the room, the lawyer's silence commanded him to be still. In a moment, Dyer said, "Indians don't count." The voice was less ironic or cynical than plain indifferent.

So far as the lawyer could determine, the Watson family had gone uncompensated for the claim on Chatham Bend, which in the aftermath of the great scandal at the time of the claimant's death, none of his descendants had seen fit to pursue. If the Watson claim was valid, the old house might still be spared, and the land awarded legal status as an inholding within the Park for which life tenure, at least, might be negotiated. Could Lucius give him family authority to pursue this matter?

"I'm afraid I can't afford a lawyer—"

"*Pro bono,*" Dyer said. "Sentimental reasons." He reminded Lucius that he had been born at Chatham Bend and had been named after the claimant. In fact, he was just the man to represent the family, since his practice specialized in real estate law. He was well-informed about inholding cases and had excellent contacts, state and federal, which might prove useful. For the moment, all he required from the family was power of attorney, in order to file for a court injunction against any attempt by the Park to burn the house before the status of the claim could be ascertained.

All right, said Lucius. But should the decision be left to him, he would gladly waive all claim to an inholding if the Park would simply restore the house and take good care of it—make it a historic monument, perhaps, to pioneer days in southwest Florida, the home of the pioneer cane planter E. J. Watson.

He awaited a comment, which was not forthcoming. Watson Dyer sighed, then proceeded to observe that this proposal would be stronger once the claim was validated, since an offer of waiver before the claim had been reinstituted could only undermine its legal standing. Lucius was not certain he had grasped just what was meant, but he promised Dyer he would do his best to enlist the support of the surviving heirs. Excited, he also assured him that any claim that would protect the house could count on strong support from the numerous local families which had occupied the house at various periods since Watson's death. Those old Island pioneers knew the historical value of that house, he said, more and more enthusiastic, and many others were bound to speak up, too! He could go talk with them!

"Perhaps even the Dyer family will speak up," the lawyer said, forcing a strange hard snort of laughter.

"Yes. The Dyers, too," Lucius said doubtfully. So far as he knew, Dyer's mother was dead, and Dyer and his sister Lucy were not speaking, and the father, Fred Dyer, had been estranged from his children for years.

In Dyer's professional opinion (he chose that phrase), the Watson Claim could not be vacated or summarily dismissed if Watson's heirs lent their support to it in writing. Well, said Lucius, Rob was dead, and Carrie and Eddie would want no part of anything that might stir scandal from the past, and Addison, who was not yet four when his father was killed, had been given his new stepfather's name the following year and might not even know he was a Watson. As for the two younger sisters—

"Looks like it's up to you, then," Dyer said smoothly, bringing the call to a quick end. "You'll be hearing from me." By cutting off the conversation before anything substantive had been decided, he made Lucius feel restless and a bit disturbed. He could not get a feel for Dyer, nor could he imagine what the man might look like. Surely he looked nothing at all like his gentle sister. How odd that neither of them mentioned Lucy, who years ago had been his dearest friend.

Arbie

Returning home that afternoon, Lucius was met on the dock by the molasses reek of a cheap stogie. In the tattered hammock on the houseboat deck, an old man in red baseball cap and an Army-surplus overcoat lay sifting pages, the bent cigar a-glower between his teeth. In the corner lay a dog-eared satchel. Before Lucius could speak, the old man removed the cigar and spat bits of cheap tobacco leaf, the better to recite from his host's manuscript notes on Leslie Cox.

" '. . . an old man known by some other name may still squint in the sun, and sniff, and revile his fate.' Same way I write! Not bad at all!" He rested Lucius's papers on his belly. "Arbie Collins is the name," he said, pointing his finger at Lucius's eyes by way of renouncing that old drunk at Gator Hook and presenting a new, respectable identity. "Yep," he said. "I had this idea about Cox before you even thought about it. Folks said Cox had been seen down at Key West, and another time right in the river park there at Fort Myers. Then I heard from this Injun friend of mine who used to be a drunk up around Orlando—"

"Billie Jimmie, you mean?"

Arbie Collins shook him off, impatient.

"—that a feller who met Cox's description had been holed up for years out on the Loop Road. That's why I went out there in the first place, to hunt down that sonofabitch, ask him some questions. Never found hide nor hair of him. Ran out of money, never made it back." He resumed reading.

"What did you plan to do if you had found him?"

Arbie Collins lowered the manuscript. "Same thing you did with that posse list of yours," he snapped. "Pass the dirty job along to someone else." Scowling hard, he hunched down again behind the pages.

"You saw that list?"

"Rob Watson showed it to me."

"I never knew that Rob ever received it!"

Arbie Collins scoffed, using the manuscript page to wave him off. Every old cracker in southwest Florida had a story about that list, he said. The only man who thought that thing was secret was the fool who made it. He winked at Lucius, blowing smoke, then claimed he'd found the list among Rob's papers.

"You're the one who showed it to Speck Daniels."

The old man nodded. One evening out at Gator Hook, noticing the name Crockett Daniels on the list, he'd called it to Speck's attention as a joke.

"Speck think it was funny?"

"No, he sure didn't."

"Mr. Collins? I'd like that list back."

The old man resumed reading, raising the page to hide his face. "That list is the lawful property of Robert B. Watson, who left his estate to me."

Lucius sat down carefully on a blue canvas chair. "Are we related? Through the Collinses in Fort White?" This old man, washed and clean-shaven, reminded him of his Collins cousins—slightly built and volatile, black-haired, with heart-red mouths and pale, fair skin.

"Sure looks like it!" Arbie waved the title page, derisive. " 'L. Watson Collins, Ph.D.'!"

Sheepishly, Lucius explained that the publishers had insisted on a pseudonym and also on citing his degree. That "Ph.D." was ridiculous; he had not bothered to attend his graduation, much less used his title. In fact, he was not really an historian—

"A historian." Arbie grinned slyly at his host's surprise.

This raffish old man was somewhat educated. He was also careless, dropping and creasing pages, flicking ash on them. Finally Lucius stood up and crossed the deck and snapped his notes off Arbie Collins's stomach, exposing the white navel hair that sprouted through the soiled and semibuttonless plaid shirt. "You certainly make yourself at home!" he said.

"Well, I'm a guest. You invited me, remember? You sure don't act too glad to see me—"

"I don't like people rooting through my notes—"

"I *found* 'em." Arbie Collins sat up with a grunt and swung his broken boots onto the deck. "Right where you left 'em, on the table inside. And they look to me like notes for a damn whitewash." He stood up spryly and performed a loose-boned shuffle, snapping his fingers. " *'Notes on the Ol' Family Skeleton.'* " He cackled. "Clackety-click." Like a skeleton danced on a string, the old man shuffled jerkily through the screen door. In a moment he was back, lugging a big loose weary carton. "The Arbie Collins Ar-chive," he announced, setting it down.

Politely, Lucius rummaged through the carton, in which dog-eared folders stuffed with clippings were mixed with scrawled notes copied out of magazines and books—mostly lurid synopses and brimstone damnations from the tabloids, dating all the way back to the newspaper reports from October and November of 1910. Most of the items were well-known to Lucius—the usual "Bloody Watson" trash, all headline and no substance. None was as interesting as the fact that this old man had made a lifelong hobby of Ed Watson.

One coffee-stained packet of yellowed clippings slid from Lucius's lap to the porch floor. Retrieving it, he recognized the top clipping in the packet, which had come from the official tourist guide to the state of Florida— ripped from a library copy, from the look of it. It described how the young widow Edna Watson, informed by her husband's executioners that she might reclaim the cadaver by following the rope strung from its neck to a nearby tree, had inquired coldly, "Where is his gold watch?" That was certainly not poor Edna's character, and anyway Papa had sold that watch to help pay off his legal debts, as Edna knew.

Disgusted, he put the packet down, asking the old man how he had met Rob Watson. Arbie explained that he had helped his cousin Rob escape his father on a freighter out of Key West after E. J. Watson's murder of those poor Tucker people back in 1901. He was the only relative, he said, whom the grateful Rob had stayed in touch with till the day he died.

"*Alleged* murder of the Tuckers," Lucius corrected him. "It was never proven. E. J. Watson was never even charged."

Arbie hurled his cigar butt at a swallow that was coursing for mosquitoes over the spartina grass along the creek. "L. Watson Fuckin Collins, Ph.D.!" he yelled. "Too bad poor Rob is not alive to hear his brother say something as bone stupid as that!" The old man was fairly shivering with fury. "Before you go to writing up this damn whitewash of yours, you better talk to the Harden men, talk to that black feller Henry Short, cause they were the ones who had to deal with the damned bodies!"

Calmly, Lucius returned the subject to Rob Watson, who had ended up a hobo, Arbie told him. "Seems to me he was always on the road. Rob never had an address, had no bank account, never paid taxes in his life. Never had to, cause they had no record of him—he was never on the books!"

For many years, Rob had worked as a "professional driver"—"the first professional in the U.S.A. to drive an auto more than twenty miles an hour." Thanks to his road flair and big company limousine, Rob had been much in demand in the night liquor trade. He had finally been offered "a lucrative position in that industry." In Prohibition, he became a trucker, and in later years, he operated an enormous mobile auto crusher in which he had traveled up and down the county roads all over the South, compacting car bodies and selling the product to small steel mills on small ruined rivers at the edges of the small cities of America.

According to Arbie, Rob had died but a few years before, in the basement of the Young Men's Christian Association in Orlando. He had left strict instructions for cremation, and the YMCA had sent along his urn. Arbie pointed at the urn in the houseboat window. Asked how the YMCA had known where to send it, the old man looked furious, and Lucius decided to let it go. "Rob never married?" he asked. "Never had children?"

"Nosir," the old man muttered, yawning. "That was the only bad mistake Robert Watson never made." Sneezing, he lifted his red foulard to wipe his bristly chin. "After Rob died, I wanted to carry him back home to Columbia County, but about that time my auto quit—that pink one in the weeds at Gator Hook?—so I never got around to it." He measured Lucius. "I thought maybe we could go up there in yours."

They went inside. Lucius poured whiskey, and they toasted their meeting silently and drank, and he poured again. Ceremonious, he set the urn on a white cloth on the small table between them, placing beside it a pot of red geraniums, grown on his cabin roof. The old man observed this ritual with cold contempt.

Considering the urn, they drank in silence, in the play of light and water from the creek. That this cheap canister contained all that was left of handsome Rob made Lucius melancholy. The family would have to be notified, but who would care? "Rob came to find me years ago but I never saw him," he said finally. "I haven't laid eyes on him since I was eleven."

"You might not care to lay eyes on what's in here." The old man picked up the urn and turned it in his hands, and a mean grimace crossed his face. "Cause it don't look like much." Watching Lucius, he shifted his hands to the top and bottom of the container and shook it like a cocktail shaker. "Hear him rattlin in there? Folks talk about ashes, but there's no ashes, it's just chunks and bits of old brown bone, like dog crackers." He shook the urn again, to prove it.

"Don't do that, damn it!"

Lucius took the urn from the old man and returned it to the table, and Arbie laughed. "Rob doesn't care," he said.

"Well, I care. It's disrespectful."

"Disrespectful." Arbie shrugged, already thinking about something else. "One of these days, you can carry that thing north to Columbia County, see if there's any room for him up that way." He cocked his head. "I was thinking we could maybe go together."

*

That evening, with a grin and flourish, Arbie produced a letter clipped from the Florida History page of *The Miami Herald.* Its author, he said, was D. M. Herlong, "a pioneer physician in this state," who had known Edgar Watson as a boy in Edgefield County, South Carolina, and had later become a Watson neighbor in Fort White, Florida. Concluding some strenuous throat hydraulics with a salutary spit, the old man launched forth on a dramatic reading, but within a few lines, he gave this up and turned the trembling paper over to Lucius.

> He inherited his savage nature from his father, who was widely known as a fighter. In one of his many fights he was given a knife wound that almost encircled one eye, and was known thereafter as Ring-Eye Lige Watson. At one time he was a warden at the state penitentiary.
>
> He married and two children were born to them, Edgar and Minnie. The woman had to leave Watson on account of his brutality and dissolute habits. She moved to Columbia County, Florida, where she had relatives.

Gleeful, Arbie watched his face. "Probably stuff like that is of no interest to serious historians like L. Watson Collins, Ph.D."

Dr. Herlong went on to describe Edgar Watson's arrest for murder in the Fort White region, and Lucius read more and more slowly as he went along. Arbie was waiting for him when he raised his eyes.

"We heading for Columbia County, Professor?"

Lucius nodded. "You think Herlong has these details right? Like 'Ring-Eye Lige'?" Just saying that name aloud made him laugh in pleased astonishment. What he held in his hand was his first real clue to his father's early years, which Papa had rarely mentioned. Since the drunken Ring-Eye, home from war, had been abusive to his wife, it seemed quite reasonable to suppose that he'd beaten his children, too.

Because Old Man Collins's bias against Watson seemed so rancorous and powerful, the historian evoked the tradition of violence in which young Edgar Watson had been raised in South Carolina. According to his research for the biography, the Cherokee Wars preceding the first settlement had given way to a wild anarchy imposed upon the countryside by marauding highwaymen and outlaws, followed by the bloodiest, most bitter fighting of the Revolutionary War, with neighbor against neighbor in a dark and grue-some civil strife of a ferocity unmatched in the nation's history. The sons of these intemperate colonials would be noted for their headlong participation in the War of 1812, then the Mexican War, while maintaining high stan-dards of mayhem there at home. In 1816, President George Washington's chronicler Parson Mason Weems, revisiting this community, which he had served formerly as Episcopal priest, began his account with "Old Edgefield again! Another murder in Edgefield! . . . It must be Pandemonium itself, a very District of Devils!" In the fifteen years preceding the Civil War, in a rural settlement of less than one hundred scattered households, some thirty-nine people had died violently, nearly half of them slaves killed by their masters. And all of this tumult, Lucius told the old man, had taken place within a sin-gle century! By every account, Edgefield District had been far and away the most unregenerate and bloody-minded in the Carolinas, leading the South in pro-slavery violence and secessionist vendettas, feuds, duels, lynchings, grievous bodily assaults, and common murders.

Edgar Watson's father, it appeared, had gone off to the "War of Northern Aggression" as a common soldier, which suggested that he had fallen from the landed gentry. Three years later, still a private, he was mustered out of the Confederate Army, by which time he apparently had lost the last of his property and inheritance. From Herlong's account, it was easy to infer that Lige Watson had been touchy, full of rage, and more likely than most to re-sent the freed blacks who were now his peers. And as a drinker, Lucius sup-posed, he might well have taken out his hatreds and frustrations on the hide of his young son who, according to Granny Ellen Watson, had scavenged the family food throughout the War while receiving only rudimentary school-ing. Even after the War, jobs had been scarce, child labor cheap, and the fam-ily poor and desperate, and the boy had toiled from dawn to dark at the whim of some dirt farmer's stick. Her son's travail and punishment had only been intensified by the return of the distempered father.

In the shadowed wake of war, its soil exhausted, the Southern countryside lay mortified beneath its shroud of anarchy and dust. And how much more galling Reconstruction must have seemed to an impoverished war veteran, for even in his reduced circumstances, Lige Watson would retain those grandiose ideas of Southern honor and the Great Lost Cause which would fire the bigotry of the meanest redneck for decades to come.

Throughout this dissertation, Arbie glowered like a coal. He did not speak.

Surely, Lucius reasoned mildly, the dark temper of this district had infected the outlook and behavior of the ill-starred Edgar, who had been but six when the War began and reached young manhood in the famine-haunted days of Reconstruction—

The old man whipped around upon him with a glare of real malevolence. "Dammit, you are just making excuses! Think I don't know what you are up to?" Gat-toothed and bristle-browed, hoarse with emphysema, Arbie yanked his cap down harder on his head. This ferocious elder might be rickety and pale, but he was no man to be trifled with. The glint in his deep eyes was now aglimmer, but his strong silver-black hair and rakish burnsides, with their hard swerve toward the corner of his mouth, asserted a wild intransigence and even menace.

"Reconstruction!" He was seized by a fit of coughing. "Mr. Ed J. Watson never got reconstructed, I can tell you that much!" He cackled savagely, hoping to give offense, but Lucius winced merely to humor him and continued his mild-mannered reflections on that dark period after the War when the Northerners ran the South, put blacks in office—

"The darkie period, you mean? Burr-head niggers in yeller boots, lording it over the white folks, giving the orders?"

Already, Lucius had intuited that despite that rasping tongue, hell-bent on outrage, Arbie Collins was an inveterate defender of the underdog, including—perhaps especially—the underdog of darker color. What infuriated this old man was any perceived defense of E. J. Watson. "Who are you to preach to me about Reconstruction?" he was hollering. "I was born in Reconstruction, practically! Scalawags and carpetbaggers! And after Reconstruction came Redemption, when we run those suckers right out of the South!" Slyly amused by his own fury, Arbie had to struggle to maintain its pitch. Within moments, his passion spent, a boyish smile broke his hunched face wide open. His quickness to set his snappishness aside, Lucius reflected, was one of his very few endearing qualities.

Arbie Collins, by his own description, was "a hopeless drunk and lifelong drifter," and Lucius Watson was coming to suspect—from the man's pallor and side-of-the-mouth speech and odd allusions—that a good part of his life had been spent in prison. For his arrival at Caxambas, he had perked up his worn clothes with a red rag around his throat like a jaunty sort of back-country foulard. Lucius was touched by this flare of color, this small gallantry.

"You're a hard feller, all right." Lucius smiled, already fond of him.

"L. Watson Collins, P-H-D!" The old man spat hard to fend off his host's affection.

Since the Herlong letter indicated that Edgar Watson had been raised in northern Florida, Granny Ellen must have fled there with her children not long after the 1870 census, when Papa was fifteen. The relative who took them in had been Great-Aunt Tabitha Watson, who had accompanied her married daughter to the Fort White region. By the mid-eighties, when Dr. Herlong's father moved south to that community, Elijah Watson back in Edgefield was already notorious as Ring-Eye Lige.

Arbie reached to take his clipping back, grinning foxily when Lucius appeared loath to give it up. "This Herlong knew about Ed Watson's checkered past, no doubt about it," Arbie assured him, "because Herlongs lived less than a mile from Watsons in both Edgefield and Fort White. Got some Herlongs in those Fort White woods even today."

Lucius nodded, intent on the details. Besides providing clues for systematic research, this Herlong reminiscence was complementary to an account of Watson's later life by his father's friend Ted Smallwood, which had turned up in recent years in a history of Chokoloskee Bay. Both brief memoirs had been set down nearly a half century after Edgar Watson's death, and yet—and this excited Lucius most—these separate narratives by two men who had never met were nowhere contradictory, and therefore more dependable than any material he had come across so far.

Returning the clipping to the old man, who was all but transcendent with self-satisfaction, the historian promised to acknowledge "the Arbie Collins Archive" in his bibliography and notes. Though Arbie would not admit it, the prospect of seeing his name in print delighted the old archivist, persuading him that he, too, was an historian of record, and that his lifelong pursuit of Watsoniana had been worthwhile research after all.

The two Watson authorities soon agreed that they must go to Columbia County to complete their research on their common subject. Given the makeshift life of frontier Florida, the chances of finding significant data by rummaging through old records seemed remote indeed. However, they might hope to locate some Collins kinsmen who might talk with them, and perhaps some old-timers who could claim a few dim reminiscences of the Watson era. But when Lucius invited Arbie to accompany him on a later visit to the house at Chatham Bend, which the Park Service was threatening to burn down, Arbie shook his head. "Not interested," he said.

It was understood (though they had not spoken of it) that Caxambas had become Arbie Collins's home. In the next days, the old man remained more or less sober, working happily to reorganize his rough data. "I been updating my archives, Professor," he might say, picking up one of Lucius's pipes and pointing the pipe stem at its bemused owner. Clearing his throat and frowning pompously, weighing his words in what he imagined was an academic manner, the old man sorted his scrofulous yellow scraps. " 'Bad Man of the Islands,' " he read out with satisfaction, " 'Red-bearded Knife Artist.' How's *that* for data?" Slyly he would frown and harrumph, pointing the pipe. "Speaking strictly as a scholar now, L. Watson, that man's beard was not real red. It was more auburn, sir. More the color of dried blood."

"Clearly a consequence of his inveterate habit of dipping his beard in the lifeblood of his victims," Lucius observed, taking back his pipe. He was having great fun with this bad old man. At the same time, he took pains not to feed an anarchic streak which flickered like heat lightning in Arbie's brain, and sometimes cracked the surface of his eye.

"That could be, L. Watson. That could be, sir."

Chapter 2

Murder in the Indian Country

Hell on the Border, *that grim compendium of Indian Country malfeasance first published in 1895, identified "a man named Watson" as the killer of "the outlaw queen" Belle Starr. Was this man one of those shadowy assassins who intervene in greater destinies, then are gone again into the long echo of history? Or did he later reappear as the enigmatic "Mister Watson," shot to pieces by his neighbors on the coast of southwest Florida in 1910?*

Edgar Watson fled north Florida in late 1886 or early 1887. In a recent letter to The Miami Herald, *which Mr. R. B. Collins has brought recently to my attention, Dr. D. M. Herlong, a neighbor of the family, describes how Watson departed their community "in the dead of night," though he relates nothing of the circumstances:*

> One bright moonlight night, I heard a wagon passing our place. It was bright enough to recognize Watson and his family in the wagon. The report was that they had settled in Georgia, but it could not have been for long.

Although there is no clear record of his movements, it appears that in the spring and summer of 1887, Edgar Watson sharecropped in Franklin County, Arkansas, continuing westward after the crop was in and settling near Whitefield, in the Indian Territory, in early January of 1888.

The period in Mr. Watson's life between January 1888 and March 1889 is relatively well documented, due to the part he may have played in the life and death of Mrs. Maybelle Reed, popularly known as Belle Starr, Queen of the Outlaws, whose multicolored myth has generated endless articles and books, poems, plays and films, to the present day. Because Belle Starr's murder in the Indian Territory on February 3, 1889, was attributed only six years after the event to a man named Watson, this name appears in the closing pages of most (but not all) of her numerous biographies, despite many doubts as to the true identity of the real killer.

In the federal archives at Fort Worth, Texas, is a lengthy transcript of the hearings held in U.S. Court at Fort Smith, Arkansas, in late February and early March of 1889, to determine if there was sufficient evidence of his guilt to bring "Edgar A. Watson" before a grand jury on the charge of murder. From this transcript, together with reports from the local newspapers, and also some speculative testimony winnowed from the exhaustive literature on the life and death of Maybelle Reed, I have ascertained beyond the smallest doubt that "the man named Watson" accused in Oklahoma was the man gunned down in Florida two decades later. Whether or not he was the "Man Who Killed Belle Starr" may never be known, but it should be noted that many of her acquaintances disliked the victim, and that almost as many were suspected of her death by her various authors.

*

Additional material from the Indian Country is taken from rough notes taken by Mr. R. B. Collins, who has made a lifelong avocation of his distant kinsman.

I went out to eastern Oklahoma in the winter of 1940, about fifty years after the February when Belle was killed. That part of the old Indian Nations is mud river and small dark gravelly buttes, hard-patched with snow—very lonely flat high bare brown country broken here and there by river bluffs, swamp forest, rock ridge, and windswept barren farms. The nearest community to where Edgar Watson lived was Hoyt, south of the highway, on a bluff on the Canadian River. I rapped on the door of the only house with a thin smoke from the chimney and inquired if I might ask a few questions.

Ask 'em, then!

This old feller makes me shout my questions through a glass storm door that would hold out a tornado. No matter what I ask him, he shouts back at me, "Shit, no!"

"Shit, no!" he hollers. "This damn place is named for a old Injun used to farm it. Hoyt Bottom! Belle Starr got killed over yonder under the mountain, by Frog Hoyt's place! Shit, no, you cain't find it! Ain't even a road out there no more! Be knee-deep in mud and water, just gettin near to it!

"Shit no. Ain't nobody knows who killed her! I'm just tellin you where she got killed at! What? Shit, no! Ain't never heard of him!"

Next, I tracked down this old widow who owns Belle's cabin site above Younger's Bend, on the north side of the Canadian. This widow has no storm door, only a rusty screen, but she won't open up for love nor money, never mind that I could walk right through it. The widow says she's been down sick so she won't let me on the property, but before I can reason with her, she decides she trusts me; if I will pay her one dollar up front, I can go trespass on her historical-type property, with a look at her old photo of Belle thrown in. The photo was kind of hazy through that rusty screen, but it sure looked like the same one you can see in every book and article ever written about Belle—egret plume hat, pearl-handled guns, and a face that would stop the Mississippi, as the old folks said.

When I shook my head over Belle's dead dog appearance, the widow thought I might be losing interest, so she told me I could take a gander at a picture of herself—the way she looked "back then," she says, meaning back in Belle's time, from the look of her. Says, "Thet's me settin right thy-ar with my hy-ar fuzzed up, way I'm s'posed to look!" Between the widow before and the widow after, there wasn't really all that much to choose.

"Now," says she, "you go on down yonder under the mountain till you see a real purty yeller trailer, and a real purty brick ranchette up in the holler, and you foller that road up to where them trespissers has destructed our iron gate." I did as she bid me and sure enough, the iron gate is face down in the mud. A path goes east along the ridge to a fenced grave in a hackberry grove that overlooks the river, which flows down around under the mountain. There's no cabin up at Belle's place anymore, and not one brick or broken bottle left to steal, which made me wonder why that widow was so nervous about trespissers. Course a body can't be too careful around strangers.

The river has been dammed since Watson's time. The dam must kill fish in the turbines, because ten or more bald eagles were flapping up and down the river or setting in the winter trees. That's a lot more eagles in one place than I have seen anywhere since a boy, and it sure did my heart good to see them. I had figured they were mostly gone out of America.

Here's the opinion of the latest book on Belle at the nearest library, which turned out to be about sixty miles east, on over the state line at Fort Smith, Arkansas:

"The case against Watson was exceedingly weak, only Jim Starr seeming anxious to secure an indictment of murder. Belle's son, Ed Reed, refused to testify against Watson, saying he knew nothing against the man, and neighbors of Watson testified that the accused was a quiet, hardworking man of refinement and education, well-liked, and never before in trouble of any kind."

If you will believe that, Professor, you will believe anything!

(signed) R. B. Collins

*

What can we conclude about his years on the frontier, apart from the widespread allegation that Watson was the "Man Who Killed Belle Starr"? At least three of Mrs. Starr's biographers declare that after his departure from Oklahoma, the same Watson was convicted of horse theft in Arkansas and sentenced to fifteen years in the penitentiary, and that he was killed while resisting recapture after an escape. (Here as elsewhere they follow the lead of Hell on the Border, *first published within a few years of the events, and considerably more accurate than many of the subsequent accounts, despite its report of Watson's death.)*

Watson's destination after his escape from the penitentiary remains unknown, though he later related to his friend Ted Smallwood at Chokoloskee that he headed west to Oregon, where he was set upon by enemies in a night raid on his cabin. Obliged to take a life, possibly two, he fled back east. Another account asserts that Watson, on his way to Oklahoma, passed through Georgia, where he killed three men in a fracas. Like the many false rumors from south Florida—including the allegation that he murdered the Audubon warden Guy Bradley in 1905—these seem to be "tall tales" unsupported by known evidence or even anecdotes within the family.

Ed Watson reappears in Florida in the early nineties, in a shooting at Arcadia in which, by his own account (as reported by Ted Smallwood), he slew a "bad actor" named Quinn Bass. In the rough frontier justice of that period, our subject was permitted to pay his way out of his troubles, according to one of Belle Starr's hagiographers, who asserts that "a mob stormed the [Arcadia] jail, determined to have Watson, but the sheriff beat them off."

As Ted Smallwood recalls in his brief memoir:

Watson said Bass had a fellow down whittling on him with his knife and Watson told Bass to stop; he had worked on the man enough and Bass got loose and came towards him and he begin putting the .38 S+W bullets into Bass and shot him down.

In a different account:

Watson and Bass, another outlaw, became involved in a dispute over the spoils of a marauding expedition, and Bass was shot through the neck.

Though Watson is rarely identified as an "outlaw," it should be noted that in those days, range wars and cattle rustling and general mayhem were rife in De Soto County, and gunmen and bushwhackers from the West found steady work. It is also true that Watson turned up at Chokoloskee Bay not long thereafter with enough money to buy a schooner, despite his alleged recompense to the Bass family. Considering that he was penniless when sent to the penitentiary and had no known employment after his escape, it is difficult to imagine where that money came from.

In his first years in southwest Florida, while establishing his plantation at Chatham Bend, Watson assaulted Adolphus Santini of Chokoloskee in an altercation in a Key West auction house, and this knife attack, which did not prove fatal, was also taken care of with a money settlement considered very substantial for that period. Again, our subject's source of funds, after long years as a fugitive remains unexplained. One cannot dismiss the possibility that from the time of his prison escape in Arkansas until the time he took refuge in the Ten Thousand Islands, E. J. Watson made his living as an outlaw.

Withlacoochee

Until his final summer on the Bend, when he was twenty, Lucius Watson had never perceived his father as other than a bold choleric man, abounding in energy and generosity, good humor and intelligence, more instinctive with crops and farm animals, work boats and tools, than any other man in all the Islands. Even today he felt haunted and constrained by that powerful human being he called Papa, the doomed man he had seen for the last time in September of 1910, waving somberly from the riverbank at Chatham Bend. But as his biographer, he understood that his task must be to set aside love and admiration and reconstitute a more objective figure, much as a paleontologist might re-create some ancient creature from scattered shards of bone, pieced together on a rickety armature of theory. Mistrusting the warp of his own memory, he hoped to collect the more critical fragments of the "truth" from the common ground in the testimonies of his subject's friends and enemies, retaining those which seemed consistent with the few known facts.

In the popular accounts (and there were very few others), the material was largely speculative as well as sparse. Most stories about Edgar Watson related to his last decade in southwest Florida, with which Lucius himself was already familiar. There was virtually no mention of South Carolina, where Papa had spent his boyhood and early youth, nor even of north Florida, where he would live well into early manhood, marry all three of his wives, and spend almost half of his entire life.

To judge from his own correspondence with the last Watsons in Clouds Creek, his father's branch of that large Carolina clan was all but forgotten now in Edgefield County. As for Fort White, the Collins cousins went knife-mouthed at the very mention of Uncle Edgar, and tracking down the last few scattered elders who might still hoard a few poor scraps of information was a poor alternative, since in Papa's day, these hinterlands had been little more than frontier wilderness, with meager literacy and without the libraries and public records already available in less benighted regions. As in southwest Florida, much local lore, with its blood and grit and smells, had simply vanished.

The biographer's difficulties were made worse by the immense false record—"the Watson myth"—and also by the failure to correct that record on the part of the subject's family and descendants, whose reluctance to come to his defense by testifying to the positive aspects of his character was surely one reason why his evil reputation had been so exaggerated. In the absence of family affirmation of that warmth and generosity for which E. J. Watson had been noted even among those who killed him, he had evolved into a kind of mythic monster. Yet as Lucius's mother had observed not long before her death, "Your father scares them, not because he is a monster, but because he is a man."

Long, long ago down the browning decades, in the sun of the old century in Carolina, walked a toddling child, a wary boy, a strong young male of muscle, blood, and brain who saw and smelled and laughed and listened, touched and tasted, ate and bred, and occupied earthly time and space with his getting and spending in the world. If his biographer could recover a true sense of his past, with its hope and longings, others might better understand who that grown man might have been who had known too much of privation, rage, and suffering, and had been destroyed.

*

Driving north to Columbia County, Arbie Collins picked through Lucius's research notes, fuming crossly over certain phrases. Flicking the pages with a nicotined fingernail as yellow as a rat tooth, he coughed and rolled his eyes and whistled in derision, all to no avail, since Lucius ignored his provocations, scanning the citrus and broad cattle country as they drove along.

" 'We cannot make an innocent man out of a guilty one!' " Arbie declaimed, slapping Lucius's notes down on his kneecaps. "Well, you're sure trying! 'E. J. Watson was known from Tampa to Key West as the finest farmer who ever lived in the Ten Thousand Islands'—*that's* what he is known for?!" Moments later, he burst out, "You're saving that house as a state monument to Pioneer Ed?" He was actually yelling. "All that house has ever been is a monument to dark and bloody deeds! As for the so-called Watson family which is supposed to help out on this land claim, some of them don't know they're Watsons and the others don't admit it, so who's going to help you?"

The old man hurled the notes onto the dashboard, and Lucius swerved the old car onto the shoulder as a few pages wafted out the window. He jumped out and chased down his work as Arbie poked his head out, yelling after him, "You're twisting the evidence to make it look like your father never hurt a fly! Well, take it from me, the man was a killer!"

Out of breath, Lucius got back into the cab. "Don't toss my work around like that, all right?"

"I know what I'm talking about! You don't! Have you ever *seen* anyone killed? It's not pretty, goddammit! It's terrible and scary! And once you've seen it—and heard it, yes, and *smelled* it!—it's not so easy to make some kind of a romantic hero of the killer, I can tell you that!"

The old man turned away from him, taking refuge in some loose pages of notes on Lucius's conversations with the attorney. "Watson Dyer!" he said, disgusted. "Jesus H. Christ!" He looked up. "I know how much you loved your father, Lucius, and I sure am sorry, but there's no way you can write your way around the man he was!"

*

Before their departure for Columbia County, Attorney Dyer had telephoned to say that court hearings on the Watson claim had been scheduled for the following week at Homestead. He also mentioned, not quite casually, that one of his "major accounts" was United Sugar, a huge agricultural conglomerate near Lake Okeechobee, and that this company had recently discovered that the first cane ever planted in the Okeechobee region had apparently come from a hardy strain developed originally on Chatham River by Mr. E. J. Watson.

"I guess they 'discovered' that in my *History*—"

"They *discovered* this fact," said Watson Dyer, who was not to be interrupted when speaking judiciously, "in *A History of Southwest Florida*, by L. Watson Collins."

Nettled, Lucius had to wonder if Dyer himself had not pointed the sugar people to the reference. He had already told him that during World War I, his friend Rob Storter and Rob's brother-in-law Harry McGill had grubbed out a mess of cuttings from old cane on Chatham Bend and run a boatload up the Calusa Hatchee to Lake Okeechobee and across to Moore Haven, where Big Sugar, as the industry became known, would have an auspicious start a few years later. Thus it seemed likely, he told Dyer, that the strain developed by

E. J. Watson had provided the seed cane for all those green square miles at Okeechobee—

"That's what your history claims, all right," Dyer interrupted. And if this claim was true, United Sugar stood ready to help in the promotion of the Watson Place as a state monument.

Lucius's pleasure in this news was tainted almost immediately by misgivings. When the Hurricane of '26 had broken down the Okeechobee dikes and drowned over a hundred souls around Moore Haven, church voices had been raised on high to blame the devastation on the curse of "Emperor" Watson, whose cane was doubtless "steeped in human blood." Even today, there were people who would say (and Lucius considered this out loud when Dyer remained silent) that cane plantations were accursed—no blessing but an abomination, notorious for the dreadful living conditions and misery of their field workers and the cause of widespread chemical pollution. To help Big Sugar grow ever more obese, no matter the cost to common citizens, the federal government was abetting the state in its rampant draining of the Glades, including the construction of immense canals to shunt away into the sea the pristine water that had formerly spread south through the peninsula from the Kissimmee River and Lake Okeechobee—

"Lord!" Dyer's bark of derisive mirth had a hard ring of anger. "Why don't we leave all that negative stuff to those whining left-wingers!" Dyer moved swiftly to his point about corporate sponsorship of Lucius's biography in progress. "Assuming of course that your book makes clear E. J. Watson's connection with the industry." United Sugar, he declared, was eager to promote any worthwhile literature about pastoral traditions on the pioneer plantations of the nineteenth century, so a book by a well-known historian that mentioned the prominence of sugarcane in Florida agriculture—why heck, that would hit the nail right on the head!

*

Setting down Lucius's notes again, the old man groaned. "I mean, what good is a land claim way to hell and gone inside the Park? Let 'em burn that damn house to the ground, if you ask me!"

Lucius ignored this. "Dyer wants to bargain for full repair and maintenance of the house as a Park ranger station or state monument—"

The old man stiffened like a dog on point. His burnsides bristled. "How about a *murder* monument? Big-time tourist attraction! First monument to bloody murder in the U.S.A.!" Unable to to maintain the huff and pomp of indignation, Arbie grinned. "Murder museum and snack bar! White rubber skeletons and black skull T-shirts, red licorice daggers! Maybe gore burgers and some nice ketchup specialties!"

But Arbie stopped smiling when he happened upon the offer from the Historical Society of Southwest Florida to pay for a lecture on the legendary planter "Emperor" Watson. Professor Collins's name, the letter said, had been suggested by one of their esteemed sponsors, the United Sugar Corporation, which had also agreed to underwrite his honorarium.

Arbie's worst suspicions were borne out. "They got you cheap." He slapped the pages down. "L. Watson Collins, Ph.D.! If it ever comes out, down the road, that Watson Dyer is your bastard brother—" The old man lifted his palm to ward off protest. "*No*, L. Watson, I cannot *prove* that your daddy mounted your attorney's mama. But I *do* know her ex-husband Fred has been hollering for fifty years: *That goddamn Watson put the horns on me!*"

Lucius was aware of Fred Dyer's claim, and his daughter Lucy had confirmed the story, confided to her by the late Mrs. Sybil Dyer. Nevertheless, he had been sworn to secrecy, which was why, in these notes on Arbie's lap, there was no mention of a Dyer son born out of wedlock.

"Course, Dyer don't want this to come out," Arbie was warning him. "According to Speck, this feller means to run for politics one of these days. It's bad enough being Watson's bastard without voters suspecting that he might have a crazy streak like his old man!"

Lucius turned to him at last. "How about me, Arb?" he said quietly. "You think I have a crazy streak like my old man?"

"Well, *I'd* sure say so!" Arbie yelled recklessly. "*Got* to be crazy to be wasting all these years trying to redeem a man like E. J. Watson! And now his bastard is slipping you right into his dirty pocket, and you so damn fanatic you don't even notice!"

"Why would he do that? Give me one good reason."

"How would I know! Maybe he wants the southwest Florida historian to clean up Watson's ugly reputation before the truth of his own ancestry gets out! By the time you boys get done with Planter Ed, you'll have all us dumb local folks rolling our eyes to the high heavens and thanking our Merciful Redeemer for that kindly old farmer who put our sovereign state of Florida where she's at today! Yessir, old-timers all over the state, reading this stuff, will repent about all their mean tales about him, and how they done him wrong: *So maybe Ol' Ed was a little rough around the edges, but so was Ol' Hickory Andy Jackson, right? First redneck president in the U.S.A. to hail from the backcountry! First of our good ol' redneck breed that made this country great!*"

*

They spent that evening at a motel camp on the Withlacoochee River. While the old man slept off a long day, Lucius drank his whiskey in the shadow of the porch, in the reflections of the giant cypress in the moon mirror of the swamp, deep in forest silence. The gallinule's eerie whistling, the ancient hootings of barred owls in duet, the horn notes of limpkins and far sandhill cranes from beyond the moss-draped walls, were primordial rumorings as exquisitely in place as the shelf fungi on the hoary bark of the great trees. And he considered how the Watson children, and especially the sons, had been bent by the great weight of the dead father, as pale saplings straining for the light twist up and around the fallen tree, drawing the last minerals from the punky wood before the great log crumbled in a feast for beetles.

Alone on the porch, he returned to that September day of 1910 when he had left Chatham on the mail boat after a dispute with his father. Not all of the story would come back to him—was he resisting it?—yet it seemed to him that the dispute had been caused by Cox, who had stood behind Papa that day, watching Lucius go. From the stern, rounding the bend downriver, he beheld his father for the last time in his life, the bulky figure in the black hat on the riverbank, fists shoved hard into the pockets of the old black Sunday coat he wore habitually over his coveralls. No, Papa had not waved to him, not in the warm way he wanted to remember. Nor was this really the last sight of Papa, although the next image to veer into his brain was not his father but a thing, a bloated slab of putrefying meat encrusted with blood-blackened sand, half-submerged in that gurried water pit on Rabbit Key.

Lucius drank half his whiskey, gasped, and shuddered hard, shaking himself like a dog shaking off water.

From the bare spring twilight came loud ringing calls of Carolina wrens. The urgency of this song from the forest pained him, and he sighed in the throes of ancient longing, mourning that bad parting. What was he forgetting? And why had he wandered so far from his own life in useless inquiry into the deeds of the lost father whom all his siblings were so anxious to forget?

He sniffed the charcoal in his whiskey. Perhaps he *was* being obsessive—that's what Eddie had once called him. Was it obsession when his father's life enthralled him far more than his own? He supposed that the ongoing search for Mr. Watson had become his solace for his life's solitude and slow diminishment, and he dreaded the hour when this quest would end. It gave continuity to his existence and even a dim purpose to his days. *Purpose to his days!* Ironic, he raised his glass to the great cypresses, but the glass was empty.

Sensing him, he turned to confront the old man in the cabin window. Arbie was watching Crazy Lucius talking to himself, watching him toast no one at all, raising an ever-emptied glass to the towering clerestories of shrouding moss and the night creatures and the black moon water.

Chapter 3

Lake City

In the early days of the Florida frontier, what was now the capital of Columbia County was a piney-woods outpost known as Alligator Town, after the "Alligator Chieftain," Halpatter Tustenuggee. A strong ally of the war chief Osceola, Alligator had been attacked by Tennessee irregulars on an expedition of "Indian chastisement," to revenge the Creek uprising against the settlers in Georgia and Alabama and the subsequent flight of Hitchiti and Muskogee Creeks into north Florida. (To the Creek people who stayed behind, these fugitives were known as the People of the Distant Fires, *siminoli*.) After the United States bought Florida from Spain, and the first pioneers rode south into the region, the Seminole chief Charley Emathla, living by the clear black pond at Alligator Town, was executed by Osceola for allowing himself to be bought off by the white men.

"Your Collins clan," the historian concluded, turning off the highway, "was among those early pioneers. They founded the Methodist community called Tustenuggee."

"Well, I never knew too much about ol' Alligator," Arbie admitted, peering out at the concrete oversprawl of strip development crisscrossed by highway overpasses under soaring signs of noble motor inns. "But I first saw the light of day in Columbia County, and rode up here to the county seat in a damn wagon. Lake City was a pretty nice town back then! Wasn't all this shit, piss, and corruption they call progress." Arbie sighed. "All the years I was on the road, I had this dream I would come home to this county, marry a local girl, you know, put me down some roots. It never happened. I never came close." The old man looked straight ahead again, contemptuous of his own sentimentality. "Just as well, from the look of the damn place, not to mention me."

From sun-glinted smog rose the billboard of the Royal Alligator Motel, where Watson Dyer was to join them the next day on his way north to Tallahassee. In their room the old man, high black shoes unlaced, reclined on the zinc green nubble of the spread while Lucius forced open a mean gimcrack window to air out the stink of sanitizing sprays and cheap cigar smoke. The old man had already closed his eyes by the time Lucius located in the phone book a grandson of E. J. Watson's sister, Minnie Collins. Asked to ring his relative, Arbie groaned and shuffled his shoulders, complaining that he had been interrupted just when he was getting off to sleep.

Lucius was still shy from the reception he'd received when he'd come north in search of Rob, decades before. To his relief, the voice cried out how much "the family" had heard about "Cousin Lucius" and bade him a warm welcome to Lake City. But when Lucius mentioned the purpose of his visit, his relative declared that even if he knew anything—which he assured him he did not—he would have to abide by the family decision never to discuss Great-Uncle Edgar.

"Look, I'm his son."

"So's Cousin Ed," the terse voice said.

"But Eddie was living here back then, he knew what happened. I never did know, and I'm trying to find out."

"May I ask why?"

A moment later, when the call was finished, Arbie sat up, holding his palms to his temples. "He may be named Collins, but he's a Watson, too!" He fell back on the motel bed. "They just won't talk about him! If you hadn't mentioned your damn biography, he might have asked you to the house, out of common courtesy, and you might have learned something!"

"I don't want to be sneaky about what I'm doing," Lucius said. "Anyway, I'm not ashamed of him!"

*

Since the library and municipal offices were closed for the day, they went to the Lake City *Advertiser*, where Lucius's ad requesting information on an E. J. Watson, "arrested for murder in this county around 1907," had failed to smoke out a response from the Collins family. However, there was one soiled letter, in smudged pencil:

Sir:

I suppose I am one of the few people still living in this area that knew Edgar Watson, having been raised in the same community near Fort White. I only know a couple of people that are old enough to remember much about those days and I do not know how well their memories are working.

As a small boy I knew the Tolens, the Getzens, and many details about Watson's reputation. The Betheas were our neighbors and close friends. I was too small to play on the old Tolen Team, a country baseball club. I picked up fowell balls and threw them in as the team could not afford to waste balls. I thought Leslie Cox was the greatest pitcher in the world. My brother Brooks was the catcher. They played such teams as Fort White and High Springs, and most always won if Leslie was pitching. The Coxs were our friends until all this trouble started.

Grover G. Kinard

Lucius's heart gave a small kick—not just that casual mention in the second paragraph—*Leslie Cox!*—but the replacement of Cox the Backwoods Killer with Young Leslie, Star Pitcher of the Tolen Team, pockets stuffed—as he imagined it—with a country boy's baseball cards and fishing twine and crumbs and one-penny nails, in those distant days before World War I when every town across the country had a sandlot ball club, when Cy Young, Ty Cobb, and Smoky Joe Wood were the nation's heroes. Leslie Cox, whiffling fastballs past thunderstruck yokels on bygone summer afternoons, doubtless bruising more batters with his untutored hurling than Iron Man Joe McGinnity himself! The crack of a bat in the somnolent August pastures, the yells of boys and cries of girls and the dogs barking, all innocent of the workings of the brain behind the young pitcher's squinted eyes in the shadow of that small-brimmed cap, which was surely all most of the teams had worn in the way of uniform.

A postscript to Kinard's letter said, "Might think about paying a visit pretty soon, because my heart is not exactly on my side, the way it used to be." Lucius telephoned at once, and Mr. Kinard came on the line. After a few alarming sounds not unlike death rattles, he advised his caller that he was feeling poorly but would agree to entertain a visitor in two days' time. Oh please don't die, prayed Lucius. Keep that ol' ticker going!

He rushed to compare Grover Kinard's letter with the Herlong clipping. "Herlong referred to the Getzens, too," he told Arbie excitedly.

Edgar and Minnie grew up and married in that section. Edgar rented a farm from Capt. T. W. Getzen. Minnie married Billy Collins and raised a fine family. . . . Watson came back to Columbia County a few months later. His closest friends were Sam and Mike Tolen. . . . One day Sam Tolen and his horse were found on a little-used road, both shot to death. Suspicion pointed to Watson and he was arrested and jailed. There was talk of a necktie party and the sheriff moved him to Duval County Jail. He got a change of venue to Madison County.

"You've read me that letter maybe three times already, and now you're reading me Herlong again!" Arbie complained.

*

That evening he called Sally Brown in Gainesville. He brought her up-to-date on the biography, and told her amusing stories about Arbie, but finally he was defeated by her silence. "You okay?" he said. No, she was not "okay," Sally said, because she had to go back south and find a lawyer and talk to Whidden Harden and clean the rest of her stuff out of their house for the divorce. "Anyway, you sure took your sweet time before you called me!"

Why, he wondered, did this pretty young woman give a damn whether he called or not? Until now, he had supposed that Sally cared for him only as a friend of the Hardens, or because he was her professor, or because the poor thing, in her distress over her marriage, had shifted her feelings of affection to a "father figure" or whatever. A little perplexed, he said he was sorry, he had not wanted to presume—"Presume!" she exclaimed. He could not tell if she were weeping, but that she had been drinking was quite clear. He told her he was headed south in a few days—would she like to come? "You and me and your mean-mouthed old sidekick? I'll have to think about it." But she took down the name of the motel.

*

Watson Dyer, seated squarely in the lobby, turned out to look like nothing so much as his own account of himself over the telephone, a major in the U.S. Marines (Reserve) and an attorney "specializing in large-scale real estate development and state politics." And in fact, his bulk was clad in the big suit and damp white shirt that Lucius had always associated with politicians. He was a heavyset man but not a fat one, with silvered auburn hair in a hard brush around a moonish face. Strong brows were hooked down at the corners, hooding pale blue eyes, and the left eyebrow but not the right was lifted quizzically as if in expectation that whatever stood in his way must now get out of it. White crescents beneath the pupils made his eyes seem to protrude, though they did not. The eyes seemed inset in the skin, like stones in hide.

"Major Dyer?" Lucius presented the old man beside him. "Mr. Arbie Collins." Though Arbie was more or less shined up for the occasion, the Major's hairline was so crisp that Arbie, by contrast, seemed disheveled, and his red neckerchief, lacking its usual flair, made him look raffish, even seedy. "And I'm Lucius Watson."

Creasing his newspaper, Dyer considered this presentation before responding to it, as if how these people were to be addressed was for W. Dyer to decide. His eyes seemed to be closing very slowly, as in turtles, and when they opened once again, Lucius noticed a rim of darker blue on the pale blue pupils, and also a delicate shiver on the skin surface around the mouth, as if within, for his own fell reasons, this man was trembling with rage. When Dyer grinned, which he did sparingly, inexplicably, those delicate shivers played like mad around a snub nose (like a wen, Arbie said later), though these phenomena had little to do with mirth. It was almost as if he laughed unwittingly, perhaps by accident.

"So you're calling yourself Watson," Dyer said finally, heaving himself onto his feet in a waft of shaving lotion. Flashing the meaty good-guy grin of the corporate executive or politician, he extended a well-manicured hard hand.

"That's his name," Arbie said sharply, glaring at Dyer with such bristling suspicion that Dyer stiffened with a bearish grunt. Stepping forward to have his own hand shaken, the old man winked conspiratorially at Lucius, who ignored this.

"R. B. Collins," the Major pronounced in a flat voice, as if scratching that name off some ultimate list. Again the stone blue eyes closed very slowly, and when they reopened, they were fixed on Lucius. The Major took the historian's elbow and guided him toward the dining room, letting the old man fall in behind. "Let's not beat around the bush," he said. "The historian I'm sponsoring—the *objective* authority the sugar folks are sponsoring—is L. Watson Collins, the noted author of *A History of Southwest Florida*." He strode a ways while that sank in, then summoned Arbie alongside to enlist his support. "Now, boys, I ask you," he complained, "if a biography of E. J. Watson signed by the well-known Florida historian wouldn't have more *impact*? Make the most of a fine reputation in the field?"

"How do you know so much about his reputation?" Arbie demanded.

Lucius said mildly, "I've never pretended to be a professional historian—"

"Avoid any suspicion that the author might be prejudiced? As Watson's *son*?" Dyer raised those heavy eyebrows, thick as wedges. He leaned in closer as if to peer through Lucius's eyes into his psyche, taking Arbie's elbow in a confidential manner. "To answer your question, sir, I know *all* about him," Dyer said in a soft voice, "and all about you, too." He held Arbie's eye for a long moment. "A routine background check." He raised both palms to fend off any outrage. "Standard business practice. Underwriting a project, you first investigate the background of all participating individuals."

"Routine background check," Arbie exclaimed later in their room, rolling his eyes heavenward for succor. *"Participating individuals."* When Lucius suggested that Dyer might be bluffing, Arbie shook his head. "You think that guy's bluffing?"

"No," said Lucius, "I do not."

*

Awaiting a table, Major Dyer explained that yes, indeed, he needed affidavits from "the Watson Boys" to expedite the claim to the Watson property, and hoped Lucius would help in obtaining one from Addison, the youngest son. Arbie shot his hand up high like a schoolroom pupil. "What makes you think Bloody Watson *had* good title? How come nobody ever heard about this title until now?"

"Let the Major finish, Arbie."

"Let the Major *begin* might be more like it," said the Major, smiling shortly in an attempt at a fresh start. "Bear with me long enough to let me finish what I drove across the whole state to explain." Again he stared the old man down. "Once our claim to a life estate is established—which avoids condemnation, in recognition of a prior right—why, we'll negotiate for preservation of the house as an historical monument or whatever."

Arbie said, "What's the 'whatever' here? And who's the 'we'?"

Dyer winked at Lucius. "Well? What do you say? First, we get the newspapers to cover the Historical Society meeting at Naples where our famous historian, Professor Collins, will demonstrate that there is no hard proof that E. J. Watson murdered *anybody*! Next, we make a fuss at Smallwood's store in Chokoloskee, get signed petitions from the locals against burning the historic home of the man who brought the sugarcane industry to Florida—"

"Oh, Lord!" Lucius shook his head. "I never claimed that!"

"See? L. Watson Collins just won't be a party to a goddamned swindle!"

Arbie barked this impudence into Dyer's face, and Lucius, afraid for him, recalled what he had witnessed long ago on a bear hunt with his father in the Glades—the morose animal biding its time, then the sudden swipe of long curved claws that gutted the raucous dog and left it whimpering, in awe of its own blood.

Major Dyer's pale blue eyes considered Arbie. He said in an intense cold voice, "Tell me, sir, what is it that you call yourself, sir? *Arbie?*"

"None of your damned business—"

"Yes, sir," Dyer insisted quietly, "it is very much my business, do you understand me?" Controlling great anger, he frowned at his watch and whacked his leg hard with his newspaper. When the hostess came for them, he tossed his loose newspaper onto the sand of the cigarette-butt canister and strode ahead.

*

At the table, Lucius showed the Major the synopsis of his notes on the Belle Starr murder, and Dyer read the entire document while the waitress stood there, awaiting their order. He paid no attention to Lucius's impatience, far less to the poised pencil of the nervous waitress, but sat hunched forward over the table, mantling the papers like a raptor.

"A preliminary hearing in Arkansas federal court. No indictment. Won't hurt us a bit." He slipped the Belle Starr documents into his briefcase. "All the same, we have to scrutinize any material that casts a bad light on our subject—discuss, I mean, whether it's fair to put it in our book."

Lucius disliked the possessive tone of "our subject" and "our book." He wanted to insist, "*My* subject, and *my* book," but not wishing to seem petulant, he held his tongue.

Arbie sat arms folded on his chest as if trying to clamp down on chronic twitches. In the silence, he demanded, "What's in this thing for you?"

"I mean, it must be a lot of work," Lucius added quickly, annoyed by Arbie's rudeness, yet aware that the old man was asking questions he should have asked himself.

"Not a thing, boys, not one blessed thing." Dyer sat back in his chair to beckon the waitress. "Call it nostalgia about Chatham Bend, call it my sense of fair play. I'd like to see the Watson family fairly compensated. Mr. Watson was lynched, and his property was appropriated by the community that lynched him. Yet his title to that property has never been waived by any member of the family—"

"Couldn't waive it if they didn't know about it," Arbie snapped. "Or if it was never nailed down in the first place—"

"That's where I come in, sir." Dyer awarded them a self-deprecatory smile, then spiked the next question before Arbie could ask it. "No fee, no commission. The family won't owe me one red cent."

Lucius waved the waitress to the table. "Who needs a drink?" he said.

"No liquor served here," Dyer said approvingly. "Nice clean place. Fine old-fashioned fundamentalist family." He observed Lucius's dismay with satisfaction. " 'God is our Senior Partner'—they put that right here on the menu! I dine here whenever I come through." He smiled at the contents of the bill of fare. "Take it from me, boys, the cheapest dinners on here are the best. Deep-fried chicken, deep-fried catfish—they do it up real nice. Crispy and golden."

Lucius muttered "Crispy and golden it is!" But Arbie cursed loudly and stood up and left the table just as the poor waitress fluttered in to take their order. "What *I* need is a good hard piss," he growled, as she backed away. When Dyer asked if they should order for him, he stopped short and turned, cocking his head. "You talking to me?"

"Might's well get your order in," Dyer said. That this man was calm in the teeth of the old man's hostility was impressive, Lucius thought, and a little scary.

"Make mine the Cheap Golden Dinner," Arbie told the waitress. He moved away between the tables, shoulders high and stiff, as if ready to fend off a blow.

Having ordered his meal, the Major lit a cigar and shuffled through more papers. "Professor, you make it plain here in your notes that the outlaw Cox was the real culprit, that E. J. Watson was a solid citizen . . ."

"Yes, in his way—"

" 'Fine husband? Excellent farmer and good businessman?' You telling me now you don't mean what you say here?" He snapped open some pages and read Lucius's words aloud: " 'The great majority of these Watson tales are mere rumors for which there is little or no evidence. To those who knew him as a neighbor, Edgar Watson was an admirable husband and kind father, an excellent farmer and fine businessman whose reputation for generosity persists even today.' "

"It's not so simple—" Lucius stopped when he saw Arbie coming back. Arbie had sniffed out some hard drink, from the look of him.

"Listen, let me ask you something. In all those old interviews of yours, back in the twenties, you never learned of a single witness to even one of his alleged murders, right?"

"Hell *yes*, there was a witness!" Arbie interrupted, even before he sat down at the table. "His own son!"

Dyer contemplated Arbie until the old man evaded his flat gaze, looking away. Then he opened his briefcase and brought out some notes. "I understand from Professor Collins," the attorney began quietly, "that you claim to have encountered Robert B. Watson back around the turn of the century? That you were present at Key West when Robert Watson turned up with his father's schooner?" The attorney held each query until after Arbie had assented to the one before.

"What the hell's all *this* about?" Arbie burst out, louder than necessary.

"And you say Robert B. Watson told you some wild story about how his father murdered somebody named Tucker?"

"Wild story? Hell, no—"

"And you say you arranged for him to sell his father's schooner? And you helped him flee Key West on a steamer with what was rightfully his father's money?" He fired his questions at increasing speed, at the same time maintaining the dangerous, neutral tone of the inquisitor. "Is *that* your story, Mr. Collins?"

Lucius said, "Now hold on, Major!"

"Is that or is that not your story? Yes or no?"

"Are you calling me a liar, Mister?"

"No. Not yet." Watson Dyer inspected his notes. "So your story is that you aided and abetted in Robert B. Watson's theft and unlawful resale of his father's schooner. And after the only witness to the alleged killing—Robert Watson, right?—was out of the way, you covered your tracks by spreading that tale about the murder of these so-called Tuckers. Is *that* correct?"

Arbie jumped up again, fuming in disgust, as if reasonable converse with this person was not possible.

"Why all this lawyerly coercion?" Lucius demanded. "What reason do you have to doubt his story?"

"None." Dyer squashed out his cigar. "I have no reason to accept it, either."

"Go fuck yourself!" Arbie yelled, as the whole restaurant turned to watch him go.

Dyer nodded. "I hope our fellow diners will forgive that. Come on, Professor. If we can get him to admit there *was* no Tucker murder, not by Watson, then it becomes arguable at least that E. J. Watson never killed a soul! Then we can claim that there were no known witnesses to even one of the other killings attributed to Watson, all the way back to Belle Starr. I mean, it's possible he never murdered *any*body, isn't that true?"

"It's conceivable, I guess."

"It's conceivable, you guess. Well, that is how I intend to argue, in case the Park Service maintains that E. J. Watson's land claim should be forfeit or invalid because he was a known criminal in that region. And I hope that no Watson nor any Watson relative"—he peered at the door through which Arbie had gone—"would contest this. Should that occur," he warned after a pause, cementing his points as neatly and firmly as bricks, "then the Watson house which was to stand as a monument to your father's reputation will receive no further protection from the courts, and will be burned down."

The Major spread his napkin as his food arrived. "The renewal of the injunction against burning runs out next week," he warned, over a raised forkful of his golden chicken. He spoke no more until he had finished eating, after which he locked his briefcase and got up. He had to be "on the road a lot," he said, "taking care of business," but in two days he'd be headed home. "Where the heart is," Lucius said helpfully, trying to imagine a Mrs. Dyer and the kiddies.

"Most Americans have faith in that," Watson Dyer warned him. But as it turned out, he had no wife or children. "I don't lead that kind of a life," he said. When Lucius requested his home number, the Major said that his home number was of little use, since his work took him up and down the state. He scribbled the number of his message service.

*

Arriving next morning at the Lake City Library a half hour before it opened, they peered into the empty rooms through the bare windows. Lucius was startled by their skewed reflection—that bad old man in red baseball cap and olive Army coat too heavy for this warming day, and beside him, returning Lucius's gaze, that odd and unimaginable person—that tall figure with the leathered neck and big hard hands of one who had worked all his life with rope and iron, now garbed incongruously in the dark green corduroy and tartan scarf of a country gentleman or old-fashioned academic. A blue woolen tie sadly twisted to one side threatened to escape his v-necked sweater, and his gray hair, already on the loose, danced in a late winter gust that spun the flannel baseball cap from the old man's head and sent it bounding off across the lawn. "Sonofabitch!" the ancient said, sidling after it quick and stalky as a crab.

Lucius turned away from the man in the reflection and led the way inside, where they sat down at a shiny maple table. While the librarian fetched the basic documents that Lucius had noted on a slip, his colleague perched erect on the edge of the next chair in sign to all as well as sundry that he, too, was on hand to inspect the data. Arbie was fairly frowning in impatience, rearing around at the delay like an old inchworm.

To expedite matters, Arbie took pains to drop the name of his eminent companion. "Professor L. Watson Collins, P.H.D.!" he said.

"The Florida historian!" the eager lady cried. "And Watson kin?" The gentle question from behind his chair took Lucius by surprise, and though he nodded, she had caught his hesitation. He wondered vaguely how many haunted kinsmen had been here before him. His *History of Southwest Florida* was in her stacks, the librarian was saying, thrilled that a genuine historian was doing genuine research in her "under-utilized facility," as she described it. Even the custodians of words, Lucius thought sadly, were succumbing to the bloated speech that was driving good English clean out of the country.

While Arbie went off to explore the old part of the town, seeking some lost corner of his boyhood, Lucius spent that soft and warm spring morning ransacking the census records for the names mentioned in the Herlong and Kinard letters. In the 1900 census for Columbia County, there was no Edgar Watson, since Papa had not returned here from south Florida until 1901. But Aunt Minnie was listed as the wife of W.H.C. Collins (Uncle Billy), together with their children, Julian, William, and Maria Antoinett, and this family included Granny Ellen Watson, born in South Carolina in 1832.

In the same census was Samuel Tolen, the man whom (Herlong said) Watson had murdered. By the turn of the century, that peculiar household consisted of Tolen and Aunt Tabitha Watson, who had given shelter to Granny Ellen after her flight south from Carolina. There were plenty of Coxes, with *e* and without, but no trace of a Leslie Cox under that name.

The librarian referred him to an elderly custodian of local history, who affirmed over the phone that Leslie Cox had been a native of these parts, "as bad as bad could be. Led a bad life and got wore out, that's all. There wasn't much left of him by the time he came back here to die, that's what we heard. Now some of those Coxes were good people, mind, they weren't *all* bad. And his kinfolks took care of him later in life, they took him in. That Cox family once lived here in Lake City, so you might find him in our cemetery, if he's dead."

Meanwhile the librarian had scuttled away to tip off her friend, the features editor of the newspaper, who came at once in quest of "an exclusive" with the noted historian from the University of Florida who was researching "our famous local crimes." Together these ladies persuaded Professor Collins that a lively interview in the paper might well smoke out would-be informants.

Since he wanted potential informants to speak freely, Lucius did not tell the reporter that his subject was his father, emphasizing instead his interest in Watson as an emblem of the Florida frontier. No, no, he protested, Ed Watson was nothing like that sick Bud Tendy, now on trial for his life here in Lake City. On the contrary, he was a family man, very much beloved—"What? I beg your pardon? *No, ma'am! Not* a mass murderer! Not a common criminal in any way!"

*

Lucius wandered down old grass-grown sidewalks to the ends of narrow lanes where the oaks had not been bulldozed out nor the street widened, where the last of the old houses tumbled down ever so slowly and sedately under the sad whispering Southern trees. He arrived at last at Oak Lawn Cemetery, the town's last redoubt of the antebellum South. Here on thin and weary grass, amidst black-lichened leaning stones tended by somnolent grave diggers and faded robins, stood a memorial to those brave men of the Confederate Army who had died at Olustee, to the east, in a small victory over Union troops. Not far from the memorial, a dark iron fence enclosed three tombstones.

TABITHA WATSON, 1813–1905
LAURA WATSON TOLEN, 1830–1894
SAMUEL TOLEN, 1858–1907

Sinking down between the dark roots, Lucius contemplated the old stones, stringing new beads of information from their dates. At some point, the former Laura Watson had married the ill-fated Samuel Tolen, born almost thirty years after his bride, and he wondered if this discrepancy in age was not a catalyst in the family feud mentioned by Dr. Herlong. Had Greedy Tolen married Foolish Laura for her Watson money, inciting her Evil Cousin Edgar?

Old Tabitha had survived her daughter by a decade, tussling along into her nineties. Her stone—much the grandest of the three, as if ordered in advance by the incumbent—suggested that this durable old lady had managed the purse strings in the Tolen household after Laura's death. Presumably it was Aunt Tabitha who bequeathed her piano and some silver to Edgar Watson's wife, a bequest which Sam Tolen had refused to honor. Had his error of judgment cost Tolen his life?

The Watson headstones were narrow and austere, as Lucius imagined these women might have been, whereas Tolen's gravestone squatted low in attendance on the ladies. Great-Aunt Tabitha's haughty monument held no message or instruction for those she had left behind, and her daughter's read tersely, "We have parted." Sam Tolen, on the other hand, was "Gone But Not Forgotten"—not forgotten by whom, Lucius wondered, since to judge from the 1900 census, Sam's wife Laura had been barren, and since both women in his household had preceded him into this earth.

Had Mike Tolen ordered that inscription as a warning to his brother's killer? And had he suspected the enigmatic Edgar, who presumably stood among the mourners gathered here beneath these ancient oaks?

So rapt was he that he scarcely noticed when Sally Brown in a blue cotton dress kneeled down in the grass beside him. When he looked up, she smiled and threw her arms around his neck and kissed him softly on the mouth for the first time ever. Startled—as if a rare small bird had just flown in—he wanted to ask why she had done that. Instead he grinned a foolish grin and asked how she was faring, and also how she had arrived and where she might be staying, and how she had managed to track him to the cemetery—

"Professor?" She raised a finger to his lips. Open-mouthed, eyes quick and bright, long blond hair straying on her face, she was open and delightful as a summer peach. Unabashed, she took his hand in both of hers and snuggled this bonding of their flesh in her warm lap. The gesture seemed innocent and simple, yet feeling his hand against the airy dress, amidst the welling thighs, he fairly trembled at its implications. A cavernous groan escaped him, and she smiled. Her green eyes had gone demure and soft, and under his gaze, she blushed and bent her head as if awaiting some seigneurial decision.

Enchanted but anxious lest he scare away the shy bird of her undefended feelings, he dared to ask, "Do you suppose you will ever call me Lucius?" But realizing how feeble this must sound, he blurted abruptly, "Did the library send you? Did you see Arbie?" She opened her eyes to gauge him, then released his hand.

"I didn't come here to see Arbie," she said shortly, rolling easily to her feet and brushing the dead grass off her backside. "I can't think *why* I came," she added, tossing her hair.

"Hey," he said. "Sit down!" But when she turned toward him, he did not dare touch her, or know what to say. *Excuse me, Miss, may I brush that naughty grass off your sweet bottom?* He laughed out of pure joy and nerves. *Yes, Your Royal Heinie, it is I, L. Watson Collins, Ph.D.! Your revered teacher!* Aloud, he said, "Phooey," and got up awkwardly and brushed off his own inconsequential ass instead. He could use a drink.

"Phooey on yooey," Sally said, still cross. "You miserable ol' fart." Then she laughed, too, she had forgiven him. A moment later, she astonished him anew with her odd mix of eroticism and innocence. "These old-time people," she said wonderingly, waving at the gravestones. "You think they did it the way we do? Oral sex and all?" Though gratified to be sought out as a person knowledgeable in these matters, he was sorry she was so casual about such a rite. He frowned judiciously, saying, "Absolutely." Laughing at him, she took his arm and squeezed his hand, and he felt an unseemly twinge in his hollow loins as they returned down the old broken sidewalks, in spring dusk. Letting go his hand, she skipped ahead over the cracks in the cement. He shifted his trousers, yearning after the fine firm bounce of her behind.

Love-besmirched, he followed the young Mrs. Harden down old broken sidewalks, in the cruel spring dusk.

In the little park beside the pond, they found the old man dozing on a bench. A rivulet of saliva, descending from a cleft in his grizzled chin, darkened his neckerchief, and in his lap was a small flask of corn whiskey—OKEFENOKEE MOON *100 Proof. Guaranteed Less Than Thirty Days of Age*. It was no good chastising Arbie, who would only yell that he had "paid his dues in life" and could therefore drink wherever and whenever and whatever—and with *whomever!*—he damn pleased. Live hard, love hard, and die drunk—that was the boyish motto he'd proclaimed in a roadhouse bar on the way north, in a transport of jukebox sadness and vainglory.

*

The Columbia County Courthouse, where they went next morning, turned out to be a fat pink building overlooking the town pond, called Lake De Soto in commemoration of the great conquistador. In the county clerk's office, three female staffers were chaffing a young black secretary who had brought in papers from another room. "Where'd you get that new bracelet, Myrtle? You being a good girl, Myrtle?" And the young woman swung a hip and chuckled saucily at her colleagues' benevolent envy of her love life.

Awaiting these ladies' attention at the counter, Lucius enjoyed the titillated banter, which he liked to think was an auspicious symptom of improved race relations in the South. But Arbie in his saw-toothed whisper bitched into his ear that the young black woman was being patronized whether she realized it or not, that all "those three harpies" were demonstrating was that old white fear of black sexuality—"of what they used to call 'hard-fuckin niggers,' " Arbie said, not quietly enough, because the young woman winced as at a whiff of some bad smell.

Arbie wasn't altogether wrong, but neither was he relevant, and Lucius wished he'd left him back at the motel. The women's affection for young Myrtle might be patronizing, but it was real. When one of them asked if she could help them, and Arbie snapped, "I doubt it," the young black woman said coldly, "That the way you were brought up to talk to ladies, sir?"

And Arbie said, "That the way *you* were brought up to talk to white men, girl?" Surprised and stung by her disdain, he had struck back before he thought, and was instantly afire with chagrin. But when red spots jumped out on his pale cheeks, what the young black woman saw was rage, as bleak and unregenerate as Old Jim Crow, and she rolled her eyes on her way through the door to her own office. Arbie started to call after her, then stopped. A little hunched, he turned away and shuffled out into the corridor.

"*Well!*" one of the women said. The others glared, offended that the old reprobate's confederate had the gall to remain standing at the counter.

"I'm sorry. It's just that Mr. Collins—" He stopped. It was no use. "I'm sorry," he repeated.

Taking a breath, Lucius inquired about documents pertaining to the murder trial of a man named Watson, back toward the turn of the century. The women informed him in no uncertain terms that deputy county clerks had more important matters to attend to than private research on some darn old jailbird. Why should they nasty up their fingernails and perms (their tossed hairdos seemed to say), digging out old dusty ledgers and disintegrating dockets on behalf of rude out-of-county people who hadn't bothered to find out the precise dates? Were these people aware, one complained to another, how busy the county clerk's office must be with the case of the real live honest-to-goodness up-to-date and otherwise outstanding mass murderer Mr. Bud Tendy, who had best-selling books and TV appearances and the Lord knows what all to his credit, and was on trial for his horrible life right here in Columbia County Court *this very morning*?

Madison County

E. J. Watson's trial, Herlong had written, had been transferred to other counties, due to the threat of "a necktie party" in Columbia. Sally stayed behind to do some further research in the library while Lucius and Arbie drove northwest across the Suwannee River to the Hamilton County capital at Jasper. The grim three-story brick courthouse with its high clock tower where Lucius's father had been tried for murder had burned down in 1929, but the old brick jail near the brick cotton gin beside the railroad tracks was dark, high, and forbidding. Part of its facade was a closed shaft like a chimney which plunged from the eave gutters to the ground—an old-time hanging shaft, Arbie explained. "Kept the hangman in out of the rain, I guess."

"Today they'd call that a 'departure facility,' " Lucius said, thinking about that "under-utilized facility" at the library where even now sweet Sally Brown sat hunched over the archives.

Arbie laughed. "I bet that ol' departure facility gave your daddy food for thought on his way to and from the courtroom!" But chastened by Lucius's bleak expression, he turned away.

Finding no old records in the new one-story courthouse, they continued west over the Suwannee into Madison County, crossing flat cattle country of small blue pasture ponds under live oaks, abandoned phosphate mines, hog farms with old corncribs and silos, and small clear black rivers winding southward from the hardwood foothills of the Georgia mountains to the marshes of Apalachee and Dead Man's Bay.

In Watson's day, the Florida Manufacturing Company at Madison had processed more Sea Island cotton than any place on earth. Today, laid low by the boll weevil, the county capital was a tranquil backwater of empty streets. The old jail where his father had been incarcerated was now the Suwannee River Regional Library, across from the Baptist Church. Presumably the trial witnesses had been lodged at the Manor House, a pink brick edifice with white columns which faced on the small park in the town square where oaks as thick as twenty men bound in a sheaf cast a soft shade. In the park stood a blockhouse from the Seminole Wars, and across from the blockhouse stood the two-story brick courthouse where in December of 1908, his lawyers had argued on behalf of E. J. Watson's life.

The county clerk, summoned forth from an inner office, was a small quick man, thin-haired, squeaky. "Yessir? What can I do you for today?" Lucius Watson explained that they were looking for court transcripts of the trial of a man named E. J. Watson, accused of the murder of a man named Samuel Tolen—a historic case which had involved Governor Broward, he mentioned quickly.

"How historical would this gentleman be talking about, girls? Older'n me?" The county clerk threw a wink over his shoulder at his middle-aged staff, and the girls laughed. "1907? Nineteen-ought-*seven*? Well, sir, I was pretty young back at that time! My daddy hadn't hardly thought me *up* yet!" Hearing no giggle, he hastened on. "Excuse me, girls, while I go peruse them terrible murders we got stored up for our perusal right outside the men's room in the basement!" Mollified by a titillated titter from the office ladies, the county clerk went whistling off, not to reappear for three quarters of an hour, by which time that ancient archivist, Mr. Arbie Collins, had nodded off on a park bench that had somehow come to rest in the outer office.

"We got us a Edgar but we ain't got no Sam," the county clerk announced on his return. "It's *D. M.* Tolen, and it's nineteen and oh-eight. That close enough?" From behind his back, as if presenting a bouquet, he whisked a thick file packet stuffed with yellowed papers.

Lucius supposed that some earlier court clerk must have made an error. He sat on the bench, passing the pages to Arbie as he read them. The file included random scraps of testimony from a jury hearing at Lake City on April 27, 1908, and also court orders for changes of venue from Lake City to Jasper and from Jasper to Madison, together with sheriff's expense vouchers and subpoenas. Though Dr. Herlong had specified Sam Tolen, all these documents concerned the murder a year later of his brother Mike. Also, there was a co-defendant, one Frank Reese. Though neither Lucius nor Arbie could recall any such name in any Watson document they had ever come across, Lucius had a dim and uneasy memory of a "Black Frank" at Chatham Bend—could Reese have been "the Negro" mentioned in Bill House's deposition?

On April 27, 1908, in Lake City, Sheriff D. W. Purvis had opened the spring term of the Columbia County Court by proclamation.

STATE OF FLORIDA V. EDGAR J. WATSON AND FRANK REESE: MURDER IN THE FIRST DEGREE

IN THE CIRCUIT COURT OF THE THIRD JUDICIAL CIRCUIT OF FLORIDA, IN AND FOR COLUMBIA COUNTY, SPRING TERM, A.D. 1908. IN THE NAME OF THE STATE OF FLORIDA:

The Grand Jurors of the State of Florida . . . upon their oath present that Edgar J. Watson and Frank Reese, on the 23rd day of March, A.D. 1908, in the County and State aforesaid, with force and arms, and with a deadly weapon, to wit: a shotgun, loaded and charged with gunpowder and leaden balls, and which the said Edgar J. Watson had and held in his hands, in and upon one D. M. Tolen, unlawfully of his malice aforethought and from a premeditated design to effect the death of the said D. M. Tolen, did make an assault, and the said Edgar J. Watson . . . did then and there shoot off and discharge the leaden balls aforesaid out of the shotgun aforesaid, at, towards, against, and into the body and limbs of the said D. M. Tolen, and said Edgar J. Watson did then and there strike, penetrate, and wound the said D. M. Tolen . . . twenty-two mortal wounds, of and from which said mortal wounds the said D. M. Tolen did then and there die. And the grand jurors aforesaid . . . do further present that the said Frank Reese was then and there unlawfully of his malice aforethought and of and from a premeditated design to effect the death of said D. M. Tolen, present, aiding, abetting, conspiring, assisting, and advising the said Edgar J. Watson the felony aforesaid to do and commit.

Identical charges had been filed against Reese, with Watson as aider and abettor.

Most of the material in the packet concerned court business in the grand jury indictment and the trial—witness selection, depositions from county residents on both sides of the question of whether or not the accused could receive a fair trial in this county, courtroom disputes over lynching threats to the defendants, motions for and against a change of venue. Following the intervention of Governor Broward, who ordered the defendants removed to "a place of safety," they were taken to Jasper on the night train, and a change of venue to Hamilton County was granted the next day, May 4. The trial at Jasper commenced on July 27 and ended with a hung jury three days later. On October 2, another change of venue moved the trial to Madison.

All courtroom testimony had apparently been sealed, but a few scraps from an earlier grand jury hearing accompanied the court documents, including a cross-examination of Mr. Jasper Cox, who testified on behalf of the defendants on the day before they were removed to Hamilton County on the night train. Mr. Cox declared that on March 26, three days after the murder of Mike Tolen, he had been approached in front of the courthouse by a member of the grand jury, Mr. Blumer Hunter, who told him "he was helping to get up a mob to get these men and asked if I didn't want to assist them, and I told him it was out of my line of business."

Q. These defendants here are under indictment for killing Mike Tolen, are they not?
A. Yes.
Q. And your nephew is under indictment for killing the other one, the brother of Mike Tolen?
A. Yes.
Q. There was no charge against Leslie Cox at that time, was there?
A. No, sir.

With this brief exchange—the only mention of Leslie Cox in the thick packet—a vital piece of evidence had come to light. Edgar Watson had never been indicted for Sam Tolen's murder. Cox was charged with it after the arrest of Watson and Reese for the murder of Tolen's brother a year later.

Lucius stifled a small yip of excitement "like a young dog on a rabbit," Arbie grumped, reaching for the page. Lucius went outside to savor the spring light. When Arbie caught up with him, they crossed the street to the old newspaper in its single-story shop, which provided three contemporary clippings.

MIKE TOLEN WAS MURDERED ON FARM

POSSE FORMED IN LAKE CITY. HEADED BY BLOODHOUNDS. LEFT FOR SCENE

Lake City, March 23.—Mike Tolen, a prominent farmer residing between Lake City and Fort White, was murdered by unknown parties on his farm about 8 o'clock this morning.

News was immediately brought to the city of the murder and a posse, headed by bloodhounds, were soon off for the scene of the murder. The authorities suspect certain parties of the murder and it is believed that arrests will be made tonight and the prisoners brought to this city. Sam Tolen, a brother of the dead man, was murdered by unknown parties last summer. The trouble is the outcome of a family feud.—Jacksonville *Times-Union*, March 24, 1908

JURY SELECTION FOR WATSON TRIAL

The special term of the Circuit Court called by Judge Palmer for Madison County convened Monday. The term was called for the trial of a murder case on change of venue from Columbia County, the defendant being E. J. Watson, a white man, and Frank Reese, a negro, they having been indicted for the murder of one Tolen, white, in Columbia County. The case is one which excited the people of Columbia greatly, all the parties concerned being prominent.

The defendant Watson is a man of fine appearance and his face betokens intelligence in an unusual degree. That a determined fight will be made to establish the innocence of the defendants is evidenced by the imposing array of lawyers employed in their behalf. . . . A special venire of 47 citizens of the county was ordered from which to select a jury and at this writing a jury is being chosen.—Madison *Enterprise-Recorder*, December 12, 1908

E. J. WATSON ACQUITTED

Defense witnesses subpoenaed for the Madison trial were essentially the same as for the previous one, with some new faces, well over thirty in all. Testimony was heard from December 12 to December 18, when the jury was charged. On Saturday, December 19, jury foreman J. R. Lang read out the verdict: "We the jurors find the prisoners at the bar not guilty, so say we all." In obedience to the verdict, the Court promptly discharged the prisoners.—Madison *Enterprise-Recorder*, December 24, 1908

Before leaving Madison, Lucius telephoned Watson Dyer, who had asked to be kept posted. He did not seem the least bit curious about Frank Reese.

"The point is, your father was acquitted," Dyer said. "He was found innocent. 'Innocent until proven guilty'—that's the American way."

"Well, I guess so. If the accused is the right color."

"What I mean is," Dyer said, impatient, "we can assume for our purposes that E. J. Watson did not kill Samuel Tolen. And if he was proved innocent of one false charge, there might be others. So in our book we can say that—"

Irritated by that "our" without quite knowing what was so objectionable, Lucius said sharply, "Let me repeat. My father was charged with killing D. M. Tolen. Mike. The man indicted for the murder of Sam Tolen was Leslie Cox."

"Is that a fact?" Mild surprise rose slowly in Dyer's voice like the first thick bubble in a pot of boiling grits.

"It's possible, of course, that both killed both."

"Or that neither killed either. Don't go forgetting what's-his-name. The nigger."

The Deacon

Awakened next morning by diesel snorts and air brakes and the howl of tires, Lucius Watson sat up with a start and gazed at Arbie, who looked dead—as flat and scanty as a run-over rabbit on an August highway. His neck was arched and his hair dry and his bloodless lips were stretched on small dry teeth, and the parched hollow of his mouth was too wide open, as if at some moment in the night he had struggled for a breath of air and never found it.

"Today we visit Grover Kinard," Lucius told him quietly.

The cadaver sucked up breath and coughed, and one eye sagged open, contemplating Lucius. The dry mouth closed and opened up again with sounds of sticking, as a spavined hand went palpitating toward the cigarette pack on the bedside table. Finally he growled in phlegmy tones that he had better things to do than waste a day with some gabby old-timer.

Lucius was concerned because the Royal Alligator was way out here near the interstate and Arbie had no transportation and no driver's license—nor social security, medical insurance, or ID of any kind, as it turned out, since he did not believe in government meddling, state or federal, far less paying taxes. There was no record of him anywhere, he often boasted.

"How will you spend the day, then?"

"Hitch a ride in to the billiard hall. Good whorehouse, maybe. None of your damn business." Annoyed that Sally Brown had joined their party, Arbie wished to be courted with more ardor, or selected in place of Sally for this outing, but having already invited her the night before, Lucius merely shrugged. "See you later, then," he said, accepting a day alone with Sally as compensation for Arbie's evil temper later on. However, Sally was not up, and he did not wake her.

*

Lucius drove south from Lake City on I-75, turning off on the old road to Fort White and working around past the 7-Eleven store to the new Honeydew Subdivision, where dust-filmed woods—"alive with redskins," according to an 1838 report—drew back aghast from the raw scraped wounds of new development.

At the specified "ranchette," he was shown inside by Grover G. Kinard, retired deacon of the First Florida Baptist Church, attired in sports jacket and open-collared shirt. Mr. Kinard did not greet his visitor nor did he present him to his wife, a pretty-pink old party propped like a doll on the front room sofa, in a bower of pale plastic flowers, hand-tinted photographs of smiling children, and a small TV. "Oriole," Kinard said in a flat tone, without a glance at either of them. In timid whimsy, Oriole Kinard fluttered fingers at their visitor as the Deacon marched him past her sofa into her spotless kitchen. He offered no coffee, just sat him at the kitchen table while he hammered out on its linoleum just what was what.

"Yessir," the Deacon said, drumming his fingers, "I knew all them people, just about the only one still living that really knew 'em all to say hello to. There may be details I won't call to mind, but I'll tell you as best as I can remember. I can show you where Edgar Watson lived, and the Tolens and Coxes, and I can tell all about the killing down in those old woods." He jerked his thumb in the general direction of the pink person on the other side of the pasteboard wall. "She ain't a Cox but she's related," her husband said. Over the loud whoop-de-do of a TV game show, a sweet old voice from the other room cried out, "No, I ain't never! Leslie's grandmother's daddy was my granddaddy's cousin, but I wouldn't know him if I met him in church!"

"It looks to me like you only know about one killing." Mr. Kinard held up one hand, spreading the fingers. "Well, five was killed down around that section 'fore them fellers got done." Lucius got out his notebook, the sight of which made the old man suck his teeth. "My information must be worth a lot to you," he said. When Lucius enthusiastically agreed, the Deacon coughed, then got it over with. "How much?" he said. "Two hundred dollars?"

"Well, to be honest, I never thought of it that way," said Lucius, taken aback. "I mean, most folks *like* to talk about old times. I guess you're the first I've come across who wanted money."

Thinking that over, the Deacon squinted, not shamefaced in the least but ready to dicker. "One hundred fifty, then," he said.

Admiring his style, Lucius forked over the money. The Deacon counted the bills minutely before getting up and going somewhere to squirrel them away. Returning, he said, "Guess we can go then, lest you want coffee."

The Deacon introduced Oriole briefly on the way out. Her TV show had a patriotic theme, and its glad light spangled her snowy head with stars. "Be back later," her husband informed her. "Next year, maybe." Lucius grinned but the Deacon did not. He marched outside and climbed into Lucius's car. "Better take your auto," he said, once he was settled. "That old rattler of mine don't run too good." The Deacon's harsh cough and painful hacking were as close as he would come all day to honest mirth. He had a certain grim mean humor, Lucius decided, but his days of open laughter were long since behind him.

They drove south on the old Fort White Road to Columbia City, which the Deacon identified as the former site of a huge sawmill. Today this pineland had been timbered out and the poor woods were second growth and Columbia City was a fading hamlet scattered about an old white church in a grove of live oak. "Ain't but that one nigra church out here today. Had a murder in there three years back, handcuffed and robbed the deacon, put two bullets through his head." Troubled, he looked over at Lucius. "Nigra, y'know, but a man of God the same as me. Don't understand that one, do you?"

A few miles farther, a dirt track called Watson Road led off toward the west, and Kinard remarked, "That's all black Watsons. All these nigras in through here used to be Watsons. Good people, too, nothin wrong with 'em. This is their descendants, and a lot of 'em have different names, but they're all Watsons far as I'm concerned. Old Bob Watson was the grandfather, hardworkin little feller, maybe five foot tall, lived back over in there. In Reconstruction, his brother Simon got to be a county commissioner, but it was Old Man Bob done all the work, put that black family out ahead. Jerusalem Baptist, there back of them trees, that's their Watson church."

Had these black Watsons arrived with Tabitha Watson, whose daughter Laura was to marry Samuel Tolen? The Deacon, startled by the question, nodded, saying, "Wouldn't surprise me," and kept right on nodding. "That's right. Old Man Sam married a Watson. I clean forgot that."

*

The Fort White Road, straight as a bullet, shot south across woodlots and farmland, a narrow county road unmarred by signs. Sixteen miles south of Lake City, a pasture pond on the east side of the road tugged at the old man's memory, making him grunt, for he patted urgently at Lucius's elbow, pointing at a grove of trees. "Where you see that grove, that was Burdetts'. Old cabin might be in there yet. I been there many a time, and Burdetts come to our place. Sunday visiting, y'know, the way us country people done back in the old days. Our house was on yonder a little ways, where them woods are now—the old house is still back there, far as I know, grown up in trees. And this land you're looking at right here"—he pointed at the open wood on the west side of the road—"this was Betheas'. Young Herkie Burdett was courting a Bethea daughter, and he was desperately in love. We thought Herkie and Edna would get hitched. Next thing we knew, this man Watson came and married her. And a couple years after that, all hell broke loose around this neck of the woods."

The community had been disappointed that Edna hadn't married young Burdett, and folks were surprised that her father, a Baptist preacher, had encouraged her to go to Edgar Watson. "He must of knowed *something* about Watson," Mr. Kinard said. "Whole county had heard tell that this man was a killer, I knew it even as a boy. So folks started in to gossiping and wondering if Preacher Bethea encouraged the wedding just because Edgar Watson was well-fixed. Their neighbors mean-mouthed Watson and the Preacher, both.

"Course Betheas never owned this place, they rented from Sam Tolen. They were sharecroppers, same as Burdetts. Right in there where I'm pointing at, that's where it was. Ain't no cabin there no more, it was tore down.

"Preacher Bethea was dead set against young Herkie. The Burdetts were even poorer than Betheas, and he wanted his pretty Edna to marry better. After Edna and Herkie became teenagers, he forbade them to see or talk to each other, so they exchanged love letters in a big stump out in the woods, one going in the early morning and the other at dusk. Edna left cookies or cake that she had made, while Herkie would leave flowers for her in a jar of water. When E. J. Watson returned to this community, Preacher Bethea was not about to let that rich man get away, and when Watson failed to take his widowed daughter off his hands, he gave him young Edna instead, and broke her heart.

"Joe Burdett's field reached almost to our ballpark, which was over beyond where that feed barn is today." The Deacon, ruminating, coughed a good long while. "The Burdett boy was shook apart when Watson took his girl away to the Ten Thousand Islands. He just moped around, he never married. After Watson's death, Edna's brothers told Herkie she had gone to stay with her sister Lola in north Florida, and he just went after her, and he never came back. His mama never got over that, nor his daddy neither."

The old man sighed. "If there's Burdetts left around here now, I sure don't know where they could be. Betheas all gone, and Watsons, Coxes, too. Ain't many of them good old families left."

*

A narrow white clay lane led west from the paved road under deepening trees. "Turn there," the Deacon commanded. "That is Herlong Lane. Still Herlongs back in there, you know. The Fort White Road has been paved quite a few years now, but all the old woods roads are white clay, same as they were when Watson came along here on his horse or buggy."

Asked about D. M. Herlong, who had written about Watson, Deacon Kinard laid a cold hand on Lucius's wrist. "Wrote something about Watson? D. M. Herlong? Must been Dr. Mark. Mark's daddy was Old Man Dan Herlong, the first one to come here from Carolina, and he never had no use for Edgar Watson. Lived right here at the head of Herlong Lane, which runs west a few miles to the railroad.

"The Collinses still live in the old schoolhouse. That's back in these woods, pretty close to a mile south of here. Edmunds's store is out there somewheres, too. Called that section Centerville, but they didn't have no post office or nothing. Watson's nephews Julian and Willie Collins lived right near that schoolhouse, and his niece May was a close friend to my sisters.

"All along this north side was Sam Tolen's place, what was left of the old Ichetucknee Plantation. Them black-and-white cattle you see in there back of them trees is just the kind Sam Tolen had here sixty years ago, so what with this old clay road and all, it's kind of scary how these woods ain't changed. Most places in this county has growed over so much I can't hardly recognize where I grew up. Weren't near so many oaks, y'know, we had open woods and great big virgin pines. Today all them big pines have been timbered out."

The car ran silently on the soft track, under the forest trees. Spanish moss stirred listlessly in hot, light air. "Had a turpentine still down by the railroad and twelve–fifteen small cabins for the workers—hard work, too. Cut the pine with a hack, make a deep V-mark on the trunk, collect the resin in a bucket. They hauled that over to the still, made turps and varnish."

Soon the Deacon signaled Lucius to pull over. "See that road that's blocked by that felled tree? That's Old Sam's road, runs a half mile through the woods up to his house. I never seen that road closed off before, and I been around here all my life." He peered about him. "I can't take you up to Sam's house with that road stopped up cause I don't walk so good. I better give you the whole story on the Tolens while I got it right here in my head."

Sam Tolen had twelve hundred acres, one of the biggest farms around. Once he got hold of the plantation by marrying the widow, he called it the Tolen Plantation, and all around here became known as Tolen Settlement, and when our post office come in, it was called Tolen, Florida. Mike Tolen's place was about a hundred eighty acres, back over to the west along the railroad. He wasn't near as wealthy as what Sam was.

Sam Tolen was in his forties, heavyset, growed a big stomach. Besides whiskey and cattle, the only thing he cared about was baseball. He didn't play baseball himself, just got het up over it. Sent all the way to St. Louis for *The Sporting News*, mowed off some of his pasture to make a baseball diamond. Might been the one time in his life that feller gave up something for nothing.

At that time, Sam and Leslie Cox was friendly, because Sam had the baseball diamond and Les Cox was the star of our Tolen Team. And our heroes was Honus Wagner, Pittsburgh Pirates, and Napoleon Lajoie, who played second base for Cleveland, Ohio. I remember that ad for Red Devil tobacco: *Lajoie Chews Red Devil! Ask Him if He Don't!* Called that team the Naps right up until Nap left, did you know that? Ain't too many as remembers that today. After that they called 'em the Indians, don't ask me why. Folks had no use for Injuns around here.

The Tolen Team would go from place to place, and teams come here to play them, had a game every Saturday all spring and summer. America was crazy about baseball then, never thought nothing about football and basketball, way they do now. It's like some big leaguer once said in the papers, baseball was played by men of normal size. Every boy in America wanted to be a professional ballplayer, and every community that could scrape up nine young men had 'em a ball club, and bigger towns that could afford uniforms might find some horn players and have 'em a parade out to the field before the game. They played some grand old Confederate marches and some new tunes, too.

The Tolen Team, as best I can recall, was Les Cox, pitcher, Luther Kinard, substitute pitcher and first baseman, Brooks Kinard, catcher, John Livingston, second base, Herkie Burdett, third base, Gordon Burdett, left field, Sam Kinard, center field. Them boys played regular. Brooks Kinard was catcher for Les Cox, and when them two played, we wasn't beat too often. Luther pitched when Les weren't there, but he couldn't pitch nothing at all like Leslie Cox.

I recall one game with Fort White, they hired two ace players from High Springs so they could try and beat the Tolen Team, and one of our players went with Fort White because he thought that this time they were bound to beat us. That feller was the only one who got as far as second base all after-noon, because Les Cox struck out the rest of 'em as fast as they come up, and we beat them boys from High Springs ten to nothing!

Les Cox never minded throwing a few beanballs, and he could throw the hardest ball I've ever heard of in my life, so none of their batters stood up close to the plate. Just poked at the pitch as it flew by, got no real cut at it. We read all about Cy Young and Christy Mathewson and them, but we figured Les had the fastest fastball in the whole U.S. and A., and I guess Les thought so, too. Sam Tolen said it was only a matter of time before the major league scouts would hear about this boy and come to get him, that's how good he was, or Piedmont League, at least. Pay him a hundred dollars every month just to play ball!

As a rule, Les Cox was kind of overbearing, and he had him a hard and raspy tongue would scrape the warts off you. Being such a fine ballplayer made it worse, because everybody bragged on him. My big brothers Brooks and Luther and them other players, they admired him so much that they copied the way Les hung his glove off his belt on his left side, kind of like a six-gun. Wore it that way even when he was at the plate. Course gloves was a lot smaller back in them days, never had all this webbing and padding that you see today.

Les Cox was lively, made some noise, but he never had too much of a sense of humor. Local hero when we won, but when we lost a game, he couldn't handle it, so he blamed the loss on Brooks or one of the other players. Took razzing all wrong, and he done that on purpose cause he wanted to fight so bad, you know, same as Ty Cobb. Leslie always figured he weren't getting a fair deal, no matter what, and that give him a real touchy disposition. Folks wanted to like him, *pretended* to like him, because he was a fine-looking feller and a star, but in their hearts nobody liked him much, and I wouldn't be sur-prised if he was kind of lonely.

I remember one time Brooks and Luther and our cousin Sam Kinard, they made these little popguns for us, shoot chinaberries, sting like anything. And Les came along, and me being the smallest one, he just grabbed my pop-gun and got into the game with 'em instead of me. Oh we was mad, all right, but there weren't nothing we could do cause we was scared of him. Point of the game was to sting the other boys, not really hurt 'em, but when Les got stung, he got mad straight off, got too excited, and after that he was out to hurt someone and generally did. So that game broke up pretty darn quick, because Les Cox took the fun out of it, as usual.

As I remember Leslie Cox, he was five foot and eleven, maybe six. He wasn't extremely tall but he was muscular, weighed a hundred eighty or one ninety pounds, would be my guess. He was only about nineteen back then, but looked much older, and I guess young May Collins was just crazy about him.

The Collinses were a very good old family around here, had a fine house, had a big land grant cause they fought the Injuns and settled this section back in the 1830s. Them were the days when Alligator and his Seminoles was raiding our outlying homesteads, murdered and scalped all around these parts for seven years! Had to run them redskins all the way south to the Peace River!

Seems to me there was always some kind of fighting going on around north Florida. Spanish, Injuns, British, then the Yankees. And after the War, them Radical Republicans and coloreds tried to take us over. My granddad, he rode with the Regulators, Young Men's Democratic Club. That started up after Reconstruction set in—Tallahassee, 1868—and later it become the Ku Klux Klan. Had to lynch sixteen nigras in the next three years, my granddad said, to get this county straightened out and running smooth again. The KKK kept going strong, and they're *still* going, cause they got all the sheriffs and state cops right in there with 'em. Them boys had things pretty much the way they wanted, and they do today.

Anyways, May Collins's daddy never liked the Coxes, and he wouldn't have Leslie in the house, but Billy Collins died about 1907, so he was gone before the trouble started. With her father dead and her mother sick most of the time, Les come after May, he hung around the Collins house, and that's probably how he got to know Ed Watson.

Now Sam drank heavy, and when he was drinking, he didn't have no friends. Sam owned a lot of cattle, and they roamed all through these woods, because all this country here was open range. He would find some of his big herd near your place, and if he couldn't spot one or two, he'd gallop that big bay horse of his up to your cabin, riding him just as hard as he could go. He'd accuse you straight out of stealing his cattle, and cuss you out, and threaten to run you off the Tolen Plantation for good. He could do that, too, because the fields and cabins was all leased to sharecropper families such as Coxes. We owned our place, but all the same, he done the same to us one time, he cussed our family something terrible. My dad was off somewheres and my brother Brooks was hardly growed, but Brooks took a rifle and went out any-ways and stood right there on the front porch, set to protect us. And Sam Tolen just sneered at him and rode away.

Well, one day Old Sam tried that on Will Cox. This man Cox leased a cou-ple hundred acres from Sam Tolen, had a log house right here on the south-west corner of this crossing, there where I'm pointing at. Old Robarts house. Ed Watson was the one who fixed it up. Watson lived in the Robarts house awhile, then lent it to his brother-in-law when he went away to Oklahoma.

When Billy Collins moved to Centerville, Watson let Will Cox have it. Them two men were friends.

Now like I say, Les was big for his young years, and he had some spirit. Hearing Sam talk so rough to his dad, he went inside and got Will's gun and come out again onto the stoop and hoisted up that gun without one word. He was fixing to shoot Sam Tolen dead and would of done it, only his daddy seen him first and knocked the gun up.

When Old Man Sam seen Leslie with that gun, he turned that big bay horse around, he just departed, but he purely hated being run off by a boy. Folks heard tell of it and laughed, and from then on, Sam was spoiling for a showdown, never mind that this young feller was his own star pitcher.

Railroad was here where these two lanes cross, you can still see that old railbed shadow through the trees. Train come south from Lake City in the morning, come back north from Fort White in the afternoon. And right here, there was cross ties piled that an old nigra named Calvin Banks cut for the railroad company. And a few days later, Leslie Cox was setting on those ties when Tolen rode up drunk on his bay horse and started cussing him. He was threatening to kill that boy, which ain't a very good idea around cracker people.

Sam Tolen never lived long after that. He was riding along on an old road that used to cut across the woods from Herlong Lane to Ichetucknee Springs—it's all growed over now—and the killers was hid in a fence corner, behind the jamb where the fence rails come together. Sam rode that bay most of the time, but the day he died he had his horse hitched up to a buggy, headed for the Ichetucknee store for his supplies. He was shot maybe half a mile west of the schoolhouse, and the horse, too. Didn't want that horse to run off home, I guess, let people know that Sam Tolen was killed before the killers had the evidence cleaned up and got away.

Watson was in on it, they say. I ain't sure what Watson's quarrel with him was, but Sam's wife being a Watson, there might been some trouble over that plantation. Or maybe Les wanted an experienced man beside him, who is to say? But it sure looks like Cox and Watson got together and waylaid Old Man Sam. They say Watson got suspected in the Belle Starr case because Belle's horse run off, and people follered back along the road to where they found her body before he got his boot tracks all scratched out, so he swore that next time he would shoot the horse, make a good job of it.

His neighbors generally were not afraid of Edgar Watson, not unless he had something agin 'em, and nobody except Mike Tolen grieved for Sam. There was no evidence, and no one looked for none. We never knew for sure who pulled the trigger, but his own family always said that it was Leslie.

Some say Les's mother was there with him. Found small boot prints behind that fence corner, looked like a woman. Never heard nothing bad about Will Cox, but we heard some rough things said about the mother's family— all mixed up with Injuns, some said. And it sure looked like Leslie had some Injun from his mother's side, that dark straight hair and the high cheekbones, too. Maybe that revengeful streak come from the half-breed in him.

Before he got suspected in the Tolen case, Leslie and his cousin Oscar Sanford used to come courting our sisters, Kate and Eva, just set and talk with 'em in the front parlor. Oh yes, Leslie was in our house many's the time, we knew him well, we was good friends with him. He come to our house once or twice even after the Sam Tolen killing, but my mother and dad and older brother had withdrawed from him by then, he weren't welcome around our girls no more. Didn't arrest him till the following year, but everybody in these woods knew who had done it.

That's generally the character of Sam Tolen and the reason he was killed. Sam Tolen loved baseball more'n he loved people, and he weren't a saint by any means. Supposed to killed a couple nigras back up toward Columbia City, and they say Les Cox was with him when he done it. Anyway, that was the end of the Tolen Team. We had to ride over to Fort White to see a ball game!

Nosir, Sam Tolen was not popular, not popular at all. I don't say people hated him or nothing, but being so afraid of Sam when he was drinking, nobody was sad to see him go. Even Mike had trouble with him, but blood is thicker than water, so they say. At Sam's funeral up in Lake City, Mike Tolen finished shoveling and mopped his brow, then announced right there over the grave that he knew who killed his brother and would take care of it. In those days, with our kind of people, you might not like your brother much but you took care of family business all the same.

Watson and Cox had nothing against Mike, they probably liked him, everybody did, but making that threat because he was upset cost him his life. There weren't nothing the killers could do straight off, it wouldn't look right, so they laid low awhile, that's what we figured. Sam Tolen was killed in May, nineteen-ought-seven, and Mike Tolen was killed in March of the following year.

Mike's killers was hid in a big live oak used to stand here at the southwest corner of the crossing. There was an old shack all sagged down, vines crawling in the windows, and one of those fellers might been hiding back in there. Coxes lived not one hundred yards from where we are this minute, but their old cabin is lost today back in that tangle.

They shot Mike Tolen square in the face when he come to his mailbox on this corner. Our mailman Mills Winn from Fort White came down Herlong

Lane in his horse and buggy, and he found Mike laying in his own life's blood right where I'm pointing at. Must been about eleven in the morning. Mike never got to mail his letter, he still had it in his hand, that's what Mills said.

Down here a little on the west side of the lane is a very old and dark log cabin in a grove of big ol' oaks—see it yonder? That is Mike Tolen's place. Them live oaks is the heaviest I know of, around here. Probably them oaks was pretty big when William Myers built this house when he first come down from South Carolina in the War. Then his young widow and her mother lived here, and then Tolens. When the Watson women had the big house built, late 1880s, Sam Tolen had already married the Widow Laura, and he let his brother Mike have this house here. It was us Kinards took it over from Mike's widow. She was a Myers, I believe, come visiting her uncle, married up with Mike against her family's wishes, wound up back home in South Carolina with nothing much to show for it besides four little ones.

When we moved here from across the Fort White Road, there was nothing left in Mike Tolen's cabin but some old broke cedar buckets and bent pots, a couple of cane chairs, and some torn mattresses that the field rats had got into. Them old mattresses was stuffed with Spanish moss right off these oaks, but most people used chicken feather down or straw or cotton, sewed up in their own homespun. Made their own clothes so everything was scratchy, didn't have none of this slick factory stuff like I got on here today. Wool in winter, cotton in summer—that was all we wore.

My dad burned Mike Tolen's mattresses, and us kids was glad about it, cause with so much blood on 'em, they drawed the ghosts. There's blood spots on the wall right now that's been there since the day they brought Mike home. That's how bad they shot him up, that's how much blood there was.

Rat smell everywhere, that's what I remember. House dead silent and so empty, only bat chitterin and cheep of crickets, and the snap of rats' teeth in them old mattresses. A house can have bloody rape and murder, or it can have folks who live good churchly lives, but rats don't pay that no attention, do they? Gnaw a hole in your Bible or your daddy's body, just depending.

Anyway, Mills Winn drove all around putting the news out, his old horse was overdrove that day. Sam Tolen's death never stirred folks up, but down deep I reckon we was worried about having them two ambushers in our community. In killing Mike Tolen, they had went too far. Mike was a county commissioner and a well-estimated man, and when word spread, this whole section was buzzing like a swarm of hornets.

Old Man Edmunds, ran the store at Centerville, he was the most religious man we ever knew about, we never heard a cussword from his mouth. But when he heard about Mike's death, Mr. Edmunds hollered, "All right, boys, let's lynch them sonsabitches!" And my brother Luther was in the store, and he was so shocked that he turned to young Paul Edmunds, to make sure what Paul's daddy had just said. And young Paul being so excited hollers, "Sonsabitches! That's what Pa said, all right! Heard it myself!" And his daddy was so riled to hear that word that he run right over and twisted up Paul's ear and whapped him one!

So the people gathering, and the men carried their firearms, ready to go. Besides being riled up, they was scared, and I believe they was more a-scared of Leslie than they was of Edgar, because Edgar was good company and a pretty good neighbor till you crossed him, whilst Cox was a lazy kind of feller with a very very ugly disposition. They figured Cox was the real killer, but they also knew Watson's reputation, and reckoned both had took a part. Cox and Watson weren't afraid of anything this side of hell. All the same, they bushwhacked them two brothers, shot 'em down like hogs.

The Sheriff's men knew before they come here that they was after the same fellers that was already suspected in Sam Tolen's death. Leslie had took off quick as a weasel, no one could find him, but they found hoofprints in the woods, and them bloodhounds went south a mile or so to Watson's place. And Edgar Watson was at home, he come right to the door, though he surely knew they would be coming for him. Either he was innocent or he had some kind of alibi he thought would hold.

Come time to step up and arrest Ed Watson, there weren't no volunteers, nobody was as riled up as they thought, So Joe Burdett—that's Herkie's daddy—he said, "I'll go get him." My brother Brooks was there, he heard him say it. Nobody asked Joe to volunteer, he just upped and done it. Small fella, y'know, very soft-spoken and shy, seemed to hide behind that bushy beard that come all the way down to his belt buckle, like a bib. He never joined in all the yelling, but when he said he would go get Watson, well, they knew he meant it. So Deputy Nance called for another volunteer, and Brooks was so impressed by Joe Burdett's courage that he piped up and said he would go, too.

Them two went up the hill to Watson's fence, went to the gate, and Joe called, "Edgar, ye'd best come on out here!" When Watson came out, they had their guns on him. Burdett pulled out the warrant, saying, "Edgar J. Watson, you are hereby under arrest, by order of the Columbia County Sheriff."

Ed Watson took that very calm, never protested, but Edna busted right out crying, and her babies, too. Edna sings out, "Uncle Joe, Mr. Watson ain't done nothing wrong! He been home here right along!" But Joe Burdett only shook his head, so Watson said kind of ironical, "Well, then, Joe, I will change to my Sunday clothes, cause I don't want to give our community a bad name by going up to town in these soiled overalls." That's how Brooks Kinard described what Mr. Watson said and the way he said it.

Burdett was too smart for that one. He says, "Nosir, Edgar, you ain't goin back into that house." Says, "Edna can bring your clothes out to ye, but you can't go in." So Edna brings out some clean clothes—she is still crying—and Watson says, "I'll just step into the corncrib there to change, I'll be with you fellers in a minute." Well, Burdett was too smart for that one, too. He told Brooks, "You search that corncrib over yonder, make sure there's no weapon hid in there." And sure enough, there was an old six-gun, loaded and ready under a loose slat on the crib floor.

So Ed Watson changed his clothes out in the yard on a cold March day, had to go right down to his long johns. And when he was near stripped like a plucked rooster, he grinned and give a wave to the armed crowd waiting on him down by the road. Joe told him he could have ten minutes to instruct Edna what he wanted done about his farm, and Edgar said Nosir, that would not be necessary. If you boys aim to arrest an innocent man, he said, let's get it over with. However, he would sure appreciate it if he could just step inside the door so he would not have to kiss his wife good-bye in front of all these men. Burdett shook his head. Let Ed Watson get a foothold, see, there wouldn't a-been no Joe Burdett nor no Brooks Kinard, neither, because Watson knew how to shoot, he didn't miss.

Edgar give his wife a hug, told her to calm herself, he would be home soon. He walked down to the fence to where the men was waiting, and they lashed his wrists. Never turned to wave to that poor girl, never looked back, but strode off down the road, until they had to hurry to keep up. It was like he was leadin 'em, and all them fellers spoke about this after. Edgar Watson had some inner strength, like his innocence and faith in God would see him through. If he was afraid, he never showed it. And that terrible calm was what got poor Brooks to worrying that Mr. Watson might be innocent after all, he got to praying by his bed at night for his own salvation. But Luther Kinard told him, "Brooks, a guiltier man than Edgar Watson ain't never yet drawed breath, not in this section, so don't you go to pestering the Almighty, cause He got enough on His hands without that."

Next thing, Les Cox got arrested for Sam Tolen, but a grand jury hearing in Lake City never come up with enough evidence to try him, so they set him free. As for Watson, he paid for fancy lawyers, got his trial moved to here and there, and by the end of the year he was acquitted.

My brothers, they was in that posse that went up to Lake City to lynch Watson, so I heard a lot about it as a boy. The posse men was the ones most angered up, but now they was the ones that was most frightened. They had wanted to make sure Watson was dead, once and for all, and when he ducked the noose, and his partner did, too, they figured that men as ornery as Cox and Watson would be honor bound to get revenge. Both them men were on the loose, and they knew just who was in that mob that had wanted to see 'em lynched, and folks around these parts was very frightened.

This was early in 1909, and I recollect that long dark winter very well. Everyone in the whole countryside was on the lookout, cause those killers could show up any evening and drill the man of the house right through his window. So when the Betheas passed the news that E. J. Watson had took Edna and went back south to the Ten Thousand Islands, folks around here was overjoyed. But Leslie Cox had come back home because somebody had seen him on a January evening, walking down the road just before dusk.

One night when my dad was away, my cousins played a trick on us, prowling around outside our house pretending to be Cox. Luther Kinard grabbed one gun and Brooks the other. Luther dropped down behind the windowsill, he was going to shoot from inside the house, but Brooks run outside, cause he was the kind that if he had to kill a man, he would do it face-to-face. And knowing how brave this boy must be, coming right out after 'em that way, them two trickers got bad scared and lay down on the ground behind the hog pen and went to hollering, "Don't shoot! We ain't Leslie at all!" That was a trick that nearly ended up all the wrong way.

A year later, our poor Brooks took sick, died of consumption. I wept in the woodshed for a week. I often told myself for consolation that a boy as honorable as Brooks Kinard was too good for this evil world and would of died or got killed anyway, sooner or later.

That spring there weren't no Tolen Team, so Les Cox tried to pitch for Columbia City. I was going on fourteen by then, I was there for his last game, and it was just so pitiful that I felt sorry for him. Nobody wanted no part of Les but nobody dared to razz that feller neither. They just sat quiet, watched him fall to pieces. His nerves was gone, he couldn't throw nothing like the way he used to, the ball hit the ground in front of the plate or flew behind the batter or whistled high over the catcher's head. He was just dead wild, and nobody wanted to go to bat against him. The worse he pitched, the harder he threw and the more dangerous, and after a while it got so bad that his own team wouldn't take the field behind him. I can see him yet today, slamming his glove down on the mound, raising the dust. So that give Les his excuse to pick a fight, and he punched some feller bloody till they hauled him off, and still nobody razzed him. He stomped off that field in a dead silence, and he never come back once all that summer.

Les finally seen there was no place for him, not around here. He wanted to go to Watson's in the Islands but he needed money, and he knew just where to go to get it. I imagine he was still feeling humiliated by the time he got there, and when that feller felt humiliated, someone would pay.

Beyond there—that line of pecan trees?—is where the Banks family had their cabin. Ain't there no more, but I remember it real good. Two rooms with a small kitchen and the shed in back, same as all the cropper cabins. I seen that old house many's the time in the days they lived there.

The Bankses, they were black people, they were old people, and they were harmless people. Calvin Banks had been a slave for Col. William Myers, but he had been more fortunate than the average black man. He had a farm, he had about eighty head of cattle, he was a pretty prosperous old man, but still he worked hard cutting ties for the Fort White railroad. He had sense enough to make and save some money but not enough to take it to the bank. Carried his dollars in a little old satchel over his shoulder, and when he bought something, he'd take that satchel out and pay, and they give him the change and he put it back in, and people could see he had money in there, silver dollars and gold twenties and plenty of green paper money, too. Calvin Banks, he reckoned the Lord loved him, so he trusted people.

I heard my dad mention it a time or two: Somebody's liable to rob Calvin for that money if he don't look out. Well, somebody did that, robbed him and killed him, and that somebody was Leslie Cox. Killed Calvin and his wife and another nigra named Jim Sailor.

Jim was Old Wash Sailor's boy and Calvin's son-in-law, and he was standing on this road passing the time of day with another black feller named May Sumpter. While Leslie was over at the cabin robbing and killing, May heard the shooting and decided he would leave, but Jim stayed where he was, so it sure looks like he might of been mixed up in it. Likely let on to Leslie where the money was or something, and was hanging around there waiting to get his share.

We figured Leslie tried to scare Old Calvin into telling where his money was and Calvin wouldn't do it, so he shot him. Calvin Banks was maybe sixty, but Aunt Celia was older, well up into her seventies—she was near-blind and she had rheumatism, couldn't run no more. Might been setting on the stoop warming her bones in that October sun, cause it looked like Les shot her right out of her rocker, but some said she slipped down out of her chair, tried to crawl under the house. Don't know how folks knew so much unless Leslie bragged on it, which knowing Leslie, I reckon he did. Killed the old man inside, killed the woman outside, killed Jim Sailor out here on this road.

Maybe Les didn't get enough to make it worth his while to divvy up, or maybe he didn't want no witnesses. If May Sumpter had stayed, he would of been a dead man, too. Whole rest of his life, that old darkie thanked the Good Lord for His mercy. Folks liked to say that Leslie Cox broke off hard straws out of this field and poked 'em right into Jim's bullet holes, for fun, but I knew Leslie and I don't believe that. First of all, he never did know what fun was.

So Leslie got his money, and we heard it was thirteen thousand dollars, but others said it weren't but about three hundred. Course in them days a field hand got paid twelve to fifteen dollars a month, so even three hundred dollars was a lot of money. One thing for sure, Les ransacked that little cabin, cause I seen it next day, but they said all he could come up with was a metal box that turned up maybe two years later in the woods. Said it contained three hundred silver dollars. Had a tough time rigging it onto the mule, and the mule had a tough time, too, had to walk lopsided. Les told that part to his cousin Oscar Sanford, who told Luther Kinard. Course we don't know for certain he found anything at all, because there weren't nobody left to tell the tale.

Our family field was directly west across the Fort White Road, so us Kinards all heard the shots, kind of far away. It was late afternoon in the autumn, 1909, and like everybody in that section, we were picking cotton. We heard one shot, then another, then in a little while another—sounded strange. We all remarked about them shots, but decided some neighbor was out hunting. Not till folks passed by next day and found Jim Sailor laying in the road did anyone know them poor coloreds over there was getting killed.

Les Cox done his killing while we was in the cotton patch, and his cousin Oscar went right by us on his mule. At the sound of those shots Oscar turned around and headed back the other way in quite a hurry, like he'd left something on the stove at home. Well, that same day my brother Luther was putting in a well for Sanfords, and he stayed that night at Oscar's house, which was across the line in Suwannee County, and who should come by that evening but Les Cox, all pale and angry, out of breath. And Luther was pretty nervous, too, because he had been in the lynch mob and he knew Les knew it. But Leslie paid no attention to my brother, just jerked his head toward the door, and him and Oscar went outside to talk. Luther and Leslie played on the same baseball team, but Luther had no use for him, and later on my brother went over to the trial and gave some testimony that helped convict him.

So Leslie got arrested in the Banks case. And sure enough, a mob formed quick and come to get some justice. But a minister was present, and that minister put his arm around that fine-looking young feller, saying, "If you take the life of this young man, you must take mine, too." Well, nobody had no use for that minister's life, so some concluded that Leslie Cox was spared by the Lord's mercy.

Leslie, Leo, Lem, Doc Cox, and Levi. I believe Leslie had three sisters and four brothers. If Leo Cox was your friend, all right, but if he was your enemy, look out! He was like Leslie that way. Sheriff Babe Douglass took Leo as his deputy so's he wouldn't be out looking for him all the time, but somebody killed Leo off—one of his own cousins, come to think of it—and darned if somebody don't come along real quick and kill that cousin! My wife's brother, who's related to them Coxes, he claims it was Leslie who came back to revenge Leo, but that might be just my brother-in-law's idea.

I guess I knew Lem Cox the best. Big likable sort of man. Lem never looked for any trouble, just lived down along the river, built him a shack, bootlegged some whiskey, sold a little fish bait for a living. Worms, y'know. Everything he could lay his hands on he spent up on whiskey. Got by best as he could, then coughed and died. Before he done that, Lem persuaded his daddy into mortgaging his farm, so pretty soon Will lost his land, then he died, too. Later on the youngest, Levi, bought back a few acres, and I reckon he is on there yet today. Got cancer, last I heard. His wife is crippled.

Yep, Levi Cox is still alive in Gilchrist County. And there may be a sister that married a Porter still living back in what old-timers call the Clay Woods. And maybe Les still comes to visit her, is what I heard. Few years ago, his brother Lem told a friend of mine that Leslie were not dead, said Les used to come around there pretty regular. Lem said he knew where his brother was hiding out but would never tell.

After they killed off the Tolens, people wouldn't hardly mention one without the other, they'd say, Ed Watson and Les Cox, or Cox and Watson. But after Calvin Banks, it was just Cox, he had the blame for Bankses to himself. And because they was nigras, he might of got away with that one, too, except that people was dead certain that this feller had took part in them Tolen killings, so them nigras give 'em a last chance to get some justice. Even Leslie's friends turned state's evidence against him. Folks wanted that mean sonofagun out of the way.

Although Will Cox was good friends with the Sheriff from way back in his Lake City days, his boy was convicted for the rest of his natural life. Hearing that, Les got very upset. He told the judge, "You got no call giving no sentence like that to a young feller who can't tolerate no cooped-up life! I weren't cut out to make it on no chain gang!" Maybe the judge winked, as some has said, and maybe he didn't. One thing for sure, the judge give Les the eye. Finally he said, "You'll be all right, boy." That judge knew what he was talking about, too.

Les Cox was sent to the penitentiary for life and stayed three months. One day he was on the road gang out of Silver Springs, and it just so happened that Will Cox was there, passing the time of day with his boy's guard. The gang was shifting railroad cars, and it looked like one got loose some way, rolled down the grade for quite a distance to a place where Les jumped off and run. That's how they told it. His guard was faced the other way, never even fired.

Leslie Cox kept right on running and never been seen since, not by the law. Les went to his uncle, Old John Fralick, who lived over near Ocala, and John Fralick brought him home one evening after dark. This was before Les went away to the Ten Thousand Islands. John Fralick was brother to Cornelia Cox, and that old woman had a piece of hell in her. Will Cox was calm as he could be, but Cornelia had a terrible darn temper. When the Sheriff came to arrest Leslie for Sam Tolen, they say that old woman reared so high that they had to put handcuffs on her till they got him safe away.

There's plenty can tell you how Cox came back in later years, hunting revenge. Course there ain't but a very few of us old-timers left that would know him if they saw him, but he ain't been forgotten around here, neither. In the family that one of his sisters married into, there was a young boy, and one day him and I were standing around waiting for a funeral over in Jacksonville. When Leslie's name come up, this boy spoke like he'd seen Leslie not too long before, which give me the idea he was seeing him pretty regular, and not no ghost nor dead man, neither. And a little later, I was setting in the congregation when the family come out of the family room to view the body, and there was one man by himself that looked the size, the build, and the whole style of Leslie Cox. He glanced over the congregation quick, then moved right on through with the three couples. I fully believe it was Les Cox, but I couldn't swear to it, because it must been close to forty years since I last seen him. But nobody around Columbia County believed Les Cox was killed, and they don't today.

*

On the dirt road near the old Banks farm, in a strand of spring woods that parted empty fields, a killdeer performed its broken-wing display to distract their attention from two puffball chicks that fluttered and clambered, trapped in the deep rut. When Lucius smiled, stopping the car and trying to point them out, Grover Kinard stared at him, suspicious, then struggled irritably to shift and peer from the car window, not certain what he should be looking for and not finding it. His frustration seemed to sadden him, or perhaps it was his inability to comprehend why others cared about these inconsequential things that he had let pass unnoticed all his life. At last he sat back bewildered, saying, "They had something pretty close to that, other evening on TV." He pinched off some loose threads in his sleeve, as if otherwise he might unravel in a blur of synthetic thread.

In silence, in their separate thoughts, they drove back to the paved highway, where they turned south again toward Fort White, then west again on the Old Bellamy Road. "This whole corner here and down to westward, that was Getzens'. Getzens was some kind of kin to Old Lady Tabitha Watson, and I guess they was pretty wealthy people. Called him Captain Getzen, from the War. Captain Tom was a one-legged man with hair as white as snow, and he had a fine two-story house, over yonder under them old oaks. Them fallingdown sheds you see, they were his, too, and he had a nice barn that some people claimed Watson set fire to. They say his hair turned white the night that barn burned and he jumped out there on his one leg to fight it. Nobody could imagine how he done that.

"This Bellamy Road goes to Ichetucknee Springs. Used to be all kinds of wild critters come in to that spring to get their water, wolves and bears and buffaloes, I don't know what. Spaniards killed buffaloes down there three hundred years ago, same thing as bisons out in the Wild West, did you know that? Nowadays young couples take truck tire tubes, go floating on the Ichetucknee, in them two–three miles between the bridges; float along in bunches, bank to bank, drinking beer, y'know, a lot of hollering, make quite a mess." He gazed at Lucius as if to learn whether Lucius would join in this horseplay, given the chance. "Four miles down, the Ichetucknee flows into the Santa Fe, which goes to the Suwannee and on down to the Gulf coast, Cedar Key. Way down on the Suwannee River. Used to be oh so shady and so quiet, but now it's all opened up from what I hear, and motorboat racket up and down, morning till night."

The weathered oak and magnolia groves where the Getzen sheds sank silently into the earth now resembled an abandoned fairground, with faded signs and weed-bound trailers, a fake tepee, shacks, an abandoned bathtub, all of these in loose association with the Ichetucknee Slammer Express Tube Co., and Granny's Hot Sandwiches and Homemade Candies, and Beer Oysters Food and Game Room: Any Size Tube One Dollar. "Can't imagine such signs back in the old days, can you? Getting to be modern times even way out here in the backwoods."

Farther west on the Old Bellamy Road, pecan trees and wisteria in the hedgerow commemorated an old homestead now long gone. "I believe Edgar Watson lived in an old cropper's shack right over by them oaks when he worked as a young feller on the Getzen place. Later on he got hold of some good Collins land and built his house, right down this road a ways."

In a mile or so, they came over a low rise. On a hilltop on the north side of the road stood a yellowing frame house with rust-streaked tin roof, a big dark porch, and a fuel tank on the open ground, under the Spanish moss of a red oak. "Oh, yes," the Deacon said, "there's his ol' pecan trees. That's where Mr. Joe Burdett served him that warrant.

"Ed Watson farmed several hundred acres, and he was a pretty good farmer, far as I know. If he'd of been a bad one, we'd of heard about it. One time I was up there with my dad, William Kinard, I don't recall whether we was driving him a well or fixing his pump, but I do recall that my dad was not too comfortable when Watson asked him to come. I wasn't old enough to do much work, I'd fetch the tools, but I remember Watson, I sure do, never forgot him. Husky kind of man, thick through the shoulders. Later Dad told me that E. J. Watson was very very strong—*unusual* strong. He was pretty close to six foot tall, big pork chop whiskers, ruddy hair and complexion. Rode a horse and had a fine red buggy, too. Good-looking man, but not so handsome as Les Cox. Course he was older."

Yes, Papa had been very strong and somewhat vain about it. Past fifty, with his son full-grown, he could lift Lucius off the ground with one hand placed under one armpit—"You get smart with your Papa, Master Lucius, you might just find yourself chucked into the river!" He could almost recall Papa's body smell, the redolence of fine Tampa cigars and shaving lotions, the charcoal in the bourbon on his breath—all rose, mysterious, from the well of memory, light as the fleeting scent of rain on sunbaked stone.

"I don't rightly know who farmed this land after Watson left," Kinard was saying. "The paper company took over most of the old fields in this section. Grew pines for pulpwood."

*

Capt. Thomas Getzen had been deacon of the Elim Baptist Church, which they visited on their way to Fort White. The old church had been replaced and the Getzen name had vanished from the region, but the Captain and his wife and those children born in the first years after the Civil War remained the most prominent citizens in the graying churchyard. The Deacon's parents, William and Ludia, were buried near the Getzens, and so was his sister Eva and his beloved brother Brooks, who had perished at the age of twenty-three.

The lettering on the Kinard gravestones had been blurred over the years by moss and algae, and the stones had shaggy grass around the base. "My people ain't had a visit in a good long while," the Deacon mourned, scratching the dry wrinkles of his cheek. He scraped at the moss disconsolately with a small penknife. "Been too long," he said, giving it up. Without a word, he headed back toward the car.

The solitary Tolen in the cemetery was D. M. Tolen, 1872–1908. His gravestone read "How Desolate Our Home Bereft of Thee"—a shard of funerary irony, Lucius thought, which Arbie would no doubt enjoy, since Mike's widow and children had returned to South Carolina right after his death.

He turned toward the car. In the car window, in spring light, Mr. Kinard's bald head shone like a skull.

*

They went south a few miles to Fort White, where the county road narrowed to a shady village street set about with high frame houses in old weedy yards.

"I'm happy to see Fort White, you know. Born right here in town." Kinard pointed through the rolled-up window. "That's Mills Winn's house—the postman who found Mike Tolen's body. Dr. Wilson had that house before him. Dr. Wilson drove his horse out our way every day for weeks after Brooks took sick, but Brooks died all the same. That was in the month of May, in 1910." The Deacon sighed. "That spring, we saw that great white fire in the sky. Some thought poor Brooks had took sick from that comet, but I guess he didn't."

Kinard gazed about him at the passing street. "I ain't been as far as here in years, and it ain't like I lived so far away, you know. Eleven miles, is all! Never seen my own family graves since they was put in there! Too busy watching that TV, is what it is. Just goes to show you how life leaks away, now don't it? One day you look up, look around, and it's all empty, cause the real life's gone. You're setting there like you always done, but your hands are empty, there ain't no color left to life, and you ain't got no more hope of nothing—cept the Lord, of course." He turned from the car window to glare at Lucius, outraged, inconsolable, waving Lucius away in case he might try to comfort him.

At a makeshift snack counter in the grocery store, they ordered barbecue ribs with soft rolls and soda pop. They carried their lunch outside to a wood picnic table by the car lot, where three old black men hitched along to one end of the bench, giving the white men the remainder of the table.

*

They headed north again toward Lake City, passing the old Tolen Plantation and the pasture pond with its red-winged blackbirds where once the Burdetts and Betheas had sharecropped both sides of the Fort White Road. Still agitated by nostalgia, working his toothpick hard, the Deacon scanned the old fields and low woods, patting the pockets of his brain in search of something lost. "Yessir," he said again, astonished. "First time in twenty years I been back to my hometown, and I don't live but eleven miles away."

When the car pulled into Kinard's yard, the Deacon sat up and looked around him as if he'd been asleep. The names of the Cox sisters, he announced, had just come back to him—Lillie Mae, Lois, and Lee. Lee had married a Porter, she was still alive: "Let's telephone, find out where she's at, see what that girl has to say about her brother."

Entering his house, the Deacon went straight to the TV and turned on the ball game, which he monitored closely throughout the remainder of Lucius's visit. Oriole Kinard, eating a soft pale meal at her kitchen table, doubted that Lee Cox was still living, but she remembered whom Lee's daughter had married. The Deacon tracked this daughter down by telephone, saying abruptly, without introductions, "There's a feller here wants to know something about Les Cox." He shoved the telephone at Lucius. "I never saw Uncle Leslie in my life!" cried the woman's voice. "Aunt Lillie Mae, she always told us that the family sent down to Thousand Islands for the body and never heard one word back about Uncle Les! That's all I know, and everybody in our family will tell you the same!"

"Course she has to *say* that in case we're the law," Grover Kinard warned. "Comes to murder, Les is still a wanted man."

The Deacon walked Lucius to his car, making sure this stranger got his money's worth and would not come asking for any of it back. "Couple years after Watson died and Edna went over to Herkie, Edna's new mother-in-law, she took and shot herself. That was Martha Burdett, who was born a Collins. Then Joe Burdett married the widow of a man who was shot by moonshiners down Ichetucknee Swamp, and their daughter married John Collins, I believe, who caught her with another man and shot her dead. There was quite a few shootings in this county, like I told you."

The old man sighed. "Burdetts moved away and tried to run a store in Columbia City. Don't know what ever happened to 'em after that. Folks have gone off to the cities now, I guess. Just gone away like they were never here at all, and most of their farms are growed over in trees, same as our old place. Fine upstanding house out in the fields and now it's lost, way back in the deep woods."

Chapter 4

The Collins Clan

Sally and Arbie had made friends at the billiards emporium and pool hall, where the aged pool shark, dangerously overexcited, had his ball cap on backwards and his cigarette pack rolled up in his T-shirt sleeve. He gave Lucius a cool nod, rack-clacking his balls for the young woman's benefit with considerably more flair than expertise.

Sally sat with one hip cocked on the corner of the table, her cerise sneaker dangling and twitching like a fish lure. She handed him the interview with L. Watson Collins, Ph.D., which had appeared that morning in the Lake City *Advertiser*. Fecklessly attributed to Professor Collins was precisely what he had denied—in effect, the reporter's stubborn notion that E. J. Watson, "formerly of this county," had been "the Bud Tendy of yore," a mass murderer and maniac unable to establish real relationships with other people.

Furious, he left the place and strode down the street to the newspaper office to demand a retraction, though he knew that a retraction would be useless, and that any chance he might have had of cooperation from the Collins cousins was now gone. But wonderfully enough, irresponsible reportage had triumphed where earnest overtures had failed. Awaiting him was a crisp note hand-delivered to the newspaper which disputed the right of this so-called Professor Collins to his opinions about Edgar Watson:

It is very doubtful that you spoke to the Collins family because those who knew of Uncle Edgar are of an older era when family business was just that and was not told to strangers. I am only writing to you to clarify a few things. I have to tell you that I greatly resent Uncle Edgar's being compared to a mass murderer. While that man in our jail is guilty of murder, as my great-uncle was, he did a great many other things that Uncle Edgar never did. If you've done any research at all, you know that my uncle could be a very considerate and courteous neighbor. What I know about Edgar Watson was told me by my mother since my father would never talk about his Uncle Edgar.

Outraged that old family detritus had been stirred into view like leaf rot from the bottom of a well, the Collins family had broken its half century of silence. Furthermore—having chastised him and set him straight—Ellen Collins had volunteered to correct his misperceptions. He rang up at once to accept her kind offer and to apologize.

She heard him out. "You say your name is Collins, Professor? Is that true?"

The sharp-voiced question took him aback, and he felt a start of panic, terrified he might lose this precious chance. Stalling, he said, "Yes, well, you see—"

"What was your father's name?" the voice persisted. Clearly the newspaper distortions had made his kinswoman exceptionally suspicious. He would have to establish himself more firmly before confiding who he really was. And so he blurted, "R. B. Collins," sensing even as he spoke that he might be making a calamitous mistake.

The anticipated outcry—*Cousin Arbie?*—was not forthcoming, only a brief, ominous pause. "R. B. *Collins,* you say?" If R. B. was a Collins, he was a very distant one indeed, her tone made clear. "I don't suppose you mean R. B. *Watson,* whose mother was a Collins?"

"Rob Watson's mother was a Collins? Really? Do you know her name?"

"Well, I used to." Ellen Collins said she'd been shown the gravestone as a child. Robert Watson's mother had been a second cousin. She was not in their Collins cemetery at Tustenuggee, she was buried in New Bethel churchyard—not the *old* Bethel Cemetery, mind, where the gravestones had been bulldozed down by Yankee developers. "Those Yankees have walked all over us for a hundred years!"

Asked about the family in the Fort White area, Ellen Collins said, sardonic, "Oh, there's still a few of 'em down there. Hettie lives in the old Centerville schoolhouse, on the last piece of the original Collins land grant. She hunts up old neighbors and collects old scraps. Knows more about our family than we do ourselves, and she's only an in-law!"

When Lucius suggested he might call on Hettie, she drew back. "I don't know about that. Probably I have talked too much already," she added brusquely. But in a while she rang back to say that Cousin Hettie would receive him the next morning on the condition that her dear brother-in-law in Lake City and Cousin Ed Watson in Fort Myers would not be told about it. "I'll be there, too," Ellen Collins warned him. And she gave directions to New Bethel Cemetery, in case he should care to stop there on his way. "You come across any 'R. B. Collins' in that place, you let us know," she added tartly.

Back at the pool hall R. B. Collins, told the exciting news that Lucius had claimed him as his father, was not amused and in fact refused to go with Lucius to Fort White, claiming he had better things to do.

"These are your *relatives*!" Lucius exclaimed.

"I know who they are." Arbie broke the rack with a furious shot which left him hopelessly behind the eight ball. "Now look what you went and done," he said, walking around the table to inspect the catastrophe from another angle. "Story of my life," he said, chalking his cue.

*

In Lucius's absence, Sally had done important research at the Columbia County Courthouse, having talked her way into a storeroom of old archives. Ransacking the musty stacks, she had found cracked leather volumes of court dockets for May 1, 1906, to June 1, 1908, with each case written out in a spidery hand upon the leaf-brown pages.

County Judge W. M. Ives had presided over the circuit court on June 12, 1907, a few weeks after Samuel Tolen's murder. On that date, the state of Florida had indicted a Frank Reese for the murder of Samuel Tolen on the basis of an affidavit from D. M. Tolen. Lucius found this astonishing. Considering the well-known family feud referred to in the Jacksonville *Times-Union*, why had Mike Tolen accused Reese and not Cox or Watson? If Reese was such a desperate character, capable of murdering a white man, why was he so utterly ignored in the Watson legend? Neither the Herlong clipping nor Grover Kinard had so much as mentioned the one man to be indicted in both Tolen murders. Were black men in those Jim Crow days so bereft of status that even black assassins were discounted?

The defendant having pled not guilty, and the state unable to prove his guilt, it is ordered that Frank Reese be discharged from custody. That court order was peculiar, too. In those days, a black man charged with murder by a well-established white would be very lucky to live long enough to be indicted, let alone have his case dismissed for want of evidence. Had this man served as a scapegoat, a decoy, until Mike Tolen was ready to act against Cox and Watson?

On March 24, 1908, Judge Ives's first case was *The State of Florida v. Leslie*

Cox, who pled guilty to carrying a pistol without a county license, and was sentenced to twenty dollars and costs, or fifty dollars, or sixty days at hard labor at the county jail. Since this case had been heard on the day following Mike Tolen's murder, Lucius supposed that Cox was already a suspect in that killing, and that this sentence was the court's device for keeping him in custody until formal charges could be brought in the Tolen killings.

On April 10, Judge Ives's court considered the findings of a coroner's hearing in late March on the killing of D. M. Tolen, for which E. J. Watson, J. Porter, and Frank Reese had been duly charged. The plot was thickening, for Watson's nephews had also been arrested: *It is ordered that Julian Collins and Willie Collins each give bond in the sum of one thousand dollars . . . conditioned to appear and answer at the next term of our Circuit Court the charge of accessories-after-the-fact in the murder of D. M. Tolen.*

On April 25, Leslie Cox was formally indicted for the murder of S. Tolen, based on an affidavit furnished on April 10 by Julian Collins. In the same court on the same day, *E. J. Watson et al. were indicted for D. M. Tolen's murder on the basis of the coroner's inquest.* Together with other witnesses, the Collins boys had been summoned to appear before the grand jury.

Sally had also come upon the "Estate of D. M. Tolen":

6	fat hogs (900 lbs. @ 12¢ gross)	108.00
1	sow and five pigs	18.00
175	bu. corn	175.00
1000	bundles fodder	15.00
14.27	lbs. cotton	206.95
4	sacks guano	16.00
1000	seed corn	15.00
50	bu. potatos	25.00
1	barrel syrup (33 gal. @ 75¢ per gal.)	24.75
20	qts. bottle syrup	4.50
23	head of cattle @ $18.00 per head	414.00
1	saddle	9.00
1	buggy and harness	70.00
1	horse wagon	30.00
	plow gear	4.50
	farming implements	27.90
1	pr. balance	1.25
1	pot	1.00
2	tubs	1.00
1400	lbs. pork	210.00

1 mule	55.00
1 shotgun	10.00

New Bethel

With Sally's help, Lucius persuaded Arbie to go to Fort White after all, but even as they set out next morning, the old man became jealous once again, squashing in beside Sally in the front rather than permit himself to be relegated to the rear. Poor Sally had been forced to straddle the old-time gearshift with its trembling knob, her left leg brushing the right leg of the driver. Her jeans were so faded, worn so thin, and her flesh so warm and firm, that Lucius fairly shimmered in the glow. "Holy, holy, ho-o-ly!" Sally sang, quite unaccountably, "All the saints ador-ore Thee!" As her leg kept time, bouncing against his, he felt the lilt of his first erection in a month of Sundays.

New Bethel Church, by a main highway, was sorely buffeted by diesel winds and the wail of tires. "New Bethel was built out of heart pine in 1854, so she's solid as ever," an elder in the churchyard assured them, shielding his eyes to admire his church in the morning light. This old man turned out to be the sexton, there to console any random pilgrim dismayed to see such a House of God beset by so much noisome progress.

While Arbie and the sexton swapped Lake City lore, Lucius and Sally hunted the granite rows for the name Watson. Eventually his eye was led by a flit of sparrows to a tilted headstone set apart by a lone juniper. The stone's lettering had been eroded by black lichens, wind, and rain, and he knelt upon the grass to piece it out.

ANN M. WATSON

WIFE OF E. A. WATSON
AND DAUGHTER OF
W. C. AND SARAH COLLINS
BORN APRIL 16, 1862
DIED AT HER HOME IN
COLUMBIA CO. FLORIDA
SEPTEMBER 13, 1879

Here were fine hard bits of information of the sort so scarce in his father's history, including the precise identity and dates of Papa's first wife, as well as what could only be the fatal birthdate of Rob Watson on that unlucky thirteenth of September. He waved excitedly to Arbie, who came and slouched around the grave, hands in his pockets. "Can't hardly read it," he complained, seeming more interested in the dark evergreen behind. "Might have planted that ol' cedar the same year he planted her," he added roughly, turning abruptly and heading for the gate.

"Arb? This is Rob's *mother,* Arb!" Lucius called after him, exasperated by the apathy of the old man, whose interest in their quest seemed to diminish by the day. "I *know* who it is!" he shouted back.

That headstone inscription was the earliest record of his father's name which Lucius had yet come across—a gravestone record in a time of family grief, therefore unlikely to be imprecise. And the initial *A* in E. A. Watson verified those court documents pertaining to the Belle Starr hearing at Fort Smith that until this moment he had thought to be in error. It suggested that *A* had been the original initial, and that the subsequent change to *J* had been intended to obscure his identity after his escape from the Arkansas state prison.

*

Arbie had not waited at the cemetery gate but was headed north on foot along the highway shoulder. When they pulled up alongside, he would not get in the car. The old man hollered that he'd been on the road all his damned life, and had pounded highways and rode rails to hell and gone across the country, so he reckoned he was tough enough to make it back the three miles to Lake City. Close to tears, he would not look at Lucius but kept walking. When Sally urged him not to miss this meeting with those Collins cousins whom he'd said himself he had not seen since he was young, he yelled, "Stop pesterin me!"

The wrongheaded old man meant what he said. Lucius waved and wheeled the car and crossed the double lines and headed south again, but in a few minutes, he turned back, for Sally was worried and had suddenly decided she would wait for the old man at the motel. Passing Arbie, Lucius slowed to give him a chance to change his mind. Arbie ignored him.

*

Driving south on the Fort White Road, Lucius realized that there was time for a brief visit to the Tolen house before his meeting with the Collinses. At Herlong Lane, he turned off the pavement onto the cool track of white clay which ran due west through the woods for a mile and a half to the plantation's southwest corner at the vanished railroad crossing. On the north side, the wall of virgin forest was parted by the old carriageway. Here he parked the car and followed the old road, still dimly defined by a woodland emptiness which parted tall spring trees. Burled oaks and hickories of the original Ichetucknee Plantation were entangled with vine-shrouded magnolias and tupelos, rising through long shafts of light to far blue patches of bright morning sky. How fresh this woodland morning air, and how delightful!—cardinal song, sad plaint of titmice, the bell note of a blue jay in resplendent spring.

Deep in the forest, the carriage drive joined a more recent track which came in from the old Junction Road off to the west. Here the fine pale clay was innocent of tire tracks, or even horseshoe prints and dapple of manure, only small heart signs made by deer, rat tail of possum, and thin hand of coon, the flutter marks of dusting quail, the wispy tracings of the quick white-footed mice.

Soon the trees parted and the carriage drive climbed toward a white-columned facade fresh-washed by morning sun, as if the forest had opened out into the lambent sunlight of an older century. The house might have arisen from Aunt Tabitha's memory of some old Watson plantation at Clouds Creek, for the high white dwelling with its hand-hewn siding was fronted by a broad veranda with square pillars which supported an upper porch and balustrade, and the columned facade faced down the drive, awaiting the gentry who would never arrive in this far country of the Florida frontier. The new house had been larger than any other in the region, but the money for construction had run out, for its grandiose facade seemed out of scale with the makeshift building and small kitchen wing stuck on behind. Its two skinny brick chimneys seemed too narrow, and the rooms upstairs under the eaves had pinched small windows.

Behind the kitchen, chinked sheds and a poor barn sagged amongst the oaks, and beyond, a worn pasture was surrounded by ragged woodlots opened up by cattle. From the distance came the groan of cows, at the feed barn on the far side of the Fort White Road.

How odd that in an abandoned place, no eave window was broken, and no stoop overgrown. The ground-floor windows were unboarded, and the grass all around appeared rough-mowed. There was no junked truck or rusted harrow, no litter of neglect, only a bareness which extended to the worn-out paint, only the silence. Everything looked tidied in the morning light, as if the house were awaiting his arrival. An unlawful occupant might be peering out at him this very moment.

Stranger still, the kitchen door stood wide, as if the inhabitants had run away, hearing him coming. Someone or something—perhaps the heartbreaking spring wind—had swept the veranda where on such a morning

Great-Aunt Tabitha Watson might have creaked in her high-backed rocker, gazing without hope at the ancient forest from which those longed-for friends from home had never come.

After her death, Sam Tolen had lived here alone. In the decades since, others had come and gone away again, and now, Grover Kinard had said, the house stood empty. It was as if, after all these years, the dank mold of the common dread of Cox and Watson had never been aired out of this countryside, where even the local people shunned this place at the far end of the dark path through the forest.

For a long time, in a silence like an echo, he stood listening. Though drawn toward that open door, he did not approach—an unreasonable fear, but there it was, of something secret, even sinister, a secret he longed not to know. So disturbed had he become that he dared not cry out, in dread of awakening the warders of the place, whether quick or dead.

Circling the house, keeping his distance, he was startled by the shriek of a red-tailed hawk, poised for flight from its nest limb in a big live oak by the house corner. So close to the building, the nest was a sure sign that the house was uninhabited, yet he could not put his uneasiness aside. That door ajar on the back steps—he scarcely dared to turn his back on it! He imagined the specter of gaunt Tabitha or even brutal Tolen looming through that opening, wiping ham fat from his mouth with hairy knuckles, demanding to know who the stranger was, what the hell he wanted, and why he should not be set upon by dogs.

Lucius walked quickly down the shadow drive toward Herlong Lane, glancing back at the lost house until it disappeared into the trees. The birdsong had stilled in the midmorning heat, there were only the dry caws of crows, the burring flight of unseen quail, a dead limb cracking, and the rush and earth thump of its tearing fall.

The Collins Farm

From Herlong Lane, he traveled south on a nameless clay track as white as bonemeal, so soft that the car tires made no sound. He passed no house, no farm, he heard no dog. The settlement called Centerville had long ago withdrawn into the woods.

In a mile or so he came to the old schoolhouse, on a knoll under great oaks in a clearing. The door was opened by a composed, iron-haired woman who introduced herself as Ellen Collins. Gazing over her shoulder from across the room were three figures in a huge dark oval photograph in a massive frame. In the portrait, between her seated elders, stood a young girl in a white dress, full-mouthed, innocent, and knowing. To her left sat a pert, quizzical old lady in white scarf and cameo brooch. On her right was a handsome and imposing man in black suit, embroidered white shirt, and black bow tie. His hair was plastered to his head after the fashion of the time, and a heavy mustache flowed sideways into heavy sideburns. His gaze was forthright and unequivocal and his brow clear.

"Great-Uncle Edgar," said Ellen Collins primly, as if introducing them, for she had missed his consternation in this sudden confrontation with his father. "With Great-Grandmother Watson and my aunt May Collins as a girl." As he recalled, May Collins had been born around 1891. Since she was a near adolescent here, the photograph had presumably been taken about 1904, before his father's marriage to Edna Bethea.

He turned as Ellen introduced two women who had now entered the room. Cousin Hettie Collins, silver-haired, had the freshness of a younger woman in the mouth and eyes. When she offered a spontaneous welcome with a warm peck on his cheek, her daughter teased her—"Are we kissin cousins?" April Collins was handsome, about twenty, with taffy hair hacked short in a no-nonsense manner, and she had the bald unswerving gaze of her great-uncle Edgar on the wall, with that crescent of white beneath the pupil shared by Watson Dyer and also Carrie Langford. When Lucius glanced back at the photograph, the young woman laughed. "Yup," she said cheerfully, "those 'Crazy Watson eyes.' Still in our family."

Ellen Collins was pointing at a chair. From the sofa, the three women watched him. "This is the first photograph of Mr. Watson I have ever seen," he explained, finding his voice at last. He searched for something "crazy" in his father's face, but there was no sign of aberration unless it was that transfixed gaze, as if E. J. Watson had never blinked in all his life.

He thought about the Watson sons, and "the blood of a killer" seeping through their veins. Perhaps his brothers, in their very different natures, shared his dread that one day, in the eruption of a gene, they might go "crazy." Or perhaps they had no wish to face that, far less understand it. Perhaps he was truly alien to all the others.

"It's the one known photograph," Ellen was saying. "How could you possibly have seen it?" She sat back stiffly, folding her arms to bar his way into the bosom of the family.

"He's *kin*, Aunt Ellie! *L. Watson Collins? Got* to be kin!"

"That might be his nom de plume," said her aunt severely. Though her brash niece mimicked her—*num de ploom!*—Ellie Collins saw nothing to laugh at. Plainly she was having second thoughts about permitting this pseudo-Collins to cross their stoop.

To confess at this point that he was here under false pretenses, that there was no such person as L. Watson Collins—that in fact he was not a Collins after all—would ruin this vital contact with the family before it started. If they mistrusted him, they would tell him nothing. On the other hand, he must declare himself before he was exposed—oh Lord! Every moment that he put it off, the more complicated it was bound to be.

The ladies awaited him in a stiff row like hard-eyed women of the pioneers, squinting over the hammers of long muskets.

Clearly the kinsman in Lake City had not passed the word that Cousin Lucius was in town. But this could occur at any time, and he frowned intently at the picture, racking his brain for some way to offset the danger of exposure. "So this is Granny Ellen," he sighed, to break the silence. "Yes. I'm named for her," his cousin Ellie said. "And Aunt May's brothers were my father, Willie, and April's grandfather, my uncle Julian. Uncle Julian's son lives in Lake City, but we rarely see him. Anyway, you could cut his tongue out before he'd ever talk about Great-Uncle Edgar." She shook her head. "The father wouldn't mention him so the son won't either. Nor my late father either, nor the grandsons. It's our male tradition."

"Collins honor." Hettie smiled.

"Collins honor!" April cried, saluting. "Watson honor, too! If it weren't for darn old Cousin Ed, down in Fort Myers, our men might have loosened up a little after all this time!"

"Well, Cousin Ed feels more strongly than anyone, and who can blame him? But Daddy told me that our cousin Lucius felt quite differently. Sometime before World War I, he actually came here just to talk about his father!"

But *I* am *Cousin Lucius*! How he longed to say that!

"Know anything about Granny Ellen's husband?" Ellen was testing him.

"Ol' Ring-Eye? Yes, indeed!" He managed a cousinly laugh, and the women exchanged glances, reassured.

Granny Ellen had left them a daguerreotype of Lige Watson in Confederate uniform, Hettie told him, handing it over. As his kinswomen observed him, he studied the brown-spotted picture for a long time, adjusting the face to the apparition of Ring-Eye Lige in his imagination.

Young Lige, gone for a soldier, had snouty, arrogant good looks, wild upright hair, and that sort of confused tumultuous demeanor that can burst forth in joy or storm with little warning. Even in the photograph, his broad mouth seemed to be shifting from a curling snarl to a grand boyish smile. And his gaze, too, had that hard white crescent beneath the pupil, that bald shine. Though the ring around his eye was still to come, that left eye loomed strangely larger than the right, as if aghast at the spectral knife that was awaiting him.

*

The women gossiped about family jewelry which Granny Ellen had brought south from Carolina—how she had hidden jewels in her hair to keep them out of Ring-Eye's clutches, and how Aunt May had probably grabbed them. Soon they fell still, joining their guest, who had turned again to the huge portrait on the wall.

Lucius found himself drawn deep into his father's eyes. A countenance which had seemed serene, without a wrinkle, was stirring, shifting, and re-settling into a hard mask swollen with intransigence—an effect, he decided, of that white crescent beneath the pupil, hard as boiled albumen. As he watched, the eyes grew unrestrained, like the glare of a trapped lunatic, peering out through the eye slits of that transfixed face. Lucius took a deep breath, then let go, and the real image snapped back into place, as composed and handsome as the mortal Papa whose memory he had cherished all his life. Yet those eyes unsettled him, stirring unwelcome recollections. In those last years at Chatham Bend, his father had often been less calm than he appeared—not tense but gathered in a deadly quietude, like a cat at a mouse hole.

Ellen Collins was saying that whenever Ed Watson became angry, he would smile. "My mother was told that all her life: *When that man smiled that smile, better watch out!* Uncle Edgar could be such a pleasant man, ever so generous and considerate, but never cross him! Oh, he had a *violent* temper! It's in the family chemistry, I guess. I have it, too, and my brother has it worse—just an explosive temper! My brother would pick a quarrel with a fence post! Away from the family, he always said, 'If I had lived in Uncle Edgar's day, I would have killed those Tolen bastards, too!'"

"If he said that once, he said it a million times," April said gleefully, wink-ing at Lucius.

"Well, a little temper goes a long long way," gentle Hettie said. "Uncle Edgar never did learn to control it—didn't have to, I don't suppose. I do know something dreadful happened in his youth, back in South Carolina. Those rumors came in with the Herlong family, who arrived from Edgefield County after he did. The Collinses would never repeat those Herlong stories because Granny Ellen wished to put Edgefield behind her. Pretty soon, of course, we had our own stories around here to take their place."

"It's told for truth in the Collins family that Uncle Edgar killed a black per-son in Lake City." April was checked by a polite cough from her aunt. "I shouldn't tell him that?"

"You already did," her aunt Ellie snapped, taking over her story. "They had wood sidewalks at that time, of course, and the sidewalks were narrow and the streets were muddy, and I guess he figured this darkie should have made way for him, stepped off into the mud. And Uncle Edgar was drunk and there were words, and then he killed him, right there in broad daylight. Now that was in Redemption times when no one paid too much attention if you killed a nigra. But you didn't go do it in broad daylight! In the public street!"

"Right in front of church!"

"April? I don't remember anything about a church." Ellie Collins shook her iron head in disapproval, worried anew about their visitor and not concealing it. "The whole thing was probably made up, one of those Watson stories. But Granddad Billy always said that when Uncle Edgar walked Lake City's streets, the nigras got clear over on the other side!"

"Well, Aunt Ellie, I would imagine so!"

This time even Ellie had to giggle.

"Years ago, somebody read someplace that Uncle Edgar had to move away to Oklahoma because he'd killed his brother-in-law!" Hettie smiled at Lucius with astonished innocence. "Seems funny the victim's family never heard about it!" she added, smiling happily when Lucius grinned. She had also read somewhere that Edgar Watson killed three men in Georgia on the way to Oklahoma and a couple more in Oregon before he returned east. "You'd think he'd say something about it to his mother or his sister if he'd gone to Oregon!"

"I suppose you know the one about Belle Starr?" Ellie inquired. "How Uncle Edgar did away with Belle in Oklahoma? When asked, he admitted it was true, but he said he'd had no choice about it. Belle would ride around his place at night, shooting guns and carrying on, spooking his horses, so one night, he said, he just 'stepped out and took care of it.' "

"Maybe he was only fooling. They say he never boasted much but he sure liked to tease."

"Well, Granddad Collins was offended by that story. He told his boys it was dishonorable to shoot a woman, no matter what. Granddad died before the trouble with those Tolens, but he had a pretty good idea about his brother-in-law before he went."

"One thing we do know, Uncle Edgar's favorite song was 'Streets of Laredo.' He used to sing it with real feeling. Said it came from an old Celtic lament which tingled up his blood—'the iron blood of our Scots Highlands ancestors,' he used to say.

"Brought that song back from Oklahoma, along with his black hat. A black slouch hat was the way it was described to us. You didn't catch him out without that hat on."

"Probably going bald," April suggested. "Wore black most of the time, sang those sad songs. Had a premonition he would die before his time and was already in mourning for his misspent life."

"Oh, what nonsense!" They all hooted in delight.

*

According to their old documents, the Collins family had descended from the brothers Charles and William Collins, English immigrants and pioneers. Charles H. B. Collins founded the section near Fort White still known as Tustenuggee. Mary Lucretia or "Minnie" Watson married Charles's grandson Billy—"that's our branch of the family"—and Uncle Edgar married William Collins's granddaughter, Ann Mary.

Asked why Grandmother Minnie was missing from the oval photo, Cousin Hettie murmured, "We don't rightly know. We have an idea—"

"Family business," Ellie snapped.

Hettie said, apologetic, "There is a letter in which Grandmother Minnie is described as beautiful!"

Ellie nodded. "We've always heard that, but there's no known picture. She *hated* the idea of her own likeness. She died a couple of years after Uncle Edgar—I was just a baby—and those who might recall her face are all gone, too. None of her grandchildren have the slightest recollection what the poor soul looked like!"

What these women knew of the years of family shame had come mostly from Laura Hawkins Collins, whose husband, Julian, with his brother, Willie, had harbored such tormented feelings about Uncle Edgar. Laura had been Edna Bethea's dearest friend, and had spent six months with her in the Ten Thousand Islands after Edna's marriage to Edgar Watson. When Laura died, her daughter-in-law Hettie had taken over her research into the family, poking into shelves and crannies, satchels and letter packets, stirring up the crusty reminiscences of ancient neighbors.

"Oh yes, our in-laws care more about our family history than we do ourselves," said Ellie, with an undisguised edge to her voice that made Hettie raise her brows. "For the blood relatives, you see, the scandals are still too painful, too close to the bone."

"All those deaths and tragedies and bitter conflicts in the family," Hettie agreed. "And then Aunt May eloping with that murderer"—"We didn't tell him *that* part!" Ellie warned her—"and Uncle Edgar's evil reputation and his grisly death. And we had a drug addict in poor Grandmother Minnie, and we had a suicide—that was our cousin Martha Collins Burdett, whose son Herkie was to marry Edna Watson. And all these tragedies befell our family in the space of a few years! The family was in shock!"

Lucius inspected the photos of Billy Collins and the two sons, Julian and

Willie—"Willie Collins was *my* daddy," Ellie reminded him. Like their father, the two Collins boys had been small and slight, with black hair and thin beards and handsome faces. What he recalled of them from his visit years ago was the pensive quality in their dark eyes, as if their young manhood had been saddened by their father's early death, their uncle's infamy, their mother's utter failure of the spirit. Like their father, they had tired early and died young.

"No one can blame our Collins men and Cousin Ed for wanting everybody to hush up about it," Hettie murmured. "My brother-in-law never laid eyes on him, but he won't mention Uncle Edgar to this day."

"No indeed! His daddy wouldn't talk about it, so my uncle knows only a little bit, but he guards that little bit extremely closely," April said. "So closely we don't even know if he knows *anything*!"

The women laughed with the affectionate malice of close families. All three seemed festive in this chance to dust and air the old closed rooms of the family past. The Collins clan, their manner said, had no reason to hang its head, even if its men were hopelessly old-fashioned.

*

Paul Edmunds, whose family had owned the general store in Centerville, had been invited by the Collins women to meet their guest. Mr. Edmunds wore his blue serge Sunday suit and high black shoes and a denim shirt without a tie. The shirt was buttoned to the top, pinching his gullet. Behind him his wife Letitia, in fussed-up hair and glinty glasses and dust-colored woolens, came in out of the sunlight like a large timorous moth.

"Your store is still out there in the woods," young April shouted, aiming her voice at his hearing aid. "I bet I could still find it for you, Mr. Edmunds!" Paul waved her aside and kept on coming. He wanted to get down to business, which for him signified men's business, and men only.

"Well, now, Mister," he began, "we hear you are some kind of a damn historian. These ladies and me have talked for years with all the old folks around here who still remember anything, and we think we've got the history down as good as you are going to get it." He bent a bushy eyebrow toward the upstart, to show he meant to brook no opposition, then cleared his throat to give himself some speaking room.

Mr. Edmunds related how Col. William Myers had come here with his slaves during the War, being scared that he might lose 'em to the Yankees. He had left his wife, the former Miss Laura Watson, back in Athens, Georgia, because this Suwannee country was still wild and life uncertain.

"Grover Kinard gave him some history, Paul. Showed him all around the old community."

"Grover Kinard? He never lived in Centerville in his whole life!" Indignant, the old man blew his nose, trumpeting for silence. "Now Colonel Myers was struck and killed by lightning. He was standing under a big tree between his log house and the old Russ cabin off southeast of it. We know that happened in 1869, cause we seen the will. The Widow Laura and her mother came down here to see to the estate, they were too grand to live in that log cabin so they stayed over at Live Oak. We found 'em there in the 1870 census."

"Colonel Myers left that whole plantation to his *mother-in-law*!" Ellie Collins was still incredulous over this outrage. "And when the old lady died, it was supposed to go to his darn nephews instead of to the Watsons! That's where the trouble started!"

"It certainly looked like Colonel Myers married poor Cousin Laura for her money, and later on Sam Tolen did the same," Hettie Collins said. "Cousin Laura was very kind and generous, but rather simple-hearted when it came to property—"

"Simpleminded," April said. "Retarded, probably."

"I don't know about all that," Paul Edmunds warned the women, harrumphing a little in impatience, fingers working like big inchworms on his chair arms.

"There's no proof of that, April dear. That's just your own idea."

"You have a better one? Why did Myers leave the whole thing to his mother-in-law, with instructions to pass it straight along to his own nephews?"

"Probably the Colonel just wanted to make sure that our Watson property stayed in the Myers family," Cousin Ellie said tartly, and the women laughed.

" 'We don't know about all that,' " April said to Lucius, mimicking Old Paul, who could not hear her. When her elders stifled smiles and frowned, this lawless person grinned at her new relative, inviting him to giggle along with them. He felt an upwelling of happiness, a return into his family, which he had not known since before his father's death.

Wishing to make some sort of contribution, he pointed out that those Myers nephews were Watsons on their mother's side. Cousin Ellie frowned at him severely. The family didn't look at it that way. It was not only his information they resisted, but the idea that it should come from an outsider, he decided later. He was not yet accepted by the family, since none of them were quite sure who he might be.

*

In 1870, the year after Colonel Myers's death, Ellen Watson and her children came from South Carolina. Granny Ellen and the Widow Laura, who were nearly the same age, had been childhood friends. "We don't know if they corresponded, or if Aunt Tabitha invited her, or if Granny Ellen just appeared and they took her in."

"Herlongs always used to say that before Edgar left Carolina, a freed nigger told him he weren't plantin the peas in a straight row, and was fixin to let on to his daddy. Well, somebody went and killed that doggone nigger." Noticing his wife fluttering at his side, Paul Edmunds scowled. "And they never knew whether Edgar shut him up out of fear of punishment over them peas or because that nigger had spoke up too smart for his own good."

"Folks say 'nigra' these days, honey," his wife coaxed him.

"*Niggera?*" Old Paul glared suspiciously about him. "Well now, I reckon there *was* some question how that niggera died—at least, that's all Edgar was ever heard to say about it. Couldn't very well deny it, knowing the Herlongs come from that same section." The old man shrugged. "Never had no regrets that Herlongs knew about." He winked at Lucius, whispering harshly behind his hand. "I doubt he give that sonofabitch a second thought, how about you?"

"Maybe the whole story was just rumor in the first place," Lucius said shortly.

"Well, darkies aren't treated that way anymore, not around here." Distressed by Paul Edmunds's way of speaking, Hettie seemed anxious to believe what she'd just said, and her pained smile entreated Lucius not to believe that this community was still mired in such bigotry. "Oh, there's a social difference, yes, but as far as mistreatment, or not taking care of a neighbor because he's black—no, not at all! The Collinses aren't like that, and they never were!"

"Not all of 'em, anyways." Paul Edmunds snorted, shrugging off all this darn folderol as pure irrelevance.

"In the old days, folks hurt black people and got away with it because nobody thought a thing about it," Ellie said. "And maybe Uncle Edgar learned that evil lesson from his father and never unlearned it."

"Old Ring-Eye conked our uncle once too often, knocked his brain askew," April told Lucius, tapping her temple as her elders hushed her. Ellie cried, "Now, April, you're not suggesting he was crazy? Nobody ever thought any such thing! Hotheaded, yes! Violent, yes! But *crazy?*"

"At least that's some kind of excuse! Anyway, there is all kinds of 'crazy.' He went crazy when he drank too much, we sure know that!"

Hettie Collins said carefully, "We always talked about the two reasons he went wrong. First, because his father was so mean to him. Granny Ellen said that Uncle Edgar started out in life just fine, but you take a good dog and you keep whipping him, he will turn bad. Another thing, he was very young when he tried to take care of his family in the War. Those were hard years of want and famine, and after the War came dreadful anarchy and violence, and those young men on the frontier had to take the law into their own hands just to survive. So perhaps he was not naturally bad, not in his young years, he just went sour after poor Ann Mary died in childbirth."

"How about that colored man the Herlongs claimed he killed in Carolina?" April demanded. "Looks to me like dear old Uncle had gone kind of sour by the time he got here!"

"Did this family ever think he was *really* crazy?" Lucius was certain his uneasiness had now betrayed him, for the room fell still, and everybody turned in his direction.

"Crazy like a fox, we used to say," Mr. Edmunds told him. "Everything that feller touched turned to pure gold. Anyways, there were plenty like Ed Watson back in frontier days! Robber barons, y'know! Killings all over the damn place! Didn't stop at *nothing*!"

"They say those darn old robber barons made this country great, and made great fortunes, but they never let too much stand in their way."

"Human life, for one thing. Uncle Edgar—"

"Well, not all men who resorted to violence were unscrupulous," Hettie warned her daughter. "In Reconstruction, the Union soldiers and carpetbaggers and uppity colored people all around made life bitter and miserable, that's all. There were *many* men who felt they had no choice but to take the law in their own hands. They weren't *all* crazy, April dear!" Hettie went pink in the face. "My own grandfather," she confessed. "There was this bold darkie who gave insult to his mother. Grandfather killed that man. Furthermore, he would not submit to trial for having done what he thought was right. They promised him the judge would let him off, they warned him he would be worse off as a fugitive than if he stayed. No, he said, what it came down to was his honor. He *knew* he would get off, of course, but he refused to be put on trial by 'those damned radical scalawags,' whom he despised! He came to Florida and changed his name, called himself Ben Scroggins!"

Cousin Ellie sighed. "No, Uncle Edgar was not the only one who resorted to violence back in those days, no, far from it. He had fine qualities, but because of his bad reputation, he was accused of a lot of things he didn't do, which made him bitter. Anyway, that's what came down in the family."

Because of his feud with the Tolens, Edgar Watson left the Myers plantation to sharecrop a piece of land for Captain Getzen, but he used the Collins store at Ichetucknee, and was good friends with Lem and Billy Collins. Hettie showed Lucius the yellowed cashbooks salvaged from the store, where Edgar Watson was one of six customers (out of twenty-two) who were identified as "good" prospects to pay their bills. In the late 1870s, his purchases included tobacco, schnapps and bitters, and a pocketknife. On different dates in 1878, he bought ceiling and weather boarding, apparently to patch his cabin on the Junction Road. "Uncle Edgar was fixing that old Robarts cabin for his bride-to-be," Hettie told Lucius.

"That same year, Minnie Watson married Billy Collins, and both couples lived there after their marriage," Ellie added. "We have a courtship letter from Granddad Billy that turned up in her things: '*Dear Miss Minnie, I would very much like you to accompany me on a buggy ride this Sunday. . . .*' Then Uncle Edgar married Ann Mary Collins, whose nickname was Charlie. We believe it was Edgar who gave her that odd name. Even on the marriage record, she is Charlie."

Lucius glanced quickly through these documents. Papa had used the pet name Mandy for his second wife, Kate for his third, exchanging the staid Ann Mary, Jane, and Edna for more "wanton" names. He considered using this esoteric theory as a deft first step in introducing himself as the long-lost cousin Lucius, but before he could do so, Ellie boasted, "I have already told him about poor Charlie, even where to go to find her grave!" She avoided referring to him as Professor Collins, lest that name prove spurious.

Hettie said that Great-Grandfather Collins died in the same year as Charlie Watson, and they had his will. Edgar Watson had bought a double-barrel shotgun and a horse from that estate, paying $10.50 for the gun and $55.00 for the horse. She passed a scrawled receipt. "Far as we know, that was the double-barrel he would use till the day he died."

"Probably used it on Belle Starr, she was the first one," Mr. Edmunds said. "I knowed a feller who read all about it in a book."

"After his darling Charlie died, Uncle Edgar went hog wild. It was five or six years, at least, before he calmed down and married that young school-teacher from Deland. Still lived in the log cabin by the Junction, the same one he rented later to his friend Will Cox. That's where our cousin Carrie was born, and Cousin Ed, who was still a baby when the family left for Oklahoma later that year. We know that was in '87, because Julian was born to Minnie and Billy just a few months later."

*

Grandpa Billy's brother Lem had killed a man in the Collins blacksmith shop behind the store. It seemed this man was angry because Lem Collins had been fooling with his wife. The Collins family put up hundreds of acres for a $4000 bond posted mainly by Laura Myers, and when Lem jumped his bond and ran away to Georgia, the family sold off most of its land to repay the debt. There was a Sheriff's sale of more Collins property in 1886, but Laura

Myers never recouped her loan, and the fortunes of the Collins clan never recovered. Grandpa Billy always said that Uncle Edgar had been a bad influence on Lem and might even have been involved in the killing, and other people were suspicious, too.

Uncle Edgar had gone away to Oklahoma, and once he was safe out of the way, Sam Tolen had married poor old Cousin Laura. The widow's marriage to an ignorant cracker almost thirty years her junior (and well beneath her social station, Ellie noted primly) had seemed to vindicate Colonel Myers's precaution of bypassing this foolish creature in his will. Sam Tolen proceeded soon thereafter with the construction of the manor house, which was scarcely finished when Laura died in 1894. Upon her death—at Tolen's urging, they supposed—Tabitha Watson, now an old lady, had transferred her daughter's "child portion" of the estate to her son-in-law, who wasted no time in selling the whole plantation out from under her.

*

When Edgar Watson returned from the West in the early nineties, he was a fugitive on horseback, passing through at night on his way south. Before he left, he gave money to the Collinses to send to Arkansas for his wife and children and to take care of them here in Fort White until he got himself established on the southwest coast. Cousin Ed was nine years old when the family came back from Arkansas, which dated their return to 1896. The next year the family left Fort White for the Ten Thousand Islands.

"Right after the turn of the century, Jane Watson died and Uncle Edgar came back here to Columbia County. Aunt Minnie got Granddad to lease him a piece of our Collins tract, where he built his house all by himself."

"Nothing but brambles and poverty grass when he took over," Mr. Edmunds said. "He brought them old fields back into production, got his place all bought and paid for, earned himself a real good reputation. Folks were ready to forgive him and forget, even the ones who had heard about Belle Starr.

"Course I lived right around here since a boy, and I seen him build that house up on the hill. Watson was staying with his sister's family. Billy Collins was grinding cane from some cuttings Watson brought him from Ten Thousand Islands, so us kids would run over at noontime from the school, drink some good cane juice. That's when I first remember Edgar Watson, must of been about nineteen and oh-four.

"Doc Straughter did odd jobs for Watson when they lived up on the hill. For the rest of his life, that niggera would talk about how Mist' Edgar worked a revolver, said he never seen anything to beat it. Set on his back porch and pick the acorns off of that red oak—that big tree is up there yet today. Course just about every man back then could work a rifle pretty good, but nobody couldn't hit nothin with a handgun. E. J. Watson could beat you and your rifle with a damn revolver, which was why they claimed he made his money as a gunfighter out in the Nations."

"Uncle Edgar was always an amusing talker and great storyteller," Hettie said. "He was invited everywhere in Fort White, which was much larger and more prosperous than it is today. Board sidewalks and tall kerosene street-lamps, two-seater horse hacks with fringe canopies. There was even three whole stories' worth of bright yellow hotel, Sparkman Hotel. Uncle Edgar went in there every Saturday to have his lunch, and Bascomb Sparkman always said he never saw a man so educated and well-dressed and mannerly. Said to hear Mr. Watson carry on beat any politician that you ever heard about. It was purely unbelievable, all the things he knew about this country's history, and not only America but Ancient Greece! Homer and the Iliad. He quoted Shakespeare! His folks couldn't get Bascomb out of the dining room on Saturdays, that's how entertained he was by Uncle Edgar!"

"Well, Mama, was he so popular? Or just notorious as the Man Who Killed Belle Starr?"

"Nobody would think such an amiable man had ever killed a woman in his life, that's what Bascomb said. But if somebody said something smart, and those blue eyes froze, folks knew enough to get out of his way. I asked Bascomb once what that look was, and Bascomb thought awhile, then said, 'He looked like God and he looked like Satan and he looked like Uncle Sam, all three at once!' Now isn't that a strange idea? Young Bascomb had a lot of imagination!"

"Probably looked like those enlistment posters where Uncle Sam is pointing at you off the wall," April exclaimed. *"You call yourself a red-blooded American? Quit skulkin around behind them bleedin-hearts and yeller-bellies! Step right up and sign your X right here!"*

"It's true," Paul Edmunds was remembering. "Warm, ruddy face and a fine lively smile, but there was a glint in them blue eyes which made most men go quaky in the belly."

"Did he ever look at *you* like that?" Letitia whispered, in honest awe of any man fearsome enough to daunt her Paul T. Edmunds. Her husband snorted and stamped crossly at her whispering, as if she were some sort of pesky fly.

"Well, most people don't recall anything like that!" Lucius protested.

"Julian Collins would tell about one night when he was going down Herlong Lane with his uncle Edgar in the horse and buggy," Hettie said. "Uncle Edgar never went anywhere without a weapon, and he would rein in before every clump of woods and peer and listen, using the moonlight to silhouette the trees, hunting for bushwhackers before whipping the horse past. That was just after the turn of the century, when he first came back here from the Islands! Someone must have been gunning for him even then."

"Could have been Tolens," Edmunds said. "Sam was starting to sell off the plantation, and maybe Edgar got riled up and said something about Watson land that made Sam think Edgar might kill him if Tolens didn't kill him first. That made for a very dangerous situation."

*

After a few years in Fort White, Edgar Watson paid occasional visits to the Islands to maintain his sugarcane plantation, which in his absence had gone back to jungle. The women recalled that in 1906, when Julian Collins was twenty, he and his Laura had accompanied Uncle Edgar to the Islands. Lucius, who was seventeen that summer, remembered his cousins rather vaguely, but he recalled that Papa had forbidden them to swim in Chatham River, saying that inland people did not swim well. Winking at Lucius, he would exaggerate the dangers of big sharks hunting upriver on the tide and the huge alligators which came downstream from the Glades during the summer rains, and the great solitary crocodile that hauled out on the bank across the river.

"In their six months in the Islands, those young Collinses heard some ugly stories about how Uncle Edgar hired loners for the harvest, people with nobody waiting for 'em back home—darkies mostly, but some outlaws, too, and drunks and drifters—and how these people would just disappear when payday came. It was true, they told us, that some of his harvest hands were drunks and drifters, but the Collinses noticed nothing wrong about how those harvest workers were paid off. They didn't know what to make of all those rumors."

"Oh, rumors went around, all right," Lucius admitted, "but I have never come across one bit of evidence that he killed his help."

Hettie Collins was silent a few moments, gazing down at her clenched hands. "My father-in-law was close to Uncle Edgar in those days," she said finally. "He would not have passed along such awful gossip."

As Lucius recalled, Julian's young wife had liked Papa very much. Laura always said he was the kindest man she ever met, kind to his own family and oh so hospitable to his young relatives at Chatham Bend. And Hettie remembered how grateful Laura was that Uncle Edgar had sat all night at her bedside when she miscarried her baby boy down in the Islands. Papa and Lucius buried the child because Julian was simply too upset. Lucius remembered that when Papa wasn't looking, he had said good-bye to that little boy by touching two fingers to the cool blue forehead. Poor Laura had been so small and frail—a dark-haired pretty little thing, with such sad eyes!

"When they came back to Fort White in early 1907, Julian and Laura moved into Uncle Edgar's house, so it doesn't look like they learned anything too terrible. They were hardly home when Grandpa Billy died, that was February of 1907, and Edgar and Edna came back north to be with the family. Edna's little Addison and Laura's little boy, who became my husband, were born in Uncle Edgar's house that same October, so those dear friends had their babies right together."

"Which means they were all in Uncle Edgar's house when Sam Tolen was killed right down the road," Lucius said, checking his own notes. "Would they have stayed if they suspected him?"

"Oh, I imagine they were *worried*," Hettie murmured. "I mean, there was *so* much talk all around the county! But Uncle Edgar was close family, so they would not believe anything said against him. At one time Julian had deeply admired his uncle, and in later years he always made Cousin Ed feel welcome. But Julian was straitlaced even then, and detested loose talk that might harm the family name. Eventually, of course, he and his brother felt obliged to repudiate their uncle for disgracing our good reputation, and they cast him out. Julian Collins is dead, and his son, too, but my brother-in-law is still adamant, up in Lake City. I wouldn't dare let on to him what we're discussing!"

"Certainly not!" Ellie's grave frown affirmed the Collins Code, as if she herself, against all odds, were its last defender. Hettie and Lucius exchanged a delicious smile.

"Julian Collins was always pretty quiet," Mr. Edmunds recalled. "You never caught Julian in too much of a conversation, he never used two words where one would do. When anybody got to talking about E. J. Watson, neither of those Collins boys would say one word."

Asked what the Collins boys had testified at their uncle's trial, the women made clear by their silence that this newcomer of doubtful antecedents was not entitled to such knowledge. But his question had caused discomfort in the room, like a woodland bird flown in through the window and fluttering distractingly behind the curtains. To put him in his place, Ellie changed the subject, reminding everyone that Samuel Tolen had lived alone with the aging Aunt Tabitha for at least ten years. "He terrorized that poor old soul! Alone in the house with that dirty brute, dependent on him for her very food and water. He might have forced her to rewrite the will, then starved her to death to get his hands on the property a little quicker."

Had Great-Aunt Tabitha, in a last-minute gesture to keep the peace, promised Edna and Edgar that wedding present of the piano and silver mentioned by Dr. Herlong, which apparently Sam Tolen had withheld?

"We heard there was some problem over cows." Ellie scowled when her niece laughed aloud at this cow theory.

"There was bad blood long before them cows," Edmunds said darkly.

"Sam Tolen kept those presents for himself? *That* would cause trouble!"

"Might cause trouble but not murder," Edmunds said. "It's land that causes murder in this part of the country—land and women. What caused the killings was Sam Tolen selling off what Watson thought was rightfully Watson land."

Lucius had to agree. A plantation owned by an elderly Watson aunt who had no heirs had seemed to Papa his great chance to restore the family fortunes. To see it usurped, mismanaged, and exploited by the Tolens could only have maddened him beyond all sense, all the more so after the bitter loss of his family property at Clouds Creek, in Carolina.

"My mama liked to recollect the day Sam Tolen died," Paul Edmunds said. "She remembered it good because them shots rung out off to the northwest of our store, on that old road that run from Tolen's through the woods and on out across the back of Watson's fields. That road's all growed over now, ain't nothing down along that way no more at all."

"Except your store," said April. "I told you I could take you to it any time you wanted. Got a nice tree growing right up through the roof."

"That's cause you know I'm too darned old to go." The old man kept his gaze fastened on Lucius.

"After Mike Tolen's death," Ellie said, "Uncle Edgar went straight to the Collins boys and asked them to back him up with a good alibi, and he also tried that on their friend, Jim Delaney Lowe. Well, those young men knew he must be guilty if he was so anxious for an alibi, and they refused to stand up and tell lies when he went to trial. And Julian's Laura, though fond of Uncle Edgar, had no choice but to stand beside her husband."

Lucius mentioned that another man besides Edgar Watson had been indicted for Mike Tolen's murder. When they turned toward him in disbelief, he told them that a black man named Frank Reese had been arrested in both Tolen cases. "That never came down in our family," Ellie warned him. Paul Edmunds agitated in impatience as if a black man didn't count, not even a black man charged with murder. Then Lucius said he supposed they knew that Julian and Willie Collins had been charged as accessories-after-the-fact in the Mike Tolen case and jailed on one thousand dollars bail.

"*Jailed?*"

As the person responsible for introducing this viper to their hearth, Ellie Collins drew herself up to stare him down. The family knew no such thing, she said, in tones suggesting it could not be true and that in grubbing through court documents, this self-styled Professor Collins had crossed the line into dishonorable behavior.

"Perhaps they were only . . . detained," Hettie said carefully.

There had been no question of Collins complicity or guilt, Lucius explained, speaking formally and even pompously in the hope that academic formality might help remove him from his own petard. Indeed, he said, court documents suggested that the state's attorney, learning that Mr. Watson had sought an alibi from the Collins brothers, had had the nephews detained as accessories-after-the-fact until such time as they agreed to testify that they had been wrongfully solicited. Presumably the boys' arrest was only the state's attorney's tactic for eliminating Watson's alibi and extorting damaging testimony for the prosecution. And in the end, the strategy had worked, since both Collins boys had testified against their uncle. Edgar Watson's solicitation of an alibi—tantamount to a confession, claimed the prosecution—turned out to be the most damaging evidence against him.

The ladies stared at him, dumbfounded. Cousin Ellie's expression seemed to say, Is this how you repay me? For Lucius knew—and knew that they knew, too—that in testifying against their uncle, Julian and Willie had transgressed the codes of those fierce Border ancestors who, despising authority, loyal only to the clan, had borne their tattered pennant of archaic honor across the seas from the British Isles into the New World. The past half century of rigid silence, however dignified and proud, had embedded that dark splinter of guilt, like a dim black line under the family skin.

In the sudden stillness of the schoolhouse, he suffered with them the inheritance of shame inflicted on the clan by Uncle Edgar. In the end it mattered little what those boys said. Through no fault or weakness of their own, his cousins had found themselves in an intractable dilemma—to swear falsely to their uncle's alibi in the name of "family honor" or to betray it out of civic duty to the commonweal.

As for that other affidavit signed by Julian Collins which had helped to indict Cox in the Sam Tolen murder, they knew nothing about it. How much Julian had known about that killing, how he had learned of it, and why his knowledge had not come to light until after the killing of Mike Tolen a year later—that information had gone with him to his grave.

*

In the three photographs which survived in the Collins family, the former Miss Ellen Addison was a wide-eyed little girl in white dress and ribbon bow, a sleepy-eyed young female in formal dress with flowers in her hair, and the elderly woman of small perky smile and wide bright eyes who appeared in the oval portrait on the wall. Despite her lifelong tribulations, Ellen Watson appeared serene in all three pictures, and indeed, she had been of good cheer to the end. "Couldn't boil an egg—that's what comes of having slaves—but when she sat down to Aunt Tabitha's piano, those delicate hands of hers were light as butterflies," Ellie Collins said.

In black church bombazine and Sunday bonnet, chin held high, Granny Ellen had made a fine impression at the trials, smiling gaily in proud witness to the fine character of her distinguished son as well as to the probity of her handsome grandsons, who were there to help establish her son's guilt. In the court recess, she beamed upon all three without discrimination, handing around nice mincemeat sandwiches in a napkined basket.

Minnie Collins did not attend her brother's trial. In her last years she was lost in grief over her dear Billy, it was said, although long before her husband's death she had scarcely spoken. In the end, nobody noticed her at all. By all accounts, she had always been a colorless person, with faint life in her, and even more entirely than her brother—who had more life than was good for him—her likeness had vanished from the family record. Indeed, the Collins women said, there were no known photographs of Minnie, as if her countenance had been too tentative to be resolved on film. There was no family memory of what she looked like, thought, or said, nor could anyone offer an anecdote about this voiceless person. The one known attribute was her rare beauty, but what form this beauty might have taken, or how she talked or hummed or smiled, nobody knew.

"It's so hard to imagine how she might have been when she was younger," Hettie murmured. "Later on, she had this malady that doctors used to call 'American nervousness.' Then paregoric was prescribed her for a toothache, and paregoric has an opium base. The poor soul was susceptible—"

" 'American nervousness'!" April cried. "I'll say! I'd have been pretty nervous, too, if I had Ol' Ring-Eye for a father, not to mention Uncle Edgar as a brother!"

"Neurasthenia was another name for it," said Ellie. "Dyspepsia, dementia, insomnia, hysteria—if it had an *-ia* at the end, Minnie Collins had it, and a bad case, too!"

After Billy Collins died in early 1907, Granny Ellen and Aunt Minnie, with Willie and May, moved to Uncle Edgar's house, where Julian and Laura were already living. Cousin Ed was there, as well, and with Uncle Edgar showing up from time to time, they were too many, so Julian and Laura built their own small house not far from the school. They wanted to put in a well so that Laura need not come down here to the school and hand-pump her water and tote back heavy pails, but just when they'd scraped a few dollars together to pay William Kinard to come and dig it was when Julian's mother became hopelessly dependent. Everything they'd saved went for her opiates, and another year went by without their well.

Once Aunt Minnie became dependent on those drugs, the family worked harder than ever in order to afford her medication. It seems she cared for nothing else. Hettie supposed it was her opium addiction which caused her family to turn its back on her, until finally it was easier to pretend that this spectral creature wasn't there than to try to include her in their daily life. By now she had withdrawn into herself entirely, drifting through her days, leaving no trace, and in her last years, they scarcely saw the figure who crept so uncertainly toward kitchen or outhouse, gently tended by old black Aunt Cindy. Only Cindy was present when she died of a failure of the spirit on a cold March day of 1912, and even her passing went unnoticed until Cindy tried to feed her a little soup.

"Aunt Cindy took care of Granny Ellen in her childhood, then took care of her household and her child rearing—she saw to everything," Hettie said. "Cinderella Myers was a good old-fashioned slave girl who stuck by her owner even after she was freed. And when Ellen and her children fled to Florida, Aunt Cindy left her own new family to come south with them, knowing that her little Miss Ellen could not take care of her life by herself."

Lucius supposed the young slave girl might have come from the Myers Plantation at Columbia, South Carolina, perhaps as a wedding present to Miss Ellen. She was about the same age as Granny Ellen, according to the census. Yet such facts told nothing about who she was, this enduring young woman with her own soft form and bittersweet desires who had used up her one life on earth so faraway from her own home and family.

It struck his cousins as perverse that Lucius should wish to know so much about Aunt Cindy. Chagrined by how little they knew themselves, they could not answer his upsetting questions. No, there was no known picture of her. After Miss Ellen and her children died—all within two years of one another—the old woman had persevered without complaint in her shack behind the house, tottering about her chores and chickens even after she started to go blind, until finally, in reward for her half century of faithful service, she was sent home. Her satchel had been packed for weeks when a stranger who had been her baby daughter long ago turned up to fetch her back to that red Piedmont country she could scarcely imagine anymore, to take such solace as she could from the voices of grandchildren and great-grandchildren whose parents she had scarcely known and whose faces she would never see.

"Nobody was home the day Aunt Cindy left, that's what my daddy told me," Cousin Ellie said. "Isn't that awful? Not a sign of her anywhere, not even a note, because she had never been taught to read or write. The poor old thing just picked up and went. As Daddy said, Aunt Cindy gave our family her whole life, and no one was there to thank her for her life or say goodbye."

*

"Well, they never arrested Cox in the Mike Tolen killing," Paul Edmunds said, compelling a change of subject. "If Grover Kinard told you that, he got it right. But Calvin Banks, he must of knowed something, cause they had that old niggera up there to the trial. Watson's revolver was the one piece of hard evidence, and it wasn't on Watson when they found it. They arrested John Porter at the start because he had quarreled with Mike, but there never was no evidence that John was in on it."

"And Frank Reese?" Lucius said. "No one recalls him?"

" 'Pin it on the niggcr,' that's all that was," April said. Hettie and Ellie frowned and shook their heads, resisting the younger generation's view of Southern justice, but so far as Paul Edmunds was concerned, the time-honored remedy mentioned by the girl needed no defense. To recapture the floor, he stuck his hand up as he must have done a half century earlier in this same room—a fresh-faced scholar in knee britches, kicking mud off high black shoes of the same clodhopper style he wore today.

"Maybe that niggera was arrested, too, but if he ever spent a day in jail, I never heard about it. Coursc hc's pretty well forgotten now around these parts—probably ain't a soul but me could recollect him." Mr. Edmunds peered about him fiercely, to discourage any further interruptions. "Now Cox and Watson had Fred Cone for their attorney, who later become the governor of Florida. Lawyer Cone had the reputation of never losing a case, and darned if he didn't get 'em off, though every man in these five counties knowed them two was guilty."

With Cox already on the loose, the family could scarcely celebrate Uncle Edgar's acquittal, so fearful were they for the lives of Minnie's sons. When Uncle Edgar was set free at Madison on Christmas Eve of 1908, the family figured he would come back through Fort White, and, sure enough, someone saw him at dusk on a back road across the county line, looking like a man who planned revenge. Another night, the Collins dogs barked violently into the darkness, and Julian and Willie were certain he was there. For weeks thereafter, they went into hiding, until word came that Uncle Edgar had gone back south to the Ten Thousand Islands. But not until late 1909, when Leslie Cox was convicted in the Banks murder case and sent to prison, did the community enjoy a good night's sleep.

A year later, when the Widow Watson passed through this community on her way to her sister in north Florida, she confided to her dear friend Laura Collins that her husband and a friend had planned his escape in case the Madison trial came out the wrong way. Who that friend was she did not reveal, but the family always supposed that it was Cox.

Edna Watson would never say whether or not her husband had acknowledged either killing. Yet he had been frank about it to Joe Gunnin, his young neighbor on the Bellamy Road whose sister Amelia would marry Willie Collins less than a fortnight after Uncle Edgar's death. Gunnin and one of the young Langfords had been visiting at Chatham Bend when Leslie Cox showed up in the spring of 1910, and had been terrified the whole time they were there for fear Cox might kill them in order to keep them quiet about his whereabouts. When they got home, they were still excited. They told the family about those three poor souls whom Cox was to murder just a few months later.

"I guess they saw it coming," Hettie said.

"I guess so," Ellie said, "if you believe my uncle Joe. Not many did."

" 'Lawyer Fred P. Cone and his assistants took every last penny that we had.' That's what Uncle Edgar told poor Edna, who confided it to her dear Laura Collins," Hettie said.

"Who confided it to everybody else," said April.

"I wonder if Governor Cone took pride in the Cox case," Ellie said. "Because he'd hardly got through persuading the jury that this good-looking young man from a churchgoing family was a nice neighbor boy at heart when that nice neighbor boy turned around and murdered those poor old colored folks right up the road here! And within the year he killed three more in the Ten Thousand Islands, and white people at that! Committed six murders *after* the Tolen deaths, and here he was, hardly old enough to vote! Murdering fool, that Cox boy was! What Fred P. Cone turned loose on our community was a murdering fool!"

Ellie glared at each of them, one after the other, to make sure they understood that such a travesty of justice was unacceptable to Ellen W. Collins of Olustee Street, Lake City, Florida.

Mr. Edmunds, still agitating for the floor, revealed that sex had been a factor in the Cox-Tolen feud. "As I recollect it, Will Cox's wife Cornelia was some kind of a half-breed Injun, which might of accounted for her boy's revengeful nature. So when Jim Tolen done her sister wrong, Cornelia could never forgive that deed, let alone forget it. She swore a feud against that family, cause nobody messed with that mean bunch and got away with it. Trouble was, one of her brothers was already killed off, and the other one in the state pen, so she mentioned to Leslie, who was her oldest, that she aimed to defend poor Sister's honor by herself, being as how she was fresh out of brothers.

"Knowing Cornelia, Jim Tolen went on home to Georgia, so Leslie consulted with Ed Watson. Didn't hardly take no time at all for them two fellers to agree that Jim Tolen's brother Sam might be better off dead than running around making a nuisance of himself."

Lucius tried in vain not to sound annoyed. "Mr. Edmunds? Are you sure all this is true?" Just when he thought he was getting things sorted out, local legend had come banging through the door like the town bully.

"That's the story, son," the old man snapped. "Take it or leave it. Don't make a goddam bit of difference, not to us home people around here."

"Now, now, Paul," Letitia murmured, patting his old knee, which twitched in fury.

"It ain't like Tolens was his first!" Giving up on Lucius, Edmunds turned back to the women. "There was two niggers—*niggeras*—killed up by Columbia City. Leslie helped Sam Tolen out with that one, is the story."

"Maybe that was just a rumor," Hettie said.

"Mr. Kinard mentioned it, too," Lucius sighed.

"Grover Kinard tell you that?" the old man said. "Well, he got *that* one right!"

"Leslie Cox would kill a man just to see him wiggle, that's what my daddy used to say."

"My daddy used to say that, too," April notified her aunt. " 'Leslie Cox would kill a man just to see him wiggle.' If he said that once, he said it—"

"April?" her mother said. "Honey, what's got *into* you today!"

"Now at the time of the Sam Tolen killing, Watson was past fifty and Cox only nineteen," Edmunds was saying. "I reckon Leslie was some kind of a hero-worshiper, otherwise that friendship made no sense. What that Cox boy seen was this big strong well-dressed feller back from the Wild West, supposed to been some kind of a gunman, supposed to killed some famous outlaws in the Injun Country."

"And what Uncle Edgar saw was a dull, vicious boy sent straight from heaven to do his dirty work. Uncle Edgar was smart and Leslie wasn't—it's as simple as that."

"No, Leslie was not well thought of around here," gentle Hettie agreed wistfully, as if still open to the possibility that the Cox boy was held in high esteem in other parts. "He was a sort of rough-and-ready person, you might say." In her wide-eyed light irony, she smiled innocently at Lucius, who was struck by how much he admired the well-worked leather of these country women and how proud he was to be related to them.

"Rough and ready! Yes indeed!" Her daughter laughed.

"Trashy, that's what my daddy called 'em!" Ellie said, cutting off her niece with a fierce look. "Coxes and Tolens were trashy people. We always wondered how Aunt Tabitha could ever let her poor dim daughter marry a trashy Tolen. But Leslie Cox! As my daddy said, 'Now there was a *real* son-ofabitch!' "

"Some of those Coxes were good people and still are," Hettie reminded her, pale eyebrows elevated in mock alarm at Ellie's sporty language. "I don't know what Leslie ever did except get in trouble, but his people were hard-working farmers, well-respected, and well-connected, too."

Everyone laughed but Mr. Edmunds, whose knobby knee jumped about to beat the band. "Connected with the Sheriff, you mean! Connected enough to get Leslie let loose off the chain gang!" He turned to address the Professor, man-to-man. "Everybody in this section knew that Leslie was dead mean, but nobody wanted to suspect Ed Watson. Cause he was real likable, and I liked him, too, from what I seen of him. I was a young feller tending store, and Mr. Watson paid his bills on time, went out of his way to help you out. I talked to my dad all about it, talked to the old-timers who knew Watson, and I never met a one who got crossed up with him!"

"Know why? The ones that got crossed up with him were dead!" said Cousin Ellie. To heal their spat, April laughed too hard at her aunt's joke, until Ellie peered at her, suspicious.

Paul Edmunds's fierce frown made it all too clear that this was no laughing matter. When he had their attention once again, he declared that after Colonel Myers's death, his coachman Calvin Banks kept the location of his buried gold from his Watson women for fear the Tolens might get hold of it. That secret hiding place was lost with Calvin's murder. Right out here this minute in these hot old woods—Mr. Edmunds was pointing through the window—that buried treasure shone unseen beneath the pine needles. "And that was the money Leslie Cox was after and never got," the inspired man told the Professor triumphantly, enjoying the expression on his face. "So Leslie come back here all his life, huntin that money, havin gone and killed the only man who could tell him where it was!"

Lucius held his tongue. What he was hearing was disgraceful fabrication, and yet it rang with a certain mythic truth.

"Some say those poor darkies were killed because Calvin testified against Uncle Edgar at his trial. Calvin was black, and he opened his mouth against a white man—that was enough!"

"Damn right, boys!" April gave a rebel yell, and her mother had to hide a smile as the others frowned. "If that ain't Southren honor, I don't know what is!"

"See, what Watson done, he got word to Cox how there was one thousand dollars waitin for him if he killed that niggera, and if he found Calvin's money, they would split it. Course that is hearsay," Mr. Edmunds went on, with a resentful glare at Lucius. "Can't put no trust in us local people that has lived in these woods all their lives and knowed every last soul who knowed anything about the truth of it."

He allowed a moment for his big barb to sink in before resuming. "The story was that at his trial, Watson made a slit-throat sign to that old niggera, drew his finger crost his throat soon as Calvin first stood up to get sworn in. And Leslie was there—he was already turned loose in the Sam Tolen case— and Leslie seen it, so Calvin was as good as dead already."

"From what I heard, Uncle Edgar liked to joke in court, to tease the prosecutor, get the jury on his side," said Ellie. "But being Leslie, he would take it seriously when everyone else knew it was a joke."

"Judge never throwed Cox out of the courtroom, just ordered Calvin not to bc scared off. Him and the public persecutor reminded Calvin he weren't no damn ol' slave no more, but a bona fide American citizen and a franchised voter, so he better stand up and do his civic duty. And Calvin bein such a proud stubborn old mule, that's what he done. Well, nobody couldn't expect a man to let no niggera get away with *that*!"

"Uncle Edgar had his good name to think about, right, Professor?" April whispered. But the others raised cries of protest over Mr. Edmunds's headstrong version of events. "Where would Uncle Edgar get a thousand dollars, Paul? He was dead broke! The whole family was poor! For a half century, we buried our dead with wooden crosses!"

"Ain't none of my damn business where hc got it! But he always come up with money, we know that much!"

There was no good evidence for any of this stuff, and Lucius sighed, disheartened. He felt suffocated.He longed to get up and stretch his legs, go out for a long hard walk in the spring woods.

*

Letitia Edmunds was marveling aloud that her own mother had attended this Centerville school with Leslie Cox. "They sat right here in this very room, looking out these same ol' windows!" cried Letitia, who promptly looked out of the windows herself by way of proof. "And Mama told me that Leslie Cox first shaved at the age of twelve!"

Hushing his wife with one terrible frown, her husband confiscated her sole contribution to Cox lore. Leslie Cox, he informed them, was a full-grown man by the time he was sixteen, and when unshaven, he looked close to thirty.

"Maybe his body grew too fast for his brain—"

"He was never nice to *anybody*, April," Ellie said. "I never heard one good thing about him, cause he didn't have a good side, just a bad side."

"I never heard about the good side of May Collins, either!"

"Now, April honey, nobody ever called Aunt May a *killer*!"

"Well, this family sure got upset when she ran off with one!"

Lucius glanced at Hettie Collins. Is that true? his expression said, and Hettie nodded. "After Billy Collins died in 1907, that's when Leslie started hanging around May. Minnie Collins paid no attention to her children anymore, she let that girl talk to any boy she wanted. May had no supervision from her mother, and meanwhile Granny Ellen was getting feeble, and poor old Cindy was half blind, and May ignored them."

According to Hettie's clippings on the Banks case, the Bankses and Jim Sailor had been slain on Monday the 11th of October, 1909, and the bodies discovered Tuesday morning. As the leading suspect in the "foul and brutal murders of three hardworking peaceable negroes" (Lake City *Citizen-Reporter*, October 19), Cox was arrested the following day when he went to the courthouse in Lake City for his marriage license. Apprised of the romantic nature of his visit, the authorities "therefore" released the young man on bond, with the understanding that he would return after the wedding in order to be charged with triple murder.

Since Cox could easily have fled after the killings instead of going to Lake City for that license, and since he passed up a second chance when he was granted a day off to get married, he was apparently confident that the whole thing would blow over and his life would go on just as before. "Never thought there'd be no problem over killin niggeras," Paul Edmunds said, "and his dad's friend Sheriff Purvis held the same opinion. Not only let him out on bail, they let him go clear across the county line to marry."

Early Thursday morning, arriving on muleback at the school, Leslie Cox had made off with Miss May Collins, escorting her straight to her friend Jessie Barr's house in Suwannee County, where the wedding took place at 3:00 P.M. that afternoon. "The Barrs were kin to us some way, and kin to Coxes, too. Evidently they sent someone to warn the family," Hettie said, "because the Collins brothers knew right where to find 'em."

"*Willie* Collins went," Ellie admonished her. "Your father-in-law decided to stay home." When April rolled her eyes, her mother raised a warning finger. "I don't know who married 'em," Ellie continued, "but somebody must have made arrangements. He couldn't just pick her up at school here and go marry her!"

"Justice of the Peace Jim Hodges married 'em!" Paul Edmunds cried, reciting his fact proudly. "I talked to Justice Jim many's the time. He says, 'Miss May, are you aware that this young man you are about to marry will not sleep in your loving arms tonight? That your newlywed will lay his head on a iron bunk in the Columbia County jail?' And Miss May says smartly, 'No, sir, Judge, I ain't aware of no such of a thing! And anyways, I aim to marry this here feller, so let's get a move on!' "

"Miss May Collins did what she darn pleased, no matter what!" Ellie exclaimed. "May was willful and May was spoiled, there was only the one way and that was her way. But Willie Collins rode over to the Barr place and warned Leslie Cox that if he tried to take his sister, he would kill him."

"Might of had his hands full, Ellie," Mr. Edmunds warned her, not unkindly. "Leslie was a big strong six-foot feller, and the Collins boys was always pretty skimpy."

"Whoever rode over there arrived too late to stop the wedding," Hettie told Lucius, "but they caught up with the newlyweds at Herlong Junction, where they went to flag the train back to Lake City. As soon as Leslie boarded the train, he was rearrested. When the bride was told she could not sleep in the jail, she decided she might as well go home." Hettie Collins smiled. "So in the Lord's eyes, and the Collinses' eyes, too, that unholy wedlock was never consummated. Even Aunt May came to believe that as the years went by."

"Don't you go smiling, Hettie Collins, because that is the God's truth! It was my daddy who went after 'em, and when he got there, they were already married—yes, that's so! But he would not let her board that train, and Leslie didn't try to fight or Daddy would have killed him!"

"Aunt Ellie? Who would have killed whom? Maybe Leslie didn't care to murder his bride's beloved brother, ever think of that? Might have took some of the fun out of the party!"

Ellie gazed balefully at her niece. "They never lived together, Miss, as man and wife. Her father was dead but her brother was there, and he would not allow it!"

"Collins gospel!" April muttered as she left the room.

In a ruffled silence, Ellie insisted that May Collins was never anything but trouble. "To her last breath, that woman expected folks to wait on her! When she was still able to get up and get around—she went three hundred pounds toward the end—she used to come over to our house and plump herself down and fan her face and wave her fingers. 'Fix me a glass of water! Peel me an orange!' Never so much as a *please*!"

Hettie was smiling. "When she wasn't claiming that Bad Uncle Edgar had led her poor young husband astray, Aunt May would tell us she couldn't be blamed for running off with Leslie Cox, because Leslie had given her a bewitched apple! Once she had eaten that terrible witched apple, she was obliged to obey his least command!"

Recalling the witched apple, the women hooted.

"Well, it weren't witched apples she got fat on later!"

"Now where d'you suppose that boy found a witched apple?" Hettie pondered. "He might have bought that darn old apple at the Edmunds store, you think so, Paul?"

Paul Edmunds cackled. "Not unless he paid down most of that Banks gold! We sold them witched apples pretty dear—the bony-fidey ones, I mean!"

Ellie giggled unwillingly with the rest, but after a moment she relapsed into restless gloom. "In later years, Aunt May would never talk too much about her husband, because she didn't *know* too much about her husband, that's the truth. Maybe it had dawned on her by that time that Leslie Cox was just as no-account and mean as people said."

*

William Leslie Cox was found guilty of first-degree murder in Columbia County Court on December 11, 1909, but the jury begged the mercy of the court in order to spare him the death sentence. Reading between the lines of these accounts—the release on negligible bond so as to marry, the jury's mercy plea—Lucius doubted that Cox would have been indicted for killing the three blacks had he not been previously implicated in the Tolen murders. His father's crony Sheriff Purvis must have scratched his head over why this dolt kept returning to Lake City—either that or the Sheriff himself was astounded by a guilty verdict in this case.

On December 14, Cox was sentenced to prison for the rest of his natural life. "But Leslie broke free right away," Paul Edmunds said. "The Sheriff fixed it. Come straight home to Ichetucknee, helped his folks with the spring plowing. This would have been late winter, spring of 1910. After that he disappeared, went south to Watson's. But he come back here from time to time in his older years. Luther Carter, who married Leslie's sister, he told me one time how he went down fishing on the Ichetucknee, and darned if he don't see Les Cox watching him from behind a fallen tree across the river. Once Luther seen him, Les lowered himself slow and eased on back into the river woods, same as a panther."

"Well, we heard Leslie never bothered to hide. Didn't see the sense in it, with the Sheriff rooting for him," April said. "Cox hunted some with Norman Porter the winter he came back here off the chain gang, and Norman claimed that Leslie bragged that he had killed both Tolens, and the darkies, too. Wanted so bad to be a desperado like Ed Watson that he took the credit for all five of 'em, which didn't hurt Uncle Edgar's feelings a bit."

"After Leslie was convicted and sent off to prison," Hettie said, "May lived awhile at Coxes because the Collins family was so scandalized that they wouldn't have her. Even after she came home, the Coxes would show up here once in a while, to fetch her. She would stay away for a few days and then come home again, saying she had visited her in-laws. She would never say that Leslie had come home, but we suspected it."

"That's right," Ellie said. "Leslie could die of old age in our county hospital and you'd never get those Coxes to admit it. They are a closemouthed bunch, and they always were." Ellie had talked to a retired police officer who had known Cox when they were little boys in the Lake City school. In the thirties, this man saw a drifter on a bench along the river in Fort Myers, and he always swore that the man was Leslie Cox. And Paul Edmunds added that Leslie had been spotted along about that time at Cornelia Cox's funeral in Gilchrist County. The friend who'd seen him said that Leslie had grown a beard as a disguise.

"What did Old Man Kinard tell you about that one?" Paul Edmunds demanded. When Lucius said that Kinard agreed with them that Cox had not been killed by Watson, Edmunds nodded for some time, well-vindicated.

"Grover Kinard said that? Well, he got *some* things right!" April was caught mouthing these words by Letitia Edmunds, who stifled a frightened smile. "The kind of person that Cox fellow was," Letitia cried, to cover her confusion, "who would try to kill him? He might kill you back!" In confusion, she rose from her chair, anxious to go home, but her husband ignored her. Not until Letitia hugged the Collinses and waved good-bye to the Professor did Edmunds grunt and get slowly to his feet. From the doorway, he told Lucius, "If Leslie's dead, he ain't been dead too many years. Wherever his grave is at, it ain't too far." He turned and went outside into the sunlight. "Probably laying in some hole out here in these old woods," his voice came back. "Just the place for a wild varmint such as that."

Eventually May had gone to live with her aunt Fanny Collins Edwards in O'Brien, in Suwannee County. There she was the postmistress for many years. Upon her aunt's death, nearly forty years later, she inherited Aunt Fanny's house, and not long thereafter, concluding she had seen the last of Leslie Cox, she married a Mr. Lee Roy Martin, against the advice of almost everybody. Martin speedily mortgaged the house and property and sold off everything of value. Before departing with the proceeds, he asked May politely for the combination of the post office safe, which he rifled to the last green one-cent stamp. Her brothers were forced to take out loans to replace the money and keep the ex-postmistress out of federal prison, and from that dark day until the day she died, they underwrote her life, then paid to bury her.

*

Hettie talked awhile about her father-in-law's first cousin, E. E. Watson, known throughout the Collins clan as Cousin Ed.

"Three of Edgar Watson's first four children were born here in Fort White, and all four returned from Oklahoma to live in this community while their father got established in southwest Florida. Then they left, in tears and smiles, all waving and calling that they would write soon, they would come visit. Well, they never did. The Collins clan never saw Rob again, nor Carrie either. Except for that one mournful visit from poor Lucius after his father's death, Cousin Ed was the only Watson who ever came back here after he was grown.

"Cousin Ed was ten when he had left here for the Islands and fifteen when he returned about 1902 to help out on his father's new farm. Both Carrie and Ed were born in that old Robarts cabin near the Junction, but the place Cousin Ed always called home was 'the house on the hill' that his father built on one hundred six acres at the south end of this Collins property. Uncle Edgar was doing very well, and by 1906 he had paid for the Fort White farm, we still have the deed. Even Grandpa Billy, who had never felt easy around his wife's brother, and never doubted that he was a dangerous killer, had to admit that E. J. Watson was a fine farmer, very fair and efficient in his dealings.

"After Uncle Edgar's death, Cousin Ed would never speak about his father. He went right along with his Collins cousins, agreeing that family silence was the best policy, and assuring them that his sister in Fort Myers felt the same way. It was only his younger brother Lucius who still lived in the past, he used to say. However, Ed mentioned that after his father's death, he had gone to Chatham Bend and searched the house in case his father had hidden some money, saying that money rightfully belonged to the eldest son. I suppose he intended to turn it over to Rob!" When Lucius raised his brows, Hettie smiled that winsome smile. "Not that he found any money, or none that he let on about—he only said those Island crackers probably took it. 'You take my word for it,' he'd exclaim, 'it's down there yet!'

"Over the years, Ed rarely spoke about his brothers, but he couldn't stop talking about Carrie Langford and her fine new house, he bragged on Carrie *all* the time. Ed brought pictures of Carrie and her little girls, so we were kind of up-to-date on the Fort Myers kin, but our family memory of Rob and Lucius more or less died out with Granny Ellen. One time when Julian's Laura questioned Ed about his brothers, he confessed that, truth be told, he knew very little about Lucius or Robert—that was the first and only time we ever heard poor Rob called Robert—because he only heard from those two when they wanted money. As for Edna's children, well, they weren't real Watsons anymore because his stepmother—he always said 'my stepmother,' although Edna was several years younger than he was—had changed their names and cut off all communication with the family.

"Now Cousin Ed's saying such a thing doesn't make it true, because much as we loved our dear old cousin, he mostly saw things in a way that suited his own idea of himself. It never occurred to him that Edna and her children were family, too, far less that *he* might get in touch with *her.* We told him where to reach her but he wasn't interested.

"Cousin Ed would visit every year on his vacations. As his insurance business prospered in the early twenties, he would come through on his driving trips two and three times in a year, and for many, many years he brought his children. They'd stop here going and they'd stop here coming. And every single visit he would tell all about yesteryear, how he went to Fort White school back in the nineties with his arithmetic, reader, and speller, and how he got beaten with peach switches when he didn't know his lessons, and all about the meat and biscuits in thick syrup that the kids brought to school in their big lunch pails, and the three brass cuspidors lined up for spitting exhibitions at John McKinney's post office and general store, and the town marshal with a club lashed to his wrist and a big pistol, and the saloon on Jordan Street where passersby might see luckless men pitched through the swinging doors. From one year to the next, there wasn't one detail of the old days that Cousin Ed forgot, not even one! And he drilled his stories into us so hard that to this day, we can't forget them either!"

*

Hearing her mother's wry account of Cousin Ed, April laughed hoarsely, snubbing her cigarette. " 'Year after year, we keep on hoping,' Daddy used to say, 'but Cousin Ed is like the elephant, he *never* forgets, not even the smallest thing!' "

"He had a sincere attachment to these woods," Hettie reflected. "He'd drive into the yard and get out and look around at these old hickories and oaks, hands on his hips, then heave him a big sigh and say, 'I sure feel like I've come home when I come back here!' We never could figure why this poor ol' place meant so darn much to him, cause he hardly went outdoors again after he got here!"

"Free bed and board, that's all it was!" Ellie Collins said. "Penny saved is a penny earned—that's Cousin Ed!"

"Put you right out of your own room because you were just a kid!" April scowled at the older women when they laughed.

Hettie said, "I guess it *was* a place where he felt welcome. After his children were all grown, and Neva died, he thought nothing of bringing a female friend, might be a week! One friend he brought before he married Augusta, she was the weirdest woman we ever saw. Before she sat down to her supper she would take her belt off, put it around her *neck*!"

"Didn't want to constrict her stomach till she had eaten up all our food, that was the only thing that we could figure!" April was doubled up with laughter, egging her mother on. "And Gussie! Tell about the one he finally married!"

"Now our Augusta didn't sweat, y'know. Too ladylike to sweat, didn't even perspire! All us poor country females, we'd be all worn out and soaking wet from the damp and heat in these old summer woods, our hairdo slack and all collapsed and *beads* of sweat, you know, on brow and lip. And here was Mrs. Augusta Watson there beside us, buttoned up tight right to the collar, sitting straight up on the edge of her chair, cool as a daffodil!"

"Those two were buttoned up, all right! I never once saw Cousin Ed without white shirt and tie, even when cooking!" Ellie said. "He was a churchman and a businessman who kept up appearances or else, and Augusta Watson kept 'em up right along with him!"

The women whooped and gasped for breath, falling all over one another now with the exploits of Cousin Ed. And Lucius was laughing, too, delighted by tales which tended to affirm his years of exasperation over Eddie, even while feeling dishonest and disloyal. Such stories would never have been told had these good women known that he was Eddie's brother.

"Oh yes, Cousin Ed dearly loved to cook! But he was like most men who get the idea that they are cooks, they make your kitchen such a mess that you wish they'd just stay out of there, go read the funnies! Before Edna Bethea came into their life, Cousin Ed cooked for his daddy in the house on the hill, that's where he learned it, and each time he returned, he'd fall back into it. March up to the stove, bang pots around, and take right over."

"Uncle Edgar usually kept a cook when he was married, but in those five years while he was a widower, he figured he didn't need a cook just for the two of them. Cousin Ed never tired of telling how hard his daddy worked him, how he had to rake the yard by moonlight after doing chores all day. And each time he told that old story, Gussie would cry out, 'Rake the yard at *night?*' And she'd turn real slow, hand to her mouth, and stare round-eyed at the rest of us, just a-marveling, you know, like she was trained to it.

"And Cousin Ed would be chuckling along, shaking his head over his own anecdote to warm us up a little bit, and let us know something pretty good was coming our way. Then he'd bust right out with it—'Well, heck! We never had free time during the *day!*' And those two would just double up with all the fun, they'd enjoy the heck out of that one right through supper! *'Never had free time during the day!'* Just couldn't get over it, you know! Year after year! And later Cousin Ed would tell us how Augusta's sense of humor was the thing he liked the best about her, by which he meant that poor ol' Gus would spare no effort laughing at his jokes. She never said anything humorous herself, not so's you'd notice."

Hettie smiled gently at Lucius, to remind him that all of this was in the family, all in fun, that none of this irreverence meant any harm. " 'Raking leaves by moonlight'—that one *never* failed! They never let that grand old story die!"

"Well, Daddy said that Uncle Edgar was a neat man in his habits, liked the place neat as a pin even out of doors," said Ellie Collins. "So I bet it was true about raking in the moonlight, because he was a stickler for getting things done right, he was famous for it all around the county. He was a hard worker, and saw to it that everybody on his place worked as hard as he did. But he never did mistreat his nigras, at least not in Fort White. Even after Uncle Edgar was safe under the ground, Doc Straughter claimed that his 'Mist' Edguh' was the best boss man he ever worked for."

"Doc wasn't taking any chances!" April laughed. "Best stay on the good side of Mist' Edguh, dead or alive!"

Hettie rummaged from her box a letter from Cousin Ed, of unknown date.

My dear folks

I know you are interested in getting up a family tree, just sorry I know so little that would be of help to you. I did not even know Grandmother Watson was buried in Columbia County. I do know Grandfather Watson's first name was Elijah, and from what I heard when I stopped in Edgefield, South Carolina, he died in Columbia, S.C. He was a Colonel in the Confederate Army and fought under Wade Hampton, which is why Lucius has that middle name. That is all I know about him. I know I know the least about my family of any person alive. . . . Neither of my brothers kept in contact with me unless they needed money.

>   Much Love
>   Cousin Ed

P.S. Dear Hettie, we think of you often and talk of the "good old days" when we were young. Much Love Gus

"Among the many things that Augusta didn't know was that Cousin Ed had had a second wife before her, nor had she been told one word about his father. He told her that his father died of heart failure down in the Islands, and I guess that was true because his heart sure failed along with everything else. But after they'd been married quite a while—she told us this herself— Cousin Ed's older daughter, who didn't care for Gussie, took her out to the Fort Myers cemetery one afternoon to show her her mother's grave. And she showed her Edgar Watson's grave while she was at it, and gave poor Gus the lowdown, too, informing her that she'd got herself hitched up to the son and spitting image of a famous murderer! Because Cousin Ed had grown up husky like his father, big man, six foot, that dark auburn hair.

"Well, Gussie got flustered up, for once, and Cousin Ed had to assure her that his Katherine had exaggerated, that his father had been innocent, that he'd only kept quiet about the scandal to spare her feelings, and so on and so forth. After that they never spoke of it again.

"For many years, Cousin Ed had his own insurance agency in Fort Myers, he was doing fine, but he still had his little ways when it came to money. Our family was dirt poor thanks to Great-Uncle Lem Collins and his forfeited bail, and even Granny Ellen and her daughter, who'd had servants all their lives, had to be buried under wooden crosses when their time came. My father-in-law died early in the thirties and there was no money for his headstone, either. It wasn't until recent years that the family recovered just a little, and scraped the wherewithal together to put some stone memorials on its graves.

"Anyway, it was untrue that Ed didn't know where Granny Ellen was buried," Hettie said sadly. "And despite all his lengthy visits, and his strong feelings about 'the Family,' and his sentiments about Fort White as 'my real home,' he would not help out with his grandmother's tombstone, nor his Aunt Minnie's, either. Now that he thought about it, Ed told us, he couldn't recall being close to either one."

*

Another letter in Hettie's cigar box was postmarked Somerville, Massachusetts, January 14, 1910, about a month after Leslie Cox's conviction for the Banks murders. It carried two green one-cent stamps bearing the profile of Ben Franklin, and was addressed to Mr. Julian E. Collins, R.D. #2, Ft. White, Florida.

Dear Julian,

Your very nice and interesting letter reached me yesterday and as usual was delighted to hear from you. Glad to hear that all of the folks are well. As to May, I have not heard from her. I am very sorry that she blames me for my opinion of Leslie, but I am sure that I have not wronged him and that he himself is to blame for the opinion held of him by all good people. She must be entirely bereft of reason if she believes him innocent. Also in this case there do not seem to be any extenuating circumstances and most assuredly no chance for a plea of justification.

The taking of human life is only justified when taken in defense of life or home. If I understand his case correctly, robbery was his motive, therefore making it a most dastardly crime. God knows I have only sympathy for her, and as she grows older she will realize the seriousness of her plight.

I doubt very much if Leslie cares for May as such people are not capable of true affection.

You spoke of my buying a place down there but I am not ready as yet. Hope that eventually I will be able to come back and settle down and probably marry some fair southern maid. I have not time to bother with the girls now as I have to work Sundays and holidays. Hoping that you will grow more prosperous as you grow older and with my very best wishes to Laura and babies I remain

Sincerely,
Rob

"We think that must be Rob Watson, though we can't be sure," Hettie told Lucius, who was startled by this unexpected word from his lost brother.

"Rob never came back here to Fort White?"

She shook her head. "Papa Julian would have said something about it."

"And that's the last letter signed Rob?"

"That is the *only* one. Rob makes it sound like my father-in-law had a regular correspondence with him, but that wasn't true. All Julian Collins ever did was notify Rob about May's marriage, and being upset, he must have mentioned something about those dreadful murders." She looked distressed. "Perhaps poor Rob pretended to be in close touch with the family because he was homesick but could not come home." She looked at the others. "Later we wondered if he might have been in prison."

Lucius read the letter again, trying to recall what Rob had looked like the last time he had seen him more than fifty years before. Lucius had been eleven at the time, and the older brother he remembered was a handsome dark-eyed youth with black hair to his shoulders like an Indian, nothing like the righteous author of this letter.

"Long ago," Hettie said carefully, "there was some trouble in the Islands, and Rob took his father's ship without permission and sold it at Key West. At least that's what Uncle Edgar told this family. He said Rob did that with the help of a young kinsman named Collins."

Lucius nodded. "R. B. Collins," he said, looking at Ellie.

The women glanced at one another. "We don't know who this R. B. Collins could be," Ellie reminded him a bit too sharply, pointing at Hettie's lineage sheets, spread on the table.

In a long and awkward silence, Lucius said, "R. B. Collins is an old man now," as if this changed things. Upset for Arbie, he resisted the intuition that was fighting its way to the surface of his mind. "He's in Lake City right this minute, he almost came with me today," he pled, as if Arbie's physical presence in Fort White might somehow validate him.

"You see"—in her distress for him, Hettie was whispering—"Rob's cousin Thomas Collins told us many years ago that *he* was the young man who helped Rob at Key West."

"There *is* no R. B. Collins in this family." Ellie said flatly. "I tried to tell you this the other night, but you didn't want to hear it." She pointed at the sheets again. "We rechecked every sheet before you came this morning, to be certain."

"Now R. B. *Watson*—Robert Briggs Watson—that is Rob, of course," Hettie said slowly. "And Rob's mother was a Collins, as you know—"

September 13, 1879. Of course. That date had nagged at the corner of his mind ever since this morning at the Bethel churchyard. The date of Ann Mary Watson's death was Arbie's birthday.

In disbelief, he studied Rob's letter. He knew Arbie's hand from the rough notes in his "archive," and this oddly familiar script, with its looping *y*'s and *g*'s, could indeed have been written by a young, stiff, priggish Arbie, working seven days a week to gain a meager living, pathetically tending the frayed threads that still connected him to home and family.

"We can't find any L. Watson Collins, either," Ellie was saying. "If that is your real name, then we have no idea who you might be."

He put the letter down. For a moment, looking away, he could not speak. Then he took a deep breath, saying, "I'm truly sorry. I am here under false pretenses, as you suspected. L. Watson Collins is a pen name." He stood up slowly and went to the window, making unnatural loud creakings on the warped pine floor. Behind him, no one spoke.

"I am Lucius Watson," Lucius said.

He turned in the sun shaft from the window and apologized for his deceit, and for imposing on them. In preparing a biography, he had needed to know the truth about his father's life here in Fort White and had feared that they might be less candid had they known that he was Uncle Edgar's son. Having failed to identify himself in the phone call to Cousin Ellie, he had decided to withhold the truth until he could learn a little more, though of course he would have told them who he was before departing. He stopped and raised his hands and dropped them in despair, sickened by his own wretched excuses.

And still the Collins women made no answer. When he went toward the door, nobody stopped him. "I'm sorry," he said again, speaking to Hettie, and seeing a mist of tears in her eyes, he felt bewildered, too. "For some reason, it seemed . . . *important*. To learn the truth, I mean." Again he stopped, unable to bear the crushed innocence of her expression. He had no place here any longer. He stepped outside and closed the door behind him.

The window beside the door was open. Inside the old schoolhouse, his kinswomen would still be sitting there in shock and ire. Cousin Ellie's voice would be the first to speak, and would not speak kindly. He hurried to his car.

At Tustenuggee

Seeking to compose himself before confronting Arbie—*Rob!*—Lucius drove to the Fort White cemetery, probing his brain for the right components to fit things back together. Who would have recognized Rob Watson in that furious, foul-mouthed old drifter in rags and scraggy beard at Gator Hook!

Was his rough crust and cryptic coloration an evidence of prison life? Had "Poor Rob" (as even the sly Arbie had referred to him) taken his mother's maiden name because he was a fugitive? It had never occurred to Lucius that a disreputable old drunk with an urn filled with "Rob's" bones might be Rob himself! That urn was simply part of his disguise!

The taking of human life is only justified when taken in defense of life or home—that tone had certainly worn off in Rob's long years as a drifter, along with the manners and good grammar that his stepmother had taught him in her years of patient tutoring in Oklahoma. But perhaps that moralizing Rob, outraged by injustice all his life, was still hidden in there at the heart of him.

I have no time to bother with the girls. Had he had time or opportunity in the years since? How could such a cautious fellow reprove wild-hearted May, borne off by the baseball hero Leslie Cox, all unaware, that morning at the schoolhouse, that her elopement would be paid for with the earth-greened silver dollars of poor Calvin Banks?

Beyond the trees at the new high school in Fort White, a boys' baseball game was in full progress. The faraway shrill of the small players, the proud cheers of their parents, flew like bird cries through the dry branches in the cemetery. Lucius Watson was swept by poignant reveries of some intimate midsummer sadness, infused with melancholy for something forever lost and far away—an innocence of "home" that he himself had never known since leaving Chatham Bend decades before.

He wandered out among the stones in search of Cousin May. Here lay Cousin Martha, Wife of Jos. Burdett, died on March 21 of 1912, shooting her broken heart out on that cold first day of spring so that she might join the sweet seven-year-old who lay beside her. Little Frank had perished in that same fateful month that his brother Herkie had left home for good to marry Edna Bethea Watson in north Florida, and the loss of both boys had undone poor Mattie, said the Collins women.

In her photograph in the Collins album, taken not long before her death, Martha Collins Burdett had sad bruised eyes and a heavy downturned mouth. At age forty-eight, she shot herself, leaving no note—proof to her sister (Hettie's grandmother) that Aunt Mattie's death was not a suicide—"Why, poor Mattie was just deathly afraid of guns!"

Aunt Mattie got her men off to the field, fixed dinner, cleaned the house, hung out the wash. On the wood porch—"She didn't want to nasty up the house!"—she spread out an old quilt on which to die. Down she sank onto this hard bed in her last lonely meeting with her Maker, clutching the cumbersome cold weapon, shivering and self-condemning even in this final act, with only a moment left of life on earth, because this good old quilt with years of life in it would be stained by her life's blood—"and bloodstains are so darned hard to get out!"—and others would be obliged to clean up after her. That's where they found her, cold and staring on the quilt, shot through the heart. A country woman, she figured out how to work the trigger with her toe.

At the far end of the cemetery, the Herlong brothers rested in peace, attended by the monoliths of kith and kin, each with its heavy skirt of well-mulched grasses. The tribe was still dominated by the patriarch, Old Dan, upon whose headstone was inscribed "AN HONEST MAN'S THE NOBLEST WORK OF GOD"—an honest man, Lucius reflected, who had perjured himself by signing a mendacious affidavit, assuring the court that Neighbor Watson could depend on a fair trial in a county already aboil with men who sought to lynch him.

On his way toward the cemetery gate, where two old men fetched in green wreaths for a fresh grave, he came upon the stone memorial to "Maria Collins Cox." Sweet Miss May of the oval photograph who had posed so prettily in her white dress lay in an untended grave, unclaimed by the Cox family, unwelcome in the Collins plot at Tustenuggee. There was no epitaph, no wire container for vanished flowers, nor a fallen vase. Because of her fatal elopement and her importunities in the years since, there had been no mourners and no witnesses, only the two thin dutiful embittered brothers, standing stiffly in hot black Sunday suits on the baked ground under dry oaks. The vast suet of their sister, wedged into a pine box in the dress she died in, had been delivered to her Maker in the July heat of Independence Day, in the racket of fireworks staccato from the dying phosphate town beyond the trees.

*

May Collins's parents and her grandmother lay in Collins ground a few miles southeast of Fort White in the Methodist cemetery at Tustenuggee, in that bare sadness of lost country churchyards which weather and woods and small wild creatures are silently taking back. The white church was spare and clear in a way that reminded him of Hettie Collins, who was fashioned from the same native heart pine. She had touched his heart, and he would not see her again. Why was he so sure that she was dying, or would soon be dead? One day she would be left behind in this still churchyard at the end of its long lane through the thin woods, in a clay earth as white as powdered bone.

Near a large cedar, under pale and shining stones which had replaced the leaning wooden crosses, the Collins clan was prominent in the small churchyard. Billy Collins had gone to his reward on February 7, 1907, three months before Sam Tolen went to his. Ellen Watson had died at eighty on June 10 of 1910, four months before her son was slain at Chokoloskee. Safe at last in the narrow grave squeezed in between them lay their Minnie, who had breathed her last on March 14 of 1912.

In no hurry to confront Rob with their brotherhood, Lucius tarried. A jay's blue fire crossed the sun from one wall of spring leaves into another. In the stillness, a stray thrush song came in wistful query from the wood, and he stopped and turned and listened. There was nothing. All he heard was time, a moment on the turning earth, a falling twig.

A churchyard in a woodland at the end of a white road where an infant's gravestone had Jesus's little lamb carved on the top. Everything in order and in place, far from the world. Old family cemeteries made him feel . . . home-sick? There it was, that old longing to go home. But as he moved among the graves, an earlier sense of buried roots which grounded him in this Collins clan of Tustenuggee gave way to an instinct—more like dread—that he had not come home after all, that this encounter with his kin could never change the fundamental solitude of his existence. Home was not these upland woods of oak and hickory in the north-central peninsula but the lonely house in the Glades rivers.

He strayed across the sun-worn grass among the gleaming stones. Solitude among lone oaks and cedars, fingertips tracing the inscriptions, brought him a kind of melancholy peace. He was moved by the pains taken with the lettering—the anonymous hand which had labored in last witness to a life now returned into the earth, to be devoured by minuscule earth demons. Respecting the dead—or perhaps Death—he did not hurry. In his odd mood, he felt humbled by the great age of the granite. Even the dry crust on the stone, touched by his blood-filled finger, was derived from black lichens millions of years old—blind algae and fungi working minutely with wind and rain and sun to obliterate man's scratchings on this upright rock hewn from granites heaved up into the sun and air by planetary fire. The industries of these lichens, their remorselessness, filled him with longing—longing for what? He supposed he missed what he had never known, the simplicity of churchly life in a small country community, the rooted peace of living day after slow day in communion with one's forebears, in the great stillness of a Florida frontier of sparkling air and crystalline fresh water, and ending one's days where one began, where one belonged.

The loss of simplicity, was that it? Loss of the simple harmonies and truths, the earth's natural order and abundance? Perhaps that ruin, mourned by the earth itself, was the most profound of all life's losses, underlying all the rest. Not fear of death, which was fear of a wasted life—that fear he would endure—but deep generic dread of the death of earth as witnessed in the despoliation of the New World, the great forests and rivers of America, the wilderness and the wild creatures, still abundant in his childhood, now fragmented and broken or bound tight by concrete, poisoned everywhere by unnameable pollutions.

Death, he supposed, was his hope of the simplicity he longed for. Therefore he was drawn to the clarity of churchyards, the solace of old cemeteries—a morbid solace, some would say, though most historians might feel as he did. If nothing else, old names and dates incised in stone were more or less dependable, preserving the critical particulars. The graveyard was the last sanctuary, inviolable, not to be transgressed. And yet Lucius had always known—or known, at least, since October of 1910—that in the end there was no sanctuary except free self-relinquishment into the eternal light of transience and change, leaving no more trace than the blown dust of an old mushroom or the glimmer of a swift minnow in a sunlit sea or the passage of a lone dark bird hurrying across a twilight winter sky.

Alachua Prairie

From Fort White, Lucius followed a thin county road which ran west across old cattle range north of the great Alachua Prairie, a meager scrub which made him wonder how the banished Coxes had even subsisted. Eventually the narrow road passed a graying church set at the scrub edge, and farther on, another mile, a few small dwellings had been patched into the wasteland.

Levi Cox was winding down his days in a little red shack in a yard full of junked trailers. "Next time you'll find my grave but you won't find me," he sang out cheerily from his shack doorway. He wore a windbreaker and had his hat on, as if this stranger had turned up very late on a visit Levi had awaited for long years. He crossed the yard slowly and got into the backseat uninvited, not inquiring who this might be and paying negligible attention when Lucius introduced himself as L. W. Collins. "Been quite a spell since I seen where I am headed for," said Levi Cox. "Let's go on up to the church-yard, have us a look."

The small graying church back up the road, a single white room with a derelict piano and small pulpit, turned out to be the Second Adventist Church founded by Will Cox not long after the family came from Ichetuck-nee. All around the building and the unfenced churchyard, the clay sand lay exposed, so hard and barren that weeds could not obscure the few small graves. No bird call brought the hot scrub wood to life, nor was there any note of color, only the sun-worn petals of the plastic flowers.

Lucius assisted the failing man out of the car. "Be up here for good before you know it," Levi Cox declared, gazing about his final resting place with sat-isfaction. "Yessir, I'll have me a one-way trip. I am just ate up with cancer, so they tell me."

He shuffled forward, removing his old hat, pointing a wavering finger toward two humble stones which marked the place where the clan patriarch and his spouse lay together. The twin stones were ten inches high and barely wide enough to carry the small initials. "W.W.C.—that's William Wright Cox. And C.F.C., that's Cornelia Fralick Cox, layin alongside of Pa where she belongs. Loved each other forevermore and died in the same year back in the thirties. Ain't got the dates wrote on there yet. I been aimin to put a big tombstone to their grave, but I been down sick about twenty years and never got to it." C.F.C.'s grave was set about with ancient jam jars that had once held flowers, and also an ancient conch shell from the coast. Lucius won-dered if that conch had come from the Ten Thousand Islands, and if Leslie lay back there in the still trees in an unmarked grave.

Leslie's brother stood there, bony hands folded like a mourner. Turning around in tiny steps, he tottered a little in the sun. Asked if he'd like to sit down in the shade, he paid no attention, pointing out the graves of the two brothers, Lem and Leo, who were here ahead of him. "Course Mama had three brothers and two sisters. All dead, too." He shook his head. "Poor Mama was just so kindly hearted. Always said she'd rather have a friend than make an enemy but she never spared nobody her true feelins.

"Our pa was the same, got along real good with people till somebody made him mad, then he meant business. Leslie and Leo was that kind, weren't scared of *nobody*. If Leslie couldn't talk to somcone, then something else had to take place. I would of loved to seen my brother Les, but I never did. People been sayin he come back when Mama died, and when Pa died, they seen a stranger at the church." He gazed around him, still expectant, as if a lone figure might appear, standing at the wood edge by the road. "But I just know if Leslie had come, he would of said something to us youngers, especially a boy named Levi that was born after he left. Can't recall if Les's wife come to that funeral, but somebody would sure have knowed if *he* was there, would have knowed him in a minute by the scar, cause Leslie had a scar up by his ear where a mule kicked him. That darn mule laid him out so cold they never thought he would sit up again. So if he had come back, y'see, they's them that would of seen that scar, they would of knowed him."

Levi Cox fell silent for a while, forgetting. He took his hat off, put it on again. "Might's well ride down to Lucas Carter's house. He's got a nicer place than me. Married my sister. Ain't nobody smarter, not out this way. Ain't a thing in the world old man Lucas don't know."

*

Lucas Carter lived in a yellow house trailer with a deep-eyed handsome daughter named Havana and a huge white-and-strawberry ceramic cat. He was lying on the sofa wearing a felt hat. He showed no surprise when Lucius introduced himself, though his daughter said, "You any kin to Fort White Collinses?"

Havana said she had been told she looked like Uncle Leslie. "Had a great big picture of him on the wall till the old house burned. Uncle Les and his wife Aunt May, they were both in it. Uncle Les had gray-green eyes, they said. Sure looked older than his twenty years of age, but that is all the age he was when he left home for good."

"Grew up in a hurry, Leslie did. Ever'body thought the world of Les." Saying this, Carter gazed wryly at Lucius. "His mama and daddy used to say he was a good boy back in Lake City days, went to church regular and done his lessons. Nosir, he weren't a bad boy at all, only mischievous. Where he got in trouble was mixin in with E. J. Watson there to Herlong Station." He gave his visitor a sharp look. "You are some kind of a Watson kin, I reckon."

Lucius nodded, glancing at the woman, whose face had closed to him. He caught a scent of backwoods menace, like the fleeting musk of an animal on the night highway.

"We been waitin on you," Lucas Carter said.

"Told me he was a *Collins*!" Levi complained.

The daughter said, "Feelin tired, Daddy?"

"I *stay* tired," Lucas Carter said, holding Lucius's eye.

"Now that is a thing I wouldn't hardly know," Levi was murmuring, in answer to some inquiry in his own head, as the woman gave Lucius a hard look, then went away into the kitchen. "It would have to be way back yonder. Long, long time ago." He gazed at Lucius and smiled, back on the track again. "But I do know Les was living there at Tolen when he got in trouble. If I understood my daddy right, Edgar Watson warned him. Edgar says, 'Now listen, Will, these Tolen boys are pretty rough, and you got to go along with it or they'll make your life pure hell around this section.' And Pa told Edgar, 'Nosir, Edgar, I don't got to go along with *nobody*.' "

"Sure enough, them Tolens showed up just like Watson said, come to the gate and told our pa what he could do and what he couldn't. Carried on like they founded the county, and every man who come in there had to look up to 'em."

"Will Cox leased his land from Sam Tolen," Carter said. "They had the rent settled, then Tolen come back, said there was more land than he figured, said Coxes better give him some more money. Will Cox told him to have it surveyed out, and if he owed him more, why, he would pay it. Said, 'We didn't move here lookin for no trouble, Mr. Tolen.' They weren't lookin for it but Tolens brought it to 'em, and Les took care of it, looks like to me."

"And Leslie killed them both?" In this house, Lucius's question did not seem to him indiscreet, since unlike the Watson-Collins clan, the Cox family was not ashamed of its errant uncle. Whatever William Leslie Cox had done, they seemed confident that it was for the best. They remembered him with pride, and fondly, too.

Levi nodded. "My pa never did declare that Les done the younger brother, not exactly. All he said was, 'From the looks of things, it might been Les'— that's what he told me when I got up big enough."

Had they ever heard that E. J. Watson was involved?

"Dog if I know if they was other fellers in on it." Levi frowned. "Our pa thought a right smart of Mr. Watson, I know that much. Had a very, very high opinion of that man. But I never heard him say Watson was in on it, nosir, I didn't."

"Les went ahead and killed some nigras, that's what got him," Carter said. "Funny, ain't it? Killed 'em for their money but he never got none."

For the first time, Levi Cox looked a bit perturbed. "Thing was, on account of rumors, folks got so unsociable about our family that our pa moved away to Ichetucknee Springs, rented a common farm. But Pa said that he always knowed that his boy Les would stand by his pa long as he ever lived, and he would stand by him. Pa went down around Silver Springs to where they had him on the road gang, and he got word to Les to get out of the way soon's the guard's back was turned. That's what he done, and after that, he come on home, worked for our pa same as he always done.

"Man who ran a little commissary at the Head of Ichetucknee, he told the Sheriff, 'Les is up to Coxes, you go git him!' Sheriff went up there, he had no choice about it. Later he'd say with a big grin, 'I do believe I could of hunted up Les Cox if I'd put my mind to it.' Cause he knowed by the smell that somebody been smokin a cigar, and he also knowed our pa couldn't afford 'em. See, my brother was up in the top of the house, they had fixed him a place where he could go up in there when somebody was a-comin. Sheriff never bothered to track down that cigar smell, but he liked a joke. He hollers out, 'Well, if I was your boy Les, I would sure head out for other parts, cause if he shows up in this neck of the woods, folks might just hang him!'

"Anyways, Les got disgusted from always hidin out. He went on down to Watson's, Thousand Islands."

"The Sheriff let him go, you mean. Never tried to catch him."

"Not so's you'd notice," Carter grunted.

"Because killing black people didn't count—that the way the Sheriff saw it?"

"Yessir, he sure did." Carter cocked his head for a better look at Lucius. "Ever'body seen it that same way, so bein Sheriff didn't make a bit of difference, ain't that right?" He set his hat straight. "Course there was family friendship in it, too."

"Les left his wife home with our ma," said Levi Cox, "on account of her own people didn't want her, and she was there when Leslie come back off the road gang. My family thought the world of Miss May Collins—well, I *mean*! Someone lookin to get my pa riled up, or Mama, only had to let on how they didn't care none for their daughter-in-law! Oh, she was a fine woman, I can tell you, I seen her myself more'n one time. Later she moved over to O'Brien to run the post office for the U.S. gov'ment. Like Havana says, we used to have May's picture on the wall. May and Leslie, the *both* of 'em was on there! Our whole gang was on there ceptin me, cause I wasn't borned yet."

Lucas Carter said, "Yep, Leslie stayed at Ichetucknee for spring planting, worked his keep, and then he went to Watson in the Islands. We never knowed another thing about him ceptin hearsays. He never come back to these counties that I heard about. I had a half brother Orbert Carter who usually told the truth, and Orbert claimed he run across him down the coast. Orbert told him, 'Since you been home, my brother Lucas married your sister.' And Leslie said, 'Well, that don't mean if you ever say you seen me, I won't kill you.'

"Another time, that same half brother showed up sayin Leslie wanted me to come where he was at, but the family said, 'Why, Lucas ain't no kind of Cox at all! He might let on about it!' That was along about nineteen and thirteen. Others has said Les been back here since that time, and some will say they seen him at his daddy's funeral up here at the church, back in the thirties. Well, they didn't."

Levi said, "I sure am sorry I never got to see my oldest brother. When Leslie bid 'em all good-bye at the head of the river, Ichetucknee Springs, he told 'em he aimed to see 'em all again someday. He went down to Thousand Islands and that was the last that he was ever knowed about. Some said his friend Watson took and killed him, but our pa said, 'E. J. *Watson?* Heck, *I* knowed E. J. Watson! Knowed him all my life! Ed Watson never done no such a thing!' "

Lucas Carter took his hat off. "We heard it was a nigger man killed Watson—any truth to that?" He turned on his side and put the hat back on, closing his eyes. "Heard nobody never raised a hand to set that right." He opened one eye a little bit to squint at Lucius. "Not even his own boys," Carter said, shutting the eye again. "Times must of changed here while I wasn't lookin."

Levi Cox looked eagerly from one man to the other. "Well, I don't know about the Watson boys, but us Cox boys was fixin to go south, get over there to Watson's island, hunt up that nigger, find out what become of Leslie or the reason why. But now my brothers are all gone, and I been down sick, and it don't look like I'm ever goin to get there, do it, Lucas?"

The man in the felt hat turned to consider Levi, then turned back again, face to the wall.

"Nosir, it sure don't," Lucas Carter said.

*

Lucius returned slowly to Lake City, sorting out what he had learned of Leslie Cox. Despite all the local speculation that Cox had been seen from time to time here in north Florida, his instinct was to accept the family's word for it that after his departure, they never laid eyes on "Uncle Les" again. Either he had lived out his bad life in other parts or he had been executed in October of 1910, as Papa claimed.

Lucius remembered Leslie's scar—"a good little scar upside his head where a mule kicked him," Grover Kinard had called it. Like Levi, he'd said that Leslie had lain unconscious for some hours and had lost all memory of the days before. Their boy had been "different" after that, so his family claimed once Leslie got in trouble.

Severe amnesia and discontinuity of thought (which had made him seem backward as a boy), indifference to the feelings of other people, coldness and detachment, fits of violence—all could be symptoms of the damage caused by such a blow. But even if that mule kick could account for his behavior, it was only one of many "reasons" why human beings reverted to animality, whether singly or in gangs and mobs, and none of these were consolation to the victims.

Cox's family seemed satisfied that "Les" had killed both Tolens. Dyer would make good use of this, yet Lucius felt uneasy. Was Papa there in the leaf shadows when those Tolens died? Even if it were true that Leslie Cox was the man most responsible for the Watson myth, it also appeared that in subtle ways, his father had been responsible for Cox—had encouraged hero worship and exploited Leslie's unstable condition, perhaps prying apart a dangerous fissure in his brain.

And what of Mr. Watson's brain? Lucius tended to discount April Collins's suggestion that his father had been brain-damaged by Ring-Eye's beatings. Violence begetting violence—that seemed indisputable—yet by no criteria he knew about had Papa seemed deranged. He had farmed successfully for forty years after leaving Carolina, and established and maintained good relations not only with his neighbors but with various women and their children. All but Rob.

*

At the motel there was no word from Arbie. What awaited him was a hand-delivered note scrawled in crude carpenter's pencil on lined yellow paper. Well, well, he thought, excited and surprised. He returned to the motel room and poured himself a drink.

Before leaving for Columbia County, he had sent a letter to the chubby shy little half sister whom he had not seen in over forty years.

> Dear Ruth Ellen,
>
> I am an older brother whom you scarcely knew and won't recall, although he recalls you fondly from Chatham Bend. I remember so well the day the skiff's bow painter came loose and you sailed away downriver in the skiff, and remember how brave you were for such a little girl—you weren't even crying when our papa found you!
>
> May I intrude upon your privacy and ask if one day soon I might pay a call? I will be traveling through Neamathla on my journey to Fort White, where you were born. I am very interested in any memories you might have about our father—I should tell you at once that I am writing his biography—but I am also interested in your branch of our family, and anything your lovely mother might have told you.

There had been no answer to that letter, nor to a postcard notifying her that he would spend a few days in Lake City before heading south. Summoning forth this secretive creature was like whistling to an unknown bird hid in the leaves, to judge from the scared and flighty silence that returned to him like the echo of a shot across the miles of silent swamp, red hill, and muddy river.

Lucius had suffered a mild paranoia. Even his stepfamily was turning away from him, cutting him off, having no wish to be put in touch with their Watson past. But now word had come, and on the very day that their brother Rob, who had never met this youngest Watson family, had risen from the dead. He sat on the bed and sipped his drink before opening the letter.

In a formal tone contrasting strangely with the writing implements, the note advised him that Mrs. Ruth E. Parker had shown his letter to the undersigned, who wished to inform him that Mrs. Parker could not imagine how she could possibly assist his research, since she'd been but five when her father died, remembered nothing, and was quite unable to converse on this painful subject.

He poured himself another drink and reread the letter, which was signed A. Burdett. He had hardly finished when the phone rang—Rob! Instead, a strange voice, gruff and heavy, said, "Did your damned attorney deliver my damned note? Because I represent the Burdett family." In grudging speech, A. Burdett said that, despite the note, Mrs. Parker would "receive" Lucius Watson after all. He did not say why she had changed her mind but merely said that he, Burdett, would be present at any meeting "to protect her interests."

"Nonnie resides in a town here in the lake country that will go unnamed," he added—for the pure love of that phrase, it appeared, since without being privy to its name, Lucius could not have sent his letter to Mrs. Parker. Downing his bourbon to calm himself, he gasped in agreement, waving excitedly for Sally's attention as she came through the door. "Where's Arbie?" she whispered, and he only shrugged, putting his hand over the mouthpiece. "It's *Addison!*" he whispered. To the telephone he said, "You want me to meet Nonnie after all."

"It's *you* who wanted to meet her, if I'm not mistaken."

"And you've decided to accommodate me. Why?"

The caller paused, taken aback. "She told me to get hold of you! Told me that before she dies, she wants to learn about Ed Watson—'the good, the bad, and anything in between,' she said!"

"Why?" Lucius repeated, groping for any sort of clue that might help to explain his own obsession.

"Now you just hold on a minute! Are you drunk?"

Sally leaned and whispered, "You trying to scare him off?" She shook her head and went into the bathroom.

"I mean, *why* does Ruth Ellen want to know?"

"What's that? Why *not*? He was her father!"

"Yours, too. Mine, too. You seem unhappy about this—"

"Look, I don't know you! I don't even like *talking* to you!" Burdett cried. "I think you're drunk! There's something funny going on! Your damn attorney showed up here day before yesterday, using your name! Not so much as a phone call! Wanted us to support some useless claim to the Watson house down in the Everglades!"

"Well, good! I hope you will!"

"Hell, no, I won't! I told my sister about it, and she got all flustered up, fished your damn letter out to show me. You claim to be her long-lost brother!"

"Addison? Yours, too."

Burdett's laugh was forced. He made no answer.

"Look, Ad, I'd like to see you. I haven't laid eyes on you since 1911. You were four."

From the telephone came trapped breathing and more silence.

"How about tomorrow?" Lucius said, banging down his glass and standing up as if ready to set off this very moment. If Burdett liked, they could meet at Ruth Ellen's house. This made the point that he knew the address and could have gone there without Addison's permission any time he wished. "I wouldn't want to upset her, of course," he added quickly. "Wouldn't want to intrude." More silence. "I have no wish to see her until she wishes to see me." Though this was calculated to dispel Burdett's wariness, it also happened to be true.

"I'll call back," Burdett blurted abruptly, and hung up.

"I'll be amazed if you ever hear from him again." Sally sat down on the bed edge, took his hand. "You drink too much, do you know that, Professor?"

"Arbie tell you to say that?" He tried to smile. "You've been known to take a drink yourself."

"What's *my* drinking got to do with it? You're supposed to be a biographer, researching a damn book! And here your long-lost brother calls and you screw it up!"

"That the tone you always take with your employer? Anyway, I didn't screw it up."

The reproof hushed her. But he was unsettled by her gaze, aware that Sally's acquiescence had nothing to do with regret, far less submission. He also knew that she was right—he drank too much, and he had probably screwed it up. However, Burdett called back in a few minutes. Without mentioning his sister, he said he would meet Lucius in two days' time, at noon, at the motor inn at the highway interchange outside Neamathla.

*

Next morning Lucius called Hettie Collins to apologize and say good-bye. She seemed relieved to hear from him, saying she quite understood why he felt he had to disguise his identity. In fact, she had worried about him all that evening, realizing how upset he must have been about "R. B. Collins." How happy the Collins clan would be to welcome Rob Watson back into the family after all these years! And Rob's brother Lucius, too, she added, her smiling voice warming his heart. He asked if one day he might pay another visit, and she told him shyly that she dearly hoped he would. "Come soon," she said, rather suddenly, and he said, "I will," and put the phone down, his heart pounding. She knew she was dying, he decided.

The police had received no report of any stray old man, dead or alive. Probably Rob was on a bender and holed up someplace, in which case he might be gone for days. When Lucius rang Sally to let her know that they were leaving, she cried, "You can't abandon that old man!"

"He's a very tough old man. He can take care of himself. He always has."

"But you saw how upset he was, leaving that cemetery! He was weeping! And small wonder!" She sounded on the point of tears herself. "Probably saw his poor young mother's grave for the first time in his life!"

"Sally, he knew I'd learn the truth, that's why he needed an excuse not to come with me. He's sleeping off a drunk someplace. He'll meet us in a day or two. You'll see."

He left a note at the motel desk in a sealed envelope containing money for bus ticket and food and the address of the Gasparilla Inn in Fort Myers. He addressed the envelope to "Mr. R. B. Collins" but the note said he would be delighted to be reunited with his long-lost brother. In an effort to cheer up the old man, he told him that, whatever his damn name was, he'd better not spend the enclosed money on more liquor, but get his old ass onto the bus down to Fort Myers and identify the occupant of that damned urn.

Chapter 5

In Neamathla

A. Burdett, checking his watch in the parking lot outside a gas station in Neamathla, turned out to be a heavy man in an ill-fitting steel gray wind-breaker, baggy khakis, and paint-splatted high black shoes. Glimpsing a female asleep in the backseat, he jerked his head away. He wore pale spectacles under a big brow with thin hair plastered back on a balding pate, and his pale auburn brows and thin downturned mouth closed a gray face. He was built like his father, Lucius thought, and earlier in life must have been strong, but now—too early—he had the hollow look of someone whose woman had left him years before. The ears and loose-skinned neck and knobby hands seemed too large for his body, and he seemed unsteady, as if he had suffered a small stroke. Without looking at Lucius, he identified himself—"A. Burdett"—at a loss as to what he might possibly say next.

"*A* for Addison, right?" Lucius smiled to make amends for having rattled this poor fellow over the telephone. Burdett looked wary. A man's Christian name was his own business, that look said, as Lucius struggled to dispel the clotting atmosphere. He said, "Last time I saw you, Ad, you were just a little boy, playing around Papa's dock at Chatham Bend."

"*Papa*," Burdett said, tasting the word. "That's what us kids called Mr. Herkie . . ." His voice trailed off and he wiped his palms down the sides of his pants, lowering his gaze in gloomy resignation. "Papa," he repeated, aimless.

A bit desperate, Lucius gazed about the little town. Was it true that Nea-mathla had taken its name from the great chief of the Mikasuki Creeks?

"How's that?"

"Do you suppose . . . I am like a bat that hangs by its claws in a dark cave, and that I can see nothing of what is going on around me? Ever since I was a small boy I have seen the white people steadily encroaching upon the Indians and driving them from their homes and hunting grounds. When I was a boy, the Indians still roamed undisputed over the country between the Tennessee River and the great sea of the south, and now when there is nothing left them but the hunting grounds in Florida the white men covet that. I will tell you plainly if I had the powers I would tonight cut the throat of every white man in Florida!"

Self-deprecating, Lucius laughed at his own recitation, inviting Burdett to cheer up, but Ad just stared at him. "My Lord!" he said. "You *memorize* that stuff?" He stared at his splotched shoes. "Might as well get going, then," he said.

Lucius tailed his lump of a half brother west on the county road, won-dering why he was looking up the tailpipe of that pokey two-tone car when he already knew Ruth Ellen's address and could probably get there faster by himself. If Ruth Ellen turned out as obdurate as Addison, he would not stay long. He would not even bother to wake Sally.

*

In a quiet street of one-story houses shaded by sycamores, Ruth Ellen Parker stood awaiting them upon her stoop. Mrs. Parker hugged her stolid brother, who said, "Hullo, Nonnie." Oddly, he introduced her to "Professor Collins." Before Lucius could greet her, Ad launched forth in sudden speech on the subject of his sister's many triumphs over adversity, blurting his words in the inchoate way of someone with a real horror of human converse. Persisting doggedly even after her hands started to flutter, speaking faster and faster to get it over with, he described how his sister had lived in this small house since her marriage to the late Mr. Parker. Nonnie had always hoped to be a teacher, and later in life, during the summers, had paid her own way to three different colleges in order to obtain a teaching certificate from the state board—

"Well, that's really something!" Lucius exclaimed, cutting him off as kindly as he could manage, for the sister had fled, leaving the brother to peer mystified at the screen door. Behind Ad, he saw Sally's blond head pop up in the backseat window and pop down again, not wishing to be observed, far less introduced.

Inside, Ruth Ellen greeted him anew, holding his *History* in both hands like a hymnal. Not having seen him since she was five, she did not really recognize him, and after five decades, he could scarcely perceive in this middle-aged woman the snub-nosed child in the sun and salt Gulf breezes at Chatham Bend, who had dressed up in her peppermint frock and bright wildflower bonnet to kiss "Woo-shish" good-bye, yet had been so hurt by the abandonment that she'd run away around the house and set up a great caterwaul behind the cistern.

Like Addison, Ruth Ellen had retained the auburn hair of their late father, and her scrubbed pink countenance was plump as a fresh bun. "I believe Mr. Watson's sister married a Collins," she told the Professor, who smiled back. It did not seem the moment to remind her that he was a Watson—in fact, her half brother. Politely she offered him a seat, but not before she had backed herself into a stuffed chair under a lamp where he supposed she passed most of her days. From this redoubt, having smoothed her feathers, she permitted herself a better look at him. What do you want with us? her scared eyes said.

On the walls all around were cheerful oils, unframed, including a painted copy of an old photograph of the Bethea homestead at Fort White. Ruth Ellen Parker thanked him kindly for gathering so much information about her family, and Lucius complimented her on her floral still lifes, and Ruth Ellen said she regretted her lack of training. Addison stood awkward in the doorway, hat in hand, anxious to be sent away. When Lucius smiled in his direction, trying to include him, Ad said gloomily, "Besides all this art, she designs and sews all her own clothes and makes fine patchwork quilts—that's another hobby."

"Addison, do please sit down," his sister said, as if he had stood up at his school desk for no reason.

They skirted fifty years of family news but soon gave up on these civilities—the ways had parted far too long ago. Lucius told them of the plan to burn the house at Chatham Bend and asked them to sign a petition which might save it. "You and Ad and little Amy were the last of our family to live there, and anyway, it would help our claim if we could show that the whole family supports it."

"Who is 'we'? You and that attorney? Count me out," growled Ad, shaking his head. His sister sighed.

On a little table set out for Lucius's arrival were a few mementos from the Watson years that Ruth Ellen hoped might make his visit worthwhile. Her pale fingertips moved these about like counters, to be offered one by one as the spring day ticked past on a big loose alarm clock in another room. The first was a gold wedding ring, inscribed "E.D. and Edna"—perplexing, they agreed, since *E.D.* had been not their father's initials but their grandfather's.

After so many years, Ruth Ellen could not bring herself to say "my father," only tweaked her pink blouse or crisscrossed her plump ankles at each mention of him. On the other hand, she betrayed no shame or resentment. Such a man had nothing to do with her, her manner said. She had led a God-fearing life, as the world knew, and had nothing to fear in the Lord's eyes. However, she asked for Lucius's assurance that he would keep her location and identity a secret.

"All those bad things happened when we were small," Addison complained, "but to Nonnie we aren't talking about the past, we are talking about her father, we are talking about horrible crimes in her own family that none of her neighbors know about even today!" His voice was rising, and his color, too. "What would they think of her? Our younger sister won't mention his name, not even to us! And you intend to *write* about it!"

"Addison? Please, dear."

Ruth Ellen touched a few mementos before tendering a photograph of a mother and small infant—"me." She smiled. Her mother was posed formally in a large round hat of black straw perched atop thick upswept honey hair—a wistful young woman, pretty enough, tense, sensual, large-featured, with a guarded smile. "Mama had hazel eyes," Ruth Ellen said fondly. The portrait studio was in Fort Myers—on the back was scrawled "Fort Myers 1906"—and Lucius supposed that "Mr. Watson," as Edna always called him, must have brought his new wife and baby daughter through Fort Myers while tending to his cane syrup business in the Islands.

"I really have no recollection of my . . . of Mr. Watson, but Mama always said I had his hair." She touched her auburn hair. "A strong and handsome man, they say! He didn't have a potato face like mine!" She blushed at Lucius's protest. "I've wished so often I could find his picture, to see if it matched the one in my mind's eye, but no one in our family kept a photo of him, not even Mama!" Eager, still wary, she was sitting forward. "Do you have one, by any chance?" Told about the Collins picture, she shook her head. "I don't suppose that I shall ever see it."

"Nonnie?" Ad growled. "Let sleeping dogs lie." She smiled at Ad briefly, out of kindness.

In two of her photos dim figures were grouped on the porch steps at Chatham Bend. The imposing man in black suit and black hat, central and dominant in both, was E. J. Watson, but the features were lost in the dark of the hat shadow. "That's all I remember anymore—that shadowed face!" She giggled uneasily. "A memory of shadows!" Startled by that phrase, she took a great deep breath. "I will tell you everything I can recall," she said. "Then we'll be finished with it."

*

"Mama's mother died when she was twelve. A few years later, Grandfather Bethea and her new stepmother encouraged her to go to Mr. Watson. They wanted the grown daughter out of the house, so her own family encouraged her marriage. Mr. Watson had a fine house and plantation, and he came courting in a red buggy with a fine big horse. They were married in May of 1904, and I was born in Fort White in May of 1905.

"Mama's half brother, William P. Bethea, is only a year or two older than I am, but he claims he remembers meeting Mr. Watson. He says that he liked Edgar Watson and so did all the rest of the Bethea family, he doesn't recall a single adverse comment. My cousin Pearl McNair felt the same way."

Ruth Ellen's curiosity about her father had been intensified a few years earlier by a letter from her Cousin Pearl. When she said this, her brother lunged forward and seized the letter from her little table and shoved it at the Professor, creasing the paper. At his needless intrusion among her things, his clumsiness and ungovernable impulse, her brow knitted minutely but soon cleared again.

Dear Ruth Ellen—

I'm going to tell you a little bit about your father.

Before your mother married him, Mama and I went to see Grandpapa Bethea. The Burdetts lived on a sharecropper's farm across the Fort White Road. Mr. Joe Burdett had a son and a daughter. Herkimer Burdett and Aunt Edna were childhood sweethearts. The Burdetts would come over and sing and play the organ, guitars, string instruments, etc., pull syrup candy. Fine times we enjoyed! We went to a Christmas tree, and Herkie gave all the kids a present. Mine was a bracelet with blue stones. While we were at Grandpapa's a Mr. John Porter came by with his wife and little girl named "Duzzie." What a name for a girl! She had a red dress on. The Porters met Mama and went back home and told Mr. Watson about Preacher Bethea's widow daughter Lola McNair visiting. They carried him back to meet Mama, but we were about to leave for home. Your father saw Aunt Edna then, fell in love with her instead, and asked for her hand.

I do not know too much about your father but I do remember him. Mama went back there to tend her little sister so we were in your home when Addison was born. Your father had a big plantation, acres and acres of land near Fort White, Florida. I can tell you about the place. You were a baby then, walking but wobbly. My brother and I loved to take your hands and walk with you.

Jane Straughter was the cook. Your father gave your mother a mare named Charlie, gray color with black speckles, a very pretty little horse. A colored man named Frank would hitch up the horse and buggy for Aunt

Edna. With you in my lap, we would drive to Mr. Edmunds's General Store in Centerville, and toffee was always on the list!

Minnie Collins was your father's sister, a beautiful lady. I dream of her house. It was a pretty place near your father's place, a large mansion in those days in west Florida.

Mr. Watson wanted to take the whole Bethea family with him to the Ten Thousand Islands. Grandpapa's wife Jessie did not want to go. Good thing she did not go, because the mosquitoes were so awful down in the Islands that they had to screen the cow stalls! But your father kept plenty of help and had two large boats. Those days men wore a gun belt and a revolver in a holster. Your father was a nice-looking man, tall and handsome. Your mother was treated like a Queen. No doubt your mother lived a romantic life, with lots of excitement. Those were the days! Ruth Ellen, I repeat so much. Take all mistakes for love always.

Pearl

On another occasion, Cousin Pearl had told Ruth Ellen that when she was a girl, a number of things happened that didn't make sense to her at all. One day at Fort White, she was riding with Aunt Edna and Uncle Edgar in the buggy when Uncle Edgar stopped at a crossroad. He had very small feet, and he put on Edna's shoes and went over to a fence corner and walked all around there making footprints. He would not explain it, just said it was a joke. Not long thereafter, they received word that Sam Tolen had been ambushed at that very spot.

In regard to her father's role in the Tolen killings, Ruth Ellen said that her mother's only comment was "He was found innocent."

*

"Addison was born at Fort White in 1907, and Amy was born in Key West in 1910. Amy was a babe in arms when that terrible Hurricane of 1910 struck Chokoloskee. I was only five but I never forgot that night at the little schoolhouse. I was sitting on a bench, children were crying. Mama was crying, too, that's how terrified we were. I asked her why she was crying and she couldn't answer. But I can remember seeing that salt water rising several inches deep over the floor. The men were building a raft for the women and children, there was a lot of hammering, and Mama said, 'Whatever happens, we will stay together.' We went up the hill. Mr. Walter Alderman lugged me and Ad under each arm, Mama had Amy.

"That hurricane frightened poor Mama to death, she was scared of bad weather the whole rest of her life. And Mr. Watson died only a few days later.

On her twenty-first birthday! The twenty-fourth of October was her birthday! And she felt so dreadful, knowing Mr. Watson had been killed because he came back just to be with her on that anniversary. Before he left Chokoloskee the last time, she begged him not to put his life in peril, she told him to go south to Key West while he had the chance. But Mr. Watson was too bold and willful, and he just smiled and kissed her, saying, 'A promise is a promise.' For the rest of her life, she would never celebrate her birthday again.

"Poor Mama was just terrified by the shooting, which sounded worse than the Great Hurricane, she said. It's very scary when a crowd of men turns violent, that's what she told me. All she could think of was getting her little ones out of those dark islands just as fast as she could go."

*

Neither Edna Watson nor her children had ever laid eyes upon Rob Watson. Ruth Ellen had a dim memory of Eddie from her early childhood in Fort White, and thought she recalled Carrie Langford from the time when her family had rested one night at Fort Myers on the way north after her father's death. However, she remembered Lucius well from her days on Chatham River. Here she blushed and fell silent, not ready yet to accept the author of the Florida history as her lost "Woo-shish." To cover her confusion, she produced a photo of Carrie Langford and her husband, Walter, which was one of her mother's few keepsakes from the old days. Carrie had been a few years older than her stepmother, Ruth Ellen said.

Lucius knew this photo well, though it had been years since he had seen it—his dark-haired and beautiful sister, with her pale skin, elegant nose, full mouth and bosom. Walter Langford, newly wed, with pale hair shining on both sides of a broad part, wore a wing collar and cravat. He looked handsome, affable, and ill at ease in a pale linen suit, much less than a match for his Miss Carrie, whose bold brows curved down around large eyes which betrayed that strange white crescent below the pupil.

"I always wondered if those Langfords gave us money for our trip north," Ruth Ellen said, returning the photo to its precise place on her little table, "because I know that Mama didn't have a penny, and we received nothing from the sale of her husband's property."

"Nonnie?" Ad barked, going quite red in the face. "Nonnie?" He was speaking loudly, like a deaf man. Hadn't Mama told them that Walter Langford sold off what was left of the property and sent the money to their family, and some of the good furniture, besides? "You said yourself that the money sent by Mr. Langford paid for Mama's house when we came here to stay!"

"Goodness, dear, I suppose I did!" she said, adjusting the white collar on her blouse.

"That's what you said," Ad persisted, looking aggrieved. "And we had a piano, and Mama saw to it that you girls had piano lessons, because she herself could only play by ear. He's after the truth here, Nonnie, not old family stories." Beset by honesty, he became short of breath. "We have to keep things straight. And we know because Mama said so that her husband lost all his money—he owed every last penny to the lawyers—so maybe Langford was being kind to send us anything at all." His voice thickened. "I guess we were kind of charity cases for a while."

Embattled by her dogged brother, Ruth Ellen showed Lucius an old schoolbook, *The History of Ancient Greece.* An inscription on the flyleaf read, *Edgar Watson, City.* "That is our only sample of his handwriting. Apparently he cherished this old history, read it over and over, kept it all his life." Lucius thought he recalled this book from Chatham Bend, and was mildly surprised that Edna had taken it when she fled north.

" 'City' was Lake City," Ruth Ellen said. "Mama told us Mr. Watson attended school in winter after coming to Florida. She said that because of the Civil War, there was never time for decent schooling in his boyhood." She smiled a little. "Mama always called him Mr. Watson. Which is why I refer to him that way," she added hurriedly.

After Mr. Watson's death, her mother refused to discuss him with her father. She scarcely visited Fort White before going to her sister Lola in north Florida. Her brother Jack told Herkie Burdett, who followed her to north Florida and stayed and married her, and gave his name to her three little ones, "to spare us scandal. Mama and our new papa were married in November 1911 by the Reverend Sidney Catts, who later became governor of Florida, and they had a little boy together, Herkie Junior, whom we always thought of as our baby brother.

"Our new papa loved my mother very much and my mother loved him. We never heard a harsh word in that house, and we had a very peaceful upbringing. Herkie Junior grew up to be a housepainter like his father, and Ad did, too. We loved our new papa very, very much. But the day before my wedding, he called us together and told us we were not really Burdetts!

"We were bewildered, we felt lost, and our new Papa was distraught. We asked, 'Who *are* we, then?' I felt as if I were nobody at all! He asked if we wished to take his name, and we all cried out, 'Oh, yes! We do!' He adopted us legally that very day, so nobody could say a word in church against my wedding. And we never let on but that he was our father, because that is what Herkie Junior thought until one of his high school classmates let poor Herkie know he wasn't one of us, and told him that our real name was

Watson." She sighed. "There's always somebody who finds a way to let you know what you don't need to hear.

"I just could not imagine a Ruth Ellen *Watson*! I had hardly any memory of Mr. Watson, so how could I think of him as my real father? Even today he is only that dark figure with the shadowed face." She picked up the group photo and peered into it. "Mama said he was always very good to her, and very kind and loving with his children, and cousin Pearl always said the same, and her mother, too. Aunt Lola never got over how much time that busy man would spend in playing with his little babies—rather unusual for any man in those days!

"For years after we left Chokoloskee, Mama exchanged letters with Mamie Smallwood, who took us in that terrible day and was so kind to us. Later I exchanged letters with the older Smallwood daughters Wilma and Ernestine. When Ernestine was eleven—this was 1918—she sent a postcard showing Charlie Tigertail's Indian trading post, way back up in Lost Man's River in the Everglades!

"A few years ago when I visited Chokoloskee, Wilma showed me clippings—showed me terrible things that had been written about Mr. Watson. I didn't ask to see them, she just showed them to me, I can't think why. I don't think Ernestine would have done that. Wilma was running the store by then, she never married. My husband and I could not help noticing how tightly she hung on to her purse, kept it right on her lap when she was eating, kept one hand on it. I guess the Smallwood family decided that Wilma was just the one to run the store!

"Anyway, I was horrified by those clippings, and later I asked Mama if Mr. Watson was the one who murdered our dear cook Hannah Smith, and those two white plantation hands, and Mama said, 'No, honey, he did not. It was his foreman, a very handsome but cold-blooded young man named Leslie Cox.' Just mentioning that name got her all nervous, and it seemed she was still deathly afraid of this man Cox, because nobody knew if he was alive or dead. Mama had asked Mr. Watson why he permitted a man like that on Chatham Bend. And Mr. Watson would not talk about it, he only said he was in Cox's debt and felt obliged to take him in.

"Mama got so upset by our discussion that she jumped up from the kitchen table, spilling the peas. 'That's a closed chapter in my life, girl! I won't hear another word about Leslie Cox, or Mr. Watson, either!' She never mentioned those two names again. But I got the feeling it was Leslie Cox, not Mr. Watson, who had truly terrified her, whose very name she could not bear to hear."

Asked by Addison if he knew Cox, Lucius told them how Leslie had turned up at the Bend in the late spring of 1910, and how he had never known much more about Leslie than he had picked up in the first five minutes. They were the same age, and he could have used a friend to hunt and fish with, but Leslie had no idea how to be a friend, he had to be in charge. He wasn't fun to hunt and fish with because he wasn't interested in wildlife or Indians or exploring back up in the Glades, all he cared about was shooting things and bringing back the meat. He stayed mostly half drunk, he liked to crowd people, he prowled around making mean remarks, poking up trouble. Anyway, he only lived there a few months before he committed the three murders which led directly to their father's death.

Lucius explained that their mother had grown up with Leslie in Fort White, she'd gone to school with him. Knowing who he was, knowing his true nature, she lived in dread of him. She implored Lucius to keep an eye on Leslie at all times because Leslie was pestering her on the sly, complaining that "a man needed a woman," and reporting how her husband was betraying her with a woman over on Pavilion Key. He was after poor Edna every time Mr. Watson turned his back, and meanwhile, his feud with another fugitive named Dutchy Melville was keeping everyone on edge.

After all that had happened at Fort White, poor Edna was so scared of more violence that she dared not tell her husband about Cox. Every chance she had, in that last hot summer, she had taken her children and gone to stay with friends in Chokoloskee. When her husband protested, she told him that the Bend was bad for little Amy's health.

"That September, I left Chatham River to fish out of Caxambas," Lucius told them. "Your mother took you children away soon after that, and a few weeks later, all hell broke loose, just as she feared. How Papa could let things get so out of hand, I'll never know."

"So those three killings were all Cox's fault. Your father . . . Mr. Watson . . . he was not to blame."

"Not as far as I know." And then he blurted, "Not as far as I want to know, might be more like it." Later he regretted saying such a thing, which told less about his father than about himself.

*

Ruth Ellen was anxious to change the subject. "When the goldenrod bloomed, Mama would take hay fever, so finally we all moved south to Neamathla." She smiled at her brother, who nodded sullenly in affirmation. "My sister Amy would become a teacher. At one time Amy worked in Lakeland, and the woman who ran her boardinghouse was a daughter of one of the House men who led the crowd which killed her father. She was actually bragging about what happened, telling poor Amy dreadful, dreadful tales. I guess that woman had to justify what those men did, but for poor Amy, it was terrifying. To this day, the poor thing cannot bear to hear one thing about her father, and her children know nothing about him. She told them their grandfather died of a heart attack!"

Ruth Ellen looked around as if hearing someone slip into the room, and when she spoke, she lowered her gentle voice to a near-whisper. "Come to think of it, I *do* remember something from Chatham Bend! I remember that my father hitched a dog to a little red wagon and trained him to pull our little boy, and the wagon tipped over, and Little Ad got scared and cried and cried. I can still hear his voice through all these years! He was only three!"

She gazed fondly at Little Ad, who was staring at the wall. "That's what Papa Burdett called Ad before he got so big! Little Ad was the first one in our family who went down south to learn the truth about our father."

"Had some time to kill," Addison grumped. "But 'Little Ad' never cared about all that, not the way you did."

She stared at him, astounded. "Didn't care? You went all the way down to Chatham Bend all by yourself!"

"That's not his business!" Ad Burdett shouted. Pointing at Lucius, he lurched to his feet, hands working, his big gray face so furrowed and menacing that Lucius stood up, too. "How do we know what you're going to write?" Ad shouted. "Why should we trust you?"

"Please stop shouting! This is *Lucius*!" cried his sister, speaking this name for the first time. "You must be more careful how you speak, dear!"

" 'It's a closed chapter in my life'—that's what Mama always said! Let's leave it closed!"

"Lucius is a *historian,* Ad! And he doesn't think Mr. Watson was so bad as a lot of people have made out. Aren't you glad to hear that?"

Distressed by her distress, Ad frowned, bewildered. "What do I care if the man was bad or good, or what was said about him? I care what people say about *our* family!" To Lucius he said, "You leave us out of your damned Watson Claim, and your book, too!" He had gone brick red in the face, with heavy breathing. "I told that lawyer I won't sign the petition! I have no interest whatsoever in what becomes of that old property! I'm not a Watson, I am a Burdett. I made a good name in my profession! I want it kept that way!"

"Those dark things happened a long time ago," Ruth Ellen mourned. "If Lucius is correct—if that house can be made into some kind of a monument—folks are bound to look at Mr. Watson in a different way! We won't have to hide him anymore, Ad! We can hold our heads up!"

"It's important to seek out the truth," Lucius told Ad. "You said so yourself."

"The truth!" Burdett said bitterly. He pointed at his sister. "She was tod-

dling around with the Smallwood girls over in the store, she never saw it! But I ran down to the boat landing to meet him! I was three years old, hollering 'Daddy! Daddy!' " Addison's eyes widened and he waved his arms. "Know what I saw? I saw my own daddy shot to pieces!"

His sister gave a little cry, longing to mother him.

Ad gasped a few breaths before resuming in a dull and quiet voice. "All I remember is that crash of guns, I thought the sky was falling down on top of me. And the dogs. Those dogs were mean and scary, they bit children. Those dogs never stopped barking all night long." His lip was trembling. "*That* the kind of truth you're after, Mister?"

"I'm your brother, Ad, remember?"

Burdett scowled, shaking him off. He leaned over to peck his sister's head, frantic to go.

Lucius followed him toward the door, where they spoke quietly.

"Why did you let me come here if you didn't trust me?"

"I was dead against it. I still am. But I knew you would find the way sooner or later." Burdett was calm again. He shook Lucius's hand, saying brusquely, "Maybe I'll think about your damn petition."

*

For a little while, they sat in silence, giving the house a chance to get its breath back. Finally Ruth Ellen cleared her throat. "Mama dragged us underneath the store, that's how scared she was those men would kill us, and her fear scared Ad, too, he was hysterical. He still wakes up smelling the dreadful odor of those dead chickens under there, drowned in the hurricane!" Involuntarily she pinched at the bridge of her nose. "I'll go to my grave with that odor in my nostrils!" She tried to smile, tried to explain how much of Ad's hostile manner stemmed from confused feelings. At one time he had actually considered changing his name to Watson—

"His name *is* Watson," Lucius reminded her.

She hurried on. "Addison is such a wonderful gardener, he grows lovely vegetables," she said brightly. "He spends almost all of his spare time out in his garden." She stared at the clenched hands in her lap before she wept. "He spoke more today than he has spoken in the last ten years together. He is very very upset, I'm not sure why." She dabbed her eyes. "He's really a very gentle man, and his life has been so sad. He was a bad sleepwalker throughout childhood, and small wonder! Then he quit school in the eighth grade. We couldn't get him to go back, finish his education. He worked as a housepainter awhile, got married, moved away. Nobody heard from him for years, not even an answer to a registered letter that we sent when Mama almost died. He only came back a while ago, after his daughter was killed in a car accident." Only now did she look up at Lucius. "Mr. Watson was a hard drinker, I have heard. Do you suppose there's a curse of alcohol on the Watson men?"

"I drink too much myself," Lucius admitted, in answer to the unspoken question, "or so I've been told."

"Lucius? Have you had a happy life? Do you have children?" She flushed and hurried on. "Addison had a few friends in the old days, but since his wife died, he has been a loner. He won't even come to family gatherings. He can't take a drink but he drinks anyway. He gets aggressive, very very angry. And we have to ask ourselves if that violent anger is something that came down from his father, and how dangerous it might be to other people." When Lucius nodded sympathetically but made no comment, she murmured, "Well. We have lots to be thankful for. I mean, everybody has to live with *something*, I suppose."

Soon after the Park took over, in the late forties, Ad had gone south to Chokoloskee, and Mr. Bill Smallwood had taken him to Chatham Bend—the first time since 1910 that any of her family had returned there. She had learned of his trip in a Christmas letter from Ernestine Smallwood, because Ad never said a word about it even after he returned.

Of course, Lucius thought. That explained a nagging mystery. "In 1947 or '48," he told her, "right after the Park announced its plan to burn all the houses and old cabins, someone went to Chatham River and gave that old house a fresh coat of white paint." He shrugged. "It might have worked, because the Watson Place is the only one still there."

"Ad never told me he'd done *that*! But of course I never questioned him about his trip. If he didn't want to talk about it, then probably he'd found out something awful. I was scared to death that what he told me might be even worse than the truth I dreaded all my life!" Yet a few years later, Ruth Ellen had made her own pilgrimage to Chokoloskee and was taken to the Watson Place by one of the Smallwood daughters and her husband.

Ruth Ellen sighed, still brooding about Ad. "He would never go see Mama in the rest home, and he was the apple of her eye! Poor Mama was nearly blind, you know, all she had was a darned old parrot to keep her company, but Ad said it made him feel too bad to see her looking so decrepit. He never thought about how Mama might feel, or how much he hurt her.

"Herkie Junior is close to his half sisters, and he tried to look out for poor Ad, too, but even Herkie gave up on Ad after a while—couldn't get close to him!

"Ad used to be such a big man, you know, and very strong—he took after his father in that way. He seems much smaller now. He was always quiet, always a loner, as I said. Even as a little boy, he never had very much to say, he was always quiet and reserved, always a little troubled. But he wasn't always off in his own head, the way he is today."

Her voice had diminished as she spoke. Soon she fell still. They listened to the ancient clock in the other room. When she looked up, she smiled at him politely, and he knew that after her brother's admonitions, she would speak no more about their father. Perhaps she had told what little she knew and perhaps she hadn't, but now she wanted him to go.

Standing in her doorway, Ruth Ellen invited him to stop by and say hello the next time he came through Neamathla, though her kind smile told him that she knew he wouldn't, which was all right, too. And still she looked at him, head cocked ever so slightly—*What do you want with us?*

South

On a green and blue day, headed south with Sally Brown beside him, Lucius reveled in a rare sense of new life, and showed off boyishly in his excitement. Crossing the Alachua Prairie, he told Sally that even in his father's day this was still a trackless country of red wolves, bear, and panthers. Half-wild cattle had wandered through this scrub since the time of the first Spaniards, who had more than thirty ranchos in north Florida by the end of the sixteenth century. Then the British came from Charleston, that was 1704, and killed every last Spaniard and every Indian they could lay bloody hands on, women and children, too—seven thousand Indians was a fair estimate. They slaughtered their fellow men like sheep.

"Fellow men," the young woman agreed, nodding sagaciously. "Like sheep."

Sally was smoking one of her "funny smokes," and now she proffered it, raising it to his lips with warm, light fingers. At her instruction, he drew deeply, holding the smoke deep in his lungs before swallowing, suffusing it upwards to his temples. When he exhaled at last, the smoke seemed to drift out through his ears. His brain was warming and his mouth slid toward a grin.

Because she had been his history student, the Professor could hold forth on Florida history to his heart's content, spilling a whole lifetime of study into her sweet ears. Yet her interest was real and her teasing of him affectionate, and in his own intoxication and plain happiness, he was delighted to babble on and on about the fugitive *siminoli* and the escaped black slaves who taught them how to grow tropical crops, and the strong alliance of these peoples against the white men who came to recapture the slaves and kill the Indians—

"Like sheep," she repeated, still back there in his earlier discourse. And now this soft, unbridled person draped herself languidly on his arm and shoulder, peering around his chin in comic awe, her shining eyes scarcely an inch from his, her lips brushing the corner of his own, until he could scarcely see the road.

He kissed her then. "Back off," he said, backing off himself. "You'll get us killed." The male voice was apart from him, not quite his own.

She whispered breathily, across great distances, "Just a-hangin on my darlin's ever' word, is all."

Alarmed, he struggled to be serious again. "The Indians had rounded up wild horses and cattle. Alachua Seminoles, they called 'em in this part of the country, ran their cattle down here on Paynes Prairie . . . biggest cattle raisers in all Florida . . ." But he was feeling neither here nor there, he was getting mixed signals, he was driving very fast, or so it seemed. Did this edible wild girl want to make love? The creature laid her hand upon his arm and leaned to blow smoke into his ear, whispering softly, "You slow down a little, hear me, darlin?"

He nodded, stirred by the fine sweet smell of her hair. The can of frosted beer between his legs moistened his jeans. "You, too," he said in a blurred voice. Realizing these words made no sense, he began to laugh.

*

Their road passed through Silver Springs, where Leslie Cox had escaped the prison road gang. Silver Springs was formerly Fort King, the historic site of one of the great episodes of the Indian Wars. On December twenty-eighth of 1835, Osceola had led forty Mikasuki in the destruction of Fort King, while on the same day, east of Tampa Bay, the war chief Alligator—Halpatter Tustenuggee—led his Muskogee in a direful ambush, destroying Major Dade's detachment of more than one hundred men. Three days later, the war chiefs joined forces in an attack on the troops of Gen. Duncan Clinch, and the Seminole Wars were under way. "Clinch is the Clinch of the Clinch River Nuclear Reactor in Tennessee, and Dade is the Dade of Dade County, Florida, drug, vice, and murder capital of America," he informed her.

"Clinch is the Clinch and Dade is the *daid.*" Relapsing comfortably into her cracker accent, Sally took another drag and passed the smoke. "Clinch is the Clinch and I don't care who knows it! Couldn't wipe them redskins out with powder and ball, so his paleface spirit has come back, fixin to *nuke* 'em!"

"How come you're speaking in the cracker tongue, Mis Sally?"

"Because under my glitterin veneer of international sophistication, a plain ol' cracker gal is what I am. First Florida Baptist bad-ass cracker, that is me."

"And how do your Baptist forebears feel about your licentious behavior and rough language?"

"It sickens 'em. Just purely *sickens* 'em. They feel like pukin." Oddly Sally's scowl was real, her mind was in a twist, she looked as if she might up and puke on purpose. Rolling another cigarette on the faded denim of her knee, licking the paper, she said quietly, "I *do* know something about Osceola which you whiteboy historians don't put in the books. Learned it from Whidden, whose grandma was descended. Osceola was a breed named Billy Powell who was ashamed of his white blood. These days there's plenty of mixed people would be better off with Osceola's attitude—ashamed of the white blood, not the dark—but that is neither here nor is it there. Osceola claimed to be pure Creek, claimed he didn't speak English, but his daddy was a white man, he was stuck with it. And later on, he took black wives along with a few red ones, probably had children on every doggone one. Most of his warriors were black Seminoles, what they called maroons, which might account for the mixed-up bunch that's running around backcountry Florida today." She cocked her head slyly. "I bet you damned historians never knew *that*!"

"Oh, we knew that. Some of us, anyway." He reminded her that mixing of the races had been widespread since colonial times—in fact, the first soldier to die in the American Revolution was a black-Indian.

"Heck, I seen Injuns got a nap so thick you couldn't put a *bullet* through it! And 'white' men, too!" Her hoarse smoker's laugh had a deep rue in it, and he laughed with her. He couldn't help it, her quirkiness delighted him, he loved her. Their mirth eased the erotic tension, and they set each other off again, over and over and over, down the road. "It's so nice to see this ol' gloom-ball professor *laugh* this way!" Sally cried happily.

But saying so put merriment to death, and she scowled crossly, banging his knee with her own. "*Anyway*, folks weren't particular in frontier days. Some of those people around Chokoloskee Bay who are so darn mean about the black people better not go poking too hard at their own woodpiles. Might be some red boys in there at the very least!" She socked his leg. "Don't laugh at me! I know what I'm talking about! Better'n you!"

A wildness had come into her eye which he sought to deflect before she blurted something angry they might both regret. "Remember those nineteenth-century edicts?" he asked her. " 'Eminent domain'? 'Manifest Destiny'? Pretending to legalize the seizure of Indian lands when we knew those seizures were gross violations of our Constitution? Even today, good jurists understand that this was lawlessness, a dangerous flaw in the very foundation of our nation's history, but no one talks about it, not even historians, it's just too dangerous—" He stopped short, for her slight smile was mocking him.

"Dangerous, huh? You some kind of *trouble*maker, boy? Some kind of a damn ol' Commie *faggot*?"

She sat up straight, trying to look bigoted, but after a moment she lay her head back and went pealing off into laughter so gleeful that she brought her knees up to her chest and kicked her cerise sneakers. She did not intend to be provocative, but that heart-shaped round of her bottom in tight jeans, the denim cleft, glimpsed on a curve, caused him to roll two wheels onto the shoulder. Since the ground was soft, he came so close to running the car into the ditch that an egret sprang skyward with a strangled squawk.

Sally took this near-disaster calmly, ignoring his apology, but her mood had swerved toward something bitter and morose. Brooding, she peered out the window. After a while, she said in a gritty voice, "Stay on the gray stuff, all right, Pop? You're getting your old balls in an uproar."

He felt the heat rush to his face. "Hey listen—"

"Student-fucker," she said quietly. "Don't you try fucking *me*. Don't even *try* it."

"Oh Lord—"

"And another thing"—she was yelling now—"I hated the way you abandoned that poor old man back in Lake City! That was the most heartless thing I ever saw! What are you, some kind of a fanatic, with all your fucking notes, your fucking boneyards! Is that all you care about? The past?"

Injured and furious, he drove in silence, disgusted with himself for even considering anything so grotesque as a romantic liaison with this dope-warped young woman. What he needed was a wise and gentle person closer to his own age, a lovely widow such as Lucy Summerlin or even Hettie Collins—Hettie was no blood relation, after all. He turned to his erstwhile admirer with as much hauteur as he could muster.

"Miss?"

" 'Mrs.' to you, Pop. I'm another man's wife, in case you were forgetting."

"I notice, Mrs., that you jumped into my car. You're not back in Lake City tending to that poor old man unless I'm much mistaken."

"You want me to get out, hitch a ride back? *That* what you're saying? Slow down, Buster!" But a moment later, weeping and snarling, she subsided. "Sorry. I'm a dope fiend. Reefer madness, Prof. I'm really sorry. I'm a mess." She fished out a pink tissue to blow sniffles.

Soon she lay her head against his shoulder. After a while, she let her fingertips trail from his knee along his inner thigh. When she sat back, sighing, into her own seat, the backs of her fingers were resting in his lap, light as a kiss.

*

They drove in silence to Arcadia, on the Peace River. That night they drank whiskey, and bad wine at supper, and made love too urgently in the farthest motel cabin from the road. Lucius had thought himself long past this grand old mix of cigarettes and whiskey and intoxicating body smells and rough wild noisy carnal entertainment, and even now, he could scarcely believe that he was back among the living. He felt rapt, shy, and omnipotent, miraculously returned into his body. He felt enchanted.

Afterwards he lay unraveled in the glow and light sweet smell of her, wondering if his desperate devouring had offended her, and knowing it hadn't when after a time she awakened gently and rolled onto her knees and bent and kissed him as he had kissed her, letting her long hair fall over her face to shroud the act because she was shy about letting him see her do what (she confessed) she had never done before.

"Well, here goes," the lovely naked creature warned him fearfully from behind the fall of hair, in a comic innocence which touched him so that he laughed joyfully, bouncing her head a little on his belly. He whispered, "Oh I love you so." Gently he caressed the crown of the small earnest head to give her the courage of her own generous desire, crying out as he dissolved in flowers of delight and earthly gratitude.

In time she crawled back up into his arms and their skins melted one into the other and they lay quiet, listening to the dawn come to Arcadia. Although more happy than he could ever remember—as if he had caught up with his real life at last—his self-doubt was seeping back, he felt himself too old to be her lover. He flinched away, deciding he had better go and brush his teeth. Still half-asleep, she sighed, detaining him, hand straying as if tracking a dropped earring. And he surprised them both with a response—"Oh-*ho*!" she murmured.

Arcadia

Arcadia had been known as plain Tater Hill Bluff until the advent of a post office in 1886 encouraged the choice of a more classic name. After the Manatee County seat was moved from Pine Level to Arcadia, this capital claimed such frontier comforts as hard drink, whoring, gambling, free-style manslaughter, and common brawling. According to one reminiscence,

"There were as many as fifty fights a day," with "four men killed in one fight alone." In addition, the untended stock on the roadless unfenced range encouraged a spirit of free enterprise in which cattle were confiscated by the herd. In 1890 four luckless strangers, denying to the end that they were rustlers, were hanged without formalities from the nearest oak. The range wars attracted desperados from the West, and revenge by knife and bullet was an everyday event when a fugitive from Arkansas named E. J. Watson turned up in Arcadia and, according to the memoirs of his friend Ted Smallwood, became embroiled with "a bad actor" named Quinn Bass.

> Watson said Bass had a fellow down whittling on him with his knife, and Watson told Bass . . . he had worked on the man enough. And Bass got loose and came towards him and he begin putting the .38 S & W bullets into Bass and shot him down.

The date of Watson's arrival in Arcadia, the length of stay, his means of livelihood—no such details were recorded, only that Watson had paid his way out of his fatal scrape with Bass before leaving town.

Since Smallwood's narrative was the only known account of his father's sojourn in Arcadia, Lucius was anxious to verify the story. Next morning, he tracked down a Bass kinsman in Kissimmee who told him over the telephone that his forebears had been cattle drovers who moved south from Georgia in 1834 and settled on the Kissimmee Prairie north of Okeechobee. "Getting killed in Arcadia don't mean Quinn came from there. Most likely he came from right where I'm at now." The original Christian name was Quincy, and the variations—Quin, Quinn, Quinton, LeQuinn—came along later. At any rate, they were all known as Quinn Bass. "The feller I'm thinking about— and I reckon he's the one you're after—is the only one I know of who died violently, but nobody in this family cares to remember how. That tells you right there he was a bad 'un and there was a scandal. His branch of the family is dying down, there's only a few old ladies left, all very testy. They hung up on me last time I called for some family information, and I was asking about something pretty small. I don't imagine they will help you out on this one."

Manatee County had become De Soto after Watson's time, and the De Soto County Sheriff's Office had none of the old records, but a deputy directed them to the county clerk's office at the courthouse, a stately edifice on the main square, where Sally located the earliest Criminal Docket Book stored in the basement. They found no mention of any malefactor named E. J. Watson nor any record of the killing of Quinn Bass. However, a LeQuinn Bass had been arrested on September 19, 1890, for carrying concealed weapons, and again on October 23 of the next year, this time for murder.

Bass had been acquitted on November 6, 1893—his last appearance in the record. Surely this man was the "bad actor" of Smallwood's account, since there was no mention of any other Bass in this record of every felony committed in this county between 1890 and 1905.

*

On the way south again, Sally spoke in a flat voice about her marriage to Whidden Harden, referring finally to the ancient feud between his clan and her own. "That old feud was one reason I married him, and also one reason I stayed with him as long as I did. I couldn't bear to have our families see us fail.

"Since we were kids together in school, Whidden and I had some idea that we could change the ugly racism in our community. But Whidden is too easygoing, too agreeable. He wants to heal the feud between our families by pretending it's all over, and that just won't work. He won't act on his own decent instincts, he stays loyal to those mean no-necks, especially the one who taught him to live his life outside the law—my own damned father." She shook her head. "Whidden is a kind good man who works with no-good people. He's not one of them, although he thinks he is, and if it comes to trouble, it's Whidden who will go to the state pen. He kind of knows that, but he's stuck in some old Island way of thinking.

"One night he admitted he didn't much respect those men because they were ignorant and lazy, always blaming the government for their way of life—that's their excuse. All they're looking for, he said, is a free ride. Too bad you don't know that well enough to quit, I said. You have no respect for Whidden Harden or you wouldn't work with them. He thought a minute and then he said he reckoned it was his wife, not him, who had no respect for Whidden Harden. This wasn't true, but I thought it might be good for him to let him think that, so I just shut up. By this time my old man was moving over into running guns, and making money off of people dying—that about finished it. I told Whidden I was moving out, and when he didn't quit, I did."

"Is that the whole story? Of Whidden and Sally, I mean?"

"It's all the story you are going to get until I'm good and ready." She tried to smile. "Why don't you tell me the Lucius Watson story instead?"

"No, Sally, I don't think I will. I'm sick of it."

"I know it anyway, at least from the Harden family's point of view." She looked him over, nodding. "As a boy, my husband worshiped 'Mister Colonel' Watson. Still does, far as I know." She was feeling guilt about the night before and so was he.

Lee County

On the north side of the Calusa Hatchee River, they stopped at a bar. Sally made a few phone calls, and when she rejoined him, said matter-of-factly that someone was in town who would pick her up and take her south for her meeting in Naples with Whidden and their lawyers.

"Today, you mean?" Stung by her willingness to leave him so abruptly, he felt abandoned, and a little panicky. He felt laid wide and as fatally exposed as an oyster on the half shell, mantle curling to escape the squirt of lemon. He knew his feeling was not reasonable—in fact, already suspected that an early parting might be for the best—but he could not endure the idea of losing her just when he'd found her. "You regret what happened, Sally?"

"I'll *never* regret it, Mister Colonel," Sally murmured, taking his hand. "But I'm going to let you go while I still can. Because I know better—and I know *you* better—than to take us seriously." Trying to smile, she sang along with the loud jukebox: " 'Ah swore ah wouldn' never be tore up bah yoo-hoo.' "

"I *do* take it seriously!" When she hushed him, he said, "When will I see you? I'll be in Naples tomorrow—" Again he was routed by her strange expression, knowing that "his" sweet Sally was beyond recall.

Within minutes, a black swamp truck crossed the windows. When a huge silhouette barged through the doorway, Lucius recognized Crockett Junior Daniels, who avoided looking at him and responded to Sally's introductions with truculent silence. Offered a drink, Crockett growled, "I'll wait outside."

Following the one-armed man across the parking lot, Sally took Lucius's arm. "Going to miss me, Professor?"

"Plain Lucius will do, I think, after last night."

"Plain Lucius, you're blushing."

"No fool like an old fool, ever hear that one?"

"Hey, I *like* that hokey kind of stuff!" She laughed, but her eyes were serious. "You think it's *easy* to give you up, a man like you?" And her eyes misted. "Do you have any idea how *rare* you are?"

On the truck's door panel, the name BAD COUNTRY had been slashed in crimson lettering. Crockett Junior hunched over his wheel, a cigarette hanging on his lower lip. Flatulent with beer, he gave Sally a befuddled squint, meant to be ironic. The big wild hair on his shaggy head tossed to the blare of music from the radio while the fingertips of his left hand tappeted on the cab roof in time to bass rhythms whappeting his brain.

"King of the Road!" cried Sally Brown, slapping the truck. "Va-*room*, va-*room*! Let's move it, Junior!" she yelled as she got in. Slamming the door, she reached over and honked the horn twice, loudly and sharply—"Toot back if you love Jesus!"—and the big black-visaged man slammed the swamp truck into gear and fishtailed around and up onto the curb and bounced it hard onto the highway shoulder.

Lucius called after her, "Watch out for his damned dog!"

"Ol' Buck? Hey, that dog *loves* me! My leg, anyway!"

Depressed by her exhilaration, he hoped she would return his wave, but she did not, only gazed back at him out the cab window, no longer exhilarated, but hollow-eyed and drained. The black truck forced its way into the traffic. The last he saw of Sally Brown was her sunny hair and soft tan arm in the southbound flow of shiny metal toward the bridge.

*

Rob was to meet him at the Gasparilla Inn, a new high-rise motel in the royal palms on the river, where Watson Dyer would join them for supper. Inquiring at the desk, he found no word. Depressed by all the chrome and mirrors, he hurried back out into the sun and walked the old riverfront streets he had known since childhood. He paid a visit to the library, then the newspaper, noting some Watson references and dates. Eventually he visited the offices of the Lee County Sheriff, where he laid a copy of his *History* on the counter to prepare the ground for his request for the old records. The huge ledgers levered from the stacks by bemused clerks had been so long unopened that their stiff leaves exhaled the breath of a half century of desiccation, and the faded ink, once sepia, was almost as faint as the blue watermark.

In the flourished script on the speckled and stained pages, the one name of interest was Green Waller, tried in 1896, 1898, and 1901 for "larceny of hog." This inveterate pig thief was none other than that Old Man Waller who later found sanctuary at the Watson Place, where he could commune with these estimable animals to his heart's content. Green's name appeared also in the Monroe County census for May 1910, where he was listed in the E. J. Watson household as "servant and farmhand." A John Smith was similarly described, and a Mrs. Smith was cook. The last entry for this household was "Lucius H. Watson, mullet fisherman." His own name startled him, flying off the ancient page of this old Domesday Book like a trapped moth.

Lucius thought he remembered Green as rather elderly, but according to the census he was five years younger than his employer, Mr. Watson, and therefore plausible if not entirely suitable as the lover of the mountainous Hannah Smith, with whom he would perish at the hands of Leslie Cox. John Smith could be the alias of someone on the run—presumably Cox himself or his third victim, the outlaw Herbert Melville, a.k.a. Dutchy, whom Lucius recalled as a lively young devil whom he had rather liked.

As in Arcadia, the strange dearth of information about E. J. Watson in these ledgers seemed astonishing. The Sheriff's records for 1910 made no reference whatever to the triple murder at Chatham Bend on October 10, nor to the violent execution at Chokoloskee of the noted planter Mr. E. J. Watson two weeks later, nor to any testimony in regard to either crime. Since Sheriff Frank Tippins had held a hearing at Fort Myers in regard to Watson's death, how was it possible that no trace of that hearing—not even a mention of the Bill House deposition—appeared anywhere in these exhaustive pages?

That the records in this case were missing (or had never been transcribed) was all the more peculiar in light of the fact that the crimes had been well covered in the Fort Myers *Press* for October 20 and 27, and in the Tampa *Morning Tribune* for October 25. True, the triple murders had occurred across the Monroe County line, but the news accounts specified that Lee County Sheriff Frank B. Tippins had traveled south to investigate both events, and that the unnamed "Negro" being held as an accessory to the massacre had spent at least a fortnight in the Fort Myers jail before being turned over to Monroe County Sheriff Clement Jaycox. It seemed incredible that in these records, where a prisoner's race was invariably noted, there was no evidence of any black man taken into custody in October of 1910, not even a brief notation in the Sheriff's fees book, which recorded the transport and feeding of all prisoners.

A sketch of Sheriff Tippins's life in a Fort Myers history found in the library had claimed that Tippins, who "arrested many desperate criminals during his career and acquired a statewide reputation for fearlessness," had been frustrated for the remainder of his days by the "unsolved killing of Ed Watson. Due to the fact that Watson was said to have killed the notorious Belle Starr and had been suspected of killing many of his employees to escape paying them their wages, his murder attracted national attention and stories about him are still being printed."

How interesting that Sheriff Tippins (or whoever transmitted Tippins's recollections to the local historian) would refer to the "murder" of Ed Watson. Since the account made special mention of the thirty-three bullets found in Watson's body, the choice of that term seemed to reflect the Sheriff's skepticism that an armed crowd of at least twenty men, putting so many bullets in the victim, had acted in self-defense, as Bill House claimed.

Had the most notorious murder case in Tippins's long career gone unrecorded simply because it was never brought to a grand jury? Or had the records been eradicated from the books? If so, the culprit must be Eddie Watson, the deputy court clerk at the Bill House hearing, who might also be able to explain why there was no mention of the notorious Ed Watson in the criminal dockets in Arcadia. He would have to go find Eddie and inquire, knowing his brother had never answered questions about Papa and was very unlikely to start now.

"Sheriff Thompson might know where them records are at and he might not," a deputy concluded, picking Lucius's *History* off the counter as if fingering strange fruit, then setting it down in unconcealed relief that he, at least, was not obliged to read it. "We got a feller in the cells back here who might know quite a lot about the Watson case, cause him and Tippins was real tight back in Prohibition. Them two purely loved to swap old yarns about Ed Watson, so what he'd tell might have some truth to it, if he's feelin truthful."

The deputy chuckled, leading the way down the back hall. "This feller ain't in jail exactly, he's just restin his bad bones in our nice facility. The feds asked us to hold him for a hearin but it ain't nothin but harassment. He'll beat the charges same as always, he can walk out any time he wants. But he won't check out until tomorrow, and that's because he enjoys livin off the taxpayers when he's up to town. Receives his business friends right in his cell, cuts deals, rigs payoffs. You'd be surprised who comes in here to hobnob with a swamp rat—politicians and businessmen, you know, that would never be caught out in broad daylight with this feller! County, state, and federal law knows all about him, but those few he ain't paid off just can't come up with him, he skitters out of it some way, time after time. Can't even get him on his income tax, cause he don't show no income on his books—ain't *got* no books! Got all his money in big croker sacks someplace, I reckon!"

Though they had arrived at the cell door, the deputy did not lower his voice but pitched it louder for the inmate's benefit. "When he come in yesterday, I told him, 'Boy, you are in *real* bad trouble this time! You are goin straight to the federal penitentiary to pay for all them felonious activities!' And he hollers, 'Nosir, I sure ain't! They ain't *never* goin to touch me, cause they know I'd take half the elected idiots in south Florida to the pen with me!' "

The deputy grinned as he fiddled with his keys, shaking his head in admiration. "Claims them feds got nothin on him, and even if they did, they wouldn't try nothin. Says Ol' Speck can chew out Uncle Sam any way he wants! In two days' time, he'll be back out in the Park, moonshinin and runnin guns and shootin the livin shit out of the gators, same way he always done."

Lucius stopped short. "Who?" he said. But it was too late, the deputy had banged open the cell door. "How many Specks y'all acquainted with? This one you are looking at is Crockett Senior Daniels, that right, Speck?"

*

Speck Daniels, sitting on the bunk edge, had been bent over tying up the laces on his sneakers, in some swamp instinct to be ready for whatever was coming at him down the hall, but when the iron door swung open, he sat up slowly, in a kind of coiling, like the sidewinding retreat of a big moccasin among the buttress roots of a pond cypress, then withdrew into the shadows underneath the upper bunk. The deputy showed his visitor into the cell and closed the door behind him.

"Goddammit, Buzz, you frisk this man?" Daniels hollered. "You pat him down good?" When the deputy just laughed and kept on going, Daniels cursed him. Green eyes fixed on Lucius, he emerged slowly and perched on the bunk edge with his hands beside him gripping the thin mattress. In the bad light from the fly-specked yellow bulb high overhead, the saturnine heavy mouth in his hard face was fringed by a dirty stubble.

"That smart-mouth peckerhead is goin on report," he muttered, tossing his bristled chin toward the door. "Prisoners' rights ain't only just the rules, they're the damn *law*!" He glowered at his visitor, who remained standing by the door because there was no chair. "What in the hell do *you* want? God A-mighty! Here I ain't laid eyes on you in twenty years, then all of a sudden you show up way to hell and gone out to Gator Hook, and next thing I know, you track me to the county jail! You paid 'em off or somethin? Let you right in and lock the door behind, don't even frisk you!"

Lucius turned his back to him and spread his arms out wide, hands to the wall. In his dislike, he was baiting Speck a little, and he was astonished when Daniels sprang and collared him and shoved his chest hard against the cement before patting him down, then gave him an extra parting shove before returning to the bunk, where he cursed some more and stretched out in the shadow, one arm flung across his eyes.

Lucius hunkered down against the wall, trying to compose himself, as Daniels shifted his arm and watched him from beneath his elbow, reading his thoughts. "I'm waitin on you, Colonel. If you ain't here to shoot me, boy, you better remember pretty quick why the fuck you come."

Lucius said he had been told that a man back in the holding cells might be able to tell him something about Sheriff Tippins's attitude toward the Watson case. "Turns out it was you," he said.

"Tell *you* somethin? Man who put me on that stupid list the way you done? I wouldn't tell you fuck-all about *nothin*!"

But when Lucius got up, prepared to leave, Speck waved him toward the corner. "You can set yourself right down on my nice toilet," he said. If anyone ended this meeting, it was going to be Crockett Senior Daniels, who wouldn't do it before gaining some advantage.

Daniels acknowledged he'd been close to Sheriff Tippins. Asked his opinion on the absence of any reference to E. J. Watson in the Sheriff's records, he sucked his teeth as if considering his right to remain silent. He rubbed his temples with iron-scarred brown knuckles, summoning up old talks with Tippins that might lead his mind back to Ed Watson. Then he put his hands behind his head and stared awhile at the straw and broken springs which thrust forth from the bottom of the upper bunk.

SPECK DANIELS

E. J. Watson got blamed for plenty killins that was done by other men along this coast—that's what Frank Tippins told me. Watson was down around the Islands long as most of 'em, but he kept hisself apart. Not many knew him good as what they claimed they did. Ed Watson grew the best sugarcane and the most, nobody near him, so the Sheriff concluded it weren't no coincidence that Old Man D. D. House who was Watson's biggest rival in the syrup business was also the leader of the crowd that killed him.

When the Sheriff brought that bunch here to the courthouse, one man, Bill House, give the main testimony and the rest just mostly backed him up. Bein so old, D. D. House got left behind in Chokoloskee, also a young feller by the name of Crockett Daniels. The Sheriff knew about me and that old man. The one he never knew about was House's nigger.

Them men thought they was bound to be indicted, so they hollered self-defense, knowin there weren't nobody would contradict 'em. Yet every last one of 'em admitted they had went to Smallwood's with guns loaded, set to shoot—malice aforemost, that's what Tippins called it. All his life, Frank Tippins swore them men should of been indicted, first-degree murder.

Bill House deposition, all that evidence, should of gone to the grand jury. Well, there weren't one. No arraignment, no indictment—nothin! So who's to say what happened to the record? Sheriff might of tossed out everythin in pure disgust after the Watson family and Banker Langford put a stop to the investigation on account of more scandal might be bad for business. And the dead man's own son was court clerk, and he backed 'em up.

In them days, Frank Tippins was still green, so he was sniffin hard after the truth. He purely hated bein whistled off his bird by Watson's family. Ever' time he thought about that so-called posse they made him deputize after the man was dead, he'd get to fumin like a big ol' bear with a snootful of beeswax, eyes full of bees and stung real smart and nothin much to show for all his trouble.

Then Tippins and his coroner went down to Rabbit Key and done an autopsy, and after he seen how much lead was shot into that tore-up body, he couldn't never swaller their damn story. For years he'd holler, Now goddammit, Speck, you was right there on the landin, son, you seen 'em shootin! Damn people must of emptied out every last load! Them bullets was just a *rollin* out! Filled a damn coffee can! Said even when his coroner quit, he figured they was more slugs left in that putrid carcass. *Thirty-three bullets!* Not countin buckshot! If thirty-three struck home, how many missed? Goddammit, boy, you goin to look a lawman in the eye and tell him that was self-defense?

Course I don't rightly know if it was self-defense or not. Couldn't hardly see nothin over the crowd. By the time I seen an opening and upped and fired, the man was fallin, deader'n a doornail.

After the autopsy, Tippins wanted to reopen up the case, but he never could figure how to go about it, not with all of 'em confessin they was in on it, and every last one of 'em in his damn posse—not your common murder case at all!

What I never could figure was why Frank took it so hard, and why he could never let it go, not for years afterwards. But I believe what dogged him most was this rumor that a nigger in that crowd had raised a gun to shoot at E. J. Watson. Now *that* would eat at Frank B. Tippins, I can tell you! Frank got on all right with Injuns but he never did see eye to eye with niggers. Course most of us was that same way, though these days some will try to tell you different.

The way that nigger story got out, a feller snuck up alongside of the Sheriff when he brought them men north to Fort Myers on the *Falcon*. This feller hinted that the man who fired first—the man who nailed Watson right between the eyes—weren't nobody else in the wide world but some fool nigger who had lost his head. Said the rest of 'em only shot afterwards, to cover up for him. Said he'd swore on his honor he would never reveal that nigger's name, and he never had to, cause there weren't but the one colored man on Chokoloskee.

Well, Tippins reckoned that this snitch was lookin out for his own skin, cause none of the rest would back that story up. Whoever told you that told a plain lie, them others hollered. Us boys don't need no goddamn nigger to do our shootin for us! Said they knew how to take care of their own business, and they done it. And the hard way they said this made Tippins conclude that some of these fellers, maybe all of 'em, knew what that day's business was before Ed Watson ever come ashore.

Tippins could not tolerate that *any* nigger would even think to raise a gun against a white man, and least of all a white man like E. J. Watson, who had every coon in southwest Florida scared up a tree. Over here in Colored Town, "Mister Watson" was the bogeyman hisself. *You doan jump inter bed dis minute, Mist' Watson gone gitcha!* Hell, he's *still* the bogeyman right to this day, though they ain't a soul can hardly recollect who Mr. Watson was or what he looked like!

So the Sheriff chewed over what he had been told, and in later years, when he heard that same damn story, he commenced to snoopin all around about that nigger, huntin up a good excuse to take that black boy into custody and work some truth out of him. By then, o' course, that boy had made himself real scarce, he was livin way off by hisself, down Lost Man's River.

Nigger Short—pretty good nigger, too, had a real light skin. Good worker, handy, got the job done, and all the while so polite and quiet it was like he wasn't hardly there at all. From what I known of him, Henry Short was about the last nigger on this earth would raise a gun to fire at Ed Watson. But first time me and the Sheriff done some business—this was five years later—he asked me straight out, Did that sonofabitch shoot at Ed or didn't he? Well, I never seen it if he did, that's what I told him, not carin to admit I was so far in the back that I couldn't hardly see nothin at all.

As for the other nigger in the case, that boy who showed up at Pavilion Key? They took him to Key West and let him off! We all thought he had fell overboard on his way down there, but Tippins had a Miami clippin the Monroe sheriff sent him, and I seen it myself in later years—Florida *Times-Union*, December first of 1910! That sonofabitch went and testified how he helped butcher that big white woman and sink her in the river, and they let him off because he claimed Cox made him do it! Even give him some clothes and a ticket and some money, sent him home to Georgia, told him to stay in touch with the Sheriff in case Cox was caught! Oh, Tippins was boilin mad, I'll tell you! *That's a Key West jury for you, Speck! Yankees and damn foreigners, is all that is! He wouldn't have got away with that here in Lee County! I mean, Good God A-mighty, Speck! He had his damn black hands all over her!* I sure heard our Sheriff holler *that* a time or two!

One night a few years later in Key West—we was in a bar down on Duval Street—a friend of mine was tellin me how they had at least two niggers there in town who was pickin up drinks by claimin it was them who escaped from the Watson Place to report the killins. And I said, why, goddammit to hell, we got one in Fort Myers claims the same damn thing! But the real one went on home to Georgia, and they never caught Cox so I don't guess he come back. Sip Linsy, he called himself, somethin like that.

The Sheriff believed till the day he died that us fellers took and lynched Ed Watson, said we was waitin there to gun him down. Said, "Maybe you held your fire till he raised his gun, maybe you didn't." Said Bill House was sincere, all right, believed the hell out of his own deposition, but somethin was missin in his story all the same. So Tippins called Ed Watson's death an unsolved crime where most wouldn't call it no damn crime at all. That was the first time, Frank would say, that he never done his duty as a Sheriff. Weren't the last time by a long shot, but he didn't know that in the early days. Might been the Ed Watson case which got him so disgusted up, when you come to think about it. The Sheriff said, "The law's the law." And killing Watson was against the law because Watson never had no chance to plead not guilty.

As for them official records of that case, here's my opinion. Eddie Watson was court clerk and he swept his daddy's case under the desk and wiped the books, and probably Banker Langford put him up to it.

Eddie, he's retired now, over here on Second Street, but that don't mean he ain't up-to-date on his neighbors' business. He is a real nosy old poop and that's a fact. Likes to fish up other people's mail out of their box. Not only reads it but jots down his personal comments on the envelope. Friend of mine was a deputy for Tippins back when Eddie started up that hobby. There was complaints, so this feller went on over, had a talk with him. Eddie denied it and promised he would quit, all in the same breath, that's how nervous he was that the deputy might get away before he could sell him this old shootin iron—single-shot, bolt-action, looked like a made-over rifle with a shotgun barrel. Hell of a lookin thing! Eddie claimed this was the gun used by the famous desperado Bloody Watson on the day he died, swore up and down that this gun was well known to be his daddy's from some kind of a black scorin on the stock. Not only that but this selfsame gun had killed the famous outlaw queen Belle Starr—no extra charge! Said it was priceless, so naturally this feller give him fourteen dollars for it. Might been priceless but it weren't what Eddie said it was.

One time I hefted the real-life gun Ed Watson was totin—I ain't rightly sure who's got her now. Twelve-gauge Remington ridge-barrel, twenty-eight- or thirty-inch double barrels, one of the earliest models ever made with smokeless steel. Didn't have no rabbit ears—that's outside hammers I'm talkin about, like on old muskets—but a real old-fashioned shootin iron just the same. Had a short forearm, wood was split but put back together pretty solid with quarter-inch squarehead screws. The safety was busted, welded back, busted again—that sound familiar? Course the wood on the stock was all raggedy-lookin from bein shot up so damn bad that day, and the barrels all pitted from layin too long in the salt water. Nobody give it a wipe of oil before the Sheriff took it for court evidence. Looks like some excited young fool flung that shootin iron into the bilges of his boat. Never stopped to think that one day that historical-type gun might be worth big money. And you know something? That fool might of been me!

*

Speck Daniels had taken off his boots and stretched out on his bunk, hands behind his head. After so much talk about the old days, he was feeling almost amiable, and sat up, annoyed, when the deputy came and opened the cell door.

"Had enough?" the deputy asked Lucius.

"Enough what?" Speck demanded. "We had enough of *you* already, and you only just showed up!"

The deputy departed, laughing, leaving the door open, and Lucius rose to leave.

"Set down a minute!"

Lucius waited in the doorway. Speck winked in a poor attempt to appear friendly and relaxed, but was scowling again almost at once. "Don't care for my company?" he said. "Well, that is natural, I reckon, for a man that's livin in the past like you been doin. But if you're still thinkin about shootin me, just remember who give you that Bill House deposition for your book!"

"*You* sent that?"

"I saved it out from bein lost, let's put it that way. Found it myself, in Tippins's desk—he never missed it. Ol' Frank is dead now, he'd of *wanted* me to have it. Ain't goin to thank me?" Speck's voice rose when Lucius did not answer. "Don't matter who sent it, it was mine by rights, and it was stole off of me! Think I don't know what that thing's worth?" He studied Lucius meanly. "As a souvenir of the famous day when us boys went and wiped out Bloody Watson?"

"You admit that, then."

Speck Daniels squinted. "When your daddy died, I was startin out as a young gator hunter, not much more than a boy. I happened to be visitin that day from Fakahatchee, and I follered my uncle Henry Smith over to Smallwood's. Figured I might's well join that line of men, see what was goin on. I never had one thing in the world against your daddy! I just hated to miss out, is all it was."

"Hated to miss out on a lynching?"

Speck was short of breath and short of temper, too, he was actually thrashing on his bunk, like a cottonmouth pinned by a stick. "I looked up to your daddy," he muttered finally.

"That makes it worse."

Speck considered this a moment. "Weren't none of us fellers was born killers exceptin maybe Horace Alderman, and we didn't know that about Horace, not that day. Even Horace didn't know it, hardly, till years later. So I was bothered some and will admit it. Your dad had daughters by two females in our family and he always helped take care of 'em, always treated us like kinfolks, in a manner of speakin. Them two ladies has been dead awhile so they can't scold me no more for takin part at Chokoloskee, but their children ain't speakin to me to this day!" Daniels laughed unpleasantly, shaking his head. "Colonel, you ain't got a thing to be ashamed about, is all I'm tellin you. Ed Watson was his own man, done what he thought was right. Never killed a livin soul who didn't need some killin." The moonshiner was grinning a sly vicious grin, as if to recover the pride lost from having tried to make excuses for himself. "Here is a nice story you'll be proud to write up your book—story my aunt Josie used to tell about how good she was took care of by her man Jack Watson.

"One fine day they was settin there eatin their supper on the Bend, had nice fresh peas. And there was a gang of cane cutters that ate at that big table, and this man was findin fault with Josie's peas. They wasn't salted— wasn't this, that, nor the other. So her Mister Jack, he started in to rumblin and he warned the man to be more careful not to hurt Miss Josie's feelins. This cutter shut up, but pretty quick he commenced to grumblin again, bad as before. Knew bad peas when he seen 'em, this feller did.

"Well, Mister Jack didn't have no more to say about it. Finished his dinner, set his fork down, wiped his mouth. Then he pushed his chair back and got up, lookin ever so calm and quiet and respectful, like a good citizen in church leavin his pew. And there come a hush, and this field hand stopped his eatin, cause he knowed that somethin terrible was comin down on him. But he was too scared to try to run, he only set there kind of bug-eyed starin out the winder, like that big ol' croc that used to hang around that stretch of river was clamberin right out onto the bank, comin to get him.

"Takin his time, Ed Watson walked around to that man's place. He laid his hand on this man's head, drawed his head back by the hair—didn't yank it, Josie said, her Jack wasn't rough with him or nothin. He laid his bowie knife acrost his throat and said, 'Folks, please excuse this unfortunate interruption.' He stood this feller on his feet because his knees weren't workin good no more and walked him outside before he slit his throat, so's not to mess up Aunt Josie's nice clean floor."

"Christ!" Lucius swore. "No wonder he's got such an evil reputation, when people like you spread stuff like that!"

Speck Daniels shrugged, not in the least put out. "Now Aunt Josie never did deny that Jack Watson put that knife to her own throat a time or two when he was in his liquor, get her to simmer down, shut up, or mind what she was told. Aunt Josie would been the first to say it—'When my Jack told you to do somethin, you done it, cause he never was a man to tell you twice.'" He spluttered, frowning hard to show that this story was serious. "See, nobody cared much for that hired hand to start with, that's how Josie explained it. He was some kind of a damn criminal, they figured, had some kind of a damn criminal mentality, and probably a damn criminal record to go with it, least that's what her Jack told them other diners when he come back in from out of doors and washed his hands and set down with 'em again to eat up Josie's lemon-lime cream pie.

"When Jack Watson finished up his pie and got done wipin his mouth, he said he were a patient man but could not be expected to put up with such a criminal at his own table. Said, 'Darn it all, the world is just plain better off *without* that darn ol' criminal!' As Josie recollected it, her Jack still had some lime cream on his mustache when he hitched his chair around to get a better look at the dead body, layin there barefaced in his boots out in the yard. Said, 'Look at that darn criminal sonofabitch! Layin out there like he owns the place!' "

Speck Daniels was struggling not to laugh into Lucius's face. "Oh yes! Them were the days when men was men! They don't make no Americans like *that* no more!" Unable to maintain his poker face, Speck doubled up with mirth, hacking and coughing with emphysema, farting joyfully, and Lucius gave up on indignation and laughed with him, a long deep hopeless laugh that came all the way up from his belly. That laugh took him by surprise— how very long it seemed since he had laughed like that! And for some reason that he could not fathom, tears rose behind his eyes.

Mercifully, Speck was too carried away to notice. "So whilst they was washin up the dishes, they all agreed it might be best to say nothin more about it, let bygones be bygones. They took that damn ol' criminal and flung him to that big croc in the river, then done their best to forget all about him and his criminal ways. Maybe somebody give him a prayer, maybe they didn't—the Watson Place was pretty busy in the harvest season. But Aunt Josie always told young Pearl that one reason she never did get over her Jack Watson was on account of how sweet he was that day about her peas, how darn considerate about her tender feelins." Speck nodded a little. "Nice romantical little story for your book."

Lucius rose again to go.

"Think I'm a liar? Think I'm makin up them stories?" Angry again, Daniels yanked opened the top buttons of his denim shirt and dragged out a heavy necklace of small leaden lumps, dull-burnished. He pushed the rough hemp string of leads at Lucius. "Count 'em. Thirty-three. Know where they come from?"

Lucius's heart stopped. The last time he had seen these lumps, they were black with coagulated blood, dropped one by one into a rusty coffee can on Rabbit Key.

Speck Daniels nodded with him. "Yep. Got 'em off the coroner's man, Willie Hendry. For good luck. I wouldn't take a million dollars for 'em," Daniels said.

Still brooding about why he had come, anxious to poke and prod his visitor to see just how he worked, what he was up to, Daniels followed Lucius out of the cell door. "Speakin of Tippins, he was the first one to show me that fuckin posse list of yours." He grinned when Lucius turned. "He was holdin it for evidence, y'know. In case you was to go crazy, start in shootin people. Such as myself." Speck uttered a snide laugh. "And you know where Tippins got it? Eddie Watson!"

Lucius nodded, hiding his astonishment. Had Eddie stolen it from Lucy Dyer or had Lucy been so foolish as to show it to him?

"Course your brother is crazier'n hell, like all you Watsons, but that don't mean that he done wrong showing that list to Tippins. Might been worried that little Lucius could get hisself killed down in the Islands."

"Eddie had no right to it. I want it back."

"You want it back? What the hell for? I ain't even got that thing no more. Cause it was stole off me!"

Old furies had struck all color from Speck's face, as if he were suffering a stroke and could not breathe. His mouth was stretched open, taut as a knothole. His hair stood on end, and his rigid forefinger was pointed at Lucius's face. The moonshiner's mahogany hide was draining to a blue-gray hue as dead and cold as gunmetal, and he leaned against the wall, wheezing and gasping. Then he reeled backwards, sat down on the bunk, and grabbed his sneakers. Breaking a rust-rotted shoelace, he yelled—"Sonofa*bitch*!"—and kicked that sneaker off. He hurled himself back on the bunk and with his sneakered foot kicked the upper bunk so hard that he split the pine slats under the torn mattress. "Ever think how a man might feel, seein his own name on a *death* list? Ever think what kind of crazy man would even *make* a list like that?"

But the fit had passed, and he sat up again, cursing his sore foot. "Might been found with a bullet in your head, back up a creek, ever think of that?"

Lucius said nothing. In this sort of man, fear was more dangerous than anger. He watched Speck's instinct to conceal that fear take over. He was grinning again, and speaking calmly. "Course that ol' list don't mean a thing no more. All of 'em's dead." He winked at Lucius. "All but the one," he added, bowing a little. "Unless you would count niggers."

Daniels awaited him with his one sneaker on. Lucius kept silent. The silence refired the man's rage, but this time the rage was low and even, cold as the strange blue mineral flame in a wood fire.

"Chokoloskee folks might be real interested to see that list, don't you think so? Cause ever' last one of them old-time families has names on there. And even if them men are gone, there ain't nothin to keep you from killin a man's son." He paused a moment, nodding a little. "Unless you was put a stop to first." He wiped spittle from his unshaven mouth with the back of his hand, which he stropped on his pant leg.

"By you, maybe?" Lucius's own voice had gone tight, and sounded frog-gish.

"All I'm sayin is, if I was you, headed down into that country, I wouldn't turn my back no more'n I had to."

Lucius said, "I lived down there for twenty-five years after I made that list and never harmed a soul. What makes you think I'm ready to start now?"

"I'll tell you why." Speck Daniels nodded cannily. "Because I seen plenty of 'em go kind of loco when their life never worked out the way they wanted. Especially queer old bachelors without no family." This meanness seemed to appease him just a little. "Fair warnin, that's all, Colonel. Here's another warnin, take it or leave it. If you're writin a book, don't go tellin no secrets on your damn attorney." Speck lowered his voice a little to draw Lucius closer. "Big-time attorney, y'know, *big*-time attorney! He's the fixer for all the fat boys in this state, from Big Sugar and the Ku Klux Klan up to the gover-nor, and he's got his own political future to look out for. He don't want no story comin out about how he is Bloody Watson's crazy bastard. He'll get a choke hold on your book in court, then hit you with a lawsuit, and if that don't put you out of business, he'll be comin after you, and he is goin to get you, and he don't care how. You might get beat up, get your house burned down, or you might get a bullet. Whatever it takes. They say he's got Cubans over to Miami will do a nice clean job for fifty dollars."

"How come you're warning me?"

"Settlin old accounts, as you might say. But don't show up so sudden next time." He nodded, holding Lucius's eye.

"That a warning, too?"

"Don't talk to me no more," Speck said, rolling over on the bunk, facing the wall.

Calusa Hatchee

Lucius headed toward the river, passing the red Langford house between Bay and First streets where he had lived with his mother in his school days. In the river park, a gaggle of pubescent girls in snowy sneakers, bouncing and gig-gling and squirting life, were observed without savor by leached-out old men, scattered and fetched up in the corners of the benches like dry leaves whirled across the hard park ground. In the river light, the tableau was surreal, as if these stick figures were arranged around the troupe of dancing nymphs like isolated pieces of a single sculpture. And one of them, thought Lucius with a start, might be a drink-worn syphilitic Leslie Cox.

Asked if anyone had seen Eddie Watson, one of the elders, taking his time, removed his toothpick and pointed it enigmatically at Lucius himself. The wet toothpick glinted like a needle in the sun's reflection off the river, transfixing Lucius for one piercing instant in the other's unimaginable vision. A second man was pointing a bone finger at a third man on a bench, who was waving gently like a pale thing in a current.

"Colonel? I sure thought that was you!" The small silver-haired man, eyes round and kindly behind glasses, shifted a little to make room on his bench. "I was savin that place for Honey," he warned, looking over his shoulder for his wife. "We sure ain't seen you in a while. We always wondered what become of Colonel." Weeks Daniels did not seem to recall that they had scarcely laid eyes upon each other in the last quarter century. "We're retired now, y'know. Tryin to get used to it."

The old friends talked at angles for a while, finding their way. Lucius mentioned Speck, and Weeks nodded with distaste. "We ain't related hardly. He's one them black-haired Cajun Danielses, look like wild Injuns and probably are. This feller fought his family from the age of one, and he weren't much more than about ten when he run off for good."

Honey Daniels, coming up behind, stood patiently, not wishing to interrupt. Like her husband, she was slight and rather frail, with the same clean silver hair and innocent gaze, and even the same style of silver glasses. As young folks, Lucius recalled, they had looked like brother and sister, making it difficult to conceive of sex between them. When Lucius stood up to offer her his seat, she smiled, uncertain.

"Remember Colonel Watson, sweetheart?" Weeks took her hand and drew her down onto the bench between them, telling her what he'd just told Colonel about Crockett Daniels. Honey nodded. "Yes, I heard you, Weeks. I believe you said that Speck was not related."

Red spots jumped to her husband's paper cheeks. "Well, I ain't so much denying him, I just ain't *proud* about him." Frowning, Weeks looked away over the river, where gulls slid down the wind between the bridges. "My dad had no use for that feller since Speck was a boy. I ain't no different. My dad was captain of the clam dredge, and he was always friends with E. J. Watson. You recall him, Colonel?"

"Yes, I sure do. Your dad was Henrietta's brother, right?"

"Aunt Netta? I believe he was." The old man glanced at him, a little guarded.

"And Josie Jenkins was their half sister, right?"

"Don't know *what* Aunt Josie was, darned if I do. Aunt Josie picked up a slew of names before she give it up, but she might of been Tant Jenkins's sister if she was a Jenkins to start off with. Mind-boggling, ain't it? Anyways, they are all kin some way or another, no getting around it. Speaking about that bunch puts me in mind of that feller got hitched so many times that one day he looked up and said, 'I'll be darned if my own dad ain't my damn son-in-law!' "

Though his joke was an old one, Honey Daniels smiled freshly at her husband, creating a little space around his dignity. "Aunt Josie was real good to you back in the old days," she reminded Lucius, not certain what he might wish to remember. "Little lady with big curly black hair, plenty of spirit? Had the same mother as Aunt Netta, I believe. They both worked awhile at Chatham Bend, and both had daughters there."

"My half sisters, you mean."

"Well, now that you mention it, I guess that's right. Aunt Netta's child was Minnie, named for your dad's sister. Married a nice man from Key West. You ever see her anymore?" When he confessed he'd never even met her, she hurried on. "Well, we always heard that Minnie had her daddy's color, blue eyes, auburn hair. She loved her daddy, he would see her in Key West, but she never wished to belong to the Watson family. After your daddy died, Netta liked to recall how Minnie's father had forced himself upon her. And when we reminded her how often she had claimed that Minnie was a love child and that Jack Watson was the nicest man she ever met, she would cry out, 'Well, that's true, too, but Jack took me by storm!' "

" 'Jack took me by storm!' " her husband marveled. "Aunt Josie, too. When Aunt Josie was drinking, she would always claim how Watson 'ravished' her."

Honey frowned a little. That word was too strong. "Aunt Josie's Pearl was five years younger than Minnie, I believe. Pretty, kind of skinny blond. She favored her half brother Lucius. You two were very close when she was small, and she never forgot that." Honey reached and squeezed his hand when he looked guilty. "Pearl always spoke so lovingly about her brother! She was so worried about you! Used to go all the way south to Hardens', just to warn you, you recall? Tell you how much talk there was, how you were making the men nervous, and how your life would never be safe, so close to Chokoloskee." Honey smiled, remembering Pearl Watson. "Tried to mother you, and here she was half your age!" She gazed at Lucius with the greatest fondness. "Know something, sweetheart?" she exclaimed, taking his wrist. "We're just tickled pink to see your face again!"

Her husband was still brooding about family matters. "I recollect how them ladies and their kids got talked about as 'Watson's backdoor family.' "

"Well, those ladies weren't ashamed about him, they were proud about him." Honey Daniels said. "They loved him dearly and their kids did, too. And at the end of it, Josie had his little boy. Poor little feller was just five months old when he drowned in the Great Hurricane."

"Ol' Speck was in the bar one night when someone was tellin about that, and Speck spoke up, said Watson's little son weren't nobody in the world but Crockett Daniels! Claimed he never drowned in the Great Hurricane because his uncle S. S. Jenkins—that was Tant—Tant upped and saved him! Them men at the bar was all agog, as Aunt Josie used to say. Speck told how Tant had hid the babe, just like Moses in the bulrushes, then got one of them Daniels girls to raise him up and give him a name to spare 'em all a scandal. Said if anyone had doubts about his story, well, here he was, the living proof, as big as life! And any man with something smart to say could step outside with him and settle it right now!

"Trouble was, the one with the worst doubts was Uncle Tant! Swore he never knew nothin about it! And Josie yelled, 'That boy's tellin people I'm his *mother*? Must of been some kind of virgin birth or somethin!'

"Speck was only havin fun, least to start off with." Weeks Daniels shook his head. "Cause them folks knew that Speck was in the gang that had shot Watson. As Tant used to say, 'I knew that young feller was born mean, but I never believed he would take a gun to his own daddy, not at the age of only five months old!'

"Those ladies weren't his only ones," Weeks cackled. "There was another backdoor boy besides that little feller. Course we won't talk about that one cause he don't admit it, but local people know who he is, and we got long memories—that's about *all* we got, seems like to me!"

"Weeks, you don't know that for a fact." Honey warned Lucius to pay no attention to her husband. "The man denies it and I imagine he should know. Better'n you."

"Him and Speck ought to get together, then, cause that feller is a Watson and says he ain't, and Speck ain't a Watson and says he is." However, Weeks Daniels raised his hand to show that, out of deference to his wife, he would make no further comment on Watson Dyer. "Nosir, Speck weren't born a Watson, he were born a liar. Ain't never had firsthand experience of the God's truth—pays no attention to it cause he flat don't care about it. Speck always took credit for bein in the posse, but what Speck mostly done that day was come up afterwards with other boys and shoot into the body. We were told that for a fact by one of them boys was in it with him."

"He's talking about my brother," Honey Daniels sniffed. "But Harley Wiggins didn't always speak the God's truth, either."

"Yes," Weeks said, "Aunt Josie and Aunt Netta called your dad Jack Watson. That was the name he brung back from the Nations. Josie claimed her Jack never done but the one wrongful killing in all the years she lived at Chatham Bend. Said he went down to Lost Man's River and shot a man who was settin in the sun patching his britches. Feller done him wrong."

"Tucker?" Lucius asked after a moment.

"We don't recall the name," Honey said carefully.

*

"Of course you know your sister Pearl married Earl Helveston from Marco." Honey Daniels smiled. "Folks called 'em Pearl 'n' Earl. If Earl ever laid eyes on Mr. Watson, we never heard about it, but he always swore he loved that man, and nobody understood how that could be. Crockett Daniels was another one claimed he loved Mr. Watson, never mind he raised a gun and fired at him. Your daddy had quite a strong effect on these young fellers."

"He was some fisherman, Earl was!" Weeks Daniels said. "But he was a cutter, pulled his knife too fast when he was drinking. Earl Helveston was rough even for Marco, and that was a rough place. Course them Marco men was always jealous they did not kill your daddy, so they went and killed a lawman later on. In Prohibition. Couple of them Helvestons was in on that one."

Lucius recalled that when Pearl first came to visit him at Lost Man's River, in the twenties, she would turn up on the runboat that stopped by three times a week to pick up fish and leave off ice. In later years, she would appear with her baby and her husband in Earl's "hobo houseboat," a little raft with a cabin perched on top, towed by an old skiff with outboard motor. Lucius felt neglectful and a bit downcast over Pearl, who had worked for years at the old Barfield Heights Hotel there at Caxambas. She was a pretty girl and a kind girl, too, but her life had always been a sad one.

Poor Pearl, he thought, had never had a chance to get her bearings. She had been born on the edge of society and stayed out there. Sometimes she called herself Pearl Jenkins, sometimes Pearl Watson. She had spent her life outside the window looking in. "Her people never had a home to call their own, and home was what that girl had always longed for," he reflected.

"She's inside of a home right now," Weeks said. He had gotten things confused and his wife hushed him. "Her mind gave out on her," Honey explained, "and they took her to some kind of institution over in Georgia." She looked down at her lap. "We never called to see how she was getting on. We don't know how to talk to Pearl when she's not right in her head."

Subdued by the story of Pearl Watson, they stared away across the broad brown reach of the Calusa Hatchee. Westward, toward Pine Island Sound, the lilting gulls caught glints of sun where the current mixed with wind in a riptide. "Honey and me moved here to live around the time you went south to the Islands, and we will die here, too, wouldn't surprise me. When Caxambas got took over for development, what was left of our old bunch come up here, too, Josie Jenkins, Tant, and Pearl, along with other Daniels kin and some old friends from that section. Uncle Tant conked out in a rest home, and Aunt Josie done the same when she come of age. That was along about 1939." Weeks Daniels sighed. "Ain't much more to say about that branch of our family, cause it's finished. Ain't one Jenkins left."

*

His old friends said they knew just where to find his brother. Honey took their arms, and they walked upriver toward the Edison Bridge. She was still rummaging around the old days. "When I was little, five or six years old, your daddy would come to our house to get his supper. Mr. Watson ate many a meal in the bosom of our family. Wasn't a boardinghouse or anything, it's only that Mama had extra room when we lived at Chokoloskee. There were times your daddy spent the night, and sometimes his wife, too—oh, she was just a beautiful young woman, very sweet. As I recall, her name was Edna, but he called her Kate. All I remember was a fine strong-looking man who wore nice clothes, he was the sporting kind. His Kate called him Mr. Watson, but to my father, he was E.J.—Mr. E. J. Watson.

"My brother Harley, who was just a boy, he couldn't get over Mr. Watson, used to spy on him hoping to see his guns, and listen to his tales of the Wild West. Mr. Watson was always kind and quiet-spoken, but all the same us little girls were all dead scared of him. We'd heard so much about how dangerous he was, and when he came, we just skedaddled, ran like quail. But Mama wasn't afraid of him—she wasn't afraid of anybody. He was always respectful and mannerly to our mama.

"One time, we children went with Mama on a visit to Chatham Bend. That must have been in 1906 or 1907. You were there, you were called Lucius then. I bet you don't recall the little Wiggins girls. We spent a week! Our daddy knew that his friend E.J. was a perfect gentleman, he absolutely trusted him to take good care of us. And sure enough, your father was so hospitable, so nice to us kids, so nice to his young wife—why, our own brother or daddy couldn't have been nicer! And the food his cook put on the table, we never saw so much food in all our life! All the same, we children were still scared of him a little bit. In early 1910, Daddy moved our family to Fort Myers so we were not at Chokoloskee that October, but I still recall how shocked we were to hear that news!"

Weeks blurted suddenly, "Your daddy was crazy some way, Colonel, only he was the dangerous kind that never showed it. That's what fooled folks. How could a body ever suspect such a fine-looking man? I guess there aren't too many like that, but every once in a while one comes along. Look and act like everybody else, joke and talk and go about their business, and all the while committing murders one after the other. Mr. Watson had a screw loose in his brain, and there wasn't a thing his family could do!"

"Weeks? You think poor Colonel likes to hear this kind of thing?" Though Lucius smiled out of affection for Weeks's inability to mince his words, Honey patted his hand in her distress over her husband, as poor Weeks stumbled forward and broke more, trying to mend things. "All I meant, folks used to tell how E. J. Watson would murder all his colored help on payday! But those women in our family who lived there at the Bend, they knew Jack Watson good as anybody, and they never recollected that at all!"

Lucius said quietly, "Those rumors about 'Watson's payday' always sounded like some local excuse for why my dad was doing better than the other planters, Houses included."

Honey Daniels nodded. "Will Wiggins grew cane for years at Half Way Creek, but he always remained a good friend to your daddy. He never wanted to believe those bad old stories."

"Never wanted to believe 'em, no, but in the end he did." Her husband cleared his throat again, frowning and worrying, torn between tact and integrity. "Our Jenkins-Daniels bunch stayed loyal to your dad, but speaking for myself—talking straight, now, Colonel—I never been too sure.

"Me and my brothers Fred and Harvey used to fish them sea trout flats northwest of Mormon Key, and one early mornin before light—we was still anchored, half asleep—we was awoke by the sound of your dad's boat, comin down out of Chatham River to the Gulf. Wasn't nobody around the Islands then who didn't know that pop-skip motor from a long ways off."

Lucius nodded. The *Brave* had been the first motor launch on that coast, thirty-foot long and nine-foot beam, with a trunk cabin forward, canvas curtains aft, hull painted black. Local fishermen nicknamed her the May-Pop, he recalled, from the eccentric popping of her one-cylinder engine.

"Well, next thing they knew, this black boat come slidin out that narrow mangrove channel. One minute there weren't no boat in sight, the coast was empty, and the next minute, there she was, popped up in front of them green islets like she had come downriver underwater. And darn if she don't swing off her course and head in our direction, never hailed us, just circled where we was anchored! Round and round she went, two-three-four times, slow and steady as a shark, and nobody on deck, no sign of life.

"Us Daniels boys had our guns loaded, cause folks was nervous around Watson territory. And we was set to shoot, that's how darn spooked we was!

And we was boys who reckoned we was friends with Mr. Watson, him bein so close to our whole Daniels family!

"I can still see that boat today, as clear as I am looking at you now. She made them circles, then come in from dead abeam like she aimed to slice our fishin boat in two. We couldn't figure what Mr. Watson wanted or what he might do next, all we could do was sit tight and wait him out. I believe he was warnin us off them fishin grounds at Mormon Key, and was just scarin us. Well, we was scared all right, we stood up and waved our guns, but Harvey had sense, he was the oldest, and he told us to lay our guns down quick, and make sure Watson seen us do it. Harvey told us to get set to jump, cause we could swim for shore if we had no bullets in us. He didn't care to trade no shots with that man we couldn't see inside that cabin. But at the last second, when we started hollerin out of our fear he meant to ram us, that launch sheered off and headed out toward Pavilion.

"After that day, my brother Fred was bone leery of Watson. Couldn't talk about nothin else but Watson, Watson. Fred Daniels weren't but nineteen years of age, afeared of nothin, so bein so bad spooked was hard for him to handle. Fred never killed a man, but you knew straight off he could do that if he had to. It was somethin you seen in certain men, he was that kind. And Fred Daniels was a feller could pick up his rifle and nail the head of a terrapin spang to the water.

"Now at that time our dad was captain of the clam dredge and my brother Harvey was the engineer on the old *Falcon,* which carried the clams north to the factory. On his day off, he worked on other boats as a mechanic. He'd done a lot of work on Watson's boat and was owed eighty-five dollars, which could buy you a pretty good motor back in them days. I recall the sight of Ed Watson at Pavilion, working on his boat with Harvey, the broad strong back of him stretchin the stripes on one of them old-time mattress-tickin shirts, and the black hat, and them sunburnt ginger whiskers. Mr. Watson was a good boatman, and generally a good man to do business with, but this was along toward his last year when he was dead broke from his troubles in north Florida, and had fell behind on all his debts for quite some while. At this time when he scared us so bad, he had not give Harvey what he owed, and had tried to put him off another month.

"So hearin that, Fred Daniels said, 'Well, now, Harvey, let's go pay that feller a night visit. We'll set in the reeds across from his damn house, and at daybreak when he comes outside, I'll pick him off for you.' He meant it, too. But Harvey was the other kind, thoughtful and careful—he'd sooner lose money than see some man gunned down. And he knew his brother was hot-headed, and might not have such a good plan as he thought. So when Fred swore he would go ahead without him, Harvey took him by the shoulder and he shook him. Said, 'Maybe you ain't doin this to settle up my debt, ever think of that? Maybe you just can't live on the same coast with a man who scared you for the fun of it.' Well, Fred gets hot and hollers at his brother, but bein dead honest, he can't fool himself, and in a minute he admits it, comes right out with it. But that don't mean he ain't still furious, and he hollers out how one of these days he'd fix that sonofabitch so he don't scare *nobody* no more!"

Weeks's eyes were wide behind his glasses. "That goes to show you how much fear and anger people felt, and just how near Ed Watson come to being killed before they killed him."

The wind tossed the royal palms along the river. As they walked along, Weeks glanced unhappily at Lucius, who showed no expression. "Folks was deathly scared of Mr. Watson, that's a fact. It was always told how killing people never bothered him a bit, he would kill women if he had to. They said Belle Starr weren't the only one, not by a long shot. Had another woman working for him, great big woman, this was in the last of Watson's days. She was the one whose body floated up out of the river, she was the one led Watson to his grave."

"He did not kill Hannah Smith, that I can promise you."

"Nosir, I ain't claiming that he killed her. But I ain't never been so sure he weren't behind it." Weeks stopped walking. He turned to look his old friend in the eye. "You ain't askin my opinion, Colonel, and likely you don't want it, but I better tell you anyways, just so we're straight about it." He took a deep breath. "I reckon the whole thing come out just about right. E. J. Watson was a coiled rattler, you never knowed when he was going to strike. I said that once where your sister Carrie heard it, and she told me she would not forgive me till the day she died and maybe a good while after!"

Honey sighed, shaking her head over her husband. "Carrie has had a dog's share of misfortune, but she's still full of life! Everyone in town knows Carrie Langford! Course we aren't in her social circle but we know her, too!"

Weeks Daniels nodded. "Yessir, your sister has plenty of spirit, and she sure needed it after Banker Langford died! Remember when she opened up the Gulf Shore Inn, down at Fort Myers Beach? That was back in Prohibition times, you was in the Islands. Had kind of a speakeasy in back, but Sheriff Tippins never bothered her at all. Carrie was along in her late thirties, she'd put on some heft, but she was a fine-lookin widder woman all the same. Anyways, she got hooked up with a fish guide at the Beach. Capt. Luke Gates on the *Black Flash*—"

"Oh goodness, Weeks!" his wife protested. But her husband wore that dogged look, having no idea how to go about not telling the whole truth and nothing but the truth, so help him God. "So one night I was in there when

Gates's wife come in—thin scratchy little blonde, she was just a-*stormin*! Run right over and tore into her husband where he was settin at the poker table. 'See you, raise you five,' he told them men. Never lifted his eyes up off the cards. And when his wife picked up his whiskey glass and let his liquor fly into Luke's face, he never blinked. Never even reached to wipe his face! Kept right on studyin the cards with the whiskey runnin off his cheeks like nothing happened, like that hard little blonde weren't even there.

"Makin no headway at the poker table, his wife let fly an ugly speech about Carrie Langford's morals or the lack of 'em, and how Carrie had come by her bad character real natural, on account of her daddy was the well-known murderer Ed 'Bloody' Watson. Well, darned if this banker's widow don't ring open the cash register, take out a revolver, and bang it down hard on the bar. And she said, 'Let me tell you something, honey, that kind of mean and dirty talk is not permitted in my place just because some little fool don't know how to hang on to her man!' And seeing that gun in the hands of Watson's daughter, that little blonde cooled off enough to run outside where it was dark. She yelled her dirty stuff in through the window, but no-body didn't pay her no attention after that, and maybe her husband least of all.

"Yes, your sister had some spirit and she had some style, and she could talk rough when she wanted. She liked to drink, have a good time, just like her daddy. She never mentioned him or tried to defend him, but she would not lie low or act ashamed about him. Some of her bootleg liquor trade might of come from the kind of nosy people who wanted to say they had a drink with Watson's daughter, but nobody said nothing bad about him around Carrie."

*

They paused at the foot of the Edison Bridge to look at the white-painted brick mansion on the corner opposite. Walter Langford had built this house in 1919 and died of cirrhosis of the liver in 1920. For a banker, poor Walter had never had much of a head for figures, Lucius recalled, and what he earned went mostly for appearances, so he'd left his wife with more debts than inheritance. Carrie got her two daughters married off, but she'd had to sell this fine brick house to do it, buying a smaller place down the street which in later years she opened up to lodgers. After Prohibition ended, and the Gulf Shore Inn, she had started a small restaurant on First Street called Miss Carrie's Chicken. Being generous, Carrie spent too much, but she made shrewd investments, too, and was comfortable enough by the time the smoke cleared.

"Methodists own that property," Honey was saying, "but Eddie Watson is so proud of it that he comes over here most every day now that he's retired. Likes to tell the tourists all about the good old days."

Shading his eyes, Weeks peered across the road. "That's him skulkin in the corner of the porch," he said, "so I reckon we'll say good-bye and let you go." Lucius confessed that he'd been estranged from Eddie, and would appreciate it if his friends would help him ease matters a little, so the Danielses accompanied him across the street. At the porch steps, Weeks doffed his hat to the bulky figure, who came forward and said good morning a bit loudly.

"Yes?" E. E. Watson moved to the top step, to bar their way. "What do you people want here, Daniels? This is private property, *church* property—" But before he could crank himself too high, Honey introduced the noted historian Professor Collins, and Eddie stepped back with a sweeping gesture of his arm. "Indeed, sir! Welcome! I am honored! E. E. Watson, at your service, sir!" He stuck out a moist hand. "Yessir, if it's history you're after, you have come to the right place." Grandly he waved them up onto the porch. "My brother Lucius, he's a historian! Comes here to consult me all the time!"

"Eddie?"

Despite the heat, Eddie Watson was dressed formally in unclean linen suit, white shirt, green tie, the whole ensemble yellowed and flecked with sad traces of repasts long forgotten. He peered at Lucius, looking worried and confused. For all his large manner, there was no life in his eyes, and Lucius pitied him.

"Eddie? Forgive me—"

"This was the Langford house, of course. My sister's house. Her Langford in-laws lived over there between Bay and First, a big pink house, it's now the Dean Hotel. Her husband was the president of the First National Bank, and Carrie and Walter entertained the Thomas Edisons and their friend Mr. Henry Ford. I believe Mark Twain—"

"Eddie? You really don't know who I am?"

"What's that?" Eddie peered again, in great alarm. "Of course I know! What do you want?"

Lucius reached out to touch his arm, trying to calm him. "I need your signature on a petition. To save Papa's house. And I'm preparing a biography of Papa, and there are some questions—"

"Oh no, you don't!" Eddie Watson pushed past him and tottered down the steps into the sunlight, where he turned and pointed an unsteady finger. "Damn you, you're just stirring up more trouble, same way you always did! It's family business, will you *never* understand? It's *family* business!" He waved wildly at the house. "You never even came to see your sister, and you broke her heart!"

"And I have to check with you about a list of men that I sent years ago to Rob—"

"I took care of *that* darned thing, don't worry! I took care of *that!*" But his eye did not hold, and he glowered at the Danielses. "None of you have any business here! You are trespassing upon church property! I am calling the police!" And he rushed off down the street, waving his arms.

They perched like three birds on the porch steps, watching him go. "Will he really do that?" Lucius asked.

Weeks Daniels nodded. "Poor Eddie's always calling in complaints. Kind of a hobby. They don't pay him any mind at all."

Far up the street, Mr. E. E. Watson, hobbling wildly, disappeared around the corner. The hollow street of the old river town stood gaunt and empty, as if that silhouette of his lost brother had lifted up into the sun like a stray cinder. He wondered if they would ever meet again.

"Eddie always tried to be like Carrie—uptown people, wealthy kind of people," Honey reflected. "Not that you ever spoke against 'em, Colonel."

"I never spoke of them at all!" he mourned. "I always thought they were ashamed because their brother was just a fisherman. Who drank too much." He smiled unhappily. "E. E. Watson and his Augusta had to keep up appearances, after all. My brother is a gentleman, as I'm sure he is the first to let folks know!"

"Oh, he's not so bad, I guess." Honey worried that she and Weeks might have been unkind. "In his younger days, Eddie was so friendly, remember, Weeks?"

"Maybe too friendly," Weeks decided, after a pause. "Big hearty man, big but not strong. Always dressed up tight cause he wanted to look like Banker Langford's brother-in-law, wanted folks to call him Mr. Watson. But I think he knew folks never took to him, not the way they took to his younger brother. Colonel was always just plain Colonel, just himself. He could go into any house in Florida and be all right." In his spontaneous surge of affection, Weeks Daniels went red, glaring fiercely at the tourist traffic coming off the river bridge, as if expecting the arrival from the north of a long-lost friend. "I never heard one bad word about Colonel Watson."

"Better go talk to Speck, then," Lucius protested, feeling disloyal to his brother and somehow fraudulent.

Anxious to finish, Weeks Daniels ignored him. "I reckon Eddie done the best he could. Having his sister here in town gave him the heart to stay. Used to let on how his rightful home was back up north where he was born, used to talk about retiring one day to Columbia County, but the years came and went and he's still here.

"E. E. Watson, Insurance. New customers would say, 'You *the* Ed Watson?

You ain't fixin to murder me, are ye, if I don't pay up my premiums?'—joking him, you know, slapping him on the back. And Eddie never blinked an eye, he made the same answer over and over—*Better watch your step, all right!*—and went right on filling out the forms. Never occurred to them damn jackasses that Watson's son might be a tender kind of feller with real feelings. The few that even noticed that the poor man minded, they would blame their own stupidity on Eddie. Said, 'Why hell, if that feller can't take it, he ought to have left town long ago, either that or change his goddamn name!'

"Mostly he stayed pretty calm about it. In his own way, Eddie Watson is as mulish as his daddy. He aimed to be a fine upstanding citizen no matter what. Got himself seen regular at church and stuck to business, went bird hunting once in a while, played golf at the new country club, tried to fit in. For a while he even headed up the Masons! Eddie would not back up, no matter what, and he weren't about to change his name.

"Only thing, in recent years, he kind of forgot to keep up his appearances. He even give up on Mr. E. E. Watson for a while, begun to call himself Ed Watson, Junior. Took a kind of pride in that—not in his daddy, not exactly, but in being the son of somebody so famous. Made him a somebody in his own right, and it brung in customers. People might stop by the agency to take a gander at Bloody Watson's son, and buying a policy was their excuse to shake his hand. Eddie was always a businessman, first and foremost, and he discovered that a nice dark past paid off!

"Them last years before he lost the agency, Eddie got to hinting to the winter visitors that he was some kind of a chip off the old block. Local folks always thought of him as pretty meek and mild behind his bluster, but to outsiders he might hint he had a violent streak, same as his daddy. Even hauled out this darn list he'd put together of those Chokoloskee men who finished E. J. Watson, and let on about how he went down there and took care of the ringleaders. 'Didn't have no choice about it,' Eddie said. 'Had to defend the honor of the family!' "

Lucius took a long deep breath but he said nothing.

Honey was getting to her feet. The day was late. "Of course one untruth leads to another," she murmured. "His Neva was hardly laid to rest before Eddie took his secretary to marry, and he hardly got that woman home before she upped and left. So he took a third one, never bothered to let on about the second!"

Weeks smiled at Lucius, clinging to his hand an extra second. "When you first went back to the Islands, Colonel, you used to say you had no family to speak of, but you always had our Jenkins-Daniels bunch. Well, you still have us, what is left of us. Come see us, hear?"

Lucius took their hands—all three held hands—so that they stood in a small circle on the sidewalk. "I was lucky to have the Jenkins-Daniels bunch," he murmured with emotion, "and I'm truly sorry I lost touch. Never taking the trouble to find out what became of Pearl—that's inexcusable! I never was the brother to her that I should have been."

Honey said, "Colonel? I have Pearl's phone number right in this purse someplace." And Weeks Daniels said, "You accepted her as your sister. That's a lot more than the others done."

Pearl

Pearl had been nine or ten when their father died, a self-starved creature, a pale fugitive from the sun. Even in those days—she clung to this sad adornment most of her life—she wore a thin white ribbon in her thin blond hair. It was that ribbon which gnawed at his heart now. Pearl had been struck speechless by her father's death, while Aunt Josie, who had lost the dead man's baby boy in the hurricane only the week before, had torn her hair and fled down the storm-rutted cart tracks at Caxambas, shrieking in woe.

His sister Pearl, he mourned, his sister Carrie. Lucy Summerlin. How would dear Mama have judged his failure to protect the tender lives and eager feelings entrusted to his care? Hearing Pearl's thin voice over the wire, he was stricken by sadness, self-disgust.

Who are you? Who is calling me?

Pearl?

Who is calling me? Hello?

This is Lucius! Your brother Lucius.

Brother Who?

Pearl, this is Lucius! This is Colonel! I called to say hello! I called to see how you were getting along!

Why are you hollering? Did you say Colonel Watson? Oh Good Lord! Oh Colonel, Lucius honey, are you sure you are all right? I was so worried, sweetheart! I went to see Miss Lucy Summerlin to ask where you were and she told me how she only wished she knew! She was so sweet to me, you know! She said I looked like you! Miss Lucy loves you dearly, do you know that? Why did you abandon her? You broke her heart! O yes I know, I know, that was some years ago. Lucius? Can you believe our life has gone so fast? Do you look as terrible and old as I do? Where are you? What are you doing there? Why are you calling me? What do you want?

I don't want anything, Pearl. Please don't be upset. I only wanted to speak to you, see how you were. Pearl honey? I feel just terrible that I haven't called before, that I didn't even know what had become of you!

Well, what's become of you, sweetheart? What are you doing?

I—well, I'm gathering information for a book about Papa.

Who?

About our father.

Our Father Who Art in Heaven, Hallowed be Thy Name, Thy Kingdom Come— that's my Father! Who Art in Heaven! Those men blew your father to Kingdom Come—

Pearl, listen, he was your dad, too—

Do you know about the J for Jack? In E. J. Watson? My mother was married to Jack Watson! She was a lovely person! My mother was married seven times—one husband twice—and she outlived the whole darn bunch! But she only had one daughter by her E. Jack Watson—that was me!

Pearl, listen to me—

Lucius? Remember how you always stopped by to see us on your way north and south from Chatham? Remember those beautiful days on the salt water? When we went everywhere by boat because there were no roads? It was hard times—a lot of work and children and hard times, remember, Lucius? When did we stop calling you Lucius? Lucius, how come you forgot about me? What do you want now?

Honey, I wanted to ask about your memories of Papa—

He's dead. I am retired now. Who gave you my phone number? What are you going to do with my information? I really don't care, I am so glad to help you. Oh, I've missed you, Colonel!

Pearl? Don't cry—

It's late in the day to try to understand what happened, but don't you give it up, you keep on trying. One man who claimed to be real close to your daddy, that was Wiley Bostic. Old Man Bostic got drunk one night at Barfield's, he told me he oiled up Daddy's shotgun cartridges so's they wouldn't fire, said he didn't want to see nobody hurt! You believe that? Because everyone claimed a lot of things back at that time.

Everyone wanted a claim on Mr. Watson, for some reason.

My mother was married to your father and you used to come visiting at Caxambas and now here we are, right on the telephone! It's a small world!

Well, yes, it is, Pearl.

Jack Watson died while my mother was married to him. He was with Belle Starr before that. Also Jesse James and that crowd. A lot of people didn't like him, but I loved him.

I imagine your mother loved him, too.

Yes, she did! The only thing, she was leery of his temper, he might put a razor to her neck. I don't know if he had a drinking problem or what. Course all the men drank. They never considered heavy drinking a real problem back in those days, not the way they do today.

Pearl, I wanted to check somebody's story with you. Did your mother ever speak about the hired hand our father killed at Chatham Bend because this man insulted her nice peas?

No, I did not hear about insulted peas. Which doesn't mean that he might not have killed somebody.

Did he ever threaten you?

No! No! No! He loved all his children! You know something? I saw the man who killed him. After we got run out of Caxambas, we were living across the canal in Naples, which was not Colored Town back then. They had real boundary lines to keep out black people. Only the whites could cross, isn't that crazy? Because our local coloreds never bothered people, it was those ones from up North who caused the trouble. Anyway, my mother pointed her finger. She said, "That mulatta over yonder killed your daddy." I don't recall his name. I do recall he was very light in color. But my mother never held a thing against him, no she didn't. Said he never would have done that on his own, he was put up to it. She blamed the white fellers.

Pearl? You must be talking about Henry Short—

That's the one. Before Earl Helveston run off on me, we had a talk about my daddy. Earl just purely loved Jack Watson, maybe because he was practicing up to be that way himself! He discussed some things, bad deeds, y'know. Swore me to secrecy! Said them Marco boys would kill him just for the knowing of it. I have got it all wrote down someplace. Earl always said, "I love that man no matter what he did." Said, "That man tell me do something, I would jump to it."

That's the effect he had on some people, all right.

One time he sent word to Lost Man's Key to tell this man to get off of his property. Said, "I will give you so much time, then you better be gone." Cause if he had something coming to him, he wanted it right then, he didn't care to wait until tomorrow. But the man sent back a sassy note—that was his finish. It's like Earl said, "If Jack Watson told you he would kill you, he would do it. Being a man of his word, he expected the same integrity in others."

Sounds like the Tucker story. Down at Lost Man's Beach.

Those young folks were killed and had rocks around their necks and they were found out in the water by the Harden men and that mulatta feller I was talking about. And after that, this Henry Short grew superstitious about Papa, he was scared to death of him. This stuff didn't come from any book, my Mama told me. Earl said to me, "Know something, Pearl? A lot of people did not care for your daddy, but I loved him!" It was only lately I figured out that when our daddy died, Earl Helveston was only ten, a kid like me! So I can't for the life of me figure out how he knew my dad so well, but he sure loved him! Earl and Speck both.

Isn't that something? A lot of young men—

My mother was in that Hurricane of 1910 and lost her baby. You know who that baby's daddy was?

Yes I do, Pearl.

It was all so hush-hush, you know, back then.

Did you ever hear the rumor that the baby lived?

Speck tell you that one? He's a damn liar, then! Excuse my language, sweetheart! But I never knew why Speck wanted so bad to join up in our family, when all the rest of 'em were trying to get out!

Hello? Are you still there? Hello? Can you still hear me, Pearl?

Who are you anyway? Whoever you are, you must be a liar! My brother Lucius would have called me before this! He would have called me! I'm his baby sister! They say I look like him! Lucius loves me more than anybody in the world!

Please don't cry, Pearl. Please don't be upset. I am ashamed I never called. I've thought of you so often—

Who are you? Who is calling me? You tell my brother to call me, hear? I'm all alone in this sad place! They won't let me go home because they say I have no home. They say Mrs. Barfield's Hotel is gone, can you imagine such a thing? They say I have no job there anymore! It's been years and years since anybody came to see me! Lucius Watson never came! And my name is Pearl Watson! I'm his baby sister!

The Niece

Lucius rang up Eddie's daughter the next morning—she who had led her unbeloved stepmother to the cemetery and told her the truth about E. J. Watson—whichever truth she had decided to bestow, since as she now declared over the telephone, she knew "nothing worth knowing" about Grandfather Watson. She had little information about family history and no interest whatever in acquiring more. "I scarcely heard Grandfather mentioned until I was sixteen, and even then, I was only told that he came from good family in South Carolina and died of a heart attack. Aunt Carrie's daughters, Faith and Betsy, they were told the same!"

Having scarcely laid eyes on him since she was a child, she did not hide her suspicion of this stranger on the telephone, who might or might not be her long-lost uncle Lucius. She finally agreed to receive him at her clothing store downtown, but when he turned up, she rushed to intercept him even before the little bell over the door had finished tinkling.

In place of the rather pretty girl he had remembered stood a cracked vessel in bony horn-rimmed glasses and a mad red dress. Katherine Watson was bitter, offhand, sharp, with a pained laugh like the rasping of a tern. "Why did you ask about my mother? If you are Uncle Lucius, then you *knew* my mother. Neva Watson died in 1924. I suppose you remember Dorothy? Your own niece? My sister was very beautiful, like Aunt Carrie's daughter, but she died many years ago in an automobile accident up north, as you would surely know if you are who you say you are. That's every last thing I know about the Watson family, so you needn't waste any more of your good time!"

"I didn't mean to upset you, Katherine. Why did you agree to see me?"

Katherine's voice went a little higher. "Your phone call startled me, I wasn't thinking! You told me you were Lucius Watson, but I have no idea who you are or what you're up to!"

His niece glared at him in alarm and dislike. He scarcely recognized the tight-pinched mouth, the worried hair, the famished shins. Was Walter's funeral the last time he had seen her? "This is family business!" she cried fiercely, darting sharp flashes off sharp corners of modern spectacles into his eyes. "I can't recall one thing worth speaking of about our family," she repeated, "because nobody bothered to remember anything. That's the way the Watsons are—indifferent!"

He could not seem to reassure this frantic person, and, in a sense, what she had said was true. Compared with his siblings and their children who had lived out their lives in the deep shadow of the scandal, he was not "family" but a feckless drifter.

"You see, I'm kind of a historian, apart from being your uncle. I'm trying to dispel some of those lurid myths about your grandfather. And I have to ask about a list of names—"

"It's family business!"

The lone customer turned to look at them. His niece gave up trying to back him through the door to the bright street and herded him instead into the shoe department.

"Did Eddie—did your father ever speak about his older brother?"

"No! I can't remember! An older brother? A *half* brother visited just once that I remember—I was still a child then, eight or nine. He didn't stay long. This man came in search of Uncle Lucius, and became unpleasant because my father didn't know or care where Lucius was. My father and his brothers were never close. My father always told us that his younger brother—is that you?—had upset the family by wasting his good education and going to live among lowlife rednecks in the Ten Thousand Islands. He said he never saw you after that. But as I said, I don't think it was hostility so much as plain indifference!"

He sought to reassure her by relating a few details of his recent visit with her cousins in Fort White. She interrupted him. "I beg your pardon? They told you my father *cooked* when he came to visit? I never knew he cooked. We always had a colored person to do the cooking. Aunt Carrie never went back to Fort White, but my father lived there for some years after his mother died.

He considered that place home, don't ask me why! We had to go there every summer, stay at the Collins farm, and my sister and I just hated it! They were nice people, I suppose, good country people, but as poor as church mice!

"My father trained us to be snobs from an early age. We were poor ourselves a good deal of the time, but he was determined to be snobbish all the same. Oh yes, he always had a darkie, to keep up appearances, but he never had nearly as much money as Uncle Walter, so he had to be extra friendly to make up for it. When he had money, he joined up—what? Just about everything there was to join! A real glad-hander. He flattered folks, he made bad jokes, he bragged.

"What's that? Why do you say that? Did *you* like him? I don't think compensating for his father's reputation had a thing to do with it! That's just the way he always was—a braggart! Yes! My father is a braggart and his wife's a fool. Augusta reveres my father for some reason, but that woman is nothing but a fool. She tries so hard to be genteel, but she never had one nickel she could throw away. And now that he's retired, of course, *I* have to help them—well, that's not your business, I'm sure," she added bitterly.

"Actually," he said gently, "I was hoping you might help me with a question that I'm afraid your father just won't answer." Had she ever heard about a list of names of the men who'd killed Grandfather Watson? A list given originally to Lucy Dyer? Lucy Summerlin? "I'm trying to find out who has this list—"

"*No!*" Katherine cried, rising abruptly in her torment, hard heels clacking on her hard new floor like hooves in a stone court. "I've already told you! I'm not interested in my family! I'm not interested in your lists and pictures! I don't even care that we are related, *if* we are related! Why should I bother my head about an uncle who fled this godforsaken family when I was a little girl? Not that I blame you, Lord knows! I don't blame you! I'd have done the same!" She gasped for breath, pointing at his notes. "If my grandfather was a monster, I can't help it! It's got nothing to do with me, that's all I know!"

"Katherine, go ahead and take care of your customer—"

"No!" Beside herself, his niece hurried him toward the door. When he turned to say good-bye, she snatched off her glasses and wiped frantically. Without her horn-rims, she looked strangely naked, like a baby bird. She blew again upon her glasses, wiped them with another tissue fetched up from the hard bodice of that cantankerous red dress, then set them on her nose again to get him back in focus. "I guess you're Uncle Lucius, all right," she complained. "But I told you I couldn't help before you came. So if you'll just excuse me, please, I have a customer!"

Was she saying that he should not wait? She nodded gratefully. "I'm sorry," she said, polite now that he seemed to be departing. And once again, glimpsing the prettiness that had forsaken her, he was touched by this bristling niece of his, though he couldn't for the life of him think why.

The customer departed and they watched her go.

"I'm sorry, Katherine."

"And don't you go pestering Aunt Carrie either! She has not been well!" She banged the door, with its small bell of greeting and farewell.

Carrie

Carrie Langford lived nearby in a small house in a court off First Street, almost in the shadow of the bank. Dreading recriminations, he had not announced his visit, and turning the corner, he found Carrie outside fetching the newspaper. In pale blue breakfast gown, she straightened by the gate of her rose fence, unkempt gray head in a bright morning aura of trellised wisteria and bougainvillea. At the sight of him, her hands rose to her hair, her temples, and she tottered a little before steadying herself on the white post.

"I was just going out. You almost missed me." Cross that her poor lie was so transparent, Carrie fussed with the pink satin on her collar. "You could have called first, Lucius."

"I'm sorry, Carrie." He paused at the fence. "I suppose Eddie warned you I was here."

"He said you were hobnobbing with those Daniels people. The Backdoor Family," she added coldly. "I never thought you'd bother to come *here.*"

"I ran into them. They are good old friends."

"Good old friends. And how about your sister?" She raised her palm to ward off any blustering. "Well, come on in, since you are here. I suppose you want something."

It made things more painful that his sister moved like an old lady. Slowly she led him up onto the porch, swinging her left leg first for each upward step, and he held the screen door as she preceded him into a small sitting room stuffed up with dark antique furniture from the much larger house at the Edison Bridge. "From the good old days," she said, with a tired wave. In the louvered shade, in the whir of fans, the dark and silent room seemed to bar the southern light, as if somewhere within, Walter's body lay in state.

Carrie indicated a hard chair by the door, in sign to him that his stay should be a brief one, and he perched well forward on the edge to show that he understood this, and would depart promptly when the time came. Carrie herself sat on the sofa, but she sat erect, hands folded on her lap, awaiting him. He handed her Dyer's petition form in regard to Chatham Bend.

"This why you came?" She glanced over the paper. "Should I trust you, Lucius?" She signed it carelessly and tossed it back.

"It was my excuse to come. I wanted to see you—"

"Spare me." She raised her hand. "No, it was not Eddie who warned me you were here, it was his daughter. You mustn't mind our poor unhappy Katherine. She just can't bear any talk about the family. Never cared for her father, let alone her stepmother, and her husband went off with someone else, and her sister died in an auto accident up north." She gazed at him. "You missed the funeral, of course. Dorothy Watson, in case you don't recall her, was the most beautiful girl in all Lee County."

"Carrie, listen, I don't want to make excuses. I know what a poor brother I have been. But I always thought that you and Eddie disapproved—"

"Don't lump me in with Eddie, if you don't mind! Whatever you may think of us, Eddie and I are not consulting about Little Brother!"

"Good." He offered a small smile. "I mean, he might persuade you not to see me."

"He knows better than to try any such thing."

To ease matters, he talked about Ruth Ellen and Addison, reminding Carrie that her Faith was about Ruth Ellen's age. Those two little girls must have stared gravely at each other when Papa's new family came through town on the journeys between Fort White and Chatham River.

"Our dear stepmother was eight years younger than I!" Carrie shook her head. "I scarcely remember their names," she added curtly. "I'm afraid I have always thought less of Edna for running away before a decent burial could be arranged. And then, of course, she changed the children's names. Made everything much easier, I imagine."

But Carrie had no heart for her own unkindness. Abruptly she faced him, her face crumbling. "Lucius, you refused to understand what I had to deal with, how much my in-laws disapproved of Papa. Walter got upset every time he came, reminding me over and over that his father-in-law's reputation 'was not exactly an asset in the banking business.' You may remember Walter as quite wild in his youth, but later on he was conservative, extremely strict." She laughed despite herself, that delighted laugh that he'd almost forgotten. "Dear Walter could be so darned *dignified* that our girls joked about it—how their daddy had ordered stiff-collared pajamas!"

Her mood shifted again, like a wind gust over water. "I honored the family decision about Papa, but those dreadful writers pestered me year after year, they would not let that scandal die a merciful death. And sure enough, someone would show me another lurid article about 'Bloody Watson,' just slapped together in a hurry to make money, no regard for truth. Well, the rest of that day I would just sit quiet, all shrunk up into myself, looking straight ahead and not saying a word. On those days I told my girls not to come near me. And it was on those days that I thought to myself"—here she looked up—"how badly I needed my dear brothers, how much I longed for Lucius to come see me.

"It made me sad, of course, that I never saw Rob either, because I loved him, too. But the little brother I adored, who lived right here in southwest Florida and never bothered to inquire how we might be getting on even when he was right here in the city!"

Though Carrie wept in her pent-up emotions, she was less sorry for herself than overjoyed to see him. "I know, dear, I *know*! I do! You had all you could handle, maybe more! I never forgot that, and I never stopped loving you all these years—"

He was close to tears himself. "I don't forgive myself, Carrie. I—"

How sad, he thought later, that just as they drew near, a visitor should come tapping on the screen, a small man in a dark suit with sallow skin and dark pouches under his eyes. Seeing Carrie, he entered, then stopped short at the sight of Lucius. Carrie introduced them, adding, "Mr. Henderson is my kind neighbor, my gentleman caller. Stops by every day to ask if I am dead, and if I am not, offers to run an errand."

Lucius smiled and she smiled back, but she was not quite ready to be mollified. She did not send Mr. Henderson on his way, as Lucius hoped she would, and the man perched himself like a chaperone on a side chair, folding cold hands together. Carrie paid him no further attention, as if he had been leaned into the corner, but her tone with her brother had turned cool. "Faith and Betsy are your other pretty nieces," she reminded him, directing Lucius's attention to piano pictures of her daughters and grandchildren.

In a photo of Walter and Carrie taken in New York City about 1917, Carrie made a handsome subject, proud-bosomed in a white dress, and Banker Langford in a houndstooth tweed appeared portly and prosperous. His hairline, slicked back hard for the big city, had receded, but his lifelong amiability seemed undiminished. If he no longer resembled the lean-faced young cow hunter of Ruth Ellen's photos, neither did he look the least bit like a man whose liver was to fail him three years later.

"You were off in the World War when that was taken. Walter had to meet people from New York City, he had to go there now and then, and the president of our First National Bank couldn't very well behave like a cracker cowboy! In New York City, he hired a governess to teach his children manners, teach his wife how to conduct a formal dinner—all of the things our family had to know in order to do well in the banking business. And we studied hard right beside our children, read the same books of etiquette, learned how to dress."

"Oh I'm sure there was no need of *that*!" Mr. Henderson exclaimed, and Carrie laughed, delighted by his consternation. She cried, "Oh yes, Mr. Henderson, yes indeed there was! Folks couldn't believe what that cowboy and that Oklahoma tomboy had turned into! We could go anywhere and feel that we belonged! But Walter never became snobbish, he always remained a kind and generous man. We had our beautiful old colonial house on First Street, then the brick house near the bridge, remember? Did you ever see it?"

"Carrie? I came to Walter's funeral! I arrived late—"

"Forgive me. Of course you did." Carrie Langford nodded. "But that was very long ago, and I don't really know you anymore." Unable to hide the tremor in her voice, she would not look at him. Then she relented, and her eyes misted. "Lucius, I needed you back then. I got almost no help from Walter's partners, and could not accept charity from others, even my own brothers. Had they offered it. Which they did not. For different reasons. You, at least, were always generous when you had anything, I will say that." Again, she raised her hand to ward off explanations or regrets. "I made my own way and did my best to be gallant in misfortune, as poor Papa had to do so often! I was never a good businesswoman, but even fools do famously in real estate. I saw to it that my daughters married well, and we came out all right in the end. Betsy was always after me for money, and she always got it."

Her gentleman caller shot a warning glance, which she ignored. He cleared his throat as smoothly as an undertaker. "Carrie Langford is one of the most gracious hostesses in all of Florida," he intoned. "Before Mr. Langford's untimely demise, she entertained Mr. and Mrs. Thomas Alva Edison in her gracious home, and also their friend Mr. Henry Ford, and many other prominent Americans."

"My goodness, Mr. Henderson, you sound like a brochure!" Bemused, she contemplated this circumspect little man before turning her attention back to Lucius.

"Two years ago I wasn't well, and I thought, Darn it all, I want to see Lucius before I die, so I told Eddie to go hunt you up. He learned you were living scarcely thirty miles away, on some old houseboat! I wanted you to come for Christmas, a real visit, but Eddie said you were drinking too much, that all you wanted was to rot on your old boat, live like a hobo." She paused, searching his eyes. "Said you seemed to think your family was ashamed of you, and that it might be best if you stayed away."

Lucius had never said such things to Eddie, whom he had scarcely seen before today, but he'd said them to others, it was true—he had said as much this very day. When he did not defend himself, she said, "Well, those words broke your sister's heart. Were they supposed to?"

Mr. Henderson hitched forward in his chair in case Mrs. Langford needed his assistance. However, he flinched when Lucius looked at him. Lucius stood up.

"Perhaps I should come back later, Carrie."

"Now, now," she teased him. "Mr. Henderson is like one of the family, which cannot be said for *you*!" More kindly, she added, "Did I ever show you what my Faith wrote about her grandpa in her school paper?" Carrie located the paper in a desk, read it aloud:

" 'I remember my grandpa with his big chest and broad shoulders and bright blue eyes and ginger brows and beard a wiry dark red, with silver in it, and his skin deep sunburned, a deep reddish brown, and always a nice warm smell of fine tobacco. He was so jolly and kind around us children— we just loved him!' " Reading this, Carrie smiled at her brother fondly. " 'He would come to our house and perch me and Betsy on each knee and tell us stories about the big old owls that lived on Chatham Bend. And as he told about the owls, he would pop his eyes open, like this!' "

Imitating her child, Carrie popped her eyes at Lucius, then gave that clear peal of delight which brought back their warm childhood days in a great rush.

With both parents dead and Rob and Lucius vanished from her life, the loss of her husband and her two girls married, all Carrie had left in the way of family was her brother Eddie. So it was fortunate, she said with a small smile, that Eddie so adored her. Lucius said with the same smile that he'd always supposed that their esteem was mutual. Carrie cocked her head. "Let's just say," Carrie said gently, "that dear Eddie felt a little more kindred to his sister's spirit than she felt to his."

As her gentleman caller peered at them, they nodded at each other. They were starting to have fun.

"Eddie can be very courtly, as you know. He has a sort of old-fashioned charm, at least he used to. And in the old days, he would laugh a good deal more, although his eyes would never, never smile. And that was because the poor old thing has never relaxed in all his life, he is always out to gain something or prove something.

"You were always the opposite—quiet, rather melancholy. But when you smiled, your whole face lit up, and your eyes, too." The memory of his smile made her smile herself, and he was smiling with her. "See?" she said, pointing at his eyes. "As a young man, you were very handsome, Lucius. You still are. All the Watsons were handsome—beautiful or handsome. But like all the rest, you drank too much." She took a deep hard breath, and her face darkened. "The Watsons were all handsome, and they all drank too much, myself included," Carrie told Mr. Henderson rather too harshly, "and I married another handsome drunk while I was at it."

*

Beside her on a bare table lay a simple leather book with a single bookmark. "I've waited for thirty years to show you this." She opened the journal to the bookmarked page and handed it across to him.

January 16, 1921

Not long after Walter died, Eddie came over with a thin bearded stranger in worn and dusty clothes. We were still in our brick house. Eddie said shortly that this man was our long-lost half brother (Eddie said "half brother" right in front of him!). Robert is not a Watson anymore, he said, rolling his eyes in suspicion for my benefit. These days he is calling himself R. B. Collins.

I had not seen Rob in twenty years, and would not have recognized him, yet the moment his name was spoken, I knew him—that jutting black hair crudely hacked off, the dead pale skin, with feverish red points on his cheeks, the big dark hollow and wild eyes, like a religious martyr in old paintings. I go by my mother's maiden name, Rob told me in a flat voice, not dignifying Eddie's contempt with an explanation.

It's you, Rob? I inquired shyly, and he nodded and extended his hand formally, making no attempt at an embrace. I said, Oh Rob! For goodness' sake! I took his stiff thin body in my arms, and he gave me a quick wiry strong hug. Oh Rob! I cried. Do you remember the last time you saw me? That afternoon before my wedding, right out here on the riverside, when you sailed away with Papa to the Gulf? We waved and waved and then you vanished from my life! Until today!

With this foolish outburst came a flood of tears. Rob looked dismayed but could find no words so he gave the poor small speech he had prepared. Sister, he said in a cracked voice, I am sorry to learn that your husband is deceased. May I meet your daughters?

He's looking for Lucius, Eddie interrupted, sulky and impatient. It turned out Rob had chastised him in front of Neva and the girls for his indifference and unloving attitude toward our little brother. I can't help him, Eddie added.

I was forced to confess that I couldn't help him, either. I felt dreadfully ashamed. We have no idea where Lucius might be living. I wonder why, Rob said, cold and sardonic. When Eddie told him that Lucius might be living in the Islands, I said how much it worried me to have my brother at the mercy of those people. You are right to be worried, Rob said. I am worried, too. That's why I came. Eddie said sourly, Sure took you long enough! and Rob snapped back that he could not have come here any sooner. He seemed just as angry and restless as the Rob of old who defied Papa every chance he got!

I gave him Lucy Summerlin's address, saying she'd been close to Lucius and might know his whereabouts. Rob said he would not stay for supper but must use this time to locate Mrs. Summerlin. That same evening, he would travel south to Marco, where a boat might be found to take him on to Lost Man's River.

To escape from Eddie, who remained sullen, we went outside. I took Rob's arm and walked with him a little way downriver. I said, Here you turn up for the first visit in many years and you won't stay for dinner!

I never learned if he found Lucius in the Islands. I never learned if he had a family, or where he lived, or what his life might be. I have never seen Rob since, or Lucius either.

Lucius set the journal down. Carrie retrieved it, holding it upright like a hymnal on her lap. "If only you'd come back from those dreadful islands and married poor dear Lucy!" She smiled, encouraging a confidence. Unable to think of one, he rose to go.

His sister accompanied him to the door, waving back Mr. Henderson, who was so accomplished in the social niceties that he could frown at Lucius without meeting his eye. "Please don't stay away forever, darling. Please come back," she whispered. "*Please,* Lucius dear." They took each other's hands. "I will," he said simply, and she knew he meant it, for she went up on tiptoes like a girl and kissed him on the cheek. At last they hugged each other. "I'm counting on you, Lucius!" Carrie whispered. "Don't forsake me." He waved from the rose gate.

Lucy Summerlin

The old Fort Myers cemetery lay within walking distance, in a faded neighborhood off the river road which ran east to La Belle and Lake Okeechobee. In banyan shade by the cemetery gate, under dark branches which extended out over the street, a small figure in Easter hat and white lace collar sat in her old auto looking straight ahead. He trod heavily so as not to startle her as he came along the sidewalk from behind, and Lucy Summerlin did not look around or even stiffen—he admired that. Even in a run-down neighborhood, her stillness said, a Southern lady waiting outside a cemetery was inviolate, and no self-respecting thug or hooligan would dare to interfere with her in the smallest way.

"Goodness gracious, Lucius Watson, is that really you?" Her voice on the telephone had faltered a moment, then returned briskly. "Have you paid your respects out at the cemetery? Well, meet me there! I'll be the rickety old contraption by the gate. Me, not the automobile—oh, don't be silly! It's high time I got out there anyway, saw to the flowers!"

At his approach, she emerged from her car, wincing a little at the loud creak of the hinge, or her own stiff joints, or both. "This pesky flivver," she declared, "is as out of date as I am!" When she slammed the door, it screeched again. "My auto and I," she said, smoothing her dress. "We're in this darn thing to the finish." Still unable to look at him, she went around to the far side and reached in through the window for her graveside flowers. Half-hid behind the shield of blossoms, she raised her eyes, then burst into a joyful smile, laying the flowers on the hood and holding out both hands. "Oh Lucius!" she whispered. "Oh my darling!"

Still at arm's length, he held her small white hands in his brown rough ones. He cleared his throat, inept and shy. "Miss L," he murmured.

"Miss L!" she cried, with a fleeting shiver of her brow. "Indeed! The very one! None other!" For all her frailty and evanescence, she was still vital, she had never lost that petal skin and delicate neck and waist. She wore a long, simple, and expensive dress of a faint shade of lavender—as faint, he decided later (trying his hand at an elegaic poem) as "the bougainvillea petal which masquerades as its own blossom—as light and evanescent as a leaf of peach hibiscus, spinning in the sunlight corner of a spider's web." In the tumult of that evening's events, this ode to Lucy, like most of Lucius's poems, was quickly put away and as quickly lost.

"For pity's sake, don't stare! It won't improve matters!" She turned away, preceding her long-ago lover through the gate. Over her shoulder, in a sprightly voice, she told him that she'd seen a notice of the forthcoming meeting of the Southwest Florida Historical Society tomorrow evening in Naples, which would be addressed—and she turned to curtsy—by " 'the noted historian and author L. Watson Collins!' " She pirouetted in a quick neat circle, dancing out into the sun on the far side of the banyan into the suspended time of the old graveyard.

He waited on the white shell path while her lavender figure turned among the stones to offer flowers at a grave under an oak—the last resting place of the late Mr. Summerlin, he supposed. She pointed him toward the Watson plot, where he went without her. "On your right, remember?" Lucy called. "Just by the path."

The stones were grouped close around a WATSON marker, and Papa lay where he belonged beside Jane Dyal Watson. The sight of his mother's small white marble headstone brought a peculiar prickling to his temples. Only once had he visited her grave since her death a half century before, in a cold north wind on the December day of Papa's burial.

E. J. WATSON
NOVEMBER 7 1855–OCTOBER 24 1910

In late October of 1910, Lucius had accompanied Sheriff Tippins and the coroner to Rabbit Key, on the outer coast south and west of Chokoloskee, and made himself look down into that hole at the crusted carcass. Returning north on the gray toiling Gulf, hearing the lumpish thing that had been Papa rolling and bumping dully in its box, assailed by that stink that would lurk forever in his sinuses, seeping forth whenever that dreadful image overtook him, he had puked and coughed into the waves that turned along the hull. At home, he discovered that none of his family wished to hear about the autopsy, and perhaps their reluctance had been sensible, but at the time—he was twenty-one—he thought it typical of the family's unworthy effort to elude scandal. Shouting back that this policy of silence served the interests of the First National Bank far better than the family honor, he had stalked out of the house, walking eastward on the river road to the Alva Bridge and west again as far as Whiskey Creek, dry-eyed and dry-hearted, heart bitter as stone. Early next morning, he and the coroner, gagging into bandannas tied bandit-style over their faces, had dragged his father's black Sunday suit onto the foul cadaver and nailed it back into its coffin for reburial. Carrie had come, and she did her best to help, though they scarcely spoke.

With no river breeze to stir the dusty leaves, the burning banyan seemed to writhe and shimmer. The thick fig leaves looked black, the graveyard white and black, no color anywhere. The air swarmed with black specks—midges or soot. In the pitiless sun on the white monoliths, the shine on the live oak leaves, the hot scent of lime and drone of bees, his brain was smitten by bare light, causing swift vertigo. He sank down abruptly on a grave.

Lucy drew near, calling a question to cover her concern. "Did you find it?"

"Find what?" Struggling to clear his head, he spoke more brusquely than he had intended.

She reached for his hand, offered an airy arm. Grateful that she asked no questions, he let her lead him toward the shade of the great banyan. "Kinfolks," she said, patting her hand on the glazed stone of a sepulchre, encouraging him to take a seat beside her. "Won't bother 'em a bit."

With her fingertips, Lucy traced the incised name, then turned and took his hand in both of hers and gazed full at him. "I was terribly in love with you, did you know that, darling? Even after you went off to war and never told me . . . never sent word. Oh Lucius! After the way we were—!" Her cheeks went scarlet but she held his eye. "I was never angry, please believe that, dearest. I knew who Lucius Watson was, even back then, I knew the man I had dearly hoped to spend my life with. And even knowing who you were, I wish you'd married your lovelorn Miss L! Have you ever heard of anything so pathetic?" In his silence, she added quietly, "People so often say they love someone. But so rarely do they really mean they love them as they *are*, including the behavior that is hurtful."

Lightly he touched her cheek, her temple. What was there to tell her? He longed to take Lucy in his arms and pretend that all that joy in life had not been wasted. He was heartbroken by their life loss, yet scared and eager, too, and also disgusted with himself, indeed infuriated— all these emotions! How could he have been such a weakhearted fool?

Lucy was studying her small livered hands as if to say, Can these really be mine? "You think I'm being foolish, don't you, Lucius? You think it's much too late for us and that we are too . . . old?" She lifted her gaze then, and her eyes pled with his. "It's just that I'm so happy to see you, dearest. . . . It's just . . . Well, I'm just babbling, I know!" But she was undone by his expression. Patting his wrist, she said, "Now never mind." She slipped a leather diary into his hands. "Perhaps you'll understand things better written down. Looking into each other's eyes only confuses things." She touched the journal in a kind of parting as she rose. "It's a love letter, I suppose. I thought about ripping these soppy pages right out of my life, but there's so much of my heart in it, and the writing it all out consoled me so, that I can't bring myself to burn it. The only way to set myself free is to offer it to the person it belongs to."

To spare them, Lucy added brightly, "I have your *History* in the car! Will you inscribe it for me?" He nodded vaguely, and she squeezed his hand and moved away among the blinding stones.

THE LIFE OF MR. LUCIUS HAMPTON WATSON
by Miss L. Dyer

Lucius Hampton Watson was born in Oklahoma in 1889 ("in the year that Belle Starr died," as my dearest of dear men declared when he'd been drinking). As a boy of seven he went to live in Columbia County and from there to southwest Florida at Chatham River. But his mother thought Mr. Watson's place was dangerous for the children, and as she was very ill and weak, she came to live at Dr. Langford's in Fort Myers and put her children into school. Her stepson Rob remained with Lucius's father in the Islands.

Lucius was twelve when his mother died in 1901. For a time, he and his brother Eddie lived with their sister Carrie Langford. In this same period, Mr. Frederick Dyer contracted as a carpenter and foreman there at "Chatham," looking after the plantation while Mr. Watson was establishing a second farm in Columbia County.

Lucius Watson spent his summers at the Bend. Even in his gangly teens, he was very strong and quiet, very handsome, with deep shadowy rather wistful eyes and the same curved lashes that I noticed later in his sister. He was always graceful, though there was nothing soft about him nor unmanly, and he was modest and soft-spoken, rather shy. Though he fished and hunted to help feed the plantation, he was merciful and quick with trapped or wounded creatures and took great pains in removing fish from hooks. He was easy and affectionate with puppies, chicks, and piglets, and tender with all of our young animals, including a certain peculiar little girl who adored the ground he walked on, imagining him to be some sort of angel. After he asked her to kindly stop pestering him, her tearstained face was poking around corners everywhere he went. The child, scarcely five, was much too young to behave like such a fool, but Lucius paid this horrid little Lucy no more mind than a grease spot on the knee of his patched britches. He never raised his voice nor became rough with her.

The one creature he treated harshly was himself. All his life, he set impossible standards for his own behavior. He prided himself—if he prided himself on anything—on making do with little, or doing entirely without, sometimes quite senselessly! For a whole year after Mama sewed new mosquito bars for everyone on the Bend, Lucius slept without netting simply because the Indians had none! He was in "life training," he would say, as if even as a boy he knew that he would need endurance.

When Eddie went north about 1904 to work on their father's farm in Columbia County, Lucius stayed on in the Islands. Boarding with the Storter family, he attended school in Everglade, but the rest of the time, he lived and worked at Chatham. After his mother died, he lost all interest in Fort Myers, though he would go occasionally to see his sister. Lucius thought of one thing only, which was pleasing his father, he revered this strange and powerful man who would do so much harm to his son's life.

Lucius closed the journal. So much harm? What nonsense! His father had loved him very much, in his own way.

Lucius had returned to Chatham Bend in 1902, not long after a new foreman had been found to replace the Tuckers. Fred Dyer, though small, was a handsome, wiry devil, with too much energy for anybody's good. When on the Bend, he worked mostly as a carpenter, building the cistern and the boat shed, and also his small family cabin just downriver, which was later taken over by Green Waller.

As foreman, Fred Dyer was away often on the schooner, trading cane syrup, gator hides, and plumes for hardware and dry goods and materials. According to Papa, who was sometimes with him, he prowled the cathouses everywhere he went, drinking more than he knew how to handle, picking fights. As long as the work got done, Papa never harassed him, though always free with harsh comment about others. Not until years later, comparing notes with Lucy, had Lucius realized that his father might have encouraged Dyer's wanderings just to get the man out of the way.

Mrs. Sybil Dyer was a seamstress and made most of the clothes—a lovely creature, "pretty as a primrose," Papa called her. This was before Papa met Edna Bethea. He had been lonely as a widower, and confessed to his son that he was "very taken with Miss Sybil," though he never presumed nor did he claim that she was drawn to him. For such a strong, hard-minded man, he would go to pieces around Sybil Dyer, chuckling and blushing, turning to mush before their very eyes. In quest of Mrs. Dyer's good opinion, he took to reading the Bible aloud on Sunday mornings, and leading them in spirited renditions of "Jesus Loves Me" and "The Little Brown Church in the Dell."

When Papa was drinking, he would talk to Mrs. Dyer about his childhood and about the loss of family land at Clouds Creek, South Carolina. He had also assured her—for she told this to her daughter, who confided it in later years to Lucius—that much of his bad reputation in the region had been spawned by envy. His innocent seamstress inevitably concluded that she alone was privy to the secret heart of Mr. Watson, so generous and kind despite his ill repute. And perhaps she imagined, as so many had before her, that "the love of a good woman" was all that was required to cause this man to mend his sinful ways.

Out of Sybil Dyer's presence, Papa was often restless and short-tempered. He could be jolly in an ironic sort of way, and he dearly loved to amuse his son with sardonic teasing, but when he was drinking, his teasing turned cynical and brutal. Upbraiding the help, both white and black, he advanced the opinion that their small brains, laziness and insatiable stomachs would send him straight into the poorhouse.

In 1905—the year Gene Roberts brought the news about the murder of Guy Bradley in Flamingo—a little boy was born to Sybil Dyer. This boy was christened Watson Dyer, known as Watt or Wattie. Lucius supposed that the foreman wished to flatter his employer, mostly because, for all his lip and strut, he was afraid. Out in the world, Dyer had heard tales of those young Tuckers who had preceded his own family on Chatham Bend, and that summer, his nerve was broken by these wildfire false rumors that Ed Watson was Guy Bradley's killer, too.

Not long after the autumn harvest, the Dyers fled, in forfeit of a whole year's pay. They left Chatham River on the mail boat, returning to Whiskey Creek, outside Fort Myers. Papa, who was absent in Key West, never forgave them, and he never paid them. Feeling bad about that withheld pay, Lucius introduced Mrs. Dyer to Carrie Langford, which led to a modest livelihood as dressmaker to Fort Myers ladies, not only the Langfords but the Summerlins and Hendrys and in the winter season Mrs. Edison, upon whose bust Sybil Dyer would make clothes to be sent north to New Jersey in the summer.

Years later, Lucy would confess that she had cried for a whole week after her family left Chatham, so lovesick had she been for her lost Lucius! She also revealed that her mother had wept when the news came of Mr. Watson's violent death. Some years later, after Fred Dyer left his family, Lucy asked her mother if Mr. Watson's feelings for her had been reciprocated, and instead of teasing back, Sybil Dyer wept anew, declaring that Mr. Edgar Watson had the most mysterious blue eyes she ever saw. Yes, he had told her that he loved her, and yes, she had loved him, though even in the early days she had heard that he would declare undying love to a lot of women. She excused him, saying that in his deepest heart was a great big aching hole which the poor man could never fill.

*

Pretty Lucy was fourteen when Lucius saw her next, at Dancy's food stand on the pier at Fort Myers. He treated her to the ice cream she was buying, and they perched on the pier end, swinging their shoes over the current. Lucy told him how sorry she had been to hear about his father, who had been so kind to her, and a moment later, blushing boldly, lifting her chin and gazing straight into his eyes, she said, "I hope you know that for the rest of my life, I shall always be devoted to your family." The next day, out for a stroll, she spontaneously took his hand and, as a young girl will, swung his arm violently out of her nervousness and high spirits as they wandered west along the river, talking of the good old days at Chatham Bend.

Though aware of the coltish tumult in her—and embarrassed by the twitch in his own trousers—Lucius had been thunderstruck when this innocent river walk caused a near-scandal. "She's only a schoolgirl! Scarcely fourteen!" he protested indignantly to Carrie after Eddie had denounced his behavior, telling him it was high time he grew up. "I married Walter at thirteen," Carrie retorted, causing her husband to withdraw into the pantry.

Eventually he and Lucy spoke of the rumors about the little brother born

at Chatham Bend. By the age of four or five, Wattie Dyer was reminding people of Ed Watson, and not long after Papa's death, Fred Dyer had confronted
his wife, mostly on the evidence of her own grief. Sybil Dyer denied that Mr.
Watson was the father and became angry that her husband dared abuse her
after all of his lowlife infidelities, which were well known. But his suspicions
rose from day to day, and his voice, too, and in the end, driven to distraction
by his hounding, Sybil Dyer acknowledged that Edgar Watson—although
never her lover—might have been Watt's father, since on several occasions
in the period in question, he had broken in and taken her by force.

Fred Dyer raged, "Goddamn you, woman, why didn't you tell me!" And
she cried out, "For the same reason you didn't want to look! Because then
you would have had to act, and he would have killed you!"

For a few years the Dyer parents chewed on their hard situation. Meanwhile the boy resembled his namesake more with every day, until at last Dyer
got sick of looking at him and drove him out. Sybil Dyer, whose dressmaking
paid their rent, ordered her husband to depart instead, and he went away
enraged, fatally bitter. For years thereafter, in his cups, he would swallow
down his last pride with his whiskey and rant about his wife's affair with
Watson—*No, no, boys, weren't no damn rape about it!*—and relate how he
would have killed that sonofabitch if the House boys hadn't beat him to it. *If
it was rape the way she claimed, how come she never used the gun he give her to
run him off when he was drinkin? How come that bitch give her bastard boy that
name of Watson?* By now poor Fred had long forgotten that the name Watson
Dyer was his own idea.

Lucius had never quite made up his mind about it. That his father had
taught Mrs. Dyer to use the revolver he had given her seemed a strong proof
of sincerity, for E. J. Watson had never deceived himself, he knew how liquor
crazed him, Lucius believed his father truly loved her, but love alone might
not have deterred rape. Papa would deride Fred Dyer's "intolerance of alcohol," but Papa himself was the most dangerous drinker his son had ever
known.

Yes, Papa was courtly with the ladies, exceptionally considerate and tender, but when he drank, he was a buccaneer and an unholy terror. Jack Watson took all he wanted when he wanted it, and he took it *the way* he wanted,
too, his Caxambas ladies whispered, with shy sly smiles which looked
strangely askew. "When *I* fuck 'em, they *stay* fucked!" Papa had shouted at
the virgin Lucius, the first time he took him to the noted palm-thatch whorehouse on Black Betsy Key. Though he made that claim in drunken brag-
gadocio, he meant it.

*

I suppose it's hard for people nowadays to imagine how awful it was for the Watson children—not only the violent murder of their father but the dreadful scandal. Fort Myers was still provincial then, a beautiful small town with white colonial houses and white picket fences to keep strayed range cattle out of the gardens. The whole downtown section was on First Street by the river, a single block along a white oyster shell road of commercial buildings, with a livery stable and a faucet for watering horses. The women convened for small talk at Miss Flossie's clothing store while the men talked under the live oaks and we children pounded up and down the new wood sidewalks.

Two days after Mr. Watson's death, I was having an ice cream soda in Doc Winkler's drugstore when Carrie Langford came in with her Faith and Betsy. Doc Winkler was the only doctor in Lee County, and his prescription shop sold ice cream sodas. Miss Carrie looked just beautiful, as usual, but that day the poor thing had gone dark around the eyes, and her wonderful thick hair had lost its shine. And little Faith whispered, kind of scared, "Mama's been crying all day long, we don't know why she's crying so!" And I came busting out with it—"She's crying cause some bad men shot your grandpa!"

Oh, when my mother heard what I had done, she almost killed me! I was only ten but that was no excuse, I don't know what came over me! Hearing those terrible words, poor Faith became hysterical, that's how upset she was, at least until she realized she might miss her ice cream soda! As for Betsy, who was only five, she started hollering, "Grandpa, Grandpa!" because she needed some attention, too.

Well, just that moment—can you believe it?—the first Indian we children ever saw came into the drugstore in a high silk hat with an egret plume and a long Seminole men's skirt. It was like he'd walked straight in out of the Glades! Faith stopped crying right away. She said, "Mama! Is he going to kill us?" Because in those days, people still talked about the Indian Wars, and most of the few Indians left were still hiding from the white settlers out in the Cypress. The Mikasuki Seminoles forbade their women to speak to a white man or even look at him. If an Indian woman had a child by a white man or a negro, both mother and child were put to death! Later I learned that this Mikasuki man at Doc Winkler's soda fountain had been threatened with death by his own people for coming in too close to the white people and learning to speak English, and for eating ice cream sodas, too, for all I know!

Anyway, Mrs. Langford comforted poor Faith about this Indian in the high silk hat, saying, "No, child, that is Mr. Conapatchie, he's not here to kill little girls but only to enjoy an ice cream soda." And Billie Conapatchie hiked up that long skirt to seat himself more comfortably, I guess, and he didn't have on a single stitch beneath! Sat down and dropped the skirt over the stool and picked his ear while waiting to be served!

A few years later, Mama sent me to apologize to Mrs. Langford for picking a beautiful rose which grew out through her fence onto public property, and Miss Carrie invited me inside for a cookie. She was gracious and well-mannered, beautiful, everyone loved her. Soft brown hair and rose complexion—oh, a lovely person, and a good, good woman. We became fast friends, and that friendship has lasted all our lives.

Since her menfolk would never talk about Mr. Watson, Miss Carrie had no clear opinion about his guilt or innocence, she only knew that she missed her "Papa" dreadfully, and was very confused and upset about what her own feelings and position ought to be. After his death, it just seemed best to hush up and go along with the men's silence. But Lucius felt no such obligation, and poor Miss Carrie became mortally upset when her younger brother became estranged from the family. She admired his loyalty towards his father, but she also felt that his refusal to be silent was a lot easier for a footloose brother who could leave Fort Myers—and go to college, go to war, and finally disappear in the Ten Thousand Islands— than for her and Eddie, married with small children, who had to stay home and suffer the stares and whispers.

Poor Lucius Watson could never settle down for long—a "lost soul," as his sister often called him. Eventually, he borrowed from Mr. Langford's bank to go to college. There he studied Southern history and wrote his thesis on the history of the Everglades and southwest Florida. For fear people might laugh at him, he told no one about it except nosy Lucy, declaring that she was the only one who would ever take him seriously as a historian!

Having been born the year Lucius's mother died, Miss Dyer was now sweet sixteen—which was when most girls married, back in those days! Lucius was in his late twenties then, still modest and handsome, with that natural ease in his own body. One would look up to find him watching from nearby, head slightly averted in that wary and quizzical way that was so dear to me. That shy bent smile (which came straight from his mother, according to Miss Carrie) was his only greeting. He would leave in the same way, slipping away without a word, leaving no trace. On the rare occasions he lingered long enough to hold a conversation, he would lightly flex fingers and knees, keeping them limber, as if at any moment he might be called upon to spring to a high perch or limb or fly away.

During World War I, only months before receiving his degree from the university, Lucius returned home in profound melancholia. As usual, he kept silent about his darkness, and soon he was drinking so relentlessly that his family more or less gave up on him. The one person he saw regularly was Lucy Dyer, who was always ready to walk with him and listen, too, on those rare occasions when he felt like talking.

This young hussy would shamelessly recount her fond memories of his father in order to win the favor of the grieving son. Thus she became his confidante and friend. She loved him dearly—so dearly that within that year, they committed "mortal sin" together. How immortal—how amazing and mysterious!—it seemed! The fond and foolish thing was overjoyed, knowing they would soon marry and have children (and live happily ever after!). She did not notice that her somber swain had lain beside her as if dead, utterly incapable of speech. And when finally he croaked a few poor words, it was not of love but only of the dishonor he had brought upon them both.

Alas, their love had only deepened the despair of Lucius Watson. Not until she pled for an explanation did her true love confess that he passed most of his days in darkness in which even the red rose and blue sky withdrew their colors and the air turned ashy, filled with fire smudge and hellish vapors. At those times he could scarcely get his breath, let alone remember joy and beauty, or maintain a thought, or rest in sleep. Though he never mentioned suicide, and assured her he was fine, he seemed to be drifting ever faster toward some fatal act. At these times he drove away his shy new lover, afraid she might be drawn down with him into that "undiscovered country," as he called it.

But we are *together,* she would cry. I am your *lover!*

One day in 1917, not telling anyone, not even lovelorn Lucy (who was mortally wounded, sobbing inconsolably, on the point of hurling herself into the river etc. etc.), Lucius joined the Navy and went off to the Great War and was gone for well over a year. When he finally came home, he seemed almost sheepish that he had survived, and his drinking was worse than ever. Asked what the matter was, he muttered cynically, A man can't even go and die for his own country anymore! In another person, this might have been self-drama, but in Lucius, that dark laconic irony—so like his father's, though it never became cruel—masked a deeply pessimistic spirit.

By now Lucius was twenty-nine years old and his life was wandering away from him. He had some education, yes (and his history of southwest Florida, still half written), but in his opinion, he had no real profession and no prospects. Even worse—as his family would ceaselessly point out—he had no ambition. "Stop this drinking, go find yourself a job, get married, go to church, get on with life!" That's *their* life they are talking about, he told young Lucy, but it isn't mine.

Lucius had always been skillful with his hands, and very competent as a commercial fisherman. In 1919, fishing was poor on this part of the coast—at least that was his excuse—and late in the year, without warning his Lucy, he left Fort Myers and returned to the Ten Thousand Islands—the last place on earth one would imagine that a son of the late Mr. Watson would care to go. His sudden departure alarmed his family and broke his Lucy's heart. When he returned the following year for Walter Langford's funeral, he discovered that his faithful Miss L had succumbed during his absence to the adoring blandishments of Mr. Summerlin, an older man with a good generous heart as well as a secure place in our society. She had done this—oh Lucius!—because once again our hero had abandoned her without a word and never written even once to say he loved her, until finally his own sister urged the girl to forget this distracted and recalcitrant young man who could only be counted upon to hurt his dear ones.

Poor dear Carrie, who worried so about her baby brother, invited young Mrs. Summerlin to tea on the terrace of the Royal Palm Yacht Club. There his womenfolk agreed that their sweet Lucius was still haunted by his father, and also by the lost home in the Islands, the only place he could remember being happy.

Poor Lucius looked so scruffy at Mr. Langford's funeral—the long wrists in the old dark Sunday suit, always too small for him, the fisherman's weather lines and lumpy hands. What a shame it was, his sister said, that such a sensitive and educated person had lost himself among rough, uneducated people who had killed his father and might do as much for him! He had banished himself, condemned himself, to exile in that lonely wilderness, and for what? for what?

One day a young woman who identified herself as Lucius's half sister came all the way north from Caxambas to seek Carrie's help in persuading "their" brother to leave the Islands for good. This Miss Pearl Watson (Pearl Jenkins, Carrie calls her) also talked with Lucy Summerlin, who joined her plea to theirs. For such a gentle and obliging person, Lucius Watson can be astonishingly stubborn, and on the question of leaving the Islands, he would only say that the Islands were his home! It soon became plain to Lucy Summerlin that he had changed entirely—not only his closed, remote expression but that coarsening of the face and hands as well as clothes and speech, and an ingrained odor of whiskey and tobacco.

Like Carrie Langford, Lucy was distressed that a man of such intelligence and promise had thrown himself away among those people, but he only said, " 'Those people' take me as I am." "So do we!" she cried. "We!" he exclaimed, waving her away. His thought was never completed, but plainly he meant that in their hearts, his brother and sister and their families—all the "good families" of Fort Myers—had dismissed Lucius Watson as a hopeless failure.

In consequence, Lucy's marriage to Mr. Summerlin was seen by Lucius as clear proof that his dearest friend had dismissed him this same way, but of course it was only Lucius who discounted Lucius. What he saw reflected in the eyes of other people was only his poor opinion of himself.

Everything she'd written in her "Life of Lucius Watson"—the girlish exclamations, the old stories, the longing and sweet lies—was a cry of pain over a bitter loss of hope for which he himself had been responsible.

Lucius sat awhile, sorting himself out.

A faded envelope had fluttered from the journal, to lie as if awaiting him in the white dust. He picked it up. The envelope had Rob's name on it, and a letter from Rob's brother Lucius was still inside.

Dear Rob,

I have entrusted this letter to Mrs. Lucy Summerlin, to hold for you in case you come back through Fort Myers. I am sorry I missed seeing you when you came to Lost Man's. I certainly hope this finds you well.

The enclosed list of the so-called Watson Posse is all I have to show for life at present. Eddie and Carrie would certainly disapprove of it, and none of us are in touch with our father's third family, who went away to north Florida and changed their names, so it looks like there's no one left but you who might be interested. You or your son if you have one might know what to do with it. I put this list together for some reason, but I never had Papa's code of Southern honor (or his guts either, if that's what's required to take a human life).

I think of you often, hoping you are safe somewhere, happy and well. Being cut off from our family, I miss you all the more. Is it true that you were searching for me? If so, that is a great relief, but it is probably just as well you didn't find me. I might have been off on a drunk someplace, and anyway, I had to lay low for a while because of rumors about this list, which has made my neighbors leery of a useless fellow who couldn't harm them even if he wanted to! (You'll think I exaggerate my drama, and no doubt I do!)

If you come again (please do), Lee Harden and family will know where to find me. (Ask for Colonel—that's what they call me these days around here.)

Hope you have more to show for life than I do.

Your loving brother, Lucius

P.S. Let's try to meet before our lives get away from us entirely.

P.P.S. I believe this list is accurate to the last name.

Lucy had rejoined him. "He never came back," she murmured. "He never got that letter." Rob had turned up just that one time, when his freighter was in dry dock in Port Tampa, looking very pale for a man who lived at sea. He had written to Lucius, receiving no response, and was concerned about Lucius's safety in the Islands. On his way south, he planned to stop off at Caxambas to talk with Pearl Watson, having learned that Pearl and Lucius stayed in touch.

"That made Carrie feel terrible, and me, too, I'm afraid. By then I was friends with Carrie, who had taken pity on me. Rob found out from Carrie that I might know where you were. He thought I might know something that the family didn't." Instead she had to confess to Rob that she had scarcely laid eyes on Lucius since his return from overseas, two years before. Very disturbed, Rob had exclaimed, "He was safer overseas than in the Islands, Miss, I will tell you that!"

"This was the first time you had met him?"

"Yes. I wrote you about our meeting, don't you recall? And after Mr. Langford's funeral, you gave me this letter."

"And the list."

"And the list," she whispered.

"Which you misplaced. In the excitement of getting married, I believe your letter said. And you never found it."

"I never lost it. Surely you knew that." Her eyes had been cast down at her lap but now they rose to face him. "Please, Lucius. This inquisition is unworthy of you. With your romantic idea of family honor, we—your family— were already terrified you might do something rash down in those islands! That list was proof!"

"I'd already given up on rash behavior. Doesn't this silly note to Rob make that quite clear?"

Lucy said she wouldn't know, since she'd never felt she had the right to read his note. She took a deep breath, contemplating her own hands. "But I saw the list, saw what it was, and I simply could not bear so much responsibility. I went to Carrie. Poor Carrie became frightened, too, and showed the list to Eddie, telling him he must bring you back at once. But Eddie only shouted, 'He won't listen to me!' He took the list to Sheriff Tippins, who would not return it, claiming he needed it for evidence—can you imagine? We had no idea that the Sheriff was still brooding over Mr. Watson's death! And finally Eddie told me that before the Sheriff retired and moved over to Miami, that list was stolen. Nobody could imagine who might have wanted it!"

Lucius nodded. "So you are saying that you never read this letter?"

"I told a lie. Feel better? I told a white lie to spare Lucius Watson his absurd embarrassment over revealing an honest sadness and affection." She took his hand. "You can still give it to him, Lucius. He's come back. He phoned this morning, asking if you'd been in touch with me. He will be at the bar of your hotel this afternoon, in case you wish to see him." And she walked away.

"Lucy? I'm sorry! Thank you!" he called after her, groaning when she did not turn. Despite all her innocence and flutter, Lucy had always known when not to turn. Once again, he had driven away the only person he had ever opened his heart to, the only one who knew who he was and loved him anyway.

*

But she returned, bringing a copy of his *History*. Watching him inscribe it— "For Dearest Miss L"—her eyes filled again. "The hole in my heart was so deep and dark!" She wept in bitterness, and when he reached to take her hand, she made a fist of it, withdrawing. "Everybody needs a place where they belong. Because of gossip"—here she glanced at him, without malevolence—"I lost what little place I had in this community. I have it back, thanks to that kind old man. And now I'm 'that nice Miss Lucy Summerlin'! The Widow Summerlin!"

She laid her head ever so lightly on his shoulder. Overcome, he did not respond, and in a moment she sat straight again, neatening her cuffs. "I have often wondered if Lucius my darling really knew the first thing about love," she murmured coolly.

He feared—indeed he had always feared—that what she'd said was true, that when it came to love, he was some sort of cripple. Hearing her speak those words aloud sent his mind spinning into that ever-waiting dread of lost love and life wasted, of a hollow old age and a long lonely death. Somewhere he had missed the point of life entirely.

Sensing the grief in him, she lowered her head to his shoulder again, hugging his arm. "Now never mind, dearest, all the girls adored you, one especially." But instead of taking her into his arms, he stared at the old hands clenched on his knees. In our need, he thought, we may draw too close before we are really ready. I may do more harm.

He said dully, "And your brother?"

"And my brother." She sat up, stung by the abrupt change of subject, and the makeshift question, as Lucius described her brother's legal efforts to save the Watson Place. "Did he ever go back to Chatham Bend?"

"He remembers nothing about Chatham. To the best of my knowledge, he has never gone back. He has no interest in the past—too busy manipulatinging the future, I suppose. My brother is a very ambitious man." She cocked her head to consider Lucius's face, then gazed away across the white haze of the cemetery. "The truth is, I don't know my brother," she continued tersely. "We have nothing in common. We lost touch years ago. I think it's safe to say that I don't interest him. He lives over in Miami now, at least that's the address that he uses. He's always on his hunting circuit, like a wolf. He has never married. As for his romantic life, if he has any, I don't care to think about it."

"You dislike your brother. Our half brother."

"Well, thank goodness I'm not your half sister!" Her laugh came as a small shriek, like a caught mouse.

"I love you, Lucy Summerlin," he said, taking her hand. "I always have and always will."

Lucy nodded, her hand cool and inert. "I understand you've been traveling with a young woman."

"My research assistant." Irrepressible Rob must have mentioned Sally Brown. "Anyway, she's gone."

"Let her stay! What difference does it make!" She turned away. Out of tact, he let go of her hand, which she raised up and inspected like some sort of curio. When he tried to return her journal, she waved him away. "It's yours. It always was. You can burn it if you want." She was in tears. "It's *this* woman you should have traveled with, Lucius! All your life!"

Sudden and silent as an owl, age had her in its grasp. Before his eyes, age bled, wrinkled, and dried her. Lucy said, "*Everyone* loves Lucius. Is that enough for you? Don't you ever miss the happy man you might have been?" She closed her eyes. "Forgive me." She gathered up her things. "Life is full of joy and anguish, wouldn't you agree?" Affecting irony and nonchalance, she was straining to subdue hysteria, and her gallantry was of no use to either of them.

"Please go," she whispered, shutting her eyes tight, gathering herself in a hard knot against his going. He touched her shoulder, rose, and moved away.

At the great banyan, Lucius turned to wave. She had not stirred. Poised on the white gravestone as if just alighted, palpitating like a rare soft moth of faint dusty lavender, she appeared transparent. In the heat shimmer of late afternoon, Death shook her small shoulders, mocking grief and laughter.

Rob Watson

At the Gasparilla Inn, he went straight to the bar, a place of refracted light and glitter which overlooked the brown Calusa Hatchee. There he found the resurrected Rob with what was left of his hind end hitched to the farthest stool toward the river windows. He seemed to have had a dispute with the bartender, who was banging bottles and wiping the bar mirror. Other than these two, the place was empty.

To give his feral brother room, he sat down several stools away, and neither spoke until Lucius was served. After his upsetting day, Lucius eased his nerves with a double bourbon, gasping in relief as the charcoal essence warmed his sinuses and welled into his brain.

"The Watson brothers," Rob muttered finally, shaking his head at the folly of it all.

"Having fun?"

"Good clean fun," the old man said, "and a lot of it." Dead mean drunk, he lifted his empty glass to toast their images. Lucius said, "Well, we have to start somewhere. Who's that in the urn?" And his brother said, "His skull. Last time I looked, it was Edgar 'Bloody' Watson."

Turning his glass to the light to inspect the amber shimmer in his ice cubes, Rob related how, in 1921, before leaving Fort Myers on his search for Lucius, he had visited the cemetery late at night with the excellent plan of pissing on his father's grave. While performing this act, he wondered if there might not be a market for the head of such a famous desperado. He broke into a caretaker's shed and borrowed a spade and chipped his way down through the limestone clay to the rotted coffin, from which he extracted the brown, bullet-broken skull, wrapping it in burlap from the toolshed. He filled and tamped the hole, returned the spade. The digging had sobered him somewhat, but he was too tired to carry out a revised plan to dig up the grave again and restore the skull. Next day, lacking any plan at all, he installed it in a Greek-type urn acquired at a funeral parlor whose proprietor had hammered the skull into small pieces.

Lucius jolted down his drink. "Is all this true? Your *father*?"

"My own father. Yep. That was the fun part," Robert Watson said. "Did my heart good. Made a nice keepsake."

"Seems like a lot of trouble," Lucius said finally. "I don't know that I believe this story."

"You might as well believe it, son, because it's true." Talking out of the side of his mouth, facing the bar mirror, Rob had yet to look him in the eye.

At a loss—what could he say?—Lucius told him about the visit with their Collins cousins, describing what their father had looked like in the large oval photograph in the Collins house. Morose, Rob said, "I *know* what that maniac looked like." Asked after another silence why he'd changed his name, Rob said he'd adopted his mother's name because he no longer wished to be a Watson.

*

After fleeing to Key West in 1901, Rob had wandered the earth as a merchant seaman. Eventually, he had learned to drive an automobile, and in Prohibition, he had found a job running trucks for liquor dealers. Unfortunately he'd become involved in a warehouse robbery—"the driver," he said—and because a guard was killed, he had done hard time in prison. He had been in and out of prison ever since. Though Lucius had suspected this, he squinted suspiciously at Rob, to warn him not to make up any stories, and after that Rob refused his questions—unwilling, he said, to discuss his life with some idiot who was calling him a liar. "You'll see," he added, ominous. "I've been writing down my side of your Watson story."

When the old man threw his whiskey back and signaled rudely for another, the bartender refused him, telling him he'd already had too many. "I notified you," the barman reminded him, "even before you was joined by this other party." Told by Lucius that the other party would take responsibility, the barman shrugged. It was true that Rob had already been drunk when Lucius first came in, but now he was in that advanced phase in which he could keep drinking without seeming drunker, except for a subtle thickening of features and a sweaty glaze. Until that point when he fell down for good, he would not even stagger.

"The Professor." Rob nodded, very, very weary. Closing the subject of Rob Watson, he asked to hear his colleague's theory on the first man to shoot a bullet at their parent. "I mean, who was Bill House trying to cover for in that deposition?" Awaiting his drink, he drummed his fingers on the bar. "That day you came hunting me at Gator Hook? Well, after you left, Speck was raging around, and he started yelling how Henry Short was in that line of men. He said he fired."

"In Jim Crow days? In Chokoloskee? I don't think so!"

"No? I read that deposition, Professor. They all admitted shooting. So why would House try to cover up for someone, unless it was a black man?"

"I'm not sure House was covering for anybody." Lucius shook his head. "I've heard that rumor about Henry Short. It might be a case of 'pin it on the nigger,' Arb."

"Rob is the name. Robert Briggs Watson. Remember me?"

"Look, I knew Henry pretty well. All his life Henry paid attention to every step he made, like a man wading a slough full of alligators. Even if he was told to follow the House men to Smallwood's landing, but he would never let himself be seen toting a gun. And even if he had a gun, he would never shoot it at a white man."

Rob had already lost concentration. "The Watson brothers," he said again, sardonic.

At the desk a message had come that Major Dyer might join them for supper on his way through town. They located Rob's satchel and took it to the room. Lucius assured him that Dyer didn't know a thing.

"Know a thing about *what?*" Rob's snarl was paranoid. Then the fight went out of him. Astonished to see those sharp old eyes go soft and shiny, Lucius approached him gingerly and drew his brother's scrawny frame into his arms. How thin Robert Briggs Watson was! There was nothing left of him.

They went downstairs and waited in the lobby. When Dyer did not appear, they left word at the desk and went into the restaurant without him.

*

The Gasparilla's Swashbuckler Restaurant had a hearty buffet topped off by a huge blood-swollen roast beef. The meat's custodian, in chef's apron and high hat, was a big roly-poly black man with a swift red knife, a rich and rolling laugh, and a rollicking line that had the whole room smiling.

"Oh yeah! Yes sir! *Yes* indeedy! Tha's it! Tha's right! How *you* this evenin? Y'all had you a good visit? You doin all right? All *right*, my frien'! Bes' have some o' this good roast! Oh yeah! Yes sir! Tha's it! Tha's right! Red for the gentleman, pink for the lady? Bes' have jus' a li'l more, now, jes' a *li'l bit*—all right? *All right!*"

"He don't know when to quit," Rob said too loudly, reaching out for his new whiskey, almost tipping her tray before the waitress could set down the amber glass. "He's playing these old tourists like a school of catfish, snuffling through the mud after a bait!"

Spoiling for trouble, the old man was still sniping when Watson Dyer came up from behind and yanked out a chair and settled on it with a heavy grunt, without a greeting. He considered their liquor glasses a few moments before noting coldly that they had gone into the dining room without him. "You boys in a big rush or what?" His smile looked terrible. "I thought *I* was the busy feller around here!"

Under the scrutiny of those hard pale eyes, Lucius could no longer doubt that this man was the natural son of E. J. Watson. It was hard to think about him in that light, since they had nothing else in common, brotherly affection least of all. Until this year, his last experience of Wattie Dyer was on the dock at Chatham Bend in 1905. The mail boat captain had been young Dan

House, a youth of his own age, and Dan's mate was another boy, Gene Gandees, and both would be present, five years later, in the line of men who gunned his father down at Smallwood's landing.

At the time he departed Chatham Bend, that hot and squalling Dyer child had not yet opened his eyes, which were never to gaze upon his natural father. According to Lucy, Watt was already a schoolboy by the time Fred Dyer spread the tale of his own cuckolding. The boy had challenged the story from the start, punching schoolmates bloody, but his fury only spread the rumor up and down the coast, until finally Watt turned his back upon his family, hitching an auto ride across the state on the new highway. Finding work in Miami, scrabbling to achieve an education, he freed himself from his own history as fiercely as a wolf gnawing its own paw to escape a trap.

Eventually people forgot about Watt Dyer, and forgot the rumors, all but those old-timers who had known Ed Watson. Years later, when Dyer's law practice required visits to the Gulf coast, certain elders might squint as soon as they laid eyes on him. "Hell, don't I know that feller?" In the time it took to wipe their glasses, someone else had whispered, "Ain't that Watson's boy?"

*

Dyer was wearing a new windbreaker with the letters—U.S.—embroidered on the breast pocket in red letters encircled by small blue stars.

"A Fed," Rob Watson said. "I should have known it."

"United Sugar." Dyer yanked out a chair. "Those men are grateful to this great land of opportunity. They are proud of Old Glory, and they don't mind showing it."

"Not surprising," Lucius observed, "considering the federal subsidies they rake in." Years before, crossing Florida by way of the south shore of Okeechobee, he had beheld those endless canefields, draining their tons of nitrates and pesticides into the Everglades, and the huge sugar factories and thick high walls of oily smoke shrouding the flat horizons like dark fronts of oncoming evil weather. Recalling this, he was ever more uneasy about corporate sponsorship of his biography of E. J. Watson. Not that Papa would have minded—on the contrary! The ruined land south of the dykes, the poor poisoned small towns of the migrant workers—the price of progress!, Papa would have said.

Dyer was rummaging intently among his papers. Finally he looked up. "Lucius H. Watson shows up on the 1910 census as residing at Chatham Bend, the last resident Watson on the property—that could help. The least we should get is a life tenure on the place, like that old man who lives on

Possum Key. That precedent is strong enough to tie this up in litigation and appeals almost forever—or long enough for our purposes, at least."

"Our purposes?"

"Let's see now." The attorney peered into his briefcase, saying casually, "You planning another interview with Henry Short?"

"I might, if I knew where to find him. Why? What's Henry got to do with it?"

"Bill House's son would know his whereabouts." Dyer scribbled the phone number of Andy House on the bottom corner of a legal pad, tore off the yellow scrap, and handed it to Lucius. "Let me know if you come up with something." He resettled himself heavily in his seat, clearing the air for a shift of topic. "Naples," he said. For tomorrow night's meeting of the Historical Society, Lucius would be listed on the program as L. Watson Collins, Ph.D.

Lucius shook his head, annoyed. "That won't work here on this coast. I told you that. Too many people know me. Anyway, I learned my lesson in Fort White." He would notify the audience that the name on the program was a pen name.

"The speaker advertised—and paid—by the Society is Professor Collins. And the newspaper is covering Professor Collins's lecture as an update on the Watson story. Also, your historian's credentials will count heavily in our favor at next week's meeting with the Park Service." Dyer was straining to be heard over the rollick of the meat carver, his irritation rising with his voice. "So why insist—Jesus! What is that damn racket!" Nostrils flared, he yanked his chair around. "What *is* that! You think he's drunk?" He glared. "He's poking fun at the damn customers!"

"He's *poking fun!*" Rob, who had been buttering a roll, parried and poked his knife toward the neighboring table. "Poke, poke," he confided with a thrusting gesture, winking dirtily at the diners, who turned away. "Poke, poke," he repeated. But already, his drunken grin was fading, replaced by that dangerous cast of eye which Lucius remembered all too well from the ugly episode in the Columbia County Courthouse. Before Lucius could stop him, Rob lurched to his feet and took off in the direction of the buffet. "Poking fun at paying customers stuffing their gullets?" he was calling. "*No* sir! Not in *this* man's restaurant, he don't! You men going to let that nigra get away with that? And still call yourselves *men?*"

By the time Lucius got there, the quick old man was well ahead of him in line. Grinning back at Lucius, he sang out to the other diners, "Oh Lordy Lordy, I surely do appreciate this kind of polite-type happy nigra, just overflowing with our grand ol' Southren hospitality!"

An old lady turned to offer a sweet smile—Ain't it the truth!—and Rob

smiled back at her. "Just so long," he told her beamishly, "as his dang ol' nigger sweat don't go to falling in our food."

"Now *that's* not nice!" When the woman hushed him, glancing fearfully
at the carver, Rob leaned toward her, cupping his ear. "Eh?" he exclaimed.
"*Nigger,* you say?" The woman was humiliated, furious. "He's drunk!" she
told her husband, whose sun-scabbed vacation pate only hunkered lower
down between his shoulders.

Rob launched forth in a homely cracker twang for increased emphasis
and audibility, though not so loud that the black man, at the head of the
long line, could make it out over his own boisterous patter. "Yes sirree, we'll
set right down to a big plate of beef that'll half-kill us! And not only that but
a heapin helpin of fine interracial fellowshipin on the side! We'll realize
maybe for the first time in our whole lives how much we love these durn ol'
Neg-ros, and why in the heck can't our durn kids see the Negro Problem the
same way we do, and what a great country we have here in the good ol' U.S.
and A., where black folks can talk to white folks just so nice and friendly
you'd almost think they was real people after all!"

The candidates for the roast beef, who had manfully resisted Lucius's at-
tempts to advance himself wrongfully in the line, realized at last that he was
trying to reach Rob, and now made way for him only too gladly. He grasped
the old man's bony shoulder, shook him hard. "That's enough," he said.
Ahead of them, the entire line looked stiff with shock. Even the carver had
slowed his chanting and was looking around with the poised knife, sensing
something disagreeable in the air.

"Irregardless of race, color, or creed!" Rob was struggling in Lucius's grip,
exalted, and again the old lady turned to him, but before she could chastise
this terrible old man about the evils of race prejudice, he checked her with a
wink and a glad smile. "Don't y'all love pickaninnies, ma'am? So much *cuter*
than them pasty ol' white babies, what do *you* think?" The woman moaned,
utterly routed.

And then, quite suddenly, Rob self-deflated, turning in upon himself,
soul-poisoned, muttering.

Watson Dyer barged past Lucius, intent upon the carver. Though wary
now, the black man was still chanting. "All right, sir! How *you* doin this fine
evenin? Care to try our beautiful roas' beef? All right? All *right!*" And the
Major snapped, in a low hard voice accustomed to command, "Knock off
this minstrel show, okay? Just carve that roast."

The man stopped carving and stood absolutely still. In the silence, all over
the room, people stopped eating, the tables wheeling in phalanxes of pale
faces, the pink-and-white waitresses clustered in bouquets.

The carver maintained his broad smile. "*Well,* now! Ever'thing all right wit' you, my friend? Y'all had you a nice day?" His eyes had tightened and his words conveyed a small hard irony, a note of warning. "What you might need is a cut of this fine beef!"

"Just carve," the Major ordered calmly, with terrific anger, solid and efficient anger, smooth as polished stone.

The carver squinted at the point of his raised knife. "Yo, Nigger! You ain't heard de man? Cut dat minstrel shit right now! You jus' carve dat meat like you been told!" The carver honed his knife, *snick-snick, snick-snick,* appraising Dyer's age and weight, the patriotic windbreaker, the cerulean hard eyes. *Snick-snick, snick-snick.* "I been where you been, man," the carver muttered, in sure and sudden insight. "Oh, I been *there*, okay!"

"This what you risked your neck for, boy, over in Asia? To come home and play the fool for these old farts?"

"Oh my goodness!" The old fart behind the Major dropped a radish as her elderly husband harrumphed in scared protest. The line, milling and wheeling, clutched its plates. "For Christ's sake, Dyer!" Lucius said, feeling oldfartish. The whole room hated them for spoiling their heartwarming fellowship with this delightful Negro personality, and their good supper, too. "Just carve, boy," Dyer repeated softly. His smile was exhilarated and his tone pitying in the purity of his cruel and righteous anger.

The carver nodded. "Playin de fool, dass it." The carver's voice was intent now, in Dyer's key. "Dass what you doin, Black Boy. Playin de fool, oh yes!" Motioning to the Major to come closer, he leaned forward with a great big grin to whisper his stentorian secret into Dyer's ear. These two had a secret, from long, hard seasons of war. "Hard to put yo' finger on de fool, now ain't dat right?" But the real secret was the carving knife, which he slid across the board on the flat of its handle. His pebbly voice grated, "Back off, mothafuck. Get outta my face." And his grin twitched as the bright tip pinked the Major's belly through his shirt.

The astounded white man sprang back, jarring a table.

The meat carver stood straight again, sharpening his knife, *snick-snick, snick-snick.* He appeared to be quaking with mirth, as if this nice customer had just told him a great story. "Yassuh, tha's *right!*" he cried, flashing his blade, dumping too much bloody meat on Dyer's plate, then more, then more. "You had enough, my friend? Don't go spillin dat blood gravy, now!" He laughed oddly in warning. "See what I'm tellin you? Lookit what you done to dat nice shirt!"

Still poised on the knife were three or four more hacked and heavy slices, which the man still threatened to heap upon the plate. The room was still but for the timid scrape of a shifted chair. But now the carver seemed transfixed by what he saw in the face of Watson Dyer, who had lifted the plate high like a pagan offering. The Major considered the red knife and its heaped meat, then raised his pale gaze to the bloodshot eyes in the carver's shining face. Patient, he watched as the black man licked his lower lip. His fury weakened and the reality of his doomed rebellion overtook him and his gaze slid sideways. In that instant the meat heaped on the knife was transmuted from bloody threat into damning evidence. The carver waited passively for what was coming.

When the Major saw that the man was defeated, he took the knife out of his hand and dumped its load and scraped most of the slices off his plate onto the cutting board.

The black veteran of Asian combat found his voice and whispered at the white one. "Just doin my job, is all it is. Jus' makin my feller Americans feel good, you know? The way they want it."

Dyer handed back the knife and moved on past. Giving his plate to a waitress, he went to the hostess near the door. Soon a manager was summoned, and he hiked his bloodstained shirt to display his stomach. All looked at the carver as they spoke.

Observing this, the black man turned a furious gaze upon Rob Watson. He slapped some meat onto Rob's plate—"Had enough now? You sure bout dat?"—then pointed the dripping knife straight at his eyes.

Then he waved Rob past, confronting Lucius. "*Yes,* sir! Them gentlemens with you?"

Lucius nodded. "They are my brothers. My half brothers."

He detained Lucius for a moment, pressing the knife blade down hard on his plate, pinning the heavy china to the butcher board. "The three brothers!" He shook his head. "Your turn now. Got anything smart you want to say to a man of color?"

Lucius flushed. "I want to say I'm extremely sorry."

"*Sorry!*" Wildly the carver slashed at the roast on the bloody board. "You sonsabitches has lost me my damn *job!*"

*

The Major brought his mood back to the table. Lucius was too roiled to speak, and only Dyer ate with any appetite. He stabbed at his roast beef, forked it away, as if oblivious of the small knife slit in his epidermis.

Their waitress wore a gold link chain on rhinestone glasses, but her ears stuck out through long and lank dark hair like a wild horse mane. With alarm she watched the Major slashing at his meat, the knife blade and fork tines grating angrily on the porcelain. "How *you* folks doin?" she ventured finally. "Everythin all right?"

"What does it look like?" Dyer snapped, not looking up. The woman fled.

Rob was intent on the carver. Beckoned from his post by emissaries from Management, the big man howled in the agony of his plight and stabbed his knife into the carving board, upright and shivering, as the food line yawed and fell away from him in fright. He stripped off his bloody apron, balled it up, and hurled it across the steam tables of vegetables onto the soups and dressings on the salad bar, then banged out of the room through the pantry doors.

Rob muttered, "I'm going to tell 'em it was all my fault."

"Save your breath," Dyer advised him. As a decorated veteran, the man had received preferential hiring, the Major had learned from Management, which soon became aware, however, that this war hero was very angry and unstable. In fact, they had expressed gratitude to Major Dyer for reporting the "assault" and providing cause for getting rid of him which could not be challenged by the veterans' organizations or the unions. Dyer had been offered free restaurant privileges for a five-year period, which would not, however, guarantee this place protection from a hefty lawsuit.

The Major forked another mouthful, chewed it up, processing his food while glancing through his papers. Officious, in a hurry now, he briefed them in a military manner. He had filed for an injunction against the burning of the house, pending a court decision on the validity of the Watson Claim. Two days hence, the judge would hold a public hearing on that claim in Homestead, without which no injunction could be granted. Once the injunction was in place, he was confident that it could be extended, several times if necessary, permitting them time to apply for permanent historical status for the house.

After attending the Professor's talk at Naples tomorrow evening, Dyer would go to Homestead for the hearing. If all went well, he would return to Everglade for a meeting with "the Watson family" and the Park attorneys. Time was short. The Park might attempt to burn the house before that injunction could be granted, which was why he had stationed a caretaker on the place, to make sure that no such "errors" would occur. What he needed at once was full power of attorney, in case his authority should be challenged and he could not reach them.

The form Dyer pushed at him to sign made Lucius feel rushed and uneasy. "This gives you authority to make all legal decisions—take any of these steps—without consulting the family?"

"Well, that's customary in these matters. You trust your attorney or you don't. And things are moving fast," he added, "so authority to act swiftly might be critical." Moving smoothly past Lucius's query, Dyer complained that he had received no response from Addison Burdett or from the sisters. Over the telephone, Mrs. Parker had told him that Addison was away, and that their sister would never cooperate. He frowned at Lucius, whom he seemed to hold responsible for this truancy, then rapped the power-of-attorney form and proffered his pen.

"My signature has to be notarized, isn't that true?"

Dyer waved him on, impatient. "I'm a notary," he said.

Something was wrong or missing here, but Lucius, rather tired and drunk, was still too unraveled by the cruel and senseless episode with the carver to think it through. To hell with it. Abruptly, he scrawled his signature.

"Oh boy," Rob said.

"I'd like this power of attorney endorsed. And the petition documents on the claim should be signed by *all* the Watson heirs. No exceptions," Dyer added, and he turned to Rob. "Not even you." Extending his pen, he contemplated Rob's shocked expression with real pleasure. "Well, Robert?" he said. "How about it?"

Rob was sure that Lucius had betrayed him. "I'm not signing a fucking thing," he told Dyer hoarsely. He rose in a lurch of plates, overturning his water glass, but before he escaped, the Major grasped him by the shirt and yanked him forward over the table, his fork points inches from Rob's face. "Sit down," he ordered. And he took out yet another document and laid it beside Rob's plate and rapped it, sharply, with his middle knuckle.

Rob glanced at the new document, dropped it back on the table. He gazed at Lucius, a heavy shadow on his face. Then he got up and headed for the door, where he paused briefly to remonstrate about the carver—in vain, it seemed, for after a noisy arm-waving dispute Rob left the room.

Dyer turned to his sour cream and baked potato, which he ate in silence. "How much do you know about him?" he asked finally. "Or should I say, How much do you *want* to know?"

Lucius struggled to compose himself. "I guess if I'd wanted to know more, I would have asked him."

"But you suspected something, right?" Dyer ate again, then put his fork down to make a note while he finished his slow mouthful. "Why did you never tell me he was Robert Watson?"

"I didn't know that when we spoke last—not that I would have told you anyway without his permission."

"And you don't know why he changed his name?"

"Hated his father. Ran away. Took his mother's name."

"He's still running away." Dyer handed him the prison record, which Lucius glanced at and tossed back at him. "Not interested in how I found this out?"

"Now that I know your cop mentality, I can guess. You lifted his finger-prints. Lake City. The Golden Dinner, right? You swiped his spoon."

"*Cheap* Golden Dinner." Dyer nodded. "Fork."

"You check everybody's prints? On general principle?"

"When it's appropriate." Dyer retrieved the sheet and returned it to his briefcase. "So you are saying you never knew that Robert Watson did a lot of time? Bootlegging during Prohibition? Driver in a warehouse robbery in which a guard was killed? Prison escape? Fugitive from justice almost twenty years?"

Lucius shook his head, disgusted. "Come on, Dyer! He was only the driver! And he's an old man! You going to turn him in?"

Dyer processed another mouthful, talking through it. "As an attorney and friend of the court, and as a reserve officer in the United States Marines, I don't really have much choice about it." And he ate some more.

"You pledged allegiance to your flag and to the republic for which it stands, is that correct?"

"Don't get snotty with me just because you're drunk." He pointed an ac-cusing finger at Lucius's whiskey. "It may surprise you that a great many of your fellow citizens are proud to pledge allegiance to our flag. And worship at church and revere our Constitution. And feel no need for intoxicating spirits." He raised his arm and pointed his finger straight at Lucius's eyes, and his own eyes sparkled with a cold blue fire. "Anyway, I sure do hate to hear any American talk sarcastically about our flag. I really *hate* that."

Lucius was startled by Dyer's face, which was actually swollen and clot-ted with a fervid hatred. He took a deep breath. "What are you saying, Dyer? If Rob signs the land claim petition and endorses your power of attorney, you'll set aside your bounden duty to report him, that what you're getting at? Let him go his way?"

"We'll see." The Major nodded as he scraped his plate and masticated his last forkful. "Tell me," he said casually, "will he be at Naples?"

"I have no idea."

"You have no idea." Dyer leaned back in his chair and suppressed a belch. "If I were you, I would see to it that he accompanies you to Naples." He nod-ded, as if falling asleep. "And when you are sure about it, I'll expect a call." He wrote a number on his paper napkin. "No need to leave your name, just his location." The Major squinted at him. "All you have to do is call and then you're out of it."

"All I have to do is call and then I'm out of it." Lucius stood up. "God, what a prick you are." And he reached down and seized Dyer's pen and criss-crossed and blotted out his own signature on the power of attorney.

Major Dyer blew like a surfacing manatee as he arose. He wiped his mouth, drank down his water. For all his self-control, he was incensed, and his napkin was still clutched in his fist when he left the table. Hearing a frightened "Sir?" behind him, he hurled the balled napkin at the waitress.

Overtaking Lucius in the lobby, Dyer took hold of the back of his upper arm. "You're drunk. You better think this over," he growled, propelling Lucius forward ever so slightly, as if he meant to run him out the door. "For your brother's sake, I mean."

"How about you? Aren't you a Watson? Shouldn't you be signing your damned documents, too?"

Releasing him, Dyer said in a thick voice, "Let me tell you something. You don't want me for an enemy." His moon face looked swollen again, and the shivers appeared in the skin around the mouth. "I'll bring fresh documents to Naples," Dyer said, and kept on going.

*

Rob's old-style satchel was wide open on the bed, and a revolver cartridge glinted on the floor. Before Lucius could react, an explosion shook the bathroom door. "Oh Christ, Rob!" he yelled, socked in the heart. But he heard no body slump and fall, only a curse, then a second shot, a third, then a wild yell. Scared voices and the screech of tires rose from outside and below as Lucius forced the door. At the window, Rob blew smoke from the revolver muzzle, gunslinger-style, then gave another rebel yell—*ya-hee!*—and broke up in hoots of drunken laughter.

Lucius leaned from the window in time to see a big black car moving out into the street with both rear tires punctured, dully thumpeting. It traveled some distance before coming to a stop at a red light, where silhouetted figures approached cautiously from the street shadows, black as ants in the pool of light. The stick figures bent to look in at the windows. Nobody got out. The green light came and then the red and then the green again.

In the parking lot, people had gathered. One man was shouting, pointing up at Lucius, who kept his head and leaned farther out the window. "What's going on down there?" he yelled, before retreating.

Rob was drunkenly crowing in the bedroom, waving the gun around. "Ran that sonofabitch clean off the property! Had him skedaddling like a damn duck!" Lucius grabbed the gun and collared the old man and rushed him across the corridor to the fire stairs. He gave him the name of a local bar where he should wait until Lucius came to get him.

"How about my stuff?" Rob yelled, back up the stairwell.

Rob's stuff consisted of a spare pair of cheap undershorts, spare socks, spare shirt, a few loose cartridges, a rusty razor, worn toothbrush but no paste, and an old sweater. Beneath these was an empty cartridge box, a large envelope of manuscript, and a folded yellowed packet, sadly stained—the list. Lucius glanced at it, took a deep breath, refolded it—there were soft torn slits where the dark creases had worn through—and tucked it into his breast pocket.

The big envelope held a handwritten manuscript with Lucius's name scrawled on the outside—had Rob written his "story," as he'd threatened? He hefted it, stood there a moment, put it back, then took the posse list out of his pocket and returned that, too. He had no right to these things, after all. He had no right to read that manuscript until Rob gave it to him of his own accord, wasn't that true? He closed the satchel and went back to the window.

A rain which had threatened since late afternoon had begun softly, shining the pavements under the hard lights. The black car had not stirred and the crowd was larger, but whether Dyer was still inside the car—whether he had gotten out or had been removed from it—Lucius could not tell. On the fire stairs, he heard loud clangorous footsteps and the shouts of people bursting into corridors. In the parking lot, as he started his car, he heard the first siren of an ambulance.

*

Lucius set his glass on the dark wood of the booth and cupped it between his hands. "I hope you missed him, Rob."

"I never shot at him. I shot his tires out, is all. Nailed both rear wheels on a moving vee-hickle with three damn rounds of a revolver!" He grinned at Lucius with wry pride. "Know who taught me? Seeing his boy shoot that way would have made ol' Bloody proud!"

Lucius nodded but did not smile back. "Why should Dyer believe that you weren't shooting at him?"

"Who gives a shit what he believes! It's the damned truth!"

Lucius nodded. "That car's still right there at the stoplight. As far as I know, nobody got out. That's the damned truth, too." They listened a moment to the sirens. "Let's go," he said, rising from the booth.

"You don't believe me?"

"You think the law is going to accept that story? Slugs ricocheting all over the damn parking lot? Suppose one hit him?"

"Lucius?" The old man retreated deeper into the booth, as if to hide himself in the warm whiskey darkness. "It was kind of a joke," he pleaded.

"Tell 'em it was a joke. See if they laugh." Lucius tossed a few bills on the table. "You have a record, dammit! You're a fugitive! At the very least they will rack your mean old ass for reckless endangerment or whatever they call it—firing a lethal weapon in a public place."

He went outside. Rob darted out behind him. "Where we heading for? I'm not going to Chatham Bend with you, I'll tell you that!"

Lucius unlocked the car door. "We're going home." He spoke without much heart. "They won't come to Caxambas before morning."

In the car, the old man was subdued. "I'm too damn old to be going back to prison, Lucius. And don't start telling me I should have thought of that!"

"All right," Lucius said. "I won't."

It was raining harder. For the next few miles, south on the Trail, they passed in silence through a wiper-washed phantasmagoria of strip development. Half-seen drowned buildings, lights, and signs streamed past in pools and glimmerings of gold-red light—as if they were newcomers to hell, thought Lucius, and were on their way in from the airport. In the tire slick and glare of the night highway, a dull dread had worn away the whiskey. He knew that Rob was doomed, and their flight useless.

Rob was banging on the outside of his door. "This here's my stop," he said. Lucius pulled in at the roadhouse, thinking the old man might need the toilet, but Rob was dragging his old satchel over the seat top. He clambered out and slammed the door. A warm waft of deep-fried foods carried across the rain. Rob spread his arms wide to the lights and rain as if summoning the night highways of America to take him back. "Don't disappear, all right?" Lucius called. "You have a home now, Rob! You belong with your own family!"

"You're my family?"

The old drifter bent to contemplate his brother, ignoring the rain that descended the deep furrows of his face. He, too, had sobered. "If they come hunting me, they'll drag you into it. You get back to the hotel, work on your alibi, okay, Luke?" Rob was the only person who had ever used that name, which Lucius had not heard since early boyhood. "*Luke!*" he exclaimed, to conceal his emotion.

"All right," Rob said, trying to smile. "I'll be there tomorrow, Luke. I'll be right there in the mob, throwing rotten eggs," he yelled, voice rising in indignation. "Us folks won't tolerate your damn whitewash of Ed Watson!"

"Keep an eye out, Rob. They might be looking for you." He pointed at the satchel. "Maybe you better let me have that gun."

Rob fished the revolver from his satchel, but after holding it a moment, he put it back. "I'd better hang on to this. Family heirloom, y'know," he added cryptically, and Lucius shrugged, handing over the cartridge dropped in the hotel room. Rob tossed the cartridge on his palm. "That's my lucky bullet. I always kept that one separate—you just never know!"

He took out the large envelope, considered it a moment, put that back, too. "Rob Watson's memoirs. For your archives. You might not be ready for it yet." He bent at the window to peer in. In the reflected light from the night neon, his cheeks and stubble glistened, and he coughed. "I'm not a killer, Luke. Just you remember that. No matter what." Then his head was gone, and a moment later he was hurrying away across oily black mirrors of the parking lot in an old man's stiff run toward the roadhouse. The door opened in a crack of light and wail of country music. Then the light closed again, and Rob Watson was gone.

*

Lucius drove south to Caxambas under a gibbous moon. Making his way out over the narrow dock toward the dark hulk of his home on the creek, he caught himself taking pains to approach quietly, as if stalking something not quite known. Down the still creek, a raccoon fishing mud clams at the water's edge sat upright and peered around at the night silence. The atmosphere seemed strangely changed by the presence of that urn—that broken skull uprooted from its grave not once but twice.

Touching the latch, he was overcome by old and unnameable premonitions. He wrenched the door like one forcing himself to jump into cold water. Framed in the window, the urn awaited him, in silhouette against the silver creek. He paused in the doorway, in a tumult of unsorted feelings.

Papa had kept a "souvenir" human skull, of obscure provenance, which Edna had not permitted in the house. Papa fastened it to the boat shed wall as inspiration to the field hands, using rough charcoal to scrawl beneath it a "classical" inscription—"from the Greek," he said.

> *I have been where you are now,*
> *And you will be where I have gone.*

Explaining that skull to the young children, enjoying their squeals of delighted fear, Papa would make "giant" noises by blowing across the mouth of his empty jug. One Sunday in the boat shed shade, gazing out over the river as the children fled toward the house, in flight from the twilight onset of mosquitoes, Papa's mind had wandered from that hollow jug to ruminations on the great hollowness of man's existence, and the horror of his isolation in the universe, alone with the knowledge of oncoming darkness— what he called "the Knowing."

Alone with that knowing, Lucius went to the cupboard and poured himself a drink. This calmed him somewhat. He set the urn outside on deck, out of his sight. He murmured, "Rest now, Papa," not certain what he meant, then returned inside and lay down wide-eyed on the moon-swept cot.

Chapter 6

Collier County

According to the morning paper, the driver of the damaged vehicle had escaped unhurt in the shooting episode the night before outside the Gasparilla. Already in custody was the enraged meat carver (the "disturbed veteran," the "furious Negro") who earlier that evening had waved a big knife at the victim and "terrified" the other diners. Apparently Dyer had not suspected Rob, for if he'd thought that Rob had tried to kill him, he would surely have reported him, citing his identity as a longtime fugitive. Or would he?

At the Naples church hall, Lucius wondered if Dyer would appear. He worried that if Rob turned up, he might not have sense enough to stay out in the dark. He hoped that Sally Brown was still in Naples.

The Program Director of the Historical Society caught up with him at the side entrance near the podium. Already upset by his tardy arrival and failure to report to her at once, this brisk thistly little person was aghast at his decision to present himself as Lucius Watson, assuring him that "her" audience had not paid good money to hear about Mr. Bloody Watson from his son! Her implication was that the son could not be trusted, and indeed, she mistrusted him herself, having caught him with a plastic glass, complete with swizzle stick. "As you know, Professor Collins, intoxicating spirits are strictly prohibited in multidenominational places of worship."

"Mineral water," Lucius advised her. "With a twist of lemon," he added brightly when she looked daggers at the citrus wedge.

She sniffed. "I see." And warned him anew that "these very unique senior citizens" (whom she also described as "very special human beings") might "not exercise the option" of "sharing their cultural heritage," far less "interfacing with the facilitator," if they suspected they weren't getting what they paid for—in short, a bona fide professor, namely L. Watson Collins, Ph.D.

Still patient, Lucius pointed out as he had to Dyer that Naples was not far from Caxambas, and that some old-timer in the audience was sure to spot him. It seemed more honest—and a great deal safer—to identify himself right from the start.

She would not listen. Closing her eyes, she shook her head throughout and then said, "No."

"I'm afraid I've made up my mind," he said.

"So have I." She waved an envelope which he took to be his check, and her thin lipstick flickered in a basilisk smile less withering than withered. "I owe it to my audience," she told him. She swept inside to greet a wealthy patron and get her settled up front near the podium.

The Gulf wind clacking in the palms unnerved him, as if all the defenses of his reclusive life were blowing away. He sucked such comfort as he could from the solid glass of ice and vodka in his hand. It was one thing to pass as a historian in north Florida and quite another to use a bogus name with a local audience which knew him well as a broken-down drunk fisherman and chronic loser.

*

The applause startled him. He was being introduced. With a murderous smile, the Program Director was summoning and beckoning "Professor Collins"—damn!—and he hurried to the podium before he had composed himself. Seeing the glass he had neglected to set down, she raised her eyebrows to the vanishing point, even reared back a little, to separate herself from any blame for his behavior. He resisted her attempt to relieve him of his glass, and they actually tussled for one hate-filled moment before she would let go.

In hard, flat light, he found himself confronted by a wary assemblage of elders, fanning the worn-out heat with their clutched programs. These old-timers had whitish aureoles around their heads like a light manna of stardust, drifted down out of the firmament in blessing. The women wore gloomy floral prints, home coifs, and pastel glasses, while their consorts—mostly smaller, as in hawks and spiders—favored thin steel specs and nylon pastel shirts, broad collars splayed to reveal the snowy singlets worn beneath. From the aseptic glint of lenses as the heads bent and whispered, he feared that the true identity of "Professor Collins" was already being bruited about the hall.

Though the back rows were mostly empty, a few young men lounged in the rear doorway—rough shaggy sunburned men in black baseball caps and black T-shirts, restless and out of place. One of them whistled and another clapped, urging the speaker to get on with it. The Professor raised his glass in a vague salute and drank off the last of it, all set to go. But when he said, "Good evening," his audience unaccountably looked elsewhere, as if he had turned up in the wrong room. Resistance to his renovated E. J. Watson would be doughty, he knew that much, for to these old-timers the truth was far less precious than the "Mister Watson" of tradition, who was not to be trifled with by some outsider.

"Tonight," he began in modest tones, "I'd like to tell you what I've learned about E. J. Watson, who he was and where he came from, and also about his foreman Leslie Cox, who as most of you know committed the three murders for which Watson was executed by his neighbors—and also, as you may *not* know, at least five other murders in north Florida. And if you folks disagree with anything I say, or have heard other versions of these stories, just raise your hand and we'll get things straightened out."

In his vodka euphoria, the silence led him to suppose that the audience was open to his reasoning if not yet entirely on his side. Filled with sudden fondness for these tough old-timers, he actually leaned outward over the podium, spreading his arms in symbolic embrace as if yearning for his flock in the manner of the evangelicals whom they were used to. As he did so, he upset his emptied glass, noting from the corner of his eye the dismay of the Program Director in the first row, who clearly imagined that her speaker was on the point of toppling off the podium entirely.

"Now you folks have read for years and years that somebody called Bloody Watson was a psychopathic killer, that he killed dozens, that he killed his help rather than pay them—you all know these stories! There's no end to them! But none of these writers ever saw Ed Watson, never shook his hand or heard him laugh—they never *knew* him! Whereas some of you folks here tonight probably knew the man to say hello to, at least your parents did. So perhaps we can clear the record just a little—"

"Now hold on a minute!"

"—because despite all these stories," Lucius persisted, holding up his hand in a plea for patience, "*despite* all these stories, there were never any witnesses, no damning evidence—in fact, no proof whatever that he killed *anybody*! On the contrary, we have plentiful testimony that he was a fine farmer and strong family man, much admired as a businessman and as a neighbor. And as you know, most of his neighbors weren't afraid of him at all!"

A stir of disbelief had charged the air. Sensing this, Lucius backed off a little, speaking briefly about Edgar Watson's early life in South Carolina, Oklahoma, and north Florida, about which almost nothing has been written. "Ted Smallwood, whom so many of you knew, wrote in his memoirs that E. J. Watson, coming from Arcadia, arrived in the Chokoloskee Bay area about 1892 or 1893. Based on my research in Arcadia, late 1893 or early 1894 would be more accurate. At some time in 1895, perhaps early 1896, down at Key West, he had a dispute with Adolphus Santini of Chokoloskee—"

"*Dispute?* I guess so! Slit his throat! Pretty close to killed him!"

"Hey! How about them Tuckers?"

"Mister, who the hell are you to come and tell us local people what we know a hell of a lot more about than you do?"

Sally Brown, coming down the aisle, lifted her hand in a small, ironic wave, as Lucius said, "Good! Good! Correct me! I welcome any information!"

An old man rose and took his hat off. On his turkey throat a green shirt was tight-buttoned, and he wore blue galluses. His pupils, enlarged by thick lenses, gave him the round-eyed appearance of an aged child. "I'm Preston Brown," he told the hall at the precise moment that Lucius recalled who he was. "I'm ninety-four and had a stroke so I ain't as good as what I was—ain't as good-lookin neither, so they tell me—but most days I got a pretty good idea what I am talking about. And these old eyes I'm lookin out of here tonight seen E. J. Watson in the flesh many's the time, and this old voice has talked with him, and this old hand shook his'n. They ain't too many in this room can say the same.

"Now Watson and Tucker had a dispute over a piece of land. Tucker and his nephew had a shack on Lost Man's Key, and Emperor Watson went down there and Watson killed him. You could see the blood. Nephew got away, tried to hide back in the mangroves, but Watson had his boy Eddie with him, so he sent Eddie after that Tucker boy, to finish him. We went over there and seen the tracks." He looked all around the room with satisfaction.

Lucius recalled what Weeks Daniels had told him—that Eddie Watson, growing older, had taken to hinting at participation in the Tucker episode, apparently to lend drama to his life. Perhaps Eddie had himself to blame for these damned stories. However, the story was untrue. Before he could object, Sally Brown had raised her hand—"Excuse me!"—and got up. She smiled briefly at Lucius, then said to the old man, "*Tucker and his nephew!* You old-timers have been trading that old tale for fifty years, and it's all wrong!"

The old man squared around to face her. "That so, Miss?" he said. He seemed to be sucking upon something.

"There wasn't any 'nephew,' " she declared. "It was young Wally Tucker from Key West and his wife Bet. They were friends and neighbors of my husband's parents, the Lee Hardens, down at Lost Man's River!"

A slim, fair-haired man who had been shaking hands with the young men inside the doorway had turned his head at her reference to the Hardens, and now he, too, slipped quickly down the aisle, and taking a seat, put a protective arm on the back of her chair. Lucius recognized Whidden Harden, whom he had known since he was born at Lost Man's River. And Whidden recognized him, too, and raised his eyebrows slightly, with a fleeting grin, careful not to draw attention to their acquaintance. His innate discretion and his implicit trust that "Mister Colonel" must know what he was doing on the podium under the name of Collins reminded Lucius of why he had been so fond of Whidden as a child.

From farther back, a woman called, "Ain't that your husband settin there beside you? He knows a lot more than you do about Lost Man's, so how come he don't speak up for himself?" Whidden Harden raised his hand in a shy wave, and the crowd snickered. The scent of old bad blood was in the air.

His wife had turned to the prim rows behind her, where the set faces made it plain that this young woman had previously rumpled up their society meetings. "Most of you know who I am. I'm Sally Brown. My mother's bunch of Browns lived in the Islands a good many years, and now I'm married to this Harden feller, so I guess I know a little bit about Lost Man's River!"

A loud harsh shout came from the men in back—"Your daddy ain't no Brown!" Sally, flustered, found no answer, and Whidden took her hand. The woman's voice said, "How come you don't use your husband's name? You shamed of him?" The crowd shifted restlessly, and a man yelled at the big man who had shouted, "That you, Crockett? What say there, Crockett? Hey, ol' buddy! Crockett Junior Daniels! American damn hero! Been over to Asie, give his right arm for Dermocracy!" The ragged cheer came mostly from Crockett's own group in the doorway.

Wigwagged by the Program Director, the speaker rapped his plastic glass down on the podium in an inaudible attempt to restore order, as Preston Brown, unperturbed by these interruptions, stood ready and willing to hold forth at greater length. "Well, I ain't no relation to Sally here," he told the audience. "Way back someplace, her mama and me might been some kind of Brown kinfolks, but I sure ain't related to her daddy! And I ain't related to them Hardens, neither!"

"Lucky for Hardens!" Sally cried. She was still standing, resting her hand on her husband's shoulder and challenging the churchly silver heads, none of which would turn to meet her eye. Whidden Harden reached and took her hand again, less to comfort her than to urge her to sit down. Failing in both, he looked straight ahead at the stage curtain. In the hush, he said in a dead flat tone, "Any man in this room under forty years of age wants to tell me to my face why he don't like Hardens, he can find me right outside after the show." The voice was quiet but it carried nonetheless, like a voice accustomed to being heard across the water.

In the stir and murmur, one of the young men called, "We sure don't know about that feud! That was way back in Lost Man's days. But we know Whidden Harden. He's all right."

"Yessir, I been fishin and guidin down there around Lost Man's all my life," Preston Brown continued. "Know all about it."

"Whidden was *born* down there," said Sally, and sat down.

"Hardens tell you to speak up for 'em? How come you know more than your husband?"

Lucius intervened by pointing at a raised hand. A Northern voice—a winter visitor—mentioned a well-known book about the Everglades in which "Luke Short, a white fisherman," was identified as the man who fired the first shot at Edgar Watson. "Whatever became of that man Short?" she said.

The men scratched silver ears, viewed liverish hands. Nobody answered. Lucius repeated the question into the microphone lest the visitor feel ignored, and after a few moments, a voice piped up, then another and another, like frog chorus.

"*Henry* Short, you mean?"

"Henry was a nigra! Still is, far as I know."

"Dan House Junior claimed *he* was the first to drill Desperader Watson, on account of Watson drawed a bead on Dan House Senior! Dan claimed that till the day he died right here in Naples!"

"Well, what *we* heard when we was comin up, them House boys covered up for Nigger Short. My daddy said, 'We was fixin to go ask him about it, get to the truth of it, y'know, but we never did come up with that sonofagun.' "

"Made himself scarce for a few years, ol' Henry did. Can't say I blame that poor sonofagun, neither, with hard-hearted young fellers lookin to hunt him down."

This last speaker, a small man in the front row with squirrel cheeks and merry eyes, smiled benignly at Lucius. His old-fashioned yacht club attire—sky blue trousers, navy blue polo shirt, crisp deck shoes with marshmallow white soles, bright sweater so yellow that the old man looked like a seated lemon—seemed rather at odds with his windburned hide and weather lines. Lucius grinned back at his good old friend Hoad Storter, whose father Cap'n Bembery had run the cargo schooner for the Storter trading post at Everglade and had been Papa's best friend. Like Whidden Harden, Hoad would be discreet, but Lucius realized that his identity might be exposed at any moment by Crockett Junior Daniels or some other person, and that as at Fort White, the longer he waited, the more awkward it was sure to be. Trying to decide how to go about it, he asked old Brown for some good evidence that E. J. Watson had killed those Tuckers. His query made him feel dishonest, since he knew there was no "good evidence" and never had been—nothing but a vague account related by Lee Harden and his brothers who (with Henry Short) had found the bodies. In his Lost Man's years, the Hardens had never spoken of the Tuckers, nor had he ever wanted to ask questions. His reluctance to know the truth had disturbed him, even at the time.

"Killed that Audubon warden, too," snarled an old man with a broken face empurpled by long falling years of drink. The man wore a soiled Panama hat and nobody sat near him or behind him. His arms were folded tight across his chest and he would not face Lucius as he spoke. "Nineteen and oh-five, that was. I was running Watson's cane plantation for him. That spring, Watson went over to Flamingo with a crate of bird plumes, and the story about Guy Bradley's murder got back before he did! That's when our family packed up and got away from there."

Preston Brown said, "Heck, I knowed Guy Bradley! Knowed him before he went over to Audubons! Him and his brother Lewis Bradley, they was partners with the Roberts boys, huntin plume birds down around Cape Sable. Ed Watson sold his bird plumes through Gene Roberts and I reckon the Bradleys done the same. Then Guy went over to wardenin, he was goin to put Watson in the jail, so Watson shot him—"

Lucius said in a flat voice, "Guy Bradley was killed by a sponge fisherman and plume hunter named Walter Smith, who was tried for that killing in Key West."

"That's right. Walt Smith. Knowed him all my life," said Preston Brown.

"Tried and acquitted," Fred Dyer insisted sourly. "Cause the word had got around that Watson done it."

"You know better than that," Lucius snapped too sharply. People stared at him, alarmed. "I have talked many times with Gene Roberts at Flamingo," he told the audience, frowning down at Fred Dyer but unable to get his eye. "Gene Roberts was Guy Bradley's friend and neighbor, he was the man who picked up Bradley's body, and he knew that whole story better than anybody."

"Gene Roberts was Ed Watson's friend, that's all I'm sayin!" Dyer cried. "Used to come by Chatham Bend when I was workin there! No wonder he spoke up for him, he had no choice about it!"

"Walter Smith never denied that he killed Bradley. He even boasted of it." Lucius turned to Preston Brown. "Another correction, sir, if you don't mind. Eddie Watson took no part in the Tucker killings."

"Yessir! Eddie Watson! Knowed him all my—"

"Excuse me, Mr. Brown. In 1901, Eddie Watson was still a schoolboy, living in Fort Myers with his mother. He never lived down here along this coast." He gazed bleakly at the audience. "I realize it's a lot more fun to implicate someone like E. E. Watson, who sits up front in church. But it isn't true."

"Well, E. J. Watson, he's the one I'm talkin about. He liked his alcohol, he visited all the bars," Preston Brown said. "My dad had nothin against alcohol, he was in there, too. One time there was a bunch of 'em around the bar, with Old Man Watson settin up the drinks. And a couple of nigra women come in there, wanted a bottle—weren't uncommon, because Key West was more a Yankee town than not. So Watson mutters, 'Well, boys, I will take care of this.' And he got up and went outside where their big ol' bucks was waitin on them women. Might of seed Watson through the window and figured it was healthier outside. One of 'em said real nervous, 'Evenin, Cap'n,' and that was about all he got to say before Watson started in to cuttin on 'em with his bowie knife. Never said a word. He had one down, pretty well killed, and the other one, he was pretty well cut to pieces. Might of finished the both of 'em, for all I know.

"So Watson had enough of it and walked away from there, but on the way over to the dock he run into some deputies who was comin to investigate all that hollerin. So Watson told 'em, 'You boys better get on up to Jimmy's Bar.' And they said, 'Ed, what in tarnation is making all that racket?' And Watson said, 'My goodness, boys, they are cuttin up a couple of perfectly good niggers over there!' Tipped his hat, climbed back aboard his schooner, and went on north to Chatham River."

Lucius closed his eyes, disgusted. He appealed to the audience's good sense. "See what I mean? These Watson tales are passed down from our parents and grandparents and we just repeat them, never bothering to find out if they are true." He was aware that his weary tone was casting a pall over the room, which had started grumbling. He could not help it.

"Who the hell is *we?*" a voice shouted hoarsely. "You come from around here?"

"Hell yes, he comes from around here! I know this feller!" Fred Dyer had hauled himself straight up in his seat and was pointing a bent arthritic claw at Lucius, who took a deep breath, braced for the worst. "That ain't no professor! That is Lucius Watson!" Dyer actually stood up, staring wildly around him, but no one would let him catch an eye, no one would look at him, as if so many years of drunkenness and reckless tirade had invalidated anything that he might say. Knowing this, he protested no further but sat down slowly, alone and aggrieved, refolding his arms upon his chest. Under Lucius's gaze, he shrugged and looked away.

"Well, it sure weren't *Colonel* Watson killed them Tuckers!" Preston

Brown declared. "I knowed Colonel all my life, and a nicer feller you would never want to meet! Colonel been on my boat about a thousand times. Sweetest person that you ever seen—*good* sense of humor! Oh yes, I fished with Colonel Watson *many's* the time. He liked his whiskey!"

Lucius had never drunk with Preston or set foot on his boat. "No, it wasn't Colonel," he said quietly, embarrassed by the old man's exaggerations and plain lies and suffocated by the greater lie he himself was perpetrating.

"How come *you* know so much about them Tuckers?" an old woman hollered at the podium. "They's only the one feller could know so much, and that's the one who done it."

"Know somethin funny?" Preston Brown was pointing at Lucius. "This feller right here, he's the spittin image of ol' Colonel Watson!"

Fred Dyer groaned loudly. "Ain't that what *I* said?"

"Well, let's see now," Hoad Storter interrupted. "Old Man Watson had four boys that he owned up to. There were just four brothers"—he paused ever so slightly—"that we want to talk about." His chipmunk cheeks rounded a little when other people laughed. "The oldest boy who ran away after that Tucker business, no one remembers him anymore"—he stopped Preston Brown with a raised palm—"not even Preston. Next one was Eddie, who stayed there at Fort Myers, wouldn't surprise me if he's up there yet. Then came Lucius—well, some of us know Colonel. Never met a man yet who had bad words for Colonel Watson, not even the men who were on that list he took so many years putting together, scaring everybody half to death, himself included!" He winked at Lucius. "Then came the youngest—the little boy who saw his daddy killed."

"How about that other little feller, supposed to been drowned in the Great Hurricane? The one Speck Daniels always claimed to be!"

"Well, Speck's mama," a woman called, "got herself hitched up to her own first cousin, and a good half of their ten, twelve head of kids come out not so smart or something worst."

Somebody hee-hawed but the rest of the hall filled with coughs and chair scrapes, whisperings, and indignation. "Well, Aunt Josie had a girl named Jenny," another woman said carefully, "and she was supposed to been a Watson, too!" And the first woman said, "No, no, honey, what they claimed, Jenny was raped by Mr. Watson!" This was vehemently disputed by a third. "Say what you like about Mr. Watson, he were not the kind to go around rapin his own daughter!"

"Ain't that Jenny Everybody we're talkin about?" Preston Brown inquired, in the first lull in the tumult. Detecting titillation, he cried out over the hubbub, "Yessir! Called her Jenny Everybody! Cause she weren't particular!" He looked confused when his joke was met with a disjointed silence. The elderly audience fretted and knitted, shifted, itched, and coughed in disapproval. "Called her Jenny Everybody cause she weren't so particular," the old man repeated without heart.

"If Speck was in *that* bunch, he got the brains of all them other ten mushed into one!" an old voice cackled. "That feller been called names aplenty, but nobody never called him Not-So-Smart!"

"Nobody that ain't lookin to outsmart hisself!" Crockett Junior bellowed. Whidden Harden gazed straight ahead, expressionless, as Sally rose and hurried toward the rear.

Preston Brown came forward to peer more closely at "Professor Collins." His prolonged scrutiny was already encouraging cranky speculation from the audience about whether this darned know-it-all professor should be trusted. Concluding his inspection, Old Preston brooded. "I always heard it was Young Ed that helped his daddy—heard that all my life. Them old-timers had no reason to lie to us. Seems kind of funny this here man would just walk in here and go to sayin that our old folks would lie to us like that." Pointing at Lucius, the old man said, "You're coverin up for Eddie Watson, ain't that right?"

Lucius turned toward the night windows, imploring forgiveness from the old man who might be out there in the dark. He said quietly, "No. It wasn't Eddie. The most likely witness—*if* E. J. Watson killed the Tuckers, and *if* there was a witness—was the oldest boy, who left this part of Florida long, long ago."

"I never heard about no older boy in that darned Tucker business." Old Brown pointed accusingly at the speaker. "You must be some kind of a Watson. 'L. Watson Collins'—they got that wrote right down here on my program!"

"L. Watson Collins is my pen name," Lucius told him. He smiled at his friends, then lifted his gaze to the whole room. "Mr. Brown is correct. My name is Lucius Watson. Most old-timers on this coast know me as Colonel." He scanned the audience for Watson Dyer. "The late Mr. E. J. Watson was my father."

The silence was broken first by a low groan, then a squeaked "I *knew* it!" then "No wonder!" An old man called out, "How *you* doin, Colonel? I'm pleased to meet up with you again! I was just tellin these folks here how much you looked like you!" But an old lady toward the back held up his *History*. "If I was to ask you to sign this book, which name would you sign? If your daddy never murdered nobody, the way you're telling us, how come you're so ashamed of him that you don't put your own name on your own book?"

In the hard light, the church hall hummed with anticipation. Preston Brown cried, "Didn't I tell you this was Eddie's brother? See why he claimed it weren't Eddie killed them Tuckers but that older boy?"

"It *was* the older boy, you cock-eyed old idjit! The man is telling you the truth!"

At that slurred shout careening through the window, the young men in the doorway rushed outside. Lucius jumped from the stage and hurried up the aisle. In the door he was blocked by the one-armed man, who grasped him by the shirtfront. Crockett Junior growled, "Don't come no further south, you understand me?" Shoving Lucius away, he went out into the darkness. Sally Brown was dragging at his arm, entreating him not to follow. By the time he fought his way outside, the men were gone.

Most of the audience, disgruntled, was rising to leave, and Preston Brown had taken advantage of the speaker's absence to regain the floor. "See, nobody wanted to go up in that wild river looking for Watson," he was shouting. "But there was one deputy was running for Sheriff, and his platform was, I will arrest Ed Watson, bring him up before the bar of justice. So he went up to Chatham River and Watson got the drop on him and took his guns away and put him to work in the cane harvest. That feller come back in two weeks' time with a neck bad sunburnt and calluses on his hands, and very very glad to be alive. Said Ed J. Watson was as fine a feller as any man could ever hope to meet, and the only planter worth a damn on that whole coast."

"That's quite a story," Lucius told the audience as he reached the podium. "Does anyone else have anything they'd like to add?" Upset by Rob's folly in coming here at all, he was anxious to bring the evening to an end.

Old Brown stood there in his high black shoes, the last of his life aglimmer in his eyes, and still he would not take a seat, as if afraid that his decrepit apparatus might never propel him back onto his feet. His fingers worked the back of his steel chair. When he raised his hand again, clearing his throat, Lucius interrupted gently, observing how helpful it would be if these old stories had any sort of documentation. He invited the audience to empathize with the frustrations of the historian, who had to be conservative about unconfirmed stories, however colorful. Lucius had hoped that this approach would be approved by an old-fashioned community which felt not only protective about "Mister Watson" but superior in their inside knowledge to people from outside the county. *Nosir, Ol' Ed weren't near so bad as what outsiders try to tell you, not when you knowed him personal the way we done.* How often he'd heard old-timers say that!

Realizing that his testimonies had been discounted, the old man suddenly sat down, and his chair creaked loudly in the hush of disapproval. In questioning an elder's recollections, consigning them to myth, the speaker had undermined the integrity of local legend and tradition, and now his hearers made it plain that any diminishment of the Watson legend, even by his son, would not be tolerated. The faces pinched closed in their suspicion that this fake professor had tried to pull the wool over their eyes. More old people tottered to their feet with a loud barging of chairs and the rest followed, as Lucius called, "Good night! Thank you for coming!"

He remained at the podium, shuffling his notes into some sort of order, upbraiding himself for letting the evening collapse so swiftly into such a shambles. The plastic glass, with its tired lemon, was a silent rebuke in the corner of the rostrum, but mercifully the Program Director had fled. Only Hoad Storter came up to shake his hand, and even Hoad, who was keeping people waiting, had to leave quickly, saying he hoped to see Lucius in a day or two at Everglade.

Last to depart was old Fred Dyer, who limped past in a syphilitic shuffle, evading the speaker's eye. When Lucius followed him up the aisle and touched his elbow, the empurpled man tottered around in a half circle with a grimace of alarm, backing like a crayfish into a row of seats. "You remember me, Mr. Dyer?" Lucius asked quietly. "I guess I wasn't much more than fifteen when your family left the Bend."

"*Family!*" The man spat upon the church hall floor. "My own children would like to see me dead, they're so ashamed of me!" He kept on going, but Lucius moved beside him.

"Your son—"

"He's your damned kin, not mine." Fred Dyer stopped short and looked Lucius in the eye for the first time that evening. "What's that ungodly bastard up to anyways? Couple months ago, he shows up real friendly where I drink, buys me a round or two while he sits there sucking a damn cherry soda. Says, 'You still tellin people that I'm Watson's son?' *Hell, yes!* 'You willin to sign that in a affidavit?' *Hell, yes!* Next thing I know, there's a legal paper settin in front of me which says it is the opinion and sincere belief of the undersigned, Fred Dyer, that Watson Dyer, born December fourth of 1905 on Chatham Bend in Monroe County, is the natural son of the planter E. J. Watson!" He shook his greasy head. "Here I been sayin that same thing for forty years, and now this damn contrary bastard wants me to *sign* it!"

Yet Fred seemed bewildered, even a little hurt. "I said, 'Wattie, for Christ's sake, what's this all about? Ain't it a little late in life to renounce your name?' And he told me, 'Fred, you got sick of living a lie, and I feel the same.' Said he aimed to live in truth just as soon as he could get around to all the paper work. Called me Fred! Made me feel funny—the cold mean way he said my name. When I signed that paper, he was grinning like a alligator. Tucked it away, stood up, and winked. Never said so much as a good-bye."

At the door, Fred Dyer yanked his bent straw hat onto a head of yellowed silver hair, which straggled to his collar. "You was always a pretty good feller, Lucius, even as a boy. Only thing, you never done right by my little daughter." He went on outside into the night.

*

Sally and Whidden greeted Lucius at the door. When he had seen Whidden last, a few years earlier, Lee Harden's son had been pretty close to thirty, a fishing guide and gator hunter and a hell-raiser. Outwardly, he had changed little—more weatherworn, perhaps, still lean and fit. The wheaten hair had iron wisps and the sun-squinted green eyes had crow's-feet in the corners.

"This here's my ex-husband-to-be," Sally said affectionately, taking Whidden's arm. "I guess you've known him a lot longer than I have."

"Watsons and Hardens always been in friendship, right back into the old century"—Harden smiled—"and Mister Colonel was my dad's best friend from 1919 until we left the Islands." As her husband spoke, Sally's expression entreated Lucius to put their recent intimacy behind him and let it stay there.

Lucius gazed down the dark street where his brother had disappeared with Crockett Junior and his men. The Hardens kept him company, peering around them. "Maybe it's all a mistake. Maybe they'll bring him back and let him go once they've had a talk with him," Sally said. Whidden shrugged, uncomfortable. "I don't think so. I believe them boys come huntin him. That's why they was here."

To free them to go home, Lucius told them he would walk down to the Gulf while he was waiting, leaving a note for Rob in his car window. But they were solicitous, and in the end they accompanied him to the beach and walked out on the long pier in the faint light of the stars, which descended to the Gulf far out to westward. By the time they returned to the church hall, the town was empty. With the crowd gone and the doors locked, there were only the caves of gloom around the streetlights, the clacking of royal palms in the Gulf wind. While Whidden went to fetch their car, Sally told Lucius she'd decided that she loved her husband after all. "That's wonderful," he said. "Any regrets?" he said. She shook her head. "How about you?" she inquired, not much interested in his answer. "I'll always love you, Prof," she said. "I mean it." And she hugged him.

Persuading Lucius to leave his car behind, they took him home to the ranch house in North Naples from where Whidden was starting a landscaping service for winter residents from up north. "Them snowbirds don't know one darn thing about scaping land," he grinned, "and I don't neither." On the way there, Whidden said that if Mister Colonel was planning a trip to Chatham Bend, they would be proud to take him on the *Cracker Belle.* "She's just settin down there rottin, so we might's well use her."

At the house, they sat Lucius at the kitchen table and asked him if he'd like some coffee. "I bet he'd like beer or whiskey a whole lot better," Whidden said, and Sally rapped her spoon. "You've given that up, remember, Whidden? We don't use liquor in this house," she told their guest, ignoring his raised eyebrows.

Still upset by the church hall meeting, Sally denounced the local attitude toward Whidden's family. "Mister Colonel ain't writin his book about my family," Whidden warned her. But when he was asked the Hardens' opinion of what actually happened to Ed Watson, Whidden said, "Well, Sal could tell you better. She talked to the old folks, hours on end, and she got the details on my family down better'n I do." Whidden waited politely for Sally to speak, and when she wouldn't, he frowned and cleared his throat, then sat forward reluctantly and folded his hands before him on the table in sign that, to the best of his knowledge, what he would say was responsible and fair as well as true.

"Lee Harden knew some days ahead that them Chokoloskee men would be layin for Ed Watson, cause even way down in the Islands rumors traveled fast. He aimed to warn him. But after the hurricane, when Mr. Watson came back to Chatham River hunting Cox, our Harden family never seen him. If my dad could have got to him first, he might never of gone back to Chokoloskee.

"Lee Harden declared for the rest of his whole life that E. J. Watson had got flat tired of running, or else he had a purpose no one knew about. Said E.J. was too smart not to know that some of them men was out to make their name by killin Bloody Watson, and that the rest was jealous because he made so much money on his syrup. They was jealous because he had ambition, and wanted a good education for his children.

"Course rednecks never give a hoot about them things. Want their kids to grow up with the same religion and the same old set of prejudices that was passed down to 'em from their own pappies. They never let go of an old notion once they got it nailed down in their brain. Ain't got no room for new ideas, and they are proud about it."

"Mr. Watson kept apart from all their lowlife goings-on," Sally said, "and they never forgave that."

"Well, I reckon that ain't fair," said her husband mildly. "The most of 'em—Houses included—are very good people in their way. Churchly people, hardworking and honest. All the same, I am very proud there weren't no Hardens in that crowd at Smallwood's landing." He winked at Lucius. "Us Hardens wanted to be redneck crackers, too. Couldn't join up because folks'd never let 'em, you remember?"

Sally cried, "How can you speak up for Houses, Whidden! They were snobs, just like the Smallwoods! Mamie Smallwood was a House, and she was meaner to your family than anyone on Chokoloskee Island, that's what your ma told me! And I bet Mister Colonel knows that, too!"

"After 1910, I hardly went to Chokoloskee," Lucius admitted, "but I talked with Sadie Harden plenty of times. Right or wrong, she had it in for Mamie Smallwood."

"You think she was wrong?"

"Mamie was judgmental, all right." Lucius shrugged. "But she was a good strong woman in her way."

Whidden put his hand on his wife's arm, to stop an outburst. "Know what my mama believed? That Mrs. Smallwood resented our family because we were kind to Henry Short. She had grown up with Henry, don't forget, and bein good Christians, the Houses might of felt guilty way down deep cause they made a good Christian eat off by himself all them long years. Mamie liked Henry well enough, I reckon, so long as he kept his place, but she never forgive us for having him eat with us when he showed up at Hardens' with her brother Bill. Bill House might of minded it some, too, but not enough to say nothing about it, cause him and Henry was good friends in their way, they done everything together since they was boys.

"Them few black people who set foot in the Islands, they never stayed no longer than it took to get away. But if one showed up hungry at the Hardens', he was treated the same as other men and that was that. Grandpa Robert said, 'Set down and eat,' and Grandma Maisie put it on the table. We was taught to believe that God made man in His own image, so He never give a hoot about the color. Any man had the right to sit at the table with the rest— that's what Grandpa said. Grandpa Robert was born ornery. He had no use for Bay people and he lived as far away from 'em as he could get. He couldn't never understand how them Bay people could call themselves good Christians, then go treat a feller Christian in ungodly ways; said *no* man was created in God's image only to sniff scraps in the corner like a dog. So rumors got back from some them fishermen who ate with Hardens, first at Chatham Bend, then Mormon Key, and later on at Lost Man's River, too. Said, 'We seen a nigger eatin at them people's table.' That's the way they put it, and word spread. Some said we was 'spoilin a good nigger,' and others called us 'nigger-lover,' and a few started in to saying that if them damn people was lettin niggers eat with 'em, they must be niggers or leastways mulattas, and bein mulattas, they didn't have no right to them good fishing grounds. Well, that was the beginning of the Fish Wars, which went way back to the turn of the century, when Hardens was workin them good sea trout banks north of Mormon Key. And that skirmishin followed 'em when they went south to Lost Man's River.

"Henry Short had to fit in with the Bay people so he done his best not to make any commotion. Because he passed most of his days steerin clear of trouble, he never talked much, and it got so those Bay folks clean forgot Henry was there. But there were times he got so lonesome for human company that he would go to visit with the Hardens, and the time came when he placed his trust in us. Took him years before he learned to do that. Our family listened to him with an open heart, and he told 'em things he wouldn't tell nobody else for fear the men would come for him and lynch him."

"He could never, never trust another soul," his wife agreed. "Maybe the House family knew Henry longer, but the Hardens knew him better, and maybe that's why Mamie House resented them."

"It was Henry Short who warned Lee Harden that the Chokoloskee people, and Smallwoods especially, resented Hardens even worse after the Watson killing. Our family could never figure out the Smallwoods' attitude, cause we were Mr. Watson's friends and they were, too. We agreed with Ted and Mamie that judging E. J. Watson was God's business or the business of the law, not something to be took in their own hands by vigilantes.

"When Ted Smallwood give his opinion that his friend Ed Watson had been lynched, the House family got very, very angry. Old Man Dan House once declared where Henry heard it that his son-in-law was two-faced about Watson's death. Said Ted always wanted to be known as Watson's friend but in his heart he dreaded him, and wanted him out of the way as bad or worse than the ones who done the shooting. What he ducked out of, Houses said, was going down there with his neighbors and looking his friend E.J. in the eye and taking his share of the responsibility for their community."

"Smallwood's excuse was, he had flu that day, malaria," said Sally. "Said if he didn't get better pretty quick, he might send Henry to fetch Sadie Harden to come doctor him. I don't know if she'd have gone or not. Sadie told me herself she would go all the way to Everglade to trade at Storters' rather than go to Chokoloskee, because Mamie flew across the store and perched right over her like a fat little old owl every time she came in for her supplies. Declared right out for all to hear how afraid she was that one of these mixed people was aiming to steal her whole store out from under her—"

"—said that to Mama! Who never stole a grit in her whole life!"

Sally looked at Lucius a long time, tears in her eyes, until he had no choice but to look back. "Does this look like a mulatta man to you?" She pointed at the fair-haired man beside her.

"Now, honey," Whidden sighed, "the man just got here."

"Talk about big frogs in a small pond!" his wife exclaimed. "And now they're all split up and bickering over their land while Hardens are doing fine. Those Bay folks can't stand it that those darn people they used to call mulattas are more prosperous than they are, all around Lee County and Collier, too!"

Sally seemed almost feverish with the injustice. "Hate and envy and mistrust! Nobody could trust *anybody* on Chokoloskee Bay, and that's because a lot of 'em came down from criminals and fugitives. Otherwise why would they settle the most godforsaken wilderness in the whole country? At least Robert Harden would admit that. He deserted from the Confederate Army and never denied it. He said, 'Why should I die for their Great Cause, which I don't believe in? Why should a poor man have to fight the rich men's wars and lose the only life he will ever have on God's good earth?' "

"My granddad took no chances, and they never caught up with him," Whidden said. "He changed his name three or four times, hid away down in the Islands and stayed down there until he died, watchin the wars go by. Before he give up in 1946—and a good thing, too, because the Park come and drove us out the very next year—he told his family how he'd lived through five American wars, not countin Injuns, and couldn't recall to save his life what even one of them damn things was all about.

"Grandpa Robert Harden said, 'I love my country! I love the U.S.A.! Ain't no place like it here on God's green earth! But all I know about them wars is thousands and thousands of poor brave young fellers screamin out their lives in woe and terror, with no more dignity than screechin hogs—shot, bayoneted, torn limb from limb in a barrage, bloody and dyin in their own mess and stink!' Grandpa took one look at that craziness and deserted from the War, lit out for the farthest frontier he could find, cause he just couldn't see no sense nor justice to it. War made him furious! Said, 'War ain't nothin to wave flags about! War is pure stupidity and sacrilege, a terrible insult to the Lord above and all Creation!' "

Whidden himself was a combat veteran. His voice had grown stony as he spoke. Not used to such intensity from her soft-spoken husband, Sally listened respectfully, but she was not to be deflected from her subject. "Oldtimers get things bogged down in their heads, and they're too cranky and worn-out to change opinions," she resumed after a while. "If their gossip was true, I could accept it, but I can't stand people slandering my husband's relatives, who were the first pioneers to settle in the Ten Thousand Islands and the last to leave!"

"Well, things are better now." Whidden grinned slyly at Lucius. "Least they ain't shootin at us."

"Don't make dumb jokes like that!" cried Sally angrily. "What was done to Hardens can never be forgiven or forgotten!"

"Not by Sally Brown." Harden closed his eyes, and his mouth set in a line, and his wife backed off a little.

"All I'm saying," she complained, "is that people who are prejudiced, and have to worry about who they are supposed to be, because that is all they have in life—well, that is pitiful!"

"Is that right, Sal?" Her husband's voice was quiet but no longer mild. He opened his eyes again. "How come it's all you talk about no more if you ain't worried about it?"

"I beg your pardon? It's *your* family I'm worried about!"

He said, "That's right. My family. And my family has been gettin by a good long while without your help."

"Whidden?" She paused. "Have you been drinking?"

"You think I got to be drunk to speak the truth?"

She rose with a bored cold exhausted look. "I was going to mention a few things," she said to Lucius, who was busy with his fork tines, tracing the lacy patterns on his plastic doily. "But I think I'll let Whidden air out his opinions." And she left the room.

Whidden drummed his fingers, glanced at Lucius, looked away again. "Darn it now if my own wife ain't put me in mind of some bush lightnin. You join me in a drop if I could find some?"

"You know something? I bet I would!"

Whidden came back with blue tin cups and a brown jug of moonshine. "Yessir, I love that pretty woman and I always will, but I might be the only one in my whole family that sees her good points, other than her looks. All that ugly hate and gossip was died right down until Miss Sally Brown come swoopin in to denounce that old-time prejudice that our younger ones never even heard about. She got that poison all stirred up again with that big heart of hers, is what she done.

"That was one reason we split up, a couple of years back—that and the fact I was workin for her daddy. I was drunk one night and told her to shut up about the Hardens, mind her own business, and she said she'd be very glad to do that, cause she weren't goin to bother her head no more with no pathetical damn drunk sonofabitch—" Here his eyebrows shot up and he whistled in astonishment, and they both laughed. "Good thing I knew it weren't her *husband* she was talkin about!" He shook his head. "No pathetical damn drunk sonofabitch so shiftless or so spineless, likely both, that after all that happened to the Harden family, he would still go out and do his dirty work for a crooked mean-mouth bigot like Speck Daniels!

"*Bigot!*" Whidden raised his eyebrows high in awe. "And she meant every word! Next thing I knew, that pretty thing had left my house and home! Went back to college for a while to pick up some more of what her daddy likes to call her nigger-lovin communistical ideas." Whidden grinned broadly. "A while ago, I sent her a nice card: *W. T. Harden has the honor to announce he has left the employ of Crockett Senior Daniels.* She didn't believe it but she reckoned she'd have a look, and day before yesterday, there she was! Peerin all around, sharp-eyed and flighty, like a wren sneakin back onto the nest. Pretended she was here to see the lawyers!

"Well, I don't say a word, not even Hi, honey! cause one wrong move and that li'l bird would fly. Her first word to her darlin was, 'Any spirits in this house?' And I says"—he reached across to slosh more into Lucius's cup—"I says, '*Spirits?*' I says. 'Good gracious, no, God bless your li'l heart!' "

Sniffing his liquor, Whidden was still smiling, but his eyes seemed sad. "Born to tell lies, I guess." He sighed in regret over his sins and slumped back with relief on the wooden chair, lifting long denimed legs and work boots and resting them on the corner of the table. His wheaten head, laid on the chair back, cocked his blue baseball cap far forward on his brow, shading his eyes, as Lucius brought him up to date on Speck and his activities at Chatham Bend. Afterwards, Whidden was quiet for a while, sipping his shine, pulling his thoughts together.

WHIDDEN HARDEN

The huntin and fishin all around the Glades was the best in the whole U.S.A., wouldn't surprise me, but when they started messin with the water flow, that was the beginning of the end. Plume birds went first, then panther, bear, and otters. Then the federal Park took over, in the same year as that first red tide—think that red tide was a warning from the Lord? Killed fish all around this coast, and the fish never come back, not like they was, cause the Glades water system they depended on for breedin was just shot to hell.

Right up till a few years ago, we was huntin gators all the year around. Had some state laws protectin 'em but nobody didn't pay that no attention, just come in and laid their gator flats right on the dock and nobody never said a thing about it. Salt down the belly flats, dry 'em in the sun, roll 'em and stack 'em in a good dry place till the day when the law gets changed and there's a market—that is their idea. Only thing, them flats don't keep good once the damp gets to 'em, so mostly all them gators was killed off for nothin.

For many years, the number-one gator poacher was Crockett Senior Daniels. Speck is still livin off the land, he says, by which he means livin off the Park. It ain't a secret, ever'body knows it, Park rangers included. Speck loves the Glades but he don't love the Park and never did—don't want to *hear* about it, even. Far as Speck's concerned, it don't exist. "That's the last of the wild country," ol' Speck likes to say, "and she's still wild, boys, never you mind how many stupid signs them greenhorns go to slappin up along their so-called boundaries. That is our territory, and Uncle Sam hisself ain't got the right to tell us born-bred local fellers what to do with it!"

Course Speck was talkin mainly about gators. By the time the Park come in, the gators was killed out about ever'where—Georgie, Mi'sippi, Loosiana, too—and after they was all but gone, the state of Florida give the gator full protection. That suited us gator hunters to a T cause it drove the price up. The state fish and wildlife boys never messed with us too much. A man on a state salary, now, he's got to think twice about riskin his neck goin up against mean swamp rats that don't take kindly to any man who gets in their way.

It ain't like the old-time gator poachin—Joe Lopez and Tant Jenkins, a few other fellers, skiff and pole and rifle and a pot for coffee. Swamp rats has to keep up with the times the same as ever'body. With gators so few, we rigged us a couple them new airboats so's to cover more country, even rented an ol' crop-duster biplane to map out every last damn gator hole in the Big Cypress. Pretty soon, them Cypress gators was all gone, the only gators left to hunt was the ones across the boundary in the Park. So one night, bouncin along over them Loop Road potholes, Speck says, "Boys, this ol' swamp over here to south'ard is supposed to be some kind of a national damn park, and what I'm lookin for is a damn boundary marker so's we don't go breakin no federal law. Any you boys see any sign of that darn boundary? Cause I can't never make it out too good, nighttimes especially."

Well, us poor fellers always did believe that the Glades was took away unfairly by the U.S. government, so when Speck said, "Boys, we best go get them gators"—well, that is what we done. Swooped in and out of there like hawks. That national park become national headquarters for poachers, to where we had strangers infestin in the Glades from other counties and from all over the South. Gator Hook was where we divvied up and where we partied, we had us a regular Redneck Riviera! Shipped hides by the damn thousands right up there to Q. C. Plott Raw Fur and Ginseng in Atlanta, which was doin real good with wild animal parts in the hide export business.

Takes a smart feller like Speck Daniels to work out all the fine points. Sets up his moonshine still and huntin camp *inside* the Park out of harm's way, where he ain't got no damn local sheriffs nor state cops snoopin around that has to be paid off. Don't hardly make no bones about it, because that's his own home territory, the way he sees it. Old Man Speck sets back on his old boat and counts his money while his lawyer takes care of somebody at Parks who keeps them patrols away from Chatham River.

I reckon you know that Speck's camp is at Chatham Bend. Works real good for his night runs by airboat. Follow the rivers back up into the Glades, head northeast over the sloughs and out over the saw grass to his drop-offs along the Loop Road. Or sometimes he uses them broad levee banks where his buyers can bring a truck south from the Trail. After the feds got on to that, Speck would be tipped off before the rangers, never lost a cargo. Stead of headin north up to the roads where they was waitin for him, he run his hides downriver to the Gulf. Hauls 'em offshore to a coast vessel that runs up a new Panama flag, crates 'em up as caiman hides marked "South America," then imports 'em back into Florida at Tampa Bay.

Course today the feds are keepin the wildlife trade under surveillance, they are crackin down inside the Park and out. But one thing they ain't done yet is catch Speck Daniels. Can't catch that man out in that wilderness, can't run him down in the shaller rivers on this coast. He drags out their channel markers fast as they put 'em in, leaves any boat that tries to chase him stranded high and dry on some ol' orster bar. No matter what they try, he stays one jump ahead.

Huntin gators was good business for a while. A lot of Chokoloskee men done that when it was legal, me included, and a few of us went ahead after it weren't. Tant Jenkins and the Lopez boys, they never paid much attention to the law, and a couple of them Browns, they was real professionals, and other fellers done it on the side. But all of 'em has quit the business now, because them poor dumb things are mostly gone.

Still got the laws but ain't got no more gators. Speck don't hardly poach no more cause they ain't enough gators left to bother with. Few years' time, there won't be no place to hunt except way south around Florida Bay, and no place to ship the few hides a man might get. But God created Crockett Senior Daniels to take and sell just about anything so long as it ain't his, so if he has to, he will rob rare bird eggs, or butterflies or ferns or orchids, or green tree snakes, or a coral snake, or maybe them peppermint-striped tree snails that's mostly gone now off the hammocks. A dealer he's got over to Miami knows how to get them pretty things to rich collectors, them very few that don't die along the way.

Case you might think I am tellin all Speck's secrets, none of this ain't no secret at all, not to nobody around the Glades country.

Ol' Speck been gettin on in years, claims he's retired now, lives on his old boat out of Flamingo on account of the heat his boys is drawing around here. Into his sixties and still gives the wardens fits. Don't need the money, he has made so much, and that ain't even where he's makin it, cause wild things today ain't nothin but his hobby. He's got his boys runnin guns for South America, in and out of the Ten Thousand Islands, just like he run bird plumes and liquor in the old days.

While Speck was over to Miami settin up deals for moonshine and gators, and payin people off, he seen that by our Florida law there weren't no kind of damn firearm you couldn't buy over the counter, and that runnin weapons to the Caribbean or Latin America, where they are kind of loose about their licenses, might be a nice sideline for a gator hunter who was huntin himself right out of business here at home. Speck went right over into haulin guns, and he's already thinkin about haulin marijuana, because that is where the real big money will be comin from ten years from now, in Speck's opinion.

You know and I know that our federal government don't put nothin in the way of businessmen, don't matter how greedy or cold-blooded dirty that business might be. If marijuana gets goin good, the big tobacco companies will take it over from the little fellers, put it out in fancy packages, you wait and see. Them corporations pays big money to get their errand boys elected, and after that, they tell 'em what kind of laws to write and how to get 'em passed. Hell, them weapons makers, they do just as good in peace as they do in war! Only hassle they might come up against is right here at the Florida end, with all the paperwork.

But ol' Speck says, "Why Godamighty, boys, them forms and export permits don't mean nothin! I aim to get them weapons out or know the reason why!" Next thing you know, he's buyin up heavy-duty ordnance that's labeled for home use or huntin or whatever kind of sportin fun us rednecks might get up to while there's still a few wild critters left to kill—assault rifles for turkey shoots, bazookas for blowin deer away. Lob a hand grenade into good cover, you might come out with a whole covey of quail! Some of that sportin hardware is so big, it comes on wheels! Truck that ordnance over here to the west coast so's not to mess with federal surveillance at Miami. Collect enough for a big shipment, haul it out beyond the three-mile limit to that Panama amigo, and run that cargo south to them poor countries where they got some kind of a cryin need to kill people.

It's like Speck told me once before I quit—"What they do with them weapons ain't none of our damn business, Whidden, on account of the customer is always right." Says, "Ain't that the motto that made this country great?" Told us about the American Dream and all like that. Ol' Speck talked so doggone patriotic, it like to brought tears to my eyes, least when I was drinkin.

All the same, I quit. I'd been thinkin about quittin anyway, because them boys was gettin too darn ornery even for me. Killed out gators all across the Glades, kept killin till it made no sense. Had gator flats piled up by the damn thousands when there just weren't no call for 'em no more. We was waitin on a market that weren't goin to come back, not before them stacks of hides moldered and rotted.

I hated that part worst—the waste of life. Felt like my own heart was leakin, some way. So when Speck's baby daughter asked me to quit and left me when I didn't, I thought about it awhile, then said okay. Sally could live with the moonshine business, she could take or leave the gators, but gun-runnin was somethin else, because innocent people was goin to come up killed.

Course Speck will tell you how some shipments of his weapons was used to put a stop to some damn revolution. Felt pretty proud about his war against godless Commonists, I can tell you. But Sally found out that most of them guns was goin to dictators and criminals, and most of the victims was Injun people down in them poor countries who made the mistake of tryin to resist gettin burned out, run off their land, maybe stomped and killed, just to make Speck's customers more money. Seems like small brown people are always in the way.

*

Whidden stopped talking to listen, then tossed off his cup as Lucius did the same. His legs came off the table and he hauled himself upright in his chair, and his boot heel nudged his jug back underneath it as Sally appeared in the door. "A while back you was askin about Henry Short. Bill House had a son could tell you something." He stretched and yawned as if unaware of Sally. "Andy House, he'd know about Henry good as anybody. Might even tell you where to find him. And Andy knows some things about your daddy, too, cause Bill House talked about Ed Watson all his life. Ted Smallwood's children would remember things, and Old Man Sandy Albritton in Everglade, and some of them older Browns at Chokoloskee."

Sally was glaring at Whidden's blue tin cup. "Smallwoods! Houses! Browns! How about Hardens? Your family knew him a lot better than these flea-bitten old-timers who are still slinging it around about Ed Watson, how their daddies told Watson this and he said that! Just to show they know something important, which they don't! The little they know that's not hand-me-down lies and bragging from their daddies comes straight out of the magazines and books, most of it wrong!"

This was true and Lucius nodded but Sally ignored him. Her gaze remained fixed upon her husband with a look that promised she would settle with him later. "Lee Harden called Old Man D. D. House 'the leader of the outlaws.' So why would you send Mister Colonel to listen to a House?"

Whidden said quietly, "The House boys thought what they done that day was right. They did not back away from it or talk their way around it, not like some."

But Sally knew he had been drinking and went storming off to bed, and after that, they remained silent for a while. Looking forward to putting his boat into the water, happy they were headed for the Islands, Whidden contemplated his guest with affection. "Seems to me," he said at last, "I been settin around with Mister Colonel Watson since the world began. And them good old times are startin to come back." Swaying erect, heading for bed, he nodded and smiled, eyes shining with fond reveries, but for an hour afterwards, before Lucius finally slept, he could hear the reverberation of their voices, rising, falling.

Next morning when Lucius awoke, Whidden's truck was gone. He listened to Sally run a bath, heard the rub of her pretty hip on the porcelain tub, and suffered a sad aching sense of loss. When she came in, she smiled affectionately and said, "Plain Lucius!" but she wasn't flirting.

Barefoot, Sally fixed his breakfast, steamy and fresh as a pink shrimp in her white towel bathrobe. Observing her movements at the stove, he longed to retreat between her legs, never to be seen on earth again. Feeling weak and hungover, he murmured finally, "You are very beautiful this morning, Mrs. Harden. And I miss you."

She turned to investigate his expression, the long fork dripping grease into the pan. "Don't, Lucius. Please." She turned her back on him. "I'll take you to Naples as soon as you're finished," she said coolly and carefully, in warning to them both.

In a while, her voice came brightly, "Ol' Mister Colonel! Whidden sure talked about ol' Mister Colonel after he came to bed! Just went on and on about the old days!" She faced him again. "Made me feel funny, as if I'd lied to him about you, though I haven't. He has never asked. I just lay there listening, as if I knew hardly anything about you!" Her eyes were misty as she turned back to his bacon.

WHIDDEN HARDEN

After E. J. Watson's death, folks reckoned they'd seen the last of that man's family. Camped and squatted in the Watson Place just as they pleased, and over the years they took away pret' near everything, nailed down or otherwise. So it must of been hard for his younger boy to come home to the Islands and see what that old place had come to.

When he first showed up around nineteen and nineteen, Lucius Watson—he was still called Lucius—spent a fortnight at his daddy's place, then kept on going south to Lost Man's River. First thing he done was offer Chatham to Lee Harden, on the condition he could live there, too, in the little Dyer cabin down the bank. Pa told him how a certain family had sold the quit-claim to the Bend to the Chevelier Corporation, and he got all hot and bothered, saying his dad's title was still good, no matter what.

Only trouble was, Pa didn't want the place, no more'n my Grandpa wanted it before him. Hardens was fishermen, not farmers. They did not care to see forty acres of good ground goin to waste. Also, most local fishermen had motorboats by then, so Chatham River was already too close to Chokoloskee. And though Pa hated to admit it, the Bend spooked him.

Lee Harden had always been uneasy on the Bend, right from a boy. Bad power there, that's what he was told by his cousin Cory Osceola. Finally Lucius Watson gave up on the Bend, moved south, built a small shack on our shell ridge back of Lost Man's Beach. And after that day, in all the times he went up Chatham River with Lee Harden, he hardly never went ashore, not even when Pa stopped to pick guavas or ladle up some water from the cistern. Fell dead silent, passin that gray house and that big old raggedy plantation out behind it, hardly never took a look in that direction. Colonel Watson was the lonesomest person on the earth, that's what my ma told me.

Mister Colonel—that's how I called him then, how I still think of him—was kind of my adopted uncle, and Lost Man's River was his adopted home. For the better part of thirty years, he lived just down the beach there at South Lost Man's. He was a well-built and good-lookin man maybe six foot tall, fair hair bleached out by the sun but thick dark brows and a brown skin from long days on the water. According to his sister Pearl up to Caxambas, he took after his mother, kind of wishful-looking, same gray eyes and little sideways smile. Spoke very soft when he spoke at all, and had real nice manners like his daddy. Mr. Lucius Watson was a real old-fashioned gentleman—a regular Kentucky Colonel, that's what my ma called him. Tant Jenkins heard that, and one day sung out, "Good mornin, Colonel!" And pretty soon the man was goin by that name, though us kids put a Mister to it, out of respect.

Mister Colonel never cared for his new name. "I am no Colonel, sir," he'd say when he was drinking. "I am Machinist's Mate Second Class Lucius Hampton Watson! U.S. Navy!" He'd put on a loony dangerous look when he talked like that, to make us children laugh, but all the same, he kind of enjoyed the sound of that old stuff. "I was born in the Indian Country in 1889, the year that Belle Starr died by an unknown hand!"—he enjoyed the sound of that one, too. I've heard him come out with it even when he thought he was alone, just to let the birds in on what ailed him.

Us Hardens sure liked Mister Colonel, everybody on this coast liked Mister Colonel, even them men who was afraid of him, but nobody could figure out just what he wanted. He was pretty close to thirty then but acted like a lanky homesick boy—a homesick boy who talked too quiet, walked too quiet, and could shoot pretty near as good as the man who taught him. He could drill a curlew through both eyes so's not to waste no meat, and that kind of shootin scared them men that was ready to be scared of Watsons in the first place. They figured Ed Watson was crazy, and if the father was crazy, the son might be, too.

By the time he come home to the Islands, the tales about his dad was worse than ever, and them terrible stories made the son withdraw from people. Even Browns and Thompsons who was his dad's friends was very uneasy around Watson's son, they couldn't figure what this man was thinking, they didn't really want nothing to do with him.

Course Mister Colonel made things worse by askin questions of anybody who might tell him anything about what happened that October day of 1910. A lot of 'em he spoke to knew more than they let on, and some knew less, but nobody didn't care none for his questions. Then one day he was seen writin somethin on a scrap of paper, and next thing you know, them rumors started that Colonel Watson was takin down the names of all the men who fired at his daddy. If Colonel weren't such a sweet-natured feller, some edgy darn fool would of put a bullet through him long ago, that's what my pa said. Said if that man don't move very careful, they might do it yet.

Every man down in the rivers had growed leery, and maybe Bill House and his brothers most of all. Once that family heard that Watson's boy was back, they kept a real sharp eye out, cause they never knew when he might be comin nor what he might do after he got there. There weren't no knowin where he might be headed, and he didn't always wave. He was a loner. A man might sense something and glance around, get maybe no more'n a glimpse of that blue skiff crossin a narrow channel between islands. Hardly no wake at all, no more'n a alligator. On land, that man could come up on you soft as a panther, even on a crunchy old shell beach, and he could disappear in that same way. You looked around and that blue skiff was gone.

Mister Colonel fished up and down the coast, but his home was with our Harden clan at Lost Man's River. The men of Chokoloskee Bay was feudin with our family, and Watson's son throwin in with us that way—though we was glad to have him—made things more dangerous for him, and for us, too.

I was born at Lost Man's River and grew up mostly with my folks, so I grew up with Colonel Watson, too. Hardens had knew his daddy well but nobody spoke too much about him, only me. After I heard about how he died I asked Mister Colonel some hard questions, sneakin up on him real crafty so's he wouldn't know what I was gettin at. And he tolerated this because I was a young boy, and also because he was good-hearted and knew the Hardens meant him well no matter what. And over the years he told me what he knew.

When he first come, Mister Colonel had a plan to repair his daddy's house for a Miss Lucy he had planned to marry, though he never mentioned her except when he was drinking. She had lived on Chatham Bend as a little girl, he said, she was his true love. Well, he weren't in the Islands hardly a year when his true love married someone else. Mister Colonel had a lovin nature, and for a long while after that, I believe he was half in love with Sadie Harden, but bein a gentleman, he never said nothin nor done nothin, so Hardens never give it no thought neither.

Lee Harden used to tell about this stranger who turned up in a skiff one time at Lost Man's Beach. Wiry feller with a black head of hair and a thin beard, spoke short and crusty. He was dead pale with smooth soft hands but seemed to know what he was doin in a boat. They said, "You off a ship someplace?" and he said, "No, I rowed down here from Everglade." His hands was raw, all blistered up, but the man was tough cause he did not complain. Pa said, "Well, that's far enough for a man ain't used to pullin oars. What can we do for ye?" He thought this feller looked some way familiar.

Feller said his name was Tucker, John D. Tucker. He claimed to be Wally Tucker's nephew, said he wanted to pay his last respects where E. J. Watson killed his aunt and uncle. So my folks took him over to the key where the Tuckers was buried back in 1901, and when they come near that burial place, this John Tucker come out all feverish and sweaty and he could not hide it. So when he asked the whereabouts of Lucius Watson, Hardens got the idea he had a feud to settle, so they told him that the last they heard, Lucious Watson had left south Florida for parts unknown. The stranger give 'em a hard eye, cross and dissatisfied. He said, "That's what they told me in Chokoloskee, too." And Lee Harden laughed and said, "Well, for once them goddamn people told some truth."

They wrapped this feller's hands in rags and watched him row away back toward the north. From his questions they had figured out that he knew more than he should about the Tuckers, considerin there weren't no witnesses that could of told him. Then it come to Pa why he looked familiar, beard or no beard. This man was Rob Watson, E.J.'s oldest boy, the one that run away in 1901.

Rob Watson had not believed them people when they told him his young brother had moved away. By the time he got to Lost Man's River, he was likely wonderin if these Island people had killed his brother and buried him someplace back in the mangroves.

When Mister Colonel come back from Flamingo, he started fishin commercial with Hoad Storter. Them fellers would always bring their catch to our Harden fish house at Wood Key, hose 'em and weigh 'em, ice 'em down, go get some rest. Like everyone else, they got their nets tore up on all them orster bars, but Colonel never minded. He'd whittle him a new needle out of red mangrove, which God made tough and limber for that purpose, then set in the sun and mend net all day long. Watchin him perched like a egret on his bow, hour after hour—that was my first real memory of Mister Colonel. You couldn't never guess what he was thinkin.

Though he never said straight out about it or complained or nothin, he talked sometimes how he come back there to represent his father's family and show the Bay people that Watson's son—or this son anyways—was not ashamed of him. Said nobody put that duty on his head except Lucius Watson, but all the same, he felt obliged to live his life there. Made a livin as a fisherman, read all them books he had there in his shack, and drank rye whiskey. Whiskey was his enemy, I guess.

Mister Colonel was well educated, he knew much more than he would ever tell, but he was modest, always set himself aside. He meant it, too, it weren't a humble show like some people. As Pa would say, "Colonel Watson is a real fine man that don't appreciate himself." In that way, he reminded us of Henry Short.

Them two good men was both close to my family but could never be friends. Mister Colonel knew about them foolish rumors that Henry was the man who killed his daddy, but he never spoke bad about Henry Short and he didn't hate him, not so far as anyone could tell. My ma told him more'n once what Henry Short told *her*, that he never took part in killing Mr. Watson, but because Mister Colonel would only nod when she said that, and never made no other sign about it, she warned Henry Short to stay away from him.

Mister Colonel never spoke against his family, never spoke of 'em at all. When he would tell us that he had no family, what he meant was, no one to go home to. All he had was that Daniels-Jenkins bunch around Caxambas that his people at Fort Myers never spoke about. Sometimes he might mention how he missed his sister Carrie or his brother Rob, especially after Hardens told him how Rob come huntin him that time, then went away again. Otherwise he never let on about how lonesome his life was, though from time to time, when he was drinkin, he would remind me and my older brother Roark how lucky we was to have such a fine family of lovin folks to raise us up. Sadie Harden said that all poor Colonel wanted was to find a place in life where he belonged. Said that all his life, all he was lookin for was the way home.

Mister Colonel wore shoes most of the time, which few men did in them days in the Islands. He stayed clean and neat in his appearance, very—that man bathed and shaved most every night! Harden women done his washing and they darned his socks. Outside, he wore a cap or hat, but always pushed it far back on his head, or rolled the front, so's nobody wouldn't take that hat too serious. Comin inside, he'd take it off, tidy his clothes. Never came to the table without first brushing his hair. He was our adopted uncle, and he brought us presents. We was poor, so if he hadn't brought some, we'd of never got any. Bring us kids a whole bushel of bubble gum—three hundred pieces!

Mister Colonel ate most of his Sunday meals with us. He kept his own shack down the beach but was always invited to Thanksgiving and Christmas. He loved to cook and was real good at it, and he canned a lot of vegetables with my ma, but behind them smiles he offered at our table, he always seemed a little sad to us, watching his own life pass him by. At Lost Man's, neighbors was few and far between. There weren't no spare women on that coast, and he didn't hunt one. He was forty or fifty when our ma told him, "Colonel, don't let the past eat you alive! You've never let yourself have any happiness, and it's time to start!" And Mister Colonel said, "Might be too late to teach old dogs new tricks, seems like to me." And he'd grin that sideways grin of his, to make sure nobody took him no more serious than they took his hat.

He would not whine. Never talked too much about his dad, only when drinking. "My dad might of been all right," he might say sometimes, "if they'd told the truth about him. It was all those lies that got him so riled up, like how he murdered his own friend Guy Bradley." Mister Colonel would never say if his dad had killed people or not, he would only relate how kind he always was to his wives and children, how he looked after 'em so well, and was always generous to his friends and neighbors. "It's so hard to believe all those terrible stories, don't *you* think so?" he might say, "How a good kind man could turn overnight into a coldhearted killer?" And Hardens could not explain that either, they could not help him.

Mister Colonel was huntin the truth about his father, he wanted to find out who he really was, but he couldn't never find a truth that satisfied him. That's why he could never let go of his death. People will tell you Colonel Watson never spoke about his father—well, he tried, but after a while he give it up. It was the Bay people who would not discuss Ed Watson, not with Colonel! Even old family friends would go dead quiet on him, kickin the ground. They were afraid of him, Lee Harden said, knowin Colonel's belief that lynch law had condemned and executed E. J. Watson. They never knew who he hated worst, the ones who gunned his father down or his father's so-called friends who stood back by the store and watched 'em do it. Hardens was about the only ones that weren't in one bunch or the other. By the end we was the only family who made him welcome, knowin he didn't hate no one at all.

When rumors started about his list of names, there was plenty of talk about gettin Colonel first. The men figured he was dead set on revenge—just a matter of time, they said, before this nice soft-speakin feller went dead crazy and picked off every man on that damn list he could draw a bead on. But years went by and nothin happened and nobody ever seen no list, and meanwhile poor Colonel never harmed a soul. Finally the Bay people figured out that Colonel Watson weren't cut out to kill nobody, he was too gentle, too kindhearted, and never meant no harm. When still in his younger years, he had come home to the Islands, and he went and become a older feller right beside 'em, and all that while, he was neighborly and friendly, even to them that spited him and cut him cold. But it was too late, they had lost their chance to be in friendship with him, so some of 'em said what a pity it was that he was so standoffish like his daddy, and never give nobody no chance to know him.

That year the Park come in, Mister Colonel had to move out of the Islands same as everybody. Most of us Hardens went to Everglade, where I took a couple years in school. From all our good tutorin at home, I could read-and-write-and-rithmetic better than anybody in my grade except a sassy girl named Sally Daniels who had a snappy brain to see her through. As for Mister Colonel, he just lived along on his little boat, went here and there— Caxambas, Everglade, Flamingo. Kind of a drifter. Lived some seasons with other fishermen on houseboat lighters back of Turkey Key, and mostly stayed clear of Chokoloskee, like before. I reckon he liked to drink as much as most. Course us fishermen didn't have no cocktails like you see today. Mister Colonel, he'd go get his pint and he'd turn it up till he got it all, then shiver hard like a wet dog and step out tall. Goin down the beach under the moon, his back looked like a block of wood, real stiff and straight!

When he moved away north—that's when I lost track of him. He was finishin up his degree at the University, finishin up his history book on south-west Florida, but he never told nobody about that, and we sure never learned it till much later. When he come back south here a few years ago is when he kind of settled at Caxambas, but I never seen him from one year to the next.

Today all them Bay families will tell you how they loved ol' Colonel. Maybe some did but damn few showed it, and that shy quiet feller never knew. That's why he come to Lost Man's River and stayed with us for most of thirty years.

*

In the phone booth on the empty mall, Lucius studied the toe of his own shoe amongst the flattened soda bottle caps and cigarette butts. Outside the booth, a shining grackle waddled on the pavement, bright cruel eye cocked for a scrap to toss and pick apart and gobble.

"You mean *Colonel* Watson?"

"That's right."

His explanation to Bill House's son—that he was writing a biography of E. J. Watson and wished to ask about his late father's conclusions about Watson's death—was met by silence. Lucius breathed deeply, trying to stay calm. A meeting with Andy House was critical, not only because his clan had been the spine of the Watson posse but because only the Houses might know the truth about the man rumored to have fired first.

Among the members of the posse (all of whom he had identified and tried in vain to question years before), only a few such as the House men had readily acknowledged taking part—not that they had talked to him about it. As for the rest, anger and guilt, fear and special pleading, had muddied their "eyewitness" accounts. A few of these men, out of pride in their inside information on the most vivid event in the region's history—or even the need of a better story with which to repay young Watson for their drink—had affirmed the rumor about Henry Short. Lucius himself thought it inconceivable that Henry Short had fired at his father, yet what had once been a stray rumor had become so commonplace that he needed the House clan to put it to rest once and for all.

Years ago he had confronted Henry—uselessly, since the man had had no choice but to deny any participation in the shooting. In those days Henry's life was still in danger, whereas now he had moved away somewhere, and many years had passed, and those who had been out to punish him were old or gone. If he was still alive and could be located, he might dare to tell the truth, and even wish to do so, to be done with it.

*

House's voice was there again, equable, mild, as if he had listened sympathetically to Lucius's thoughts. "Just so we understand each other, Colonel. My granddad and my dad and Uncle Dan and Uncle Lloyd, they was all in on it, and none of 'em decided later they done wrong." The voice paused a moment to let that settle. "I don't reckon I'm the one to decide that for 'em. I ain't glad about what they done but I don't aim to tell you I am sorry, neither." Another pause. "Still want to come all the way out here?"

Lucius said yes. Queried nervously by a woman in the background, House asked if he had any reason for coming that he had not mentioned. Lucius said simply, "I hoped you could help me locate Henry Short."

"That's honest, anyways. Maybe I can help, maybe I can't. Depends on what you want him for." The voice paused again. "Come ahead, then, Colonel." There came the clatter of a dropped receiver, then the same calm voice, soothing someone else. "It's all right, sweetheart. Yes, he's on his way." The telephone was fumbled roughly while being hung up, and House's voice continued through the bump and clatter. "Now, Sue, no need to be afraid of Colonel just cause he's a Watson . . ."

*

Golden Years Estates, in the Big Cypress country between Naples and Immokalee, was a vast pale waste in the flat landscape. Everywhere, the broken forest had been bulldozed into ramparts of tree skeletons and blackened stumps, leaving dead white clay where fossil limestone seabeds lay exposed. Fires smoldered in the desolation, and thick smoke rose to a thick and humid sky. In the near distance, ancient cypress trees in funereal Spanish moss drew back affrighted from the earth-mauling machines, which brooded among white sterile pools like yellow dinosaurs. In a litter of raw pipe and tubing, plastic cups and mud-stuck newspapers, and scraps of pine lumber crusted with gray cement, stood a lone outhouse of a bad zinc green with a stink of carnivores and a rusted door which banged in the wet wind. Here and there in this desolation, a hard-edged house perched naked on a "crescent"—Cypress Crescent, Panther Crescent, Sunset Crescent. Andy House had said laconically that his "retirement estate" could be found on Panther Crescent, but these streets seemed makeshift and unfinished, and the street signs still lay scattered on the ground.

The only living thing in sight was a big florid man in khaki shirt and trousers peering outward from a doorway. He stood like a sentinel, staring away over the white waste as if in hope of rescue, or reinforcements at the very least. "I'll be on the lookout," Andy House had said, but this man gave no sign that he awaited someone. Only when Lucius drew off the crescent onto the short driveway did he lift a vague hand in the car's direction. The last time Lucius had seen this man was when the Houses lived at Chatham Bend back in the twenties.

"Notice any panthers crossing Panther Crescent?" Andy House had grown from a sturdy straw-haired boy to a big ruddy man with blue eyes in a steadfast gaze which went right past Lucius's head toward the surrounding distance. Not until he thrust out his hand, which his visitor caught after some fumble and adjustment, did Lucius realize that Andy House was sightless.

"I chose this here retirement estate on account of all the panthers," House said wryly. "Hoped I might hear one screamin in the night." Holding on to Lucius's hand, the blind man was still facing outward, as if trying to fathom the great silence of his surroundings. "Funny, ain't it? They been sellin this swamp-and-overflowed to suckers since before I was born, and I never caught on to the deal till a few years back when I bought some myself. They couldn't find no more darn fools to buy land underwater, so they dredged out ditches, laid roads on the fill, then called them ditches 'bayous' and 'canals' and sold 'em off as prime waterfront property. Done that first at Miami, Naples, then up and down both coasts. Today there ain't hardly no coast left in all south Florida outside of the Park, so they're doin the same darn thing back up inland! All you need is some old tract of swamp and you are in business. All you got to do is dredge and fill.

"Well, don't let me get started blowin off steam about what they're doin to the backcountry just cause I ain't got nothin else to do!" He raised big heavy arms and let them fall. "One of the big attorneys makin a fortune on this mess you're lookin at, he's supposed to be some kind of kin to Watsons. I won't say a word against the man cause he is a big shot over to Miami. Might send some Spanish over here to beat me up."

"Watson Dyer?"

"You said the name, not me. Called him Watt or Wattie in the old days."

"Well, at least he's trying to help stop the Park from burning our old house," said Lucius, sounding more loyal to Dyer than he felt.

"You mind tellin me what's in it for him?"

"He was born there," Lucius said finally.

"That might be reason enough for you or me." Andy House rocked a little on the heels of high square-toed black shoes which looked more like shoe boxes. "Hell, I don't know a thing about it. Just bitchin, is all. Don't you pay this mean old sinner no attention."

A woman poked her head out of the door but Lucius's smile only scared her back inside. "Good thing God struck me blind, I guess," Andy was saying. "What I figured I was buying in this 'planned community' was a little house out in the Cypress, surrounded by green woods and fresh water. Can't see the trees too good no more, but I sure could enjoy them musky smells and swamp cries in the night, maybe the roarin of a big bull gator in the spring-time. Sound just like a ol' outboard, crankin up!" The blind man nodded. "I guess you heard *that* racket plenty times!"

He turned toward the door. "Well, it ain't likely I'll be hearin no bull gator, nor no panther neither, cause after I had this place all bought and paid for, they changed the plan, drained off the swamp, stripped off the cypress. Had to make some room for more retirement estates, I reckon. Tore out every tree they could mangle up with their machines, smashed the country flat. And before they could clean up the mess they made, they run out of money, and before I could get out of the whole deal, I run out, too."

He waved vaguely at the wasteland all around him. "These eyes can't see what all that money went for, and I reckon that's a mercy. Can't even smell it. Ain't nothin left alive out there to smell. But I can hear the deadness of it, night or day." He rapped the thin wall of his house. "You ever need you a re-tirement estate, I reckon I know where you could get one pretty cheap."

Inside, the house was neat and comfortable, with all blinds drawn against the desolation. "This here is Colonel Watson, Sue." House spoke in the gen-eral direction of the kitchen, where a pretty white-haired woman, wiping her hands upon her apron, peered out at their guest. "Don't you make no false moves, Colonel," the blind man whispered for his wife to hear, "cause that poor little lady in the kitchen is deathly afraid of Watsons. Scared you might of come out here to bump me off." He shifted a chair in Lucius's di-rection, then lowered himself with a heavy sigh onto the sofa. "Speaking about bumping off, you might be doing me a kindness," he confided. "You make a nice clean job of it, don't make no mess for poor Sue to clean up, I might throw this here retirement estate in on the deal."

"Andy, you just stop those kind of jokes!" his poor wife cried, and he said sheepishly, "Now, Sue, you know I'd never leave you out here all alone. Not with all them panthers!" Hearing Lucius laugh, Andy smiled for the first time, and his wife looked reproachfully at this stranger for encouraging her husband's wry despair.

"Never sat still in my whole life, now I sit all day," Andy House said, still surprised. "Can't get the hang of it. Nosir, God struck this sinner blind, and I don't know why." He waved a big hand toward the kitchen where his wife was preparing lemonade and cookies. "She hauls me off to church, y'know, morning, noon, and night, but I don't think that'll change His mind, do you?"

Unsettled by House's wide clear gaze, Lucius could find nothing comfort-ing to say. And the blind man spared him, folding big gold-haired hands upon his lap. "So," he said. "I remember that day many years ago when you come to Chatham Bend to speak with Houses."

Lucius nodded. "Your dad didn't care to speak with me, remember?"

"Colonel, my dad liked you fine. He felt real bad about what happened, as far as the Watson children was concerned. He weren't naturally unfriendly, you know that—just the opposite. But I reckon he figured that if Watson's son was out to take revenge, Bill House would probably serve as good as anybody.

"W. W., known as Bill—my dad—looked just like me, remember? Big nose and ruddy, not what you'd call top of the line for looks. That second time you come, huntin for Henry, Dad weren't so much unfriendly as plain frustrated. This was mostly because of his own brother-in-law—don't you put this in your book!—who every year was growin to be more successful in his store while poor Dad endured one failure after another. He was still swallerin the fact that he had ended up in middle life as caretaker for the Chevelier Corporation on that half-overgrowed and godforsook plantation.

"One time my dad went to see your brother Eddie. Had the money saved for some insurance, and he aimed to show him there weren't no hard feelings, nothing personal. Told him he wanted to let bygones be bygones, and Eddie acted like he felt that same way. But I bet you won't drop dead from surprise if I tell you your brother could be, well, kind of malicious. For all his friendly words and jokes, he talked bad about most everyone behind their back. Eddie was very polite that day, and he took Dad's business, but after that insurance was all bought and paid for, he stood up from behind his desk and he let Dad know that E. E. Watson was a good Christian businessman who done his best to practice his Christian forgiveness, but still and all, Mr. House should of took his business someplace else. And Dad come out of there red in the face, never got over it! He said, 'See that? Good Christian businessman, practicin forgiveness! Forgive me for just long enough to take my money!' "

Andy House fell quiet, as if giving his visitor an opportunity to defend his brother. With his clear eyes, he seemed to measure not only the workings of Lucius's brain but the world beyond. When Lucius remained silent, Andy shrugged. "Took you a good while to show up at the Bend to talk with Dad, as I recall. We wondered why. Saved Bill House for last, is what we figured, and that kind of spooked us. I wasn't but a boy back then, but I can still see your blue cedar skiff coming down the river under sail, how she turned up-current, lost her headway, and touched at our little dock light as a butterfly. I don't believe you ever used an oar!" He shook his head with pleasure in that memory.

Hearing his wife fixing a tray, Andy included her in his account of Lucius Watson, knowing she had not missed a word. "Colonel sung out a hello, and he waited right there for an answer before coming any closer to the house—

that was Island custom—and when he got it, he come up the path unarmed. All the same, Dad had his rifle loaded, not rightly knowing what Ed Watson's son was after. Maybe Colonel didn't know himself, is what my Dad thought. All we knew about this feller, he was keeping some kind of a list, and Dad was on it, maybe number one.

"Dad told us to get out of the way, there might be trouble. He stood in the doorway, offered our visitor a seat on the screened porch. Colonel said 'Thank you, much obliged,' but never crossed the sill. He stood there in the sun on the porch steps, turning his straw hat in both hands, and inquired real quiet and polite if Dad would care to tell him exactly what led up to E. J. Watson's death that day at Smallwood's landing."

House turned toward his guest. "My dad did not care to talk to you, not really. Granddad House was dead, and Dad had the responsibility for the House family, and here was Watson's son right on his doorstep. This was more'n fifteen years after the shooting, and by that time the Watson story was all turned around so that Ed Watson was a real fine feller who got murdered because them House people was jealous of his cane! Houses was the ringleaders in a darned ambush, they shot Watson in the back—that story was started up by our own kin!"

Andy ruminated bitterly, almost as if—because he could not see him—Lucius were not there. "No, Dad never had no argument with Colonel Watson. He felt bad for you. But having heard about that list, he was leery, too.

"See, Dad never took to Mr. Watson the way Smallwoods done, never pretended to. I believe he told you short and plain how he fired at your dad and probably hit him, and how that was all he aimed to say about it. He would not tell who else was present, let alone who fired the first shot. And he told you you were a damn fool to keep that list. Spoke pretty rough, as I recall, and you went redder'n a redbird. Next, you asked to speak with Henry Short, and I guess you did. That was twenty-five years ago, and now you're back, wantin to speak with Henry Short again! Don't look like we're making too much progress!"

"It's just that I'd like to understand things better—"

"That day Henry stayed out of the way until you asked to see him. When you went over to the boat shed and talked to him alone, Dad kept a close eye on you from the screened porch. Had his gun handy in case you lost your head, tried to shoot our nigra. I reckon Henry was uneasy, too." The blind man thought awhile. "But you must of come to some kind of understanding, because Henry wouldn't never tell what Colonel Watson asked nor how he answered. I reckon Henry had lived long enough to know that anything a nigra said could be turned against him."

Lucius told Andy that Henry had been tense, which had made his account cryptic and unsatisfactory. If he could locate him, he would like to try again. When the other remained silent, Lucius added, "I was told you might know where to find him."

"I might," the blind man said, still noncommittal. He raised a big hand in a plea for silence while he considered this. Finally he said, "And I might not." The blue eyes were unblinking, and the silence grew. Lucius knew that any effort to assure House about his good intentions would only make him appear more intent on Henry. Finally he stood up, saying thank you. He fully understood, he said, why Andy had to be careful, but reminded him that if he'd wanted to harm Henry Short, "there were many years down in the rivers when it would have been easy to catch Henry alone. And nobody would have said a thing about it."

Andy raised thick colorless eyebrows. "I reckon that is correct," he said. "Sit down, Colonel. I'll tell you what I know."

ANDY HOUSE

Henry Short was a very uncommon man. His mother was the daughter of a well-to-do planter from my granddad's district, out of Spartansburg, South Carolina. She was a white girl but the father was brown—mostly Injun with some white and nigra, what country people used to call red-bone mulatta.

Now this was in the early years after Reconstruction was got rid of and what they called Southern Redemption had come in, and Redemption was the worst of times for any nigra who still hung on to any notion he was free and equal. Henry's father was one of that kind, very brave and foolish. He was a handsome kind of feller, and he had him a fine horse from his days out west as a buffalo soldier in the federal militia. Fought Comanches in Texas and the like. He got dead sick of killing Injuns, that's what he told people, cause in his opinion, it weren't the Injuns who deserved killing. Talk like that made folks uneasy, black folks, too, and this young feller never fit with neither. He would not learn that a colored man could no longer speak out in the same manner he had got away with during Reconstruction, even in the Indian Territory, where his breed was common.

That buffalo soldier was not ashamed about his blood, and his pride cost him his life. He rode too hard and talked too much, he figured that was his bounden right as a cavalry soldier and new citizen. Henry's daddy was just the kind them redshirts and night riders would come after, and when he got mixed up with a white girl—well, that finished him. The girl denied that he had raped her, but nobody paid that no attention. That baby was all the proof they needed that this nigger was too big for his damn britches. Folks never give a thought back then to a brown baby with a white daddy, but a white mother was another thing entirely, never mind that the baby might be the exact same shade, same sound, same smile and smell.

Henry's daddy would not repent or beg, and for that he was punished something terrible. A merciful death was about all of the Lord's mercy he could hope or pray for, but them men tutored him about repentance first—whip, knife, and fire. Them good Christians was just plain "indignant," that's what their weekly newspaper reported. But after a while, the evening was gettin late so they give up on his education, just gelded and burned that poor young feller and went home to bed.

The baby boy was give to a wet nurse and hid away on the next planta-tion. His mother would slip over there to visit, help as best she could. But Henry weren't but four years old when that planter moved away and took his nigras with him. It must of broke the poor mother's heart to see her first-born carried off just like a slave child! That little boy was riding up behind the man and crying for his mama, so the man got tired of his yowling and threw him down and made him walk. When he couldn't keep up, the man commenced to whipping him along, and right about then, Mr. D. D. House come down the road.

My granddad Daniel David House was fiery and stubborn, no one jostled him or told him what to do. He was the black sheep of a well-to-do family, ran away to the War Between the States with his daddy's favorite horse, went north and south with it. When the War was over, he returned that horse somewhat the worse for wear, and his father cared more about that horse than he did about his boy safe home from war. He was disowned.

Granddad had two wives as a young man, lost 'em both in childbirth. Bein D. D. House, he figured the mothers must be faulty, so he dumped them children off on their maternal grandparents and hunted up another female that might suit him better. Granddad House was hard that way, though a good man in most respects. When he got married that third time, he headed south to the Florida frontier to change his luck.

See that old photograph across the room? That fierce-lookin feller in the round black hat is D. D. House, and that scared young thing beside him is the former Miss Blanche Ida Borders, who knew everything there was to know about Christian worshiping. Mamie Ulala and my dad were already in the world when that was taken.

Riding down to Florida, Granddad seen one of the many things he would not tolerate. This little brown boy on the high road was so scrawny and so weak, and here was this jackass whipping him along. So Granddad rode up, told the man to quit, and when he refused, he knocked him sprawling. Feller hollered, "That there pickaninny is lawful mine to do with what I please!" And Granddad said, "Nosir, not no more he ain't." He set that little boy up on his wagon and took him on south to Arcadia. Give him the last name of Short because he was so small and puny, and after that, he pretty much forgot about him. But that little boy never forgot. Far as Henry was concerned, Daniel David House was right up there with God.

Now Granddad House fought Abolition in the War but he didn't hold no more with common slavery. He never seen Henry as no slave, and I sure would hate to think we ever owned him. But Henry Short was with my family from the age of four years old, and people always spoke of him as "Houses' nigger."

The family stopped off in Arcadia on the Peace River, homesteaded 160 acres, improved it up, had 5 good acres of bearing orange grove. In them days plenty of kids died off, got pinworms, got big bellies and went all yeller-looking, turned up their toes. But when they went with Granddad over to the coast, ate plenty of mullet, why, they would get well. So he decided to live near the sea, and he loaded 'em all into the wagon, went to Punta Gorda and took ship to Everglade, and farmed for a few years up Turner River. Had to board the hogs up every night, that's how thick the panthers was in them days. And the kids got well, got meaner'n the devil, and Grandma raised Henry right along with 'em. Henry and my dad was the same age, them two come up together.

D. D. House raised his boys up to be honest, and most of 'em stayed that way, least till he died, but there wasn't a one of 'em except my dad was as dead honest as Henry grew to be. He was the most honest man I ever knew, never mind all the pretendin that nigras had to do back then just to stay healthy.

So Henry started out in life a scared and puny little feller, but later on he grew into his own, six foot two and solid. Had the skull and features of a white man, and his skin stayed light. He had bushy eyebrows, too, and a mustache. He was very clean and neat, shaved every day—Henry Short wore out a lot of old straight razors!

In his younger years, Henry was well-esteemed in Chokoloskee. Never had no trouble with white folks before Watson died. Ate apart and slept apart—that's how he wanted it—because Granddad's family back in Carolina always had nigras and knew how to treat 'em, so Henry Short was treated that same way. He was the only colored on Chokoloskee Island at that time, and there ain't been one since, not so's you'd notice. Even today, you can walk around that island for a month and never spot one.

In Jim Crow days, right up into the thirties, good Christian men was terribly concerned, saying nigras was too primitive to handle their black animal natures around white women. Burnings and lynchings was still popular all around the country, to teach 'em a lesson for their own darn good. That's what become of Henry's daddy, and lynchings by fire was all the rage in Henry's day. So Henry Short always made sure he was never alone with no white woman, no matter what. White woman might holler an order to come help her—even Grandma Ida!—and he'd go stone-deaf on her unless other folks was there to witness it. A woman wanted Henry Short to do something, she would have to get her man to tell him, that's how very careful Henry was.

One time our men was out huntin in the Glades, and Henry was hunting right beside 'em, so it bothered Dad to see Henry always eatin a ways off and by himself. So my dad said, "Henry, you just bring your plate on over here, you set with us." Well, Henry went deaf on him, pretended he didn't hear. So Dad said, "Come on, boy, dammit, ain't nobody lookin, we're out here by ourselves!" And Henry just shook his head, he would not do it, not until Dad got mad and *ordered* him to do it—then it was okay. Dad told him, "Boy, you best look out you don't get yourself whipped for disobedience!"

Later Dad felt sheepish and pretended he was joking, but Henry knew he wasn't joking, not entirely. After that he would eat with the House men when they were out somewhere away from everybody, but always setting just a little bit off to one side, and not until he'd fixed our dinner first. Finally Dad give up on him, let him eat by himself if that was what he wanted.

No, Henry Short never forgot what they done to his father. He was a man who knowed his place, and probably that's what saved his life, more'n one time. Henry fished and farmed right alongside of us, but he wanted to be treated like a black man. Ate apart and slept apart and never talked to no one, hardly, cause there weren't hardly nobody he could talk to. I reckon he figured that loneliness was his punishment in life for what his mama done, his punishment for being Henry. I don't reckon he ever once looked up to ask his Merciful Redeemer if he himself done a blessed thing to deserve such a lonesome fate. Henry would figure he deserved a nigra's life, so he just hunkered down and took it.

In the year after Mr. Watson's death, some of them men weren't so proud no more about that killing and were looking around for somebody to blame. That was when that story started that Henry Short had fired the fatal shot, because being a nigger, he had naturally lost his head. Next, they wanted an explanation of how he got there in the first place, and why that black sonofabitch was armed, and what made him think he could get away with it—they were all for getting to the bottom of this thing right then and there.

The only trouble was, Henry was gone. Being leery of the atmosphere around that place, he had left Chokoloskee quick and he never went back. He went to fish with the Hardens around Lost Man's, and got himself hitched up to Libby Harden. Henry was lighter than his wife, but he was supposed to be mulatta and she was supposed to be a white, so there was talk. It tore up Henry, broke his heart, when she run off with another man. That feller was certified white, I guess, but that was about all.

Some time after that, he left Lost Man's for good. Came back to our family, worked with my dad who was caretaking at Chatham Bend for Cheveliers and worked his own patch at House's Hammock, up the river. One time I said, "Henry? Ain't it lonely over there?" And Henry said something peculiar. He said, "Mist' Andy, it's less lonely alone." First time in all the years I knew him that I picked up a hair of bitterness in that man's voice.

In them days, this was up in the late twenties, we had lots of bananas on House Hammock, we grew ninety-pound heads! Bananas just went wild down there, you took a cane knife and chopped around 'em to clear off the vines a little, then just stood back and let 'em go! Henry had a rusty old five-horse Palmer engine in an open boat, and one day he loaded a cargo of bananas, thinking to run 'em up to Everglade next morning. But when he come down at break of day, his boat was gone! He had her tied up with a new piece of line, so he knowed for a fact that his line had never parted. He made his way across to Chatham Bend, wading and swimming, and we come back with him and we searched hard for that boat all around the bays and never found her. A few days later he found her tied up in the same place she had disappeared from. By that time his banana crop was sunburnt black, couldn't be sold.

That's the kind of tricks them brave young fellers done to That Nigger Who Dared to Raise a Gun Against a White Man. Don't rightly know which boy it was, but Shine Thompson always flared when we asked questions. I never heard of any family that resented Henry for himself. Every soul that knew that man before the trouble had a very high opinion of him as a nigra. But he left Chokoloskee after Watson died, and the younger ones had never hardly known him, only his name. So when they come across him in the rivers, they might yell at him over the water. "Hey, boy? We'll git you one day, boy, see if we don't!"

*

Andy's wife brought lemonade and cookies. The blind man thanked her and took the glass into his hand but he did not drink it, not a drop, just held his glass tight and sat in silence, working through some thought or other. Over the air-conditioning, an old-fashioned clock ticktocked in the kitchen, reminding Lucius of Ruth Ellen's house in Neamathla.

Lucius said, "At the time of the shooting, your dad signed a deposition.

Ever hear about it? It seemed like he was defending someone against rumors." Lucius paused. "Was that Henry? From what you tell me about Henry, that rumor never made very much sense."

"No sense at all. Henry was dead scared of E. J. Watson, and he wasn't crazy."

Andy's tone seemed slightly enigmatic. Lucius said gently, "No. But did he do it?"

"What are you after, Colonel? What do you think I been trying to tell you here?" The blind man turned a dangerous red, and his wife came trembling to the kitchen doorway. Sensing her there, Andy waved to reassure her.

"I'm not sure *what* you're trying to tell me," Lucius said carefully, and the blind man nodded. Aware of his wife hovering, he said in an even voice, "I don't know where Henry is living, Colonel. Last I heard, he was someplace over near Immokalee. I have the name of some people in his church. You want to run me over there tomorrow, we might try to find him."

*

According to the newspaper, there was a second suspect in the Gasparilla shooting, but there had been no formal arrest, and the victim—"the noted east coast attorney Mr. Watson Dyer"—had announced that for the moment he would press no charges. Since Rob had been kidnapped by Speck's men, and since Speck was Dyer's man on Chatham Bend, Lucius had to conclude that Dyer himself had arranged the abduction.

At Caxambas, Lucius passed an unsettled evening with his father's urn, which stood in the window like an art object or vase. At sunset, it appeared to glow in a bronze fire. He could not sleep. Feeling ridiculous, he draped the urn with a white cloth, which gave him a start when something awoke him in the night. Hearing only the soft riffles of the tide flooding the salt grass, he got up and placed the shrouded thing in a far corner before stepping outside to urinate off the deck under the flying moon.

*

On their way to Golden Years Estates next morning, Sally questioned Andy House's objectivity about Henry Short. "If you go listening to people who raised him up as a near-slave, then you'd better learn how his real friends felt about him!" And she told Lucius what she knew of Henry's friendship with the Harden family.

Henry Short had first visited the Harden clan before the turn of the century, on Mormon Key. He went there the first time with Bill House, when they worked for Jean Chevelier, collecting bird eggs. After the Hardens sold Mormon Key to E. J. Watson and moved on south to Wood Key and Lost

Man's River, Henry still came to visit when he could, because that family made him feel like a human being. Henry trusted Lee and Sadie Harden, who were to become his lifelong friends. After the death of Mr. Watson, Henry assured them that he had not taken part, but he also said, "They will hang it on the nigger."

Lee Harden said that Henry Short could swing his rifle up so fast that it would scare you, said this man was the best shot on this coast, Watson included. But he never believed that Henry shot at Watson because Henry would never line a man up in his rifle sights and pull the trigger. "Henry loved the Lord, and he lived by the Ten Commandments."

When Henry started courting Libby Harden, nobody but her brother Earl paid much attention. Libby was a beautiful coffee-colored girl, while Henry was the color of new wheat—lighter than any of the Hardens except Lee and Earl and the youngest sister Abbie. He even had blue eyes, like Mr. Watson! Henry told the family his mother was a white, and that on his daddy's side he was mostly Indian. As Sadie Harden used to say, "Henry Short is a lot more white than some of those who call him a mulatta." Except for Earl, the Hardens never thought about his color, all they saw was a fine man and a friend.

Robert Harden was mostly Choctaw with some English and Portagee mixed in, but he never cared too much what people called him so long as they let him live in peace. Some of his children favored his wife, Maisie, whose mother was Elizabeth Osceola, a granddaughter of the great war chief. So the Hardens were white and Indian on both sides, and they had nothing against black people—that much was true.

Henry Short and Libby Harden were married by the constable at Cape Sable, but pretty soon Libby ran off with a white man from Mound Key. This man told her he had money. He did not. Libby claimed her marriage to Henry Short had been performed outside the Catholic Church and was therefore officially annulled, but she never claimed that anyone annulled it. Being strong-minded like her mother, she probably just annulled it by herself.

Now Grandmother Maisie was a cruel, strong-hearted person, but she worshiped the ground that her boy Lee walked on. That old lady never did believe that his "conch bride" was good enough for Lee, and as for Sadie, she could not stand her mother-in-law, though she did her best not to say so. But even Sadie would admit that Mother Harden stood up strong for Henry Short, no matter what, and never had much use for Libby after she ran off with that Mound Key man, who had the habit of picking up anything loose he could lay his hands on, Libby included. Lee Harden said, "He might be a fine feller, but I never met a single soul who really liked him."

That pretty Libby had been Henry's consolation for a lonely life. He was heartbroken when he lost her and never got over his abandonment. He followed the Hardens to Flamingo, fished for some years around Cape Sable, but when he returned to Lost Man's River, who should he find living there but Libby and her husband. They were not happy to see Henry, and Henry couldn't stand to be so near, and he took to drinking for the first and only time in his whole life. He couldn't handle moonshine, and one night when he was drunk, he was heard to mumble that somebody ought to take and shoot that Mound Key cracker. The Hardens knew that Henry's threat was only a way to ease his torment, but they had to hush him up for his own safety. Because of the rumors about Henry's part in Watson's death, it was worse than dangerous for this man to talk this way against a white man.

Not that he talked much, having never had much practice. Libby dearly loved a conversation, and she always complained that Henry never gave her more than the bare facts even when he talked about the weather.

Before she took up with Henry Short, some of the Bay women called Libby Harden "white trash." None of their slander changed the fact that every man along the coast would have sold his soul for a bite of that golden apple, and those women knew it. So they were happy when she humiliated her family—as they saw it—by marrying Henry Short and delighted anew when she abandoned him. It did their hearts good to see the Lord humble that mulatta who had married that supposed-to-be white woman.

Henry Short was a high type of man who had a low opinion of himself. White people had robbed him of all hope for a decent life, and they took away his self-respect right along with it. That's what we did to him, the Hardens said. But Lee Harden believed that losing his Libby to another man might have saved his life, because it got the young men cracking mean jokes instead of shooting off their drunken mouths about a lynching. "When there is enough lynching talk, it is going to happen," said Lee Harden.

Sometime after World War I, Henry told Lee Harden he would not remarry and would never return to Lost Man's River. Though his grief had something to do with that decision, he also knew that his presence might draw more trouble to the Hardens, who had plenty of trouble without that. And perhaps he'd heard that Ed Watson's son was on his way back to the Islands.

*

The blind man was waiting in his doorway, a small suitcase beside him. His wife was off at church, he said, otherwise he would ask them in for a cup of coffee. Reminiscing with Colonel had made him kind of homesick, he confessed, and he wondered if—after looking for Henry at Immokalee—he might travel on with them to Chokoloskee, to visit with his relatives and friends. "As a boy, I knew your family on both sides," he told Sally politely. "Your mama's brothers were my friends down in the Islands."

"Is that a fact," Sally said coolly, as Lucius slid the blind man's bag into the trunk. She opened the front door for Andy, but the big hand fumbled deftly for the other handle and he climbed into the back over her protests. "Can't see much anyway," he told her cheerfully, "so I might's well ride in style."

They headed eastward past the Corkscrew Strand bound for Immokalee, at the edge of the Big Cypress. On the narrow road across the rough savanna, Lucius slowed to pick up a black man, although the man had not stuck out his thumb nor even turned to observe the car coming up behind. Lucius had murmured, "Must be hot, walking the road," and Andy House said, "Let's give him a ride, then."

"It's only a field hand, Mr. House—" Sally checked herself, annoyed. "I thought you might have some objection."

"If he can take it, I guess I can," Andy said easily. "I rode with plenty of 'em."

With a rattle of limestone bits striking the fenders, the car slowed and drew up on the shoulder. The stringy figure sprang sideways as if startled by a snake. Alarmed that these whites had stopped, he was smiling hard, as if resigning himself to some rough joke. When Sally offered him a bright Good morning! the black man doffed a dusty cap. "Yesm," he said. Even this single word was guarded, all one blurred and neutral syllable. He took out a bandanna and wiped his brow, glancing over his shoulder at the pine woods.

"We're headed for Immokalee," Lucius told him. "Care for a ride?"

"Hop in," said Andy, reaching across to find the door handle, patting the seat.

The man raised a hard-veined gray-brown hand to the bill of his soiled cap. Slow and careful as a lizard, trying to enter without touching anything, he eased into the car in a waft of humid heat and hard-earned odors. He could scarcely bring himself to close the door.

Asked how he liked living in Immokalee, the man chuckled, *cuk-cuk-cuk*, like a dusting chicken. " 'Mokalee." He nodded, feeling for safe ground. He would not look at them. "Any man ain't been a nigger in 'Mokalee on Sat'day night, dat man ain't *lived* right!" He chuckled a little more, *cuk-cuk-cuk-cuk*. "Dass what us niggers say."

"Oh Lord!" said Sally, when her companions laughed. She faced around toward the front.

The black man hummed a little, peering outward at the pine savanna. Over the woods, vultures circled like swirled cinders on a smoky sky. "Gone be fryin hot t'day." The black man sighed deeply, hoping for the best. "Deep-fryin hot."

"Ever come across a colored fella name of Henry Short?" Andy House asked him.

"Henry Sho't, you said?" He looked alarmed. "Nosuh I sho' ain't, nosuh. I sho' doan know no nigger by dat name."

At a main corner in the outskirts of the town, the man tapped a gray fingernail on the window, saying, "Thank'ee kin'ly, kin'ly," soft as a lullaby— *kin'ly, kin'ly*—until the car stopped at last and he got out. He was recognized at once, and cheered, by a pair of morning celebrants leaned on a wall, who brandished small flat bottles in brown paper bags. He turned to wave. "I'se in good hands now as you can see!" he cried, no longer hiding a sly smile. "I thank'ee kin'ly, white folks!" he called cheerily.

"Kin'ly, kin'ly!" Lucius repeated, not unkindly, as he drove on down the street, crossing the railroad tracks. But Sally Brown, watching the men grin, just shook her head. "Perhaps that performance still amuses your generation," she snapped tartly, "but it isn't funny, Professor, you know that?" She frowned, seeking a way to say this clearly. "I mean, if they go *calling* themselves niggers, *acting* like trashy niggers, then that's the way they're going to be seen!" This was well-intentioned, Lucius decided, but in her distress over the man's manner—his protective coloration—she had missed not only his mischievous irony but his profound rebuke, and the great poignance in it, and a dogged love of life, and beyond everything, that brave cheerfulness and in-the-bone endurance which Lucius found so moving in such people.

Eventually they tracked down a black family named Cooper which worshiped at Henry's former church. The Coopers lived in a small house at the north end of town. After consultation with their neighbors, measuring the white folks from their stoops and dooryards, they all agreed that Deacon Short didn't live here anymore, having taken work in the cane fields around Moore Haven. Yes, United Sugar. No, he had no phone and they knew no address. Their reserve seemed a sign that others had come looking for him, for these people were certainly protecting him. After another consultation, Mr. Cooper mentioned worriedly that the Deacon might be in the hospital over there. With the meeting with Dyer and the Park attorneys scheduled for next day, Moore Haven was too far out of their way. They decided to visit Henry Short on the way back.

*

They headed east on the main street, past dealerships of bright green farm machinery and auto junkyards and car body shops and whistle-stop brown saloons. Still brooding, Sally pared her nails. In this damn redneck town, back in the twenties, she had heard, a local man entered the hardware store and took a revolver from the showcase, saying, "This one kill niggers?" Then he stepped to the door and shot a field hand at the end of the pay line. "Shoots pretty good," he told the storekeeper, "I'll take it." Though the black man died, the man was never arrested, far less taken to court.

Sally stared outraged from one man to the other, awaiting their horrified reaction. When they could find nothing to say but only shook their heads, she cried out, "Can you believe that? *Shoots pretty good! I'll take it!*"

"Found the model he was looking for, I reckon," Andy said.

Speechless, Sally scrabbled for a hankie in the old straw bag that served her as a purse. Dabbing tears, she stared stonily ahead. In a bad silence, in the growing heat, the old car crossed grassy railroad tracks past stranded freight cars, then turned due south, and all the while Lucius frowned mightily in order not to smile at the sight of Andy's innocent wide eyes in the rearview mirror.

The blind man had cauterized the wound of Sally's outrage with a darker fire even more outrageous, and his boldness, under the circumstances, was breathtaking. However, he had gone too far, and both men knew it. "That weren't funny, ma'am. I know that. And I sure am sorry." The blind man frowned at the big hands in his lap, sincerely penitent. "It was just . . . you were so . . . *serious*, Miss Sally. Beg pardon? No, ma'am, I ain't makin excuses. I was wrong."

Southeast of Immokalee, where the county road made a big bend, Andy tried again to make amends. "I lived down this road in the late twenties when the KKK was cranking up, Miss Sally, and that story you told don't surprise me one little bit. That was along about the time of the Rosewood Massacre, remember that one, Colonel? When they burnt out that nigra community down west of Gainesville?" He took a great deep breath. "Folks don't care to remember no more how it was for black people in this part of the country. Still pretty bad today when you scratch down a little."

Lucius observed that Jim Crow days might have been worse around this south part of the peninsula than almost anywhere, because so many Florida pioneers had been fugitives from the Civil War or Reconstruction, bitter and unregenerate men who identified the freedmen with their loss of home. That was why so few blacks had drifted into southwest Florida, and why so few besides the migrant field hands at Immokalee had settled in this region even today.

Andy nodded. "Course in recent years, the law there in Immokalee has been a nigra. Call him Big Boy. Ain't too many, black or white, that cares to go up against this Mr. Big Boy."

"But black especially."

"But black especially. That sure is right, ma'am."

"Because blacks know that in the end your Mr. Big Boy will do what white folks tell Big Boy to do."

"Reckon that's right, too. But you got to start somewheres, I reckon."

Sally seethed and brooded, then spoke all in a burst. "I hear you've talked to Mister Colonel about Henry Short. I bet you told him Henry Short was a mulatta, and here was a man who was no more mulatta than the Hardens! Robert Harden had some Portuguese blood, and Portuguese people have that tight curly black hair—the so-called kink you people tried to pin on him!"

"You people?" The blind man raised his thick colorless brows, tugged his red ear. Anxious to be fair but unwilling to retreat, he finally said, "So far as I know, Miss Sally, I never set eyes on a Portagee even in the days I could still see one, so I don't know much about Portagee hair. But it could be that Henry told the Hardens what they wanted to hear from a brown feller who was aimin to marry up with their pretty daughter."

"Oh Lord!" said Sally. "Your family may have left there a long time ago, Mr. House, but you're still Chokoloskee through and through!"

*

The county road south to the Tamiami Trail and the Gulf coast at Everglade, fifty miles away, ran through the flat palmetto scrub of the Big Cypress. The two-lane asphalt, straight and shiny, writhed and shimmered in mirage toward its point of disappearance on the low horizon. Across the white sky, dark-pointed as a weapon, a swallow-tailed kite coursed the savanna for small prey.

"Cattlemen held a big panther hunt out this way a few years ago—that about finished 'em—but there's still more panthers here in the Big Cypress than anyplace in Florida except maybe my front yard on Panther Crescent."

They rode for a long while in silence without meeting or overtaking other vehicles, as Andy kept track of their southward progress through his own dead reckoning. "Deep Lake," he said after a while. He pointed off toward the west, where a lone vulture tilted down along the cypress wall. "Ever seen it? Deep small lake in a two-hundred-acre hammock. Seems like I can *feel* that water back in there. Twenty miles inland from the Gulf but connected some way to salt water. There's been tarpon in Deep Lake as far back as any old-timer can remember."

In the days of Billy Bowlegs, in the Third Seminole War, Lucius told them, the Indians had kept large gardens on that hammock. After the band gave itself up and was shipped away to the Oklahoma Territory, Deep Lake knew a half century of silence before Walter Langford and his northern partners learned of that rich ground and rode over from Fort Myers to plant citrus."

Andy nodded. "Why do you think Sheriff Tippins put his prison camp way out here at Copeland? Langford paid next to nothing for that convict labor, and Sheriff Frank held back the little that they made, being as how it was against state law for them terrible black criminals to receive payment." He grunted. "Big businessmen don't worry much about whose sweat and blood makes all their money—don't even *know* about it if they can help it! So maybe Langford knew how Tippins worked things, maybe not. But a lot of sweat and a lot of blood was spilled out in this scrub, I will tell you that."

He seemed subdued. "Deep Lake had a bad reputation right from 1913, when they laid that rail line north from Everglade to get the citrus out. Them nigras workin on that line was kept at Weaver's Camp, and every little while when some run off, they'd take and shoot a few, make an example, and bury 'em in that nice soft fill on the railway spoil bank. Later years, when they was surfacing that old rail bed for this county road, they dug up so many human bones it was embarrassing."

"Is it possible," Lucius said, "that those bones were the source of some of those bad stories about E. J. Watson? About those skeletons supposedly dug up on Chatham Bend?" Sally Brown nodded a little, ready to accept this possibility, but that lake-like gaze in the blind man's blue eyes was unrelenting. Clearly he thought the question disingenuous.

"Well, we blame too much on your daddy, that is correct," Andy said finally. "We forget how much competition that man had, and I'm not talking about common criminals nor backwoods varmints like that feller Cox. I'm talking about ordinary business people who let poor folks get worked to death to make more money. At Deep Lake, them miserable lives was all wrote off to free enterprise. E. J. Watson might of called that progress, and he weren't the only one, not by a long shot.

"Right up to the twenties, the Sheriff supplied convict labor to them Deep Lake partners—bankers, railroad men, and such. When convicts tried to run away, they paid Injuns to track 'em. All swampy country out here then, so them runaways never got too far in chains. Left tracks or sign that any Injun could follow blindfolded, and miskeeters and thorns and heat and snakes just took the heart out of 'em. Time they was finished, they was beggin to be caught—hell, they got *rescued*!

"When we was farming down this way at Turner River, Dad would get deputized sometimes to catch them runaways. He took that work tracking for Tippins cause we needed the money, but he never liked it. Tippins kept up his friendly reputation in Fort Myers, same way your daddy did, but he didn't behave right at Deep Lake, where nobody was watchin. He'd handcuff them prisoners, knock 'em around, give 'em a taste of what was waitin for 'em if they didn't go out and work in that swelterin heat until they dropped. And finally Dad swore out loud and said, 'You goin to abuse a handcuffed man that ain't done nothin wrong, you better find some other stupid feller to do your trackin for you.' But then Dad would go broke again, and he'd come back.

"Course the Sheriff was never friendly with my dad on account of what Bill House told him in Fort Myers Courthouse back in 1910—that the men who killed Watson were not criminals, and that he wanted a grand jury hearing to clear his name. Tippins likely agreed with him, cause he never cared for nobody coming in to meddle with the law, not in his early days. But he had pressure from Langford and his friends to let the case slide beneath the surface—that was that. Pretty soon, he become a real politician, he wanted to get reelected worse than he wanted to be honest, and after a while, he got the habit of sellin his public service to the highest bidder, same as the rest of 'em.

"When the Florida Boom collapsed, the Deep Lake plantation went down with it, but the Collier Corporation took over that convict labor, making logging roads to lumber out the Cypress. The prison camp weren't but four miles from our farm, so they made me captain of the road gang when they was shorthanded. Them nigras never run off on me, neither, seein how nervous I was—scared my gun might go off, kill somebody by mistake!

"The bookkeeper was bragging all the time about how much work they got out of those convicts, how every week they'd flog a man whether he deserved it or he didn't, to improve the attitude among the rest. Course road gangs was very bad all over Florida. Black convict or white, it made no difference, not when it come to chains and rawhide whips. Road gangs was why so many outlaws run away to Watson's—Leslie Cox, y'know, and Waller and Dutchy that was killed by Cox, and plenty of others, too, from what we heard.

"No, we never thought much of the Sheriff's Department. Dad only let himself get deputized to do the dirty work cause we was poor. One time he went after a man who had killed a mess of people, brought him in meek as a lamb, because Dad was amiable but he was also a dead shot, so nobody wanted to trade bullets with him. A lot of men thought Bill House was the feller who put the first bullet into Watson, but Dad always left that claim to my uncle Dan. Said he didn't want to make a liar out of his own brother.

"In them years our Sheriff made his peace with Prohibition, and him and Dad's bootlegger brothers got together, cause a man can't go far in the bootlegging trade without some friendly understanding from the law. Frank Tippins learned a live-and-let-live attitude, long as the man's skin were the right color.

"One time Tippins killed a prisoner in his own cell. Might of saved that unfortunate nigra from committin suicide, but he called it an escape attempt, as I recall. Claimed this man was the only prisoner he ever killed in the line of duty. Never thought to count all them poor devils that never went home from his labor camp here in the Cypress.

"Yessir, when it come to nigras, Collier County was very hard, Lee County, too. A free black man down here in south Florida would of been far better off being a slave. Right up until recent times, any black man not attached to a white family, the way Henry was, he'd get grabbed right off the street and charged with loitering or vagrancy and sentenced to farm labor or the chain gang. A nigra that belonged somewhere weren't never bothered, not even when he done something pretty serious, because folks won't stand for messin with private property, not in this part of the country. No fool lawman who tried that could get reelected. So if you was black with white people behind you, you could murder your wife if you didn't make a racket, and the Sheriff might look the other way. After all, he weren't never elected to go spendin up the taxpayers' money for nothin.

"Nigras was free men but they belonged to you, right up into the thirties and the forties. The only black in Everglade was known as Storters' nigger, same way Henry Short was Houses' nigger to some people. Sounds awful, don't it? But that's the way it was around the Bay. And you know something? Them boys was *glad* about it! Any nigra that wanted protection, wanted to get along, he was very very glad that he belonged to somebody."

*

Of the old prison camp at Copeland, little sign was left but overgrown rough thorn and lianas, and shadow ruins on white limestone sand back off the roads. A pileated woodpecker's loud solitary call rang strangely in the high noon heat, over the dead scrape of palmetto, in the sunny wind. The Copeland settlement, named for the Trail engineer, had become field headquarters for Lee Tidewater Cypress, which in recent years had been logging out the last of the great strands. Copeland's journals, which contained a brief account of E. J. Watson's death, described the group which confronted him on that October evening as D. D. House and Charley Johnson and three transient fishermen. "When D. D. House told him to hand over his gun, Watson raised the gun, growling, 'I'll give you my gun,' and pulled the trigger." Paraphrasing this passage, Lucius turned to watch Andy's expression. "Where did Graham Copeland get that stuff? Is that how your dad told it?"

"Mr. Copeland was particular about his facts, that was his training, and what he wrote was accurate, far as it goes. Course it don't go far enough. The names, I mean. He only mentioned Charley's name because Charley wanted his name mentioned. Charley used to boast how he took part."

"Any idea who those transient fishermen might have been?"

"Ain't got your list on you?" Disliking his own sarcasm, Andy frowned. "Course there was always drifters down around the Islands, but I believe Dad told me them three fishermen was Frank and Leland Rice, who showed up most years in the mullet season, and Horace Alderman from Marco, who was over visiting his brother Walter.

"Before he was done, Horace Alderman made his name as 'the Gulf Stream Pirate,' smuggling bootlegged liquor and Chinese. Them Orientals was kind of a nice sideline, cause the new railroads needed 'em for coolie labor. Took all their savings, up to five hundred dollars a head, to smuggle 'em in from Cuba or someplace. Unload 'em off ships, sneak 'em ashore a few head at a time. Sometimes they ran 'em right up Taylor Slough, dumped 'em off in the Glades and pointed 'em northeast, told 'em Miami was just up the road, if they could find a road. But Immigration was keepin a sharp eye on the east coast and the Key West railroad, so Horace might come in off Cape Sable, scan the shore for any sign of trouble, then land his cargo at Middle Cape and move 'em over the old Homestead trail to the east coast.

"As a businessman, Horace Alderman was prudent, out of respect for the law. If he seen something wrong, he'd holler a order to transfer the cargo to a smaller boat, then knock each yeller man over the head as he come on deck, relieve him of his valuables, and slide him overboard. Other times, they might chain the whole string to a heavy anchor, and if the federals was gainin on 'em, they'd destroy the evidence, let 'em go rattlin over the side. Might waste a cargo if they dumped 'em too quick, but better safe than sorry, that was Horace's motto. Anyways, he had their money, so it weren't what you would call a total loss. So Horace was doin pretty good in that line of business until that night the Coast Guards come up alongside. Bein after him for bootleggin, they only found them Chinese when they searched his boat. Horace said, 'There must be some mistake.' He had a weapon hid under his mattress, and he come out shootin. Killed two Coast Guards and a Secret Service man and commandeered their vessel, but later one of his own men lost his nerve and they got captured.

"Horace's mother always said her poor boy was a real nice feller till he married up with a greedy woman and went for the fast money. The Law hung Horace in Fort Lauderdale around 1925. Before he went, Horace wrote up his life story, explained all about it, but maybe his mama never got around to readin it. That old body puzzled and prayed but never did conclude where her boy went wrong.

"And the Rices? Wasn't there something about a bank robbery, and a shooting on Chokoloskee—?" Lucius stopped short, glancing at Sally, as Andy frowned and cleared his throat.

"—and Speck Daniels?" Sally finished.

"The Rice boys come to a bad end, too. I reckon God is done with them three now, so mentionin their names ain't goin to hurt nothin."

"I had those names already. I was just confirming."

"Just confirmin. You got your list all learned by heart, wouldn't surprise me." The blind man's smile had an edge like a broken knife. "I sure hope there ain't nobody named House on there."

"I'm not gunning for anybody," Lucius said crossly.

"Well, Bill House never thought you was real serious about it, neither, but having young children, he couldn't take no chances."

Lucius appraised Andy's expression in the rearview mirror. "Bill could never be sure, though, could he, Andy?"

"Nosir. You was a Watson. He never could be one hundred percent sure."

*

The sun was high and the hot noon road empty, boring ever farther south into the swamp country. On the spoil bank of the black canal that paralled the road, a thick gator lay inert, like a log of mud. Gallinules cackled in primordial woe, and long-necked cormorants and snakebirds, like aquatic reptiles, rose in the canal and sank away again. A cottonmouth lay coiled in a rotted stump along the water edge across the canal, and farther on, a bog turtle had climbed to the pavement edge to point its snout at the howl of passing tires.

Across an old railroad-tie bridge, the wall of liana, vine, and thorn was broken by a sagging roadhouse, in a yard inlaid with broken glass and bottle caps and flattened beer cans, motor oil, lube buckets, tires, defunct batteries. Big-finned autos and rangy motorcycles baked in the Sunday heat, and men in dark glasses and motorcycle boots, attended by scraggy kids and hounds and dragged-out women, leaned back on their elbows, watching strangers pass.

Among the decrepit vehicles were two big swamp trucks, one red, the other black. When Lucius braked, Sally said tersely, "Don't even think about it. Don't even slow down."

*

At the crossroads, they turned left onto the Tamiami Trail, passing the few cabins at Ochopee and continuing on a little distance to the low shaded bridge where the Trail crossed the headwaters of Turner River. Here Capt. Richard Turner had guided a punitive expedition against Chief Billy Bowlegs at Deep Lake; here Big Hannah Smith had farmed awhile before traveling down to Chatham Bend to meet her Maker; here the House family and Henry Short had raised tomatoes for the Chevelier Corporation; here the Mikasuki Seminole, protesting this highway which had split the Everglades wide open like a watermelon, had made their last desperate plea to the encroaching white men. *Pohaan chekish,* the Indians had said. "Leave us alone." The Trail engineers had commemorated this historic death song with a nice roadside picnic table and a sign.

When Sally read the sign aloud, the blind man nodded. "Yes, ma'am. 'Leave us alone!' " He told them how the Indians had spied on the House family when it pioneered out this way during the Depression, how they had felt those black eyes watching from way back in the trees, or peering through the grass tips from a dugout—how they might get that feeling ten or twenty times for every Indian seen, until they realized that everywhere they went, the Indians watched them. Lucius remarked that Indian scouts had tracked white strangers day and night since the first Spaniards came ashore on this peninsula. " 'We are your shadow'—that's what Indians say."

"Course the red man favored black men over white men, least in the old days," Andy said. "The red men—I ain't never seen a red one yet, have you?—they give shelter to runaway slaves and also white fugitives and outlaws who hid out in the swamp. Any man the white people was after deserved help—that's how the Injuns always seen it. That is why folks around here thought Leslie Cox might of gone over to the Injuns.

"Them Government Injuns ain't so sure of who they are no more, so they look down on black people because the whites do. That way they might feel a little better about being nobody in their own land—land of the free and home of the brave but NO INDIANS AND DOGS ALLOWED. Might still run across that sign back in this country."

*

Lucius led Andy to an opening in the trees. At Andy's request, he described the southern prospect out across the blowing grasses and sun-glittered waters which under the broad Atlantic light slid slowly, slowly south toward Shark River. White egrets in breeding plumage lifted airy crests to the Gulf wind, and white ibis crossed the sky over Roberts Lake, where Bill House and Ted Smallwood and their partners, Andy said, had killed the thousand alligators that paid for most of Smallwood's land on Chokoloskee. "I still see this place! Still got our Turner River shack in my mind's eye!"

In the Florida Boom, back in '24, the Chevelier Corporation had sent Andy's father to this Turner River land to demonstrate to the Trail settlers how tomatoes could be grown commercially on palmetto prairie. "Once the company learned how Dad done that, it took that fine new farm right out from under him. That's when he had to go back to Frank Tippins. Dad worked this prairie so darn well he worked himself right out of his job!

"Turner River was a clear wild stream before the Trail construction broke her. There's a little lake back in this strand where fish are plentiful, but because there's no trail through that hot thicket no more, nobody don't even *know* about that lake, let alone go there! Why go sloggin through the back-country when you can ride in a nice auto to Miami or sit on your sofa, watch your new TV?"

Back at the picnic grove, the blind man raised his hands in a vague gesture. "Right about here where they got these roadside tables, that's where Henry raised his watermelons—"

"Darkies love watermelons," Sally said, laying out forks.

"Sally? You plan to jump on Andy every time he opens his mouth from now on?"

"Well, she's right, Colonel. Maybe I talk too much. Talkin about old times makes me happy, and when I'm happy is when I tell all the old stories." For want of a way to give vent to his well-being, he circled the table, sniffing the air, lifting his big arms, letting them fall. And in a while, finishing his meal, he was reminded of Henry and his brothers.

ANDY HOUSE

Henry Short come to Turner River with our family, and this is where his long-lost past caught up with him. This was in 1928, maybe 1929, because the Tamiami Trail was just put through. Well, one day two white fellers showed up in a old flivver. Never mixed words about who they was and what they come for. Got out of their car and told my dad that Henry Short was their half brother and they come to visit with him. If they was ashamed of it, that never showed.

First time them brothers tried to find him was way back before World War I, a couple years after Ed Watson was killed. They tracked him all the way south to Lost Man's River. Henry was living at Lee Harden's then, but he hid back in the bushes, never showed himself nor talked with 'em at all, because he believed them men had come to kill him. Hardens was pretty leery, too, so they said nothin to help. Them big barefoot men just stood there with their guns, set to run them strangers right back where they come from.

At Lost Man's them brothers left Henry a letter, and when he come in out of hiding and he read it, that poor feller wept. He kept that letter all them years, he must of read them words one thousand times, but he never showed it to our family, only said politely that his letter was them brothers' business.

I reckon he didn't want to take a chance that some word or joke or maybe just somebody's expression might go spoiling something. But over the years, he referred to it some—he had it memorized—and finally we had the story pieced together.

After the lynching of Henry's father, his young mother was punished severely, but her father kept his ruined daughter, he took her back and her child, too, least till the age of four, when he got rid of Henry in the way I told you. Once the child was gone, he found some feller to marry her, and she give her husband them two sons, as white as you or me. And them two come south just to make sure their half brother was getting on all right. And when they showed up on the Trail, Henry's eyes was shining like he seen a miracle. I met them men myself, four or five times. The name of those two brothers might been Graham, and they had settled some good land west of Arcadia, around where the old settlement called Pine Level used to be. They were ranchers—they owned cattle, they weren't ranch hands—and both of 'em were good steady men, polite and very quiet like their brother.

Well, our House family could not get over that. We used to wonder if Henry's mother sent 'em. Her community had made her witness it when Henry's daddy was burned and killed, and she never forgot it. She was yearning to know where her firstborn was, and if he was all right. In the eye of God, she was a sinner, but to us mortals she must be a good woman if she could raise up two white sons to take responsibility for that half brother they had never seen and never *had* to see, him being a poor colored field hand way off in some godforsaken part of Florida who didn't even know them two existed.

Granddad House told his boys many's the time what that lynch mob done to Henry's daddy, but I'm shamed to say I never give much thought to it. It's sinful how we shut things out that we don't care to look at! But after I met his two half brothers, I had a gruesome dream about Henry's father, a man of flesh and blood like me who *become* me in my dream, or I was him, nailed up to that oak in that night fire circle, sufferin them torments of the torch and rope in woe and terror, looking down into the howling faces of them Christian demons. That dream has come back all my life, no matter how hard I try not to think about it.

One night before his white brothers showed up, Henry whispered, looking deep into the fire, "If there is one thing that is sorrier than a nigra, it is a white woman who *traffics* with a nigra." We never did know if he meant his mother or his wife, but we was shocked to hear such bitter words. After his brothers come and claimed him, and told him how much his mother missed him all her life, I never heard him speak such words again. I believe he was tore up and sick at heart that he had said something so cold and hard about his mama.

If Henry understood why his half brothers stayed in touch with him, he never said, but knowing Henry, he probably thought them men was plain darn crazy to go up against the common prejudice that way! All the same, he was very very grateful, he would whistle and smile for days after they left, we never seen him look that way before nor since!

I was always sorry I never knew them two men better. What they stood up for, so simple and so clear, made me ashamed of my whole way of thinking about nigra people, it woke me up and turned me right around. Yessir, I was mighty impressed, and I am today.

The last time Henry's brothers came to Turner River, we was real happy to see them, and we invited 'em to share our supper. We meant well, but it didn't sound right, it felt funny, and it made 'em uncomfortable, so they would not eat with us. They didn't act angry or upset, they were polite about it, but they said, No thank you, they had come there to see Henry, and they built their own cooking fire off a little ways. I never got over the sight of them three men setting on their hunkers by their fire, chuckling and trading stories while they cooked and served each other, like Henry had ate with other people all his life.

After they left, Henry never said what they had talked about, it was too precious. That was *his* life, the only family life he ever had. And the following year, Henry left the House family for good, and we never saw them Graham men again.

Sometimes Henry rowed down Turner River and headed north or south along the coast, hunting for gold. That feller was a fool for gold since way back in the nineties. Picked up tales of buried treasure from Old Man Juan Gomez on Panther Key, who claimed he'd sailed before the mast with Gasparilla. The God's truth never did catch up with that old Cuban. Drowned in his own net off Panther Key but his lies are going strong right to this day.

One time Henry worked for strangers who come to Everglade in a old schooner, hired a crew and went prospecting on Rabbit Key. Took ranges all over the place and worked like beavers for two-three days digging up that island. Well, E. J. Watson had been buried on that key, and Henry was scared to death of Watson's spirit. He knew the body had been dug up and taken to Fort Myers, but he weren't so sure Watson's spirit had went with it. A hoot owl was calling from the mangrove clumps, and Henry knew there weren't no owls out there, he knew that owl weren't nothing in the world but a wandering spirit.

Henry had the ghost of Watson on his mind when a shovel struck something deep down in the sand on the third evening. It was close to dark, so the men was ready to knock off, but first they wanted to dig up whatever the heck it was that shovel scraped on. But the strangers told 'em to go back to camp on Indian Key, they would set a guard and start fresh in the morning. And when the men come back bright and early, thinking to finish up, get paid their wages—yep! Them strangers was all gone. The schooner was gone, and their wages was gone, too. There was only this square pit in the sand, shaped like a chest.

Henry never got over being so close to Gasparilla's treasure, he was prospecting gold for the whole rest of his life. Seemed like there was rascals setting up all night making genuine parchment maps to sell to Henry. He drilled on Pine Island, Sanibel, wherever Gasparilla might of gone ashore. Sent away for a certified surefire drill and drilled up and down the coast, he was hot for gold. Even drilled on Chatham Bend when nobody was looking, cause there was rumors that your daddy struck Calusa gold or maybe Ponce de León's gold when he first plowed that place. As Dad used to say, "Henry Short is a smart man, but that gold fever has diseased his brain."

After the Hurricane of '26 Henry went over to Pelican Key, and there he seen these lumps of metal laying on the sand where the storm cast up big slabs of coral rock. He could have had 'em for the picking up, he told me, but he thought they was scraps off an old engine block half sanded up out there. Later a feller showed me scraps from the same spot, said, "Looky here what I just bought! Pieces of eight them Spaniards buried out on Pelican Key!"

Never come out until years later how Gasparilla the Pirate weren't nothing but a publicity stunt thought up by some city slicker to fool tourists. To this day you can read about Gasparilla's buried treasure right there on your lunch mat in your Sun Coast Restaurant while you're waiting on your jumbo shrimps and key lime pie. Wipe off the coffee spill and ketchup and that mat will tell you all you need to know about how Emperor Napoleon patted Juan Gomez on his head back there in Madrid, Spain, and how Juan sailed with Gasparilla, who become so famous that all kinds of tourist enterprises got named after him. Yessiree, that Sun Coast menu got a real nice picture of Gasparilla in his official pirate hat with skull and crossbones and a eye patch and a sword between his teeth. You got that authentical evidence right there by your plate alongside your home fries and red snapper, and a lot of other history thrown in for free.

Henry Short was the most able man in this coast country, so my dad always found some work for him to do. Bill House was a good man, kind to black men, and they give him back a lot of work. Treat 'em like fine horses and they'll run for you, is what he said. He always had a nigra to help out, whether we needed him or not—it just come natural to him. If Henry Short weren't nowheres around, he'd find another, but he always said he liked Henry the best.

In the Depression when it got so hard to make a living, Dad sent Henry with a bunch of men who was going to Honduras hunting gators. Well, Henry didn't want to go. He was near to fifty now, and he'd heard life was dangerous in them Spanish countries. Dad told him not to be a fool, this was his chance, and after so many years, it never occurred to him not to do what my dad told him. But when I took Henry to Immokalee—he was going to Fort Myers to board ship—he got out at the bus stop with his little bindle and stood a minute looking down the street. Then he turned slowly and he said, "Your daddy's tired of me. He's getting shut of me before I get too old." He said good-bye and walked over to the bus and went down to Honduras.

Them hunters like to starved to death, couldn't find no gators. They never come close to making their expenses, couldn't pay for their own beans, so bein Spaniards, the authorities locked 'em up without no food. The American consul got some grub in to 'em, bribed somebody, finally shipped 'em home. Henry Short came back from Honduras but he never came back to Bill House. He was very bitter. Lived mostly at Immokalee, La Belle, ricked charcoal and cut cane, done what work he could find. The House family ain't heard from him in years.

But God works in mysterious ways, and God saved Henry Short at Turner River, because after Henry left for good, he was tracked here by that stranger he had been afraid of all his life since Watson's death. We caught this man skulking around toting a rifle with a hunting scope. Dad hollered, told him to lay down that rifle and step out where we could see him. Well, he steps out from behind that bush but he don't put that rifle down. Seeing none of us is armed, he rests that weapon back over his shoulder. He was a city feller from the poor color of him. He says real bold, "I ain't here to hurt you people, and I ain't broke no law. I got some business with a nigger name of Short." Claimed he had something for Henry but would not say what.

Dad never took his eyes off him. He had the idea this man was sick inside his head or some way crazy. I was whispering how I better run and fetch his gun. Dad said, "Don't try nothin." He told the man we didn't know where Henry Short was at and wouldn't tell him even if we did. He said, "Mister, you are trespassin, and trespassin is breakin the law. Don't never come back onto my property." And the man laughed at him. He said, "It ain't even your property! I know all about you, Bud!" Then he walked off down the Trail to where he'd hid his car and headed back east where he come from.

When I finally got out of the convict labor business, I drove a school bus,

I become a carpenter, I went back farming just so I could eat. Then I quit farming, went over to Miami, built me a gas station, and a few years later, this same man rolled in there. Course he was older, but I knew him—same ice blue eyes with that dark ring, same solid set to him. He said straight off he was still huntin that nigra, said this man Short was kind of like his hobby. I told him to get his automobile out of my station.

This feller nods but he don't go no place, he's setting there lookin me over out his window. And I'm getting edgy, I'm starting to get mad, when he says to me real soft, "Back up, my friend, don't get your pecker in the wringer. Let's say some nigger shot *your* daddy, and none of your brothers had guts enough to go take care of it. Now what would *you* do?"

I guess he figured he had brung me around to his own way of thinking, cause he flashed me a bad grin like he had proved his point. And damn if he don't hand me this card with a phone number—no name, only that number. And he says, "You understand me, Mr. House? All you got to do is call and then you're out of it." Lifted his fingertips to his brow in a kind of a salute, and winked and drove on out of there, screeching his tires!

Not long after that I left Miami, because all them Cubans that was taking over, they wouldn't buy no gas from us poor Angle-os. Spanish-American War all over again, guns and all, only this time them Spaniards run us Angle-os right out. My last customers give me a nice sticker to put on my rear bumper when I left for good: LAST AMERICAN OUT OF MIAMI BRING THE FLAG.

Chapter 7

The Ten Thousand Islands

South of the Tamiami Trail, the road entered the coastal mangrove, arriving at last at a humpbacked bridge over the tidal creek called the Haiti Potato River, from which, in the late nineteenth century, black muck had been heaved to build a patch of high ground for a hunting camp. The Haiti Potato became the Allen River, after William Allen, the first settler, then the Storter River, after the family which established an Indian trading post and post office in 1890. Before 1913, when Walter Langford and his partners dredged a canal from Everglade north through the swamps, using the spoil bank to support a railway to Deep Lake, the shack community called Everglade, three miles inland from the Gulf of Mexico, had only been accessible by sea.

The original idea for that small gauge citrus railway came from E. J. Watson, who had offered to manage the Deep Lake Plantation in a letter that his son-in-law Banker Langford never answered. George W. Storter, Senior, had driven the first spike and George W. Junior drove the second, and the rest of the fourteen-mile track was laid by convict labor. Four years later, 17,000 crates of citrus were shipped out by sea. When Deep Lake Plantation collapsed in the early twenties, the railway was used to haul construction materials eight miles north to the Tampa-Miami Trail. Subsequently the rails were removed and the rail bed surfaced for this county road.

From the small bridge across the tidal river, Lucius described to Andy House what was left of the old landmarks. In the period of Trail construction, a small community of black laborers known as Port DuPont had sprouted up across the river from the fish docks. "Looks like this river isn't wide enough," Sally commented, "because with all this new talk about civil rights, the white folks here on the south bank aim to move the black ones to the old construction camps back north at Copeland. As long as they stay ten miles out in the sticks, they'll be free to enjoy any civil right they want!"

"Folks on the Bay don't take to nigras and they never did," Andy admitted sadly. "Black feller tries to catch a fish anywhere down around these islands, he might get a bullet past his ear to run him off. Ain't one black man lives today at Everglade or Chokoloskee, neither one." He looked troubled. "Course there's good folks that don't feel that way, but they don't do nothin about it—they just don't speak up. And you know something? I might been one of 'em."

On the south side of the bridge, behind the seafood-packing sheds along the river, small, low houses were scattered loosely like spilled produce, and beyond them rose the ornamental palms in the civic center of what was now Everglades City. "A lot of these old cottages through here, that's my kinfolks," Sally said. "Got 'em in Everglade, got 'em in Chokoloskee, all hitched up to one another like stuck dogs. When she married a Harden, this li'l ol' gal got disinherited from the whole bunch. Got disinherited from an old nail-sick hulk that's sinking away into a mud bank back upriver, and an old step-side pickup with a paint job that never did get past the prime coat, and maybe some kind of measly share of one of these old shacks with the tin roof sagging from rain leak and mold, and mosquitoes riding mean dogs through the busted screens, and crusted plastic dishes and grease-stained unpaid bills on the kitchen table.

"And they don't give a damn. They are *proud* to be broke and out of work and never know where the next payment is coming from, they damn well *like* it that way! There's not a Harden in south Florida who lives in the sorry way of some of these damn lawless know-nothings who used to give the Harden family so much hell!

"But my old man and his kind, they aren't poor white trash, the way people say. They are *rich* white trash who aim to live in the same poor-white-trash way their daddies did. Those shacks might look like they're ready to fall down, but the occupants are in there sitting on big bank accounts from gator hides, guns, moonshine, God knows what. You fight your way through the tin door of that li'l doodad trailer over there, you'd be blasted back out by a new TV the size and voltage of the electric chair up there at Raiford, spang in the middle of their six-pack redneck mess!"

When disgusted, Sally dropped her educated accents and spoke with a harsh and grotesque humor which (though he knew better than to mention it) reminded Lucius of her rich-white-trash daddy. She stared out of the car window like something trapped.

"Whidden Harden married me because I had some spirit. My batteries weren't dead the way they are in most of the worn-out females around here." She tossed her chin at the dilapidated houses. "And he married me because I felt ashamed about the way the Hardens had been treated, and because he hoped our marriage might help heal the feud between our families."

Lucius glanced back at Andy, who had closed his eyes.

"Yes, the feud! Are you two going to pretend you don't remember how my damned uncles murdered those young Hardens at Shark River?"

Andy House opened his eyes again. "That was back there in the Fish Wars, Sally. Very hard times and hard feelins. Them young Carr boys lost their heads. That don't mean there ain't plenty of fine men in your family. I've known 'em since I was a boy, and most of 'em are First Florida Baptists who don't touch a drop—honest, self-respectin folks who are trying to get by best way they can, same as they always done. Most of 'em ain't smugglers nor 'rich white trash,' neither. They are poor people. And they are poor because this is a fishing village where the fishing has died out and the huntin along with it, and even tourists stay away because there ain't no bathing beaches back here in the mangroves, not even a Gulf breeze, only mosquitoes.

"So men gets desperate to support their families, and some of 'em turn to night trades like their daddies done, and their granddaddies, too. This town is getting a rough reputation, cause moonshiners and smugglers don't like outsiders. Honest citizens who got lawbreakers in the family don't like 'em neither, so why would any visitors want to come here, let alone come back?"

"Mr. House, your dad left the Bay when you were still a boy, and most of the other Houses are gone, too!" Sally cried shrilly. "Gone to someplace civilized like Naples or Fort Myers where there's something to do after supper besides screw your sister! Something besides high-school basketball and church bingo, is what I mean!" she finished desperately, raising her hands up to her face. The break and tearing in her voice startled them more than what she'd said, and all three fell quiet, not knowing what to say.

*

In midafternoon there was no one in the street, and no car moving, only a dusty road-gang truck manned by a plier-faced guard whose sunglasses twitched in their direction like the hard eyes of a fly. Two black convicts and two white ones, in juxtaposed pairs, stood on the truck bed. The young whites swayed recklessly in the center of the bed, thumbs hooked in the hip pockets of their jeans, while the two blacks, indifferent, maintained easy balance with one fingertip each on the high side boards. When Sally Brown looked out her window, the black convicts looked past her, while the white boys cocked their pelvises and whistled.

She gazed about her at the empty streets. "Great to be back home," she said, "if you like home." She was watching the black pickup truck, which came up from behind and slowed, then rumbled past, leaving a loud wake of country music.

The huge mahogany that had volunteered along the Haiti Potato River in the nineteenth century still guarded the old Storter trading post, now the hotel. The rambling white building was the last of the Old Everglade that Lucius had known at the turn of the century when he came from Chatham River to board with the Storter family during school days. Here they left Andy, who hoped to find Hoad Storter. "Don't have to walk me," he protested at the door. "My old shoes still know where to go."

*

Sally Brown would stay with Sandy Albritton, one of the last old-timers who had actually witnessed the shooting of Ed Watson. The Albrittons lived at Half Way Creek, an old Bay settlement east of the new causeway built in recent years to connect Chokoloskee Island to the mainland. In front of the house was an old sign reading COLD BEER AND BAIT. A faded mullet boat was up on blocks in Sandy's yard, and beside it sat an ancient coupe whose paint had been beaten to a grainy brown by years of sun and rain. The front porch screen was diaphanous with rust, and the porch space overflowed with yellowed newspapers and assorted litter.

A woman with gray-streaked raven hair down to her hips and a prominent mole under her left eye appeared at the front door in a mauve bathrobe. "That you, Sally? Don't know no better than to come in at the front? Who's that old feller fetchin your valise? You got you some kind of a sugar daddy or somethin?"

Annie Albritton waggled her fingers at Lucius Watson from behind the screen. "Only foolin, Colonel, darlin!" she said coyly. "I knew that you was who you was soon as I seen you!"

"*Cousin* Sally," came an old man's voice. "That purty little gal and me is kissin cousins."

"Maybe she don't admit to it," said Annie, unhooking the screen and waving them inside. "What y'all waitin on? You like miskeeters?"

Sandy Albritton said, "Colonel? Is that really you? We heard you was here some place but we never believed it!" The two men exchanged a bony hand-shake. "I knowed this feller from way back when we called him Lucius! We used to visit at the Bend, see Mr. Watson's trained-up pig by the name of Betsy! Ain't that somethin?" He stood back a little, hands resting on Lucius's shoulders. "Well, time ain't been kind to you, it sure ain't, but you look bet-ter'n me, I will say that!"

Sandy Albritton was frail and pale-haired, with hard drink marks. His wife was younger, a whiskey-voiced wild swamp darling of yore gone slack and rueful but still itched by her old demons. She jumped right in, beating her husband to their common memories.

"Well now, let me think back. After 1910, the Willie Browns who were my Brown cousins—Sally here don't think too much of 'em, but I enjoyed 'em—they got the quitclaim to the Watson Place, cause they was very best of friends to Mr. Watson. Us kids got to visit Chatham every summer! I recall one time we come in without warning, scared poor Aunt Fanny so darn bad she dropped a whole pot of fresh milk. She said her nerves was shot to hell around that place, cause she expected Leslie Cox at any minute! Us little girls was always scared down there, wanted to sleep in bed between the bigger kids. The boys wanted us in there, too, but their reasons was different, if you get my meanin." Pinning her hair with a rhinestone barrette in the form of a red-eyed alligator, she winked at Sally. "Nosir, they never got the blood up off that floor."

Sandy said, "She ain't even from here. She's one of them damn Lowes from Marco. I don't believe she ever went to Chatham in her life." He glared balefully at his wife. "So I can't figure your damn story out too good."

Sally asked, "Has he always been as rude as that?"

"*You* know why I'm rude." Sandy's sneer expressed the sincere disgust in which decent men viewed the deceits of women.

Annie shook her head. "He was all lovey-dovey when I married him. He was after young meat, that dirty feller. I didn't know what I was in for, mar-ryin a fisherman. Up at three A.M. to get his breakfast for him, that was the worst part, and even at three A.M. he was all over me—"

"She's still doin it," Sandy confided to Lucius. "Makin my breakfast, I mean." He contemplated his wife with mixed emotions. "Before she got so fat she looked all right—hard to believe that, ain't it? I don't guess nobody would have her now," he added gloomily.

Holding Lucius's attention, Annie waved him off. "The days I'm talkin about, o' course, was when Walker Carr was on Chatham Bend in the De-pression. His boys was all after me—"

"Listen to that! Them Carr boys wasn't after you, they was after Edie Harden, same as I was!"

"Now in them times," his wife persisted, "there was still a lot of Injuns coming into Chokoloskee, used to set around that great big pot of sofkee grits, pass the wood spoon. The women had their babies under Smallwood's store, they'd go out in the water to wash off—I seen that a time or two myself. My husband here—he married me when I turned thirteen, filthy old feller—he used to sell moonshine to the Injuns, then go drink with 'em till he got back most of what he sold!"

She gazed at Sandy, who gazed right back with the same rancorous affection. "I think you was a drunk," she said. "You used to scare me. His best friend was the medicine man, ol' Doctor Tiger, remember, Colonel? Still wore that old-time Injun skirt and neckerchief and blouse, and Injun turban?"

"When he got drunk, Doc Tiger used to hint how he knew what become of Leslie Cox." Sandy Albritton coughed up some catarrh. "I seen that feller Cox a time or two, so I was fixin to ask Doc Tiger all about it, but that ol' Injun's secret went down with him, if he ever had one."

"Oh my, them were the days! That night this old man settin here, he was so darn drunk he was snowed under, and Doc Tiger right along with him. That ol' heathen was down to just a-mumblin. Sandy jumped up hollerin how that mumblin must mean that Doc Tiger wanted to head home, so we pushed him off in his dugout, aimed him east. Might of pushed too hard, cause darn if that ol' dugout don't turn turtle! First time we ever seen a Injun so drunk he capsized his dugout! We kept an eye peeled for a while, but nope, there weren't no sign of him. That old medicine man weren't nowheres to be seen, just his poor dog swimmin round and round, barkin, you know." Annie chuckled at the memory, shaking her head.

"I think we drowned him," her husband agreed. "That old redskin was never laid eyes upon again." Lucius searched their faces for some sign of irony or regret and felt a little chill when he found nothing. "Them were the days, all right," Annie repeated.

"Now them old-time Injuns," she said, "they wasn't just dirty redskins, they was our friends. Them days we didn't have nothing but a skiff and a set of oars. This old man here would take me coon hunting down around Chevelier Bay, go up them creeks. Prettiest sight in all the world, to see them Injuns setting quiet around their fire, and the firelight glinting off them beads that their women wore in stacks around their necks." Her fingers played a little at her throat. "My life with the Injuns was the most beautiful time of my whole life. If I tried till doomsday I could never tell you how beautiful it was or what it meant to me." She looked momentarily confused. "Even I don't hardly know what all it meant to me, I only know it tore me up and broke my heart."

"Well, she had *me* tore up a good while before that, so she had it coming," her husband said, sour again.

Annie ignored him, still thinking about Indians. Her face, which had been close to tears, turned sullen. "Colonel? You been up on the Trail lately?" she said accusingly. "You seen them faked-up Injun villages they got there for the tourists? Rasslin alligators? Genuine-type Injun jewelry from Hong Kong and New Jersey? Well, them people ain't beautiful no more! They ain't even real Injuns no more, and that's the truth!"

*

During their visit the phone rang twice, and Annie Albritton's response made clear that these callers wished to know exactly what their visitor was up to.

"Why he ain't no such of a thing! Just asking a few questions, is all. What? Not *nosy* questions! Asking about his daddy, s'all it is. Old-timey things! What's that? *Course* I'll be careful!" She listened a moment, then put her hand over the mouthpiece. "You ain't workin for the federal gov'ment, are you?"

"You've been spotted for a fed," Sally whispered, gleeful.

Sandy frowned and muttered. The feds were not a joke. "Way them boys figure, you might be informin. Revengin on your daddy that way," Sandy said.

Annie put down the phone with care and picked her way like a sick cat back to her place. The little house had fallen silent, all but the relentless tick-tack-ticking of that rickety alarm clock in the kitchen that seemed to be dogging Lucius's steps all over Florida. The Albrittons stared imploringly at Sally, who was enjoying the whole business and perversely refused to clarify the atmosphere.

Annie hummed a little, kicked the bent dog away—"Spot's just the lovinest dawg!" Settled down again, she marveled, "Colonel Watson!" and hummed a little more. "I like to eat good, don't you, Colonel? That's all us old folks can still do, so we might's well do it good."

"I been thinkin I'll prob'ly take up sex again," her husband said.

"Now *Lucius* Watson was a fisherman for years," Annie told Sally in a dreamy voice. She glanced at Lucius slyly, humming a bit more. "It was only later on they called him Colonel. I was scared of him because he was exactly like my daddy said *his* daddy was—bow to you, wouldn't let you pay for nothing, too goody-goody altogether. One time he bought me a ice cream, I weren't but fourteen-fifteen years of age. Bought my husband here a beer while he was at it. Oh, Colonel was always so polite, like his daddy before him; do anything you want, then he might kill you. Colonel Watson's manners, they was just upstanding."

Her husband ignored her. "I got bunions, do you?" he said to Lucius. "Want to see 'em? Worstest thing I ever got, and I had plenty."

"My dad said he was always scared of Mr. Watson, said they all were. They knew a desperado like Ed Watson would never let himself be taken, never had and never would, so every man on that landing knew what was coming. When E. J. Watson swung that gun up, them men froze."

"Colonel come here to find out about his daddy, and all you want to talk about is your old man, who was over to Marco and weren't nothin much to talk about in the first place!"

"So *anyways*"—Annie rolled her eyes—"Mr. Colonel Watson made him up a list of all them men." She gave Lucius a crafty look. "Colonel? Where d'you suppose that list of yours has got to?"

"Hardly anybody on that list is still alive," Lucius said casually. The very mention of the list made him feel weary. "Anyway, it never meant much. Kind of a hobby."

Sandy Albritton looked skeptical and somber. "The sons are still around, and grandsons, too. Man lookin for revenge would not have to hunt far to find a target, especially a man who shoots like you done, man and boy—"

"He's not looking for revenge," Sally declared in a firm voice. She had been smiling at Lucius's discomfiture, but now she saw that the atmosphere was shifting and that the Albrittons, infected by small-town paranoia, were growing uneasy and afraid. "We had one of the sons in the car with us all morning, and if Mister Colonel wanted his revenge, Andy House was probably the one to start with."

"Hell, I trust Colonel and I always did." Sandy got to his feet, motioning to his old friend to follow him outside. "That woman don't know nothin about E. J. Watson," Sandy told him, plenty loud enough for his wife to hear. The screen door banged behind them. He led the way down the rain-greened rotten steps and crept into the colorless old car, where he cranked the windows tight against mosquitoes. "My office," he explained. In the stifling heat, through the cracked windshield flecked with broken insects, he glowered at the hulk of his rotting boat. "A man don't need no aggravation whilst he's talkin, that is all I'm sayin."

Old Man Sandy scrunched down in the seat, hiked his knees high as his nose, swung his black shoes onto the dashboard, and recited his eyewitness impressions of Mr. Watson's death. When he was finished, he turned his head to see how his friend had taken it. When Lucius asked calmly if the men had planned it, Sandy gave no sign that he had heard this question, gazing out past his old mullet boat toward Half Way Creek.

Eventually he said, "That feller who rung my telephone just a while back? Crockett Junior." Again he turned his head to peer at Lucius, to see how much he knew. "And that woman settin in my house is his damn mother. Sally tell you?"

Lucius was astonished. *"Annie?"*

"Annie. Yessir. That's her name, all right." He rolled down the window, spat, rolled it up tight again. "Life is a bitch, now ain't it?"

"Sally has never said a word. I even forgot until just lately that Speck Daniels was her father—"

Sandy Albritton held up his hand. "Nobody mentions *that* name without my permission!" He worked up more phlegm and spat it forcefully out of the window, remaining silent until satisfied that Colonel Watson was ready to hear his story without interrupting.

*

"Back in the Depression-time, we was pret' near starvin around here, so me'n a couple of other boys, we took and killed a steer to feed our families. We was turned in, turned over to the law, and me and them other boys, we done a year at Raiford on the chain gang."

"I remember something about that," Lucius said.

"Well, you don't remember what I aim to tell you, cause you never knowed about it, nor me neither. The baby boy that welcomed his daddy home from Raiford was still all red and wrinkled, hot out of the oven. But the mother told me, 'No, no, honey! He is goin on three months of age, he was born just nine months to the day after our sweet partin!' I was fixin to name the little feller Crockett Albritton after Speck, cause Speck was my best friend since we was boys, and he'd promised to look out for Annie while I was away. But my wife said, 'No, no, honey!' Said this baby boy was a chip off the ol' block and she wanted his name to remind her of her darlin! Said her lovin heart was dead set on the name of Sandy Junior.

"Right about then, the news come out how that damned Speck was the one who told the owner how he seen us boys butcher that steer. We done it, all right, cause times was hard, but Speck Daniels never seen us do it, he just heard about it. Nobody couldn't figure out why he was so willin to make trouble, knowin it wouldn't earn him one thin dime. Well, not long after that, ol' Speck was found half-dead back in the bushes here, boot treads all over him and a mouthful of broken teeth. I believe he spent a pretty good while in the hospital. Anyone else would of left the Bay or tried to make amends. Didn't do neither. He took his punishment, never spoke about it, went right on like before. Takes a real ornery sonofabitch like him to stick around a place where nobody had no use for him at all. Didn't need no friends in life, I guess."

Albritton glared at him, in pain. "I never talked to *nobody* about this stuff!" he said, resentful.

"Sandy, you don't have to tell me—"

"I told you it already. Anyways, if I don't tell, they's other ones that will. Might's well hear the truth." He hawked and spat again. "So years fly by the way they do, and next thing you know, this Sandy Junior and Speck's daughter Sally, they get goin pretty hot and heavy in the high school. Annie got wind of it and done her best to break it up without spillin no more beans than what she had to. That Marco woman that I got in there"—he pointed at his house—"interfered so bad she almost caused a feud in the two families, cause only Speck knew what she was up to, and Speck never cared to admit nothin nor get drawed into the mess in any way. Them two kids could hump theirselves to death for all he cared. But Annie nagged and threatened him so much that he got fed up and tossed poor little Sally into his truck and hauled her away to some kinfolk in Fort Myers.

"Only thing, them kids had no idea what they done wrong. The boy was rarin to foller her, he just weren't aimin to be stopped, so that female in there, she feared the worst. Finally she come blubberin to me with the whole story about how my ol' partner Speck Daniels was the natural born daddy of the *both* of 'em."

He nodded for a long while, looking grim. "I put a stop to it. I notified Sandy Junior Albritton how his rightful name startin that day was Crockett Junior Daniels, and I sent him off to live with Crockett Senior. And his little sister that he loved so dearly and wanted so bad to put his dingus into was told the sad news as soon as she come home."

They sat in silence for a while, out of respect for this disagreeable life situation.

"So that poor girl settin inside was so darn horrified by her own daddy, and so tore up in her feelins about her brother, that she run out of her house, never went back. Took her mama's name, but her mama bein dead, she didn't rightly have no place to go. Well, me and Annie, we was scrappin all over the house, but we always been so fond of our almost-daughter-in-law that we put her in Sandy Junior's room in place of him. Probably been in there with her panties off a time or two already, but none of us didn't say nothin about *that*.

"That's how come that girl got married so fast, sheerly out of her terrible mortification. Sally got scarred up pretty bad, and she ain't over it. You ever notice she got kind of a sharp tongue? She is still pretty hot under the collar, and she's out to prove somethin, don't ask me what.

"I never blamed Annie all that much. I wore out a stick on her big butt so's she couldn't sit down for a month and let it go at that. I understood her, see. She was full of life to overflowin back in them days, and Speck bein her husband's oldest friend, he sidled up while I was in the pen. Got some liquor into her, to comfort her, y'know, and next thing you know, she had to have it. They's fellers will take advantage of a sad and lonesome female, especially females that look as good as Annie did. And anyways, it weren't nobody but me that asked that bastrid to look out for my darlin while I done my time. I kind of knew who Speck was before then, but I didn't think he'd do somethin like that to the last friend he had left in southwest Florida.

"I never took a stick to Speck, in case you're wonderin. With Speck, there ain't no halfway measures. You shoot at Speck, you best not miss, cause he ain't goin to." He squinted at Lucius. "Sure, I thought about it. But I knew I couldn't kill him, not in a fair fight, and I also knew I weren't the kind to shoot him from behind. Not that there's many would of minded. Folks would of stepped right up and shook my hand, I reckon, stead of laughin behind my back all my whole life. But I made my choice and I have lived with it, and I'll die with it, too, one of these days.

"Know somethin? I don't hate that man no more. As the years go by, it's him I miss the most out of that bunch I was raised up with! Crockett Daniels is a lot of fun to get rip-roarin drunk with, I will tell you that. A *lot* of fun! He was right there when we drowned poor ol' Doc Tiger by mistake! Ain't hardly got a enemy that won't admit that ol' Speck was his drinkin buddy to start off with. Yessir, we had wild nights together, Speck and me. I get to thinkin about them times we had as boys, huntin and drinkin, chasin after the bad girls, we just never seemed to stop hootin and laughin. Life was real long back in them days, and the nights never seemed to end. Funny, ain't it? I been thinkin lately that I miss Speck more than I would of missed that woman in there if she got drunk and fell into the river. But all them good old times we had never meant no more to that damn feller than the fish gurry in the bilges of his boat."

Watching the women come out onto the porch, Sandy raised his voice to drown out his wife, who was railing at him for taking Colonel outside. When Lucius rolled his window down, Annie Albritton told him to return next morning when her husband was out if he wanted the real lowdown on his daddy—"no ifs, ands, or buts!"

"Might give you more butt than you bargained for!" her husband shouted for her benefit, but his voice was muffled by his rolled-up window.

"She was brave to come to you that time, to protect the young people," Lucius reminded him before leaving the car.

"Well, that ain't none of your damn business, Colonel, but it's true. That's why I'm still settin here thirty years later."

*

Sally pointed across a weedy lot toward the small houses on the creek. "You can go visit those old friends of yours," she said ill-humoredly, as if suspicious of what Sandy might have told him. "One of those damn Carrs who shot the Harden boys, I mean. See that purple house, the one on posts? See that chain-link fence he's got around it? It's Sunday so he's probably in there right this minute. Afraid some Harden might come by and blow his head off before he can get safely to his grave."

*

Lucius climbed the outside stair to the door of the purple house. At his knock, a reedy voice told him to come in. Mr. and Mrs. Owen Carr, seated in their front room, were intent on a small black-and-white TV, and neither rose or offered him a seat, or seemed to hear his apologies for the intrusion. He thought at first they'd been expecting someone else, since Owen Carr, looking thin and sickly, was staring at him with that horror of mortality which seemed to anticipate a dark old age. Eyes and nostrils reddened, thin arms twitching, he clutched his chair arms as he might a wheelchair. His wife was an ample pinkish woman, uncomplicated in demeanor. Her face had betrayed a tremor at Lucius's intrusion, then composed itself as smoothly as a pond. She continued knitting.

A little tall for the low room, Lucius seemed to loom over the inhabitants. Penny Carr pointed her baby-blue needle at a chair, but not until he was moving toward it of his own accord. "We got word you'd be coming," she told Lucius, her voice flat, without inflection.

Before he could ask how they had learned so fast, Owen Carr burst out, "I was just tellin Penny how Walker Carr was your dad's best friend, right from the day a stranger name of Watson first showed up at Half Way Creek and bought a schooner from William Brown, who was my granddad on my mamma's side. My daddy and Ed Watson, they was *real* good friends! Watson visited regular, liked to talk crops, and our whole family had a high opinion of him, a *very* high opinion!" Carr talked faster and faster. "Colonel, if I said it once, I said it a thousand times, I don't believe the Watson family got one thing to be ashamed about!" By now he was glancing wildly at his wife.

Lucius was astonished by Carr's fear of him, which he worsened inadvertently by saying, "I believe you were a witness to my father's death—"

The man's stare reflected his belief that Colonel Watson must have come in search of vengeance. Racing to disassociate himself from that event, he quickly became short of breath, in fact looked ill. "In 1910, I was only a little feller, Colonel! Only nine years old! I was over on the island, stayin with kin. Whole island knowed trouble was comin!

"My dad was dead set against that killing, and I sure hope nobody ain't told you different! Him and Willie Brown yelled at them men to go to Everglade, see Justice Storter, see what they should do accordin to the law. Tried and tried but he couldn't head 'em off, it was too late. Every man there knew what was goin to happen! They aimed to shoot Ed Watson dead no matter what! I heard it was Old Man Henry Smith spoke up and said, 'Let's draw straws, put a live round in only the one gun, so's nobody will know for sure who done the killin!' But no man there thought one bullet would stop him!"

Lucius nodded. "How about Henry Short? Was he there with them?"

Owen Carr winked slyly. "Now don't you go fallin for *that* ol' rigamarole! Them men was hunters, they could clip the plumes off an egret's head, never draw blood! They never needed no damn nigger to take care of nothin!" He uttered a derisive squawk, meant to be laughter. "Colonel? You still keepin that ol' list? Cause if I was to think back on it a little, I bet I could name you every last man in that crowd!"

"You already named one," his wife warned him. "Anyways, the man didn't ask you about names." Coolly she met Lucius's gaze, her needles feeding swiftly on the wool like the quick mandibles of a blue beetle. "He can read the names off of his own list any time he wants."

Owen spoke again, in gusts of breath. "Course I don't rightly remember now just who was in on it. All us boys runnin around—Crockett Daniels, Harley Wiggins, Sandy Albritton—Jim Thompson might been with us, come to think about it."

Here he glanced at his wife, who said, "*Might* been, is right. Jim weren't but six years old."

"Well, I was there and don't deny it! A eyewitness! I seen your dad's old shotgun comin up, double-barrel shotgun! I ain't never forgot that sight! Then a rifle cracked out of the dusk, and after that, all hell broke loose, just a hellacious racket, I can sit back and hear it still today! Cause if all of 'em shot, then who would know who done it? I reckon that's what they settled on beforetime!"

"According to your daddy," his wife said.

Owen Carr's testimony, which directly disputed the posse's claim of self-defense, was too significant to be accepted lightly. Lucius gave the man a moment to calm down. Then he said carefully, "So the killing was planned in advance. You are quite sure of that."

The Carrs looked at each other. "That's what come down in our families," Penny said.

"That's right! It come down in our families!"

"Did your father tell you which men planned it?" Lucius paused. "Or when the killing was discussed? You can tell me, Owen—they're all dead now—but accuracy is important."

"Important to who?" the woman said coldly. "Not to us folks around here."

Lucius ignored her, trying to hold the eye of Owen Carr, who twitched in consternation. "I was there that day," he muttered. "I weren't but nine years old. I remember a heck of a racket and dogs barkin. Mrs. Smallwood sent after his gold watch for Mrs. Watson, and Isaac Yeomans laughed and said, 'Tell the Widder Watson that we sure are sorry but that nice gold watch has been blowed to smithereens.' "

"That's two," his wife said.

"I had those names long ago," Lucius assured her, keeping his gaze fastened on her husband.

Carr cried out eagerly, "One thing our family always did agree about, Colonel Watson was a real fine man, same as his daddy! I was younger'n you but we knew you good because you was in friendship with our family before the trouble!"

"The trouble," said Lucius, to encourage him.

"He never asked you nothing about that," his wife warned Owen, who gave her a panicked look. She was knitting more rapidly, quick-fingered, impassive, and Lucius decided to back off a little.

"You say someone told you I was coming here today?"

"Now, honey, who was tellin us about Colonel Watson?" Owen looked furtive again, and his voice had lost all animation. Trying to dodge his visitor's gaze, he whined a little like a dog in nightmare, as if racking his poor brain for names was exquisite torment.

To give them a chance to smooth their feathers, Lucius asked after Penny's father, Jack Demere, who had worked at Chatham Bend in Papa's time—did she think he might sign a petition? "Nosir, I don't think he will," she said. "He's dead." When he said he was sorry to hear that, she shrugged. "Oldest man on Chokoloskee. Couldn't hold that job forever, I don't guess."

While she talked, her husband twitched and brooded, frowning hard. As if unable to bear so much suspense, he brought up the Harden feud again of his own accord, but so obliquely that for a moment Lucius had no idea what he was talking about. "I already told folks all I know about that, Colonel. You was there. You come there to the Bend that day, come with the Harden men." Having blurted that out, he looked confused and gloomy, lifting his arms from the chair, letting them fall again, then falling still except for spasmodic twitching of his hands. "Life happens to a man, is all it is," he mourned.

"I went there with the Harden men when you boys still denied it," Lucius said gently. "I never did hear your side of that story."

Penny's needles paused as if the mandibles had stopped while the beetle listened. "What story might that be?" she warned again, as her frail husband took cover in a coughing fit. She took a deep breath and put her needles down entirely, smoothed her lap. She stood up. "Well, we won't keep you," Penny said, compelling Owen's silence with a needle pointed at his eye.

Before departing, Lucius asked them to sign his petition to the Park to save the Watson house, since both members of this household had known Chatham Bend well during their youth. Mrs. Carr glanced at her husband, who seemed unnerved by their visitor's request. She said, "Nosir, we won't sign nothing in this house. Not today."

*

Entering the dark pine lobby of the Everglades Hotel, with its yellowing marine charts and huge mounted fish, Lucius stopped a moment at the desk. The blue-haired receptionist, engaged in her own telephone gossip, was utterly indifferent to his presence, and he waited at a discreet distance, hands clasped behind his back, flexing his legs a little with small knee bends. When eventually he cleared his throat, the woman looked up, battle ready. The color of her eye makeup was running, and she seemed to be biting the telephone as she talked. Finally she tucked it under her ear and waved him forward. Perhaps, he thought, she would be less haughty if she knew how much lipstick was smeared like gore across her teeth.

Asked if there were any message for L. W. Collins or Lucius Watson, Bluehair snapped, "Which?" When he gently persisted, the woman yawned with that red grimace, like a carnivore. "No messages," she said, without a glance at the scattered memos on her desk. He wondered how to tangle with this brute. "From Mr. Arbie Collins? Or a Robert Watson? How about Watson Dyer?" She ignored him.

Disgruntled, he went out onto the porch overlooking the water, where Hoad Storter was describing the river scene to Andy House with gestures which the blind man could not see. Lucius listened with pleasure as his old friend portrayed the crab boats passing down the tidal river and the gold-and-purple bronzing on the heads of pelicans on their nests on the bright mangrove wall across the water. Although aware that his listener was dozing, he urged the blind man to listen for the silver mullet, flipping upward toward the air and light, then falling back to the surface of the channel with that dainty smack so mysteriously audible from far away. Lucius suspected that these wistful sketches were for Hoad's benefit, too, imprinting images against the day when he could no longer come to Storter River to witness these common miracles moment by moment as they rose and vanished in the great turn and glisten of his passing world.

Hoad greeted Lucius with that chipmunk grin, pointing to an old green wicker chair. "I come back every year just to remember! Course Andy knows everything I'm telling him, but he might have forgotten a few things about this coast after so many years as a city slicker in Miami." He chuckled when the blind man grunted in comfortable protest, refolding his big hands on his stomach.

Hoad was a small man with round red cheeks and a seraphic smile, and his transparent girlish skin appeared to have gone unshaven throughout life. In fact, he looked much as he had when they were boys, fooling and fishing in small boats along this river. "Speaking of mullet, you recall them schools we seen south of Caxambas? Remember, Lucius? Two-three miles across!"

When Lucius nodded, his friend laughed out of sheer pleasure in the sight of him. "Andy told me you'd be coming, Lucius!" Having known him since boyhood, Hoad used his given name. "I expected to see that professor who spoke at Naples, all dressed up in navy blue jacket and linen trousers like those Yankee yachtsmen who tied up to this dock back in the twenties, you remember? And what do I see but the same good old feller I remembered! Same old sun-bleached khakis and salt-rotted sneakers and faded shirt buttoned at wrists and collar against insects—'so's the dirt won't show,' you used to say, though all of us knew that Lucius Watson wore the cleanest shirt—maybe the only clean shirt!—in the Ten Thousand Islands!

"I remember your daddy, too! Other night there at the church hall, I was thinking how my dad Cap'n Bembery always saw the good side of Ed Watson. Harry McGill who married my sister Eva, he might of been in the crowd that day at Smallwood's, but there weren't no Storters mixed up in it, not one. It was only when my uncle George got old, after so many years of telling newcomers about Ed Watson, that he concluded he had took part, too. Lucky thing we had written proof that Uncle George was on jury duty at Fort Myers or he might have wound up on some darn old list!"

Lucius laughed unhappily—"Oh Lord!"—and Hoad reached and patted his friend's arm, to take any sting out of his teasing. "Yep, Storters stayed friends with everybody—those who took part and those who didn't—and we're friends today." And he offered a fine friendly smile to prove it.

On this afternoon beside the river, Hoad was happy to be reminded of the very little that he had forgotten. Together, they regathered the details of how they had netted pompano off the Gulf beaches, mostly at night in the cool season, following the fish schools from Captiva Island all the way south to the middle Keys. When they wanted sea trout, they fished the grass banks and the current points. For snook, they worked the channel edges, and the deep holes around a river mouth for the big grouper.

"I was telling Andy what a fine life it was, to have your own boat at your own dock, and go to work when you felt like it and not before!" Hoad cried. "Sometimes them mullet jumping was as thick as raindrops, Andy, so many that it sent the price down! We left off netting, hooked up mullet strips, hand-lined redfish and big trout, two-three hundred pounds a day! This man here could tell you! But mullet strip don't work no more, got to use shrimp, and you're very lucky if you catch enough to pay your bait!" He laughed. "I quit when the fishing got so poor that I had to eat my own bait for my supper, to get some use out of them shrimps 'fore they went bad!

"Yessir! Mullet schools two and three miles across! Won't never forget that! I tell my grandchildren all about it—got me some pretty nice grandchildren, Lucius! I'm a lucky man! You got you any, Lucius? No? I think grandchildren are pretty nice! I tell 'em all about the mullet, and how the noise of millions on the surface, it would deafen you! And know what them children told me? Said when they grow up, they aim to take good care of the wild things, and bring 'em back to the way they was, so they could see what their granddad was talking about!" Hoad sat back sighing, shaking his head. "Well, them poor little fellers ain't never going to see nothing like we seen. It's a pity, ain't it? And all because that good Glades water is pouring away through them canals. How long can we go on wasting God's good water, instead of taking care of it for our grandchildren?

"The Glades is getting bled to death by all that draining! At low tide at the end of rainy season in October, especially in a northeast wind, a man could lean out of his boat and drink the water in any inside bay along this coast, remember? Freshwater pressure flooding them rivers held the salt tide out where it belongs. Today you might have a quarter of that volume, and the brackish waterline where you find fish has moved back up into the creeks, way back up inside where a net fisherman can't work!"

Lucius told Andy about setting net off the oyster bars at Lost Man's, sliding up to the bars at night and punching down into the bilges with an oar blade and listening for the mysterious grunt of startled fish. The volume of the grunt would tell them whether there were enough fish around the bars to bother striking—fish enough to make the set worthwhile. Sometimes mullet would skip out nearer the shore, and he and Hoad would set around them with a gill net and smack the oars flat on the surface to drive the schools into the mesh.

But Andy had never been a fisherman and he dozed off again, and though Hoad smiled at Lucius's evocation, nodding his small head, his reveries had strayed. Talking about his grandchildren had saddened him about the future of the Glades, which in their youth had been immense and inaccessible, mysterious. "Ducks by the thousands! Clouds of 'em! Now they're all gone, too! Even the wasps are gone, you noticed? Them big hives along the mangrove channels? Darn it, boys, our good old earth is just fading away! Seems like we don't know what we're doing to this country, and we don't care neither, long as there's money in it. Seems to me that this country used to have more honor than you see today! I mean, what do *you* think, Lucius?"

But Hoad's nature was too cheerful and inquisitive to stay depressed for long. Fed up with "old men who nagged after the past," he talked about the Storter trading post, which was passing itself off these days as a hotel. The original house had been built by William Allen—twice, he said, because Allen had rebuilt on stilts after the Hurricane of 1873. He got engaged to the daughter of the French consul in Key West, but for some reason—and Hoad's eyebrows rose in mock astonishment—she was so set against her banishment to this mangrove paradise that she threatened to destroy herself if she were brought here, and being a young woman of her word, that is what she did. William Allen sold his holding to the Storter family and went off to Pine Level, where he married a Mrs. Ellen Graham, a widow with two sons.

"I was telling Andy some of that old history here a while ago, and he got real excited, wondering if those sons could be the Grahams who turned out to be half brothers to Henry Short. I knew Henry well, fished with him often—good fisherman, too!—and he never breathed a word about those brothers!

"Plenty of Injuns around here at that time, but this place never had no nigras to speak of. In the early days, William Allen moved a mulatta cropper off his property for taking up with a white woman, and not long after that, the body of their little boy came floating down this river, right out here. Folks said that woman killed her boy, out of her shame, you know, but more'n likely it was her brothers who done it. No place for that poor little feller in their family line, I guess.

"A young black boy from the Cayman Islands, Erskine Rowland—we called him Dab—he turned up as a stowaway out of Key West. Lived in the jelly house, where we stored cane syrup and our jams and jellies, but some way he never felt that he belonged. At that time, Henry Short was the only other nigra on the Bay, but Henry was over on Chokoloskee and anyway, he moved south to the Islands after 1910. Dab got lonesome, he wanted to leave, he tried to stow away on my dad's boat even after my Aunt Nannie took him into her own house. Course Dab didn't eat with the family nor attend our school, but Aunt Nannie taught him to read and write, and Uncle George give him a banjo, he'd sit up practicing so late at night they had to holler at him. Dab Rowland became an expert banjo picker and an expert syrup maker and a fine all-around hand, he used to set net down in the Islands with me and my brothers, sometimes Henry Short. Yessir, them two boys was real fine fishermen, they done their work as good as anybody and a lot better'n most. It always did seem funny when you come to think about it—one of 'em lighter than most of the white men around here and the other one black as black can be, but both called niggers cause the way folks looked at things, there weren't no difference!

"Dab and Henry fished with me and my brother Claude right around the mouth of Chatham River, this was 1910, and Henry would carry his rifle in the boat, never went without it. He had worked for Mr. Watson, said Watson always treated him real fine, but he purely dreaded him. Thought the world of him and scared to death of him, Claude always said. Mr. Watson might been the one man in south Florida on which black people and whites seen eye to eye.

"Later on, Dab got in trouble, had to move away. That was before you came back to the Islands. As for Henry, I don't know what become of him— probably dead someplace. Seems like nigras couldn't never get adjusted to our ways."

The blind man grunted. "Amazin, ain't it? How them darned nigras couldn't never get adjusted to our ways?" Hoad stared at him, cheeks coloring, but Andy's eyes remained closed, and in a moment he softly snored once again. He seemed to have spoken from deep in his dream, making Hoad uneasy.

Hoad spread old fingers on his knees and got carefully to his feet. "Feel like stretching your legs? Have a look at the old town or what is left of it?" He asked the waitress to notify Mr. House as soon as he awakened that they would be back in a short while. "I ain't likely to skip town," the blind man murmured.

Walking along under the old-fashioned streetlamps toward the former Collier County Courthouse on the circle, Hoad and Lucius were passed by the road-gang truck from Deep Lake prison camp. One of the whites now sat up front with the plier-faced guard, while on the truck bed, the other white boy stood apart from the two blacks. Any of them could have jumped and run, but the only way out of Everglade was that narrow road which ran eight miles north through water, mud, and mangrove before striking the higher ground along the Trail, and presumably the convicts knew that Plier Face was not a man to pass up a chance for a shot at a human target.

Tattooed arm stuck out the window, the favored con in the front seat was wearing the guard's black cowboy hat. He raised his hand above the roof and erected his middle finger toward Hoad and Lucius, as if contemptuous of everything his elders stood for, and Lucius was glad that Storter hadn't noticed.

HOAD STORTER

At Half Way Creek somewhere around the early nineties, Cap'n Bembery Storter met Mr. E. J. Watson and became his friend. This was before Mr. Watson's family come here from north Florida. Every Tuesday Mr. Watson came in his boat to Everglade, picked up his mail and his supplies from Uncle George Storter at the trading post, and consigned his packet to Cap'n Bembery on the *Bertie Lee*. He made it over to our house long about noon and ate at our table almost every week.

Mr. E. J. Watson was not a man you were liable to forget. I could draw his picture! Being his son, you probably thought he never changed, but over the years my dad had watched him thicken—still very strong but tending more toward stout. E. J. Watson had a deep red-brown hide—"That's fire, from a life of sun and drink," said Cap'n Bembery—but his auburn hair was grizzled in those later years, with gray mixed into a heavy mustache that tangled with long bushy sideburns and made him bristle out like a wild boar.

In those days, Mr. Watson was a friendly man, a jolly man, full of ginger, full of get up and go. Always had something funny to tell, good sense of humor, and always carrying on about the future of America—*"the greatest nation in the history of the world!"*—and also about Hawaii and the Philippines, and land claims in the Islands. He aimed to file a title claim on Chatham River, as Storters had done in Everglade and Smallwoods on Chokoloskee. It was only a matter of time, he declared, before this southwest coast was developed, and maybe he was just the man to do it. He'd laugh a little at his own ambition, but nobody had any doubt that he meant business. Uncle George always claimed he was the one who nicknamed your dad Emperor Watson, but Bill House said no, it was the old Frenchman, Jean Chevelier. Whoever it was, that name never bothered the Emperor one bit!

Mr. Watson also loved to talk about strains of sugar cane that might do better here in the subtropics, how many gallons of syrup per acre and all that—he was getting close to 700 gallons at that time. Had a ten-horse engine with steam coils that fed into a 150-gallon kettle, twice the size of our Storter kettles, and Wiggins and House, too. Used fine Cuba cane, not our Georgia cane, and his syrup came out amber-gold in color, clear as fine honey. *Island Pride*—that syrup was famous! Got a good price for every gallon he could make, and he made 333 gallons every day! Old Man House, he would complain how Watson bought that good equipment with bad money, not honest money made by the sweat of his brow. And my dad said, "Well, Dan, maybe that's so, but I never seen a man work harder than Ed Watson."

Mr. Watson had been on this coast as long as most, but they still called him an outsider and standoffish. Claimed he wouldn't hardly associate with nobody except Storters and Smallwoods cause he wanted to stay on the good side of the traders, who were the most well-to-do and influential. Well, that don't seem fair neither. Your daddy liked people and most of 'em liked him. The William Browns at Half Way Creek who sold him his first schooner, they always said that E. J. Watson was a good man to do business with, and they wouldn't hear a single word against him. It was only those ones scared of him who claimed he was aloof, and that was because they steered clear of him themselves.

Your dad was always well-behaved on Chokoloskee Bay and at Fort Myers, very careful about his family and good name, but in Key West and Port Tampa, he was a hell-raiser and no mistake. Cap'n Bembery brought back many a wild story about shooting the lights out in the bars and such as that. My dad was a loyal friend to him, no matter what, but sometimes he seemed leery of him, too.

One night in Eddie's Bar—this was Key West—Mr. Watson grabbed a revolver away from some drunk young feller who was waving it around. "How in the hell do you work this thing!" he hollers, pretending he never shot a gun, and he shoots a half circle right around this feller's toes as if the gun was just shooting by itself and he had lost control of that darned trigger. But when the chamber was empty, this young feller came up with a derringer he had hid in his boot, told E. J. Watson to dance in that same manner!

"Ain't many men would try that trick with me," Mr. Watson warned him, "let alone boys." But this young feller only laughed and went ahead and made him do it. And that was the first we ever heard about Dutchy, who killed a deputy later that year. Dutchy was an arsonist, for hire, and the lawman caught him setting fire to a cigar factory. Went on the chain gang, got away after a year or two, and went and hid out at the Watson Place.

When Mr. Watson tried that shooting dance in Tampa, he got thrown in jail. But Key West was a wilder kind of place, seamen and soldiers, ships from all over the world. DINING AND DANCING, NINE TO ELEVEN; FIGHTING FROM ELEVEN TO TWO—that was the sign in Eddie's Bar! There were so many fights that Mr. Watson could cut loose all he wanted, he just fit right in.

For many years Ed Watson was the bad man in that town. But until that extra drink when he got unruly and the crowd was looking for the door, they all wanted to step up and drink with him, they all wanted to trade stories about him, they were proud as pelicans about good ol' E.J., so my dad said. The men told strangers in the bar how their ol' pardner here, Ed Watson, had killed tough hombres out in Oklahoma where he had that famous shoot-out with Belle Starr. And Ol' Ed, he'd just sit there looking dangerous, and finally he'd drawl out kind of modest how Belle and her foreman rode him down, had him cut off in a narrow neck of woods, so he had no choice but to swing around and drill 'em both.

There'd be a wild cheer for frontier justice, and right while those men were cheering he would turn to Cap'n Bembery and give him that slow old wink of his, hiking his thumb over his shoulder as if that bar crowd was the dumbest bunch of hayseeds he had ever come across. Them onlookers might not care for that, but they kept laughing anyway, pretending they knew right along it was all a joke.

Maybe five years after your dad's death, before you came back to the Islands, my brother Rob was fishing with Harry McGill, and they went upriver to the Bend and took some cane cuttings. That plantation was already growed over, very rough and shaggy, but new cane sprouts were still volunteering through the tangle. They grubbed 'em out, stacked 'em on deck, and carried a boatload up the coast and on up the Calusa Hatchee to Lake Okeechobee. They say that small boatload of cane from Chatham Bend was the start of the Big Sugar industry as it is today. Probably your dad is rolling in his grave over how his cane—after his years of hard struggle—has made fortunes for other growers at Moore Haven, because those Watson cuttings stretch today from Okeechobee south to the horizon. Many's the time I've thought about how Emperor Watson could of stood up on those dikes and enjoyed a grand view of that sugarcane plantation he had probably dreamt of all his life.

*

The white courthouse building on the circle reminded the old friends of Barron Collier, a New York businessman who became interested in Deep Lake through Walter Langford. Talk about enterprise! Now there was a man whom Emperor Watson himself might have admired! When Langford died in 1920, Barron Collier acquired the Deep Lake holding, railroad and all, then bought up the whole south half of Lee County, more than a million acres of unbroken wilderness, the biggest private empire in the U.S.A. By then the Trail was under way, and it looked like the authorities had been paid off to get the section coming due west from Miami turned northwest beyond Forty-Mile Bend, circumventing the Chevelier Road and Monroe County in favor of Barron Collier's domain and leaving the Chevelier Corporation stuck in the mud. Meanwhile Collier paid off politicians to get his empire set aside as a whole new county, which he named in honor of himself—"the biggest landowner in Florida," Hoad said, "if not the country!"

When the Storters sold most of Everglade to Collier, the Storter River became the Barron River, and Everglade was renamed Everglades City. Because Collier needed a county capital that was more than just a trading post and a few shacks, he brought in twelve-inch suction pipe and dredged enough mud out of the river to make a channel for large boats and build up spoil banks and high ground to enlarge the settlement. This was 1923, when the only other settlements in his new county—Naples, Immokalee, Marco, Chokoloskee—could not claim a thousand souls between them, even with outlaws and Indians thrown in!

That same year, Prohibition became law, and one of the "Pro-hi" agents who came here hunting moonshine stills never made it back out of the Islands. Bahamas rum came in at night and was stacked in Collier's pasture, Hoad recalled. The Deep Lake railway was extended to Immokalee by 1928, the same year the Trail was finally completed, and distilled spirits loaded here in Everglade traveled straight from Immokalee to Chicago on the Atlantic Coast Line. "I don't know if that's true or not," Hoad Storter said, "but men who knew something believed that Barron Collier paid for his new county during Prohibition by running contraband liquor to Scarface Al Capone. That is none of my darn business nor yours neither, but it goes to show you what your daddy knew so well, that a businessman who aims to make his mark here in America can't let no finer points of law stand in his way."

With the completion of the cross-Florida highway, modern times thundered right past Everglades City, down there in the mangroves eight miles off the Trail, and this community died back down to nothing. In the Depression, the Collier Corporation dumped its brave new county back on the federal government, and as usual, the taxpayers picked up the bill. Some of it was set aside as the Big Cypress preserve, and the rest would be called the Everglades National Park. The Park dedication in 1947 was the first ceremony of significance ever held in this Collier County Courthouse, and the last one, too, because the county seat was moved to Naples.

They contemplated the white courthouse on the empty circle, the sterile facade set about with planted palms. They recalled the brass band and the flags and windy speeches, and also the stony grief of the Mikasuki—the ragtag "Cypress Indians"—who stood off to one side, watching the Muskogee Creeks in their bright-striped blouses who stood beside the white people hailing the new Park. These government-sponsored "Seminoles," who had never inhabited these southern Glades, ignored the silent witness of the Mikasuki, who long ago had withdrawn into the Grassy Waters, *Pa-hay-okee*, still undefeated by the U.S. Army, only to be vanquished by bureaucrats a century later. Excluded from their hunting and fishing grounds around Shark River, they camped like refugees on the north boundary of the Park, along the canal banks of the Trail. The president of the United States was declaring the new park a grand beginning, but for the silent Mikasuki, this great day was the beginning of the End.

Lucius never forgot the bitterness in those black eyes, tight as currants stuck into brown dough. One big strong Indian had drunk too much and fallen off the bridge before he had hardly set out on his long walk home, and Lucius and Hoad had waded in and dragged him out. This man was said to be descended on his mother's side from the "Big People"—the vanished Calusa, later called Spanish Indians, because a few found refuge with the Spaniards in Cuba. This despairing man was in spiritual training, and not long thereafter he had disappeared, taking along the sacred Green Corn Bundle. What became of him the Mikasuki did not know, they only knew that without the sacred bundle, the old ways must wither. The story was that he had gone to Oklahoma in search of the Creek Nation elders, whose counsel might teach him how to help his people find their way in a time of change and terrible desecration of the Mother Earth. Not until some years had passed had the man returned with the sacred bundle, and not until this moment—he recalled that dim sense of recognition at Caxambas—did Lucius realize with a start that the Indian could only have been Billie Jimmie.

"Billie Jimmie. Yep. That was him," Hoad agreed.

The Miami Herald had sent a reporter to the Park ceremony. Inevitably, she had dragged Lucius's father into her article, reporting that he was still "a touchy subject." Lucius quoted from memory: "If everybody who says he shot Watson actually shot him, the dock must have been a frightful mess." This reporter would write a fine book about the Everglades in which E. J. Watson was awarded three whole pages, including the misinformation that Watson shot and wounded C. G. McKinney (who had not been present), and was thereupon killed by a white fisherman, Luke Short.

"So *that*'s where Ol' Luke came from!" Hoad cried, remembering the query from the Naples audience. "Luke Short! He on your list?" The old friends laughed.

*

At the bridge, they circled back downriver, passing the fish houses and the stone crab and mullet boats along the docks and the stacked crab pots, gray-green with dried algae. It was near twilight. A few old cars came and went.

"Uncle George was Justice of the Peace when he sold out to Barron Collier, so he was made the first county judge there at the courthouse. Funny thing was, the two cases that most interested him never came to trial. The first one was the Watson case—was Watson lynched?—and the second was the mystery of those two young Hardens who disappeared in the late twenties down around Shark River."

Lucius nodded. "One was Roark, Whidden's older brother. Roark and his cousin were murdered."

"That so, Lucius? It's like the Watson case—depends on who you talk to. Suspicious circumstances, Uncle George called it. Maybe those boys had it coming, maybe not."

Lucius changed the subject. "Lots of For Sale signs around here. Looks like too many houses up for sale and too few takers."

"Naturally. The place is dead. Only reason I come back here is because I'm homesick, but I sure don't care much for this 'Everglades City.' Can't hardly find old Everglade no more, can't hardly make head or tail of the whole place. Big trees gone, old houses, too, got all these power lines and trailer homes and plywood houses that look more like chicken coops. Instead of citrus, bougainvillea, they pave the whole yard, nothing but driveway. Brick barbecues, y'know, and tin flamingos. Got their plastic boat parked on the concrete alongside the car.

"Can't hardly tell boats from cars no more, with all the shine and chrome. And the noise of them big outboards—Lord! Scaring the last fish out of the bays! Hit the throttle when they hit the water, take off howling, throw up waves that bash our old wood boats against the bulkheads. No experience of fish or tides or weather, no knowledge of the backcountry, no idea where in heck they might be headed for, let alone why, just roaring around bouncing off each other's wakes like damn fool chickens with their heads cut off!"

Stopping to get a breath, Hoad glared at Lucius, poking his stick at the insolent hard weeds that pushed through big cracks in the broken sidewalk. "Even this darn *weed* only come here lately!" He smiled unwillingly. "Well, dammit, Lucius, a man's boat has no business in his yard! *That* ain't Everglade! Might be Everglades City but it sure ain't Everglade! That Yankee never done this place one bit of good!"

Hoad stopped waving his thin arms and resumed walking. "Lord!" he groaned, disgusted with himself. "No wonder people hate crabby old men! I can't live with what I'm turning into! Heck, my family got nothing to complain about—I know that. Storters sold our old home place, so it's our own darn fault! Sold out our paradise for paper money—not greenbacks even, just numbers in the bank that only exist in thin air! Traded in our fine old home for a pink ranchette on a grid street in a new subdivision on a hot bare stretch of bulldozed scrub inland. The same thing Andy done! Big show window with a ugly view of the same darn ugly thing cropping up next door!"

He frowned and smiled at the same time, trying to air out his dyspeptic humor. "Ranchettes sure ain't much to leave your grandchildren. They sure ain't nothing much at all when you go comparing 'em to the wood homes we used to have here on this good old river. The mullets jumping and the pelicans, and all that good ol' family living that we lost."

He paused again to stare balefully at Lucius, who could think of no way to console him. Torn and incomplete, the two old friends stood ruminating in the dusk. At the end of every street, the encircling green mangroves lay in wait, as if this dense forbidding growth might come in after dark to smother the small town, returning the former Haiti Potato Creek to coastal jungle. "Our family had our good out of this place, and we never came back," Hoad Storter said. "My dad died the year the Park came in—good thing for him!—and my brother Claude's gone, too. That sign might still say Storter Avenue, but there aren't too many living there today who would even remember who the Storters were."

*

Taking cold bottles of beer, they sat on crab pots on the dock, looking out across the tidal river, where the sun falling to the Gulf out to the westward was firing the highest leaves on the mangrove wall. When darkness came, they went up onto the hotel porch, where Andy joined them for a stone crab supper. There was still no word from Rob or Dyer, and in the absence of word about his brother, the talk made Lucius unbearably restless. He said good night and went into the bar, which was almost empty.

Sally Brown lay drunk and half-reclined across a tiny table. She must have heard some rumor about Lucy Summerlin, for she was regaling the barman in her local dialect about "Ol' Colonel" and his "widder woman."

"Now this here widder woman's friend run and told the widder, says, 'Guess who I seen only this minute, down to the Jif-Quik Convenience Store! Your ol' schooldays sweetheart Mr. Lucius H. Watson, buyin hisself a six-pack of Ol' Fishhead Beer! He come a-slippin through the vestee-bule as I was leavin!' So that ol' widder jumps into her finery and runs down to the Jif-Quik for a look! Sure enough, there's good ol' Colonel, homin right in on the chunky peanut butter plus the high-grade cat food that's one hundred percent certified safe to eat by senior citizens!

"Well, that smart widder props her hair up, dabs her lips, and comes sailin right on down the aisle, big bosom first, she plows smack into him. Pops her big eyes open wide and hollers, 'Oh my goodness!' like this Mr. Lucius Watson were some kind of a visitation that the Merciful Lord sent down to that convenience store. She went all soft, fell up against him bosom first, till he had to grab her to keep her from swoonin dead away and bringin down a few racks of comestibles right along with her. When she come to in his manly arms, she batted her eyes like just the cutest l'il girl and sighed and thanked him ever so sweet for savin her pore life, and when she recovered, which she done real quick, she struck up some of that snappy conversation she is knowed for. Well, poor ol' Mr. Lucius Watson—who might not of talked to nothin but stray dogs for a month of Sundays—poor ol' Lucius never knew what hit him. Next thing he knew, she had him wrapped up like a ham, ready to take home and eat for dinner!"

Hearing Lucius laugh, Sally whirled and glared, embarrassed but too dazed to be apologetic. As he came forward, she sat up straight and crossed her legs and produced a sort of smile but did not ask him to sit down and have a drink with her. "Don't tell Whidden, for Christ's sake," she said. She lit a cigarette, her crossed leg twitching like the stiff tail of a cat, eyes looking past him toward the door. "You see Mr. House out on the porch? He's waiting for you." Then Crockett Junior filled the doorway, and she closed her eyes and groaned and said, "Oh boy." She blew her cigarette smoke from her mouth, watched it disperse.

On his way out, Lucius told Crockett that if Rob Watson failed to show up by tomorrow, he would call the Sheriff and report a kidnapping. "Call him, then," said the one-armed man and shouldered him aside. He crossed the room and yanked out the other chair at Sally's table, shouting roughly at Lucius that somebody was expecting him at the front door.

*

The black car had its motor running, and the passenger door swung open when Lucius appeared. They drove in silence down along the riverfront, under the moon. Where the tidal river widened near its mouth, Dyer swerved and stopped with a hard yank, so close to the bulkhead that the large eagle ornament on the front of the car hood stuck out over the water. He did not turn the motor off and he left the car in gear, foot on the clutch. Fists clamped on the top rim of the steering wheel, he confronted the wide portal in the mangroves where the river opened out onto the Bay.

Beyond the portal, a moon-spun silver tide hurried west between pale spoil banks of the channel to Indian Key Pass and the barrier islands on the Gulf horizon. He's looking right at everything and he sees nothing, Lucius thought. This strange brother of his, staring right at it, had never seen that brilliant tide in all his life. And he had to wonder if their father had seen it, either.

"I guess you know that crazy old man tried to shoot me," Dyer said at last.

"Shoot out your car tires, you mean? How can you be certain it was Rob when so many others seem to have it in for you?"

"Brother Lucius," Dyer pronounced slowly, still facing straight ahead. In the glare of the old streetlamps, his face was a fungus white. "Brother Lucius knows about my tires. Brother Lucius knows all about that shooting." Dyer turned to look at him. "You knew Robert Watson was armed and dangerous. You didn't warn me."

"Old and harmless, you mean."

"Aiding and abetting in a double murder? No jury in this state is going to call that 'harmless'!"

So Dyer had seen that packet in Rob's satchel, or had heard about it, probably from Crockett Junior. Lucius said carefully, "Even if Rob happened to be present, whatever occurred took place more than fifty years ago, and nobody can show what preceded it—what caused it."

"You know what I'm referring to, I see. And probably you also know that there's no statute of limitations on first-degree murder."

"Nobody was ever charged with murder. That case was never on the books. No hearing, no indictment, and no evidence."

"You've read the written statement? The confession?"

"Yes," he lied, feeling all twisted. Perhaps he did not *want* to read Rob's statement (though it had his name on it). Why read the thing? He saw no point in it. Even if Rob had his facts straight about the Tucker case, it might only mean that Papa had lost his senses on that one occasion—temporary insanity or something. One could scarcely dismiss his whole career on the basis of one aberrant episode!

Dyer's bloodless hands clenched the top rim of the steering wheel, as if, at any moment, he might release the clutch and let the car lurch off the bulkhead into the channel. He was relating in his courtroom tone that the police had found a cartridge casing "consistent with" the slugs taken from Dyer's tires. That evidence cast strong suspicion on Robert Watson, but probably insufficient to convict, without the weapon. "There's other evidence, of course. The suspect's brother Lucius had pointed the finger at Robert Watson at a public meeting in Naples before a hundred witnesses. It's on the record. However," Dyer added coolly, turning to Lucius, "we might not use your . . . testimony? . . . unless we had to, since drawing attention to the Tucker case could be counterproductive in our effort to rehabilitate your father."

"Our father, you mean."

"There you go again." Watt Dyer's eyes closed in his slow tortoise blink. Otherwise his face showed no expression, only that queer shivering of skin above his lip. Slowly he looked back along the riverfront toward the hotel, then gazed fixedly again at the night river. There was no one in the street, and only Crockett Junior, Lucius realized with a start, knew where he'd gone. But for the moment, Lucius was much more concerned about the purring motor, still in gear—he shifted a little in his seat, opened his door a little.

Dyer noted this. He said, "At any rate, we now have the revolver. If Robert Watson is turned over to the law, he returns to prison automatically as an escaped felon. If I turn the weapon over to the police, the ballistics tests will show that Robert Watson was guilty of attempted murder. He will be sentenced with due consideration of his prior record and will finish out his life in federal prison."

He drew a power-of-attorney form out of his briefcase. "On the other hand, if you people cooperate, the gun will be returned. That eliminates the ballistics evidence, without which there can be no case, even if I press charges, which I won't."

"And the so-called confession?"

"You can have that, too."

"How can I be certain you will keep your word? What if I refused to sign until this so-called evidence was returned?"

"In that case, you will certainly delay—and jeopardize—the Watson Claim. Meanwhile you will endanger your brother and ensure my ill will, which as your attorney I do not recommend." Dyer almost smiled. "You might as well cooperate, since you have no choice."

"And if I do sign, then you will release him?"

"I haven't got him. But if the men who have him know you are cooperating—"

Lucius took the form, scribbled a signature, and sat back, strangely out of breath.

Dyer snapped on the car light and put the document into his briefcase. He withdrew a clipping and read aloud from a newspaper feature about "Emperor Watson's" frontier house on a "lost" Indian mound in a remote region of the Park where "most authorities agreed" that the legendary Fountain of Youth had been located, where Ponce de León had been slain by the Calusa, where the giant Chief Chekaika (who massacred the whites at Indian Key back in 1842 and was later caught and hanged on a Glades hammock by the noted Indian fighter General William Harney) had made his hideout— "This is all nonsense!" Lucius protested—and where the pioneer planter E. J. Watson had first developed the fine strain of Cuban sugarcane that seeded the vast agricultural empire at Okeechobee which helped put the sovereign state of Florida where it was today.

Dyer thrust the clipping at him and he scanned it quickly. Quoted throughout was the well-known Miami attorney Watson Dyer, who had lately obtained a temporary injunction against the proposed burning of the house, citing the unextinguished land claim of the Watson heirs. According to the article, the Park was contesting the injunction on the grounds that any land claim E. J. Watson might have made was no longer valid, and that the historic traditions being ascribed to this site were "unproven or demonstrably untrue." Nevertheless, attorney Dyer had expressed full confidence in the claim, which was supported by an *amici curiae* motion from several esteemed colleagues of the presiding judge. Leading businessmen and political figures in the state had interested themselves in the case and stood ready to endorse the Watson claim, attorney Dyer asserted.

Unless the taxpayers protested the senseless burning of the Watson Place, the article concluded, what Mr. Dyer termed "the only tourist attraction in the whole Park" would be destroyed by the same technocratic lack of vision that was already obliterating the wildlife of the Everglades and the world-famous marine fisheries in surrounding waters. In that event, the journalist suggested, it was time to recommend that this tragically degraded region should be taken away from a remote and foolish federal bureaucracy and restored to the people of Florida before its utter destruction was complete.

"How's that?" Dyer grinned with satisfaction. Nevertheless, he had wanted to make sure that the Watson Claim was unassailable, that it would be sustained by the court in perpetuity. A preexisting building helped the claim, he said, because without the house, there was no historic monument. Since any man-made structure within Park boundaries could never be repaired or replaced, and because Park land could not be used for private purposes, the loss of the house might weaken the whole claim by making it appear frivolous, in fact pointless.

"With your endorsement of the claim"—he tapped his briefcase—"we should win an indefinite extension of the court injunction against burning. Meanwhile, your biography will establish Watson's prominence in our state history and provide good cause to make the house a monument. With public opinion in our favor, it becomes unlikely that the Park will continue to contest our claim. We'll have these family affidavits, we'll have your petitions from the local families, and we'll have favorable publicity from the newspapers which will save face for our farsighted Park officials by giving them all the credit. I'm even arranging the requisition of a new military helicopter to junket them across the Glades in a few days for our official meeting at the Bend!"

Dyer put his clipping away, and still they sat there on the moonlit river with the car still running. Beside himself, Lucius burst out, "Goddammit, what about Rob? How can I be certain they'll release him?"

"Why don't we simply assume that he will be turned over to you at Chatham Bend. All he has to do is sign our documents."

And still they were dissatisfied, not finished. Lucius said, "How about Fred Dyer's affidavit that you are E. J. Watson's natural son?"

For the first time since Lucius had known him, Watson Dyer was taken by surprise. Clearing his throat, Dyer said finally, "Just wanted to cover all contingencies. In a tight decision, it might be helpful to make the formal claimant a Watson heir who was actually born on Chatham Bend—"

"How about Pearl and Minnie? They were born there, too."

"—but as long as you and your brother are present at the meeting," Dyer continued, "I hardly think such an affidavit will be necessary."

"Formal claimant. That the same as the sole claimant? Under your new name? Watson Watson, maybe? You could hyphenate it!" He brooded bitterly. "Something's missing, Dyer. The truth, maybe? If the house is set aside as a historic monument within the park, what does it matter whose name is on the claim? Am I missing something? What do the Watsons have to lose by making you the 'formal claimant,' if that saves the house?"

"Precisely. The point is to win the claim. If the claim is denied, then the Watson family loses. Not that you've welcomed me into the family."

"And you're going to all this trouble out of sentiment? Out of the goodness of your heart? I don't believe it!"

"You have a better explanation?"

"Not yet. But I will."

Anxious to catch up with Crockett Junior, Lucius got out of the running car and hurried back to the hotel, walking upriver, but Crockett and Sally were no longer in the bar.

Chapter 8

To Chokoloskee

Lady Bluehair at the desk impaled his frugal breakfast check upon a spike, in a manner suggesting that solitary elders who dined sparsely were not to be taken seriously as clientele. "Enjoy your little snack?" she said, not looking up. Between black roots of hard blue hair, the pallid skin was taut over her pate, and he wondered if Papa, provoked beyond endurance, might have seized up a blunt instrument and obliterated this creature at a blow. "Thank you," he said, with a courtliness entirely lost on her. "Thank you kindly," he repeated vaguely, turning away across the lobby where huge tarpon leapt in painful arcs high on the dark wood walls. The ocean pearliness on the Triassic scales of the great armored herring had been transmuted to an opaque dull yellow, and the huge jaws, stretched forever in pursuit of that last fatal lure, were gray with spiderwebs.

Out of the east, in brilliant morning, the sun roared up out of the Glades, filling the great mahogany at the front door and flying in wild shards from the black palm fronds. That woman's spite, compounding the evil feeling left by Dyer, had soured his morning before it was half-started. At a loss about Rob and growing desperate, he felt assailed by the hard light which smote his eye.

Sandy Albritton cracked his door but would not unlatch the screen. "The wife ain't home today," he said, ignoring the cigarette coughs in the background. "Tomorrow neither." Through the rusty screen, he observed Lucius with glee.

"I wanted to get your signature on my petition. To stop the Park from burning down the house on Chatham Bend."

"I ain't feelin good," said Sandy, eliciting a cackle from the room behind. Abruptly, he closed the door, lest Watson attempt to force an entry. "Don't bother comin back here, Lucius," came his muffled voice. "If I was you, I would head right out of town."

A woman's face withdrew from a small window next door. The kitchen door creaked at the back. Sally Brown did not greet him but marched straight to the car. When he opened the front door for her, she climbed into the backseat, and he felt the heavy stir of paranoia—the Albrittons' refusal to let him in the house, then Sandy's contemptuous use of "Lucius," now Sally's coldness. "They have their orders, that's all," Sally said, closing her eyes. Knowing he was watching her in the rearview mirror, she snapped irritably, "Don't you *ever* give up? When are you going to learn?"

Driving back to the hotel, he tried to justify himself, which annoyed him further. Unsupported versions of long-ago events (including her own renditions, though he did not say this) were unacceptable, of course. But if a certain story was confirmed repeatedly by different people, an echo of the truth might still be heard. One way or another, all these local families had a part in the Watson legend, and their memories and opinions had to be considered. . . .

The peremptory gesture of her hand, glimpsed in the mirror, dismissed his entire quest, and not politely. "No Albrittons were in that posse, yet even Albrittons don't want to talk to you!" She opened her window to get some fresh air. "You're not going to get straight answers from these people! They're all related one way or another, they're all snarled up amongst each other like a tub of snakes. Every family on the Bay has relatives on that list of yours! Why should they help you?"

Sally looked drawn and tired as well as irritable. He supposed she was upset because he'd seen her drunk and in the company of Crockett Junior. He had to know if she had anything to tell him.

"About Crockett? Yes. Mind your own business!"

"About Rob. Dyer told me last night they would release him."

Her eyes shot open. She sat forward and laid her hand on his arm. "Oh sweetheart, don't torture yourself this way! You can't count on that! They don't like Dyer and don't trust him. They don't owe Watson Dyer a damn thing!"

Andy was awaiting them beneath the great mahogany. "Later," she murmured, but she held his eye. "In case you're worried, Prof, I didn't do it. With Crockett, I mean. I hoped to find out something about Rob." She shook her head. "He wouldn't say a word, he only growled. Said, 'That fuckin Mud has talked too much already.' "

With Andy House, they headed south toward the new causeway that connected the mainland with Chokoloskee Island. The fire color of the sun had turned ash white, boiling the humid air. Told what had happened at the Albrittons', Andy nodded, unsurprised. "Folks are wondering why Colonel Watson came to town. They're leery, that's all," Andy said finally.

"Guilty, you mean—"

"You're too rough on 'em, Miss. When these Bay folks know you, they are kind and generous—too darn generous! My dad used to buy his gator hides from Sandy, so when I'm visiting, those Albrittons won't let me pay for one darned thing. Bought some mullet from Annie years ago and she wouldn't take my money, so I never bought from them again. It hurts me when poor people give away everything for nothing! I can't let 'em do that, so I don't announce my visit! But I like to sneak back this way once in a while, just to remind myself how much I like these people after all!

"Course Sandy was a terrible drinker. I always liked that sonofagun but when he drank, he had some hell in him, I'll tell you! Albrittons always like to say how much they liked the Injuns, but them poor Injuns was plain scared to death of him, and nigras, too! He used to hang out with Speck Daniels, and them two together was a public menace. One time when our family was livin at Ochopee, them boys come along to where some nigras with long bamboo poles was fishing perch along the Trail canal, and they shot rifles from the truck, made them black folks dance till every last poor soul jumped in the water!

"Frank Tippins, now, he was another one had a high opinion of the Injuns, it was only black people he had no use for. My aunt Mamie Smallwood was a wonderful, good, generous woman, but she was that way, too—always very concerned about the Injuns. Ever notice how popular Injuns can be with folks who are mean-mouthed about blacks? Maybe liking Injuns that way is proof to their own selves that despising black people don't have nothing to do with anything so ignorant and ugly as race prejudice—proof that they are fair-minded Americans, I mean, and that being so fair-minded in the Land of the Free, they are free to despise the colored people to their hearts' content."

*

Andy's words were lost as the black truck came roaring up behind on its huge tires, filling the rearview mirror to bursting before veering onto the road shoulder and buffeting them as it passed on the wrong side. A moment later, it swerved across, filling the windshield, then bounced over the divider in the middle of the road. It rocketed ahead down the wrong-way lane before careening in a crashing turn back over the divider and hurtling back in their direction, wrong way and head-on, running them off the road as it blared past.

In the howl of knobbed tires biting at the concrete, rags of shouted filth drifted past their ears. Shaken, Sally cried, "He warned you! *Don't come farther south!* And you came anyway!"

Lucius's nerves gave way, too, and his temper spilled over. "It's *my* fault, what that maniac just did?"

"That's the message them boys give to strangers," Andy said, trying to smooth things. Despite his calm demeanor, his own voice was tight. He peered away over the Bay—the broad low-tide flats and the reflected clouds, the channel markers, oyster bars, and tall gaunt stalking herons—as if, in this crisis, his blind eyes might read that mirror of the sky for signs and portents.

"I'm sorry, Mister Colonel." Sally pressed her brow on the cool glass of the window as if resting up after the effort of apology. "Know what his everlovin daddy said to Crockett Junior? 'You're pretty handy with that big toy truck, leastways for a cripple with one arm.' "

Chokoloskee

The causeway went south past Half Way Creek and bent offshore from the mangrove wall at the mouth of Turner River. It ended at the round high mound of Chokoloskee, which had risen forty feet above sea level, Lucius told them, before this new road had laid it open to the bulldozers. Excepting the Caxambas hills on Marco Island, Chokoloskee had been the highest Indian mound along this coast. Andy observed that the Islanders had started selling off their land, and that speculators were leveling the mounds to create "prime water-view properties." Within a few years, what the Calusa had built slowly over centuries would be graded off as fill for new development.

The old Lopez graveyard was an abrupt rise which had been ground level for this part of the island before the land around it had been carved away. The cemetery reminded Andy of that time some local boys had rustled a Lopez cow to feed their families. "Joe Lopez wouldn't listen to one word about them boys paying it back," Andy remembered, as Lucius cast about for a quick change of subject. "Nosir," said Andy, "they brung in the Sheriff. The families was ready to start the Spanish War all over again, run that Lopez bunch right back to Spain, they were that angry! Old Man Sandy ever tell you about that, Miss Sally?"

Sally's face had closed as tight as a persimmon. Knowing Old Man Sandy's reckless tongue, she doubtless suspected that he had been indiscreet in his talk with Lucius, who might have passed the story on to Andy. At the blind man's question, she flushed with emotion, and her answer, intended to be casual, came out wavering and crushed and close to tears. "The year Sandy went to prison was the year my brother Crockett was conceived and born. That what you're getting at?"

"No, it sure ain't! Oh Lord, Miss Sally, I just clean forgot! Us Houses was mostly gone from here by that time!" Chagrined, he stuck his little finger in his ear as if scraping his brain for a new topic. How had she met Whidden— were they schoolmates in Everglade after the Hardens came north from the Islands? "I heard he was put in with the white kids—"

"Mr. House? Excuse me! They put him in with the white children because he was a white child. He was *born* white, Mr. House! The Hardens are white people, white and Indian—the rest is slander!"

The blind man groaned. "Heck, it sure don't matter none. I was just—"

"Nosir, it sure don't matter none," she said—not to mimic his unlettered speech but to confront this local man on common ground. "Nosir, not one little bit. Less you're a Harden."

House was red-faced and nettled. "Might not matter much to Hardens neither, not no more, Miss," Andy warned her.

*

Beyond lay the wooded Smallwood cemetery, where they all got out. Looking around him, Andy smiled, saying that some way he could see everything better when he was standing up on his two feet. He made a slow circle on the grass, getting the feel of things, as a big dog makes its turn before lying down. Long ago, with other boys, he had played in this canal and its deep inner basin, which was perhaps fifty feet across, ringed around by trees. Canal and basin had been excavated by the Calusa, whose seagoing dugouts had been hewn and fire-hollowed from great cypress. "You could lay a long rifle in the bottom crossways," Andy said.

"My dad moved us off this island when I was still a boy, and it sure don't look like I'll be comin back. The House family was close-knit once, but we're scattered now, we're all over west Florida. Smallwoods stayed, the most of 'em, but they're squabbling over what little land is left. The rest of the old families don't hardly own no land no more, they got just about everything sold off to strangers."

Lucius could recall the abounding gardens and fine avocado groves which the early families had hacked and hoed from the old shell. Already those gardens were disappearing, and a few years from now, this island, beaten flat, would disappear beneath the tar and concrete, the tourist courts and house trailers, the noisy cars of vacationers with their red faces, funny sun hats, candy-colored clothes. Here and there, some faded figure might be glimpsed along the weedy edges—a relict islander, living along on government handouts and thin reminiscence of the way things were.

"It's important to line up the old frontier families behind the petition," Lucius said. "Smallwoods. Browns and Thompsons. Carrs."

"Browns and Thompsons. Carrs!" Sally rolled her eyes and went ahead on foot.

Andy turned toward the sound of her retreating steps. "Well, I'm kin to all them families, kin to *all* these folks down here," he reminded Lucius. "And they're all related to each other, back door, front, and every whichy-way, which is why they all think the same when they get around to thinkin, which ain't often." He smiled with wry affection. "No sense thinkin if you know what your daddy thought. Just get yourself all flustered up for nothin.

"What Sally forgets, there is a difference between ignorance and evil. I'd like to take and shoot some of these Chok folks for being so ornery and cranky, but I love 'em, too—I do! It's only a crowd of 'em that bothers me. I take after Bill House, I guess. Whenever he spoke about that day your daddy died—well, he never regretted it or nothing, but he'd sure mutter some about the way us rednecks act when we're in a crowd. Different animal altogether, Dad would say."

Lucius said, "I was talking with Hoad Storter yesterday about those Harden boys killed at Shark River."

Andy stopped short, pointing his cane at him. "Colonel? You best not stir up that ol' mud, not if you're huntin up support for that petition." He resumed walking. "I was heartsick for them Harden families when them boys come up missin, same as you were. Roark and Wilson was close to my own age, so I knowed 'em good when our family was living at the Bend."

"And you don't think all that bad gossip about the Harden family was involved."

"Nosir, I sure don't. Them two cousins was wild and angry boys. They was looking for trouble, and you know that good as I do."

"Are you saying they got what they deserved?"

"Darn it, Colonel, I never said nothin like that! Don't you go to cornerin me like she done, just cause I ain't educated good!" He fumed and stumped along. "Sure, Hardens had some Injun, like the girl says. But that ain't all they had! I ain't sayin that is bad nor good, but facts is facts! And when they commenced to shootin rifles over the men's heads, folks just naturally got their dander up against 'em!"

"That's not all they had—you sure about that, Andy?"

"Hell, Colonel, everybody was sure about it! I never heard my daddy say no different!"

"No sense thinking if you know already what your daddy thought. Get yourself all flustered up for nothing."

"Hell, I'm flustered up right now!"

The blind man headed down the road alone. When he heard the motor come up slow behind him, he waved it off, using his cane. "Leave me be! I see the sun and I see this white shell road—don't need much else to find my way on my home island!"

Lucius caught up with Sally Brown, who had paused to watch Andy's slow progress. "Think he'll be all right?" she said, annoyed by her own concern. She would keep an eye on Andy, see him safely to the Smallwoods. Whidden, she said, might turn up at the Smallwood store toward noon.

*

Lloyd Brown was one of the last full-time fishermen on the Bay, and his backyard was cluttered with crab pots, buoys, sun-bleached netting, rusted gear, dead outboard motors, a big mushroom anchor.

A gray head peered at Lucius from behind a curtain of blue plastic lace. Then the head vanished, and the kitchen door of the old cottage opened slowly. "I know who you are," the woman said, to warn him, and he came no closer. Still yanking at her hair, she did not invite him in. The last time he recalled seeing her, back in the twenties, pretty Mary Hamilton had been one in a long line of towhead kids.

"You remember me, Mary? You were pretty young—"

"Nobody forgot you around here." Arms folded on her breasts, she smoked and squinted. "Bet you made 'em kind of nervous over yonder," Mary said wryly. She cocked her head, the better to enjoy his consternation. "You still messing around with that ol' list?" She squinted at him through a shroud of smoke, then turned and went inside without a word, leaving the door open. By the time he entered, knocking lightly, she had resumed her place behind her coffee cup and ashtray on the far side of the linoleumed kitchen table. "You want coffee, it's in the pot," she said, in a fit of smoker's coughing. When he brought his coffee to the table, she whispered hoarsely, "I been thinking about writing up *my* memoirs, too."

"Is that right?"

"Yep." She snubbed her cigarette, lit up another. "And all that Watson stuff is going straight into my story." She nodded a long time, looking him over. "Course some folks were resentful of Mr. Watson right from the time he started out at Half Way Creek, cause everything he touched just turned to gold. And he'd been in trouble, and he found some more, so of course they made up stories just to pull him down. You ever hear about old bones that somebody dug up on the Bend back in the thirties? Supposed to been Bloody Watson's victims?" Seeing Lucius's expression, she added quickly, "Well, you can rest easy on *that* one, Colonel, cause those were the bones of old-time Indians that had a village on there long ago, or maybe some bones from a hog barbecue or something. What people tell about your daddy is a crying shame!

"My husband's aunt—the husband I have now, I mean—she was a McKinney, and she went down there and visited with Edna Watson for a week. Old Man McKinney, who was very strict, would never have allowed that visit if he didn't have a lot of faith in Mr. Watson. Mr. McKinney took no part in the shooting, said he never messed in other folks' affairs. For the rest of his life, he would remind those men that his friend Watson never killed nobody from our island. Might of cut Santini's throat, but as Ted Smallwood used to say, 'He never killed that old Corsican completely.' That business happened at Key West, where there were always foreigners and knife fights, and anyways those darn Santinis were some kind of darn Catholics to start off with."

Her voice died to a whisper as she stopped to listen, turning her ear with the precision of a cat. Uncoiling slowly, recoiling again, Mary Brown pulled her wrap close and sat up primly at the table, raising her voice as her husband reached the kitchen door. "I was just now telling Colonel Watson how I don't believe C. G. McKinney would have let his daughter go to Chatham Bend, not if he thought Colonel's daddy was a killer!"

The man in the doorway had dark frown lines in a weathered face and curly hair blown back across a brow crusted by sun. "I seen a car out there," he told his wife. Despite Lucius's warm greeting—he had always liked Lloyd Brown—Brown made no answer but appraised his visitor, making certain who he was. "How-do, Colonel," he said finally. "Been a very long time since we seen you on this island."

His wife observed both men obliquely through her long strayed hair, her expression ironic and affectionate at the same time. "He says he's only interested in old-time stuff," she told her husband, who slopped himself a cup of coffee and sat down glowering.

"Well, your family took no part in the killing, I know that much," Lucius said.

"My aunt seen the whole thing," Lloyd Brown recalled. "She was visiting that day with Mrs. Watson there at Smallwood's, and she had a pretty darn good view down through the trees. Said Watson run his boat aground, then jumped ashore with Cox's hat in one hand and his double-barrel shotgun in the other. When the crowd didn't believe his story, he snapped off both barrels, which misfired. Went for his .38 but never got to it, because a man who had no business there, he put a bullet right between his eyes."

Lucius said, "Henry Short?"

"I don't recall no names no more," Lloyd said. He stared his wife down when she piped up, and she looked away with a miffed expression, like an ousted cat. She blew thin smoke, drowned her cigarette in the spilled coffee in her saucer, and tamped a new one, bouncing it on the table.

Lloyd Brown was still glowering at Lucius. "How come you're askin about Henry Short? He on your list?" He looked resentful. "What you up to, Colonel? You already know all there is to know about your daddy. Know it better'n we do, very likely, cause we was youngsters when you first went around askin all them questions."

They nodded over that awhile, until Lucius said, "I'm trying to learn who lived on the Watson Place in the years I was away—"

"Let me think back a little, Colonel," Lloyd Brown said. "For the first years after your dad died, there weren't no one on the Bend at all, that's how scared of Leslie Cox the people was. Weren't till about 1913 that Willie Brown moved on there the first time, and it might been Willie who sold it to the Chevelier Corporation. Bill House was the first caretaker, then Henry Thompson, that's how I remember it.

"My uncles took over in the early thirties, and I lived there awhile. All the outbuildings was swept away in the '26 Hurricane, but some of the old dock platforms was still there. Had to patch the screens, douse 'em with cylinder oil, cause the mosquitoes was terrible, worse than ever. That was Depression times, no work anyplace and the net fishin poor. Mostly we cooked shine and gator-hunted, ricked some charcoal, lived off of the land. A bear broke into the kitchen wing, come in after our venison—that bear sure made a mess, I can tell you that!

"Chatham Bend is where me and my cousins learned to hunt, and we always thought of it as home. Still do, I guess. I never heard nobody around our family run down Watsons. No matter what he might of did, E. J. Watson was E. J. Watson. Like my dad said, 'That man was who he was! He weren't like some!'

"About 1934, I reckon, Chatham Bend was turned over to the Audubon warden Charlie Green. Mac Johnson and his wife come on there after that but didn't last long, because Dorothy lost her mind down there, tried to burn them bloodstains off the floor and near to burned down the whole house while she was at it. She was ravin that the ghost of Mr. Watson would come get her, on account of her daddy Henry Smith was in the posse."

"Oh, my," said Mary Brown. "It takes all kinds, I guess."

"After Mac Johnson, it was mostly gator hunters, moonshiners. Some common drifters. None of 'em stayed long, and none of 'em loved ol' Chatham the way we done, they just used it hard. Just before the Park come in, some Miami politicians got the use of it for a huntin camp. Done more drinkin and screwin than huntin and fishin, left the house a mess." Lloyd Brown lifted his eyes from the petition. "Know who brought them sports there in the first place? Same lawyer who got up this here paper!"

"So I have heard," said Lucius.

"That Great Hurricane might been the worst one, but last year's storm took out all them giant mangroves down around Shark River. You hear about that, up there to Caxambas? Got to be a good blow to do that, cause some of them trees went eighty-foot tall, must of been back there since Calusa days. But it never done real damage to the Watson house, not the way Parks claims. She's as strong as ever, from the look of her."

*

"We heard you come here to the Bay with Andy House—we think a lot of Andy," Lloyd Brown said. "Course his family wasn't so much liked because Old Man House taught all his kids how they was some way better'n the rest of us, and Mamie House took that attitude over to Smallwood's. But one of my McKinney cousins married young Dan House, and I always got on good with Smallwoods, all but that one who claims his daddy started up the post office—well, we know better. C. G. McKinney was the founder, and Mr. Ted Smallwood took it over from him later."

"Probably Ned gets those ideas from his sister Wilma," Mary said. "Visitors come into their store to find out who they should ask about the old days, and Wilma never mentions the name Brown, although Browns and McKinneys were on this Bay a good ten years before her own family showed up."

"Old Man McKinney's heart failed on the dock at Everglade, 1926, and his only boy never had nothin but daughters, so that good old name is almost gone from around here. His boy Charlie was all tore up about not havin no sons, cause he was a feller had his heart set on the past. Uncle Charlie went barefoot year in and year out, would not buy shoes nor get into a car. His wife put in some indoor plumbing but he never lost faith in his outhouse. Passin in my boat, sometimes, I'd see him settin in there peerin out like a old possum.

"When the new causeway come along and let the world in—that about broke him. He never been much good for nothin since that happened. Still pines away for the grand old days of the Florida frontier, don't care for modern times at all. Takes out most of his disappointment on the automobile, says he wouldn't get into one of them damned things if you paid him. Ain't *never* goin on no auto ride till the day they ride his carcass to the cemetery, and even then, he wants a wheelbarrer if they have any respect for his last wishes, which they won't."

Cap'n Lloyd relaxed a little when his guest laughed. He poured more coffee. "It was Mamie pushed so hard to get that causeway, she was always lookin to escape off of this island. Us Browns was more like Charlie McKinney, we liked this good old place the way it was. All them autos honkin around, stinkin up the air—I reckon progress was the last thing our home people needed." He waved his arm, indicating the out-of-doors. "Hell, that ain't Chok! It ain't even an island, not no more!"

Lloyd took a deep breath. "What you here for, Colonel?"

His wife winked at Lucius Watson. "What Colonel wants to know is, honey, will we sign this paper. He aims to circulate it over to the store. Wants our old families to help protect the Watson Place, especially them ones like us that used to call it home."

Captain Lloyd signed the petition without reading it, then shoved it at his wife, who did the same.

*

Ernestine Thompson, who lived on the last high mound on Chokoloskee, was a small, owlish lady in thick glasses who reminded Lucius of her mother, Mamie Smallwood. Indicating a chair, she returned to her place on the sofa, where she was joined by round-faced Roy, her spouse. When Lucius grinned at him, he beamed. Roy Thompson and Lucius had been friendly in the twenties, but his wife introduced them anyway, on general principles. Lucius said he was sorry to impose on them with so little notice, and she said, "Nobody's going anyplace. Not on a Sunday."

Ernestine Thompson offered no refreshment. Neither friendly nor unfriendly, she sat waiting for their visitor to state his business. No, they would not sign the petition without consultation with her cousin Bill Smallwood. As for family memories of Mr. Watson, her mother had always told the children that he was a fine-looking man with bright blue eyes and dark red hair. "That's temper." Mr. Watson was courtly in his manners, acted like a gentleman, but there were awful stories. "As Mama always said, she liked him very much but didn't want to!"

"You couldn't *help* but like him!" Roy piped up. "He was interested in everybody and he made 'em feel good. Life got a spark when Mr. Watson was around! He would of made a heck of a politician! Could of run for president!"

His wife closed her eyes for a long moment in sign that she, Ernestine S. Thompson, did not necessarily agree that E. J. Watson could or would or should have run for president. When she opened them again, she said,

"Everything went along all right until that man Cox showed up at Chatham River. Leslie Cox was Edna Watson's age, she had known him since a child, had gone to school with him, and he took advantage, that's what she told Mama. So most of the time, Edna and her little children stayed on this is- land—stayed with Smallwoods, stayed with Wigginses, stayed with McKinneys."

"Cox took advantage, you say?"

"He tried to."

"*Sexual* advantage?"

"She stayed with Aldermans sometimes," Roy Thompson said, hurrying them past his wife's curdled expression.

" 'Stayed with Aldermans,' says Roy, who wasn't here."

"Ain't that who she was staying with, time of the hurricane? That's what your mama told us."

His wife's demeanor made it plain that no matter how plausible her hus- band might appear, he had a lamentable tendency to be mistaken. "Roy? Whose mother are you speaking for?"

"Old Man Watson now, he was in Bonita Springs, night of the storm. Bonita was Surveyor's Creek or Survey back in them days."

"He's not here to inquire about Survey, Roy."

"All I'm tellin is, Mr. Watson stayed over that night with Postmaster A. M. Smith at Survey. Had to go by boat, Marco to Naples, then to Survey by horse and wagon, sand track through the woods. Next morning, the Postmaster got somebody to take him as far north as Punta Rassa, where a feller called Bill Leitner run him up the river to Fort Myers."

"I never heard until this moment who took him upriver!" Lucius noted down the name, astonished anew by the tenacity with which old-timers clung to their precious scraps of the Watson legend. He spared Roy Thomp- son what he already knew, that Papa had spent that stormy night with the Naples postmaster Pop Stewart and headed north by way of Survey the next day. In any case, legend foreshortened time, as dreams did. There was no coast road in those days, only poor trails, and considering the distance over- land, and the strong weather, his father's journey might well have required stopping over one night in each place.

"Well, I guess they ain't too many left that knows the Survey part of the Ed Watson story." Roy looked proudly at his wife, who sat eyes closed for a lit- tle while, perhaps in prayer. "Uncle Dick Moore, he was from Survey, told me all about the Survey story! Used to visit his friend Lucius Watson at the Bend! Went down there about 1909, worked there the best part of a year, never changed the opinion that Mr. Edgar Watson was the nicest man he ever met in all his life. Later years when Uncle Dick and me was working the clam flats off Pavilion Key, we went up to the Bend to fetch some water, and we took some of his alligator pears, which was still pushin up out of the overgrowth. I don't believe I've had a pear so good, that day to this one!

"My Uncle Dick was on Mormon Key in the Great Hurricane, and a feller yelled, 'Better lift your hands and pray to God!' and Uncle Dick yelled, 'The hell I will! I need 'em both to hang on to this tree!' " Roy Thompson laughed, and Lucius laughed, too, happy to hear about his good old friend Dick Moore.

Raising thin eyebrows at her husband's language, Ernestine said, "The man did not call on us to hear your jokes, Roy." And she cleared her throat rather testily before resuming.

"Now when the shooting started, Edna Watson threw her hands up, crying, 'Merciful God, they are killing Mr. Watson!' The Smallwoods never forgot that woeful cry! Millicent was three years old and not in bed yet, so she heard the shooting, and surely the little Watson children heard it, too. Wilma was a little older, that's why she remembered."

"*Merciful God, they are killing Mr. Watson!*" Roy Thompson marveled. "Heck yes, I bet them Watson kids remembered something! Just don't *remember* they remembered! And how about the little feller? Was it Addison? He must of remembered, honey, cause he *seen* it!"

"And that was Edna's birthday! October the twenty-fourth of 1910! The poor creature was twenty-one years old *that very day*!" Ernestine laid a firm hand on her husband's forearm to put a stop to any further contributions. "Edna Watson and her three little ones were staying with Marie Alderman. Marie was a Lopez from Lopez River, Old Man Gregorio's daughter. She married Walter Alderman in 1906."

Now it was Roy Thompson's turn for a warning look. "Honey, like you said yourself, we ain't so sure it was the Aldermans they stayed with. . . ."

"Goodness gracious, Roy! Wasn't it you who told us it was Aldermans? Anyway, there was so much fear on this little island that after her husband had been murdered, that local family was too scared to take her back— whichever family Mr. Thompson thinks it was, him being only a young boy down in the Islands."

"Walter Alderman went up to Columbia County to work for Mr. Watson, and came home in a hurry when Watson got in trouble up there around nineteen and oh-eight," Roy said, hot on the scent. "And I always heard he was right there in that crowd! Might been why he wouldn't keep Edna and the children in his house! Might of felt ashamed, bein around her!"

"Those were the very words our Mama used: 'They wouldn't take her back'! They couldn't look her in the eye, they were so ashamed!"

Roy Thompson said, "Course it could be that the widow had seen Walter in the crowd and didn't want to stay there at his house no more. Or maybe

Aldermans was scared that Leslie Cox might come there huntin her and make more trouble."

"Anyway, our Mama took 'em in. She said to Edna, 'Don't set there weeping, girl, we got plenty o' bedding and there's beds upstairs.' Her new kitchen had been flattened down by hurricane, her new woodstove and new set of dishes all destroyed—she was just heartbroken. Even so, she took those Watsons in. She fed and tended them until Edna was well enough recovered from her shock to leave forever.

"All that water through the house, all those drowned chickens underneath the store that raised up such a smell—poor Mama was sorely depressed by so much rot and wreckage, she thought she'd never get that reek of death out of her nostrils. Then came Mr. Watson's death, when they'd hardly started to clean up after the storm—that uproar finished her. Mama knew the man, knew who he was, but she felt such terrible disgust about the way he died, and so much pity for that young widow and her little ones, and so much anger against those men who terrified them, including her own father and three brothers, that she vowed to run off and leave this place forever.

"First that comet like a warning from the heavens that painted the night with ice all that long spring! Then that huge black storm that descended in the autumn! Then the bloody slaughter of the sinners—signs of Judgment Day! A final warning from the Lord before he wiped this godforsaken coast off of this earth. Mama said, 'Let's leave this accursed place!' And Daddy said, 'Mrs. Smallwood, we have everything all bought and paid for. We'll fix the place right up before you know it, we'll restock and we'll start again.' So the poor thing never got away, she was condemned to a life sentence on this little island.

"Three murders, then that doomsday hurricane, then the Watson killing—those terrible events occurred on three straight Mondays! No wonder everyone felt that they were doomed! And after those Black Mondays came a drought. People forget about the drought, which dragged on forever. This was deep in the autumn rainy season, yet there was no rain for weeks and weeks, into December! It was spooky! Cisterns went dry and such little water as we had turned green and poisonous. Had to go up Turner River to find water!

"Well, all of these calamities were seen as signs of the Lord's wrath. Watsons won't recall because you left the Islands, but all folks here could talk about was Revelations and Apocalypse, bowl of wrath and rain of fire, poisoned water and the darkened sun."

"Heck, they *still* talk about it around here!" Roy Thompson cried, unable to contain himself a moment longer. "But things simmered down after that death. We got religion and life was quiet for the next few years. The first Pentecostals to show up were Babe and Sallie Whidden out of Venus, Florida, who was shocked to learn that the dreadful sinners on this island had no House of God. So Charley Johnson who was in the Watson posse and never minded bein first and foremost, he stepped right up, shouted loud and clear how Charles P. Johnson was 'the chiefest of the sinners,' a rum runner who had done the Devil's work! When it come to sinners, there weren't nobody *near* him, Charley hollered, he was in a class all by himself! Yessir, he was burnin to repent, ol' Charley was, he aimed to get Saved or know the reason why. So what he done, he took his rum boat, took some wages of his sin north to Fort Myers, brung back a cargo of lumber for the church! When it come to saving souls on Chokoloskee, as Tant Jenkins used to say, the Good Lord got a helping hand from the Demon Rum!"

"Are you finished, Roy? I suppose my husband was trying to explain that after 1912, Sunday was Church Day. There's been a Church of God here on the island since that year. And other missionaries heard about our need, and the next year they held a regular revival. Forty souls—about all of Chokoloskee—were baptized in the Bay, right out in front of McKinney's store."

Roy laughed out loud. "First to be dunked were Mrs. McKinney and Mrs. Ida Lopez! C. G. McKinney looked kind of uneasy, he did not care to join in, he just set there fanning hard with his wild turkey wing. And I think it was Rob Storter—Rob got saved, too—who claimed he heard Old Man McKinney mutter how all them people, his own wife included, should of went elsewhere to get purified. Said a man had enough to worry about in life without having them ol' hand-me-down sins washed up at his front door!"

"Well, Roy, you got *that* story from Mr. Smallwood. He always did enjoy telling that story! Not that he was baptized—not that day! Because every last one of our customers had come in from the out islands to be baptized, so Ted Smallwood kept his store open all day."

"Ted sure hated to lose even one customer to those McKinneys! And Mamie was furious that he never closed the store to observe Church Day. He handled money seven days a week, and evenings, too." Roy Thompson chuckled. "Fisherman passing through at midnight, if he happened to need something, all he had to do was sing out from the landing, and Ted went 'Ho!' and rolled right out of bed!"

"First time I ever heard Roy Thompson refer to the senior Smallwoods as 'Ted and Mamie'!" his wife said tartly, as if daring her husband to try minding any more of her family business. Roy rushed on gleefully.

"Course most of them ones in the posse was fishermen and farmers, they wasn't hard like them Marco men who come over and joined in. In fact, bein so close to that killin scared 'em so that they jumped right up into the strong arms of the Lord!

"The Marco men 'came over and joined in'? Does that mean the people here knew what was coming?" But the question was lost in Roy's eagerness to tell him more.

"Mac Johnson was just a youngster at the time, but he always claimed he was with the gang that done the burial on Rabbit Key. No prayer was spoke, there weren't no box, only the bloody body. Lookin down on him, Mac was scared to death that Mr. Watson might come back to haunt 'em. Before the first spade of gravel sand was throwed on top of him, Mac looked down into the hole and hollered, 'I sure hope you are goin where I ain't!' "

"Roy? Do you think Mr. Watson cares to hear these tales about his own father's remains?"

"All I mean to say, Mac looked right down into them eyes! Ted Smallwood claimed he had went there and closed 'em, but maybe the man had enough life left to open 'em for the last time! Course them wild blue eyes was rolled back hard, the way they do, they were gone kind of a bad purply gray, Mac Johnson said."

"At Rabbit Key, the eyes were closed," Lucius said quietly. "I saw the corpse."

"For pity's sake, Roy! As I was saying—Roy? As I tried to tell you before my husband interrupted, the Lord heard our prayers and folks got religion all around the Bay, and naturally they flocked to the brand-new gospel that came here all the way from California. Pentecostal and the Second Coming— that's how desperate for salvation people were! Course we never could keep a minister nor schoolmarm very long, not in the early days. In summer this climate weighed down something terrible on those poor outsiders, as thick and heavy as the black mud in the Bay, and the mosquitoes and no-see-ums were even worse. Even folks who hardly ever left this island took to going off in summertime to worship at big prayer meetings in central Florida."

"Camp meetins! Yessir! Done that every summer! Went by wagon, brought their hogs and vittles, held three services a day for weeks, with all kind of religious fellowshipping in between. As Mr. McKinney wrote in his news column in the papers, a dose of religion strong as that would stand 'em in good stead with the Lord for a whole year!"

"Johnsons! McKinneys! He came to hear about *my* family, Roy!" She frowned at her husband until order was restored.

*

"Our Mama always told us girls that our Chokoloskee men had some kind of a pent-up need to kill someone. Hunting and fishing were dying out, folks were poor as poor, and some of the men were just itching to make somebody pay for their hard life, get that misery and crankiness out of their system. She said Mr. E. J. Watson was killed not because he was a killer but because he was a gentleman who kept himself apart. He was not their kind.

"Well, the House men grumbled but they only said that our Mama had forgotten how scared she'd been of Mr. Watson. Forgot how sometimes while he was alive, she had wanted him dead—she confessed it later in her life, when she was an old lady. There was too much dread around that man, too much suspense. But all the same, she was horrified by how he died.

"Mama always hated all the violence, all the fighting and the senseless feuds. The young men had nothing to do at night, no electric light, no radios, just hung around the store and talked loud talk and swatted mosquitoes in the dark. So they made their own moonshine and got drunk and cussed and fought bare-knuckle out behind the store, those crazy Danielses and Yeomanses, the Lopez boys, and plenty of others, too. Mama didn't like it, it plain scared her. She always said, 'The way those boys are carrying on, one of 'em is bound to come up killed!'

"Yes, the drinking and fighting had resumed, church or no church, and Mama said, 'They're getting set to kill another one.' And sure enough, there was another killing on this island—this was along about 1915, when you were living at Fort Myers. Two of the older boys bushwhacked a bank robber named Leland Rice who came to Chokoloskee to hide out. This young man had been a fisherman, he was well thought of around here. Young Harley Wiggins was about fifteen, and Crockett Daniels not much older, and the women said, 'That goes to show you how boys can take to killing if the men are going to set 'em that example!'

"Anyway, our Mama grew to despise Chokoloskee! In her last years, she never stopped campaigning for the causeway, she longed for some connection to the outside world. But by the time that road came in, the poor thing was dead and gone. The last time she got into the boat to go visit her brother up in Sarasota, she'd been sick from Christmas until August, and her legs were all swollen and full of water from heart dropsy—oh, it was pitiful! Saying good-bye to us girls, she looked up with her big blue eyes and she said fervently, 'I hope I never see this place again!' And she never did. But she never escaped, either, because her husband brought her right back home here to be buried. She's over in the Smallwood cemetery right this minute!

"My sister Wilma became postmistress before her father died, and ran the store, and people would come in and ask questions, and sometimes she'd answer a question about Mr. Watson and it got in the paper. So your brother

Eddie would get very upset, drive all the way down here from Fort Myers to see Wilma, ask her to please stop stirring up all that old scandal. And Wilma would say, 'Well, now, it's a little late to put the lid on, don't you think?' Your brother never wished to know what really happened, he wasn't the least bit curious about his father, he just wanted Wilma to keep quiet."

"Well, Eddie Watson was already in his twenties when his daddy died," Roy Thompson said, "so he might of knew as much about him as he wanted."

"The younger son was just the opposite, they say," Ernestine reflected. "Just couldn't hear enough about his father. He must have realized who his father was but could not live with that hard truth. Went around for years and years asking dangerous questions." Only now did she raise her eyes and look straight at him, as if mildly surprised to see Lucius Watson there. "And I bet you wondered why no one would talk to you!"

"No, they sure wouldn't!" Lucius smiled. "Made me wait another thirty years!"

Ernestine harrumphed as she got to her feet, permitting herself a ponderous sigh as she left the room. Roy Thompson smiled to reassure his guest. "Going back to the hurricane," Roy said hurriedly, speaking in a whisper while his wife was absent, "Henry Thompson and his family was camped over on Wood Key not far from Hardens, and that terrible storm washed right over the island. Dad got us all into his boat and tied her up into the mangroves and put a washtub over the baby, trying to keep him dry. Baby Wesley was saved, grew up to marry, but the hand of God was on him, he was first to go. Mama had eleven kids and that baby boy was the only one she lost, the only one that never did survive her."

"Hard to think about ol' Shine as Baby Wesley!" Lucius exclaimed, and Roy Thompson laughed. "Shine was a good name for a feller in that business. Only thing, he drank most of his product, got rambunctious. A few years back, he pulled out blind in front of another pickup on the Trail, and that was the finish of Shine Thompson.

"After the Great Hurricane, us Thompsons went to Fakahatchee, came back to this island in 1917, stayed on here for good except that one time in the twenties when we were living on the Bend. You were at Lost Man's at that time, but you showed up at Chatham now and then, remember, Colonel? And Henry Short came and went in those years, too. He was drawn back to the Bend the same as you were, Colonel, couldn't stay away. I believe he was huntin for Calusa gold—that was his dream—but Dad reckoned that nigra was trying to make his peace with Mr. Watson's ghost—not that he ever talked to Dad about it. Dad got on all right with him, but my brothers might have teased him some just for the sport of it. He was the first nigra man I ever laid my eyes on, cause coloreds weren't never seen so much around these islands.

"After a few years on the Bend, we came back to Chokoloskee, and in the thirties, they made my dad superintendent of the little school. Not much of a job but he held on to it twenty-two years. Later on in life, he fell back into quiet and never hardly raised his voice again. Lived out his life like he was sentenced to it. He just faded out. Spent most of his last years in Everglade, looking out his little window in Bet's Trailer Park, there by the bridge. One time he had an abscess tooth and no darn money, so he went after that bad tooth with his own pocketknife. Took him to Naples to let a dentist clean up after him, and this man yanked every last one of Dad's teeth while he had the old man sitting in the chair. The rest of his life my dad would say, 'I got a toothache but I got no teeth!' and suck his gums to prove it.

"Henry Thompson was the last man on the Bay could remember every hurricane of the twentieth century, and he always said that the Great Hurricane of 1910, that was the worst one, even worse than '26 and '35. Told how they boiled up mullet heads and snook roe to make cooking oil, that's how bad off our folks were for common stores.

"My dad never knew his father, so he was grateful when Mr. Watson treated him like his own son. Said nobody never treated him no better. But Dad never let his children know him—not me anyways.

"Toward the end, Dad mostly listened to his radio. Sat hunched up over it like a old blue heron, like any moment it might give a message, tell him what his life was all about." Roy smiled a wistful smile. " 'This all there is?' he'd say, looking out his little window. 'Well, it sure ain't much.' And we never could think up a good saying that might tide him over."

Roy Thompson grinned at his guest in open pleasure. "I sure am tickled to welcome you to Chokoloskee, Colonel! Us fellers that knowed you pretty good, we knew you never meant no harm with your ol' list. But them ones that took part needed time to learn that. Them men couldn't never be easy around you, Colonel. And in the Fish Wars, they thought you was on the Hardens' side, so that made folks leery of you, too."

Lucius nodded, standing up to stretch. "Roy, I wanted to ask you if you ever heard any resentment of Henry Short."

"Henry Short? I don't believe that nobody resented him." Roy Thompson looked guarded as his wife returned, bringing some coffee.

"Resented who? For what?" she said, poised in the doorway with the pot. "You leaving?" she said, because Lucius was still standing.

"What I mean is, folks liked Henry," Roy continued as his friend sat back down. "Folks didn't go against him just because he was a nigger. If you was a nigger and they liked you, everything was fine."

"Nigra," his wife corrected him. "Times are changing, Roy, in case you haven't heard." She sat down slowly, tugging at her skirt to smooth it. "The trouble was, this nigra man married a woman who was white, to hear her family tell it."

"Now, Mama—"

"Long as those two stayed at Lost Man's, nobody said much. It was God's Mercy that they had no children. Then the younger sister married Storters' man—not a light mulatta this time but a coal black darkie. And after all that, Mrs. Sadie Harden dared to march into our store, expecting to be served like anybody else—"

Lucius stopped her with a harsh noise in his throat. Coolly she awaited his protest. He recrossed his long legs, loath to spoil their meeting, yet feeling obliged to protest that Henry and Dab were both good Christian men, and that anyway, Sadie had no say about whom her husband's sisters chose to marry.

In his sweet high voice, Roy Thompson struggled to mute his wife's insinuations.

"Now, Mother, that ain't fair! Up till the Fish Wars, us fishermen used to camp at Hardens', ate with Hardens, went to all their parties down at Lost Man's! And here's Colonel, setting right here, he lived with 'em for many, many years! Sure, Hardens was always kind to Henry Short. But I never seen Henry go near their table, not when they had visitors, never mind how loud we hollered at him to sit down. Yessir, I sure liked them Hardens, and I liked Henry, too. I never could figure what all that spite and meanness was about."

"Roy? Mr. Watson came here—"

"The Hardens was all fine fishermen and hunters, they was real nice Christian people, very generous people. And I don't care to hear no more against 'em." He looked resolutely at his wife, who seemed astonished by this insurrection.

"Well, those people never learned their lesson. They became very unfriendly to their neighbors," she complained, "all except Earl. Earl Harden would play up to our community, joking and smiling, but he looked like he might bite at the same time."

Roy said, "Well, I got on with Earl all right, he was a good fella when he wanted." He looked delighted when Lucius Watson laughed.

"Those Hardens are everywhere these days, up and down the coast. The woods are full of 'em." She shook her head.

"The Harden kids have come right to the front, grandchildren, too. Fine-looking people," Roy said joyfully, casting his henpecked condition to the winds. Yet a certain doomed cast to his eye betrayed an awareness that he would pay dearly once Lucius left the house. "Nosir, they ain't callin 'em no names, not anymore."

"Edna Watson moved far, far away," Ernestine said, returning to safer ground, "but she never did forget our Mama's kindness. They corresponded till poor Mama's death. Even then, Edna kept on writing to my sister Wilma, and her oldest daughter stays in touch right to this day."

"A few years back, we took Ruth Ellen down to Chatham River! She never been there since a real small girl!"

Coming upriver to the Bend, Ruth Ellen had been stunned to see that lonely house. It seemed to her she had seen it in a dream. Ruth Ellen had known almost nothing about her father and did not ask too many questions, but finally she said, very low and shy, 'What did he look like?' And when she saw the big old cistern on the east side of the house, she recalled in a faint voice how one day she was picked up off the ground and held way out over the black and murky water. And she heard a deep voice warning her she must never play around the cistern, because if she fell in, she would surely drown, and her soul would be lost forever. For long years after, she imagined that this voice was God, but now she believed it was her father, holding her out over the dark waters.

More and more, her childhood days were starting to seep back. Returning downriver, she recalled a morning when she was playing in a skiff tied to the dock. The children were warned they would be punished if they played around the boats because of the giant crocodile which was often seen in that part of the river. The skiff came loose and drifted away with her, and the poor thing was so terrified of that huge crocodile that she could not even cry out. She crouched down in the bottom of the skiff and did her best to pray. As the boat drifted downriver, there was nothing left in all the world but the blue sky above and the sun and silence, and the swift current whispering among the mangroves, whispering and whispering, telling that dreadful monster where to find her. She saw a white bird crossing the blue, the sun piercing its wings, and she prayed that it might be her guardian angel. Then there came a great bump against the boat, and she started to cry, knowing the crocodile had found her. She closed her eyes and scrunched down tight, holding her breath, hoping and hoping it was all a dream.

A blackness crossed the sun, and she thought, Death. But when she gasped for breath to scream, she caught a smell of spirits and tobacco—a half century later, that's what she remembered. This was the only time in all her life she recalled seeing her father, and what remained with her was the great strength of him, and the warmth of his arms as he lifted her from the bottom of that skiff without a word. She couldn't remember the face leaning over, only the circle of fire on the rim of the black hat shutting out the sun.

*

At the old McKinney store, moved to a higher ground from the island's northwest point after the Hurricane of 1926, the two swamp trucks, dark gurry red, dull crankcase black, were parked outside the small and faded building. On their huge tires, which jacked the beds high up off the shell road, the new machines seemed top-heavy and out of place in this island backwater of sand tracks, shacks, and ancient autos, loose-fendered, with fallen mufflers. The old broken boats nearby were gray-bearded with dried algae. Scummed rainwater bred mosquitoes in the bilges.

Mud and Dummy lounged against the trucks, watching him come. On the red truck's door was painted in black lettering—WILD HOG JAMBOREE—and on its rear bumper was a sticker with blue stars and red stripes—WHEN YOU TAKE MY GUN, YOU TAKE MY FREEDOM. Below the rifle rack in BAD COUNTRY's rear window was this printed notice:

GOD, GUNS, AND GUTS
MADE IN AMERICA
LET'S KEEP ALL THREE

In the flat light on the Sunday island, Lucius felt thirsty. His first impulse had been to keep on going, but he had taken a deep breath and slowed and turned, and parked.

Bare-chested, in greasy overalls and soiled red galluses, the silent Dummy appeared torpid and indifferent, but Mud grinned like a hound. Both men wore black buckled boots, black baseball caps, rough beards. Mud had one boot hitched up behind on a rear fender.

Crockett Junior lay sprawled across BAD COUNTRY's hood, using a big hunting knife to scrape crisped insects off the windshield. Unaware of Lucius, he wheezed with his exertions, levering his torso with bare and hairy shoulders, thrashing on the stump of the lost arm. A heavy key chain at his belt scraped the truck paint as he shifted position. "This sucker don't go nowhere at all he ain't got a beer can stuck into his face!" Crockett was yelling. "He don't know fuck-all, this stupid fuck! I ain't lettin him nowhere near my rig, not in no truck-pull! Wouldn't have fuckin nothin left of it, time he got done!" Lucius supposed that Dummy was the man referred to, but if so, he seemed utterly indifferent, kneading his testes in a languid manner.

Through the window, Lucius said, "You damn near ran us off the road this morning." Mud Braman hooted. "We'll do better next time." He glanced at the one-armed man for his approval, but Crockett neither turned nor laughed, just kept on scraping. Behind his head, the crude head of his dog loomed in the windshield.

"Dyer says you're supposed to let him go."

Crockett Junior Daniels lay his knife down on the hood and hiked himself onto his stump. Then he took hold of his big belt buckle with his freed hand the better to hike and shift the belt and jeans, in what looked like an instinctive move to free a weapon. The maneuver took considerable effort, and he gasped noisily, a wet snarl twisting his stubble. Then he said in a low voice, "Fuck Dyer. That old man is goin to get his fuckin neck broke. Maybe you, too."

Mud Braman whinnied. "Hell, Colonel, you ain't the only one out huntin him! Come on the radio this mornin!" He squinted one puffy eye. "Ol' Chicken sure turned out to be a *mean* old feller! Armed and dangerous! Attempted murder! He's getting too damn old for stuff like that!"

Lucius got out of the car. "I want to know where I can pick him up."

"You got a boat?"

Crockett pointed his big knife at Mud. "Motor Mouth here don't know nothin. He talks." He gazed malevolently at Mud, who cursed and kicked the tire. The knife point switched toward Dummy, who appeared to be in suspended animation. Crockett said, "Looks like a idjit, don't he? But the real idjit is this one can't keep his mouth shut."

"Hell, Dummy ain't no idjit! He ain't even extra stupid. Only quiet. Quiet as the grave." Mud winked at Lucius. "Good soldier. Very *very* good. But one day when us three boys and Whidden was on patrol, over there to Asie, this man stopped talkin. Said 'Fuck it'—them were his last words. I believe he has lost the hang of human speech."

Dummy said nothing, then or later, gazing past Lucius's head, but the corner of his eye tracked every movement.

Crockett growled, "Get goin, Mister." He turned to his scraping, as if unable to endure Lucius's appearance. In the sun-shined air and Sunday silence, the knife blade squeaked on the dry glass.

"I could charge you guys with kidnapping—that what you want? You know how serious that is?"

Mud jeered, "How come you ain't done that before now?"

"Dyer—" Lucius started, and Mud said, "Fuck Dyer," and the one-armed man slid off the hood and backed Lucius up against his car at knife point. "You don't listen good," he murmured, moving forward.

Lucius let all expression leave his face, averting his eyes like a dog showing its throat. Dummy was watching now, his mouth half open, while Mud stood ready to snarl or jeer according to the one-armed man's first shift in mood.

Mud yelled at Lucius, "Never heard Junior tellin you, 'Get goin?' You keep pesterin with them stupid-ass questions, he might set that dog on you, run your sorry ass right off this island!"

Cocking the knife blade back under his wrist, Crockett used this knife fist to punch Lucius's chest, driving him back against the car. He went back to his work and did not speak again.

Mud Braman took a long swallow of beer and came up gasping with relief, shaking his head over Lucius's close shave. But when Lucius asked where he might find Bill Smallwood, Mud merely belched, wiping his bearded mouth with the back of his hand. "Nosir," he snarled. "Nosir, we cain't help you. And that is because we are dumb-ass fuckin rednecks that don't know fuckin nothing about nothin. Only fuckin thing we know to tell you is the fastest fuckin way off this here island!"

An amorphous form loomed in the store's screen door like abyssal life rising palely from the deeps. "We sure don't care none for that kind of talk, not on a Sunday. You boys was sure raised up better'n that." Slowly the man came outside, blinking in the hard noon light, an elderly, clean-shaven man with thinning hair slicked down on a pale scalp and a line of white skin along the hairline. "Well brung-up young Christian men, talkin like New York City or some darned place," he complained wearily. "How-do, Colonel," he said.

"Cap?" Mud complained. "He's lookin to pester Cap'n Bill, is what it is."

Cap Brown ignored this. "You want Bill, you foller that white road around to the marina. Likely find him in a trailer house up from the office." To the three young men, the storekeeper said, "I knowed this man since I was your age. He ain't out to harm nobody." Contemplating the huge new trucks, he shook his head before going back inside.

Crockett climbed into BAD COMPANY and slammed the door, yanking the gargling dog aside by its leather collar. Dummy got into the red truck beside Braman, who eased WILD HOG JAMBOREE into gear. Gunning his motor, Mud jolted ahead as Lucius yelled and stepped forward to detain him. Dummy's paw shot out and seized his shirtfront and yanked him hard against the truck door. Though he fought to get loose, he was dragged out onto the road before the hand released him, sending him spinning hard to the hard ground. BAD COMPANY honked in approval and salute as both trucks wheeled away, the triumphant jeers commingled with bare sunlight and white Sunday dust.

The air turned black, came light again. His forearm was scraped and his brain ringing. He rested on his knees a moment before staggering to his feet.

"You hurt?"

He shook his head. He could not make out the storekeeper through the dark mesh, only the paleness of his shirt. The paleness brought back an odd memory from the old days: Cap had always enjoyed a meal of mayonnaise, spooned from the jar.

Cap said, "Been a few years, ain't it? You sure don't change much, Colonel. Only thing, these younger ones don't know you good as we do. You snoop around askin them questions, how they s'posed to know you ain't a fed?" When Lucius shrugged, the voice behind the screen continued, "What they mainly heard about is that ol' list."

Lucius spat out dust. "A list of dead men!"

"Crockett's daddy ain't dead, lest he died yesterday. And there's another one. If he ain't on there, he sure ought to be."

"I haven't kept that list in thirty years, goddammit, Cap! If revenge was what I'd wanted—" But not knowing what he'd wanted, he fell silent, slapping angrily at his dusty pants.

"That a fact? If you was Speck, would you take a Watson's word for that? After *another* Watson showed up here just lately, wantin to be took down to the Bend? Where Speck is caretakin?"

"Wait a minute! What—?"

"All these brothers slippin around all of a sudden has got to strike folks kind of funny, Colonel, when we ain't hardly seen a Watson on this island since your old man was shot in 1910. Also, we heard how you been askin whether them men *planned* to kill your daddy."

Lucius stopped slapping the white dust. He straightened and moved slowly toward the steps, trying to locate the storekeeper behind the screen. "Cap? Does everyone know where my brother is except for me?"

"Them boys won't hurt him none without Speck says so."

"I can't count on that. I'll have to call the state police."

The storekeeper was silent a long moment. When he spoke again, his tone had shifted and turned cold. "Let me tell you somethin. With boys like these, all war-wounded, kind of half-loco, I would not call in no law if I was you." The voice diminished as it withdrew from the screen and the paleness faded back into the gloom.

"Cap? I'm thirsty. I could use a soda pop or something—"

"Store's closed," the voice said.

*

It was now midmorning. In his desperate need to act, he drove at high speed north and east to Gator Hook. There were no trucks or autos and the place looked closed. The door at the top of the roadhouse steps was padlocked, and a yellow rat snake, gathering sun into its coils on the wood stoop, slipped without haste into a rain-rotted crevice. He called out, but there was no answer, only frogs chugging in the cypress, and forlorn odd cries of gallinule and limpkin.

Nailed to the door was a stained scrap of paper reading "Gone to Church." In the same scrawled hand, splotched with spilled coffee, were rough directions to a "wild hog jambaree and truck pull, free 6-pack with admission." The truck pull would take place this afternoon off the Copeland Road in the Big Cypress, at the same roadhouse where BAD COUNTRY had been parked the day before.

He drove the eight miles east to Forty-Mile Bend, then west again along the Trail to the first Indian camp, a collection of palm-thatched *cheke* roofs mostly hidden behind a high stockade fence. Knocking at the gate, he asked the woman who eventually appeared where he might locate Billie Jimmie. A small crowd gathered, mostly children. After a long silence in which nobody would look him in the face, he was pointed toward his car and told to wait. When Lucius said he could not wait, the command was repeated and the gate was shut. Within a few minutes, Billie Jimmie emerged, wiping his mouth, and squashed into the car without explanation.

He had not seen Chicken, Billie Jimmie said, before Lucius could ask him. Yes, he had been brought to Gator Hook, just as Lucius suspected. The Indian ignored the white man's question about how he had found out. Knowing Chicken was there, he had walked cross-country through the Cypress, coming in behind the roadhouse. Driven off by drunks, he found no way to talk with him. Now the old man was gone. Asked how he knew, the big man winced again. "Indin business," he said this time, wanting nothing to do with the dangerous incredulity of white men.

Lucius wondered aloud if the old man might be found at that wild hog jamboree on the Copeland Road? The Indian sat expressionless. "South," he said finally, with a hand gesture indicating distance. "Pavioni." Lucius recognized the Mikasuki word for the vanished Indian village on Chatham Bend. After that, they sat in silence for a while, contemplating the purple morning glory blossoms on the stockade wall.

"No damn good," Billie Jimmie pronounced gloomily. He was worried, too.

*

Lucius reminded him that they had first met on the occasion of the Park inauguration at Everglade. "Drunk Injun," Billie Jimmie grunted, relating how he owed his life to Chicken, who had cured him of drink and returned him to the spiritual path of the Old Way.

"Rob cured you of drink? Returned you to the spiritual path?"

The Indian waited politely for the white man's amusement to subside, then reminded Lucius that the Park ceremony at Everglade had been a very dark day for his people, who were banned forever from Hatchee Chok-ti, or "Shark River." And he related his own grief and his flight into spiritual darkness. All this had ended one hot summer afternoon on the roof of the Young Men's Christian Association of Orlando, where his friend Mr. Collins had provided a fresh jug of his favorite corn whiskey, Okeefenokee Moon. "Only white feller I ever come across could drink himself drunker'n a Indin and still sit up straight," Billie Jimmie marveled, with a fine mix of admiration and disgust.

Tongue loosened by the Okeefenokee Moon, Billie Jimmie had confided to the white man his undying shame that a hereditary chief and spiritual leader, entrusted with an ancient deerskin containing the medicine of the Green Corn, had hidden this sacred relic in a hollow tree "back in the Cypress," then abandoned his people to become a drunkard. From that dark day onward, he had taken refuge from his life in the white man's cities, yet had never ceased to be tormented that the Green Corn Bundle was deteriorating in its hiding place, and the tribe's spiritual power along with it. To drown his sorrows over this calamity, he had taken a mighty slug of Okeefenokee Moon, set the jug down on the roof cinders with a doleful sigh, and cursed the fate that had afflicted him with a flawed character. But when he wiped the tears out of his eyes and was reaching once more for the jug, he found his solace out of reach and the old man pointing at him in a fury. "You're a damn disgrace," his friend had yelled. "A big sloppy Injun drunk, and a disgrace!"

Billie Jimmie was too flabbergasted to respond. He felt as if his soul had been struck by lightning. Furthermore, his incensed companion was by no means finished with his abuse. "You get the hell up off your redskin ass," this terrible old man was yelling. "You go get yourself sober and cleaned up, and then you go out in the woods and find all that sacred heathen crud and clean the dirt off of it! And from now on, you take care of your spiritual duties like your people told you!"

The Indian rose to his full height, ready to kill. He lifted the old man right off the cinders, prepared to cast him from the rooftop to the concrete sidewalk five stories below. "You crazy old sonofabitch!" he hollered, or words to that effect, "you ain't never drawed a sober breath in all the time I knowed you, you are the most unmercifullest drunk I ever come across, and I seen plenty! Who are you to talk that way to a hereditary chief!"

"You sure don't act like any chief I ever heard about," Old Man Chicken told him, "and your breath ain't so hot, neither. Anyways, Bill," the white elder continued, rising up and brushing cinders from a bloody elbow where the Indian had flung him down, "that ain't the difference between you and me." And he drew Billie Jimmie down beside him, keeping the corn liquor out of reach. "The difference is, I don't drink because I *have* to drink, like you. I drink because I *like* to drink, I'm a drunk because I *enjoy* being drunk, and I ain't all weepy and full of guilt about it, neither. I *like* bein a drunk, you understand? I *like* it! And the older I get, the *better* I like it. And if I die early, that is all right, too, cause old age ain't all that it's cracked up to be." The old man said this more or less cheerfully, gazing out over the hot smog of the town. Then he added in a quiet voice, "If I thought I could do it, I would drink it all."

"Might kill yourself," the Indian warned him.

"You find a better way, you let me know."

Cheerful again, Chicken waved a bony arm toward the city. "Life is great and life is terrible, there's just no end to the damned possibilities!" Then he turned to the hereditary chief and said in a stern voice, "You do like I tell you, Bill. You haul your redskin ass right off this roof and don't come back." And when Billie Jimmie got riled up again, and demanded to know how the hell he could straighten himself out when the forked-tongue white man would not offer him so much as one puny hit of Okeefenokee Moon, to tide him over—just when, in fact, he was considering taking the jug by force— the old man polished it off himself, without haste or undue ceremony. "Let that be a lesson to you," he said. "No more. Forever." And with that, he slipped a green bill from his shoe into the Indian's hand. "Now you go get yourself cleaned up, get a new shirt," Old Chicken said. "Invest in a toothbrush and a fresh pair of socks while you are at it."

Rising to his feet, the Indian cast that money down with a great shout of contempt. Only then did he see that this frogskin was a century note, a hundred-dollar bill. Enraged, he went storming off the roof and down the fire stairs, reaching the bottom floor, still shouting, before it came to him why Indians so rarely got ahead in life, or even home. True, he had made some sort of moral point, but what good would that do him or his lost people? With not one penny in his pocket, nothing left him but his pride, he booted the fire door and banged out into the street, hoping his brave repudiation of white-man corruption would ring forever in that old man's ears.

Down from the heavens came a shrill whistle—like the voice of an eagle, Billie Jimmie said. He looked up in time to see the old man peering down over the roof edge. With the sun behind his head, his silver hair burned like a halo on the summer blue. "Looked like the Great Spirit," the Indian said, still reverential. For between the old man's eyes and his own, a leaf-like thing was lilting downward, downward on the eddying breeze.

A moment later, the burning halo disappeared, the sky was empty, there was only that crisp ticket to the future, palpitating like a green butterfly on the hot sidewalk.

Billie Jimmie sighed, gazing at Lucius. He could never repay that good old man, not only for the money but for the dignity he had been granted, the solitude in which to stoop to pick it up. He had been sober ever since, he said, all thanks to R. B. Chicken, and had been restored as a spiritual leader of his people. "He is a very good old man," Billie Jimmie said fervently. "A *very* good old man. He is not honored in the white man's world the way he should be."

*

Ernestine Thompson had told Lucius to talk with her cousin Bill if he wanted their family to sign his petition. Hurrying back to Chokoloskee, he went straight to the marina, where through the slat windows of a wide-load trailer, he discovered the corpus of Bill Smallwood lumped on his sofa. Beyond the sofa stood a TV screen, fuzzed white by the hard sunlight through the metal blinds. Knocking again without much result, he rattled the aluminum door, and finally Smallwood sat up slowly, overweight and wheezing. "Who's that?" he growled, putting his straw hat on. Surly, he tottered toward the door and peered out through the screen as he tucked his shirt in. "Godamighty! Will you look at that pathetical old coot! I sure do hate to think what I must look like when I see ol' Colonel lookin poor as that!"

Bill opened the door and came outside and they shook hands. "Been expectin you and I don't know why," he said, "except one time I was married to the sister of that feller where you was at yesterday. You a tourist these days, Colonel? Come to have a look at Smallwood's store? You tourists always want a look at the old store." Doggedly sour even when Lucius laughed, Smallwood peered around him at the day. "Well, it sure looks like Sunday, don't it? Wilma's off to church, unless hell froze over. Keeps the store tight closed on Sundays, which would of been a sacrilege to our dad. Maybe he'll forgive her when she gets to heaven, maybe not—depends. But you being the famous history writer, I might pry the door."

Bill Smallwood hadn't changed a bit, he was ornery as ever, with the same ironic turn of mind as his cousin Andy. But while Andy's irony was gentle and laconic, Bill's was almost always harsh and mordant. "You want me to sign your damned petition? That why you're creeping around pesterin everybody? Well, I don't reckon I will do it, Colonel. They can't burn that place down too soon for me."

The two walked slowly up the white shell road. What was left of Ted Smallwood's land had been broken up into a small trailer park, a motel, and a marina, and Lucius supposed Bill was aware that he had not set foot on that store property since 1910 and might feel some reluctance even now. "You might not remember our old place too good," Cap'n Bill reflected.

They passed the Blue Heron Motel. "Andy's in there hobnobbin with my younger sister. She runs the motel. You already talked to Ernestine, I heard, but I bet you ain't talked to young Ned. Might not care to. Ned'll take for you or he'll take agin you. He missed out on my sunny disposition. No trouble to find him if you want him, but you might decide you don't.

"Course you never heard me say none of this stuff. I'm the oldest male in the Smallwood clan, so I'm bound to get in trouble if I talk too much." He shook his head, dyspeptic. "Don't look like I'll kick up trouble too much longer. Got me a cancer of the exhaust system, y'know. They made a expedition up in there, took something out, I don't know what; I told 'em they were more'n welcome to anything they come across." He winced without self-pity. "The less I know about what's happening back there, the better. Course my innards work somewhat different now than the way God rigged 'em, but I'm gettin used to it even if God ain't. A man can get used to pret' near anything, I guess, if life is worth it to him. Got to go runnin to the hospital every two minutes, get up on a cold steel table to get probed and fingered and slapped around like an ol' piece of dead meat, so I ain't made up my mind about that last part."

Bill Smallwood stopped to get his breath. "We heard you was still asking around about the whys and wherefores of what happened that day down here on the landing—same questions you asked back in the twenties! Well, I'm warnin you, Colonel, snoopin ain't a good idea even today."

"I asked questions, all right," Lucius agreed, "but nobody was answering."

Bill Smallwood grunted once and changed the subject. Mr. Watson's fourth son by his final marriage, he said, had come here from north Florida some years ago. "Big feller. Housepainter. Don't go by the name Watson, but hinted who he was. Never knew nothing much about his daddy, so I let on how E. J. Watson was a famous planter in these parts and let it go at that. Figured that's what the man had come to hear."

"Addison Burdett?"

Smallwood's expression closed. "I never caught the name. All I know is, he shows up with a whole car full of paint and a big supply of grub. This was not long after the Park took over, they was already talking about burnin down every last shack in the Islands. I run this man to Chatham Bend and dropped him off. He was real nervous about varmints, gators especially—nervous about *everything*! He was pecking at his grub all the way down there, had the most of it already et by the time I set him on the bank!

"Well, that house looked all gray and busted, jungled over. Hunters and such had left everything a mess, and the place stunk like a bear den. This man decided to sleep out on the porch. Says, 'Wish me luck,' by which he meant no diamondbacks nor scorpions nor panthers. But I knew what would plague him most was the miskeeters, cause the porch screens was all storm-torn, shot to hell. I sure hope you won't need no sleep, I told him. Uncle Bill House used to say them skeeters on the Watson Place was the worst he come across in all his years out in the Glades. Said he had to chaw a whole plug of Brown Mule to fight 'em off.

"I went back for that housepainter four days later. Naturally he was half-crazy from bad dreams and bug bites, but damn if he don't have that paint job finished! Even knowing what that man was up to, when I come around the point and seen that house, I let out a whoop he could hear over my engine. The Watson Place weren't gray no more, she was settin up there on her mound so fresh and white, looked like a castle! That's what I told him when I hit the bank, and he give me some kind of a grin, but even that grin looked like he was hurtin.

"So I said, 'Boy, I sure do hate to see so much good oil paint wasted on a house that Parks aims to set afire before the year is out.' And he told me he wanted folks to know that the Watsons had pride in their old home, no matter what. Said this was all he could think up to do to pay his daddy his respects. On the way back up the coast, he said that maybe if the old place looked like new, Parks might think twice about burnin her down. 'Nosir,' I said, 'cause them damned feds don't never think at all, let alone twice. Don't want to waste their good time thinkin, with so much stupidity just a-cryin to be done.' But this feller was smarter than I thought, cause that was some few years ago, and Parks ain't burned her.

"At Chokoloskee, he got right into his car. I said, 'Come back and chew the fat another day, cause I'll be thinkin up some more nice lies about E. J. Watson.' And he don't give me so much as a smile, just shakes his head and says, 'I won't be back.' "

Bill Smallwood stopped dead in the road, still troubled by the flatness of that statement. "Leavin a place, a man's heart might tell him that he won't never get back there in this life. He was the first I ever heard admit it. Very very peculiar kind of feller." He wheezed a little more and resumed walking.

"Has he come back? Cap Brown just told me—"

"Showed up here a few days ago, Ol' Won't-Be-Back himself! Same old ugly car, same carload of white housepaint and big yeller junk-food packets! Piled the whole mess into one of my skiffs, said he didn't need to pay no guide, said he reckoned he knew the way now by himself. I hollered, 'How about my boat? You know anythin about boats?' And he sings out, 'Heck, yes, Mr. Smallwood! I seen people boatin on the Lakes!' "

Bill Smallwood shuddered. " '*Lakes!*' " he grumbled. "So I give him a chart, showed him how to read it, warned him not to tear her bottom out on no damn orster bars, and pushed him off. If that fool ever made it, he's on the Bend right now, slappin the paint to that old place just like before."

Ernestine Thompson had mentioned to Bill that the housepainter's sister had visited there, too. "Said the sister was real sweet and friendly. Well, her brother might been sweet but he sure weren't friendly. Hell of a good painter, though, you got to give him that." He shook his head. "Funny thing how a brother and sister would get a notion to find out about their daddy, come all the way down here in their later age and ask their questions, then go on home to the same town and never even tell each other that they went!"

Smallwood peered at Lucius as if to descry whether queer behavior might not be endemic in the Watson family. "His bunch changed their names after they left here, and we was noticin you done that, too, least on your history book. You ashamed of your daddy?" When Lucius denied this and explained the pen name, Bill just grunted. "None of my damned business, Colonel. All I know is I'd never change my name, no matter *what*. I was borned right here and raised right here, and raised my children, too. I couldn't never answer to no name except Bill Smallwood."

*

A thick strangler fig and the old cistern were all that remained of the hurricane-battered homestead where the Smallwood and Watson children and their mothers had huddled and wept during the shooting. "Our old house had the store on the ground floor," Smallwood was saying. "Three windows on the second floor, three bedrooms. That's where Mama put the Widow Watson and her children. Ground floor in front had a long porch with high dark skinny chairs, case you don't remember. Walk up some steps and cross that porch, go in the front door to the trading post, had a real long counter. But them steps weren't nearly high enough to keep the Gulf out, not in the Great Hurricane of 1910.

"Dad had his ditch dug from the bay side right up to the store so's the Injun dugouts could unload the furs and gator hides onto his dock, all set to trade." He pointed out a leaning shed in the undergrowth close to the boat ways. "That's where we stored tomatoes and some produce before it was loaded on the boats bound for Key West."

A clearing on the Bay was set about with palms and sea grape, buttonwood, tall coco palms, and airy casuarina. "Weren't none of these Australian pines back in your daddy's day, nor this store neither." He pointed at the barn-red building high on posts under the trees, with a steep stair to the second-story entrance. Above the door was a faded sign, SMALLWOOD'S STORE

AND POST OFFICE. "People are still reading in their magazines and books where Watson died inside of that red buildin, or under that red buildin, or on this open shore on the east side. But he was buried seven years before this store was built, and the buildin weren't raised up this way till just before the Hurricane of '26. Wilma tried to set them writers straight, and tourists, too, but all she ever done was disappoint 'em."

Lucius nodded. "A picturesque old store would illustrate their story, so they changed the story."

"That's about it. Don't want nothin to do with the hard truth, no more'n the rest of us. Anyways, Wilma give up on the truth, cause she seen that truth was very bad for business." Smallwood gave a small pained grunt which was as close to mirth as he could manage. He turned back toward the building and climbed the stairs, fuming and puffing, clutching the railing at the top. "Call this exercise! Don't make a damn bit of difference if I get exercised or not, you're lookin at a feller might be dead next year!" He rummaged a padlock on the door. With his back to Lucius, he paused and said, "Ever think about that, Colonel? Death, I mean?" Without waiting for an answer—it was not a question—Smallwood pushed the door open and went inside.

At the far end of the dark room shone a bright rectangle where a rear door opened on a second-story balcony over the water. In the light from both ends, the store took a dim shape. The inventory of E. J. Watson's day was still in place. The dusty shelves, Lucius realized, could offer nothing to those visitors who arrived over the causeway—no camera film or sunburn lotion, no sunglasses, no souvenir T-shirts, no bright postcards. Instead it catered to the old spare needs of local customers—dry goods and staples, canned foods and lard, turpentine and linseed oil, storm lanterns, kerosene, paint, rope, boots, buckets, burlap, barrels, cook pots, kettles, pans. Over all was a stale mousy smell and a dry moan of wasps, from the white nests plastered hard to the bare rafters.

Bill Smallwood dug out ancient ledgers and spread them on the counter, inviting Lucius to inspect Watson accounts—grits at five dollars a barrel, venison and bacon at seven cents a pound. For coffee, the green beans in a sack were beaten up fine with a marlin spike. Grated cassava and ground coontie roots dug in the piney woods inland supplied the starch. Lard tubs were saved for keeping matches and tobacco dry out in the boats, and spare clothes, too. Almost everything had found a use, nothing was wasted.

Smallwood dragged a canvas boat chair out onto the balcony over the water. In the corner leaned a bamboo fish pole with a piece of clam dried hard as yellow wood on its rusty hook. White bits of broken shellfish baits lay scattered in the cracks of the weathered deck. "I bet them ol' baits been there since I was little." Smallwood sighed. He patted a rust-locked gas pump that in other days had served the boats by gravity feed. "Runboats coming in to pick up mullet brought our gasoline and kerosene and oil, maybe fifty drums. My dad had a hoist rigged up, to lift 'em." Bill Smallwood nodded at this memory, resting quietly in the bay heat, gazing out over the channels between oyster bars where the fishing boats of long ago had anchored. Most of the old-time boats were white, he reminded Lucius, with bright blue trim along the gunwales and the red copper of the bottom paint showing along the waterline.

"Red, white, and blue. Don't know if them boats was patriotic-meant, but they sure looked cheerful," Smallwood said, not cheered much by the memory. "Them were the cheerful days, all right, all but that one." His slow arm rose to point across the glittering gray water. "See where I'm pointin at? Them real high trees where that dogleg channel off Rabbit Key Pass comes out back of them bars? Hard to make out sunken bars in the late dusk, so not all of 'em would try it, but that's the way your dad come in on that October evenin. Come north on the Gulf far as Rabbit Key, cause the inside channels was all choked with broken trees after that storm. East up the Pass, took a 'ninety' north up that short channel, follered it around them bars and clumps and on in to our landing.

"Course I was only a little boy and don't recall much, but I have listened all about that evenin over and over. The men was strung along this shore, right below where we are sittin at this minute, and the rest was back up there by the old store."

Lucius imagined Billy Smallwood and Little Ad Burdett, at play in the old store back from the water. Those quick little boys in their noisy play, forever running—who could have foretold the heavy dour men they would become?

All around this south end of the Bay, white egrets were pinned like ornaments on high green walls of the encircling trees. The view of the shoreline and the open water which his father had crossed on his last evening on earth brought Lucius a cavernous sorrow even now. Though he had learned all— or almost all—the details, he found his father's final minutes unimaginable. Why he had returned at all was a true mystery. Surely it could not have been simply to celebrate Kate Edna's birthday! The other unknown was the terrible miscalculation—if such it was—which had brought down on him that dreadful crash of fire, the burning blows of volley after volley, the long falling to earth, the staring end.

"Nobody said a word when it was over," Smallwood was saying. "Some men took their hats off, my dad said, but they put 'em right back on when others growled at 'em. Pretty soon, the men who done it went off in the dark, just shadows in the trees, then they were gone. My dad come down here to the shore, straightened him out a little, crossed his arms, y'know. Toward daylight, a few men come back, hauled the body out to Rabbit Key."

Smallwood stifled a dyspeptic grunt. "I heard your daddy killed a few. Them people needed some killing, wouldn't surprise me. They say he shot a couple niggers, too—probably had it coming. This far south, there weren't no law cept what you made. But he never killed all them men that people said. He just got the credit, you might say. Like my dad told us, 'Ed Watson never was so bad as he was painted. But you try to push him, he'd push back, only he'd push harder.' Watson was always honest with my dad—*a fine man to do business with!* I heard Dad say that, many and many's the time."

Smallwood's ruined breathing came and went like the slow and shallow sucking of the tide at the shore below. "I believe his foreman was behind most of the trouble. I believe Ed Watson was a pretty good man. There was just too many killed down there, and folks got tired of it."

Not wanting to impose on him, Lucius asked him if he wanted to go home. "Home to what?" Bill Smallwood grumbled. He leaned forward again, arms on the rail, chin on his clasped fingers, looking out over the silvered glitter of the turning water. Then his laboring harsh rasp came again, in elegy and reminiscence, his arm waving in vague arcs toward the south.

"A few years after your dad died, them Chevelier people was looking to buy the rights to Chatham Bend. The feller livin on there then, he pipes right up, says he would accept some money for the quitclaim. Maybe he sold 'em something that he never owned.

"Cheveliers laid out all them plots and dug all kinds of canals to drain them islands before they seen they was only letting in the tidewater. Pretty stupid, you might say, but developers are still doin that today. Another outfit, Tropical Development, they claimed the rights to Lost Man's River, got themselves a big write-up in *The Miami Herald*, big pictures of this paradise they had discovered, royal palms all along the banks and steamships going up and down flying red-white-and-blue flags! Ain't a steamship on earth could make it into Lost Man's crost them orster bars, and the royal palms was all gone by that time, they was all dug out for them new tourist boulevards, Naples, Fort Myers.

"When Barron Collier made a harbor there at Everglade, that was the end of our fish business over here. And after the Trail went through a few years later, our Injun trade was pretty well finished, too. Course we blamed everything on Collier and the Depression, but we was already dead by then, just didn't know it. Nobody except maybe the Injuns ever looked ahead and seen how that cross-Florida highway would be the end of us. That so-called progress was the end of the Everglades, and the end of the Injuns, and the end to all us old-time people, too.

"In '27, I become a eyewitness to history when the old Orange Blossom Special come a-chuggin into Naples. That was the first train I ever seen. A few years after that, my cousin Andy House give me a auto ride over the Trail to the east coast, right to Miami! Looked like the future of Florida laid out before us, that's how fast we crossed the state, that's how shining the world seemed to us poor country fellers! Andy stayed in Miami most of his whole life trying to catch up with that future. Next thing he knew, them Spaniards come swarmin back from Cuba, and they run him out."

*

"Used to be some good small pieces of high ground down in these Islands, and E. J. Watson had the biggest one at Chatham Bend. Parks took them pieces from the pioneers and never paid 'em, called them people squatters. Damn tourists was more important to 'em than home people, and they are today. A man can't hardly build a dock on his own waterfront no more without them nature-lovin sonsabitches comin in here, wavin papers in his face! Want to protect every last varmint in Creation cept us common people!" Bill waved his arm at the mangrove forest which surrounded them in all directions in a wall of green. "Look to you like we're running short of them damn mangoes? And now our old families are gettin pushed right off this island. Strangers and developers come swarmin in over that causeway, buy us out cheap cause we are poor, and it looks like we just got to set and take it."

Smallwood's breath was erratic and too heavy. Abruptly he took Lucius's pen and reached for the petition, scratched a signature. "Local people would be sad to see ol' Chatham burn. The Bay families are all behind you, Colonel. Only thing, we don't much trust your lawyer."

Lucius kept his expression noncommittal. "Dyer is interested in helping out because he was born there. Says he wants to see the place preserved 'for sentimental reasons.' He's not charging us," he added.

Smallwood snorted. "You know Dyer?" When Lucius nodded, Smallwood nodded, too. "If he ain't chargin you, there is a reason, and it ain't no sentimental reason, neither. Man over here at Parks told me one time that Dyer been snoopin around that Watson Claim since the Park took over back in '47. Got a dirty finger stuck in every pie in southern Florida, got big shots behind him all the way to Washington, D.C. Miami politicians and state legislators, lawyers and lobbyists for Big Sugar, big development. Them kind ain't sentimental about anything on God's earth except more money.

"Us local people got no love for Parks, but it ain't the Park deserves the blame nor the federal government neither, they're just doin what they're told to do by the politicians, and politicians gets their orders from big business. That's the mistake that is always made by ignorant fellers like Speck

Daniels, who hates the Park, hates the government so bad for movin him out of his home territory that he can't see them ones who are behind it, can't see who's spoilin this whole country, or what's left of it."

Bill shook his head over the nation's prospects. "Your attorney is the mouthpiece for big developers on the east coast that fought the comin of the Park for years and years. I'm already seein a few signs that them men might be tryin to get it back. The waste and ruination of this Glades country might be just what them boys want—I believe they might even be behind it! You seen this stuff in the papers lately? You notice who's runnin down the Park—'the big dead Park'—to the newspapers and politicians, plantin the idea with the public about the state gettin all that Park land back and sellin it off, supposedly to create jobs and help the taxpayers? Nobody else but the Big Sugar people and Watson Dyer! Get the voters talkin and writin to the papers about them tragical dead Glades out there, get editorial writers snipin back and forth, and pretty soon there'll be a referendum on the ballot.

"Idea like that would draw plenty of support amongst the voters, cause the great part of 'em ain't home-born in the first place, they are mostly all invaders from the North, and them retired people hates to see so much real estate rottin away that could be sold off to lower taxes and pay for more conveniences and damn 'facilities'—more highways and development, more shoppin malls, y'know. Don't care nothin for our old-time Florida! Nothin at all! Them Yankees are takin over this coast country like them walkin catfish or Australia trees that every hurricane spreads faster and farther out acrost the Glades till pretty soon that wild country back there won't even look like Florida no more!

"Next thing you know, the federal government will dump the Park back on the state, same as was done with Collier County when the Colliers seen that their swamp empire weren't payin off. Next, they call in flood control, build some new canals to get more land drained off at public expense while it's still public land. And finally, once all that's out of the way, them corporations lean on their pet politicians, advise 'em how state can't let all that empty land just set there earnin nothin, and how they owe it to the voters to sell it off to folks who know what to do with it, namely big agriculture and big development. Before you know it, the last of that Glades country out there will be drained off for retirement homes and golf courses and malls. Lay concrete and spray poisons over the whole works while they are at it so no damn bugs nor snakes nor lizards can go to pesterin the senior citizens. *Yessir, folks, we guarantee our oldsters 100% security and comfort all the way down that sunset trail right smack into the casket! Might not be America no more but it sure is comfy!*"

Smallwood spat over the rail, leaning forward in time to watch the dull phlegm falling through the air to vanish into the bright water of the tide. "You just wait and see," he said. "Ain't goin to be one bright-eyed bit of life left in south Florida."

*

In the rusty sunlight in the screen door entrance at the top of the stair, Andy House appeared with a slow old lady on his arm. They seemed confused as to who was helping whom as they shuffled through the dim and narrow store toward the balcony. More old folks were entering behind them, peering and poking in a beehive hum of gentle converse.

Barging out onto the balcony, Andy announced in a loud voice, "My cousin Bill Smallwood is a fine feller, all right, except one thing: I never could figure what give him the idea that he was irresistible to women."

"I reckon they's one or two could resist me now," Smallwood admitted. "But if my young cousin here keeps speakin up so smart, he might get a whippin." He didn't stand up to greet Andy or even look around, but in his distempered manner, he was smiling. He leaned toward Lucius. "Between a blind man and a dying one," he whispered loudly for his cousin's benefit, "you might get you a pretty fair scrap."

Inside the store the old folks, brisk as sparrows, perched on crates and barrels, and elderly voices, crying out more loudly than they knew, carried outside onto the balcony.

"—so Colonel told Parks, 'If you people set fire to the Watson house, you will have to set fire to a Watson!' Says he never did find much to live for, but now he's found somethin he will *die* for! And you know something? He'll do it! I fished with Colonel plenty times, I knowed ol' Colonel *good*! He'll *do* it! So we got to help out on his petition! Don't want ol' Colonel goin up in smoke!"

"Hush! He's outside! Want him to hear you? Colonel never said no such fool thing as that! That's only *your* idea! If you ain't aiming to hush up and behave, I'm taking you home!"

"What we heard was, Colonel took his daddy's schooner and sold her at Key West, and maybe he took Cox with him, turned him loose. Them two fellers was close to the same age and they might of been partners all along. Don't seem likely but it makes some sense, cause after that black October day, the ol' *Gladiator* weren't never seen again, nor Les Cox neither."

"Well, that ain't the way it come down in our family. Cox snuck back into the Glades, lived with the Injuns, him being part of a Injun himself—least that's what Walter Alderman always told us, and Walter knew Cox from his days up around Columbia County when he worked for Watson. No tellin who lives back in them rivers, and they ain't too many has went in there to find out."

"Oh yes, I fished with Colonel Watson many's the time! Sweetest person I ever knew—*good* sense of humor! I never seen him riled in all my life! He liked his whiskey, too, ol' Colonel did!"

"Still do!" Lucius called cheerily, stepping inside.

The abashed assembly looked shy, but most of the men offered warm smiles, and a few slipped forward to shake his hand. No one seemed surprised to see him, since all had known that Watson's son was on the Bay since his first hour in Everglade the day before.

Though Andy House had been away for years, he had no trouble identifying voices. "Look here who we got with us today!" He welcomed Lloyd Brown and Owen Carr, Charlie McKinney and two Hamiltons, Hoad Storter and assorted Smallwoods, the Roy Thompsons, Lopezes, and Johnsons, a Demere, Weeks and Honey Daniels, down from Fort Myers on a visit—Lucius was grateful for their smiling wave. Over twenty elders were installed—the last of the last generation whose childhood had been lived in "Mister Watson"'s shadow.

"Last time so many of our old families got together," Bill Smallwood said, "was October twenty-fourth of 1910."

"Come to give another Watson a warm welcome!" one man called. There came a cackle of malevolence, but the others looked relieved when Lucius laughed.

Holding up a copy of Lucius's *History*, Andy introduced their honored guest. "As you folks know your old friend Colonel Watson is the famous book author Professor Collins!" He added that Colonel deserved their support in his fight to save his daddy's house at Chatham Bend, and that he was completing his research for a biography of his father and would welcome reminiscences from his old neighbors.

Doing his best to appear harmless, Lucius offered a self-deprecating smile. He said they should think of E. J. Watson not as "Colonel's daddy" but only as the subject of a book, and must not worry that they might hurt his feelings.

For a long moment, no one spoke. The few guarded asides were meant for one another. Then talk burst forth like sun through rain and clouds.

"I guess you knew your dad had him a $500 watch, that was a lot of money back in them days. Hunting-case repeater watch, with a thick gold chain that was worth even more! Ever find out what happened to that watch? Ted Smallwood get it? Might be hid down here under this counter right this minute, come to think about it! Ol' Man Ted tucked so much away, he could never recollect where he had it hid!"

"Yessir, that man was all business. They say Ted's spirit is what made this country great."

"Well, come to spirit, I would have to choose Ed Watson, cause he never let nobody stand in the way of progress."

"If ever'body goes to makin speeches here, we ain't never going to figure out about that watch. But what we heard, the Sheriff put that evidence in his own pocket for safekeepin."

"That poor young woman was afraid for her very life, and her children's life. That poor soul drug her kids under the store, and when they come out, they stunk to high heaven from Old Man Ted's drowned chickens! The kids was just whimpering like puppies under there, that's how scared they was, with all the gunfire and them dogs howlin . . ."

"Was Charlie Boggess in on it or wasn't he? Some say he sprained his ankle in the storm but hobbled right over anyway, cause he was a feller did not like to miss out. His family claims he took no part, on account of Ted was his best friend, but he must of been of a mixed mind, because the rest of his life, he wouldn't say about it, one way or the other!"

"Well, my mama come up as a Boggess, and she recalls how Grandpa Charlie told 'em to stay at home that day no matter what. Said they never seen the shooting but they heard it."

"One day Grandpa Charlie was out on the store porch talkin about old times a mile a minute, and a feller asked him what he recalled about the death of Watson. Well, that old man stopped his rockin and he fell dead quiet. From inside the house all you could hear was that kind of soft croonin from the chickens. But after a while, his old rocker started up, commenced to creakin, and pretty soon his visitor worked him up to the same subject, said, 'Well, I bet *that* day was somethin to remember!' And the creakin stopped, and Boggess clammed right up, same as before. He never answered, not a single word!"

"Well, one man said, 'Let's put a live cartridge just in the one gun so's nobody has to know who shot him.' But none of them others had no confidence that one bullet would do the job, so they loaded their guns and emptied 'em instead."

Lucius raised his hand and cleared his throat. "If that story is true, doesn't that suggest that everything was planned beforehand?"

"Nosir," Andy House declared, in a stiff silence. "The House family never knew about no such plan."

"My dad said the shooting never stopped till them guns was empty. A couple of 'em might even of reloaded, shot again."

"Them men never took a live shell from this place, that's what Ted Smallwood told me."

"How did Ted know? He was back there in his house!"

"Well, *I* seen it, cause I was here! Regular Fourth of July!"

"And I seen *you*! Your ma was nursin' you!"

"Them men might of panicked—"

"No sense stirring up all them old lies! Them men weren't panicky! Had something they had to take care of, that's all! Didn't hang back, let other people do the dirty work, like some!"

Hoad Storter said quickly, "Well, for this part of the country, Mr. Watson's house was a good big house!"

"We had pictures of it, boat sheds and all! Hurricane of '35 took the last sheds off the riverbank, cause we have a photo from '38, when Mac Johnson and his Dorothy was on there, and they ain't no sign of them outbuildins, nothin but that bare old house and a few coco palms, and the jungle creeping in over them cane fields. Jungle comes back so fast down there, it's like the tide, you can just set back and watch it come."

"Dorothy went kind of crazy on the Bend, tryin to burn out them old bloodstains in the front room. Some victim or other, I imagine. Then her brother run off with this young woman, then she run off with a young man, and people laughed at him. So he puts a gun up to his head and dials her number on the telephone. He says real calm, 'You better hear this, sweetheart.' And darned if she don't hear a *bang*—that was his finish!"

"Yep, Henry Smith's young 'uns had a lot of trouble. And some would say this was because their daddy raised his hand against Ed Watson."

"Oh what nonsense!"

"We have a historic letter in a box here someplace, came from the Surveyor, Joseph Shands, in 1904. I guess this was when E. J. Watson filed his land claim, because Mr. Shands makes mention of 'friend Watson,' which goes to show that important men of that day estimated Mr. Watson as a friend . . ."

"He was friendly with the governor, too, they say."

"Yes, he was," said Lucius, making a note of that Shands letter. "He knew Napoleon Broward in Key West before the Spanish War, when Broward was running contraband arms to Cuba. He talked with Broward about building Glades canals . . ."

"That why Parks never burned your house, the way they done the shacks of us poor common folks that never knew nobody? Took years to gather boards enough to put 'em up, but Parks didn't take ten minutes burnin 'em down!"

"Remember Chevelier's old shack on Possum Key? Never burned, because some feller took that shack down for the lumber, took her right down to the ground. That was a while back—"

"We got a pretty good idea about that, don't we?"

"Hardens, you mean?"

"Nosir! Nigger Short! Can't blame *everything* on Hardens! Henry took that lumber and built him a little cabin way back on the inside of North Cape Sable, laid low a good long while down there, all by his lonesome."

"Whoever taught a colored man to shoot as good as Henry done has got to answer for it to his Maker."

"Henry Short put his bullets in so close, you could lay a dollar bill acrost the holes—"

"Heck no! They say he never fired but the onct! He hit ol' Emperor right between the eyes!"

*

Nobody had noticed Sally in the doorway. She said, "Henry Short was there, all right, but he never fired."

Hearing her voice, the blind man welcomed her. "Folks, you all know Sally Brown. Come sit here, Sally." Andy stood up and offered her his place. Considering how abrasive she had been, his gentle use of her first name made Lucius's temples tingle. "We was having a good talk about the old days," Andy said, with a warm smile in the general direction of the door.

"The good old days," said Sally, edging no farther into the room than a stray cat. Her gaze had fastened on Owen Carr, trapped in the corner. "I don't sit down with murderers," she said.

Penny Carr's tone was a sharp warning. "You're Speck Daniels's girl, ain't that right, Miss? Married a Harden?"

"That is correct, ma'am. And you know which Harden, too, and probably a lot else that is not your business." Her gaze remained fixed on the old man in the corner. There came a scattering, a shifting, as the old people rearranged themselves, like setting hens shuffling feathers when the coop door is thrown open to the sun and air. "Roark Harden was my husband's older brother. Roark was shot down in cold blood by that man and his brothers, and nobody on this Bay said a word about it."

Owen Carr twisted on his seat like a thing burning. "Old Man Owen," Sally said finally, "who lived to tell the tale, and even brag about it."

"That was a long time ago," Hoad Storter said. "And he is kinfolks to your mama. Your kin, too."

"The Hardens let it die, girl," Lloyd Brown told her, not unkindly. "It ain't your place to stir it up again."

" 'The Hardens let it die!' Of course! Because otherwise they might have died themselves! Might have been burned out one fine night by a nice Pentecostal lynching party, the sons of the same bunch that lynched Ed Watson!"

The door screen whacked behind her like a pistol shot, and her sandaled feet fled lightly down the steps.

"My, my, my," sighed Penny Carr, still knitting.

Owen Carr let a tight breath escape, trying to smile. "Her husband's daddy was Lee Harden, he had a temper, too!" He smiled still harder. "Might been my brother Alden made a joke about Lee's sister at one of them old-time Harden shindigs down at Lost Man's. Called her Nigger Libby. And darned if Lee don't take out after him, run him all the way down the beach to where Alden got away into his boat at Sadie's Hole!"

"Guess everybody has their own idea of what's a joke," the blind man said.

Penny wove a determined stitch and purl. "Honest to goodness! You never told *me* about those Harden shindigs, Mr. Owen Carr!"

"Owen was chasing Edie Harden!" Mary Brown exclaimed, as Owen snickered. "And my brother, he was chasing Edie, too!"

"Edie's aunt Libby was a golden kind of color—a real smooth yeller gold, same as a mango. It was Libby who married up with Nigger Short."

"*Henry* Short." Andy bowed a little, in the certain instinct that all eyes in the room had turned toward him. "Times has changed," he persisted, addressing the darkness with those clear wide eyes. "Even if we ain't."

"Well, her sister Abbie run off with Storters' man, who was black as they make 'em! 'Black as Dab's ass'—remember that? I recall that sayin from when I was a boy!"

"This is Sunday, Mr. Owen Carr, case you don't know it!"

Andy persisted in that stolid voice, "Now how come all those boys was courting Edie Harden? Sandy Albritton, too! Wanted to marry her, at least Bob Thompson did. That sure strikes me as peculiar if Hardens were mulatta, like folks called 'em" A bad silence was filled by loud keening of the wasps in the low rafters. "How come nobody thought twice about accepting Hardens' hospitality, sitting right down, eating up their food—same men who wouldn't *never* sit down with Dab or Henry?" He looked all around the room as if he could see deeply into every heart. "Don't make too much sense when you come to think about it."

The plaint of wasps was audible throughout the room.

"You're the one ain't makin too much sense," Bill Smallwood warned him. Bill was breathing heavily again, shifting his cramps and pains.

"Well, answer me, then, Bill. Explain it to me."

"Seems like you changed your thinking in Miami," Smallwood said sourly.

"That's where I *begun* my thinking. I ain't done yet. Maybe I had to get struck blind to make me see."

*

"One night Old Man Carr was headed back to Lost Man's, stopped by here to pick up his supplies, caught them same two Hardens right here in this store! They busted in!"

"Well, Old Man Carr was your friend Owen's daddy, ain't that right? And nobody never heard that story you just told till after you boys was accused," the blind man said.

"Andy, whose side are you on?" Owen Carr cried desperately. "Them sonsabitches, they would shoot at your damn boat! Fishermen had to carry guns around that Lost Man's territory! And after they was put a stop to, there weren't no more trouble. Don't that prove somethin?"

"Proves they was dead, I reckon."

"Proves Lee Harden was gettin old, that's about it. Losin his oldest boy that way just took the fight out of him."

"Didn't take no fight out of Lee's wife! For years and years, Sadie Harden would put a bullet in your boat if you drifted too close inshore around South Lost Man's!"

"Earl Harden lost his boy, too, don't forget. I liked Ol' Earl all right, most of the time. He took it hard. That brought them two brothers back together for a while."

"Goddammit to hell! Are you fellers on *their* side? Men I growed up with on this island? Goddammit to hell—"

"Owen, this here's Sunday, and there's Christian ladies present—"

"Anyways, we know your side of the story. Been hearin it thirty years and more. What's past is done with."

Owen Carr looked at the floor between his shoes, then rose, unsteady, and went reeling past his neighbors as if running a gauntlet. His calm large wife took plenty of time to fold and tuck away her knitting before following him out of doors into the afternoon.

*

The atmosphere was shifting and uneasy. Lucius changed the subject. "After so many years, I've never learned where my stepmother was staying when my father died."

"Aldermans," Smallwood said wearily. "Smallwoods took 'em in after Aldermans threw 'em out."

"Well, Alice McKinney was her good friend, too."

"It weren't my mother she was staying with. It weren't McKinneys." Lloyd Brown peered suspiciously at Lucius. "How come you're writing down all this old stuff?"

"Firsthand accounts help me understand things better." Lucius put his pen away when nobody returned his smile.

"Alderman knew that feller Cox, he knew how bad he was," Bill Smallwood said. "Knew Cox had his eye on Watson's wife and might come lookin for her. Walter had a young family startin up, didn't want no trouble."

"Marie had her new baby just a few months later, so she was well along when all that happened. Her husband was afraid for her and he was right to be," Bill's sister said.

"Walter come right out with it," Bill said. "His nerves was shot that day. He was even scared some of them men might take it in their heads to bust into his house and finish off them Watsons and have done with it. Don't seem possible, setting here today, but I do know Mrs. Watson was plain terrified of that armed crowd, cause Mama said so."

Andy said, "Bill? You aimin to stand there and tell me your House uncles would of let that happen? Let that crowd murder the young widow and three little children?"

Smallwood growled stubbornly, "Some of them men had drunk somewhat to steady up their nerves, and once that crowd of men had got their blood up, got the killing instinct, your dad and his brothers and Grandpa House might not of had much say. After what happened, and all that racket, I sure ain't surprised the young widow was nervous."

Lucius said, "Did Alderman join in the shooting?"

"You're the man to tell us, Colonel. All you got to do is check your list."

Again, the blind man mended a tense silence. "Walter might of went along but I don't believe he fired. He was always a nice quiet feller. Moved away from here soon after that, become a fish guide at Fort Myers Beach. He guided them writers, Hemingway and Mr. Zane."

*

A heavy step banged up the stairs and kicked open the screen door. Crockett Junior Daniels, fulminating beer, came straight at Lucius, tugging crumpled yellow papers from beneath his stump and thrusting them into his face. To the elders he bawled, "This here is his damn list of your kinfolks in the crowd that put Ed Watson out of his damn misery!"

Lucius snapped the list out of his hand, intending to tear it into little pieces, but voices protested, calling out their right to see it first. Relinquishing the list to Smallwood, he followed the one-armed man outside, yelling after him down the steps. "He's too old to harm anybody, Crockett! Let him go!"

Crockett Junior lurched around at the bottom of the steps. "If that old loon weren't gunnin for Speck Daniels, how come he was packin a loaded .38 and some spare loads, never mind that fuckin list with all the names scratched out but just the one?"

"He never cared about revenge! He hated his father all his life! Just ask him!"

Batting the words away like gnats, the one-armed man kept on going toward his truck.

*

Bill Smallwood declaimed the list aloud, as people groaned. Those familiar names, read out like a list of dead, had exhumed ancient guilt and fear which people imagined had been safely buried under the old leaf litter of the years. Once Smallwood had finished, the people rose, forcing Lucius to pitch his last entreaties over the commotion, and he lost all hope of signatures for his petition. His audience made their escape, hurrying one another through the doorway. One old man muttered crossly as he passed, "Us people know who was here that day! We don't need no darn ol' list!" Even Hoad Storter and Weeks Daniels, Lloyd Brown and Roy Thompson, scarcely looked their old friend in the eye. Lloyd muttered regretfully, "Trouble is, that list makes our old-timers look like a damn lynch mob."

Then all were gone. The screen was empty and the old store silent, in the hum of wasps. When Bill Smallwood, waiting at the door to lock up after them, gave him his list, Lucius tore it in half and tore the halves in quarters. Hearing the papers rip, Andy looked alarmed, and his big hand flew up and outward, finding Lucius's arm. "That list is history! You aim to write the whole story or just part of it?"

"He got the names about right," Bill told Andy, as Lucius folded the torn posse list into his breast pocket. "Sure took him long enough." And Andy said, "Bill, that list don't *mean* nothin no more and you damn well know it!"

Smallwood squinted at his cousin. "Your own family got four men on there, and they got sons and grandsons, and you're one of 'em. You fool enough to tell me that don't *mean* nothin?"

"If I thought for one minute he was after Houses, or after Henry—even if I thought he was after Speck—you think I would of rode down here in his car with him?"

Bill locked the door behind them and descended ahead of them. "It sure is pathetic to see you so mixed up in this," he told his cousin from the bottom step. "You've growed so goddamn open-minded since you went over to Miami, I'm startin to think that all your brains fell out." He walked away.

"Bill?" Andy one-stepped down the stair, using the rail. He looked more vulnerable than before, and he flinched when Lucius took his arm to steady him. "Well, Colonel," he said, "I'm the oldest son of the oldest son of the oldest member of the posse, and you got me all alone right where your daddy died. Might be a pretty good chance to bump me off." He tried to smile. "I reckon you can't blame these folks for being leery." The blind man turned toward him. "See, it ain't that you might be gunnin for Speck Daniels that's got people upset. It's the *idea* of it—the idea of *any* man, even Speck, bein shot down by a Watson for takin part in what was done for the common good."

"Not everyone agreed."

"That so? A lot of your dad's friends was standin where we are standin right this minute, and nobody disagreed enough to try to stop it. And none of 'em hollered out a warning, neither, when he come near shore."

"He would have come in anyway. That's the way he was."

"Bill House always said the same." The blind man shrugged.

"Just now, you said, 'what was done for the common good.' I keep hearing things that sound as if the whole business was planned. Sheriff Tippins spoke with all those men, and that's what he believed. Malice aforethought," Lucius paused. "First-degree murder."

"All I know is, the House men never planned nothin aforetime."

The sun was hot. Lucius finally said, "I meant to ask where my father came ashore."

The blind man turned without a word, using his cane to poke his way toward the west side of the store, as if guided by the splash of wavelets off the bay. "The old boat ways are still here under the mud, cause I can feel 'em, but the dock was tore out by the hurricane. The stumps of the old pilings might be out there yet."

In the shallows, the outlines of the silted rails emerged from beneath the marl, in the glimmerings and glints beneath the surface. Andy's shoe had located a rusted section that lay under dead turtle grass along the water's edge. "Colonel? You see my toe? Go west about fifteen feet"—he pointed his cane tip. "That's where your daddy run his boat up on the shore. That's where he jumped out. That's where he died." Out of respect, the blind man stood there quietly a moment. "My dad drove a stake into that spot when we come home to bury Grandma Ida."

"You going to tell me your dad's version of what took place here that afternoon?"

"*Version?*" Andy raised his pale eyebrows high on his pink brow. "You talked all these years to all these people and *still* you ain't heard the story you want to hear?" He turned and started back toward the road.

Lucius explained that all he could expect was a general agreement on what had happened. So far, accounts differed on whether or not there had been a dispute, and whether E. J. Watson had been shot down in his boat or on the shore. Was it self-defense or according to a plan? Did Henry fire? And who fired first?

"You ain't never goin to arrive at no agreement, not if you nag folks for a hundred years. The only man who could walk you through it is the man whose lifeblood soaked into this ground, and even your daddy might not know just how it happened." He sighed. "Let him go, Colonel. For your own sake."

"Can't you tell me just what your father told you? About Henry, for example?"

Andy shook his head. "You keep coming back to Henry Short. I tell you what I know. You ask again." He resumed walking. "I told you, yes, Henry come here with Houses. I told you, yes, he had his rifle with him. That don't mean he raised that gun and aimed it at your father."

"Your dad told you that Henry Short did not fire at Ed Watson?"

Andy flushed. "Ain't you kind of calling me a liar, Colonel?" He pointed a thick finger toward the place where Watson died. "My dad was lookin down Ed Watson's gun barrels! He was raisin his own gun, pullin the trigger! There weren't no time to keep his eye on Henry!" He tried to calm himself. "Henry was standin right here in the shallers, like I told you. Bill House was standing right beside him. He said your dad was killed by the first bullet. That is all he knew and that is all I know!" He stumped ahead.

They sat down in the thin shade of a casuarina. Leaning back against the leafy bark, facing the water, the blind man breathed deeply for a long, long time. "I sure do like that south wind in my face, don't you? I can smell that Lost Man's country all the way from here!"

*

Whidden Harden came down the road from the motel and joined them at the tree. "Mister Colonel?" He kicked at the dust, clearing his throat. "I seen Crockett. He told me the story." Andy groped and put his hand on Lucius's arm, tugged him down beside him. Whidden settled on one heel on the other side.

"The other night, them boys got word from Dyer to go and grab some crazy old feller who would likely be hanging around outside the Naples church hall. Said this man was a fugitive from justice, 'armed and dangerous.' As soon as the old man hollered through the window, they knew that must be him. They went and grabbed him, grabbed his satchel, slapped a gunnysack over his head so's he wouldn't know where he was headed, then hustled him into the truck and hauled him over east to Gator Hook. Said he kicked and bit—he give 'em a real scrap—but bein old and drunk, he didn't change nothin.

"Maybe halfway there, the old feller sobered up enough to recognize their voices. So he pipes up in his sack, yells 'Don't you know me, Boys?' They open the sack and sure enough, the armed and dangerous fugitive from justice is Old Man Chicken! He was shaved and washed, which they sure wasn't used to, so they never recognized him in the dark. So they all have a good laugh over that, give him a little shine to make him feel better, and pretty soon he's as drunk as before and hollerin how he wants to talk to the man in charge! 'Where's that damn Speck at? I got to talk to him!' But when he learns that Speck is on the Bend, he yells, 'Hell, no! I ain't goin!' Said he'd prayed to God to strike him dead before he ever set foot on that place again!

"At Gator Hook, where they go through his stuff, what do they find but a revolver and some extra rounds and the list with all the names crossed out, all but the one." Whidden studied the casuarina needle that he twirled between his fingers. "They brought your brother here next day. But them boys weren't in Everglade an hour when Mud went blabbin the whole story to his girlfriend. The news that the Gasparilla Gunman was in town was all around the Bay before the day was out, and naturally someone called the Lee County law."

Andy nodded. "I heard the same story. Moved him out before the cops come, from what they was telling me here at the motel. I didn't say nothin about it because there ain't one thing you can do about it, Colonel, without riskin his life. If the law gets in too close, that old man might fall overboard or something. You best let them boys cool off a little. You don't want to push that kind, not when they're jumpy."

Whidden told him that finding that stuff in the possession of a Watson gave that gang a lot more excuse than such men needed. Asked if he meant "excuse to kill," Whidden nodded, though he doubted they would go that far without clearing it with Speck, who was at the Bend. Probably they were headed down that way already. "From what they was sayin, I figured out that they got some kind of business on the Bend that they have to finish before the Parks people show up for Dyer's meeting. You go to crowding boys like that when they don't want no witnesses around, they might just shoot somebody. So we better give 'em another day, then run on down there first thing in the mornin, see if we can talk some sense into their heads. Speck won't take a human life without he has to, that's the difference between a mean old moonshiner and these loco war vets who was trained to kill." When Lucius gazed at him, inquiring, Whidden looked unhappy. "Crockett and them took a lot of human lives. They won't mind doin it again. We all signed up together, got to serve together. I done my duty, too, right alongside 'em. But I never got the taste for it, not the way they did."

When Whidden fell quiet, Andy asked if he might go with them to Chatham River. He confessed to an unexpected yearning to visit that old Watson place just one last time. "You never know, a blind man might come in handy," he said wryly. "With me along, they might shoot over your head, at least the first time. I was born on Chokoloskee, and Mud Braman is kin, and Speck and me always got on pretty good, don't ask me why. Flaw in my character, I reckon."

Lucius and Whidden glanced at each other, and both shrugged—why not? They told Andy they were much obliged.

"I reckon my family owes something to Watsons," Andy mused as they walked back up the road. "The House men done what they thought was right, and I ain't backing off it, but they helped kill your daddy all the same."

*

ANDY HOUSE

Bill House swore Henry never fired at Ed Watson. Said he only fired past his head tryin to distract him.

Whether Dad's own bullet struck home, Dad never knew. All he knew was, a red hole jumped out on Watson's forehead. He was done for. That double-barrel was already comin down.

One thing Dad never forgot, and Granddad neither: Ed Watson's hand reached and broke that gun as he was fallin! That takes a man that's been around guns all his life. But later some said that a man killed quick as that wouldn't never have no reflex time to break his gun. They said he must of been breakin it already, must been gettin set to hand over his gun when he was gunned down.

That's what Uncle Ted told his boy Ned, according to Ned Smallwood, but I don't know how they knew so much, do you? Uncle Ted was over in his house, and Ned, he wasn't nowhere near to being borned yet.

Exceptin Ned, no man can say whose bullet killed Ed Watson. Only Ned knows for a *fact* that Watson never pulled his triggers, never even raised his gun to fire! Well, maybe Watson pulled his triggers, maybe he didn't. Anybody check for firing-pin marks on the caps of them dead shells? All we know for sure, them shells was damp, and they come apart. He broke that gun and them long barrels tipped down and that buckshot rolled right out onto the ground.

When he gets cranked up, Ned enjoys tellin how his own House cousins shot Ed Watson in the back. Now it could be that all that gunfire spun Watson right around. Might even kept him upright for a moment, cause the way some tell it, he was staggerin and spinnin, he was pitching towards 'em! They said he circled thirteen times before he fell! Thirteen times! Now I don't know who was in that crowd who could count up to thirteen, let alone keep his head in all that noise and do the counting. But I do know this, that a man who spins all the way around, spins thirteen times through a hail of fire, might get a bullet in his back if he ain't careful!

Course Cousin Ned, he likes to say that his daddy knew Ed Watson better than anybody on the southwest coast, so naturally would know the most about the case. Says his daddy weren't no liar, neither, not like some. Comes to my house maybe once every two years, gives me that message, turns purple in the face, and drives off snap-cracklin like a bucket of blue crabs. He'll be back next year a-cussin and a-hissin just so's he can tell me it again. I never figured out why Ned comes so far to see me just to do that. That feller will pick a fight with anybody in the family who might care to have one.

Before he died a couple of years back, my dad remarked how some folks were still busy twisting up the truth, never mind all the long years in between. "Don't pay no attention to young Ned," he told me. "Ask the opinion of them men was in that line, dry-mouthed and miskita-bit and all set to soil their pants from staring down the gun barrels of E. J. Watson. Us House boys was scared from start to finish, same as all the rest, and we never denied it."

It's true most of 'em lost their heads, kept right on shooting after Watson was down and stretched flat on his face. Done that to ease their nerves, I reckon, out of pure relief, but it made my dad ashamed he had took part in it.

Funny thing how a man's reputation changes once he's dead, according to the need—not his own need, I don't mean, but just so folks can feel a little better. My dad thought on this a lot, and I did, too. Because a few years after Watson's death, when this community was pretty well recovered, folks' notions about Mr. Watson begun changin. Them Pentecostal missionaries, Church of God, they come in here and baptized the community, purified the sinners, told 'em they was born again and marchin alongside of Jesus on the road to Glory. All them dark and fearful days seemed like some hellish fever that had broke with that man's death. Next thing you know, your dad was gettin credit for turnin the Lord's attention to our sinful ways and bringing in salvation, you would almost thought he died to save us all.

Most settled for makin him some kind of a local hero. *Ol' E.J. was pretty wild, all right, he probably killed a few, but so did Wyatt Earp and Wild Bill Hickok!* —that's the way some of them men commenced to talking. They wasn't ashamed of E. J. Watson, nosir, they was *proud* about him! Used to brag on their friend Ed to every stranger who come down the coast! And some of 'em are proud about him yet today. But when writers came in to get more dirt on "Bloody Watson," "Emperor Watson"—his neighbors never used them names, only the writers—them ones who claimed to be so proud about him was the first to repeat all the worst stories, cook up a lot of stuff that never happened. Some would tell any damfool thing to make it seem like themself or their daddy was the only man Ed Watson would confide in, the only one who knew what really happened. Do that to get their picture in the paper pointin out the spot where Watson died: *Muh daddy was Ed Watson's drinkin buddy, and he always did say Good Ol' Ed was the nicest feller you would ever want to meet. Give ye the shirt off his back with the one hand, slit your damn throat with the other—that was Ed!* Oh yes, that sayin was famous around here. I bet you heard that one a few times—two thousand, maybe? And they'd cackle and squawk at that old sayin like it had just popped out like a fresh egg!

Well, Bill House *did* know Watson pretty good, knowed him eighteen years from when he first showed up down in the Islands. Kind of liked him, too, the same as everybody—said you couldn't help it. But Bill House made no jokes about him, cause E. J. Watson weren't no laughin matter. My dad never forgot how it was that dark October, that black drought hanging over this coast like the Almighty had given up on us forever.

A lot of people who was secretly relieved to see their friend Ed Watson shot to pieces was the same ones who hollered later on how he deserved a trial—the same ones who pointed fingers at the House family and called us lynchers. That cousin of mine is still sayin that today, don't know the first thing about the truth and don't care neither. Well, the House men never lynched nobody. Never had no plan to kill Ed Watson in cold blood, and never fired till he swung that gun up.

All his life my dad would talk about that piece of history that happened here on this little stretch of shore. Talked about that October twilight, talked about that death like it happened yesterday—"clear as stump water," them was his words. What he meant by that: when the sun catches it right, the little pool of water in the heart of an old stump shines as deep as a black diamond, dark silver black but full of holy light, like that shine in them little limestone sinkholes in the hammocks. In them deep small holes, they ain't a breath of wind to rile the surface, nothin but some little leaf that might drift down and float on that black mirror just as light as teal down or wild petal or dry seed, with the treetops and clouds and the blue sky all contained in the reflection. "Clear as a deer's eye"—that's the way Bill House described how clear that moment was, every detail, right to the bright red of Watson's blood flecks on his rifle barrel, right to the hairs the evening wind was stirring on the dead man's neck where he lay face down.

That's the way Bill House recalled the death of Mr. Watson. He never mentioned Henry Short at all.

The Harden men weren't there that day but later years, they asked Henry for the truth about what happened. Hardens weren't liars, neither, they was honest people, and from what Henry told 'em, they concluded that Henry never fired at Ed Watson. Course bein a black man back when lynchin nigras didn't hardly make the papers, he would never admit to shooting at a white man, not to Houses and not to Hardens, neither. Not to God in Heaven! Because if that one he told ever let on, them men would say, "That dang nigger bragged he killed a white man"—say that real sweet and soft, you know, which is the sign amongst them fellers that some poor nigra is headed for perdition. But so long as he never bragged on it, it was all right, because he had the whole House clan behind him, seven men and boys.

Now them other men was very glad that Henry Short was in that line, and his rifle with him. Later years, a few of 'em took on about it some when they was drinking, but they liked Henry and they was grateful, and I don't believe they would of raised their hand against him. It was them men's sons who hated to admit that a black man had took care of Watson while the white men only finished off the job. So pretty soon certain ones was saying that Henry Short had lost his head and murdered Watson. *We gone to stand for some damn nigger shootin down a white man? Who in the hell give him the idea he could get away with that? Who give him that damn rifle in the first place?* And maybe, they said, Henry's bad attitude come from the way them Houses spoiled him, and anyways, Houses done wrong to arm that nigger, never mind lettin him foller 'em over to Smallwood's. The way some of the younger ones was carrying on when they got drunk, you would have thought that Henry Short was the only armed man there. Then someone would say, *Ain't he the one married that Harden down to Lost Man's River?* And a few of them fools started in to saying, *"Well, who's going to teach that boy his lesson?"*

Course they was not so much bad fellers as big talkers. They never rightly understood what a terrible fear had weighed on our community. And their daddies went along with it, they kind of nodded. In their hearts, they knew Henry was there that day because they wanted him there, but bein a little bit ashamed, they would not discuss it in the family. The fathers never admitted to the sons how scared they was of Watson—scared enough so for that one day, they forgive a man his color because that man could shoot better'n they could and might of kept some of 'em from getting hurt.

So Henry Short never told nobody he fired that gun, not even my dad, who was raised with Henry and was standin right beside him when he done it. And Dad would never think to ask, because Henry was dead honest all his life, and Dad would never want to be the one to make a liar of him. Henry Short never had no choice about what he had to do. From the very first minute after Watson's death, he was setting a backfire, trying to keep that firestorm away.

That same evening after dark, Henry slipped away to Lost Man's River. Before he left, he told my dad he might be gone awhile from Chokoloskee. Far as I ever heard about, he never come back. Never said nothin about Mr. Watson, but Dad knew. He said, "Them men ain't goin to bother you none, Henry. Hell, they *like* you!" And Henry nodded, give a little kind of smile. Then he said, "Spect so, Mist' Bill. They liked Mist' Watson, too."

THE WATSON POSSE

Daniel David House

Bill, Dan Junior, and Lloyd House (the oldest boys)

Harry McGill (married Eva Storter, whose dad, R. B. "Bembery," was best friends with Papa. Harry told Eva's brother Hoad that he had fired, but he said he was not proud of it and hoped he'd missed.)

Hiram McGill (always tagging after Harry; probably missed, too)

McDuff Johnson

Charley Johnson, his son

Isaac Yeomans

Saint Demere (his daughter Estelle D. Brown says he took part)

Jim Demere

Henry Smith (visiting that day from Marco)

Gene Gandees

Young Gene Gandees (later let on to his wife, Doris, that the so-called posse was planning to do away with Watson "no matter what"; he was not alone in this opinion.)

Crockett Daniels (over from Marco that day with Henry Smith. "Speck" was only twelve or so, but some say he fired; others say he was also with those boys who came up later and shot into the body.)

Walter Alderman (worked for Papa in Columbia County; probably in the line of men due to social pressure, but would later claim he never pulled the trigger.)

Horace Alderman (his brother, visiting from Marco; joined in "for the heck of it," Walter said. Hanged in Fort Lauderdale in 1925 as "the Gulf Stream Pirate.")

Andrew Wiggins (his parents, Will and Lydia, were good friends of Papa, but Andrew apparently took part. He was renting the Atwell place on Rodgers River but had come back north after the storm.)

Leland and Frank Rice (three transient fishermen took part, including the Rice boys, according to reports. Both now dead.)

Note: According to rumor, the third fisherman was that John Tucker who showed up a few years later with the Rice-Alderman gang and drowned while trying to swim across the Bay.

All agree that "about 20 men" were in "the posse."

SUSPECTS

There are stories that the following took part—in one case, his participation was confessed by the elderly suspect himself! But it seems more
likely that these men were not involved, or if they were, that they did not
pull the trigger.

C. T. Boggess (Most people agree that Charlie was across the island with a
swollen ankle sprained in the hurricane and couldn't have limped that
far in time. Asked about it, he always harrumphed, wouldn't say a word.
He never objected when, years later, a story started up that he was in
on it.)

Judge George Storter (Liked to display "the gun I used that day," but nobody
recalls him being there. In 1910 he was Justice of the Peace in Everglade,
but on the date in question, he is listed in the Sheriff's records as a juror
in Fort Myers.)

Claude Storter (Now deceased. Most people say Claude was away on Fakahatchee.)

Old Man Gregorio Lopez (C. G. McKinney's column of Chokoloskee news in
the *American Eagle* puts him in British Honduras at the time.)

Joe, Fonso, Greggy Lopez (in Brit. Honduras with their father)

Note: Apparently the Lopez clan was sorry to miss out on the shooting, and
Joe and Fonso were among those who would imply in later years that they
had been present.

Jim Howell (As father-in-law to Bill House and Andrew Wiggins, Jim might
have gone along, but he once worked for Papa on the Bend and stayed
good friends with him, and nobody believes Jim pulled the trigger.)

Henry Short (He accompanied the House men to the landing, and all agree
that he was armed, but whether or not he fired is another question. In
view of the Jim Crow climate of the time, and Henry's famous prudence,
it scarcely seems credible that he aimed his rifle at a man such as E. J. Watson. Short has assured L. H. Watson and the Hardens that he did not fire,
and has never wavered in that story.)

Frank B. Tippins (For the record, a reliable source reports the following:
"When I was a teenager, Frank Tippins stood on our back porch and told
my folks and me how he and three other men killed Mr. Watson, how they
put four men in the mangroves, two on each side. Mister Watson came in,
standing in his boat, his double-barrel shotgun laying beside him. He
heard something, reached for his gun, and then Frank shot him—they all
four shot, Frank said, but he shot first." However, it is very well-
established that Sheriff Tippins, who wished to take Watson into custody,
did not arrive at Chokoloskee until the following day. Like so many
others—among them Justice Storter, Old Man Lopez, Nelson Noble, per-

haps Charlie Boggess—he appears to have been afflicted in his later years by a need to have participated in the Watson myth, at least among Fort Myers people unacquainted with the facts.)

Certain boys, including Crockett Daniels, were said to have shot into the corpse there at the water's edge.

WITNESSES

Ted Smallwood. Ted had malaria that day, and anyway, he always said he had nothing against his old friend "E.J.," wanted no part of it, never stepped out of his store to watch. Despite their long friendship, some people claim that Ted was as relieved as all the rest to see Watson killed.

Willie Brown. Old friend of Dad, dead set against the shooting.

Walker Carr. Old friend of Dad, dead set against the shooting.

Nelson Noble. Rowing around the point as the shooting started; his daughter Edith's claim that he took part appears mistaken.

George Storter. Justice Storter's nephew; in boat with Nelson Noble.

Granger Albritton. Came up from Islands after the Great Hurricane. Did not take part. His sons Sandy and Baxter were also witnesses.

Henry Thompson. Present but did not take part.

James Hamilton, and sons Frank, Lewis, and Jesse. Came back from Lost Man's with Henry Thompson; present but did not take part.

Walter and Fred House; Alvin Brown and Owen Carr; Rob Thompson; Dinks and Tony Boggess, also younger Howell, Smith, Brown, Yeomans, and Johnson boys, also a few young girls and women, including Alice McKinney, Ethel Boggess—claim (or are said) to have been among the onlookers.

ABSENT

At various times, the following were reported to have been present. They were not.

C. G. McKinney (across the Island in his store or absent in Fort Myers on jury duty with Justice Storter)

Charlie McKinney, his son (out fishing)

John Henry Daniels, Phin Daniels, Cap and Jack Daniels (at Fakahatchee)

Tant Jenkins (ditto)

Old Man Robert Harden, and sons Earl, Webster, and Lee (all at Lost Man's, though Earl always claimed he would have shot had he been present.)

Gene Roberts (was renting Andrew Wiggins's Chokoloskee house, but after the storm, he went home to Flamingo.)

Adolphus Santini (a rumor persists that Old Dolphus took part, although he never returned to Chokoloskee after moving away to the east coast, soon after his near-fatal encounter with E.J.W. back in the nineties.)

To the best of my knowledge, this list is accurate and complete.

(signed) *Lucius H. Watson*
Lost Man's River
Spring 1923

Chapter 9

Southward

The *Cracker Belle*, which Whidden Harden kept upriver near the bridge at Everglade, was a thirty-two-foot cabin boat with a long work deck for commercial fishing. When Lee Harden owned her, Lucius recalled, she had been white, with that old-time blue trim at the red waterline, but after years of disuse, her hull was a flaking driftwood gray.

The engine started with a cavernous rumble. "Sounds pretty good, Cap," Lucius said, and Whidden said, "Sounds good because I tinkered all this mornin. We'll see how good she starts tomorrow."

"He talking about his wife or his old boat?" called Sally, who was guiding Andy to a canvas boat chair in the aft end of the cockpit. In blue sweatshirt and torn-off jeans, she swung gracefully to the cabin roof and leaned back against the windshield, raising her pretty face up to the sun.

The *Cracker Belle* idled down current past rusty fish houses and a sagging dock and stacks of sea-greened crab pots. On a warehouse wall a notice read DON'T EVEN THINK ABOUT STACKING YOUR SHIT ON THIS DOCK. "Nice," Sally said. She fluttered her fingers at the men in rubber boots, packing ice and fish into slat boxes. Straightening, they squinted at the *Belle* from beneath their caps. They did not wave back.

Beyond the hotel, the tidal river turned west through the mangrove wall toward the Gulf, and the *Cracker Belle* set out across the bay between the sparkling white spoil banks of the channel. On the tall navigation markers, ospreys had assembled their huge nests, and cormorants, uttering low cretaceous grunts, fled their pedestals and beat away like ancient flying lizards, down the long channels between islets and out across the shallow reaches where oyster bars and mangrove sprouts and stalking egrets broke the gleam of the marl flats, all the way south to Chokoloskee Island.

Facing aft over the wake, Andy was identifying the side channels, and he grinned when they asked him how he did it. "The nests is where you hear them fish hawks, and nests in Chokoloskee Bay means channel markers." He pointed toward the peeping osprey overhead. "In my mind's eye I can see that bird pretty near as clear as you can, them black burnsides and that sharp crook in the wing!"

On the spoil bank stood a pair of bald eagles. The great white heads with their massive beaks like yellow ivory gleamed in the fresh sun and sparkling water. When Lucius described how unperturbed the eagles were by the boat's wake, which washed up the shell bank, bathing their mighty talons, Andy cried out happily, "I can just *see* 'em!"

Folding his big hands on his gut, he nodded in contentment. "I recall when they tore down every eagle's nest on Marco Island. Claimed them big ol' nests was unsightly and unsanitary. Said they'd improve on them old sticks with some nice new plastic nests, but what the eagles thought of that, I just don't know."

Andy shifted in his canvas chair, to converse better. "I was visitin with my niece's son last time I come here. He'd shot a eagle and had plans to stuff it, but never got around to it. When that beautiful bird commenced to stink, he threw it out." He banged his hands down on the chair arms. "After the law went through protecting 'em, Henry Short got offered some nice money to poach two eagles for this veterans' club. They aimed to make the bar lounge atmosphere more patriotic. What was wanted was a breeding pair with nice white heads, a pair like that would likely have chicks back at the nest. Henry said all right, just to go along—he had no choice—but some way he never could come up with any eagles. Them red-blooded Americans hooted him, y'know! They got abusive! *This boy was supposed to be a dead-eye shot!* Never understood that this nigra man was more loyal to the national bird than what their club was!

"Henry plain hated any waste of the wild creatures. Probably spent less ammunition taking care of his own needs than any hunter in south Florida, because you could spin a clam shell up against the sky and he'd clip it every time with that old Winnie. How Henry learned to shoot like that, Dad never knew, and they were raised together. Way back before the century turned, Granddad House give his young nigra that old 30.30, and it wasn't long before this colored feller could outshoot anybody on this coast, the Harden boys and E. J. Watson included. Your daddy did not care to hear that and would not be teased about it. Other men started complainin, too. Said, 'Niggers ain't *s'posed* to shoot as good as that. Got too much white in him.' "

*

Rabbit Key was a gravel bar with a lone mangrove clump on the west point. Watching the barren key as it passed astern, Lucius asked Andy if he'd ever heard why E. J. Watson's body had been brought out here instead of being buried on Chokoloskee.

Andy thought a minute. "I recollect Dad sayin that nobody could rest easy while that body lay there in the dark down by the shore, and nobody wanted to go near him in the nighttime. Superstition. What they thought they seen during the shooting was beyond all nature. That weren't their neighbor anymore but a bloody-headed fright out of a nightmare, lurching at 'em through the dusk with enough lead in him to stop ten men. A man who come ahead ten yards when he was full of bullets might not pay much attention to natural laws, not after nightfall. They was terrified that gory thing might sit up in the dark, and look around, and maybe come huntin 'em again."

Here was the seed of legend, Lucius thought, sprouted into darkling flower from the grit and blood and filth on the shore at Smallwood's, like the white lotus sprung up from the mud. He thought with a shudder of his father, fastened by bullets to the earth, eyes turning to blue ice in the rigid face.

"Next morning, the men was still leery about touchin him, so they took a hitch around his ankles, snaked him off the bank. Towed him all the way out here and buried him four feet down under sand and gravel. They knew Ed Watson was too full of lead to crawl, let alone swim, but they went and piled big coral slabs on top, just to make sure."

Whidden Harden laughed out of nervous awe. "Might sit up in his grave and lurch into the channel and swim on back to Chokoloskee underwater! Me 'n' Roark dreamed about that as kids—the gray-blue face and the sea grass in his bloody hair, turning and bumping up the Pass on the flood tide!"

"What's the *matter* with you two!" Sally cried. "That's Mister Colonel's *daddy* you are joking about!"

"Well, we wasn't jokin, not exactly, Sal." Whidden smiled apologetically at Lucius, who could not smile back. Though he understood that his efforts to appear objective encouraged a certain disrespect toward the dead man, and was content that his companions felt they could speak freely, he also knew that with the making of the myth, his father was diminished as a human being.

Whidden said, "My dad would tell us that after the Great Hurricane, there weren't nothin left here except one big tree in a clump of mangroves where them little sprouts are takin hold right now. Rigged a noose around his neck, run the line to that lone tree. Course Chokoloskee people will deny that."

"What I heard," Andy said, "them fellers run that rope so Watson's family could locate the body if they come to claim it, which they did."

"Rigged a noose?" Lucius said sharply. "Dragged him out here underwater, scraping on the bottom, instead of laying his body under a canvas in the stern?" He shook his head, outraged. "I think they needed to degrade him in order to feel better about what they'd done."

"I always heard you come down here with Tippins," House said carefully. "You remember seeing any rope?" When Lucius shook his head, House said, "Well, maybe there was a hanging rope and maybe not. Maybe they dragged him on the bottom, maybe not. The main thing was, they didn't want no part of him on Chokoloskee. Some will tell you they aimed to bury him outside the county line, just south of where it crosses Rabbit Key. But back in them days, this was all Monroe County, so maybe that outside-the-county stuff was like that rope—somethin folks might of spliced on later to spice up the story.

"Easier to dig a grave out on this key, that's all it is. These little islands on the Gulf, they come and go from year to year in storm and current. This year that bar might be hard gravel, but that year it might of been white coral sand. And even gravel digs easier than shell mound, cause them shells compact so hard, it's like chipping concrete. Old Man Tant Jenkins used to say how Mr. Watson was an inspiration to a young man's life. Said that all his valuable experience of farmin that shell-packed soil on Chatham Bend was what inspired him to a life of huntin and fishin."

Whidden said, "That old tale about the hanging rope come straight out of the magazines," and Sally called from the cabin roof, "I always suspected there was one of those darn Hardens who could read!" She laughed at Whidden as he reached and tickled her. "*All* us Hardens could read pretty good," he said. "That was one reason—aside from bein Catholics—that all the ignoramuses around here had it in for us."

Andy was pointing. "Pelican Key must be someplace over this way. Charlie McKinney got a lot of sea trout right back of that key, he sometimes took four hundred pounds a day. He was some fisherman, that feller. Fished by the tides like everybody else, but mostly he fished in the daytime while other fellers had to work at night. And that's where he was that October afternoon, watchin Watson's boat pot-pottin by on her way to Chokoloskee!"

*

The Gulf of Mexico was lost in sunny mist, soft silver gray. In the mute emptiness, in soft risings of the water, three porpoises parted the smooth pewter surface, drawing the hunting terns.

Traversing the shallow coastal shelf which ran north from Lost Man's River to Fakahatchee, they swapped stories about the clam shack village on Pavilion Key, a low green island off the starboard beam. In the clam crew days, Pavilion had been stripped of every tree and shrub for cooking fires, until finally it was little more than a broad sand spit. Here two hundred people lived in makeshift shacks, including E. J. Watson's "backdoor family," which awaited his comings and goings out of Chatham River. The clam skiffs were staked out off this lee shore, Lucius told Whidden, who was still young when that era ended.

Andy recalled "a day in '26, when we was living on the Watson Place, a day of hurricane when twenty-five men from Pavilion Key come up the river to find shelter. They had to stand up in the boat, they was that crowded. That clam skiff was sunk right to the gunwales, and the river lappin in, we couldn't hardly see no boat at all. Coming up around the bend, them men looked like they was walkin on the water.

"By then, the clams was pretty well thinned out, and in the Depression, the cannery jobs at Caxambas and Marco was real scarce. The white fellers claimed that the nigra hands had undercut their pay, so they lynched a black feller at Marco to teach the rest a lesson. Only thing that poor nigra done wrong was try to make a livin. Them white boys had no education, no ambition, just wanted to feel they was better than somebody else. Cowards, you know, always in a gang. They was feelin frustrated, was all it was."

"Frustrated." Sally brought her knees up to her chin and put her arms around them, rocking a little. "Is it true that Old Man Speck was in on that one?" She expected no answer and she did not get one.

"That nigra had a job at Doxsee's clam factory, which them boys didn't," Whidden said, as if that might explain it.

"Later they claimed this black boy looked crossways at some white woman, but most folks believed that was only their excuse." The blind man slapped his big hands on his knees. "Them fellers knew before they done it that most of us good Christian folks wouldn't bother our heads about it, and even them few that had doubts wouldn't never stop 'em."

In recent years, the Caxambas factory had been moved to Naples, where it failed for good, and the local economy had been struck down by the Red Tide. With the whole coast stinking of dead fish, and the clams dying, the Red Tide seemed an unnatural affliction associated with the coming of the

Park, since both had descended on this coast in the same year. When the last clams died off in epidemic, with stone crabs, conchs, and sponges close behind, there was fear that this was no red tide but something much more evil and mysterious. Eventually the blame was put on Capt. Bill Collier's big clam dredge, which dragged up five hundred bushels every day and tore up and disrupted the sand bottom.

The vast clam flat had never recovered. Today this shallow shelf was so plagued with sharks that men disliked going overboard to wade. Nobody knew what drew the sharks from deeper water. It wasn't fish, because the fish had never returned after the tide, not the way they were. These days, there was talk of a shark fishery. "Imagine our granddaddies goin after sharks!" Whidden exclaimed. "I ain't never et a shark, and I sure ain't aimin to start now!"

"The Lord's Creation is too old to adjust to all our meddlin." The blind man had heard that down on Northwest Cape, two hundred killer whales had run aground and died—who had ever heard of such a thing? They all fell quiet, wondering if those doomed leviathans were a sign of the Apocalypse, a signal that the old ways of the earth were near an end.

*

Where islands shifted in the mist, Whidden called to Sally, who had remained on the forward cabin, hair flying in the salt Gulf wind. "That's Mormon Key, there where I am pointin at!" Mormon Key was where his grandfather had settled after turning over Chatham Bend to the old Frenchman. "Course Mormon was closer to the Bend than Granddad Robert might of liked, bein just off the mouth of Chatham River."

"Well," she cried, "Mister Colonel's daddy was never their real enemy along this coast!" Whidden nudged Lucius, then hollered back, "How come you know so much about them old-time Hardens? You think you know my family history better'n me?"

"Yes, I sure do! I spent evening after evening talking with your family when you were out in the swamp breaking the law!"

"Well, the family had our Harden story taught me pretty good by that time!"

Sally clambered back into the cockpit. "Those older Hardens always said they kept a sharp eye on your father but they learned to trust him," she told Lucius, "and they certainly trusted you." She helped Andy bring his chair forward to join them.

Whidden said, "Well, they didn't care to have E. J. Watson as their enemy. And he was always generous to 'em, very kind. Never thought about 'em as mulatta people, the way some did."

Sally groaned. "Whidden? Maybe that's because they *weren't* mulatta, ever think of that?"

"Them men from Chokoloskee Bay harassed Whidden's family something unmerciful," Andy said tactfully. "Once they seen how many sea trout come up on these banks on the flood tide, they aimed to run that pioneer family right off Mormon Key, and was very indignant when the Hardens would not let 'em do it. I heard this from my dad, y'know, because I'm talking about way back, now, when Colonel here was just a boy, up in Fort Myers.

"The Hardens all knew how to shoot, and they held this place with guns. Mormon Key was the real start of the Fish Wars. Men from the Bay would come down here"—he waved his arm with that uncanny orientation—"and fish this northwest side, stake gillnets all around the grasses, catch sea trout coming off the flats on the falling tide. But sometimes they left them nets too long, and couldn't lift until the tide come in again, and by then they was lucky to save a third of the fish caught, because the rest was dead. And the Hardens hated being crowded out, hated that waste, and they would put a bullet past those fellers' heads, to scare 'em off, and the boats took to shooting back as they departed.

"Robert Harden give up on Mormon Key because he was fed up with being harassed by the Bay people. It was only a matter of time, he reckoned, till them men bushwhacked one of his boys when they went north for their supplies. He sold the quitclaim to E. J. Watson around 1899 and bought Nick Santini's claim to Hog Key and Wood Key, down around Lost Man's. Stayed for life. All that old man wanted was his peace and quiet, which meant plenty of space between Hardens and Chokoloskee."

Andy said, "Bill House got his fill of Chokoloskee on the same day Colonel's daddy did, October twenty-fourth of 1910. Just took him a few years more to realize it. All the same, my dad loved that island, loved them people. I do, too. Can't tell you why, cause a lot of 'em ain't lovable. I guess Chokoloskee's in my blood, like my cousin Ned. I just can't get him out."

Lucius nodded. Not willingly, he was fond of those people, too. In his long decades on this coast, he had come to admire a frontier grit, a wry integrity born of endurance, a cranky generosity and hard-grudged decency in the Bay people, including some who had been present in the crowd which killed Ed Watson, and some who harassed the Harden family later on.

"The Fish Wars was still going strong when me 'n' Roark was growin up," Whidden was saying. "One time Old Man Walker Carr come in off Lost Man's Key and set his nets. He had his gun with him. The very first night, Earl Harden come up on him out of the dark. 'What's the matter with you, old man, never seen our sign?' So Walker said, 'I thought I'd help you fellers catch a fish.' Earl hollers out, 'We don't allow nobody fishin in this territory!

If I was you, I'd head on home right about now!' Old Man Carr put his gun up in Earl's face. He said, 'I come here to make my livin, Mister, mind my own business, and I don't know of any law which says I can't fish any damn place I please.' And Earl said, 'Look here, Walker, let's you and me get along!' I guess Uncle Earl liked that old man's style, because the Hardens never bothered him no more." Sally yelled out, "Too bad he didn't shoot him." And Harden nodded. "It was Carrs and their Brown kin who give the Hardens so much trouble later on."

*

The *Cracker Belle* was the lone boat on this empty coast. Passing north of Mormon Key, she neared the stilt-root mangrove islets that camouflaged the broken delta at the mouth of Chatham River. What Papa had liked best about his river was this hidden entrance. The deep and narrow channel sluicing through the islets was all but concealed from the Gulf, so that any stranger unfamiliar with this coast would pass right by the mouth and never see it.

"Dead reckoning," Harden muttered, cutting her speed. "Got to go by your old bearings, your old courses, listen to what's under your propeller. Used to be markers, but I reckon them terrible moonshiners and smugglers ripped 'em out." He had to grin. "Come in off the Gulf at night, hit this narrow channel at high speed, and any law that tried to follow 'em, lookin for markers, would go buckin aground up on a flat or tear out the bottom of their boat on one them orster bars."

"You suppose any of those smugglers might answer to the name of Brown or Daniels?" Sally inquired. "Used to be one by the name of Harden, I know that much."

Harden laughed. "Might come across one-two Danielses, Sal, now that you mention it. I don't know about no Browns unless you would count them few that went to jail."

"The cargo changes, but the smuggling sure don't!" Andy reflected. "It's been a way of life here on this coast since pirate times, and Spanish times— since white men first showed up on the horizon! My uncle Dan and my uncle Lloyd, they was both rum runners, and Old Man Nick Santini done plenty of night work out of Estero Bay, there at Fort Myers Beach."

"Is that the man Mister Colonel's father—?"

"His brother," Lucius told her. He did not feel like explaining. The knifing of Adolphus Santini at Key West had been witnessed by a dozen men and could never be argued away, and it did no good to explain that it was but one of hundreds of near-fatal knifings on this coast, long since forgotten. What he would state in the biography was true, that there was no witness to any *killing* ever attributed to E. J. Watson, or no *known* witness, at any rate. He thought unwillingly of that "memoir" in Rob's satchel. If Rob had died far away and long ago, as his family had supposed, the biography could make that claim without hesitation.

*

Inside the delta lay the mangrove archipelago of Storter Bay, where years ago the Storter boys liked to net mullet. In Chatham River, the incoming tide swelled upstream between the gleaming walls of thick-leaved seacoast trees, meeting and turning back upon itself the fresh flow from the Glades, and carrying the brackish mangrove fringe far back inland. By his own reckoning—elapsed time, shifts in boat speed and direction, scents of dry ground vegetation on the air—the blind man navigated the old river of his youth as intently as an eel nosing upstream, tracing the minerals and shifts of current toward the mouth of the home creek from which it first descended to the sea.

Where broken trees had stranded on a shoal, the thin bare branches dipped and beckoned, slapped by brown froth in the curl of the boat's wake. Two miles above the river mouth, they neared the bar off the north bank where the bodies of the two men killed by Cox had nudged aground. The rotted cadavers had been too loose to take into the boats, so the clammers from Pavilion Key had rigged soft hitches to the remains of Green and Dutchy and towed them slowly out across the river. "Buried what was left of 'em up here a little ways on the south bank, longside of Hannah Smith," the blind man finished. Asked how he knew where that place was, Andy supposed his father had shown him Hannah's grave when the House family was living on the Bend, but he looked surprised by the questions, as if he had always known the answer in his sinew. Like fish and tides, human deaths and burials were in the grain of local knowledge—signs to mark the passing years and commemorate those corners of this silent landscape where old-time people had left small scars in the green and gone away again.

"About all us local people got is our long memories, along with the history that come down in our families," Whidden agreed. "Bad hurricanes and feuds and shootings might roil things up now and again, but otherwise our seasons stay mostly the same. That's why we remember deaths and the old stories, and carry that remembrance back a hundred years. And that's why the Watson Place is so important, Mister Colonel, even to the younger ones who never seen it."

The burial place lay close to Hannah's Point, which was downstream and across the river from the Bend. Maybe thirty feet back from the bank, the blind man said, was a square dent in the ground about one foot deep, "as if you had crowbarred a half-buried barn door out of the ground."

"You mean you can still see it?" Sally wrinkled up her nose.

"I imagine so. That's one of the things still spooks people about this place. Burial ground will generally sprout up in heavy weeds, but nothing has growed over that square patch in fifty years. Them three sinners is still there unless the river took 'em."

"No coffin?"

"No time for coffins. This weren't hardly two days before the hurricane, and the sky was very strange and murky, in the darkest October ever recollected, so them men was certain a bad storm was on the way. Another thing, that nigra who helped Cox sink the bodies had escaped to Pavilion Key, so they knew that Cox was still there at the Watson Place, not a mile upriver from this grave. Them men was clam diggers, they was unarmed, and they didn't want to mess with Cox without the Sheriff.

"Anyways, the poor lost souls that was fished out of the river never had no family to come after 'em, nobody who cared enough to build a coffin or mark the place where they had died. But the burial party kind of hated to throw earth on their bare faces, so they laid a scrap of canvas down, then let the dirt fly fast as they could, holding their breaths so's they wouldn't puke into the grave.

"Course them victims was lucky they got into the ground at all, let alone stayed there. If they was still in the water, their bodies would been lost after that storm. I was on this river in the Hurricane of '26, and the Gulf rose up and washed way back inland, and when that rush of water come back down out of the Glades on the next tide, it sounded like thunder rolling past the Bend. *Nothin* could of stayed put in this river! But the Watson Place stood up to bad hurricanes in 1909 and 1910, and again in '26 and '35, remember, Colonel? And she done just fine!"

A snakebird fled from a low snag, brushing the surface before beating away over the water. At a rounded point on the south bank where buttonwood and gumbo-limbo rose from higher ground, they eased ashore and tied up to the mangroves. Leaving Andy in the boat, they hunted along the riverbank through broken thicket until they found a rectangular indentation in the marly soil. Already one corner of the common grave was eroding bit by clod into the river.

"Won't last too much longer," Andy whispered, when they described it. "That grave is closer to the water than it was." In the heat and silence, he listened intently to the flood as it curled past, a *lic-lic-lic* along the waterline, a relict sound of those ancient far millenniums when briny rivers poured from the wave-washed limestone of the great peninsula as it inched upward, upward, parting the surface of the silent seas.

In sun-tossed branches, in the river wind, black pigeons with sepulchral white pates bobbed, craned, and peered like anxious spirits. From upriver, others called in mournful columbine lament, *woe-woe-wuk-woe.* "This stretch of river can still spook me," Andy murmured, when his friends came back aboard. "Poor Hannah's bones are right there in that marl, along with Waller and young Dutchy. Won't do no harm to give 'em a nice prayer, in case that burial party was in too much of a hurry."

Woe-woe-wuk-woe.

Bending their heads, they joined the blind man's meditation. "Hear us, O Lord. One of these years, this river will take these poor lost souls and carry their poor bones down to the Gulf. And we pray You will have Mercy, Lord, and lift them from the Bosom of the Deep and give them rest." The words were intoned slowly and mindfully—the one prayer ever offered on behalf of Hannah Smith, Green Waller, and young Herbert Melville, alias Dutchy.

"Amen," they murmured.

*

The Watson Place lay on the point of a large island between rivers, a higher ground where the mangrove along the river edge gave way to subtropical forest and salt prairie. Perhaps the Calusa had built up this ground on the shoal of silt which would have formed on this big bend. Upriver at the eastern end of the great island was House Hammock Bay, where Andy's family had grown sugarcane for many years. "I sure come up this river enough times," Andy explained when Sally complimented him on his close knowledge of the river after years away. His face turned a gold red like a rare apple in his gratification that this thorny young woman whose face he could not see had offered a conciliatory word. "I'm sure tickled you folks let me come along," he blurted, heaving his canvas chair around to smile toward the khaki haze which was Lucius Watson.

"Now Henry Short was working at House Hammock while we was living on the Watson Place, remember? Raised fine tomatoes, and a world of bananas to go with 'em. Slept in Granddad's old shack, cracks in the walls, plenty of snakes and spiders. That Hurricane of '26 had blowed the roof right off the cistern, and this moonlit night he was awoke by somethin out there, lappin at the water. Peekin through the cracks, he seen this real big panther, and he got so excited by the size that he raised up his rifle and fired without thinkin, shot it through one ear and out the other. Made a bad job because the blood spoiled the cistern, you'd of thought the lifeblood of every panther in the Glades was in that water.

"Henry hoisted that big cat out of the cistern and rowed him around to Chatham Bend. Laid straight, he went eleven feet counting tail and whiskers. Henry and Dad skinned him out, they got twenty-five dollars for that hide. Should have got more, but as usual, my dad was took because he couldn't read.

"Oh, that was a beautiful animal! I never in my life seen a cat that size, and I never heard about one like it since. Course back in them days, panthers was still common in the Islands, swam from island to island same way deer will, used to catch 'em in a bear trap baited with fish. Sometimes one'd kill a hog or take some chickens. Kill a dog, too, if they got the chance. Panthers will eat a dog, all but the head. They'll bury that dog head but they won't come back for it.

"Them big cats is all but gone out of the Everglades, gone out of Florida, and the bears is close behind. What bothers me today is all them ones we wasted. Shot 'em on sight, never give it a thought, cause folks was poor and their stock was precious, and they naturally thought that them beautiful things was only varmints."

*

Lucius tried to envision "the Watson Place" as seen in his first impression as a child—the roof peak of "Papa's new house in the jungle," rising out of the green river walls as the small schooner called the *Gladiator* rounded the broad bend, then the white beacon of the house itself, miraculous and bright as any castle.

The year was 1896, when the new house prepared for the family's arrival was barely finished. They had sailed down the green and silver coast from the railroad terminus at Punta Gorda and tacked up Chatham River with the tide. Like Mama and the other children, he had never seen the sea and became seasick, but the shining waves sweeping past the bow had been magnificent, and the children cried out at the bronze porpoises gleaming in the sea under the bowsprit, and the swift white birds dancing upward from the whitecaps. Papa and his young crewman Henry Thompson had rigged troll lines, and the children caught silver fishes—kingfish or Spanish mackerel, Lucius remembered, and barracuda.

He had never forgotten the Watson Place as it was on that first arrival, the red blossoms of the twin poinsettias between the white house and the river, planted years before by the old Frenchman, and the smell of fresh paint which scoured his nostrils in the hot small children's rooms upstairs. He was seven then, rushing pell-mell into boyhood, and a great new passion for small boats and fishing would sweep his dimming memories of Oklahoma and north Florida into the past.

He had wept that day they were taken from the Bend to be put into the day school at Fort Myers—all but Rob, who stayed behind to help on the plantation, only to disappear for good a few years later. After his mama's death in 1901, Eddie had gone north to Columbia County to help his father while Lucius returned to live here in the Islands. The only house ever built on Chatham River was also his first real and beloved home.

*

A half mile above Hannah's Point, a roof peak emerged slowly from the ragged tree line, sinking away again as the river turned, then reappearing. Below wind-warped shingles like saw teeth on the roofline, the house was a brilliant white against the trees behind. Whidden burst out, "I'll be damned!" as Sally cried, "It's beautiful!" But to Lucius, his old home looked stunned, as if blinded by the sun, like a senile person dressed too festively and trotted out uncomprehending for an anniversary.

All by itself, stark on its mound, the Watson Place was eerily identical to the house first beheld in 1896. Only gradually, as the *Belle* drew closer, did he see that fresh paint could not disguise the sag of old wood weariness along the peak. The windows without glass or shutters were gaunt naked holes, as black as if burned through the white facade.

Between the river and the house, the two great twisted royal poincianas, thick roots exposed by decades of erosion, were the last of the old trees planted by the Frenchman. And soon these, too, would lean away and follow the old sheds and docks and the last of Papa's coco palms into the current.

Whidden slowed the boat to scan the banks. Nobody had appeared out of the house. Lucius had told them about Addison Burdett, and now they saw across the river an old skiff with a scabby outboard motor tied up to the mangroves, which formed a thin wall between the current and the salt prairie of white marl muck, hard scrub, and bitter grasses. They crossed the river and eased the *Belle* up alongside. Except for bilge water and empty paint cans, the boat was empty, yet all agreed that Burdett had not gone ashore. There was no destination here, nothing but wasteland of salt prairie and dead marl.

Harden rerigged the skiff's bow line to the branches. "Whoever tied her up as poor as this never cared whether she drifted off or not. This boat was towed across the river so nobody could escape off of the Bend." Grumpy with uneasiness, he straightened, the line still in his hand, and gazed back across the water at the silent house. "Maybe like they took him someplace else," he said.

Lucius thought, *Or he is in the river.* Whidden must have considered this, too, for he added quietly, "Well, I reckon they ain't harmed him, Mister Colonel, or they wouldn't leave his boat where somebody who came lookin for him would see her." Whidden's instinct was to wait awhile for someone to appear before they went ashore across the river. "If them boys catch us snoopin at the house, they might shoot first and ask their questions after, especially if they been drinkin." He looked around some more. "I want to sniff things out a little, keep my distance, till I get the feel of it." When Sally asked him what that meant, Whidden was unable to explain, but Lucius thought he knew. He felt the same.

*

Lucius sat cross-legged on the bow, staring at the shining house across broad soft swirls of current. At one time he had known every eddy and hole in this stretch of the river, on those long-ago slow summer days when a deft hook might land half a hundred fish of a half dozen species in an afternoon, more than enough to feed the field hands in the harvest. In later years, as a commercial fisherman, he and his partner—usually Hoad Storter, sometimes Lee Harden—might come upriver to draw fresh water from the cistern, which Fred Dyer had built to hold 10,000 gallons. They would scour the overgrowth for the last guavas and alligator pears and slip through the old cane fields to the salt ground known as Watson Prairie to shoot one or two young ibis for their supper. The grass was low and sparse on that marl ground, which held fresh puddles where the wild creatures could come get their water. Papa had burned his prairie every year to keep its small ponds open for the ducks and rails, ibis and deer. Occasionally they took a black bear or a panther.

Behind him, the muted voices rose and fell as the wind shifted. Andy was pointing down the river. From here, he was saying, they could probably see that bar off the north bank where some fisherman come across what was left of a dead colored man, in that last summer before all hell broke loose in that black October. "The way Ed Watson used his field hands, people said, was like something out of the old century. Replaced a hand like you replaced a horse."

They were all gazing at the house. "Back in the early days," Whidden told his wife, "an old nigra got his sleeve caught in a cane presser. He lost his arm and he bled and bled, all over everything. Mister Watson couldn't take the time to run him to Key West, not in the harvest. Anyways, it wouldn't do no good, he said, that boy is done for. The women took him to the house, laid him down in the front room, but they couldn't stop it, he just bled to death while he lay there watchin 'em. Couldn't never get that stain up, couldn't never paint it out, now ain't that something? Cause sooner or later that blood rose through the paint. Still there today! You can go through that door and see it for yourself!

"That nigra blood was like a spell on that old house. After Watson's death, folks would go ashore and point to it—'See there? That's a *murder* victim's blood!' Well, it weren't no such a thing! It were only the lifeblood of that poor feller whose arm got overtook by that machine!"

My God, Lucius thought, they have heard that tale so often, and *still* they are reciting it, like myth or scripture—not that the story was untrue. He recalled Sybil Dyer hurrying her Lucy away from the dreadful sight of so much blood, and Papa mopping his brow by the shed, knowing how that dying black man would come back to haunt him.

"*The only way that blood is going to come out is burn it out.*" Lucius called this from the bow, to close the story in the traditional way in which local people had always closed it. Not wishing to eavesdrop, he came back astern, inquiring if anyone recalled the name of the black man who had gone to Pavilion Key to report the murders. He vaguely recalled the name "Sip Linsy," but he needed confirmation.

"I don't believe I ever heard his name." Andy's fair skin was deep red with chagrin that he and the Hardens had been overheard. "We was told he showed up at Pavilion with the flap of his forehead skin hanging down where a bullet creased his scalp—had to hold that flap out of his eyes. Claimed Cox had shot at him as he took off."

Whidden was skeptical. His cousin Weeks Daniels, who had seen the man that day, had always described him as dark and husky, very calm and "cunnin-lookin." He had not mentioned any wound. Whidden said, "It ain't so easy to look calm and cunnin with a flap of skin hangin down into your eyes."

Whidden's wife gazed disgustedly from face to face as the men laughed. "You know something?" she said. "There's something cruel and hateful in the whole male sex."

*

In the years after E. J. Watson's death, before Lucius came back to the Islands, these rivers had been all but empty. The settlers had been flooded out by the Great Hurricane, all but the Hardens, and none of them ever found the heart to accept such hard loss and discouragement and return to the ruined clearings to rebuild. There was also a dread of Leslie Cox, who might still be lurking somewhere in the Glades, might still come prowling down around the coast, to be glimpsed toward dusk of some fateful day when an unknown craft slipped behind some wooded point, leaving the frightened settler to wonder if that silhouetted figure in the stern might have been Cox, if Cox were stalking him, if Cox were watching at this moment from the mangrove shadows, ready to trail him back to his defenseless family.

The dread of Cox would fade as years went by, but not the dread of hurricanes in these barrier islands. Many of those who ventured south were not settlers but fugitives and drifters, content with makeshift shelters and hand-to-mouth existence, with no ambition to help them endure the dull humidity and biting insects which made existence here all but unbearable. The only inhabitants who had prevailed year after year, setting out smudge pots for mosquitoes and taking hardship and contentment where they found it, were Robert Harden and his three strong sons and the pioneer women of that family.

"Course plenty of strangers tried camping in your house, but no one stayed long," Andy said. "Seen that place in the parlor where somebody had fired off a shotgun. That charge of shot chewed up one corner pretty good, and was always connected to them bloodstains from that black man's death, which was took to mean that somebody got in the way. Folks wondered was that some of Cox's work, when he killed them people? Or was that your daddy killing Cox? Cause nobody knew for absolutely sure that he never done that.

"So people got the shivers from them bloodstains, never liked the feel of the whole place. You didn't sleep good in that house till you got used to it. I ain't the only one had nightmares. Mac Johnson's Dorothy went wild down here, tryin' to burn that blood out, and Bill Smallwood wouldn't hardly go ashore, slept in his boat, though he wouldn't admit that them bloodstains was the reason." Andy laughed. "Ol' Bill! Come down here to fish-guide for some northern people who was anchored off Mormon Key on a big yacht. Bill was still in his late teens, but he had him a twenty-six-foot launch with a Model-T Ford marine-converted engine. I recall we took all the snook we wanted over there front of the house, and plenty of small tarpon, too. Best tarpon bait he ever found was a strip of mullet on a green parrot-head feather. 'I ain't failed with that ol' parrot-head too many times,' Bill used to say. And every time he never failed, we had to hear about it!"

Andy shook his head in the glow of reminiscence. "Remember that day you come visitin, Colonel? Huntin Henry Short? Good thing you didn't stay the night, cause there weren't hardly no place to lay down, weren't a mattress left. Hunters and moonshiners had took every last one. But some of the heavy crockery was still there, and that big pine table. Sat fourteen, cause your daddy fed a lot of hands at harvest time. My dad took it with us when we left.

"Hurricane of '26, the Watson Place rode this wild jungle river like a ship at sea, stood up just fine. Next year, Henry Thompson took over as the caretaker. He wasn't paid but fifty bucks a month by the Chevelier Corporation, cause developers was losin faith in the Florida Boom. Anyway, we was all loaded in the boat but we couldn't take off till Thompsons come, cause we wasn't supposed to leave the place untended. Left three dogs behind for Thompsons because we had too many, and if I know Henry, he shot one of 'em before he set foot on the dock. Big yeller hound that liked to run them bobcats off the chickens. One day at Chokoloskee, that yeller dog had bit him pretty good, woke that man up a little. I heard him mutter, 'Dog, I'll git you one day, see if I don't.' Well, I bet he did!

"As I recall him, Henry Thompson was a tall thin kind of a feller, kind of a far-off person, you might say. Sandy hair bleached whitish by the sun, but his hide would bake brown as a bun, where mine boils up hot red, like a boiled crawfish. I don't guess him and his Gert Hamilton never bothered nobody, but they didn't much approve nobody, neither. Not even God!"

Lucius grinned. "Well, that atheist streak Old Henry had came straight from his old boss! When pretty ladies were around, my dad might get religion, but he never found much use for God at other times."

"Henry Thompson never talked too much when he weren't talking about Watson," Andy said. "I guess he was the authority on Watson, but toward the end he got tired of what he knew. Drank quite a lot, kept his own company, got skinnier and skinnier like an old white leghorn. When he did speak, he had a way of trailin off, shruggin his shoulders, like havin any opinion about life plain wore him out.

"Henry Thompson always claimed that Ed Watson had been good to him, he had nothin against the man whatever. Said he never had no reason to be scared of him, and neither did his half-uncle Tant Jenkins, cause Ol' Ed never hurt a fly that didn't hurt him first. Only thing was, in later life, Henry needed a little drinkin money, so he give an interview to some magazine writer about all of his close shaves with Bloody Watson. Got paid cash money for his firsthand knowledge of the cold cold heart of that terrible desperado, might of threw in some gory details he made up, to keep things lively."

Intent upon the silent house, the others were content to listen as Andy rambled on. "What d'you reckon happened to your daddy's schooner?" Andy said after a while, as if to make sure the others were still there. "I been puzzling about that since you mentioned her. She was tied up here at the Bend during the hurricane, then disappeared. People talked about Cox sellin her, and they talked about how Watson's boy might of helped him get away—"

Lucius shook his head. "I never took Cox anywhere. That was another rumor, like the hanging rope. And Cox never took the schooner, either. That summer of 1910 was his first time off the farm in Columbia County. He couldn't swim, much less handle a schooner. He was afraid of the water and plain terrified of crocs and gators, and back then we had both. As for the launch, my dad brought her to Chokoloskee on the day he died, so the last I heard, she was right there at Smallwood's. Local people must know what happened to her, but by the time I came back—that was nine years later—nobody seemed to recall. Strange, don't you think? Folks can remember all the lies, like the hanging rope and the gold watch, but nobody recalls what happened to those boats."

"Weren't no Watson sons around to keep an eye on 'em," Andy reminded him, and Lucius changed the subject.

"I guess that after they calmed down a little, most folks decided that my father must have killed Cox after all," Lucius suggested.

"Is that a fact? Us Hardens never thought so. A few years after your daddy died, the Rice boys claimed they seen Cox on the east coast near Lemon City. They said Cox recognized Leland Rice, slipped away quick. Hardens decided that sonofagun was still holed up someplace back in the rivers, because one day that old cabin we built for Chevelier just disappeared off Possum Key. No fire or nothin, she was just tore down and took away, probably hammered back together someplace else.

"Course some claimed it was Henry Short done that. Claimed he moved that cabin board by board way back up inside of Gopher Key, where he was kind of hidin out from some of them younger fellers around Chokoloskee. Spent his days diggin for Calusa treasure, which the Frenchman always did believe was there. But some concluded it was Cox who took that cabin. For a little while in the late twenties, when Roark and our cousin Wilson come up missin, there was rumors that Cox had done away with 'em some way. Course Hardens never took that serious, cause we *knew* who done it."

Sally said, "Probably those Carrs spread that rumor about Cox, trying to cover their tracks!"

Whidden shrugged, still studying the house through his binoculars. "I recollect one time Fonso Lopez was tellin how Desperado Cox was put to death by Mr. Watson. And Mama said, 'Why, Fonso, you know better than that! That man is living along somewhere just as mean as ever!' "

"Anyway, if Cox cleaned all the stuff out of that house, folks would have heard about it," Sally declared. "Sadie Harden told us that Mr. Watson had some good silver and crystal, and she always declared it was the Carrs who cleaned him out. Probably claimed that good old E.J. left it all to them!"

"Well, that's just gossip, Sally," Andy said. "Sadie always had it in for the Carr family. It might been anybody who came here after the shooting."

"People felt free to lug away all they could carry!" Lucius said. "Why was that, do you suppose? Because of my father's reputation? Because they thought that he deserved no better?"

Andy looked impatient. "Because he was dead, and because you Watsons had abandoned the damned place, and because if the first comers didn't take that stuff, the next bunch would. You take them thieving Houses, now, them people stole Ed Watson's pine deal table!" Andy's laughter was infectious. "Course he'd been gone for sixteen years by the time we done it."

*

It was getting late. Harden lowered the binoculars. "Okay?" he said. "We better have a look." Gunning the engine in reverse, he backed the *Cracker Belle* into the current, then drummed upstream while letting the current carry her across the river. Wide of the dock, he cut back on the throttle, taking the binoculars from Sally.

"Nobody home," she said.

"Got to be sure."

As the boat lost headway, drifting back downstream, he studied the frame house. In its fresh paint, the old building on the mound looked stripped and naked on its cement pillions, which lifted the main floor two feet above ground to permit high storm water to rush beneath. Loose roof shingles lay scattered on bare earth from which most of the vegetation had been scoured by the high salt tides of last year's hurricane.

"In the late thirties some Miami sports come over here, used this place hard, remember, Mister Colonel? Huntin and fishin, plenty of booze, and loud blond women. Them men had no respect at all, and the place was pretty much let go. Nobody fixed no broken screens nor windows, let alone rain gutters. All the same, I seen this house after last year's storm and Parks could of touched her up without no trouble. Storm damage is only their excuse for doin somethin they been itchin to do for years."

Whidden eased his boat upstream again, letting the current sweep her in against the leaning skeleton of the old dock and leaving her engine running even after Lucius took a turn around a post. Lucius made no hitch or knot, making sure the line could be slipped quickly.

> DANGER. TRESPASSING FORBIDDEN.
> BY ORDER OF SUPT.
> U.S. NATIONAL PARK SERVICE

Near the official notice, nailed to a stake jammed into the bank, was an unofficial sign painted in rude black letters on a driftwood board:

```
KEEP OUT!! THIS MEANS YOU!!
```

"That sign weren't put up by no damn Park Service and it ain't meant for tourists," Whidden said, "cause nobody never seen no tourist back in here." He cut the engine. In the wash of silence came that hard licking at the bank as the brown current searched along under the branches, in the whisper of leaning trees in the river wind, and the boat's exhaust stink was replaced by the musk of humus and that scent of hot wild lime in the dry foliage which stirred Lucius Watson's heart and brought him home.

Lucius went forward to rig a bow line, and Whidden jumped ashore, running a stern line to a mangrove. In the noon silence, the only answer to their shouts and calls was the dry, insistent song of a small bird from the wood edge. A heavy odor came and went on the shifting wind. "That ain't the housepainter, if that is what you're thinkin. That is gators. Might of shot one or two of 'em myself." Whidden whispered this in Lucius's ear, keeping a wary eye on Sally, who had guided Andy onto the bank, and led him toward the house. "Gator hides!" he yelled when they stopped short and turned and looked back, uneasy.

Whidden had been with the Daniels gang when it first came to the Watson Place, which Speck liked to refer to as "my huntin camp." Because a tight roof and dry ground-floor rooms with solid floors were needed for heavy storage, they had boarded up and nailed the windows and installed big chains and padlocks on the doors. On the south side of the house, facing the poincianas and the river, was a screened porch from which the screens were missing. Whidden went up onto the porch and checked the padlocked door. He knocked and hollered, "Anybody home?" He spat away the bad taste of the stench. "I never thought they'd cure them hides as poor as that!"

When Speck was around, the hides had been cured properly, said Whidden, but his men had let things go after he left. They knew little about the Watson Place and had no curiosity about its history, and they had used it in the same hard way as the Miami men, ripping off porch steps and posts and the old storm shutters for their cooking fires. Meanwhile, they ranged out into the Glades country, killing every last gator they came across, big and small. "Course gator poachin was only part of it. Speck's distillery ain't a hundred yards back in the bushes. Ran his barrels of shine by airboat far as Gator Hook, and from there by truck east to Miami. He found customers as fast as he could brew it, never stored a pint. Never got caught neither. Same thing for the gator hides while there was a market."

Circling the house, checking the ground-floor windows in search of some way to get in, they paused to see if the cistern still held water. Whidden hoisted the corner of its green tarpaper roof, which was splatted white with bird droppings and scattered with dry leaves and twigs, red-seeded coon scat, bright coral bean in long hard pods, owl pellets, spiderwebs, a bobcat feces woolly green with mold.

"This cistern is twenty-four foot by sixteen—pretty fair size for the Islands," Lucius said proudly. "We dug her down into the ground, the way she should be—that's why there's water in there now."

"That ol' water must be pretty rank. Ain't nobody has fixed them gutterins in years." Harden pointed at the rotted rain gutters, split and half fallen. "They tell me the brackish-water mosquitoes which breeds in this here cistern are the worst in all the Ten Thousand Islands.

"At Lost Man's, after Parks took over, a real big gator got into our cistern. Found him there when we went back to visit, couldn't get him out. Still there, I reckon. And there was a drowned deer in the one at Possum Key, still had his hide on. Parks claims they want things back the way they was, and burnin our old homes was kind of fun, but I notice they never get around to digging out old cisterns or coverin 'em or fillin 'em—might be hard work!" He shook his head. "Don't *have* to fill 'em! Just knock a hole into one side so's a wild thing can go get his water, climb back out again."

When Lucius looked up, Harden was watching him. "The man who built this cistern was Fred Dyer," Lucius said vaguely, struggling to recover the feel of the lost conversation. For some reason, he had been daydreaming about Lucy, wondering if they would find each other before it was too late. "His daughter married a Summerlin, but she's a widow. I believe she is still living at Fort Myers."

Whidden Harden laughed. "I believe that, too! On account of you already told me about her yesterday. You met her at the cemetery, remember?"

They had a piss before returning to the others, and facing the woods, Lucius located the bird which made that small, insistent song. "White-eyed vireo!" he blurted, wondering if Papa had ever heard its ancestor, or rather, listened to it.

"*White*-eyed? You sure?" Whidden was shading his brow like an explorer, staring purposely in the wrong direction. "Sure looked like a wall-eyed to me!" Affectionate, he patted Lucius's shoulder.

On the porch, Andy was talking to Sally, instinctively keeping his voice low as if there were somebody asleep inside. "When we come here in 1924, this good old place was already stunk up by every kind of varmint, not just humans. Coons and possums, sometimes a bear, all kinds of snakes and lizards—I seen a rattler by the cistern one time, big around as my arm. Upstairs, all kinds of bats and rat snakes and swallers flying in and out all them empty winders, and ceilin wasps, and some of them big narrow black hornets, flickerin their wings under the rafters—you never knew what kind of varmint might be layin for you up that stair, that Cox included!"

Whidden went up on the porch again and put his ear to the door. "Thought I heard creakin." Again they called, and again they got no answer. "I don't reckon this new paint will keep them people from burning this place down," Whidden said. "The Island homes was mostly lean-tos and old shacks, whacked together any whichy-way, ain't that right, Colonel?— palmetto fan thatch, driftwood scrap, patched out with tarpaper and tin. Weren't much lost when Parks destroyed 'em except lifetimes of hard work, which don't count for nothin these days, it don't seem like." In his quiet way, Harden was very angry.

"Setting *this* old house afire, that is something else," Andy House said. "Dade County pine, cures hard as iron, so her frame and flooring is as sound as ever. Likely Parks don't even know that, and don't care. Why them people are so hot to burn this good old house is hard to figure. Got the rest of 'em destroyed already, I suppose. Want to look like they're doing somethin to earn them government salaries, is what it is."

Lucius told Andy about Fred Dyer, who had built the porch and cistern. Andy nodded. "I sure heard about them Dyers from an early age. Back in 1905, my uncle Dan ran the mail boat, Punta Rassa to Cape Sable, and he had young Gene Gandees as his crew. Them boys was maybe fifteen at that time. So one day they turned up here when Mr. Watson was away, and the Dyer family come flyin out with their little girl and baby boy, leavin toys and clothes all scattered out behind. Never went back for that stuff neither, just jumped aboard the boat and yelled, 'Let's go!'

"On the way downriver, Uncle Dan asked 'em why they was in such a hurry. They admitted that they never seen no bad deeds while they was here, no sign that Watson killed his help on payday, the way people said. But they knew somethin very bad had happened to the young couple that was here before 'em, and they was worried about their little children. Around that time, rumor come about Watson murderin the Audubon warden at Flamingo—well, that done it. The woman seemed calm enough, Uncle Dan said, but her husband was sick afraid.

"Mrs. Dyer let on how it was her who wished to leave, and how she was always scared in this wild country, what with all the snakes and panthers and wild Injuns. But Uncle Dan believed she only said that to cover up her husband's fear of Mr. Watson. On the way north, she mentioned that in her estimation, Mr. Watson was a good and generous man, a gentleman, and a good Christian. Every Sunday morning without fail, they would all sing hymns in the front room and Mr. Watson would read aloud out of the Bible.

"Twenty years later, Dan House saw the husband in Fort Myers, and he said to him 'Well, Mr. Dyer, you might not be walking around this town if it weren't for me.' I reckon Fred Dyer thought so, too, cause seein Uncle Dan, he whooped for joy and hugged him like a long-lost friend."

Sally Brown said shortly, "Maybe Dan House and Gene Gandees made so much of that story because both of 'em were in the Watson mob a few years later, and they wanted to justify the execution of a neighbor who helped folks out when times were hard and never did a bit of harm to either one of them."

"Well, Miss Sally, that is possible," Andy House said.

*

When Lucius Watson first returned to the Ten Thousand Islands, people made sure that he heard the rumors about Henry Short and the death of Lucius's father. Though he thought these stories dangerous and absurd, he eventually decided to seek out Henry and hear what he had to say.

Henry had not been easy to track down. He no longer visited the Hardens, who claimed they did not know where he might be found. This was more or less true, but it was also true that, much as they liked Lucius, they could not be sure of his true intentions. Only later did they tell him that Henry Short, still feeling unsafe, had dismantled the Frenchman's shack again and moved it by skiff piece by piece from Gopher Key all the way south to Cape Sable, where he lugged the boards three miles or more inland to a desolate area of scrub and brackish water ("That whole cabin traveled on that one man's shoulder," Lee Harden marveled) only to have it blow away in the Hurricane of '26. Meanwhile he worked from time to time for the House family here on the Watson Place, and learning of this, Lucius came to see him. Not wanting to scare Henry into hiding, he slipped up Chatham River with the tide and was at the dock at daybreak. Trying to calm the House's mean dogs, he walked unarmed toward the house, careful to keep his empty hands out to the side.

Bill House was already on the porch. In his nightshirt, he stood like a ghost in the porch shadows. Warning Henry, he sang out, "Ain't that a Watson?"

"Morning, Bill."

"Lookin for me?"

"Looking for Henry."

"What you want with him?"

Henry Short appeared at the corner of the boat shed, holding his rifle down along his leg. When Lucius said good morning, Henry Short lifted his hat a little but did not come forward. He was a strong, good-looking man with blue-gray eyes, composed and very clear in his appearance. Like most men in the Islands, he went barefoot, but unlike most, he kept himself clean-shaven, and his blue denims were well-patched and clean.

Lucius drew closer, out of earshot from the porch. He had planned to open this difficult conversation with a few civilities, but at the last second he came right out with it. "There's been some rumors, Henry."

Oddly, Henry chose this moment to lean his rifle against a sawhorse by the boat shed wall. His face was set, without expression, like a prisoner resigned to a harsh sentence.

"Some say you took part in my father's death," Lucius continued, keeping his voice low. "That you were first to shoot."

The night before, camped under the moon at Mormon Key, his purpose had seemed clear, but standing here in the new heat of morning, with the Houses watching from the porch, he no longer knew why he had come nor what he might be looking for. He had finally caught up with Henry Short, yet within instants his whole inquiry seemed empty and unreasonable—what was the man to say? How could he act on anything this man confessed to, since even if Short's bullet was the first one, striking Papa dead before the others fired, that astonishing circumstance could not have changed the outcome in the slightest way.

"Well?" he demanded stupidly. "Is it true?"

The man's headshake was scarcely more than a twitch, as if he were bone tired of telling a truth which had never been believed—tired of lying, tired of running, tired of an unfulfilled existence. He seemed to indicate that the white man could do anything he liked, and Henry Short would go along with it out of indifference. "Your daddy always treated me real good," Henry said politely, not to ingratiate himself but to ease the ridiculous situation in which Lucius had put them.

Lucius saw that he and Henry Short could have been friends. He had an impulse to offer his hand, but under the sharp eye of Bill House he could not bring himself to do that, knowing how weak and sentimental it would appear. Instead he told him, "You have nothing to fear from me," and Henry nodded. "All right, Mist' Lucius," he said simply. They did not say good-bye. Lucius turned and walked toward the dock.

"Well, that was quick!" Bill House called out as he went by the porch. Lucius raised his hand, taking time to smile at the husky blond boy who stood close as a calf at House's elbow. The boy had to subdue a friendly grin. This chip off the old block had his gun with him, too—the oldest boy, named for Bill's cousin Andrew Wiggins.

"How's your list coming, Colonel?" Bill House called after him. "I sure hope you got *my* name on there!" When Lucius kept on going, he yelled angrily, "You hear me, Watson? Next time, don't try slippin up on us so quiet!"

*

Lucius Watson's visit to the Bend fired up old rumors in regard to Henry Short and did nothing to resolve the ambiguities. He had been too circumspect, failing to demand that Short refute the story in so many words—not that his denial would signify a thing. But in that case, why had he gone there in the first place?

Lucius recognized that the Bay families, despite their wariness of "Watson's boy," had done their best to welcome him when he came back—that it was his own ambiguous behavior which had scared and angered them. Even the Hardens had warned him from the start that in asking his questions, he was making a serious mistake. The Harden clan was already shunned at Chokoloskee Bay, and Lucius Watson's presence made their danger worse, since it was believed that in any showdown, Lucius Watson would throw in with the Hardens, and would bring his gun. Except for Earl Harden, they had not complained, for they were tough and independent, but feeling guilty about worsening their danger, and trying to ease the tension on the Lost Man's coast, Lucius would leave from time to time, live on his boat and fish out of Flamingo or fish-guide out of Marco or perhaps go on a long bender at Key West. Yet he never strayed from the Harden family very long. For thirty years, until the Park came in, the wilderness at Lost Man's River was his home.

*

Two years later, the House family had gone north to the Trail to grow tomatoes and the Thompsons had replaced them on the Bend. "Probably heard there wasn't much hard work involved in caretaking," Andy said, "or maybe Thompson believed those tales about Watson's buried gold. Henry Short must of heard them stories, too, because he stayed behind here after we left, kept right on diggin.

"Bein friends of E. J. Watson, Thompsons resented Henry Short. They believed he had raised his gun against a white man. Told him to start his digging over here back of the cistern, and when he was done, Gert made that place her kitchen garden, which she had planned to put in all along. Had him dig a pit for a new outhouse that bein a nigra he was not allowed to use."

Lucius visited Henry Short again after the arrival of the Thompsons.

"He's hidin on ye," Thompson told him when Lucius showed up at the Bend—his way of hinting without saying so that Yes, indeed, Henry Short had been involved. Thompson shooed his girls inside without offering help, and Lucius hunted Short down by himself.

It was the first real autumn day, a norther, when mosquitoes seemed listless even at dawn and dusk. He found the man mending net around the corner of the boat shed, perched on a sawhorse in the October sun, out of the wind. The ancient Winchester was leaned against the shed, well out of reach, though Short had heard his motor on the river and could have kept that gun at hand if he had chosen to.

Henry Short laid down his net needle and touched his hat. He rose slowly, ceremoniously, standing not stiffly but dead straight, and as before, he appeared resigned to anything his black man's life still had in store for him, including its relinquishment here and now at the hands of Watson. Had Lucius put a revolver to his temple, he might have flinched but would have remained still, less out of fortitude than fatalism and perhaps relief that his trials were coming to an end.

Henry brushed coon scat off a fish box for his visitor. Yes sir, he agreed, he had gone down to the shore that day. He had done so because his Miz Ida had told him to go keep an eye on Mist' Dan Senior.

"Why did you carry your rifle down there if you never meant to use it?"

"I don't know, suh."

"If you don't know, then why should I believe your story?"

"I don't know, suh." Neither insolent nor evasive, careful to speak in an open, earnest manner, Henry had looked his inquisitor straight in the face.

Lucius tried to be hard-minded and objective. "My father knew that Mr. D. D. House adopted you when you were little, and that you owed a debt to Mr. House. And we can assume that my father saw you standing in that crowd of armed frightened men who might panic and gun him down at any second. He knew that you were a crack shot, and he knew you might feel obliged to shoot if any of the House men became threatened. That correct so far? And being afraid of him, you probably feared that he might shoot you unless you shot him first—was that your thinking?"

"Nosuh," Henry mumbled, suddenly retreating into negritude. "Wouldn't nevuh shoot Mist' Edguh Wasson, nosuh, wouldn't nevuh shoot no white mans, nosuh." When Lucius gave him a severe look, he hunched a little in subservience, neck bent, eyes cast down. "White folks 'customed to seein Nigger Henry with Mist' Dan's old rifle. Maybe dat las' afternoon, dey imagine dey seen Henry raise it up like he fixin to shoot." He shook his head. "Jus' mistaked dereself, dass all. Dem mens was busy watchin yo' daddy, see what

he might do, dey nevuh paid no mind to no ol' nigger. Anyways," he whee-
dled, "dem white folks roun' de Bay was allus good to me. Dem Chrishun
folks wouldn' nevuh tell no lies 'bout po' Henry."

Lucius had jumped up in a rage. This man had lived his whole life among
whites, and spoke like one, and furthermore, Henry knew well that Lucius
Watson would never be taken in by this performance. What Henry was saying to him was, *Is this minstrel show what I must offer before you will let me live
my life in peace?*

Henry Short stood motionless, staring straight back at him. Then he
blinked and slowly shook his head. That might have been all the denial Lucius needed, but Henry, reverting to his normal voice, resumed, unbidden, as
if alerted long before to Lucius's coming, and to the inevitability of his questions, and to the necessity of answering him, at whatever risk. Very carefully, Henry said, "Mist' Edguh knew as good as anybody that Henry Short
would never raise a gun against him." Lucius searched his face for any sign
of ambiguity. It remained impassive. They held that gaze and then, minutely,
both men nodded.

After that meeting, their paths would cross from time to time along the
rivers. They would lift their hats or make a vague half wave. Rarely, they
smiled, then looked away and kept on going. Both were outcasts, taken in by
the same outcast family, and that alone should have disposed them to a common trust, yet they shared an instinct not to seek the other out. They had
spoken together only twice, yet felt no need to speak, because they *knew.* And
though neither man would have referred to this odd bond in terms of friendship, a friendship was what, in its mute way, it had become.

*

High cirrus. Sun. A strange loud racketing, rising and falling, coming downriver.

"Ah hell." Whidden stood up. They hurried the blind man back toward
the boat.

Ibis and egrets scattered out across the sky, their squawking lost in the
oncoming noise, which grew violently loud, as if the airboat had sprung free
of the river surface, to rise over the treetops and crash down on them.
Though it had not emerged from behind the bend, leaves shuddered and
spun where the windstream from its airplane propeller tore at the trees.
Then the motor howled—"They seen the *Belle!*"—and the airboat skidded
into view, skating out wide onto the open river. There it idled, slopped by its
own wake. When it circled back toward the bank, the metal hull pushed a
bow wave crossways to the current.

Perched on a platform raised above the propeller, which was housed in a heavy wire cage over the stern, Crockett Junior in black T-shirt and dark glasses yanked at the controls with dexterous grabs and swings of his good arm. Dummy and Mud on the deck below were jamming clips into their carbines. On the bow, straining to jump, crouched the brindle dog.

"Ah hell," Harden repeated, cranking the engine.

Andy and Sally were already in the cockpit, and Lucius was ready to let go the lines when Whidden raised a hand to check him. He cut the engine and, in no hurry, joined Lucius on the bank. An attempt at flight could excite a predatory instinct which might get them shot at, and anyway, the airboat could overtake them within seconds.

That they were so suddenly in peril, that the battering wind and awful racket might end in senseless violence, seemed incredible to Lucius, who could scarcely take it in. In this instant, there was less danger from the guns than from that dog—a large knob-headed male, squat and tawny, patched with brown, as if hacked rudely from a block of tropic wood. "He ain't tied," Whidden's mouth was shouting, over the airboat's roar.

Crockett Junior spun the propeller in reverse, and the roar died in a buffet of hot wind as he killed the engine. In the stunned quiet, the airboat lost headway, riding its bow wave toward the bank. "You huntin trouble, Whidden boy? You come to the right place!" And Sally shrieked, "Junior? Take it easy, honey! There's no need to act crazy!"

Mud and Dummy had lowered their automatic rifles but neither made a move toward the dog. The pit bull, shivering, strained forward on the bow, tendons, jaws, and dirty gold eyes taut. As Whidden yelled, "Mud, grab that fuckin dog!" it sprang, striking the bank with an audible hard thud of bone-filled paws.

Stiff-legged, the dog circled the two strangers, leg by leg, the bristles of its nape as stiff as wire. A rank canine smell rose from its hide, and from its clamped jaws came a low steady rumble. Lucius's instinct was to freeze and not look down, as if the least twitch might betray his fear to this morose animal. That in these stark instants he could still hear the light *tsik-teriu-tsik* of the vireo would strike him later as the furthest reach of hallucination.

Sally had sunk onto the gunwale, weak with fear, perhaps trying to defuse the situation. Not sure what was happening, Andy House folded his arms and clutched his elbows, as if holding himself quiet by main force.

"Junior," Crockett mimicked Sally. He jumped down from the pilot seat as his men swung aboard the *Cracker Belle.* Covered by Dummy, Mud pushed Andy aside and poked the muzzle of his carbine into the boat cabin.

"We're not armed," Whidden said, face set and drawn. The pit bull turned toward his voice and jammed its snout against his calf and left it there.

"If I tole him to," Crockett muttered heavily, "that dog'd go for a bull gator."

"That a fact?" Whidden's voice was amiable and easy, but their eyes were locked like adversaries in a fight. "Yessir, you stupid fuck," growled Crockett, "that is a fuckin fact. I lay a T-bone by Buck's nose and go out to the store, he won't never touch it."

"You got him trained up good, all right." Whidden risked a downward glance at the rigid dog. "Course I ain't seen Buck since a pup. Might not remember me."

"Buck don't forget." Crockett's voice had turned aggrieved and bitter. "Buck don't never forget. He ain't like you."

"We're supposed to meet Watson Dyer here, and the Parks people," Lucius explained. As Sally hissed at him to stay out of this, he pointed at the skiff across the river. "My younger brother—" But he stopped as the one-armed man yanked a third carbine from a rack on the helmsman's platform and the dog turned toward him.

Whidden whispered, "You shut up, okay?"

"No safety on this thing," Crockett warned Lucius, "cause I ain't learned to work a safety with my teeth." He swung the short rifle like a crutch and pointed the black hole of it at Lucius's eyes.

"We ain't lookin for no trouble, Junior," Whidden said. The rifle swung toward him, and again the pit bull pushed its muzzle hard into his leg, bulk shivering. Whidden let all expression fade. With his eyes half closed, he looked almost sleepy.

"Whidden boy? You never read our sign?" The carbine swung toward the sign reading KEEP OUT and swung right back again. "You're lookin to get some people killed," he muttered.

House cleared his throat. "You don't mean that, son."

The one-armed man breathed noisily. "Mr. House?" he grated. "No disrespect. You shut the fuck up, too."

Mud's head emerged from the cabin of the *Belle*. "Nothin down here, Junior," he told Crockett, who tossed his head sideways toward the house itself. Mud circled the house, checking the doors and windows. "Okay," he called. Reboarding the airboat, he leaned his gun against the platform. "Your old home sure stinks," he said to Lucius.

Crockett whistled to the dog—"Come in here, Buck!" He climbed back up onto his seat, yelling at Whidden. "Get off this river, boy!"

When Lucius called desperately, "Now wait a minute!" Sally cried, "Let Whidden handle this!"

"Let Whidden handle this!" But there was no heart in Crockett's sarcasm. He seemed to brood, easing the airboat slowly off the bank. To his own men, his quiet appeared ominous, for both moved aft, out of Crockett's line of fire.

Whidden spoke quietly to Mud Braman, "How come you fellers won't tell Mister Colonel his brothers is all right? That ain't askin so much."

"Dammit, Whidden! Just do what he says!" Mud was very uneasy, and even Dummy adjusted his genitals through his greased coveralls.

The gorgon head of the one-armed man high on his perch was cocked back oddly on his shoulders as he spun the airboat. "You Watsons are a bunch of lunatics, you know that? I ought to take and blow the heads off them two crazy brothers, and yours, too!" He revved the airplane motor to a roar so loud and battering in its own wind that they could hardly hear him in his maddened howling, then slowed the engine to a sudden idle, as leaf and bark bits torn from the old poincianas spun down into the water, to drift away in the slow spirals of the current.

Crockett sat motionless against the sky. In the river light, the world seemed fixed in a frieze of stillness, a silvered dance of death. The pit bull's hackles rose, and its nails clicked on the metal deck. The pit bull whined. Crockett leaned and said something to Braman, then looked sleepily away. In a hoarse whisper, Braman said, "Get goin, Whidden. Make camp on Mormon so we know right where you're at, then head for Lost Man's first thing in the mornin."

The airboat, taken by an eddy of brown current, drifted gradually from the bank. Lucius shouted, "But we have to be here day after tomorrow!" And Mud screeched back, "He ain't talkin about day after tomorrow! He is talking about *now!* Get movin *now!*"

Lucius cast off the *Belle*'s lines and followed Whidden aboard. He shouted, "Why the hell can't they at least tell us that those men are alive!" Sally seized Lucius's arm, but he wrenched free of her, as Whidden gunned the engine of the *Belle* to blur his shouting and the old boat's bow swung off into the current. "He *told* you," Whidden said. "Sayin he ought to blow their heads off was Junior's way of saying he ain't done it yet."

Even now, headed downriver, they were scared and agitated. In the stern, the blind man sat unnoticed. No one felt like speaking. Finally Sally went aft and hunkered down beside his chair, to draw him back into their company.

Below the bend, Harden cut the motor, letting the boat drift in a slow orbit as they listened. "They ain't leavin. We would hear that motor. Only pretended they was takin off to see if we'd try sneakin back. And Crockett is listenin the same as we are, right this minute, and when he don't hear our motor, he might come have a look." He cranked the motor and, shaking off Lucius's questions, ran his boat downriver toward the Gulf.

Whidden guessed that both brothers were in the house, tied up and gagged. "Probably heard us callin but they couldn't answer."

Andy House agreed. "When Sally and me was settin on the porch, there come this little kind of thump and scrapin. Figured it must be raccoons, but now that I think about it, that don't seem likely."

Whidden supposed that the Daniels gang was clearing its contraband out of the house before Parks arrived the day after tomorrow. Lucius scarcely listened. He was trying to imagine his two misfit kinsmen, born more than a quarter century apart. One called himself Burdett, the other Collins. They had finally laid eyes upon each other for the first time in their lives only to find themselves—if Whidden was correct—bound captives in their father's house, perhaps entirely unaware that they were brothers.

*

Crockett Junior Daniels, Sally said in a tense flat voice, had been exposed all his life to an evil influence. "Speck was smart and Speck never got caught. He let his big dumb son get caught instead! Know where he spent his sixteenth birthday? In the county jail! Judge released him on probation if he would join up in the Marines, go get his head blown off for God and country." He might have come out all right, she said, if he had not gone to war, since he'd always hoped to attend college, but when he returned from Asia, he was angry and bitter, boozing and brawling and breaking things and doing harm. It was only a matter of time before he sank back down into the swamp beside his goddamned father.

"Whidden honey," she finished bitterly, "you are so darn smart for a man who has wasted the best years of his life making moonshine and skinning alligators! I bet you were the brains of that whole outfit!"

"This fine young woman here got me back on the straight and narrow path, and bound for Glory," Whidden told the others. Holding his wife's eye, he added, "We wasn't such terrible bad fellers, Sal. Only kind of crooked."

"Crooked," she said. With Lucius watching, she went stiff when Whidden put his arm around her shoulders.

The *Belle* anchored off a little beach in the lee of Mormon Key, where Sally said she needed some time alone. Whidden tossed the dinghy overboard and she jumped down neatly on the thwarts, pushing off at the same time, taking up the oars. "Look at that Sally Brown!" her husband called. "Real old-time Island gal!" He opened a beer and sat on the boat transom and watched his darling row away to Mormon Key. Finally he turned and said to Lucius, "Mister Colonel? I don't believe them boys will hurt 'em lest they has to."

Crockett Junior is messed up and he is violent. He killed plenty over there in Asia, but he weren't a natural killer before he went and he ain't today. When he first come home, Junior used to say, "Them flag-wavin old farts up there to Washington, D.C., has lost me my damned arm, but that don't mean they can take away my livelihood." That poor feller is so angry that he can't hardly get his breath, and I don't see how any good can come of it. Got a terrible need to blow the head off somethin. That's what Speck knows and that's why Speck stays away.

Dummy now, he don't care if he kills or if he don't, he don't care nothin about *nothin,* and that's dangerous, too. But most of the time Dummy ain't there. He's still in Asia, talkin to them voices in his head. So Mud is the feller that we have to work with. Ol' Mud is tough and he is wild, but he is pretty good-hearted behind all his hot air, and he tries to keep them other two out of trouble. Mud has hero-worshiped Junior since a boy and he'll go down in flames with Crockett if he has to, and Dummy will go right along with 'em for the goddamn hell of it.

I ain't sayin that Junior ain't pretty good at his daddy's business, never mind that he ain't got but the one arm—fact he's better'n most that has all their equipment. But when Old Man Speck first seen the way them boys was spendin up their money, he made hisself real scarce from that day on. Sally's mother was long gone by then, and Sally, too, so he turned his shack over to Junior, threw his gear down in his boat, and run her south around Cape Sable to Flamingo. Meets those boys on business at the Bend or Gator Hook, then disappears again. "I ain't doin no association with known criminals," is what he told me. "I told Junior I don't aim to be around when they run up against the law and start to shootin. I'll turn my back on 'em like I never seen 'em in my life and head on down my road, same as I always done."

Speck is out for Speck and always has been. Even his own family never put no trust in him. But I will say this for Crockett Senior Daniels, he knows every last foot of this Glades country. Learned it the hard way, which is just about the only way a man can learn it. Put in many a long day alone out here, and long nights, too. I admired that when I threw in with him, and I still do. This wilderness out here, or what is left of it, might be the one thing in his life he loved, when you come to think about it. Speck don't know he loves it, naturally, and wouldn't hardly admit to it if he did.

Course he always poached and smuggled and made moonshine, always broke the law. But you fellers know as good as I do that Speck ain't only just a common outlaw. He was a expert hunter, too, and a expert fisherman, until Parks come along and put him out of business. He can tinker motors, pretty fair country mechanic. He builds good shacks and boats and traps, and hangs nets, too. If Speck ever decided to go straight, he's got a half dozen trades that he could choose from. That's another difference between him and them. Cause unless there's some kind of a call for a militia, mercenary soldiers, them boys of his have no idea how to make a livin. They'd have trouble makin a day's pay inside the law.

This new breed don't care nothin about wilderness. All they know is how to use it hard, same way they use their women and their gear. Shoot everythin that moves in case some other feller beats you to it, find out later if it's any use—that's their damn attitude. That's why they got all them gator hides rottin in there. Never look ahead and don't look back, got no respect at all for land nor life. Maybe this country could use a dose of Speck's old-time outlaw spirit, but not this kind.

Them boys got handed every bit of that man's hard-earned knowledge, and they don't appreciate it. Sure, Speck is dead ornery and ignorant, and greedy, too, but he been known to leave a little room for other people long as they don't get in his way. These younger ones don't leave no room for nobody, and their war experience give 'em their excuse. To their way of thinkin, the country owes 'em a free ride for sendin 'em halfway around the earth to get mangled up in some stupid Asia war that nobody give a shit about in the first place.

Like I'm sayin, that is only their excuse, because long before they went off soldierin, them kind done what they pleased around the backcountry. And that is because they know for a damn fact that the Everglades is their God-given inheritance. Got it straight from the Bible, Faith, and Revelation that the Merciful Lord hates nigras and won't stand for Yankees, turned His back on Injuns and despises Spanish. The Almighty, He detests a Jew, the same way they do. Nosir, their Redeemer won't put up with nobody who ain't Old-time Religion, which is why it's okay to go persecutin in His Holy Name.

So when them fellers say, "This here is God's Country," what they mean is, it is *their* country, and not only the Park but the Big Cypress. Not countin Injuns—who just naturally don't count—their granddaddies was the first to hunt out here in the last century, so these boys don't give a hoot in hell whether it's state, federal, or private-owned. A man who ain't local born and bred tries to build him a legal huntin camp back in the Cypress—well, it just don't matter if he paid his lease, paid up his taxes. If he ain't one of 'em, they burn him out, cause he don't belong out there no more'n them Australia trees or them walkin catfish that come in from Louisiana. Them boys get wind of that invader, they'll grab their guns and a few six-packs of beer, go roarin over there, swamp buggies or airboats, high-power rifles and bad dogs, throw gasoline and torch that camp right to the ground. Maybe they'll look-see who's inside, maybe they won't. And what's to stop 'em, way to hell and gone out there back of that Glades horizon?

Tryin to deal with that mean kind is like baggin up a bunch of bobcats. Older generation now, they played hell with a new warden or park ranger, but they wouldn't kill him, not if they could help it. These fellers here, I ain't so sure. Older ones, if the warden was a local man, they'd tease him, play along with him, maybe throw a scare into him so next time he might shy away, all the while knowin that no local jury would convict 'em.

A few years back, this young ranger spotted Ol' Man Speck in his binoculars, slippin across between two hammocks in the sloughs. Speck was mindin his own business, just huntin along in his own private preserve, maybe two-three miles inside the Park boundary. He was snarin his gators, so's not to create no disturbance. This ranger used a scullin pole to sneak around the backside of a hammock, took him half the mornin probin through the saw grass, but finally he was set. Let Speck work his way to him, he had him dead to rights—*Mornin, Mr. Daniels!* Speck's rifle was layin where he couldn't reach it, and havin the drop on this bad ol' feller, that ranger laughed at him, feelin real cocky. All that sweat and nerves and plain hard work had made him the first man and the only man who ever brung this wily old rascal to the bar of justice.

When that young ranger comes up alongside, Speck is shakin his head real pathetic, doin his best to look old and slow and heartbroke, is what he told me. Real wore-out and discouraged. He takes this three-foot gator by the tail, says "Ye ain't fixin to run a old man in for this here *lizard,* are ye?" Distracted that ranger for one second, which was all Speck needed. Before the poor feller could speak up and say, "Yessir, I sure am!" Speck is uncoilin like a cottonmouth. Brings that young gator up off of the deck, whaps that feller upside of the head and knocks him sprawlin. Grabs that boy's rifle, pumps the cartridges into the water, jams the muzzle deep into wet mud, then lays it back real careful in the ranger's boat so's nobody can't never say he broke nor stole no gov'mint property. Ol' Speck cranks up and heads for home, and no hard feelins. And sittin up watchin him go, that poor feller felt so sheepish and so stupid that he clean forgot to report his great adventure with Speck Daniels!

In the old days, we had a tougher breed of warden. A lot of them men was hunters theirselves and knew the country, and generally they had a local clan behind 'em. You messed with one, you was messin with 'em all. You take and hit one them old wardens with a gator, you better finish it. You best leave him out there.

*

Whidden watched Sally's boat on its way from shore. "Before them other boys come home from overseas and Speck went over into runnin guns, we was just your common moonshiners and gator hunters, puttin to use what Speck was taught by his uncle Tant and Old Man Joe Lopez. We never bothered with no gator longer'n eight feet, cause after that they grow these hard buttons inside that spoils the hide. No market for that hornback, not no more. We stripped off the belly flat and left the rest, except for maybe a few tails to sell to restaurants. Any damn fool can shoot a gator, skin it out, but strippin that flat quick without nickin it or tearin it, that's another breed of gator man entirely.

"Big gator now, before you cut that tail, you have to cut the back open, use a stick to pry the spinal cord and twist it out, otherwise that tail could spasm, break your leg. But gator tail is 'larripin good,' as Old Man Smallwood used to say! Tastes somewhere between frog legs and a rattler, so they tell me."

Andy said, "You never et one, Whidden?"

"Never et them crawly things, nosir, I didn't. Ain't one gator hunter out of five that cares to try one. We had our fill of 'em already, from all that raw meat and guts and blood smell, skinnin 'em out."

"Well, I weren't never a real gator hunter," Andy said, "so I always et a piece if someone give it to me. Them crawly things is pretty good when you know how to fix 'em like the Injuns done. You get hungry enough, a nice fat rattlesnake can put you in mind of some lean chicken."

"Mikasukis eat them cold-blood things but they won't touch a rabbit. Claim it takes away your manlihood. Can't get your courage up, you know." Whidden leaned down to help Sally aboard. When he hugged her, she grumped, "I'm going to fix you some nice rabbit then. Get me some rest."

For supper, they fried small jack and mangrove snappers, and two blue catfish, pin-hooked by Andy from the stern. "Better'n ladyfish, I guess," he said, to disguise his pride in them, "but them sail-fin cat in the deeper channels eat a little better than these blues. Course in the old days, we wouldn't touch these things. We'd have a good snook or a pompano, maybe trout or grouper. All them good kinds was right here for the takin."

Because of mosquitoes, they prepared to sleep aboard. Whidden said, "Sally and me'll sleep here in the cabin, and you two fellers can lay out on deck in this nice Gulf breeze. I got some mesh, so miskeeters won't be too bad. We'll give you a blood transfusion in the mornin." He put his arms around Sally from behind, but she was still brooding, and was cool with him. "Or maybe I can take turns on deck with you two fellers," Whidden sighed.

*

Sally said she had been told by Sadie Harden that whoever last pillaged the Watson house had stripped out the only built-in cabinets in all the Islands—

"You sneakin up on those bad ol' Carrs again?" Whidden was cross. "Dammit, Sally, them young Carrs killed two young Hardens in an argument over some coon skins. We *all* know that, known it for thirty years! That don't mean that all that family are no good from here on out!"

Sheepish, she said in a whiny cracker voice, "Honey, ah ain't nevuh said *all* of 'em was bay-yud! Ah jus' said the *mos'* of 'em, is all!"

"Killed a couple of dirty Hardens, that's all," Whidden said.

" 'Dirty Hardens'! That's exactly how they talked! There was still lynch talk when I was in school!"

"Even in the thirties, lynching was common all around the South," Lucius reminded them, "and up north wasn't much better. And there were massacres."

Andy nodded. "I guess we all got our bad story. Cousin of mine was in Tavernier around 1933 when some sports fishermen went in and gunned down an old black man and his family. Didn't like what the old man charged for bait and didn't care for the expression on his face when they cussed him out. Went back for him after dark, of course. Drank some shine to get their courage up and found some more brave fellers to help out. The son got away, come running with his baby to get help. They was the only survivors."

"And nobody was charged, I don't suppose."

"Well, the Monroe Sheriff done the sensible thing, to keep the peace. He charged that hysterical young nigra with massacring his own family, and nobody bothered their heads no more about it."

The blind man stared away into the night, as if awaiting the judgment of the heavens upon Florida. "I ain't too proud about them days, are you? God Bless America, we say, but I'd hate to think that God would bless the ignoramus gun-crazy Americans that done things like that." His words were uttered quietly with a terrible finality, as if he had slowly opened up his hands on his stigmata.

*

Lucius lay down on the cabin roof with a life jacket under his head and hunted the Southern Cross in the Gulf sky, but fear for his brothers, seeping back into his lungs, made him sit up again. How long could an old man survive, tied and gagged in the suffocating heat and stench inside that house! The image wrenched a small cry from his throat, and beside him, the blind man's eyes opened wide under the starry heavens.

Considering the poor alternatives of flight or prison, was an octogenarian such as Rob better off dead? If that old man were killed, he would be grief-stricken—oh God! of *course!*—but would he also feel that Rob's end might be a mercy? *No!* He denounced himself for an unworthy idea which he vowed never to recognize again.

Above the bank of thunderheads to westward, the Gulf night was clear, and heat lightning flashed across the firmament as if shot from the farthest bright clear stars of deepest heaven. That lightning shimmer would be followed in a day or two by a southwest blow, after which the wind would back around to the northwest. The winds came and went away again, with more wind at certain times of year, more heat and rain, but fundamentally the Island seasons remained monotone, as they must be, Lucius imagined, in the realms of purgatory.

*

The *Cracker Belle* headed south at dawn toward Lost Man's River. Off to the eastward the sun swelled behind the night wall of coast jungle, and the rim of the coast forest was a band of fire.

Cryptic fins of porpoise parted a silken sea. The faint smudge of a freighter on the Gulf horizon was the only sign of man. "We're comin up on Turkey Key," Harden told Andy in a while. "I heard the clams was startin to come back behind Little Turkey."

"Turkey Key, Plover Key, Wood Key, Hog Key," Andy said, counting his fingers. "Don't all of them islands have a high shell beach tossed up by storms? The pioneers chose these windward beaches because the sea wind kept the mosquitoes back in the bushes, and the shell ridge behind was higher ground in time of hurricane. I reckon the Hardens tried out every one!"

Whidden nodded. "Hardens liked being far away, farther the better, so the Great Hurricane never drove 'em from the Islands, it just scattered 'em. Earl rebuilt on Wood Key near his daddy, and Lee moved our bunch over to South Lost Man's, and Webster went four miles upriver past First Lost Man's Bay. After that nobody saw him much. Slim, quiet feller. Stayed up in the river. Made moonshine back in there and done some voodoo."

Sally said, "Whidden's mama told me that Webster lived apart because Earl made him feel bad about his color. She said Webster was dark but had good pointed features and straight hair, and was very handsome. Some men who work all of their lives out in the sun go very dark, that's all."

Andy agreed. "Some men just take the sun that way. My own cousin Harley Wiggins was as dark as Webster Harden, nobody never questioned Harley cause he was a Wiggins!"

"Back in the old days," Sally said, "the Hardens gave a square dance once a week, and people came in from all over the Islands. Mr. Watson came, too, and he always sat with his back to the corner—had his place saved for him. If he went outside, he never came into the firelight where somebody might shoot at him out of the dark. That man was wary!"

Listening to his wife talk about his family, Harden winked at Lucius. "Yep, Harden men all played some kind of music," he recalled. "Lee Harden called the dances, played the fiddle. He'd put a keg of moonshine on his elbow and throw it down. Uncle Earl picked the guitar but he couldn't sing, and Uncle Webster played fiddle and mandolin. My pa's favorite tunes were 'Sugarfoot Rag' and 'That Dear Old Gal of Mine.'

"Pa burned his linings out so bad on moonshine that in later years he went all numb, didn't feel a thing. He could take and lift a coffeepot right off the fire and drink black coffee right out of the pot, was famous for it. He never let moonshine get the better of him, the way most did, but he had that temper and he had that Injun in him and he wouldn't take no nonsense, not from nobody. He was tough, all right, and so was Webster, but them two never turned mean when they was drinkin. I mean, they never killed nobody, not completely."

"Not completely, no!" Andy smiled broadly. "Oh my, oh my," he said with a happy sigh.

Sally contemplated the three men. " 'Oh my, oh my' is right! This man's father was supposed to be a famous killer, and this one's daddy helped to kill him, and the third one's brother was killed by my cousins—dangerous bunch here!"

Though her husband laughed, he was quick to change the subject. "My pa knew them men would be layin for Ed Watson because rumors traveled fast even in them days. He aimed to warn him. After the hurricane, Mr. Watson come back south, hunting for Cox, but the Hardens never seen him. If Lee Harden could have got to him first, he might not of gone back there and got shot to pieces.

"Pa always said that E. J. Watson knew a whole lot better than to return that day to Chokoloskee. He must of got tired of running—either that, or he had a purpose no one knew about. Said E.J. was just too darn smart not to suspect something. Them men was scared of him as well as jealous, and scared men are the most dangerous, and E.J. knew that."

"Well, Mr. Watson never stooped down to their level," Sally said. "He kept apart and they never forgave it. They were out to revenge that and make their name by killing a famous desperado. That's why Lee Harden called 'em outlaws. Called 'em the mob."

The blind man stifled a red-faced retort. He cleared his throat. "All the same, them fishermen-farmers you call the mob was your family's neighbors, and good people, too."

"Good people? Let their young boys run over there and shoot into that body?"

"You sure of that?" The blind man grunted. "One of them boys you always mention was eight years older'n me, and I reckon he stayed that way till the day he died. That would make him about six years of age when he was puttin all them bullets in that body. Course he might of had him a durn popgun or something. Might of shot a cork." Andy turned his sightless gaze in Lucius's direction, and his heavy sigh was open warning to distrust anything this young woman might say about the Bay people.

"What was unforgivable," she persisted, "was putting the blame on Henry Short for shooting Mr. Watson. Henry Short, who never raised his gun!"

Like a manatee breaking the surface, Andy emitted a short emphatic puff. Even her husband protested, "Honey, you don't know that! Not for sure!"

"Well, that's what Henry told your father, who told me. Henry swore on his Bible that he never raised his gun."

Andy leaned back with his hands behind his head. "You're sayin Henry swore that on the Bible? You pretty sure of that?"

"No, I'm not!" she blurted, close to tears.

"Because Henry was standing right beside my dad," Andy said carefully, "and my dad told me he seen that rifle comin up, longside of his own."

Lucius peered at the blind face for some sign of ambiguity. "Why would he raise his gun unless he meant to fire," he said carefully.

"Maybe he meant to bluff your dad," Andy said gloomily, looking out to sea. "I never asked him." He shook his head. "If you don't believe me, Colonel, then quit askin!" He closed his eyes.

*

Whidden was eager to show Sally his home coast. Taking advantage of fair weather, they continued south to Lost Man's River. The water of the Gulf was cloudy green, and its long slow swells swept inshore from distant storms of the Antilles.

A low island rising dead ahead stood out a little from the shore, in the middle of the Lost Man's River delta. "My dad bought the claim to Lost Man's Key but built his house south of the river mouth on Lost Man's Beach," Whidden told Sally. "Built again after the '26 Hurricane, built again after the tornado, 1940. He farmed his corn and peas there where I'm pointin at.

That little cove back over there was full of fish, so he called it Sadie's Hole, after my ma."

"The Carrs called it the same thing," she said, "because any Carr who tried to sneak in there to fish was asking for a bullet hole from Sadie Harden!"

"Well, after 1929, you might be right, Sal. Course I ain't no authority on my own family."

Bougainvillea was resurgent in its red-lavender bowers over the charcoal shadows of Lee Harden's cabin. There was no trace of Lucius's small shack, only coast undergrowth. Behind the white ridge of storm-washed shell and sea grape rose the black columns of the coco palms burned by the Park.

"Pioneer families might have no news for many months, the world went past them," Sally said solemnly. "But those folks knew every shift of wind and turn of current, they could see and smell and listen, and they *knew*." She looked from one man to the other, misty-eyed in her evocations of the old traditions. "They just *knew*."

"Knew *what?*" Lucius could not hide his impatience. Yet seeing her so moved by this wild coast, and so embattled by her demons, he stifled his annoyance at her tendency to instruct them in a place and way of life that all three men had known before she was born. Sally was principled and gallant, but her need to right old Island wrongs had killed the fun in her—the tart observations and the goofiness and whimsy which had so delighted him on their journey south.

Whidden was pointing out old landmarks. "See that little stretch of sand nearest the creek mouth? That's where the Tuckers farmed, and my family, too. Call it Little Creek, had a freshwater spring that Mr. Watson had his eye on. That's where Tuckers had their garden and that's where my folks had their farm after 1910."

"Jim Daniels and his family were living down this beach because his daughter was married to Frank Hamilton," Lucius reminded them. "His son recalls that the Tuckers were living here on a little sloop. James remembers hearing shots, at least he thinks he does. He says the killer put the bodies aboard Tucker's little sloop, set her afire, drifted her out to sea. James told me once he'd seen that burning boat himself, he'd seen the smoke of her, off-shore."

Harden shook his head. "Easterly wind might of drifted off their sloop, but my dad and his brothers found the bodies in the shallers off the Key. That's where Tuckers had their palm-thatch hut, in the Gulf breeze."

Andy said, "I sure do like James Daniels, and I always did. But James weren't but a little feller then, and he might recall most of it all right and still be wrong about the bodies. Nobody wrote nothin down about it, only Ted

Smallwood, who weren't here, and Uncle Ted had to think back a half century by the time he done that. There weren't no hearing, nothing in the papers. Two dark stains fading down into the sand was about all them young folks left behind to show they ever walked upon God's earth."

No matter what the circumstances of the killings, these could only seem inconsequential when set against the horror of the act itself. Yet Lucius disliked this discussion very much, and his own part in it seemed to him dishonest. He had encouraged objective discussion of his father, trying to learn something—to remain equable and simply listen—but his companions were talking more freely than he liked about E. J. Watson, as if his own feelings were beside the point, as if Papa were no longer his father but a figure of legend, therefore in the public domain. On the other hand, any comment by the son appeared self-serving and beside the point, no matter what that point happened to be.

Having defended the Kind Parent, the Good Neighbor, the Inspired Farmer for so long, he was feeling tremors of unhappy dread and self-deception. Even those well-disposed toward his father seemed in agreement on the menace of him, and the pall that his violence had cast over this coast. As the beloved younger son, safe under Papa's roof, what could he know of the long nights and days—and months and years—which others had spent in this lonesome mangrove wilderness in the shadow of a man allegedly involved in cold-blooded murders in at least three states?

"Them bodies with their eyes wide open underwater give Uncle Earl a fright he never got over," Harden was saying. "Once he made sure Watson had gone north, he went to Key West and give an affidavit. Swore on his oath that the three men and one nigra who found them murdered had recognized the keel mark made by Watson's boat. Uncle Earl claimed his whole family had read Tucker's note defyin Watson that was found on the kitchen table at the Bend. Well, where was that note now? the Sheriff asked him. How could he show a grand jury an underwater sand track nearly one month old, off of Lost Man's Key, forty miles north? Anyway, no self-respectin jury in the sovereign state of Florida would accept a Harden's testimony against a white man.

" 'You sayin I ain't white?' Uncle Earl yelled, as if this was the first time he'd ever heard about it. And them lawmen said, 'We know who you are, boy. Now go on home.' So Earl went home humiliated, and dead cold furious at everybody.

"Earl Harden hated the prejudice against his family, but not as bad as he hated his family for lettin Henry Short eat at their table. He hated nigras so darn bad that some of the Bay folks took a shine to him, decided he must be a white man after all. He was good friends with Browns and Thompsons, and with Fonso Lopez, too. Them families liked him somewhat better than his own did." Whidden sighed, avoiding his wife's glare. "Uncle Earl weren't all bad by no means, and I felt sorry for him—got to be sorry for any man who don't feel easy in his skin.

"Ed Watson had been good to us, and very generous, and nobody but Uncle Earl would act against him. They give Earl credit for sticking to his guns, but they knew he done it more out of his fear of Watson than in public duty. And after that year, Earl was more afraid than ever, in case that man might come back to the Islands and get wind of what Earl Harden told the law.

"Once Watson was dead, Uncle Earl got drunk and started hollerin about how he wished he'd been at Chokoloskee, how he would of been first man in line to shoot that sonofabitch, and all like that. Kind of surprised people, I reckon, because while Mr. Watson was alive, he never talked that way. And he was still talkin that way when Mister Colonel come back to the Islands a few years later."

"Couldn't shake that habit, I guess." Lucius tried to smile. "Earl made sly remarks where I could hear 'em, and when he was drinking, he got abusive to my face. In all the years I lived at Lost Man's, I never went near him if I could help it. If he was at one of the Harden parties, I just stayed away."

"Well, after he heard about your list, Uncle Earl stopped shootin off his mouth about Ed Watson. He got over all them kind of speeches!"

*

Lost Man's Key lay straight across the mouth of Lost Man's River, hiding the broad shallow bay inside. Whidden said with a shy pride, "Lee Harden came here after the Hurricane of 1910, and he swore that nobody would ever run him off. Well, Pa was wrong. But it took pretty close to forty years and it took the federal government to do it."

The boat approached the river mouth by the south channel. Black skimmers lilted over the swift eddies that ran between the gold-brown oyster bars and channeled into the Gulf on the ebb tide. The purling cries of oyster catchers came and went across the bars, rising and falling.

"Hear that orster bird? He always been here." Andy House smiled. "Got a big red bill, the same as me. I bet that bird been makin that lonesome sound at Lost Man's River since before the Injuns first come, in the old centuries."

The southwest shore of Lost Man's Key was a crescent point of fine white limestone sand. Easing the *Belle* past the bars, they set out a stern anchor in the cove behind the sand point. Lucius ran the bowline to a driftwood tree so that the *Belle* could be pulled in close to shore, but even so, Andy lost his footing and got soaked to the hips. "Guess I'll go swimming," he said happily, sinking down in all his clothes, sending up bubbles. When his big face broke the surface in a joyful smile, the Gulf sky sparkled in his eyes.

From upriver came the loud and hollow knocking of the great black woodpecker, and from much nearer, the hoot of a barred owl—*hoo-hoot, hoo-haw*. In the silence, the large forest birds seemed far away and also very near. "That hoot owl ain't so usual in daytime," Whidden said, sheepish in his uneasiness. "Any Injun hearin that hoot at noon, he'd take that as a sign. Jump back in his dugout and keep right on goin."

When Lucius asked where the Tuckers were buried, Whidden led him off into the thicket of dense buttonwood and bayonet plant, strap fern, marlberry. In the hot undergrowth, Lucius caught the skunk smell of white stopper, the antidote to dysentery at Chatham Bend. Everywhere, the sea wood's sandy floor was marked by deft hands of raccoon, the swathe and claw prints of a gopher tortoise, the whispery traces of wood mouse and lizard, a single gray-green bobcat scat, hair-packed, ends twisted up into long points.

Harden crawled ever deeper into the tangle, and Lucius followed, brushing at the tiny flies which sought the stinging sweat around his eyes. Thorn-lashed, gasping, he felt dizzy with the humidity and heat, and clawed at a disconcerting numbness at the forehead—the heavy web of the golden orb spider, like a tight plaster.

Soon they came to a dim clearing in the wood where the Tucker cabin had stood years before. "That's where they was put." Harden seemed uneasy, still troubled by that owl. "Way back in there." Where he pointed was impenetrable thicket.

A man patching his britches in the sun . . . Aunt Josie had mentioned that detail to her poor Pearl. Here at Lost Man's, even Lucius could imagine the fell imminence of the killer, like a bruised cloud come swiftly from an unknown quadrant, crossing the dawn to break the burnished edge of a clear sunrise. Perhaps poor Tucker, in his final moment, had heard a lizard jump and scutter in dry sea grape leaves—had stopped his needle, held his breath as he half-turned, sensing those bare eyes in a shadowed visage under a black hat, and the fatal shift of light in the morning leaves, in the sweet scent of lime . . .

*

On the sand point, Sally Brown was making camp. Andy lay spread-eagled in the sun, drying his clothes. Hearing their sneakers squeeze the sand, he raised his hand in contented greeting. "Call this sunbathin," House called, laughing happily at the very idea. They unloaded supplies from the boat, and swam, and stretched on the warm sand.

Whidden and Lucius went fishing for supper, heading east up the mangrove river—the home river, Whidden called it—crossing the vast expanse of silver bayou called First Lost Man's Bay. In the twenties, the Hardens had been threatened when this lower river was surveyed by the Tropical Development Company of Miami. The more intrepid prospective buyers had been bounced in jalopies over the Chevelier Road to its dead end in the Glades savanna, then poled in dugouts by "genuine wild Indians" some six miles southwest to upper Lost Man's River, where they were met by a launch from the company camp at Onion Key. A few plots were sold before the scheme collapsed when the Onion Key headquarters were destroyed by the Hurricane of '26, which also removed most of the outbuildings from Chatham Bend.

Farther east, they passed Alderman Point, then the charcoaled ruins of Webster Harden's homestead, on a high bank under buttonwood and figs and tall black mangroves. From there they returned down Lost Man's River, trolling the current points and inner bends. Fishing was slow. "It's like Speck says, them sport hunters have killed the game out, and the sport fishermen will do the same for fish. Maybe we're ignorant crackers around here, but we never fished nor hunted nothin that we didn't eat."

"Plume birds and gators?"

"Well, them things was our livelihood! Anyways, we never took much, only the belly flats and plumes!" Harden grinned, clearing a backlash from his reel. "Couldn't let all them poor Yankee ladies pine away for egret bonnets and nice alligator boots!" But while he picked and fiddled, his mood changed. "Ain't that somethin, what we done, and our forefathers, too? Leavin all them carcasses to rot day after day? Ate at my gizzard every time I done it. I purely hate to think about them hides stacked in that house. I do. But if them wild critters ever come back the way they was, I reckon I'd do the same damn thing all over."

Whidden cast a bright white-feathered lure across the broad expanding smiles of turning water. The disks of current moved downriver, slow as planets, and the tide changed, and the wind shifted. They drifted downriver toward First Lost Man's Bay. Like an ancient fort in the river mouth, Lost Man's Key rose in black subtropic tangle, eclipsing the sun as it started its slow fall to the Gulf horizon.

WHIDDEN HARDEN

Alderman Point upriver there got that name back in 1915, when you was in Fort Myers. That year, times was very hard—the fishin poor, no jobs to speak of, nothin but clammin, rickin charcoal. But the Ashley boys was getting by, robbing banks and such on the east coast. So Leland and Frank Rice and

Hugh Alderman, along with a stranger name of Tucker—them four fellers give it a try and robbed the Homestead bank. We always heard them Rice boys was in the crowd killed Mr. Watson, but I reckon you know all about that, better'n me.

The Rice-Alderman gang escaped after a shooting scrape at Jewfish Creek, over in the east of Florida Bay. They killed two deputies. A fisherman took 'em as far west as Flamingo, where they hired a boat to take them north around the Cape. Man dropped 'em off at a place up Lost Man's River—Alderman Point—and probably these boys bought some supplies off our Harden family. The Rice gang didn't want to stay no place too long. Knowin the back creeks, they rowed as far as Lopez River. Hugh Alderman's cousin Walter had married Marie Lopez, and they figured they would get a little help. All they got was water from the cistern, cause the Lopez Place was empty. Next thing, their skiff drifted off, and they had to clamber through the mangroves all the way downriver to the nearest point across from Chokoloskee. By that time a reward notice was posted on the door at Small-wood's post office.

At dusk, Leland swum over to the island. Two boys seen him swimming and bushwhacked him when he come ashore. Harley Wiggins and a younger boy. Remember Harley? Big, dark-complected feller? And that younger boy was Crockett Daniels—Speck. Them boys was nervous, they just shot and run, and Leland crawled away. The sun went down before the word got out that a wounded bank robber was out there in the dark. Only ones who weren't scared to death were Rob Storter and his pretty Cassie who come in late from fishing and never knowed a thing about it. Next morning Old Man McDuff Johnson come pounding on the door, informin Rob he had a dead man on his stoop. It was Leland Rice with a pistol in one pocket and five thousand dollars in the other.

It bothered people that them boys killed Leland Rice for the reward. Everybody knew the Rice boys, they were real nice fellers, never made no trouble. They weren't local men, they come from up around Lake Okee-chobee, but they fished around here for some years and they had kinfolk on the island.

Them boys always claimed they tried to arrest Leland, but he went for his gun and so they had to shoot him. Maybe that's the way it was. I wasn't there. But shooting a feller for a cash reward? Weren't nobody felt good about that killing. Harley's sister *still* don't like to talk about it! Maybe twenty years later, when that Rice story come up in a conversation, she sat up very straight and stiff and tugged her skirt. *"Harley Wiggins is my brother and he never said a thing about it, not to me!"* That was the last we ever heard on *that* subject!

The men wrapped Leland in a canvas shroud and buried him. They took Leland's money to Ted Smallwood, thinking the postmaster would know what to do with it, but Ted was a stickler for minding his own business, he didn't want the responsibility. Ted weren't one to turn his nose up at five thousand dollars, but he knew it wouldn't be much use to him if he was dead. Some tough hombre with a gun was bound to come hunting for that money, and he did not care to be the one holding the bag. When Ted said that, the rest decided they didn't want nothing to do with that blood money. They turned it over to the captain of the *Pal*, a big old boat that run produce once a week to Punta Gorda.

Sure enough, Frank Rice swum over from the east side of the Bay and asked after his brother and they told him that since he seen him last, Leland was dead and buried. So after Frank had blew his nose and put his neckerchief away, he asked where that money might be and was told he could go claim it on the *Pal*, which was tied up to a fish house off of Smallwood's. But when Frank rowed out, tried to climb aboard, a sniper hid back in the mangrove put a bullet in his back, and he dropped back into the water. He was hauled aboard and patched up some, and he lived long enough to die in prison.

Next day Hugh Alderman decided to swim over, and the fourth man, Tucker, followed. Told Hugh he'd rather go to prison than spend another day with them damned miskiters, and anyways he was dog sick from eatin raw orsters morning, noon, and night. Those were John Tucker's last complaints, cause he didn't swim good and he didn't make it. The mud bar where his body came ashore is still Tucker Key today. He lay in the sun quite a good while, and by the time Ted Smallwood whacked a box together and they got him buried, he had turned black as any nigra that you ever seen.

Some claimed that Tucker was the brother of that feller who got killed at the turn of the century at Lost Man's River, because once before, when this same man come through Chokoloskee on his own two feet, he said he was gunnin for Ed Watson. Must of stayed away a good long while, getting his nerve up, cause by the time he got here, his intended victim was five years in the grave. Maybe the poor feller went over to bank robbing because he had all that nerve saved up and didn't want to let it go to waste. Then Bill House took a good look at that body and come up with the opinion that the dead man weren't nobody but young Rob Watson, who had ran away at the time of the Tucker killings, but it looks like Bill might of been wrong, as usual.

Who ended up with all that money no one knows. There's some will tell you Sheriff Tippins kept it so safe that he could never find it, and others spread stories how Ted Smallwood offered to hold it for Hugh Alderman. Smallwood kept all of his own money rolled up in deep pockets sewed inside his coveralls, never got separated from his greenbacks for two minutes, and maybe that measly ol' five thousand dollars got lost way down inside. Anyways, when the banks come looking, them fellers scratched their heads, tried to think back about it, but none of 'em could rightly recall where that durn money could of got to.

Most folks believed that the ones who shot Frank Rice and near to drowned him were the same ones who killed his brother Leland, and they never did forgive them two young fellers. Some said them boys picked up their bad attitudes from seeing Ed Watson shot to pieces, because both of 'em was among them ones who run down there and shot into the body. Anyways, folks were ashamed of them young bushwhackers. This is a coast where moonshining and smuggling go back a hundred years and more, but there never had been no local crime to speak of. Cash could lay for a week on the kitchen table, wouldn't nobody touch it.

Leland lay on that doorstep all night long with five thousand dollars in his pocket and nobody touched him. Might of took his life for a two-hundred-buck reward, but nobody stole that feller's hard-earned money. He had a big diamond on his finger when they buried him, and nobody touched that diamond neither, though there was talk about a feller who might of gone back with his shovel later on.

*

All Whidden and Lucius had brought back to enhance a supper of dark bread and baked beans was one thin sea trout, a small jack, and a pail of oysters. "Beans and mullet, grits and mullet—*that* sticks to your belly," Whidden commented. "Trout and jack don't scarcely do the job." They squatted at the water's edge scaling and cleaning fish and shucking oysters while Sally scavenged driftwood for the fire.

"I was tellin Sally," Andy said, "that the ones who lasted in the Islands was hard men—they had to be. Lee Harden and his brothers was as tough as knotholes and Lee had that temper. All the same, he was kinder and broader in his mind than most. My daddy knew him from way back, in the Frenchman's time. His Sadie was a strong woman, too, and she was kind—she was just wonderful! Fine people! Hung on here at Lost Man's till the end. Hardens lived here more than seventy years, the first real settlers to come here and the last to go—the greatest pioneer clan in the Islands!"

"Hear that, Mr. Whidden?" Sally cried, delighted, throwing down her driftwood. "That sure is right!"

Her husband nodded. "My pa always said that the one thing he was glad of, his daddy wasn't here to see us leave. Granddad Robert died in the nick of time, at 106 years old, and Parks run us out of here the followin year. For a little while, we come back in the summers, set some nets from May until September. Pa was the only Harden who had title to his property, a lifetime right, but we weren't allowed to build nothin nor plant a garden. Pa got him a little houseboat we could camp on, cause we couldn't set up so much as a lean-to on the shore. Couldn't hunt nor trap nor gather nothin—all we done was fish. The more Pa visited, the more he'd grieve, and pretty soon, he give it up for good. Lost Man's was what he worked for his whole life, and the loss of it took the heart out of him, though he lived along in Naples for a few more years. I will say for the first park ranger, he knew how hard it was for the old-timers. He'd turn his head if Sadie Harden took sea turtle eggs or netted terrapins. Before that, he worked as an Audubon warden and had made good friends among the Island people."

Sally laughed. "If I had worked as Audubon warden back in those days, I'd have made good friends among the Island people, too! Made all the friends that I could find, and then some!"

"This ranger, name of Barney Parker, never noticed if we shot for the pot. Might been too busy chasin gator poachers. One time he come up alongside a young Brown that had him a mess of gator flats under a canvas, and gator blood all through his bilge water. That ranger just set there looking at that bloody water, never says one word, till that young Brown was set to jump out of his skin. Finally Barney looks up and says, 'Well, son, it sure looks like the time has come for you to try another line of work.' That was partly a warning and partly good advice, because the way them reptiles was disappearin from slough after slough, there weren't no more future in the gator business.

"Exterminatin the last gators was what stopped the slaughter, cause the rangers couldn't. The gator hunters knew every meander of these creeks and rivers, knew every backwater of the Glades country south to Cape Sable and Florida Bay, and the good ones always slipped away without no trouble.

"It used to be that every point and river mouth and key, and any piece of higher ground along this coast, had a family living off the water and farmin their little bit of soil to get their greens. Hard to believe that, ain't it? Parks tore out everything—houses, fruit trees, little docks, every sign of man. Course there's plenty of sign if a man knows where to look, all the way back to the Calusas, but folks today will never know what we knew about these islands, never know how beautiful they were. Used to be wild limes everywhere, smelled like pure paradise, and every little bay was full of mullet.

"Parks couldn't believe how many old trails and clearins that last hurricane uncovered, how much rusty metal and crockery and glass. The pains taken by them old-time settlers to haul their poor old stuff all them miles down here, mostly by rowboat! The lives that was used up clearin jungle, hackin furrows in the rock-hard ground on these old shell mounds! Well, all that labor never meant a damn to them officials. Come ashore and ate up their nice lunch, set down and rustled a few papers, then destroyed what it took years and years for us poor folks to scrape together, rough shacks and home-built beds and tables and chairs and cisterns and fish houses and docks! Even our gardens! 'This here is an American damn park, so you folks just rip out them guavas and papaws, them ol' gator pears, cause them foreign damn things ain't got no business here!' "

Harden smiled but in his quiet way, he was bone angry. "Maybe all our families had was quitclaims, but we paid for 'em in blood! Ask the miskiters! We was the pioneers here, the first settlers, but we had to watch this deputy with a gun on his fat butt come waddlin up the beach with some damn vacate papers. Tossed some gasoline and burned our cabin to the ground, then went down the shore and done the same at Mister Colonel's. They got back in their big-ass boat, but before they left, that feller hollers out across the water. 'Real nice fire, folks! Too bad we forgot to bring the marshmallers!' Had to listen to 'em hee-haw. Left us in the rain with no roof over our heads, just settin on that beach there like wet possums!

"Our old homesteads is all grown over now, and Wood Key, too, you'd never know that human beins ever lived here. They was worried that our poor ol' shacks might spoil the scenery for their Park visitors. Never gave a good goddamn for those who was born and lived their lives here and was kicked out without one thing to show for it!"

Whidden swore with such uncustomary violence that the others fell silent, giving him some room. After a long while he said somberly, "I was tellin Mister Colonel about Leland Rice, how he come through Lost Man's with his gang after the bank robbery. I never got to the other half of that old story."

"Whidden? I'm sure Mister Colonel knows the rest of it—"

"This was back in World War I, when he was gone." Stolid, stubborn, Whidden said to Lucius, "When them fellers come through here, Abbie Harden fell in love with Leland, wanted to run off with him. Well, her parents said no, and next thing she knew, that young bank robber was killed on Chokoloskee. Aunt Abbie was wailin and screechin how that tragedy would not have happened if she had been allowed to go with that young man, and she threatened she might destroy herself almost any day. Course Abbie weren't a young girl no more, and she might of thought that Leland Rice was her last chance in life. And Leland bein dead and buried, we never got to hear his side of the story.

"Abbie Harden was tall and slim, she never got heavy like her sisters, and she had them nice manners that she learned in Key West convent school. You might recall her helpin out at some of your daddy's parties, makin sure that everything looked nice. A lot of local boys was after her but she weren't interested, she had her own romantical ideas.

"Abbie took after her brother Earl, she was ashamed of the dark ones in the family. Probably it was Earl taught her to think that way. Whenever she went up to Chokoloskee, folks would find ways to humiliate her because her sister had married Henry Short, and she was furious because her own family saw nothing wrong in that. 'It's not bad enough,' she screeched, 'that we're called mulattas up and down the coast, without Libby marrying up with some darned nigger?' Well, Grandmother Maisie grabbed her daughter by the scruff of her white neck and washed her mouth out with lye soap. Yelled, 'Girl, are you fool enough to listen to them mean-mouth hypocrites up on the Bay? Didn't Henry tell us he was part Indian, the same as us? He is a good Christian man and would not lie about it!' And she told Abbie she should count her blessins, having such a fine man in the family, told her she didn't care to hear no more about it.

"You recall my grandma, Mister Colonel? From her Seminole side, Grandma Maisie was darker than anybody in her family except Uncle Webster, but because her daddy was John Weeks, the first pioneer to settle Chokoloskee, she was a white woman and that was that. She never paid her own color no attention, so nobody else did neither, only Earl and Abbie. Abbie Harden vowed she would never forgive her family, she was out to spite them. And what she done, she run off with the Storters' man Dab Rowland, from Grand Cayman Island. This young Carribean man at Everglade was the only other black person around the Bay, and he weren't wheat color like Henry, he was black—"

"*Other* black person?" Sally looked cross. "You're saying Henry Short was black?"

"In them days Dab was fishing with Claude Storter, and he played the banjo for our Harden parties. Well, one night Abbie drank too much, which she weren't used to, and she grabbed that banjo picker and run off with him and got married by the Cape Sable constable, same way Aunt Libby done. Maybe she told Dab she would holler rape and see him lynched if he didn't go along, because Abbie was as headstrong as the rest of 'em. If Abbie had married out of love instead of spite, things might been different, but Dab was so black that it seems like she picked him out for his wrong color. Poor feller must of woke up in the mornin and knew he was fixin to get lynched no matter what. Some folks wondered why that nigra would let that wild young woman risk his life, but one way or another, I don't reckon he had no say about it.

"Aunt Abbie announced that marryin Dab Rowland was all she could think of to get even with her family for ruinin her life by lettin Libby marry

Henry. Because, said she, Henry Short was a nigger just as much as Dab, a nigger was a nigger, there weren't one speck of difference between niggers."

Andy said sorrowfully, "That's the way folks seen it—there *weren't* no difference between Henry and Dab."

"Whatever he was, Granddad Robert disowned her, not so much for marryin a black man as for marryin him out of spite to wreck her family. Granddad Robert knew who he liked and who he didn't, and family had damned little to do with it. He never liked his oldest boy and never pretended that he did, which is probably why Uncle Earl always lived near that old man hopin to change his daddy's poor opinion of him.

"Dab and Abbie went to Key West for a trip, then back to Everglade, where Dab had some protection from the Storters. But Earl believed that Abbie was flauntin her black husband on the Bay to pay back her family for disowning her, and some of our Weeks and Daniels cousins came over from Marco with a plan to string Dab from the big mahogany out front of the trading post, same ol' tree that is standin there today.

"My pa was about the only one took up for Abbie. When his brother Earl was fixin to join up with the lynchin party, he stepped in. He told him, 'That man's wife is our little sister, so Hardens will stand by 'em.' And Earl paid some attention, too, because Pa was very strong, with that fiery temper. If Lee Harden give you his word, you could lay your life on it, men always said, so I guess Earl figured if he took a part, he could lay his life on his brother's promise he would kill him. Earl Harden never forgive his brother for makin him back down about Dab Rowland.

"Course the Bay families liked Earl better'n Lee because he was more like them. Earl was friends with the same folks who became Hardens' worst enemies and whenever my pa run into trouble, it always seemed like Old Man Earl was hid behind it.

"Lee Harden went to Everglade and warned his sister that the lovebirds better fly, so they went over there to Arizona. Wrote back to inform us that out in the West where nigras ain't so plentiful, the Injuns and Mexicans are treated even worse. Just ain't enough black people out there for good Christians to get worked up about, cause they already have their hands full, bein mean to Injuns. Aunt Abbie never had no children, but they adopted a little black boy and they sent his picture and we sure liked the look of him. She ended up enjoyin her black family."

Whidden stopped to sort his feelings. "In some way, the Hardens' troubles went back to their friendship with Mr. Watson," he said finally. "I ain't blaming him, Mister Colonel—I said, went *back* to him. Because his friendship with Hardens was a warning to the Bay people: *leave these folks be.* Maybe all he wanted was the support of Harden guns, like some has said—that worked both ways. As long as Mr. Watson was known to be our friend, nobody messed with us. But after his death, the Hardens was resented worse than ever, especially Lee Harden, who called the men who gunned down his old friend 'a mob of outlaws.' Even the ones who took no part had kinsmen in that crowd, and they resented it. Mamie Smallwood purely hated what her dad and brothers done that day, but she never forgive Lee Harden for them words. That woman had it in for Hardens till the day she died.

"Once Mr. Watson was out of the way, the men took to fishing farther and farther south toward Lost Man's River, and pretty soon, the Fish Wars started up again. The Harden clan was outcast more than ever, and when one sister married Henry Short, it got worse still, and when another run off with Dab Rowland—well, she ruined her family. Aunt Abbie give our enemies all the argument they ever needed that Hardens must be some kind of mulattas who had no right to run no white men off that Lost Man's coast. The Bay fishermen and the trappers, too, was after our Harden territory, and it got so they were huntin an excuse to come down here in a gang and wipe us out."

"My cousins! Carrs and Browns—!"

"Your line of Browns had nothin much to do with that feud with Hardens. Matter of fact, your uncle Harry stayed pretty good friends—remember Dollar? Called him that name because back in the old days, he sold his Lost Man's Key claim to my dad for one silver dollar. Dollar was always selling somethin, he was full of big ideas, a real finagler. It was Dollar who invented commercial stone crabbing, he was the first man around here to set him a line of deep water traps floored with cement that would sink to the bottom and set upright in fifty foot of water. Stone crabs crawl better in winter and rough water and at night, and they are partial to a good tough bait like stingray.

"Anyways, it was Dollar Bill who warned my pa that the Lopez bunch might try to run him off this Lost Man's claim. Lopezes lived at Mormon Key for quite a while, raised some sugarcane because fishin was so poor—two cents a pound was all we was gettin for pickled mullet—and they was very jealous of our territory. Pa always believed it was one them Lopez cousins who caught him from behind one night at Chokoloskee, cut him up like pork chops with an ax. Pa went to the hospital for the first time in his life, and when he got out, he stopped off at Smallwood's on his way home. Didn't suspect Old Man Ted was behind it, just pretended that he did, knowin Ted was friends with the ones who probably done it. Stood there awhile not sayin a word, just watchin Ted tryin not to look at him, cause his face was all ripped up and swollen purple. He was waitin to see if Ted would come apart, and he damn near did, he couldn't hardly speak. So finally Pa said, 'The day I catch up with the man who carved this Halloween mask you are lookin at' "—and Whidden tapped his own face, his eyes squinted—" 'that man is as good as dead.' Old Man Smallwood says, 'No, no, no, Lee! I never knew a thing about it!' And he probably didn't. But he spread the word about what Pa said, until even the innocent ones got nervous, in case Lee Harden decided it was them." He shook his head. "Pa wore them heavy face scars all his life. And every year the tensions between Hardens and the Bay kept growin worse.

"Takin a life was about the only way them wars was goin to end, and both sides knew that. Even the weather give us warning signs, like that strange cold breath out of the sky before a thunderstorm. That atmosphere along this coast had to bust like a woman's water before anybody could breathe easy again.

"Seems terrible to say it but my pa said this himself: if them ones that tried to kill him with an ax had knowed their job, and drawed off that dangerous head of steam by killin him, my brother Roark and my cousin Wilson might not of lost their lives down at Shark River.

"Dollar Bill might been the only Brown who ever did our family a kind deed, and the only one was welcome at our musical parties after them murders. But one day Dollar got drunk and run his mouth off, trying to patch the feud. He was lettin on how it weren't nothin but a tragical misunderstandin, and how Hardens should quit holdin a grudge against his young Carr cousins. Pa run him right off Lost Man's Beach, told him he weren't welcome anymore."

"Why should the Hardens begrudge the Carrs a couple of ol' murders?" His wife glared at Whidden, who lay back on the sand again, looking resigned. "Damn it, Whidden," Sally said then, "Mister Colonel better hear our side of that old story!"

"Honey, he already knows our side." Whidden pointed across the river mouth toward Lost Man's Beach. "He was livin right down the beach over there when it happened." He folded his arms across his knees, his expression enigmatic in the firelight.

It was true that Lucius knew the tragic story. He did not know how the Hardens perceived it decades later, and when Sally looked at him, he urged her to go ahead. Anxious to pull herself together, to set her emotions aside, she folded her hands upon her lap and for almost a minute sat in silence, in her instinct that the recounting of human death deserved formality.

"Roark Harden was eighteen years of age and his cousin—Earl's boy Wilson—was just one year older. One day Wilson came over from Wood Key to pick up Roark in his skiff. They sailed out to the Gulf sky to pick up wind, then took a bearing southward. Sadie Harden was worried by bad dreams, and she watched from shore until they disappeared.

"The family knew that the two boys planned to spend their first night at Shark River Point. Nobody owned that country down around Shark River, that was Indian country. The boys hoped to make a grubstake trapping coons back of Cape Sable, then go hunting crocodiles out of Belize."

"They was going across to Belize in a sailing skiff?"

"Mr. House? They were going to Key West, catch a coast trader!" She took a long deep breath.

"Now this was the worst time of the Fish Wars, too many bullets too close to people's heads, and Roark decided to leave Lost Man's River before he killed somebody or somebody killed him. Roark and Wilson were real hotheads, they wanted to get away for a while until they simmered down, but they weren't out hunting trouble, they were avoiding it.

"Those boys were never seen again except by those who killed them! But Roark's daddy knew who trapped around Shark River and which ones had it in for Hardens. He had no proof but he was sure it was the sons of Walker Carr, who was living at the Watson Place on Chatham Bend."

Once again, the Bend had been involved in a dark and violent episode in Island history. Lucius wondered if this thought had occurred to Andy House, who lay beside him, staring sightless at the canopy of ocean stars high overhead as if to receive some vision of existence. When the blind man shifted with a weary sigh, Sally stopped talking and awaited him.

"If they was headed for Belize, Mis Sally, and they never come back home, how did their families learn that they was missin? How did Hardens know them boys never got no farther than Shark River? You ever talk to your *own* family about this?"

"I never talk to my 'own family' at all!"

Andy sighed again and lay back on the sand as if expiring, and Sally waited pointedly before resuming.

"The Harden men had hunted for their sons for two long years, even visited a Georgia prison on a rumor. With each failed search, they became more convinced about what actually happened, and Lee Harden was so upset that he swore when he was drinking that he was going after those damned Carrs and no more talk about it. By that time there were plenty of rumors, and Walker Carr had removed his family from the Watson Place, and his sons steered clear of Harden territory, never went south of the fish house at Turkey Key.

"Sadie Harden never doubted that her missing boy was right there in Shark River, killed by Carrs. One time she shot at Cap Daniels's boat because it looked like a Carr boat."

Whidden laughed, "Poor Cap went back to Fakahatchee and painted that darn boat of his a different color!"

"For years those Carrs denied the rumors, just barefaced denied them. I believe it was the youngest brother, Alden, who spat up the truth. He was camped there at Shark River with his brothers Owen and Turner, and he'd seen what happened. Couldn't live with it, I guess, he was having nightmares. He did not know that the Johnson boy he was drinking with at Tavernier was a Harden cousin.

"Alden Carr told the Johnson boy that some coon hides had been taken from their camp. They thought the Harden boys must have them, so they went over there to take them back. Owen Carr was leader, and he crept up and shone a carbide lantern, and when Wilson heaved up on one elbow, he shot him in cold blood where he lay there on the ground under his mosquito bar. Later he claimed the Harden boys were threatening to fire, and another time he kind of hinted that his little brother Alden got buck fever and fired that first shot. But Alden claimed he never fired, he was screeching at his brothers not to shoot.

"Roark sat up at the noise and turned to face them. Seeing his gun was out of reach, and seeing poor dying Wilson there beside him, he was very frightened. According to Alden, he put his hands up, begging them to spare his life. The panicked Carrs yelled and argued right in front of him, waving their guns around. 'We don't kill him, he'll run home and tell, and them Hardens will come gunnin for us!' Can you believe it? While poor Roark huddled in the light beam, awaiting their decision? Can you imagine anything more terrifying for that poor boy?

"While they were yelling, Roark bolted, scrambling away into the dark. They had that lantern and they chased him down and started shooting, but being scared, not wanting to get close, they just kept firing and wounding him as he crawled away under the stilt roots of the mangroves, until finally he lay down from loss of blood and finally died. They dragged those two boys into their skiff and towed that skiff all the way upriver to the saw grass, then way on up some little creek. They were thinking to bury the bodies, set the skiff on fire, but they were so frightened that they made a mess of the whole business and never finished it. First they heard owls and then a panther screamed, and they just cut and ran!"

Lucius said quietly, "Well, that was Alden's story, all right." He gazed across the firelight at Sally. "That's what he told me, too. Panther scream and all."

"I don't believe that Alden fired. It was Owen and Turner!"

Andy House grunted unhappily, sorting his own memories and ruminations. He cleared his throat. "Sally, I ain't excusin what they done. But when Turner grew up, he married into our House family, and we never found nothin the matter with him. You are tellin this story only from the Hardens' side, which is all right, but like I say, somebody should speak up for *your* family if you won't do it."

"The *Hardens* are my family," Sally cried, as if he were being dense. Upset, she rose and walked off down the beach, and after waiting a little to give her dignity some room, Whidden rose and followed her toward the point.

"Well, Colonel, you was here at Lost Man's then. You know the story." When Lucius urged him to tell how he perceived it, Andy cleared his throat, frowning in his determination to speak responsibly and to avoid contradicting Sally's story more than he had to.

ANDY HOUSE

In the first part of the Depression, young Roark Harden and his cousin Wilson come up missing. Because they was known to be coon hunting around Shark River, their daddies suspected the young Carrs, who was camped nearby. Only trouble was, they had no evidence. Up to here, Sally and me don't have no problem.

That year I was seventeen years old, so I can recall about it pretty good. Our family was truck-farming up near the Trail, so all we had was hearsays, but we knowed Walker Carr's boys was suspected, knowed all hell broke loose anytime a Carr tried to net mullet south of Turkey Key. And we heard how them Carr boys was claiming that five hundred dollars' worth of coon hides had been stole out of their camp—a lot of money in Depression times, for folks like us.

Maybe you was too close to 'em to notice, Colonel, but a lot of men said those Harden boys was not only hotheads, they was troublemakers. There was angry talk how somethin had to be done to put a stop to 'em, because them two cousins was the ones most likely to wing a bullet past the ear of any fisherman who came anywhere within two miles of Lost Man's Beach. After so many years of bad talk and harassment, Hardens was bitter, you can't blame 'em, and they aimed to scare Bay fishermen off that territory, because Lost Man's River was the last wild heart of the last wild country left in southwest Florida.

On their side, the men resented Hardens for puttin signs up, tryin to keep others off so much good fishin ground. All the Bay families had it in for 'em, not only Carrs. The fishermen would tear their signs down, cuss 'em out, yell filth across the water at their cabins, hollerin how these Island waters was free territory and how no damn half-breeds weren't goin to get away with hoggin the whole coast for theirselves.

Us Houses knowed somethin was up pretty soon after it happened. Walker Carr rowed up Turner River to where we was farmin near the Trail.

Showed up one night, never said what he was after—might of muttered about hard times and prospectin for gator holes or somethin. At first light, he walked off toward the east. He was a strong little feller but not young no more, so my dad was worried and he follered him a ways before he give up and let him go.

Back then there weren't much traffic across Florida, and the few trucks and autos never picked up drifters, not in the Depression, not way out there in the middle of the Glades. Anyways, he must of walked a good ways east over the Trail, cause he never come back through till near a fortnight later. Might of spent that second night at Monroe Station, then headed off on some Injun path south and east across the Cypress and out across that long pine ridge on the old Chevelier Road and on down into the Shark River Slough. That's hard goin, bogs and saw grass and limestone solution holes that slash your boots, never mind the varmints, and no dry place to sleep after the summer rains.

That's a big country down there, so Carr must of had a rough idea where he was headed. But why he would take that hard overland journey is a mystery, unless he was aimin to make sure that there weren't no bodies layin out in the Shark River savannas where turkey buzzards might find 'em, maybe draw some Injuns that was out huntin. Wouldn't want to go in there by river in case he might run across the Hardens, who was out searchin for them bodies, too. The difference was, the Hardens had nothin to hide. They was searchin for sign along the edges of the creeks in broad open daylight. They wanted to find their boys, take 'em home for burial. I reckon Carr wanted to bury 'em for good right where they lay.

Them Hardens had a heavy cross to bear, and we all felt bad about it. Lee Harden lost his oldest boy, and Earl did, too. Earl could be likable, but he was hard. All his life, he seemed kind of discontented, and he complained a lot as he grew older. Rounder than Lee, a little shorter, but not fat. Lee was a big man, and he looked real tough and craggy with that ax-scarred face, but he was easygoing, he could laugh at himself, which Earl could never do. All the same, nobody messed with Lee, because when he drank, he had that dangerous temper.

For a few years, Lee come up to Everglade and haunted them young Carrs. Never harassed 'em directly, just anchored his boat in the river off Carrs' fish house. Couldn't shoot 'em only on suspicion—though men done a *lot* just on suspicion, back in them days! Never called out, never said a word, like he was studying on what to do and had probably come to the right place to do it. That big boat anchored out front was Lee's way of saying that Carrs and Hardens had unfinished business, and it might of been what caused one of 'em to crack.

Well, the truth finally come out, like Sally says. The Carr boys said they never meant to shoot, they was just nervous, and when Wilson Harden heard somethin and reared up under his miskeeter bar, a gun went off. They claimed they thought the Harden boys was up and shootin so they fired— a pure case of self-defense, to hear Carrs tell it. They admitted they run down Roark in the swamp, admitted they was shriekin at each other, tryin to decide what they should do, because Roark Harden wasn't likely to forget what he had witnessed.

Those Harden boys was angry wild young fellers, no doubt about it, but Walker Carr's boys, they weren't angels neither. One of 'em was always fidgetin his eyes, and I reckon he's still doin that today. Got so you always had to watch what was laying around loose—life weren't never that way in the old days.

Whatever them Carr boys done or didn't do, they are the ones who has to live with it, die with it, too. But it was a shame, the way they killed that poor young feller beggin for his life—that was the part that ate at Turner Carr. Said shootin Roark Harden while he crawled away was the worstest thing he ever had to do. Well, I sure hope so!

I won't speak for Owen Carr, but I known Turner all my life and I don't believe he ever bragged about that killin. Nosir, he was real upset and very close to tears just in the tellin of it—this was two years later! Told me that all they wanted was their coonskins, and how when one boy got shot by mistake, they went ahead because they could not leave a witness. I warned young Turner that he better keep his mouth shut, pray for forgiveness, but he could not stop talkin—not braggin, the way Sally tells it, only talkin, like confessin his sins over and over was his only hope of getting shut of what they done.

After the news got out, the whole Bay hunkered down, expectin trouble. The guns come out every time them Harden men come up from Lost Man's, and them young Carrs was pretty hard to find.

Outside of their family, most people took that coonskin story with some salt. Roy Thompson who married my cousin Ernestine, he fished with Lee Harden for some years, and fished with one of them Carr brothers, too, so he heard the inside story from both sides. Roy Thompson told me he did not believe them Hardens stole no coon hides. Whether he'd say that to the Carrs, I just don't know.

What it comes down to, the Carr boys knew that no matter what, the community was behind 'em. There weren't no law south of Caxambas, that was understood by everybody, Sheriff included. Carrs knew they could take the law in their own hands, like was done with Guy Bradley and the Rice boys and Ed Watson and a lot of other men who come to a bad end down in this country.

Like I say, Earl and Lee was tough old boys, and crack shots, too. Robert Harden was an old feller by that time, might not of known what he was shootin at but could still hit it if you got him pointed in the right direction. Even the women in that clan were as handy with shootin irons as they were with hoes. Besides that, they had Webster Harden, who usually finished what he started, and a feller named Watson right next door who could shoot as good as any of 'em and maybe better. Altogether, that was not a gang you would want to mess with.

So everybody on the Bay was set for trouble, but the years went by and not a thing was done about it. Maybe Lee and Earl was startin to get old, or maybe too much time had passed before they learned for sure what really happened, or maybe they never did agree on what to do. They was good brothers as boys, is what my dad told me, but later in life them two men could not agree on the best place in the woods to take a piss.

*

Crossing her ankles, Sally Brown sank down on the sand. Hands in hip pockets, Whidden stood behind her. In the Gulf wind, they had come up quietly, and Andy House, not knowing how long they had been in earshot, looked chagrined.

"What was done to those Harden boys," Sally said brusquely, "was what those people wanted to see done. The whole community was behind it, as you say. And those murders were excused by calling the Hardens mixed breed or mulatta. Well, if Hardens are mixed, then the Bay people are, too, because most of those families are blood kin to the Hardens whether they admit it or not. Sandy Albritton is not ashamed of it, but the rest will try to let on to this day that they are no kin to Hardens whatsoever. Probably think that after fifty years of telling that old lie, it might be true."

Andy House said carefully, "Them young Carrs were not the least bit proud about what happened."

"Back then? I'm not so sure."

"You weren't born back then."

Cutting off their wrangling, Whidden sounded tired. "Owen Carr was hot after my sister Edie. He never came around, not once, after Roark disappeared, that was one reason our family suspected him. But we knew that if we done anything about it, we would give 'em their excuse to stage a raid down here and lynch them mixed-breed sonsabitches once and for all. My mama *heard* that lynch talk. Folks made sure she heard it. In the store."

"And even if Hardens got the case to a grand jury," Andy said thoughtfully, "they knew that the Carr boy would testify how he never confessed to no such thing. And they knew a jury would accept that coonskin story whether they believed it or they didn't because no self-respectin jury was going to sit still for no supposed-to-be mulattas takin white folks into court, not in Collier County nor in Lee nor Monroe neither."

Slowly he turned toward the Hardens. "I sure do hate to be the one to say that, Whidden, but ain't that about right?"

Whidden and Sally stared into the fire and did not answer, and Lucius did not know what to say to make things better. Andy's conclusion was also self-condemnation, a gagging down of bitter medicine, but unable to see anyone's expression, hearing no comment, the blind man, too, seemed cast down, filled with despair. Even in firelight, Andy looked ashamed of his own need to hammer out his "truth." Yet his calm and measured voice would not relent. "And even after it come out who done it," he resumed, "I never heard no Harden claim they was deprived of legal justice. Why?"

Sally burst out, "I know what *you* think, Mr. House, because people like you all think the same! You think it's because the Hardens knew that as 'supposed-to-be-mulattas,' they were not going to get justice, no matter what!" Sally Brown was very close to tears. "On the other hand, they couldn't claim race prejudice, because claiming prejudice would seem to be admitting that there might be something for people to be prejudiced *about—that about right?"* She mimicked him sarcastically, voice quavering.

Yet a moment later she spoke to him without rancor. Picking up cool sand, watching it pour away between her fingers, she blurted finally, "Oh, I guess what you've been saying is 'true' enough, Mr. House. A half-truth, anyway."

*

Whidden hauled the bow of the *Cracker Belle* onto the sand. Followed by Lucius, he clambered aboard and ducked down into the cabin, where he fished a bottle from beneath the coils of anchor warp in the forward cuddy and brought it back on deck. Each took a snort and gasped as the liquor eased him.

"Like Andy says, they was wild and they was angry, they sank boats and broke up traps, they was reckless with their mouths and with their guns. And knowin how people talked about our family, that made 'em angrier than ever. Them boys swore over and over they would never be run off their home territory without a fight. Roark and Wilson was the most ornery amongst the Hardens—or bravest, depending how you look at it." Whidden paused, observing Lucius. "So you might say—and people did say—that they had it comin."

"Do you believe they had it coming?"

"I guess I do. If you believe them Carrs about them coonskins." Whidden shrugged. "Carrs are my wife's kinfolks. I sure do hate to call 'em liars as well as murderers." He smiled with Lucius but his eyes were serious. "Sally wonders how them Carrs could shoot another boy while he was beggin for his life—she can't get over that! Well, don't let on I said this, Mister Colonel—and I'm not just sayin it, I have done some thinkin on it—but I never wondered about that, not for one minute. Back in them Fish Wars, in the Depression, with poor people so hungry on this coast, and all the ugly bitter feelins that there was? In them Carrs' place, so scared and angry, I might of done no different than what they done."

"Are you saying the Hardens have forgiven it?"

"No, I sure ain't. I'm only sayin that most of us can understand how it could happen. That make sense?"

Lucius supposed that the Bay people had suspended the feud after those deaths, since Whidden had been accepted when he courted Sally.

"Not by all of 'em. Someone seen us holdin hands and commenced to holler and take on, tell the old bad stories. The Carr cousins said, 'Why, honey, he's a *Harden!*' And Sally said, 'That's right, folks, and I'm fixin to marry him, cause I just dote on this here Harden boy for his sparkly green eyes and his blond hair!' Well, she had 'em there, they couldn't say too much, they just kept bleatin at her, 'He's a *Harden!*'

"I loved that sweet Miss Sally Daniels right from school days, she was the prettiest girl I ever seen and she still is. When I asked her to marry, she said no but I kept at it, and finally she took a real deep breath and told me what happened about Crockett Junior. For a while, I was pretty jealous over Junior, bein as how I seen him every day, worked alongside him. But I told her I could handle that, and asked her again to be my wife. She said Nosir, not unless you leave off workin for a certain sonofabitch name of Crockett Senior, and I said, No, Sal, I can't just quit on him, and Sally said, 'You will, just wait and see.' Then she leaned over to whisper in my ear, said, 'That means "Yes, I'll marry you," case you don't know it!' "

Whidden smiled with pleasure at this memory. "So I went to Speck and I said, 'Well, Old-Timer, I aim to marry your fine daughter if you give her to me.' I was aimin to marry his fine daughter whether he give her to me or he didn't, but I never told him about that part.

"Speck Daniels was in Everglade that day, whilin away the afternoon drinkin beer in his bunk on his old boat upriver by the bridge. Looked me over for quite a while there with just one red eye, gettin his brain together. Liked a Harden better as his moonshine partner than his son-in-law, I seen that straight off. Sat up finally and finished up his beer and spat most of his chewin tobacco through that little slot into the can. Then he squints at it and says, 'This here looks like some kind of a dang twat. What's your opinion, boy?'—them was the first words from that man's mouth, hearin the news that his sweet daughter aimed to marry. Then he looks up and he says, 'Our family don't tolerate mixed people, Whidden, you know that.'

" 'What's that got to do with me?' I says.

"Speck looks me over for a minute. 'Heck if I know,' he says. Next, he says, 'You're a bad drinker, Whidden, I been watchin you. Old days now, a man that spent up all he made on spirits and weren't loyal to his family might get him a whippin. What's your views on that?'

" 'Who's gonna give me that whippin, Speck?' says I.

" 'Heck if I know,' Speck says again, and he cracks us both a beer. 'I got no say about it anyways, so you are welcome to her. Don't even know where she is livin at. Her and me been lookin crossways at the other from the first time she opened up her eyes in her layette. Weren't for me, that gal would of married her own brother, so I reckon she can't be too much worse off hitched up to you.' Rolled over then and closed his eyes, wavin me the hell out of his cabin. 'Just mind she don't go gettin you so pussy-whipped that you can't work nights, that is all I'm askin.'

"That was Speck Daniels's way of saying, Let's you 'n' me forget it, son, cause I don't give a shit."

Whidden tried to laugh at his father-in-law's low-down ways, but he didn't have his heart in it, and stopped.

"Course Sally herself ain't got it all doped out yet. But in my opinion, this grudge of hers, this refusin to forgive what was done to Hardens—well, that ain't only just her kindly nature." Whidden lifted his gaze from the night water and held Lucius's eye. "She turned her back on her own family, and not only her own family but her own kind. She blames this on their bad attitudes, but she's too honest to pretend that's all it is."

Whidden sighed. "She can't abide her daddy. Even before she got mixed up with Crockett Junior, she could not tolerate Speck Daniels, and that goes way back to the time she heard how Speck and his brother-in-law helped lynch that nigra man at Marco. Course he done that as a young feller in the Depression—"

"That made it all right?"

"No, but he's changed some. Might not do nothin such as that today." Whidden cast again, hard, with a light whipping sound. "I ain't goin to criticize Speck Daniels, Mister Colonel. I knowed all about that Marco business when I went to work for him, and it never kept me from feelin proud about my job with the number one moonshiner and gator poacher in South

Florida. I never thought too much about the right and wrong of it. Never thought much at all, and that's the truth, not till Sally come along and woke me up." He considered Lucius with a rueful gaze.

"But why does Sally—"

"The Hardens are her family now cause she ain't got one of her own, so she's bein fierce, she tries to take on all the pain our family suffered. She can't make these people say they're sorry, or apologize, though she's sure tryin—you seen her in Naples!

"In her heart, Sally wants me to be white, wants our kids to be white, not only because that is right but because our kids will have a better chance that way. But she is ashamed of wanting that so bad, cause it makes her feel disloyal some way to those old-time Hardens that were so discriminated. That's why she's so ready to scrap with folks like Andy who might still think that the Hardens were . . . mixed.

"What I'm learning is—real slow but deep—It just don't matter. *It don't matter!* There's a *lot* of families on this coast got a little color that they ain't owned up to. Well, that ain't nothin to be ashamed of! It comes from the wild nature of our Florida history. You take them Muskogee and Mikasuki Creeks, some were mixed-blood when they first come down here out of Georgia, and the early pioneers had children with 'em, and with runaway slaves, too. *In thees meex blood ees foking gee-nee-us of America!* That's what old Chevelier used to holler at my granddad. Claimed there weren't one white man on this earth who didn't have some black or brown in him, because all mankind got started out in Africa!

"You got a million drops of white, one drop of black, and you're supposed to be a nigra, accordin to that old redneck arithmetic. Well, in a century, that one drop can travel a long ways, and these local families are so much intermarried that whatever is true of one is true for all. That one little drop is just a-spreadin all the time, but it stays hid, like a molasses drop in milk. Most of the time you never notice, and then you might get a glimpse of it, one little trace, or one person that's too dark in a fair-haired family, or might be bad hair. Most likely that family never knew that it was there, so they don't even recognize it when they see it. Depends how strong your family is in your community. If you are strong enough, it just don't count. Nobody sees it.

"Our pastor and his wife was narrow-minded. They would not accept a boy from Marco that their daughter wanted because he weren't raised up Pentecostal Church of God. Weren't one thing wrong with that young devil that a bullet wouldn't cure, it was only he was runnin kind of wild. So that girl done what Abbie Harden done, she run off with a young black feller, to spite 'em. And now them poor worshipful folks got to smile until it hurts, cause that black son-in-law is just as God-lovin as they are, and not only that but a decorated American hero, a veteran of the United States Marines!" Whidden laughed quietly. "If that preacher had a second chance, he'd take and hogtie that wild Marco heathen to his daughter, never mind if they took their vows in jail. But bein a good Christian, he must stand up and be proud that she married this patriotic soldier boy from the black community, this fine upstandin young American that risked his life for freedom and democracy. They *got* to be happy about that boy—ain't that a terrible thing? They *got* to be happy! Whether they like bein happy or they don't!"

But in a moment, his jaw set again. "Yep," he said. "Miss Sally Brown is still burnt up over the old days, and she's over there at the Historical Society every year, fighting her heart out for our family name. And everyone wishes—Hardens especially—that that pretty little gal would just shut up, because all she is doing is stirring up old gossip.

"Today Hardens are doin fine all over southwest Florida, ranch homes and new pickups and fair-haired kiddies everywhere you look. They have left most of them old Baptists who looked down on 'em back in the dust. These new Hardens have forgot all that old bitterness, if they even knew about it. Wouldn't of never doubted they was white people if that darned female Cousin Whidden married didn't stir up so much sand tryin to prove it."

Whidden smiled faintly. "Got this big fight goin against herself, and they ain't no way she can win, poor little sweetheart. She wants it both ways, same as the rest of us, but can't admit to it. That's why you see her strugglin so hard."

"And that's hard on Whidden," Lucius said.

"I wanted to think we could heal things some between our families by bein together, bein who we was. Sally agreed with that idea but she don't cooperate. She's been to college, takes it real hard about race prejudice, she just despises people for despisin nigras. Sally says over and over that the color of your skin don't matter, it's your heart and mind that count. Trouble is, at the same time she is sayin skin don't matter, she is out to make them old-timers admit that the Hardens weren't mulattas, but only had some Injun in their blood. She even wants 'em to admit that Henry Short was probably Injun, to show the world that Libby Harden never run off with a colored man.

"Well, them old-timers ain't going to admit no such a thing. That generation got their idea about the old-time Hardens and they ain't goin to change it. And with the world they knew changin so fast, you can't hardly blame 'em."

"You don't blame them?"

"Aunt Libby married a brown man, Henry Short, then Aunt Abbie run off with a black one. Can you blame folks for thinking the way they do?"

"Blame," Lucius said shortly, tasting that word.

"I been talking about Sally, ain't I. But it looks like I am fightin that hook, too."

*

Lucius Watson had helped raise Roark Harden. He knew Wilson, too, since these cousins had been inseparable. Because of Earl's hostility, he had never been quite comfortable with Wilson, but had always very felt close to Roark, who was nine when they first met, and who, even as a boy, had been generous and dead honest like his father. However, Lucius was also fond of Walker Carr's son Alden, who had remained friendly throughout that period in the twenties when almost everyone except the Hardens was avoiding him.

When the Johnson boy brought word from Tavernier that Alden Carr had made a drunk confession in a bar, the Harden men had loaded up their guns. Even Earl, who took such pride in his Bay friends, was raging around about a raid on Chatham Bend. Lucius went to Lee and offered to go instead. He would talk with Alden, make sure they had the story straight before steps were taken that might get the wrong ones killed. Suspicious, Lee had studied Lucius's eyes before he nodded.

By the time Lucius turned up at the Bend, poor Alden was more frightened of his brothers than he was of Hardens, but he took responsibility for what he'd said at Tavernier and did not try to contradict that story. When Lucius confronted the others, both denied it, saying that when Alden was drunk, he sometimes made up crazy stories to get attention to himself, which, alas, was true. Then Old Man Walker, who had been listening behind the door, blew up and came bursting in, yelling at the visitor to ease his nerves. Before his boys could hush him, he hollered out that those damned Hardens had stolen five hundred dollars' worth of pelts, then threatened his boys when they went to get them back. One of their guns must have gone off, and his sons, afraid they were being shot at, had no choice but to return their fire, "not intendin to *hit* nobody! It was self-defense!" After firing that one wild volley in the dark, his boys had hurried back to their own camp. So far as they knew, the Harden boys had left Shark Point early the next morning, for their skiff was gone.

When their father started hollering, Owen and Turner slipped away, but Alden trailed Lucius to the dock. He asked whose side Lucius was on, and Lucius asked how he could take sides without knowing the truth. Alden squinted at him. "What Pa told may not be the God's truth, Lucius," Alden said coldly and carefully. "But it's our Carr truth. This year, anyways."

Lucius was already cast off when Old Man Walker roared down to the dock and cuffed poor Alden out of the way and bellowed at Watson's son across the water. "I was very old friends with your dad! You know it, too! Done my best that day to stop that crowd. So if it comes down to some kind of a showdown, Lucius, are you on your old friends' side or ain't you?" Next, he hollered, "Lucius, boy, for ten years now you been wanderin around these islands askin a whole hell of a lot of stupid questions, and it sure looks like you're doin that again! If it weren't for me tellin the men you was only a heartbroke poor damn fool that meant no harm, it's *you* who might of come up missin, boy, not no damn Hardens!" Red and sweating, Walker Carr turned his back on him and stumped away. Within a day, the Carr family was gone from Chatham River.

Lucius reported the Carrs' account in the same words it was told to him, Lee Harden asked if he believed their story, and he admitted he did not. At the same time, he reminded Lee that the Hardens had no evidence whatever, which meant they had no hope at all of seeing the Carr boys prosecuted in a court of law. And if they took the law into their own hands, they would bring a firestorm down on their clan which would destroy it.

Lee Harden thanked Lucius gruffly, saying that his family would take care of the problem in their own good time. For the moment, all Lee needed to know was what Walker Carr had effectively admitted, that his sons had fired at the Harden boys down at Shark River.

After Carr moved his family back to Everglade, a silent tension would pervade the settlement whenever the Harden men came north from Lost Man's River. No one spoke to the Hardens, not one word, as if they were trying to "hate" them out of the region, a traditional remedy in the old Border lands from where most of their clans had come.

One day Lee Harden ran into the culprits, down the street from Barron Collier's new courthouse. Though the Carr boys were frightened, they did not run because a small crowd gathered. They stood with eyes down when Harden circled them twice, three times, as if consigning some unpleasant scent to future memory. Abruptly he broke off his circling and walked away.

In later years, as the tension eased, folks started saying that those Hardens had it coming and that everything had worked out for the best. Owen when drunk would even hint behind his hand that you-know-who had put a stop to those damned mixed-breeds. And young Turner went along with it, confiding that he had fired, too—in fact, how he was probably the one (though he sure felt terrible about it) who had finally put that Roark Harden out of his misery.

*

A month after the young Hardens disappeared, Henry Short rowed his skiff down Turner River and on south through the inland bays, coming ashore and walking up the beach as Lee Harden jumped up and went to meet him. Shaking hands, kicking the sand, Henry asked if there was any way that he could help. Even Earl Harden finally agreed to let Henry go, look for the bodies, knowing that Short was the best tracker on the coast.

Henry Short knew plenty of reasons why it was a poor idea for him to go. He owed a lot to the Harden family, but he also knew how dangerous it was for him to get mixed up in this at all. "Lordy, Lordy," he kept saying, tugging on his earlobe. Lee decided it was not fair to ask him, but Henry decided that he had no choice.

At Shark Point, Henry located a rain-rotted pelt salted and stretched in the painstaking way that Henry had taught those Harden boys himself. Another camp not far away had been abandoned in a hurry. He poled upriver, checking the mangroves on both banks for any small sign of disturbance. He poked and prowled and pried and peered till he found overhanging willow branches, bent and broken, in a small hidden creek on the east side of Shark Lake. All alone, far back up in the Glades, he pushed upstream.

At the head of the creek the Harden skiff, charred by a hasty attempt at burning, lay half-sunk and half-hidden beneath hacked-off branches. Taking his shovel and a length of rope, rigging his shirt over his nose and mouth, he followed the mud smear of the gator's belly and great tail, matting the saw grass. Vultures flapped aloft as he drew closer.

The bodies lay on the open savanna, bloated so badly and so torn that he could scarcely tell which boy was which. He buried what was left of the boys' bodies. Then he said a prayer under the sun and returned to the main river. On his way north, anticipating what Lee Harden would do, and fearing the certain retribution which any such action would bring down upon the Hardens—and knowing, finally, how often black men had been put to death for the mere witnessing of evil acts they had no part in—he decided that no good could come from telling the Harden clan what he had found.

Arriving at Lost Man's after dark, Henry stopped at Lucius Watson's cabin. Asked about that second camp he had located at Shark Point, he would only say that three trappers had used that place and that they had broken their camp in a hurry, and that their prints were also present in the Harden Camp. He did not identify the Carrs by name. Lucius agreed with Henry's instinct not to tell what he had found, because that would leave the Hardens with no choice but to load their guns and take the law into their own hands.

Keeping their secret from this family which had been so good to both of them became one of their uncommon bonds. By the time Alden Carr blurted out the truth a few years later, Earl had renewed his Chokoloskee friendships and his invitation to maintain them. Even Lee resigned himself to the fact that there was no way to avenge his son and nephew without inviting the annihilation of the Harden clan.

Chapter 10

At Lost Man's Key

Toward sundown an ancient cabin boat came down the river. Though the estuary tide was low, she made her way at near full speed, her wash carving the oyster bars as she circled up into the current with a grumpy gurgling. With her engine cut, her bow coasted ashore on the sand point with a hard crunching scrape.

A loud hoarse voice hailed the men around the fire. "You fellers seen any fish around this river that might like a ride in this old boat?"

"Oh Lord." Sally rose and moved away toward the point.

"Heck, I know that feller," Andy said, surprised. Whidden was yelling, "Well now, old-timer, are you lost or what? Maybe your eyesight ain't so good no more. This here's Miami!"

"That a fact?" The boatman heaved out a stern anchor—*ker-plunk*—then put his hands upon his hips, looking around him with proprietary satisfaction at the evening river. "Well, if I am lost, which ain't too likely, I found the right place to be lost in, looks like to me!"

"Well, come ashore, then! Got good fish to eat!"

The boatman kicked old sneakers off and rolled up baggy coveralls on scrawny legs, which contrasted oddly with the thick brown arms matted with hair. "Sure it's safe for a old feller over there? Don't that ol' scow belong to one them Hardens? What you damn fellers doin this far south? You fixin to run some of that marijuana dope?" He sat on the gunwale and swung over, lowering himself carefully into the water. "Be in over my diddley here before I know it. Don't want to hurt my pride and joy, y'know." He sloshed ashore, handing Harden his bow line, and pointed at a driftwood tree worn silver by coast weather. "Case you boys don't know it, that snag is private property. There'd be hell to pay if I was to find your line hitched onto it!"

Under stained brown galluses, Speck Daniels wore a long-sleeved undershirt of soiled white cotton. On his head was a broken Panama with a tropical green feather that Lucius supposed had been scavenged from a parrot until he saw that it was painted on. Daniels gave Lucius a cold nod and shook hands with Whidden without looking either in the eye, but a grin split his face as he went to Andy House, who was grinning, too. "That you, Speck?" he called. "You making all that noise all by yourself?" And Speck yelled back, "God struck you so damn blind you don't know who the hell I am no more? Well, that is *pitiful*!"

Andy, who had gotten to his feet, was tapping his sunburned nose. "Don't need no eyes! I'd know you anywhere! Lord A-mighty, Speck! I sure would hate to smell as bad as you!" Laughing outright, he hung on to Speck's hand with both his own.

"Well, for an older feller, I still smell pretty sweet, I reckon!" Speck took a long pleased sniff under his own arm.

"I want to talk with you," Lucius said in a cold voice.

Daniels hawked and spat but otherwise ignored him. "Know somethin, boys? The goddamn Park is tryin to run me off of my own territory! Damn helio-copter come racketin down on me this mornin—first helio-copter I ever seen over the Park! Told me I got to have a permit to come on this here public property! Never thought they'd pick on a poor taxpayer just livin his life away back in the rivers.

"Then it come to me! Parks don't *have* no helio-copter! This damn thing was military, what my boys call a gunship. Had some kind of a Marine officer settin up there alongside of the pilot, ribbons all acrost his heart, looked just like eagle shit, and two Parks greenhorns settin in the back. This officer tosses me this stupid-ass salute, two fingers to the brow, y'know, and I says to myself, Don't you know this fancy skunk from some damn place? I says, Speck boy, it's goin to come to you, just in a minute, soon's this sonofabitch opens his mouth. Well, maybe he figured out my thinkin, cause he never spoke! Turned away while them greenhorns searched my boat, like he had more important stuff to think about than old swamp riffraff.

"Naturally, they come up empty-handed, so they got ugly with me. Wanted to know what I was doin in the Park. I told 'em I was out here in the great outdoors enjoyin our great American damn Park on the advice of my personal physician: 'You're dead within the year, Speck Daniels, lest you don't stop drinkin'! Better go back out in the swamp if that's what it's gone to take to make you quit! 'Well, men'—this is still me talkin to 'em—'Well, men, that is exactly what I'm doin! Follerin Doc's orders! Cause if I go back to humankind, I get just a terrible ringin in my ears, and I got to drink up every last drop I can find, just to drown it out!'

"Well, they wasn't used to smooth talk such as that, not from a swamp rat, it was pretty plain they was startin to come around to my way of thinkin. All but one, dang foreign-lookin cuss, might could been some kind of a dang Jew from New York City. This Jew says, 'See here, old feller, what's all these orchids and damn ligs doin in your boat?'" Speck fished a striped tree snail from his pocket. "*Liguus*—sounds dirty, don't it? That's what my customers call this purty thing, don't ask me why. So anyways, he's hollerin, 'Don't you know them ligs is federal property, old feller, property of the American darn people? Ain't never heard how them darn things is gettin more rare by the minute, just on account of darn rascals like you?!'

" 'Nosir,' says I, 'I never knew no such a thing! Why, hellamighty, if I'da knowed ligs was so scarce, I'd of searched them hammocks top to bottom, stole every Christly one I could lay my hands on, make me some *money*!' Well, none of 'em thought that was so comical, so I frowned at 'em, real serious. 'Nosir,' says I, 'What I am doing is observin lig *behavior*!' Didn't want 'em to think they was dealin with some dumb cracker. And what they was messin with, I told 'em, was a famous lig o-thority, and a leadin orchid fancier to boot!

" 'Nosir,' this Parks greenhorn says, 'what you are is a liar, cause ligs ain't *got* no dang behavior! Ligs just sets there mindin their own business! What *you* are is a scallywag by the name of Daniels!' Called me a scallywag! Dirtiest name that you could call a man, back in my granddad's time! I told that Jew I aimed to take him into court, jail him for slander, but it didn't do no good. They stole my ligs, they stole ever' damn orchid, and after that, they run me off with a last warnin. Didn't care to look foolish draggin a crippled-up old alky into court, is what it was. Ligs and orchids ain't the same as guns or gator flats, not when you aim to persecute in court. Them greenhorn sonsabitches seen right off that Old Man Speck had given 'em the slip! Done it again!"

Speck's humor was cruel and his style mock stupid, and the laughter he elicited would always be uneasy. The man's mood veered swiftly even while his closed face remained deadpan, that green stare flicking from one person to the next, showing neither warmth nor interest, missing nothing. "I'd help a few snook escape out of this Park, if I could find some. Sell 'em to the restaurants, y'know. They can't catch a fisherman that can't catch fish, now can they?

"Helio-copters!" he suddenly burst out, slamming his hat down on the sand. "Until today them rangers in this Park knew Speck Daniels by name only. Ain't hardly ever seen my face. I come and go. Don't roil the mud nor break no twigs, don't leave no more track than a ol' wood mouse. That's the way I learned the trade from Joe Lopez and Old Man Tant, and I trained up Crockett Junior that same way. Course, it don't look like he'll need it, not the way he's goin. Junior is lookin to get killed, and he'll take them others with him, more'n likely." Speck was matter-of-fact. He squinted bitterly at Whidden. "Course I trained up this Harden feller, too, only he quit on me—the one man with sense enough to keep them shell-shocked morons from bustin out their guns where another man would run or look for cover."

*

"One time a feller from St. Augustine, had him a zoo, he paid me to hunt him up some crocs. Sure enough, he shows up at my house at Flamingo—'Got muh crocodiles?' I says, 'Sure thing, got sixteen right out back.' Only thing, all he had out front was a pink Cadillac. 'What in the hell you aim to *haul* 'em in?' I says. 'Muh crocodile car! That's her you're lookin at!' 'Why hell,' I says, 'I got me a croc back here that goes twelve feet! Fill that whole limmo-zeen!' '*Twelve feet?*' he hollers. 'I want that 'un *now*!'

"So we jump on that croc and rassle him around, roll him up into a ball, get him humped some way into the trunk, and that ol' tail whacked that Cadillac a lick that rung out like a dang mule in a tin stall. I fling the smaller ones in the backseat, they hit that velveteen just a-snappin and a-crappin, and this croc fancier don't mind one little bit. Takes off for St. Augustine bumpin the ground with the load of crocs he's got in there, left a big ol' ugly cloud of smoke right in my yard!

"Next time he showed up, he bought him a hen crocodile. Had a big hump on her shoulders, big as a coconut. Said, 'That 'un don't look so good, my friend, I'll give you ten down and twenty-five on top if she goes two weeks.' So he sent a letter with no money in it, notified me she had upped and died. Well, the next year I was passin through St. Augustine, dropped in to see him, and there she was, my humped-up crocodile! Star of the show!

"So I says, 'My, my, that sure is a purty little hen you got in there!' " Speck nodded a little at this memory. "Well, you fellers know somethin? Darn it all if I ain't went and hurt his feelins! Cause he hollers out, 'No, no, no, *no*! That ain't your purty little hen! Ain't her *at all*!" Speck nodded more. "That's the way we left it, cause she didn't have no pedigree nor nothin." He shook his head over life's vicissitudes. "That feller had him a good head for the croc business, is what it was. That's how you get you one of them big Cadillacs, I reckon."

Watching the others laugh, Speck remained somber. "If crocs was rocks, Christ could of walked acrost the water on some of them coastal bays east of Flamingo. I guess I could still find a few crocs in the Park, but I'd have to hunt for 'em. Today any crocodile you show me in the Park, I'll take you outside and show you five." He spat into the flames. "I told them so-called scientists, 'You're worried about them crocodiles but you're the ones to blame, cause you went down there and went messin with the nest. It's just like birds, you keep messin with the nest, they're goin to leave it. You went there and caught them crocs, put beepers on 'em, electrical fuckin apparatus to where you can hear 'em fart two miles away. It's like a horse, you tie a kerchief to his tail, he'll run hisself to death trying to get rid of it. Can't find no crocs to hang beepers on no more, but you still got the guts to wonder what become of 'em!' "

Back in the forties, a man could see crocs from his car window on the Key West Highway, Whidden commented, poking the fire. When Andy teased him—"Probably gators!"—Whidden laughed, saying crocs weren't all that hard to tell from gators. Their range was coastal, and most were a green-gray color that was rarely encountered in a gator, even those that wandered down around salt water. True, the few crocs that turned up on the mangrove coasts north of Cape Sable were mostly the same black-brown color as the gators, so one had to look for the narrow snout and the big teeth protruding from both mandibles.

"Pertrudin from both manderbles, you said?" Speck's jeering was a reminder to his son-in-law that there was a real croc expert in this outfit who did not need these half-ass interruptions. "I might not know much about manderbles," Speck said, "but I do know that to see a croc today, you got to organize a damn safari, and even then, you got to night-light 'em, and even then, all you might get is a puff of mud or a little far-off ripple out acrost the water. Them big old crocs are few and far between, and they ain't the only critters that are disappearin. Look at your sawfish, sea turtle, your mana-tees! Them big kind of wild critters was dirt common all around these rivers in our daddies' time! And plume birds—egrets! Since the Park took over and messed up the water, they are more few and far between than what they was back when they had the shit shot out of 'em by every cracker in south Florida! It's like I told Parks, If you go on like this, you'll have a big dead country on your hands, dead, dead, dead!—just dirty water and dry mud, and nothin stirrin in the saw grass and the mangrove, only wind.

"Us fellers finally give up on the poor fishin, give up on tryin to make a livin obeyin all them laws put through by them outsiders. Them fools love the heck out of Mother Nature, but they don't know nothin about the backcountry, and never give a hoot in hell whether us damn natives lived nor died.

"We felt real bad when we had no choice but to go back gator-huntin, cause it's gators that digs the water holes that sees the fish and birds and snakes and turtles through the dry season. Trouble was, with the terrible drought brought down on 'em by all that drainin, even them scaly dinosaur damn things was startin to die out, so they shut down our markets for the hides. So us poor raggedy-ass home fellers, we had to go back to the midnight export business, same as our daddies and granddaddies done, bird plumes and liquor. Today it's mostly ordnance, munitions, tomorrow it might be marijuana dope—hell, it don't matter. The law can't catch us back amongst these mangroves and it never could."

Moving sideways into the sea grape to relieve himself, Speck kept an eye on them, not in modesty but because in his swamp nature, with its wariness of a concealed presence, or anything approaching from behind, he would never be caught unaware out in the open.

Andy whispered, "Know something, Colonel?" He had intuited Lucius's torn mood. "I *do* like that ornery sonofagun, I just can't help it! I got to like just about anybody these days who cheers me up! But I never took him for a good man, cause he ain't."

"Speck's some talker, all right." Concerned about Sally, Harden peered off down the beach. "Enjoys hell out of his own stories, so everybody else gets a kick out of 'em, too. And he don't hide his thinkin, he tells it to you straight, least when he ain't lyin."

"Straight and dirty," Andy House agreed.

Daniels came out of the bushes yanking his zipper. Jerking a thumb in Whidden's direction, he bent to speak into Andy's ear, lowering his voice to a loud hoarse whisper. "One of them damn Hardens, now—and I ain't sayin which one, case he feels shy about it—we made him some big money before he quit, but he won't settle up the $700 he still owes me for nothin in the world but gas and groceries!" Daniels raised his eyebrows in disbelief, peering from one face to the next for a clue to such perfidious behavior. "Last time I seen him, he told me, 'Speck, you'll get that money, don't you worry!' " Here he paused to give Whidden a deadly smile. "And I told him, 'Boy, I might *look* like a spring chicken, but I ain't gettin no younger and I want what I got comin!' Know what this young Harden says to a poor old man? Says, 'Speck, if you kick the fuckin bucket fore you get your money, you won't have a worry in the world, and I won't neither!' "

Andy said, "Your language ain't improved, I see."

"Weren't *my* language! That was *Whidden* talkin!"

"There's a young lady down the beach, is all."

Daniels lurched drunkenly around to stare off down the shore. Blinking to adjust his sight, he took his hat off and wiped his mouth roughly with the back of his hand. Sally had her back to him, and when she bent over from the waist, picking up seashells on the sandy point, Speck shaded his eyes against the sinking sun, the better to appraise the finer points of her hindquarters. When she straightened, he turned back to the men, visibly moved. "Well, she's a lovable little thing, I can see that." He hitched at the crotch of his disconsolate old pants. "I sure hope I don't steal her off you fellers."

"I hope so, too, cause that is your own daughter."

"Good God A-mighty, Whidden! I forgot!" In prayer, Speck put his hand over his eyes. "Ain't life a pity? I mean, what is the world comin to when a man is begrudged a piece of his own daughter?" He watched Whidden's grin as it twisted off his face.

"That ain't no way to joke!" Andy protested.

"Ain't no way to joke?" Speck studied the blind man like a specimen, nodding his head over and over. In a cold flat voice he said, "I believe you was jokin some just now about my smell. You recollect that day over to Miami when I come into your gas station and you done the same? Well, next time I come to town, I dropped by to say I had a bath and lived to tell the tale! What do I find? A whole swarm of Cuban Spanish—loud radios, babies, big-fin cars, the whole fiesta! So I says to 'em, 'Now what in the name of Jesu Cristo have you spicks gone and done with Andy House?' And one of 'em shows his teeth in a gold smile and lays his thievin fingers crost his eyes like the blind monkey. And he says, '*Finito!* See Seen-yore! Seen-yore Andy ees *finito!*' "

Speck nodded some more, undaunted by Andy's wide blue gaze. " 'See Seen-yore.' Them Cubanos told me all about you. So what you got to say about it? You *finito?* Struck blind for your sins by your First Florida Baptist God—I bet that's what your nice little missus decided! Probably decided you was spendin too much time layin on top of her—"

Andy grunted as if his wind had been knocked out. His big face looked slapped red. "Ol' Speck," he said, tasting that name. "You sure don't change much." He drew closer to the fire.

Daniels drew his flask out of his coveralls and helped himself to a hard snort before passing it around. Nobody took it. "Since when?" he challenged Lucius. "Since Gator Hook? Ain't gone to drink with a man that's on your list?" He took a few turns like a dog before settling slowly. Raising the flask, he toasted them all in an ironic sweep, and when he lowered it, he fastened on Whidden Harden, seeking a purchase. "That li'l Sally is a tough customer and then some," he began. "Too tough for *me*. And she got you pussy-whipped, just like I warned you. Otherwise, you'd be back workin for me.

Workin out what you still owe me," he added quickly, lest Whidden imagine he was wanted on his own merits, or that Speck Daniels might excuse old debts just because he was his son-in-law.

Whidden said, "You'll get your money. Comes in slower in the landscape business. Slow but sure."

"Landscape business," Daniels said, disgusted. "Whole fuckin state of Florida is in the landscape business."

He gazed balefully at his own flask, turned it in his hand. When he spoke again, he tried halfheartedly to patch their mood. "Speakin about tough customers and pussy puts me in mind of one of Andy's cousins. Tried that stuff myself one time, didn't get nowhere! As Mud Braman's daddy used to say, 'That darn ol' critter, she's so tight, her pussy gets to squeakin when she walks!' "

"Speck?"

"Told me he *heard* it! Sound just like a mouse!"

"Speck? We all know you don't mean no harm, but don't go givin my cousin a bad name!"

"Well, she would of give *me* a bad name, Andy, and I didn't need it. I already had one!"

"Still takin care of the ladies pretty good, I see," Whidden said, to smooth things.

"Ain't been no complaints, not lately." Conspiratorial, Speck spoke from behind his hand. "Don't know too much about *ladies*, now, but I had me a certified piece of ass, I don't believe it was more than maybe four-five years ago. Ol' Diddley here stuck to my leg like a wet leaf for two weeks after, that's how whipped he was." Cocking his head, Speck scanned their faces avidly for signs of outrage. "Schoolteacher, y'know. *Skinny* damn thing! I was pickin the bones out of my prick all winter!"

*

Speck accepted a tin plate of food and poked at it suspiciously with his tin fork, then brought it up close under his nose, green eyes watching them over the plate.

"Our kind of people likes good fish to eat, ain't that right, Andy? Won't eat shark nor manatee, and ain't all of 'em will eat a sea turtle. Won't eat conch neither—call that nigger food. Course over to Key West and the Bahamas, they eat conch and glad to get it. That's how come we call 'em Conchs, I reckon."

He sniffed his plate again, then shrugged and started eating, but his eyes kept moving and he ate quickly, tossing scraps and spitting bones over his shoulder. Once again his mood was changing for he ate and talked ever faster and more angrily, eyes snapping, mouth opening and closing on white food, pausing only for a gasp of moonshine. "Hell, there's more fish on this plate than I seen all week. In this damned sorry day and age, a man can't hardly get enough to feed his cat. Never seen fishin poor as this since the Red Tide. Them fish is fed up with the Park, the same as I am.

"What's happenin to our local fishery is just a crime, and it's bein committed in broad open daylight! You know why? Because the law's behind it. Some of us fellers might be moonshiners today, and poachers and gunrunners, too—how come? We started out to be hunters and fishermen like our daddies, ain't that right?

"Fifty years ago when Robert Harden first come to Lost Man's River, sea trout and snook and mullet was so thick a man could dance on 'em, it was a pure astonishment to the heart and eye. The fishin was somethin wonderful, and the trappin and huntin, too. But now the wilderness is bein hammered and the wildlife with it, and before them people are done messin with our water, the fish all around this coast will be gone, too!"

He set down his plate to roll a cigarette. He inhaled raggedly, blew it out, gauging their expressions through the smoke, coughing, nearly out of breath, yet talking rapidly, gathering intensity and rage as he went along.

SPECK DANIELS

Before Parks come in, a man might land a half million pounds of fish each year along this coast. Today he would be doin good to land one tenth of that amount, and tomorrow is going to be worse. Because Parks is diggin all them ditches and canals, lettin the fresh water out and the salt water in, and they will end up ruinin the spawnin grounds of one of the great fisheries of the whole world! And they are doin that to drain the land east of the boundaries for the big farmers, same as Flood Control already done north of the Park. They are destroyin the rightful property of the common people. Give 'em two dollars an acre, take it or don't, for a century's worth of clearin and improvement. Parks burnt their fish houses, hundred-foot dock and all—that hurt, you know, to see all that hard work wasted.

I never knew the U.S. Gov'ment would tell us barefaced lies like that, did you? If them damn bureaucrats and politicians can get away with it, they'll steal you blind. Two-faced lyin bastards, right up to the president, tell the stupid-ass damn public any ol' fool thing that might keep their asses covered till the next election! Here I grew up thinkin—wasn't we taught this back in school?—that the U.S.A. was the greatest country in the world! It purely *hurts* me to speak bad about my country! But the truth's the truth, at least it used to be.

Hell, boys, I ain't *talkin* to my country, not no more! A man can't trust a single word that ain't writ down in black and white, signed, sealed, and hand-delivered, and even then it don't mean diddley-shit. If you ain't some kind of a big corporation that helps to grease their skids, get 'em elected, they'll weasel around and break their promises, they'll screw you every time. I finally realized how them Injuns must of felt about all them broken treaties, bein lied to and stole off of and cheated for two hundred years! Well, you know somethin? All us old-time pioneers are disappearin down that Injun road!

Weren't that the way you was brought up? To trust the Gov'ment? Hel-lamighty, they ain't done *nothin* for us common people, not around the Glades! Too busy throwin the taxpayers' money at developers and farm corporations like United Sugar that wanted Okeechobee diked and the Glades drained and the Kissimmee River funneled away through concrete sewage pipes so's rich men can get richer every day growin cane and citrus on the public land. Same way all over the damn country! Well, some of us don't aim to sit and take it!

Since Parks come in, they been playin right along with Flood Control and the growers and developers that's behind it. That good water overflowin Okeechobee don't come south no more, and this part of the Glades here in the Park is starved for water. Pretty soon all this wild country over here will be layin dead under the sun, no more use than a old gator carcass with the flat stripped off the belly and guts fallin out. Might still look like a live gator from a little ways off, till the stink hits you, and you hear the flies. Well, this wild Florida that was our home country and got took away from us is goin to wind up as dead and stinkin as that gator! Might look like Florida to tourists drivin past, but they better not stop or look too close!

Man like me never got much education, never needed it. Never knowed no other way than huntin and fishin, usin a boat. We done that all the year around. Then the Big Cypress and the north Glades started dyin, to where they ain't hardly nothin left to hunt. Don't see no game from one year to the next! Finally we said to hell with it and went over to huntin in the Park. Got to take what's left before the gator holes dry up and the last life dies away for want of water.

Goin to sleep nights, starin straight up at the stars, I pine away for the Glades the way they was. I know in my mind it would all come back if them sonsabitches would just leave this place alone. You take that bad storm last September—that one them lyin bastards claimed done so much damage to the Watson Place! Come in after midnight, hit Florida Bay, lashin along at 150 miles an hour, pulled all the water off them flats, mile after mile, dead dry as far out as the eye could see. When them seas come back, they was fourteen foot above mean high water! Struck Flamingo at daybreak and broke most of the trees, all the way up and down that low flat coast, carried milky marl inland ten miles, all the way to the Nine-Mile Bend! Left long drift lines of dead fish and birds when the tide went out again—miles and miles of dead-lookin gray swamp and not so much as a buzzard in the sky. That country laid there so still and ghosty that any stranger comin through, he'd say, It's finished. This Glades country is deader'n a dead man's dick.

Well, the greenery and the birds, too, is startin to come back, and it ain't a year yet! Had to learn all over again what our granddaddies been tellin us since Nap Broward started messin with the Glades when we was boys. This big ol' swamp got nothin in the world to fear from hurricanes, not in the long run. Only thing it got to fear is two-legged idiots screwin with the water, and doin it legal with the help of politician-lawyers. Destroy the whole damn Everglades for profit, then turn around and call a man a criminal who is huntin gators in his own home country, same as his daddy and granddaddy done before him! That seem right to you? You call that justice?

Them corporations and the lawyers and the politicians on their payroll—the bigger they are, the more the Gov'ment rigs the laws for 'em so they don't pay taxes! Grab the whole pot for theirselves! Big Sugar and them others, hell, they're already so fat they don't know what to do with all their profits, but even so they will still move in on every square mile of the Glades they can lay their hands on! Same thing everywhere! Call themselves "big businessmen"—fuckin stupid hogs is all they are! Never raise their snouts out of the trough for long enough to see what their hoggishness is doin to our great country!

Know how they get away with it? They get away with it because they own the government, state government and federal both. Them so-called elected people, they're just overhead! Now what the hell kind of a democracy is that? All them bought-and-paid-for politicians ever done was sell the people out, then holler about progress and democracy and wave the American flag over their dirty dealins! Get us into their damn wars so they can make more money for the arms industries and oil and chemicals that paid to get these chickenshits elected!

Them businessmen and their lawyer-politicians who work our federal government like some old whore—*them* kind are the real criminals in this country! If we go to talkin about betrayin America, them powerful sons-abitches at the top are the worst traitors in the whole history of the U.S.A.!

That whole gang deserves to be took out and shot, or at least have their ears cut off so's the common man could see 'em comin!

You know who pays for all them profits with their lives? Same ones that always pays—the little fellers! All us pathetical damn fools that don't know how to do nothin about it! Fools like Crockett Junior Daniels who are dumb enough to sign right up to go and fight their wars for 'em! Go get their heads blowed off or arms blowed off for a tin medal, while these fat boys stay home livin high off of the hog!

Before Junior went overseas, he'd talk real serious about fightin for freedom and democracy. Frown a little, y'know, squint off into the future like he seen in the movies, let on kind of quiet and modest how he aimed to serve his country. And I said, "No, boy, that ain't what you are doin, cause this *ain't* your country! It's *their* damn country, right up to the White House! Them greedy sonsabitches owns it *all!*"

*

Panting for his breath like a thirsty dog, Daniels glared about him, fire-eyed with drink. His weathered face was dark with blood to the point of stroke, and no one spoke as he wound himself down, snarling and muttering. All were astonished by the passion in this man who had never been suspected of unselfish feelings or even the smallest deference to the common good.

Speck glared into the fire while he wiped his mouth and otherwise composed himself, too unraveled to focus. When he spoke again, his tone was low and bitter, and his green-eyed head hunched down between his shoulders like the head of a swamp panther, sinking all but imperceptibly into the undergrowth. "I'm still fightin 'em and always will." Speck's voice was hoarse. "I always stood up to their law—home law, school law, church law, state and federal. I only got the one life, same as you, and I never liked nobody tellin me what I must do with it, specially when ever'thin they're tellin is plain lies and bullshit."

Speck Daniels looked them over, as if daring them to dispute what he had said. When they awaited him, respecting his strong feelings, his dark aggrieved expression gave way to sly amusement. He winked at them conspiratorially, as if all his grief and fury over the ruination of the Everglades and the despoliation of America and even the maiming of his son had been no more than cynical performance.

Hearing him laugh—more like a bark—the blind man burst out, "Goddammit to hell!" and Harden growled and turned away, disgusted. Lucius watched coldly as the gator poacher, to burlesque things further, attacked his food with loud and sloppy chewing. Peering gleefully from beneath his heavy brows, he ate ferociously, and because he was grinning, pieces of fish protruded and fell from both sides of his mouth. In inspired perversity—to spite his listeners, making their awe of his populist eloquence seem idiotic—the man was mocking them. Yet even his mockery was ambiguous, since plainly he believed what he had said, and was only jeering at it—and at himself, and at them, too—because he saw sincerity, even his own, as foolish weakness.

Belching, Speck picked his teeth with a fish spine, in no hurry. Tossing the bone away, he spoke again, so softly now that he was almost whispering. "Old feller asts me the other day, says, 'Speck? Don't you pine for our old life? Don't you wish them days was back the way they was?' And I told him, 'Yessir, Lee Roy, I sure do.' Said, 'If I had my life to do again, I would live it right here where I'm at, live off this land same way I always done, huntin and fishin, and lawbreakin, too.' I told him, 'Lee Roy, I ain't *never* goin to be drove out! Goin to live off this Glades country till I die! U.S. Gov'ment wants to run me out, they'll have to come in after me, and they better come in shootin, cause I aim to be.'"

*

"Runnin guns to the Spanish countries, now that is a good business," Speck said cheerfully when nobody else spoke. "Course some say it's a cryin shame to haul that ordnance so far south and come back with a empty hold. Might's well find you a return cargo, might's well haul some of that marijuana weed and make you a nice livin. First feller who done that, over to the Keys, the other men looked down on him somethin terrible, but now there's more of 'em startin up into that trade, so I been thinkin it couldn't be too bad. And we got us a smuggler's damn paradise here in the Islands, least for the ones like Whidden here that knows these shaller waters."

He eyed Whidden, still picking his teeth. "What you think about you 'n' me runnin some of them drugs? Want to try it? I'm studyin up a little bit about this dope business, cause ten years from now, there ain't goin to be a fishin family on this coast that don't have men in it. Young fellers has to support their families, ain't that right?" When Whidden said nothing, Speck sucked the last fish bits from his teeth and spat into the fire. He drank from his flask while his eyes searched anew, and this time his gaze came to rest, with shining hard malevolence, on Lucius Watson.

"I reckon you knowed Colonel from the old days," Harden said warily, trying to head him off.

"Knowed him all my life," Speck said in a voice as hard as gravel. "He is the feller I am here to see." He nodded. "Still diggin up your poor dead daddy, Lucius? What you want with him?" Speck gnawed off a chaw of bread and masticated with his mouth open, awaiting him.

"I want the truth, I guess."

"You want the truth. Where you aim to find it at?" He pointed his fork at Andy, then Whidden, and finally at his own chest. "He'll tell you his truth, he'll tell his, I'll give you another. Which one you aim to settle for and make your peace with?"

Daniels switched the fork toward Lucius's eyes. "Maybe nobody don't *want* this truth, ever think of that? Maybe your daddy weren't so bad the way he was." Putting his hands behind his head, he lay back on the sand, one leg cocked across the other knee, old sneaker swinging. "What I'm saying, Lucius, you'd be very smart to let sleepin dogs lie—*well*, now!" Speck sat up again as his daughter approached the fire. He adjusted the small hat with the painted feather as if sartorial precision might tend to sober him a little. "Evenin, Sally! You remember me?"

Sally said shortly, "Yes, sir, I sure do."

Her father had actually heaved himself onto his knees, but seeing her hostile expression, he gave up the struggle to be courtly and sank back down beside the fire. In doing so, he tipped over his flask. Cursing, he brushed sand off its mouth, nodding in Sally's direction as if his daughter could be depended on to bring him this bad luck. "Baby daughter," he said. "Ain't she sweet? Got herself hitched to this young Harden that was borned right here on Lost Man's Key. At that time, I was settin net around Shark River, so I been acquainted with my son-in-law all his whole life."

He contemplated Whidden with a curious mix of indulgence and malevolence. "Us fishermen was always friendly with you Hardens. Went huntin with you, ate at your table, never thought a thing about it. Only time there was hard feelins was one night when you made Nigger Short set down at your table, eat his food with us. Give that boy the wrong idea"—and here he shifted, leaning on one hand to observe Lucius—"cause next thing we knew, he killed this feller's daddy."

Harden said flatly, "It weren't Short who killed his daddy. Anyway, you wasn't never at our table. You just heard about it."

"And anyway," Sally Brown added, "Mr. Henry Short was *not* a 'nigger.' "

"*Mr.* Henry Short?" Speck glanced incredulously at Andy House, who was not quite smiling. "*Mr.* Henry? Weren't a nigger?" He grinned at each of them, hunting the joke, and finding none, he cackled anyway. "All right by me." He scratched his ear. "Never too late to learn, I guess! One time Mr. Robert Harden was lettin' on to Mr. Henry Short how Hardens was Choctaw Injuns at heart—"

"Speck?"

"—and Henry says . . ." Daniels thought better of this. "To hell with it," he said, setting his painted hat upon his head. "One thing I *do* know, ol' Desperader Watson took some killin. Old Man Gene Roberts, now, he was close with Watson, and pretty friendly with the House boys in that crowd that lynched him—"

"One of those House boys was my daddy," Andy said. "And they didn't lynch nobody, and you know that, too, because you was right there with 'em."

"Well, now, let's see." Speck squinched his nose like a cat straightening its whiskers. "I never had no bones to pick with Nigger Henry—*Mr.* Henry. I recollect we used to speak about Black Henry, so's not to confuse him with Henry Smith and Henry Thompson. Used to chuckle because both of them White Henrys had hides that was somewhat darker than Black Henry!" Speck Daniels cackled. "I do know Mr. Henry moved south for a good while after Colonel come skulkin back here to the Islands. He was scared to death of Colonel for some nigger reason. Lived on False Cape Sable and up Northwest Cape, some little lakes way back in there that us old-timers call Henry Short Lakes yet today.

"That country back over by Whitewater Bay is sparse and lonesome, so he must been afeared someone was after him, likely this same Watson we got settin here this evenin. Mr. Henry fished and hunted, took care of his own needs—very good hunter and tracker, got to give Mr. Black Henry his due. Dug him a sand well for his water—ever try that? Put a barrel in a sand pit with the bottom knocked out and small holes drilled into the sides? Get brackish water?"

Not interested in their response, Speck lay back again with his hands behind his head, watching the night fill to the brim with stars and wind. "Some used to say Mr. Henry Short was huntin the gold that Ponce de León hid on Northwest Cape. Don't know why ol' Ponce would hike way out across them salt flats and clear on over to Henry Short Lakes, do you? Prob'ly said to himself, Now darn it, Ponce, it stands to reason that the Fountain of Youth is right next to them Henry Short Lakes over yonder!"

Speck Daniels's chest heaved in waves of drunken mirth which he did not care if the others shared or not. "Ol' Ponce!" he exploded. "Probably lookin for that fountain cause his pecker weren't so perky. Let him down too many times when he was out rapin Calusa princesses and such. Likely that's what Ponce was up to when them redskins come along and put a stop to that greaser sonofabitch once and for all."

"Speck? You got your daughter settin here."

"That's why he talks that way," she said.

"When Short was livin at the Fountain of Youth, he never come around the Cape far as Flamingo. Went back north when he went anywhere." Speck winked at Sally. "*Mr.* Henry Short, we're talkin about here."

"Sadie Harden told me that Henry did not banish himself because he was afraid," Sally told Lucius. "He needed solitude because he was recovering from a broken heart."

"Broken heart?" her father marveled, as if this affliction had been heretofore unheard of among black men. "Mr. Henry Short?"

Lucius demanded, "What makes you so damn sure that Short killed E. J. Watson?"

"Common knowledge. *Got* to be common, if I got it." Speck laughed some more.

"It might be common," Sally said, "but it's not the truth."

"No?" Speck Daniels measured her a long hard moment. "If I was you, Miss, I'd speak more respectful to your own blood daddy."

"Your dad witnessed it, Sally," Andy cautioned her.

"That never made him tell the truth before."

Speck lay back again, ignoring her. "I seen this famous female on a TV show on the Wild West, and they claimed she was killed by a Florida desperader by the name of Watson. Clamanity Jane or some such of a name— called her Clam for short, wouldn't surprise me." He winked dirtily at Whidden. "When Mr. Nigger Short killed Mr. Desperader Watson, they found Clam's name wrote down in Watson's diary. Seems like there was fifty-five names in there, one for every last soul that he sent howlin to perdition."

"It's *Calamity*," Sally informed her father. "Anyway, you're thinking of Belle Starr."

Lucius said, "My sister kept a diary because our father did, and he showed her what his journal looked like. She described it as a rawhide leather book with a small clasp lock and a title burned onto the cover. *Footnotes to My Life.* I don't recall seeing that journal, but it seems unlikely that she made that up."

Whidden said, "Mister Colonel? My ma seen that same journal once. Leather book with them same words burned on the cover. Said when he was drinkin, your daddy liked to tease. Claimed he'd took a life for each year of his own. And he called them deaths the footnotes to his life."

"Fifty-five human beings? Does that make sense to you, goddammit, Whidden? I mean, why would the Hardens remain friendly with a maniac who had killed fifty-five people!" Lucius rose abruptly and went off down the beach in an effort to control an immense frustration. "And that ain't countin niggers!" Speck called gleefully.

Lucius turned around to find Speck grinning at him. "Now let's don't tell him that I said so, but this Watson we are lookin at right here this minute ain't but the shadder of his daddy. Course it's possible"—Speck held his eye—"that Colonel Watson would do you hurt if you pushed him hard enough. Leastways that's what he wanted us to think, back when he was makin up his list. But I believe this feller is weakhearted. Just wants to live along, get on with ever'body." He paused again, then added meanly, "Wants to keep lookin for his Lucius truth and just make goddamn sure he never finds it."

Lucius stood transfixed at the edge of firelight. He could not seem to think, far less move away or return into the circle.

"One time a feller was tellin me how Mr. Watson took his boy to the red-light district in Key West, this was in the last years of Watson's life. Lucius must been twenty years of age, but this was the first female he ever fooled with, and damn if he don't get a good dose of the clap the first time out! Now I heard plenty said about Lucius Watson, but nobody never said he was a lucky feller."

Sally muttered something and her father turned on her. "Excuse me, Miss? You sayin, Miss, that *Mister* Colonel is not a man that would catch a dose of gonorrhea? Well, I might not know so much as you about gonorrhea, Miss, but he sure had the clap. What them Navy boys down to Key West call 'a chancre on your anchor,' ever hear that one, Miss? While you was studyin up on gonorrhea?"

Startled by this attack, Sally's sharp tongue faltered, and she groped for a response, flushed close to tears. "Have you ever felt the least respect for women? Ever in your life?"

Speck dismissed her with a grimace and turned back to the men. "See, folks was only scared of Colonel on account of his last name. Even Flamingo people was a-scared of him when he fished down there in the twenties, after his fool list made things hot for him up around home. Feller name Maxwell was Parks ranger up Little Coot Bay, and he was gettin on to Colonel for some reason. And a feller says to him, 'Maxwell, you best leave that man alone! You keep on messin, one of these days you gone to come up *missin*! Don't you know who that man is? Hell, Desperader Watson was his *daddy*!' Well, that news took Maxwell's cold, cold heart and turned it right around, and after that, them fellers always said, they never seen nobody nicer than what this Maxwell was to Colonel Watson."

*

"I believe Sandy Albritton was the one who told me how when Edgar Watson first come to southwest Florida, the train stopped someplace—was it

Arcadia?—and there was a man had another feller man down and was beatin on him somethin pitiful. So Mr. Watson swung down off that train and he walked over there and said, 'How come you onlookers don't stop this man from beatin this here feller half to death?' 'No, no,' they said. 'They ain't *nobody* can't stop him, cause that is Quinn Bass, the meanest hombre in all Manatee County!' So Desperader Watson said, 'Well, I can stop him.' And darned if he don't step over there and shove his revolver into the burl of that man's ear. Never advised him to quit or nothin, he weren't the kind to tell another man his business. Just squeezed the trigger and climbed back on the train and went on south."

Infuriated, unfairly defeated, Lucius had returned and sat down across the fire. Sally leaned toward him and whispered, "I don't believe Sandy Albritton ever told any such story!" Her father gave her a funny smile, then reached and whacked her blue-jeaned thigh above the knee. She reared around at him, tears in her eyes. "Keep your cotton-picking hands to your damned self!" Father and daughter measured each other, tasting old bad episodes in their past history, and he raised his brows in unabashed appreciation of her pretty bosom, which was heaving in emotion, Speck picked a broken horsefly off the sand by the gauze wing and turned its glass green body between thumb and forefinger, catching the firelight. "Sharpshooters," he said. "That's what old-timers used to call 'em." He turned to Lucius.

"Anyways, your daddy had no chance that time Mr. Short killed him, cause when he come ashore, them men was waitin on him. Old Man Lloyd House, had a fish dock at Flamingo for a while—Barrelhead House, we called him, cause he liked hard cash—Mr. Barrelhead was in on the whole plan, and in later years he told me all about it." He cocked his eye to observe Lucius as a hawk might eye the creature in its talon prior to feeding. "Course I was in Chok that day myself, I was what you might call a eyewitness. But bein so young and comin there that day from Fakahatchee, I weren't asked to join up, so I follered my uncle across to Smallwood's landin and joined up in that crowd all by myself."

Andy said, "Lloyd House told you they *planned* it? That sure weren't the way his brothers told it!"

"I can't he'p it," Speck said airily, waving off the interruption. "Talkin about Fakahatchee, Aunt Emmeline Daniels over there is one of the last ones left alive around south Florida who knew Mr. Desperader Watson from the early days. They give her a family party every year since she broke ninety, and some years she will draw three hundred head, all kissin kin. Don't have no idea at all who the hell they are but gets into the spirit of it all the same. She used to say Ol' Desperader Watson had the neatest foot in all the world, looked like a ought-seven shoe, she couldn't get over it. Smallest foot for a man his size I ever saw, she'd say, and a sparklin personality to go with it."

His daughter demanded, "Do you *ever* speak the truth?" He rumbled like a sleeping dog but would not look at her.

"Back in the last years of the century, Mr. Watson would come through Flamingo on his way to Key West, stop over sometimes to sell bird plumes to Mr. Gene Roberts. Mister Gene and Desperader was the best of friends, and when Mr. Gene was rentin Andrew Wiggins's place on Chokoloskee, he always stayed at Chatham Bend on the way through. Mr. Watson would say, 'What time do you aim to get goin in the mornin, Gene?' And next mornin he would wake him up, shake him real gentle. That's what Gene remembered—the gentle way that Desperader shook him. 'Come on, Gene, time to get up!' Didn't hurry him off or nothin, just woke him up and give him flapjacks, put him on his way. I reckon that's where Colonel got them fancy manners.

"Yessir, ol' Mr. Gene thought the world of E. J. Watson. Later years, when Colonel Watson showed up at Flamingo, the Roberts boys told the local men not to run him off or sink his boat but let him fish that country. Gene Roberts said, 'Boys, I fished with Colonel Watson many's the time, and drank his whiskey with him, cause he likes his whiskey and a lot of it, same way his daddy did.' And Gene would say how E.J.'s boy had the sweetest nature he ever come across, said he never seen him mad in all his life. Never caught on that this man's sweetness weren't but weakness."

Speck met Lucius's eye. "I always heard you was a alky-holic," he said softly. "Any truth to that?"

Sally cried out, "Oh for God's sake! Why can't you men stand up to him?" To her father, she said, "You're a brutal and cynical and vicious man and you always were!"

And still her husband and the blind man remained silent. All four men knew that Lucius had to deal with Speck in his own way.

"Come to think about it, might been Mr. Gene who told this story," Daniels was saying. "Ol' Desperader had two niggers stackin cordwood on a payday, and one nigger said, 'All right now, Cap'n, we is about done!' And Watson said, 'Well, you better stack it straight, cause that's your last one.' And he give Gene Roberts a big wink when he said that. The next week when Gene come through on his way back south from Chokoloskee, them two black boys was gone, there weren't a sign of 'em. Ed Watson's Nigger Payday some men called it. Mr. Gene admired hell out of Colonel's daddy, but he never doubted that ol' Desperader done away with 'em. And them two weren't the only ones, not by no means."

"That's the rumor, all right," Lucius snapped. "I've never seen a single scrap of evidence!"

"Me neither." Speck yawned at him, indifferent. "I just heard about it."

"So you pass along vicious lies."

Speck Daniels sat up on his elbows for a better look at him. "You callin me a liar, Colonel? Can't swaller the truth? How come you wasted all these years in diggin up the truth if you cover it right up again when you come across it?"

Speck reeled to his feet and jerked his head in the direction of the point. "We got some business." Lucius followed him a little distance down the beach, and they talked standing.

Speck said, "We got Old Man Chicken in the house, him and his damfool brother. You people wasn't ten feet from 'em when you was on the porch the other day."

*

When Lucius had gone hunting him at Gator Hook, day before yesterday, Rob was already on his way to Chatham Bend, where the men meant to hold him until Speck arrived. Coming downriver from the inland bays, Speck's men had heard a helicopter in the distance. Next, they came around the Bend to find a skiff tied up to the old pilings. The Watson Place was as white as a lighthouse, and the painter was up under the eaves on the west wall on his high ladder, paying no attention to their arrival.

The three men gathered at the ladder's foot, staring upward, as Speck put it, "like red-tick hounds with a fat coon up a tree." The bulky housepainter would not even look down but instead cried cheerily over his shoulder that the old place would look a whole heck of a lot better once he had finished this second coat of paint. Next, he asked if there was anything that he could do for them. "For a start," roared Crockett Junior, "you can haul your ass down off that ladder and tell us what you think you're doin on this posted property! Never read our sign? Says, 'This Means You!' " The stranger kept right on with his painting, promising he would be with them shortly. Not until Crockett shook his ladder hard would he finally look down, and even then they could not make out whether the big man was snarling or smiling. Lucius concluded that Ad's fearful grimace was intended to disarm them, or possibly persuade himself that he'd only imagined the apocalyptic roar of an approaching airboat and that ugly dog built like a keg which was circling the ladder and these hard-looking men with heavy boots and automatic weapons who had swarmed ashore like drunken militia at a public hanging.

On pain of death he gave his name as A. Burdett of Neamathla, Florida, come to give his childhood home a coat of paint. Despite his name, Ad cried, he was a Watson. He said he'd been urged to come here by his brother Lucius, and assured them that a venerable institution such as the Park would never destroy such a fine-looking house once it realized how much the old place meant to the Watson family! Surely that sign saying KEEP OUT must be illegal, since everyone knew that all Park land belonged to the American people. Also he'd been unpleasantly surprised to find the doors padlocked and the windows boarded, thwarting his plans to sleep beneath his father's roof. Furthermore, there was an awful smell which seemed to come from behind those boarded windows—one would almost suspect something had *died* in there!

Having started, Addison could not stop talking, until finally he said with a forced laugh more like a shriek that he hoped that what he was smelling in there was not bodies!

"Shut the hell up!" Crockett Junior bellowed, at wits' end. To make his point, he shoved the ladder hard, sending it scraping down the house side in a long slow arc. "Hey, wait!" the painter hollered. The ladder described a crescent down the wall, then fell to the hard ground, where the pit bull Buck, awaiting orders, took up a position at the stranger's throat. Still clutching his brush, unhurt except for splotches of white paint and his bruised feelings, he picked himself up and pointed at the unsightly gray scrape marks made by the ladder. "Let's not go spoiling my nice paint job, fellers!" They watched in astonishment as he poured new paint and raised the ladder and clambered up with a fresh bucket and set to work at once, painting out scrapes.

Apparently, Dummy had raised his gun, intending to shoot this loony off the ladder like a big turkey, but Mud deflected him, warning the stranger to get the hell off this river before that helicopter arrived with the outlaw gang which would put him to death at once because he knew too much. But seeming incapable of leaving his second coat unfinished, the man only increased his pace, burrowing deeper into his work like a child pulling the covers up over its head. If that "whirlybird" arrived, he cried, he would do his best to talk some sense into the heads of those darned criminals! With this, Speck's men abandoned hope of reasonable discussion. The *real* whirlybird, as they now recognized, was this wild-eyed Watson on the ladder, slathering paint on that doomed house as if his life depended on it, which it did.

Speck's men soon realized that they could not let a witness leave before their cargoes were safely off the Bend. Also, it seemed easier to let him flap along under the eaves than to have him descend and get in their way. For the moment they went on about their business, lugging Chicken ashore—he was bound and gagged because they were sick of his abuse—and setting him in the thin shade of the poincianas. Then they unlocked the house and heaved outside the stacks of reeking gator hides, which stuck together in various states of putrefaction from mold rot and roof leak and humidity as well as maggots.

The gator hides were camouflage for the tarpaulins and heavy crates beneath—contraband weapons and munitions, Lucius deduced, recalling what Whidden had told him, which had to be lugged out one by one and stacked along the bank, in preparation for airboat transfers to a second depot.

From Whirlybird's peculiar expression, Speck's men suspected that his docile return to work was a ruse to throw them off the scent of some escape plan. (Lucius imagined Addison's plan as strange, formless incipience, spinning in his white-speckled head like primordial matter in the cosmos.) When they went inside for the last crates, they sat down for a smoke, and watched through the door as Whirlybird executed a stealthy descent and tiptoed toward the old man under the trees.

"How does she look?" he was heard to whisper, turning with his hands upon his hips to sincerely admire his own handiwork, as the old man, still gagged, glared at him in hatred. Knowing Rob, Lucius could well imagine the beetling brows and sparking eyes of that infuriated oldster, gargling at the mad housepainter to free him. "What in the heck is going *on* around this place?" Ad wished to know. Rob rolled his eyes and eventually Ad freed him.

Not long thereafter, they discovered they were brothers—nearly thirty years apart, Lucius reflected, and irrevocably opposed in temperament, but sired by the same red rooster, E. J. Watson. During their long conversation, Rob was seen to weep a little, though whether this was exasperation with his brother or fear for his own life, the onlookers were unable to determine.

When the *Cracker Belle* arrived toward noon next day, Speck's men were on their way upriver with a cargo. The bound-and-gagged brothers were lashed down on bunks inside, unable to signal their rescuers a few yards away. Once the *Belle* had departed for Mormon Key, they were set free long enough to eat and stretch their legs, then bound again while the exhausted crew got a little sleep. This morning, when Speck arrived, Whirlybird was sent back up his ladder, while Rob was settled on the porch, in the musky and rain-rotted ruin of a plush settee.

Having heard the report of the abduction from the Naples church hall and the various disreputable adventures since, Speck contemplated his irascible old friend, shaking his head. "Public Enemy Number One!" he said. "Ol' Chicken-Wing!"

"The same," Rob Watson said. He accepted a jam jar of Speck's moonshine and raised his glass to the man under the eaves—"To my long-lost baby brother Ad Burdett, a painting fool out of north Florida!"

While his crew ran another cargo up the river, Speck poured himself more shine, and Chicken, too. "One for the road," Speck teased him, lifting his glass, and the prisoner cursed him. They sat on the porch in the dead quiet of the river day to think things through. When Whirlybird descended and nagged at Speck to return him to his boat and let him go, the older brother backed him up, declaring that the Watson heirs did not care to be ill-treated in their own ancestral dwelling, especially on their first visit home in a half century. Surely, Rob said, Mr. Daniels owed some consideration to the sons of E. J. Watson, having helped to kill him. Whirlybird stared in disbelief as these two laughed.

However, not knowing what to do with these damned Watsons, Speck was growing irritable. "Ain't *you* here to kill *me?*" he jeered. "How about that weapon and that list?" Unlike his men, Speck doubted very much that Chicken Collins had ever meant to kill him, but whether or not he could keep them from killing Chicken was another matter. He tied Rob up again, gagging his snapping mouth so tight that his bloodshot eyes bugged out. "I always enjoyed the hell out of old Chicken," Speck told Lucius. "Us two fellers got along real good yesterday evenin, considerin he might wind up gettin shot."

Ad Burdett, upset when his skiff was towed across the river, expressed his sincere disapproval of his old brother consorting with known criminals, and demanded to know what gave these men the right to take him prisoner on these Park lands. Offering him moonshine, Speck cheerfully agreed that they had no right whatever, but pointed out that a caretaker's solemn duties included protecting the place from whirlybirds and vandals. To illustrate, he pointed at the paint job. "If that ain't unlawful vandalism of federal property, I don't know what," he said, winking at Chicken.

"I traveled a long way to paint this house," Ad moaned, in an onset of self-pity, "and I spent up all my vacation time and all my savings, so I deserve a better explanation than that one you gave me."

Fed up, Speck snarled, "Try this one, then. This damn ol' house is goin up in smoke in a few days, and your paint job with it—all your hard work and time and money, and your stupid vacation, and maybe your own self if you're tied up inside, ever think of that?"

This morning Speck had left there before noon, to make his way south by the inland creeks to Lost Man's Key. He had not gotten far when he was apprehended by the helicopter, which he had not heard over the din of his own engine. Circling in the high distance, the machine had picked up the white wake of his boat when he left the Watson Place. From the shrouded sun, tracking his propeller roil across the copper bays, it finally descended in a tree-shattering racket to run him aground against the bank at Onion Key.

There the Park rangers searched his boat and confiscated his tree snails and his orchids. (They were dead anyway, said Speck, who had had no time to tend them.) Finding no gator hides or guns or moonshine, they had let him go.

*

Lucius said finally, "If you came here to let me know they were all right, then I'm much obliged."

"That ain't why I come here, and they ain't 'all right.'" Speck whistled in amazement. "Are *all* you Watsons crazy? Between Chicken and that Whirlybird—"

"Rob got off to a rough start in life. Addison, too. It's not their fault."

"Ain't Junior's fault, neither," Speck said grimly. "But that ain't goin to help him, vet or no vet, not when that last screw lets go and he starts shootin at them fuckin helio-copters!"

"Rob's not going to shoot anybody! He was drunk—"

"I am drunk right here this minute, you stupid bastard, and I ain't shot you yet! In the old days, *you* was drunk most all the time, but you never shot nobody I ever heard about!" His voice rose to a shout. "I mean, goddammit, if you was them wild boys of mine, outside the law, what would *you* make of a man carryin a list like that, and a loaded weapon?" Before Lucius could speak, he said in a hard voice, "You might figure his crazy brother Colonel Watson put him up to it! I mean, it ain't like we're talkin about some poor old alky. It ain't like he never killed before! Killed right here at Lost Man's, for Christ's sake! Killed right here on this key where we are standin on!" Speck raised his hand to block Lucius's protest. "So you're tryin to tell me it weren't him took a shot at Dyer? And if he will shoot at Dyer, why not me?"

Lucius said, "Rob's not a killer. He never wanted to kill anyone. Not ever." But there was no way to explain why he believed this, and he did not try.

"You can deny it all you want. Chicken don't deny it." Speck would not explain this. Morose, he was gazing back toward the silhouetted figures at the fire. As suddenly as it had flared, his rage had guttered out, and his voice was quiet. "Anyways, we can't let him loose till we are finished, and even then we got a problem cause he seen too much. We ain't got time to mess with him, is what it is. Junior and them got their own idea how to clean up this damn mess, and you don't come up with a better one pretty damn quick, that's what has to happen."

"Cold-blooded murder? *That* what they're talking about?"

"They're through talkin, Colonel," Speck said quietly, folding his arms upon his chest.

Then he said, "Let's say we turn ol' Chicken loose. The law is after him. You was mentionin that nigger cook—"

"Oh hell no! It wasn't him!"

"Well, you know that, and Dyer, too, I reckon. All the same, the law told Dyer they would settle for the nigger. They got all the witnesses they need— all them scared old people who was up all night with heartburn. Them kind will want somebody to pay. And Dyer says it's a nice tight case that will teach them kind of smart-mouth niggers a good lesson."

Speck's mean chuckle came from down deep in his belly. "I asked him, Do you really want to go after that man, and he says, 'Hell yes, I'm a law-and-order man, I don't believe in coddlin no criminals.' Respects the hell out of the law and never seen a jail he didn't like. Says, 'I'm out for justice or my name ain't Watson Dyer.' " Speck emitted a low, hard bark of derision. "Sure hates to mess with our American justice system, Dyer says. And otherwise he'd feel obliged to testify against ol' Chicken, who don't stand a Chinaman's chance of gettin off. Man out in the parkin lot, he spotted an old white man in a red neckerchief shootin at the victim's car from a hotel window. Seen him plenty good enough to testify that it weren't no black boy in a chef's outfit who got loose some way in a whites-only room on the sixth floor."

"Rob shot at the car tires. He never shot at Dyer."

"Pretty hard to sell that to a judge, with Chicken's record."

"My brother will confess before he lets that black man go to jail for him. That's who he is."

Speck Daniels snickered. "Specially when all that poor coon ever done was go to cuttin on a white customer with a damn carvin knife!" He heaved around and squinted at Lucius in disbelief. "Chicken was tellin me just yesterday how he wasted maybe half his life in one pen or another, and you're goin to set there and tell me you would let that old feller get locked away for the rest of his natural life? For a crazy nigger?"

Daniels searched Lucius's eyes for doubt and nodded when he found some. "I was warnin Chicken only this mornin how we might have to kill him, and he told me that was fine by him. He meant it, too. Said he had his fill of this shitty life and couldn't tolerate no more hard time in prison, so it was no use wastin time tryin to scare him. He was scared to death of death, all right, but was scared a lot worse by the future."

"He's better off dead than going to prison? That what you're saying?"

"That's what *he's* saying." He held Lucius's eye for a long time, nodding minutely. "What do *you* say, Lucius?"

"He's my *brother*, for Christ's sake!"

Heart jumping, sick and dizzy, he reeled to his feet. Driven by urgent pressure of the bladder, he staggered off toward the sea grape. But he had scarcely opened up his fly when he was punched between the shoulder blades by what turned out to be the muzzle of a hand gun.

"Let's see them hands before you turn around."

Startled, hurting, and incensed, Lucius took time to finish and get things straightened out, ignoring the emphysemic hacking close behind him and the steel prod nudging his bruised back. Finally he stuck his hands out to the side. "Kind of jumpy, aren't you?" he said then, with as much contempt as his shaken voice could muster.

"Kind of jumpy, yessir, I sure am. Which is why I'm still doin pretty good after thirty years in my same line of business." For the second time in a fortnight, Daniels frisked him. "I have growed a nose for a certain kind of a cock-eyed sonofabitch that you give 'em any room at all, it's goin to cost you." He spun Lucius around harder than necessary, slapping at his chest and front pockets with the back of his free hand. "Next time, do your pissin out where I can see you."

Lucius struggled to remain calm. "You're the one who's armed, god-dammit!" His voice still trembled in his shock and outrage. "You're the one talking about eliminating witnesses! How about Addison? He gets shot, too?"

"Shut up and listen." In the moonlight Speck was squatted on his hunkers, using his knife to draw a quick map in the sand. He spoke quickly, coldly. "Maybe when we get our business finished up tomorrow evenin, we'll put your brothers aboard Whirlybird's skiff, point 'em downriver to Mormon Key. Course Junior will blow another gasket. But I'll remind him there ain't nowhere they can get to, not before we're gone."

"Crockett will do just what you tell him, right?"

"Junior?" Daniels snorted in a surprised response that was not quite affection. "We're like buck deer in the rut, Junior and me. Every year the old buck stands there just a-shiverin, knowin in every snort and hoof, bristle and tine, that he can still run all the young bucks off his does"—Speck chuckled—"includin this big stupid-lookin one high-steppin towards him right this very minute. Only this time, after the dust clears, he finds himself bad hurt and all alone. He ain't even allowed in his own herd no more." Speck scratched his stubble. "Might happen to me the first time Junior gets it in his head that he ain't takin no more goddamned orders. Might be tomorrow, if he don't like my plan. And it ain't goin to be like no damn buck deer, neither. I'll be lucky if that sonofagun don't kill me."

"So you'll let them go?"

"Depends," Speck said, ambiguous again. "Can't promise nothin."

"You were saying Rob was sick of life—"

"You back on that again?" Speck was enjoying this.

"—and suggesting that his death might be a mercy. Might be preferable. Something like that." Hating Speck's knowing grin, he could not go on.

"That's what *I* say. That's what *he* said. What are *you* sayin? You don't want us to let him go?"

"I never said that!"

"Not in them words, no."

"You say he *told* you he killed someone here at Lost Man's?"

"Damn fool had it all wrote down on paper. Had it right there with the list and the revolver. With your name on the packet." He cocked his head. "You sure you didn't know?" The moon glint caught his tooth when Daniels grinned. "Dyer now, he was real excited when he heard about it. Told Junior to hold that stuff for him, it might come in handy. In case Watsons didn't cooperate or something."

"You're giving Dyer the gun?"

"I already give it back to Chicken. Without no loads, of course. He told me to bring that ol' packet to you."

"What's in it for you?"

"Well, me 'n' Chicken—you know. We go back a ways. Gator Hook and all."

"I thought you worked for Dyer."

Daniels nodded. "But I never owed him nothin, no more'n he owes me. Once his land claim's settled, he won't have no use for me, won't want to be tied in with me at all. Won't want nobody around who knows too much, can't take no chances. And if he's goin into politics, the way it looks—well, any dealins with the Daniels gang might cost him pretty dear, on down the road."

Before coming south, Speck had phoned his contact man at Parks headquarters, trying to find out when the Parks meeting at the Bend could be expected. The official told him that Watson Dyer had failed to appear at the court hearing at Homestead, and the judge had suspended the injunction against "the demolition of the Watson premises." It now appeared likely that demolition would be carried out before another motion for an extension or a new hearing could be filed. Why Dyer had not filed earlier, citing his emergency at Fort Myers, the official did not know. All he knew was, things were moving fast, and a large-scale operation was underway which included the requisition of a helicopter.

His Parks man warned Speck that this operation might be more ambitious than an expedition to burn down a house. A confidential federal report had advised the Park authorities that an armed and dangerous fugitive named Robert Watson might have joined forces with the Daniels gang to engage in felonious activities at a remote location in the Lost Man's region of the Ten Thousand Islands. Attorney Watson Dyer, the intended victim in a recent episode of attempted murder at Fort Myers in which this Robert Watson was the leading suspect, was quoted as speculating that he had known too much about the fugitive's participation in a double murder in the Lost Man's region many years before.

Daniels seemed flattered that the federal agencies were using a U.S. military "helio-copter" to come after him. "Joint federal secret big-ass operation! Goin to cost us poor ol' taxpayers maybe a million dollars, and we ain't even going to know one thing about it! Anyone questions it, them bureaucrats will paper 'em to death, spread the responsibility all over Washington, D.C. Bureaucrats can't pour piss out of a boot without the instructions wrote onto the heel, but when it comes to coverin their butts, you just can't beat 'em!"

Daniels had told his man at Parks to damn well finagle them enough time so that his depot could be cleared before the raid—either that or his official ass would fry along with theirs. " 'You fellers can't prove nothin on me,' he says. 'You sure?' I says. 'We kept a fuckin *ar*-chive on you, Bud!' So then he says, Well, that bein the case, he might screw up the paperwork a little, maybe delay the burnin permit for a day or two. 'Good idea,' I says. But he hung up on me, and I couldn't get him back."

Lighting a stogie, Speck let his news sink in. "When Parks hung up on me that way, I seen straight off that Dyer sold me out. Sold you out, too. He's changed his plan some way. He was in Everglade the other night, so he could of made that court hearin at Homestead. Watson Dyer is a very efficient feller, he ain't the kind to miss a hearin, so when he don't bother to show up in court, that tells me he must of cut a deal. Dyer knows right now the injunction ain't no good, he knows that Parks is gettin set to burn the house, but in Everglade he was still talking to Junior like he's comin in with Parks to meet you, settle up the claim for the Watson family."

"He told me that, too."

"He ain't comin in to meet you, Colonel. Know what he's doin? He's settin up Speck Daniels for this raid, under the cover of burnin down the house. Rob Watson, too. Crime fightin, y'know—look real good on his record. And when it's all over, and the Major gets the credit for bustin up them criminal activities out in the Glades, nothing that low-down Daniels bunch might say won't never hurt him."

Daniels seemed honestly admiring, as if Dyer's dealings throughout their acquaintance had been handled impeccably and with dispatch. "If I was him, I would not want me alive, knowin what I do. Dead would make a hell of a lot more sense, and Dyer is a very sensible type of feller. Plays his cards right, plays percentages, don't go off half-cocked." He nodded. "They'll be lookin to catch Speck nappin on the Bend. But I aim to stay one jump ahead of 'em. Ol' Man Speck will have flew the coop, as usual."

"You think all that talk of preserving the house as some kind of pioneer monument was only to line the Watsons up behind the land claim?!"

"That plan didn't work out. He made a deal. You really thought he *cared* about that house? He ain't set foot in that old house since he left there half a century ago!"

"He was born there!"

"Colonel, they don't make your kind no more! Wake up, boy! What we got here is a whole new kind of human bein! To a man like that, the house-where-he-was-born don't mean no more than the crap that he took yesterday!" Speck shook his head. "It's that forty acres of high ground he must be after. But all that time he was dickerin with the feds, he didn't want to throw away no cards. He knew they was hot to burn the house cause it don't fit in with their idea of a wilderness, and he knew he could hold 'em up for years with legal diddling. They knew that, too. Well, now he has stepped out of their way. They will burn the house but recognize the land claim."

"This is all wrong! There's nothing he can do with it! That's Park land!"

"Well, I admit I ain't got that part figured out. I will."

Lucius stood up. "They can't burn down the Watson house with Watson standing in the door."

"I wouldn't count on that if I was you. Old house all by itself, way to hell and gone out in the backcountry? Swoop in by helio-copter? They can get away with anything they want."

"This is the U.S. Government, dammit! This isn't some crime syndicate or something!"

"You don't learn good, Colonel. Who's goin to read 'em the Constitution way out here?"

Speck heaved back to his feet, a little creaky. "At our age, now, a man gets stiff all over," he grumped, "ceptin the one part that might be some use." He was set to leer, but met by Lucius's bleak gaze, he did not bother. Slowly they returned toward the fire.

"If everythin goes right, your brothers will be comin downriver in that skiff tomorrow afternoon. You fellers wait for 'em at Mormon Key, and keep 'em at Mormon tomorrow night, give us a little more time in case we need it. Still with me, Colonel? You're lookin kinda peaked, boy. Okay so far?

Whidden can take that skiff in tow next mornin, run your whole bunch back north to the Bay. And after that, you get in your damn car and you drive that old man out of southwest Florida and keep him out."

At the boats, Lucius waded out with him and boosted him over his gunwale. A minute later, Daniels emerged from his boat cabin with the packet marked LUCIUS H. WATSON that had lain at the bottom of Rob's satchel.

Drunkenly Speck swung back overboard and splashed ashore. "You ain't goin to enjoy his story, Colonel. Might be more truth in there than you was wantin." Saying this, he leaned way forward to peer into Lucius's eyes. "Less you been lying to yourself all these long years? About how much you *really* knew about your daddy?" He winked at Lucius and set off again, hailing the others, usurping the conversation even before he reached the smoke swirls and blown sparks at the driftwood fire.

Lucius climbed aboard the *Belle* and lit the kerosene storm lamp in the cabin. Building a pillow out of life jackets, he lay back with the opened packet on his chest, weighing Daniels's insinuation: *All these long years—* that was unfair, of course. But was it true?

*

To My Little Brother "Luke":

Here is the truth about what happened early in 1901 at Lost Man's River. I hope this will help you understand my sentiments or lack of same about your "Papa." I am writing this in the sincere hope that it will end your well-meant but mistaken struggle to restore his reputation.

I know (because I saw them, too) that our father had bold, generous qualities. I also know that he adored my mother, perhaps more than he adored yours. I don't say that out of pettiness, I hope, but only to clarify what I say next—that he was mortally embittered when she died, and made an enemy of his firstborn throughout childhood, into early youth. Such kinship as we had came to an end on the first day of Anno Domini 1901.

Late in 1899, Wally Tucker and his bride Elizabeth, lately of Key West, came to work for E. J. Watson at Chatham Bend. At age fourteen, Bet was no more than a child, but Tucker was close to my own age, we were twenty-two. Wally was "the driver" in the cane field, Bet helped Aunt Josie Jenkins with the housekeeping, and the wash and yard chores—slopped the hogs, tended the bees and poultry and the kitchen garden—while Josie was tending her little Pearl.

Late in the next year of 1900, the Tuckers fled from Chatham Bend in their small sloop after Papa's hogs sniffed out two shallow graves way out in the northeast part of the plantation. Bet had wandered out there, calling in the hogs, which were penned up at night on account of panthers. She discovered the remains of two black field hands whom she had befriended in the months before. These hands had confided that they wished to leave the Bend. They were owed more than a year in their back wages and could not get Papa to pay attention to it.

I ran into the Tuckers dragging their stuff down to their boat. Someone killed Zachariah and Ted, they cried, almost hysterical. I told them this was impossible, since I knew my father had paid off those hands and carried them back north to Fort Myers. Wally told me I should go see for myself, and poor Bet wept some more. Though they didn't dare say so to his son, they seemed scared they might be next if Mr. Watson found out what they knew, and so had decided to flee the Bend at once.

I ran out past the cane fields to the place they had described. I smelled those corpses long before I got there. I put a neckerchief to my face and went in close, and I had to get away on that same breath to keep from puking. The bodies were all bloated up, half-eaten by the hogs, and the ground chopped up by hog prints all around. I recognized the clothes. There was no question.

By the time I got back, the Tuckers were gone. Papa was dead drunk in the house. According to Aunt Josie, who came flying out to warn me, Wally had finished loading their sloop, put Bet aboard, then took his gun and walked up to the house and demanded their year's wages, saying not a word about the graves. Papa was incensed because they were quitting without notice, right at the start of the cane harvest, and furious also at the gun raised to his face when he threatened Wally. Being drunk, he shouted, "Shoot me, you conch bastard! You don't dare!" It terrified Aunt Josie because it was so crazy, but as usual, E. J. Watson knew his man. Wally Tucker was not a killer, never would be. Lunging for him, your father spun and fell down hard and fell again when he tried to get up, so lay there cursing.

Aunt Josie and poor pale little Pearl were hidden someplace in that silent house. I remember a shaft of sunlight through the window that struck an open jug of shine on our pine table, and I had a gulp of it to get my nerve up. Then I went to my father, who was snoring like a bullfrog on his bed, with muddy boots on. I opened up the storm shutters to have some light, then shook him awake and said, "Forgive me, Papa." I was scared to death! Then I took a deep breath and told him about those colored boys. "The hogs found 'em," I said, to fill an awful silence.

Papa opened up one eye, so red and raw it looked like the slit throat of a chicken. Then he heaved away, dragging a pillow over his head, he couldn't take the light nor stand the sight of me. But after a while his voice growled out that he knew nothing about it. Next he snarled that Mr. Wally

Tucker better be damned careful about spreading slander against E. J. Watson. He asked if I knew that those damned Tuckers had forfeited back wages by running out on their damned contract? This reminded him that he was shorthanded for the harvest, and he reared up with a roar and hurled himself out of bed as if he could still catch them, but he blacked out and crashed against the wall and sagged down in a heap behind the door.

At these times, "hair of the dog" was all that helped. By the time I came back with the jug, he was sitting on the bed edge holding his head, wheezing for breath. He stunk like a bear and his skin was blotchy and his breath was terrible. I was very much afraid. I whispered, "You told me you paid them, Papa, took them to Fort Myers." He opened his eyes and looked me over and then he shook his head. "Those two owed me money, they were thieves." He took a last big slug out of his jug and sighed. "I couldn't pay 'em, boy," he muttered. "Nothing to pay 'em with." He shoved the jug at me. "I have some business to take care of. Hide this jug from me." He pulled it back and gulped at it one last time before handing it over, and I went outside and hid it on that ledge under the cistern cover where we placed the buckets when we fetched water, remember?

I missed those Tuckers badly, they were my good friends. Without them, the Bend seemed very grim and lonely. Even Tant had gone away, there was no one to talk to but Aunt Josie. My father went out with me to rebury Ted and Zachariah, even mumbled some kind of a rough prayer. I wanted to believe what he tried to hint (not very seriously) that other field hands must have killed them for their pay, and meanwhile he instructed all of us to forget this. There was nothing to be done about it, he said.

After their long year of hard work, the poor Tuckers had departed unpaid and penniless, without stores, in worn-out clothes. They got no farther south than Lost Man's Key. They lived there in their little sloop while they built a shelter, borrowing a gillnet and a few tools from the Hardens while they farmed a piece of ground across the river mouth, back of South Lost Man's.

Toward the end of that year, Winky Atwell from Rodgers River showed up at the Bend with his younger brother. He wanted to let Mr. Watson know he was moving his family back south to Key West—was Mr. Watson still interested in buying up their claim on Lost Man's Key? But after he had bought and paid for it, and everyone was celebrating, the Atwells advised him that the Tuckers had been camping there to get away from the mosquitoes, though Wally rowed across the channel every day to tend his crop. They had a little shack there on the shell ridge, and a small cistern and a little dock. Since Bet was in a family way, perhaps Mr. Watson would not mind if those young folks got their little harvest in before they had to leave. Papa roared that he would mind that very much. Being drunk on that day, too, he sent a rough note back with Atwells notifying the Tuckers that by Monday next, they must get off his paid-up claim at Lost Man's Key.

Two days later the Atwells, very nervous, brought an answer from Wally Tucker reminding Mr. Watson that they were owed a year's back pay and would not leave there "until hell burns over." Those back wages amounted to full payment of a five-year lease on Lost Man's Key. My heart sank when I saw what Wally wrote, because Mr. Watson took that as a challenge and a threat. He muttered something about hell burning over somewhat sooner than some people might think, and he didn't seem to care that Josie heard him.

That woman was so crazy for him that nothing bothered her, I guess, and no secret that would do him harm ever passed her lips. Even if Josie knew about those hog-chewed cadavers in the woods, she would have claimed she didn't know a thing about "those darned ol' niggers," all she knew was that her "Jack" Watson had had a showdown with the Tuckers because they were squatters on his claim who insulted and defied him when he sent word to get off.

The truth was, their defiance had reminded him of what those young people knew, and reminded him, too, that feeling wronged, they might take their story to the Sheriff at Key West, who had always welcomed evidence against Ed Watson.

On New Year's Eve—the last night of the old century—Papa broke out a new jug of Tant's moonshine, but we didn't celebrate. He sat down heavily at the table and studied Tucker's note over and over as he drank. Aunt Josie came in with Pearl, in hope of a little cheer, but she took one look at his grim face and went right out again and sat in the gloomy kitchen in the twilight. She knew better than to speak to him, and she signaled me to keep my mouth shut, too.

Aunt Josie fixed some supper but he hardly ate. He drank and brooded until nearly midnight. Finally he rose and went outside and looked at the full moon and came back in and got his gun and said, "Let's go." Praying he would pass out and sleep it off, I said I was tired and that one night made no difference, we should wait till daylight. But Aunt Josie in the doorway put a finger to her lips, fearful of the consequences if I protested.

We took the sailing skiff. There was no wind. In the light of the moon, I rowed him upriver on the incoming tide and on past Possum Key to the eastern bays. In all that long journey, he never twitched, never uttered a sound, but sat there jutted up out of the stern like an old stump, silhouetted on the moonlit water. That black hat shaded his face from the moon, his eyes were hidden.

Some time after midnight, we went ashore on Onion Key and slept a little. I was exhausted when he woke me in the dark, and I asked why we had to leave there before daybreak. His hard low grunt of warning meant I was not to speak again.

It was cold before daybreak, with a cold mist on the water. I rowed hard to get warm. Descending Lost Man's River, there was breeze, and I raised the sail. That old skiff slipped swiftly down the current in the early mists and on across the empty grayness of First Lost Man's Bay, with the dark bulk of him, still mute, hunched in the stern.

At first light, we slid the skiff into the mangroves and waded around to the sand point on the south end of the Key. Already afraid, I dared not ask why we were sneaking up on Bet and Wally when our mission was to run them off the claim. I guess I knew he had not come there to discuss things. In that first dawn of the new year, my teeth were chattering with cold and fear.

We slipped along through the low wood. Soon we could see between the trees the stretch of shore where Tucker's little sloop was moored off the Gulf beach. His driftwood shack with palm-thatch roof was back up on the shell ridge, in thin shade. Like most Islanders, the Tuckers rose at the first light, and Wally was already outside, perched on a driftwood log mending his galluses. He must have been expecting trouble, because he had leaned his rifle against the log beside him.

Papa gave me a kind of a funny wince, like he had no choice about what he had to do. Then he moved forward out of the sea grape with his old double-barrel down along his leg, crossing the sand in stiff short steps like a bristled-up male dog. He made no sound that I could hear, yet Tucker, being extra wary, must have picked up that tiny pinching of the sand. His gallus strap and sail needle and twine fell from his hand as he whirled, already reaching for his gun. At that instant he stopped that hand and moved the other one out to the side before slowly raising both.

Wally swallowed, as if sickened by the twin muzzle holes of that raised shotgun. Seeing no mercy in my father's face, he did not ask for any. He held my eye for a long moment, as if there were something I could do. He spoke to me while he watched Papa, saying, "Please, Rob. Take care of poor Bet." Perhaps he forgave me, knowing I was there against my will. Then he looked his executioner squarely in the eye, as if resigned to his fate. Papa knew better. Cursing, he swung the shotgun up in a quick snap as Tucker spun sideways toward his gun, and the scene exploded in red haze as Wally, blown clean over that log, fell twisted to the sand. A voice screamed, "Oh Christ Jesus no!" It was not Bet as I first thought but me.

Bet ran outside, holding a pot, and she screamed, too, at the sight of her beloved, kicking and shuddering on the new morning sand. Surely they had expected something, for she kept her head and did not run toward her young husband. She dropped her pot and lit out for the woods, very fast for a woman so close to term. I see her still, her white shift sailing over that pale sand like a departing spirit.

Your father—our father—murdered Tucker in cold blood. I never knew till he had done it that this was his intention even before we departed Chatham Bend. And perhaps he hadn't really known it either, for his face looked unimaginably sad and weary, as if the last of his life anger had drained out of him. He seemed bewildered, like someone arrived in a dark realm of no return. In that moment—for all took place while the ghostly form of that young girl was still crossing the beach ridge into the trees— what struck me as most strange was his quiet demeanor, his unnatural and horrifying calm.

"You see that, boy? He tried to kill me," he said dully.

Leaning his shotgun on the driftwood where Tucker himself had perched moments before, he eased himself down, seating himself, and planted his hands upon his knees, his boots not two feet from the body, which was still bloody and shuddering like a felled steer. Then he reached into his coat and took out his revolver, extending it butt first. In my crazed state, I imagined he was inviting me to execute him, and I took the gun and pointed it at his blue eyes. I was gagging and choking, knowing there could be no future, that my life was finished. I think I might have pulled the trigger if he had not smiled. I stared at him, and my arm lowered. Then he pointed at the sea wood, saying, "If she gets too deep into the brush, we just might lose her." And he mentioned that the families who lived down South Lost Man's Beach who might come to investigate that shot. We could not lose time hunting her down.

I stood stupidly, unable to take in what he was saying. Patiently he said that Bet Tucker was a witness. I must go after her at once. "We cannot stay here," he repeated gently, and still I did not move. "You came this far, Rob. You better finish it."

I gasped, teeth chattering, whole body shivering, I was fighting with all my might not to be sick. I yelled, "*You* finish it!" He gazed where she had gone. "I would take care of it myself," he said, "but I'd never catch her. It is up to you." I started yelling. Shooting these poor young people in cold blood was something terrible and crazy, we would burn in hell!

He was losing patience now, although still calm. He folded his arms upon his chest and said, "Well, Rob, that's possible. But meanwhile, if she gets away, we are going to hang."

I would not listen. I couldn't look at Wally's body without retching, so how could I run down his poor Bet and point a gun at her and take her life? I wept. "Don't make me do it, Papa! I can't do it!"

"Why, sure you can, Son," he told me then, "and you best jump to it, because you are an accomplice. It's your life or hers, look at it that way."

"You told me we were coming here to settle up our claim!"

"That's what we did," he said. He stood up then and turned his back to me, looking out toward the Gulf horizon. "Too late for talk," he said.

I was running. I was screaming the whole way. Whether that scream was heard there on that lonely river or whether it was only in my heart I do not know.

Being so cumbersome, poor Bet had not run far. In that thick tangle, there was no place to run to. I found sand scuffs where she had fallen to her knees and crawled in under a big sea grape. Panting like a doe, she lay big-bellied on her side, wide-eyed in the shock of what had happened. I stopped at a little distance. Seeing me, she whimpered, just a little. "Oh Rob," she murmured. "We did you no harm."

I called out, "Please, Bet, please don't look! I beg of you!" I crept up then and knelt beside her, and she breathed my name again just once, softly, as if trying to imagine such a person.

I never expected death to be so . . . intimate? That white skin pulsing at her temple, the sun-filled hair and small pink ear, clean and transparent as a seashell in the morning light—so full of life! Her eyes were open and she seemed to pray, her parted lips yearning for salvation like a thirsting creature. She never looked into my eyes nor spoke another word on earth, just stared away toward the bright morning water.

Raging at myself to be merciful and quick, I grasped my wrist to steady my gun hand. Even so, it shook as I raised the revolver. Already steps were coming up behind, crushing the sand, and hearing them, her eyes flew wider and her whole body trembled. Before she could shriek, I placed the muzzle to her ear, forcing my breath into my gut to steel myself and crying aloud as I pulled back on the trigger. I pulled her life clean out of her. My head exploded with red noise. Spattered crimson with her life, I fainted.

For a while after I became aware, I lay there in the morning dance of sea grape leaves reflected on the sand. Light and branches, sky and turquoise water—all was calm, as in a dream of heaven.

I forced open my eyes. I yelled in terror. She was gone. Closing my eyes again, I prayed for sleep, I prayed that nothing had taken place, that the dream of trees and sky and water might not end.

He came and leaned and shook my shoulder. Gently, he said, "Come along, it's time to go." He had already hauled the bodies out into the river. Alive and unharmed in the warm womb of its mother, the unborn kicked in blind foreboding beneath the sunny riffles of the current.

I struggled to stand up but I could not. The weakness and frustration broke me, and I sobbed. I saw the boot prints, the sand kicked over the dark bloodstain, like a fatal shadow on the earth.

He leaned and took me underneath one arm and lifted me easily onto my feet. He used a brush of leaves and twigs to scrape the brains and bloody skull bits from my breast, for I had fallen down across her body. Never before had this man touched me with such kindness, nor taken care of me in this strong loving way. I actually thought, What took so long? After all these years, he loves me! But his compassion—if that is what it was—had come too late. My life was destroyed beyond the last hope of redemption. What had happened here had bound me in a shroud. I was a dead man from that day forward, forever and ever and amen.

I retched and fought away from him but fell, too weak to run. He bent again and lifted me, half-carried me toward the skiff.

With hard short strokes he rowed upriver, against the ebb tide. His heavy coat lay on the thwart beside me. He himself seemed stunned, half-dead, and he had forgotten the revolver. My hand found the gun furtively, over and over, whenever he turned to see the course ahead. I wanted to take it, cover it with my shirt, but I felt too shaken and afraid. In that long noon, ascending Lost Man's River, I realized I should have killed him when he first gave me that gun, sparing Bet Tucker and her baby. Now I had taken those two lives and lost my own.

He told me on the long row home that the delta tide would carry the bodies off the shallow bank into the channel and the deeper water, where sharks following the blood mist in toward shore would find them. I did not answer him. I could not. I felt a loathing as profound as nausea. I never spoke a word to him again.

By oar and sail, he returned to Chatham Bend, using the inland passages to avoid being seen by the Lost Man's settlers or the Hardens on Wood Key or the few drifters and net fishermen along that coast. He told me to keep my head below the gunwales, so that if the bodies were discovered and Watson's skiff had been reported in that region, the son would not be implicated in the alleged crimes. That was his word that day—"alleged"—and that is the word that you, Luke, are still clinging to.

All that New Year's afternoon, curled up like a hound on the bilge boards near his boots, I observed that murderous drunkard at the tiller, the blue eyes squinted in the sun, the ginger beard under the scuffed black hat, against the sun shafts and dark rising towers of far cumulus.

At the Bend, Aunt Josie was nowhere to be seen. He resumed drinking. Before he finally lost consciousness, he reviled me for ingratitude and cowardice and shouted threats against imagined enemies, while saving his vilest curses for the Tuckers. I found the revolver and I aimed it, but I could not fire.

That evening I slipped the schooner's lines and drifted her downriver on a falling tide. At first light, I worked her out beyond Mormon Key, where an onshore wind was chipping up the surface, and ran a course south for Key West, where our cousin Thomas Collins worked in a shipping office. Tom found a buyer right away because I sold the schooner cheap, aware of the one who, even now, must be in hard pursuit of me, to claim her. That same night I shipped out as a crewman on a Mallory steamer, bound for New York City.

In this way, your brother forsook home and family. My history in the half century since (under an alias) is not worth recording, having no relevance to your Watson archive.

(signed) R. B. Watson

For a long time Lucius lay inert in the mildewed cabin. His heart felt like a core of lead with flayed nerves stretched around it, and its beating hurt him.

Some time later he arose and took the bedrolls over to the beach. He spread them at a little distance from the fire, not far downriver from the place where Rob and Papa must have slipped ashore. The Tucker shack had been around the point, on the west shore, and he dimly recalled the great hardwood from some tropic river, cast up by hurricane, against which Wally Tucker must have leaned his rifle while he patched his pants.

In the firelight, Andy and Whidden were laughing warily with Daniels. Instinctively, Sally sat behind her husband's shoulder, keeping Whidden between her and her father. By reputation, the hard-drinking Daniels would remain upright and articulate to a point just short of brain death before passing out.

"Course my daughter here got the queer idea that her daddy prefers gators to niggers—hell, that ain't right at all! I was brung up with old-fashioned views but I kept up with the times better'n some." Daniels glanced slyly at Sally Brown, whose face was closed. "If I go in a restaurant, Key West, and a nigger comes in there and sets down, I ain't gone to open my damn mouth, cause I respect the law. But far as one comin into my own house and pullin a chair up to my table, well, I weren't raised that way. After we're done eatin, he can come on in, case of a 'mergency, to use my phone—

that's different. But as far as settin down just like a white person? Nosir! I don't hold with that. I weren't raised that way, and it's hard to change so much after all these years."

Sally burst out, "Don't let him get started! He just bullies everybody with his viciousness. And it isn't funny just because he's drunk!"

Speck Daniels turned slowly to confront his daughter, looking her over in the same judicious way in which earlier he had met criticism from the blind man. "Course my daughter here was raised up with her daddy's views, ain't that right, Sally? When she was young, some people name of Hyatt come to town and word was going round they might be colored—"

"Oh don't!" begged Sally, jumping up. "I was only twelve!"

Speck kept nodding. "So this Hyatt girl told her best friend Sally Daniels she was white, and I guess she was, to look at. But my daughter was kind of a mean girl back at that time, talked and thought like her own kind of people. So Sally would not let it go, and them two had a catfight in the school yard every day. Sally called the other girl a dirty nigger, and other kids got into it and then the grown-ups. Finally it was settled, Hyatts was black. Wanted to be white in the worst way but people wouldn't let 'em. So they got moved acrost the bridge and their kids was sent to the nigra school, and Miss Sally Daniels got most of the credit."

Her husband put his arm around her but no one could protest, since Sally did not deny that it was true. "That was the way he brought us up!" she cried. Speck contemplated his daughter while she wept. He said, "Them people suffered somethin terrible, y'know. I was almost sorry it was me let on to Sally how they might be niggers."

Nobody spoke. The blind man, who had propped himself onto his elbows, let himself down again and folded his big hands over his eyes.

"I will say this much, when it come to looks, that Hyatt girl was about as cute as us fellers ever seen in our hometown. Had a couple of state cops hangin around there a good while that wanted to shack up with her, that's how pretty that girl was, but her people proved to be niggers all the same.

"Black nor white, a person can't control what he was borned to be. It's like a dog or cat. A good cat's a good cat, and a good dog's a good dog. I like a good dog, but a sorry one is about the sorriest thing there is on God's good earth. You take a good nigger, it's the same. But a sorry nigger—"

Whidden said, "Speck? Let's—"

"All I'm sayin is, God give His own strength to the white race! And the strong ones eat the weak ones and they always did, that's the way of fish and the way of man and the way of God's Creation—dog eat dog! And for all us poor fools know about it, this dog-eat-dog might just be the way God *wants* it! Might be His idea of *justice*, ever think of that? Keepin His Creation strong? Might be God's *Mercy*!"

"I'm ashamed," Sally murmured, weeping. "Truly ashamed." She got up and headed for the boat, and her father leaned forward around Andy House to admire her movements. "Ain't she sweet?" He sighed when he sat back again. "I got another daughter in Miami just as purty, only this girl purely *loves* her daddy, loves to set on her bad old daddy's knee." He winked at Whidden, who looked past him, watching Sally brush her teeth and crawl into her bedroll. Her father nodded in approval, as if she were being a good little girl about her bedtime.

"Speakin of that other daughter, you fellers hear about them black boys that busted in when I was over visitin Miami? When my little grandchild run outside and left the door unlocked while I was layin on the sofa? These two snuck in and when they seen me, they run right over and started in to beatin on me. One straddled me and broke my nose all up while the other was yankin at my pockets, huntin my wallet, and neither of 'em spoke a word the whole time they was there. Money for dope, that's what the cops told me, but it seemed more like plain old hate to me. Old man that never done a thing to them damn people, and here they're invadin in broad daylight, just *a-beatin* on him? *Got* to be hate! I sure don't know what's the matter with that kind, with all our tax money they are gettin free on nigger welfare!

"Had a stray bullet whap into my daughter's house, fall on the floor, when the cops was runnin dopers there on the back avenues. This is dangerous stuff that's goin on! Used to be you could leave everythin unlocked, now you have to guard your house twenty-four hours a day. I ain't so much a religious person, but I think that the Old Man Up There, He'll have to take and thin some of this out. The world is gettin so wicked, y'know, something has to stop. They talk about old-time desperaders like Ed Watson, but the killin back then ain't nothin like it is today. See more killed in one week on the news than Watson done away with in a lifetime!

"Miami now, there's a barbecue on the next block has a nigger in it who just thinks the world of me. Said he'd find them ones who beat me up, get 'em took care of. Good nigger people, they don't want that kind around no more'n we do.

"Next day a man drove right up to the house. Very easy and polite, like he was in some kind of law enforcement. Handed me a card without no name on it, only a Miami phone number. Says, 'Mr. Daniels, I seen in the papers where niggers invaded into your home and robbed and beat you. You think you would know them ones that done it? Cause if you ever run acrost 'em, you can call this number and describe 'em, say where they are at. You can reach this number twenty-four hours a day, you understand me, Mr.

Daniels? Twenty-four hours every day. All you got to do is call and then you're out of it.' Got back in his big car and went away. Don't seem like that man worked in law enforcement, what do you think?"

Asked what the man looked like, Speck said, "Well, I ain't forgot him. Heavy-set strong-lookin feller, pale moony face, dark jowls, y'know, but clean-shaved all the same. Had these pale blue eyes with a dark outside ring. Why I recall 'em, I seen that same dark eye ring on a panther that come prowlin into camp one night, took my best hound. This was back before the Park, up Lost Man's Slough. I heard somethin and sat up and worked my flashlight. This big cat had my best dog by the throat, haulin him off. Had that hound killed on the first jump, hardly made a sound. When the beam hit him, he dropped that dog and crouched. Didn't back up, he didn't want to leave it. Stared down my light beam all the while I was fumblin for my rifle. Then he was gone, weren't nothin left, only that circle of the beam with the dead dog in it."

Lucius called, "That man look anything like Watson Dyer?"

Speck relit his cigarette before he answered. "I ain't never laid eyes on Watson Dyer," he said, expelling smoke. "Him and me done all our talkin on the phone."

"How about that military officer? In the helicopter?"

Speck chewed on this idea. "With the sunshine blazin up the wind-shield—oil haze and smashed bugs and scratches on that plastic—I never got a good look at the face. All the same, he looked some way familiar." He nodded a little. "Might been that same man but I ain't sure."

Speck finished his jug and tossed it aside and tottered to his feet. "Got to get goin early in the morning." He said this to all of them, by way of parting. He was already headed for his boat when he stopped short and wheeled so fast he almost fell.

"Colonel? I believe you might be right. He might been Dyer. Same real deep calm voice, like a old-time preacher. And that military man, I never got a good look at his face, but I seen his hind view when he got out to take a leak. Same set to his walk as that Miami feller, back on his heels with his boot toes pointed out, like a bear reared up on his hind legs. That sound like Dyer?"

"That's the feller in my gas station!" Andy exclaimed. "*All you got to do is call and then you're out of it*—the selfsame feller!"

Speck had come back and was swaying over the fire. "I ain't so much for coloreds, now, don't get me wrong. But a growed man runnin around on his own time and money, huntin down niggers he ain't never even seen? That is a man with a bad case of race predu-juice or somethin!" Speck looked sly again, and not wishing to encourage him, the others went off to their blankets, leaving him tottering and hooting by the fire. But soon, he pitched his voice toward their blankets, and his tone grew angry as his oratory rose. He was still ranting at the world when Lucius fell asleep.

"—yessir, Friends, them Glades today is layin out there DEAD! No use to NO-body! A big ol' godforsaken swamp, ain't hardly fit for rep-tiles nor mosquiters! And these here Islands goin to wind up the same way! Don't you dumb-ass taxpayers realize how much prime tourist coast is goin to waste right here in southwest Florida? When we could pump white sand out of the Gulf where it don't do a single bit of good, make gorgeous beaches, dredge nice cocktail-boat canals right smack through them mis'rable ol' mangroves, throw up deluxe waterfront condoms just like we got right here in ol' Miam-uh? Condoms a-risin on the Sun Coast Skyline in just a thrillin silver line, all the way south around Cape Sable! If *that* ain't the American Dream, I don't know what! Sunset on the Golden Gulf, just a-glintin off them condoms, turnin 'em from silver into gold!"

*

Lucius Watson tossed on the hard sand. Had he lived his entire life in dread of awful revelations which in some realm below consciousness were already known? Rob's tale seemed so utterly remote, corresponding but faintly with his own sun-filled memories of Papa and the Bend—had memory betrayed him? Had there been no shadows? Had he never wondered ?

He felt gutted. So near its finish after all these years, his biography of E. J. Watson seemed invalidated, wasted, in the half-light of Rob's story, with its implicit validation of what Daniels had so vilely called "Watson's Nigger Payday."

And Rob? If Rob survived and were miraculously set free to be a fugitive, where would he hide? There would be no sanctuary at Gator Hook, far less Caxambas. The old man would be entirely dependent on his brother, for who else would look after him? Next week? Next month? Next year?

Lying there hour after hour, his mind struggled against Speck Daniel's insinuation that Lucius . . . that in the end, it might be best for everyone—Rob in particular—if Rob Watson were . . . to disappear? How could Daniels imagine that Rob's own brother might harbor such an unnatural idea! Surely this came from his own ugly misanthropy and bitter feelings, his disappointment in his own half-crazed, doomed son!

But after midnight, started up from restless sleep, Lucius was breathless with deep anxious guilt that in his heart, at least, he had betrayed his brother. Why had Speck's insinuations so upset him, unless his shock and outrage were not honest? Was a craven and exhausted hypocrite named Lucius Watson so willing to believe that death would come as a relief and mercy to Rob Watson, setting him free from a badly broken life?

Speck Daniels had forced his nose into an unsuspected seam in his own nature, an inadmissible twinge of regret over the fact that someone—Rob— had survived to bear witness against their father. Would Daniels have hinted at Lucius's ambivalence if the scent of that ambivalence had not encouraged him? Did he truly intend to set Rob free or—imagining he understood Lucius Watson's secret wish—did he mean to let those others kill him? This would have to be settled first thing in the morning. Lucius tossed and twisted, only to sink away toward the night's end, harried by dreams. Across the cove where moonlit water danced like crystals in the mangroves, a night heron gave its strangled *quock*, to unknown purpose.

*

At first light, he awakened, unsure where he was, cobwebbed by dreams. The mangrove delta, still guarding the nighttime, lay in darkness. Squatted on his heels by a new fire, Whidden Harden was making coffee. The blond head at one end of the bed rolls would be Sally, and the blind man was the amorphous lump beyond.

Speck Daniels's ancient cabin boat was gone.

Lucius dragged himself half-sick from his damp bedding and wandered clumsily toward the point. Far out on the Gulf, the dark cloud rims were edged with pewter, and the sea, roiled to a smoky green by distant storm, was smooth after night rain. On this shore where the innocent young victims had been lifted from the sandy shallows, he mourned for Rob and for the waste of his own life, which over the night seemed to have lost all purpose.

At the fire, without looking up, Whidden Harden handed him hot coffee. Respecting each other's silence, warming their hands on the cups, they hunkered together as they had so often when Whidden was a boy.

"Does he ever say good-bye?" Lucius said at last.

Whidden shook his head. "Likes to stay one jump ahead and sometimes two."

Awakened before daybreak by the kick and quiet burble of Speck's motor, Whidden had gone down to the water and unhitched the bow line from the driftwood stump and waded out with it. In cool water to his waist, he stayed the old boat against the drag of current while they shared a smoke. Speck told him he was heading for the Bend to help his crew with the last loads. "Keep these people away, you understand me?" When Whidden nodded, Speck insisted, "Don't you cross us, boy. This ain't no kind of picayune deal we're talkin here. With all the money and big men that's tied up in munitions, it ain't got to go very far wrong before somebody comes up killed." He flicked his cigarette butt toward the blanket lumps by the dead fire. "Them, for instance."

"Your own baby daughter, Speck?"

"Maybe her first," Speck said with a sour smile.

Sifting this, Lucius found no clue to Speck's intentions. He dredged his brain for the worst implications of what he'd said to Speck, and the way he'd said it, down to the last inflection, knowing the while that none of this mattered, it was all too late. Rob Watson's fate was in Daniels's hands, and Daniels was on his way to Chatham Bend. The one hope was the plan to release the hostages this afternoon. Was it only despair that made him certain that for whatever reason, this release would not occur, and that Daniels had known this when he proposed it?

When Lucius questioned him about Speck's promise to let his brothers escape to Mormon Key, Whidden looked doubtful. Maybe Speck's men would go along with that, and maybe not. But in case there were six mouths to feed at Mormon Key this evening, Whidden said, they should go fishing.

*

Over the Glades as the skiff moved up the river, the purple sky went the bad yellow color of old bruise. The mangrove delta seemed gray and dead and the current empty, turning and turning with the earth in great slow spirals, wandering ever westward down First Lost Man's Bay. "Comin off the Gulf, headin upriver, the first bay you would come to"—Lucius imagined this was how, in the old century, this vast, uninhabited mangrove reach had got its name. The lost man, the man lost—who might he have been? What age and color, origin and destination? Indian, Spaniard, castaway, slave—where was his lost voice now? And where his bones?

For the first time in all the years he had inhabited this region, he found himself disturbed by the river's name. In this gray void of silent water and dark forest, the lonely intuition came that he had strayed into some Land of the Lost where the man lost was the man doomed to apprehend his ultimate solitude on earth as his ordained existence. And again he recalled his father's fascination with "the Undiscovered Country," which signified not wilderness, but death.

Perhaps Whidden Harden sensed this dread, perhaps this was why he seemed so sad and shy. Drifting downriver, avoiding Lucius's eye, he whistled and picked and chirped and trilled, invoking river spirits. He muttered as he rigged the lines, he uttered incantations. "Got to coax 'em on there," he sang to the river over the soft purl of the outboard. "Got to *coax* 'em."

At sunrise, the flood quickened with life, the smooth swift surface of descending current broken now by myriad swirls and slits cut by scaled creatures. Working the current points for sea trout, Whidden coughed softly, sun-up cigarette in the corner of his mouth.

Lucius cast his lure with a quick whisk, dropping it beneath the branch tips. He worked it in an arc across the current, awaiting the strike from hidden depths that might reconnect him to the heart of the world. In sleepless exhaustion, needing an end, he asked Whidden's opinion of what Speck Daniels had said the night before about "Watson Payday." Perhaps this was what Whidden had feared coming, for he grunted. In a little while, with no changes of expression, he began speaking.

"Early thirties, now, before the Park come in, a few men was still shootin plume birds for the foreign market. Late as '35, a seaplane come in and cleaned out the last egrets, Whitewater Bay, and them Audubons was tryin to put a stop to it. Back at that time, a feller name of Charlie Green was Audubon warden up the coast at Duck Rock rookery. Remember Charlie? Pretty good feller, never paid no mind if a man shot a few white ibis for his supper, cause curlews was common. Well, one fine evenin the head Audubon, a Yankee from New York, come with Charlie on the Audubon boat—the old *Widgeon*, cabins fore and aft, remember her?—to where the fishermen was living on these houseboat lighters back of Turkey Key. They heard somebody shootin in the bayou, and when that man learned how us local boys was takin a few curlews, he cussed out ever'body, Charlie included. So later that night, around the moonrise, them two turned in. And knowin Charlie's cabin was up forward, some of us boys circled that boat, shot the portholes clean out of the after cabin. And you know somethin? That head Audubon never poked his head out once to tell us ignorant local fellers we done wrong!

"Course them old-time wardens was laid off when the Park took over. Charlie Green was a local man and knew how to act proper, but most of these Park greenhorns is outsiders, like Speck says. One time a couple of that kind come to Turkey Key and told us we had to pay cash for federal licenses to fish commercial 'in Park waters,' never mind that back in them days, folks never had no cash money at all. So one of them young Browns sings out, 'Well, we been here since 1880, and you been here since 1947—now which one do these Everglades belong to?' Then his brother hollers, 'How fast will your boat go?' And when the ranger told him, young Brown says, 'If you get goin right this minute, that might be about fast enough to haul your dumb ass out of here before it gets shot off'—"

"Whidden? I'm serious. I want to know if the Harden family ever heard or saw any good evidence that E. J. Watson killed his help rather than pay them."

Risking his teeth, Whidden bit off a rusty knot of linen line and spat the bitter end into the scuppers. "Charlie Green had a young helper on Duck Key, and somebody had lent this boy a contraption to try out—early-type metal detector, not even on the market yet, might been the first one ever made, for all I know. I seen it once, hell of a lookin thing—heavy ol' black box with tin earphones, wouldn't hunt down but about two feet.

"This was still Depression times, and very few jobs anywhere. Henry Short had no steady work, so he spent a lot of time huntin for gold. Henry had heard about this new-fangled machine, and he got the loan of it for a few days, wanted to try it out. He was convinced that the Calusa—or maybe the Frenchman, or maybe Mr. Watson—had left buried treasure on Chatham Bend.

"One day Henry shows up at South Lost Man's. I believe you must of been away. For such a calm man, he was fevered and upset, but finally he sat down and ate something. Lee Harden said, 'How come you're so worked up? You find your treasure?' Henry shook his head. He shoved a rusty ax head and a big ol' screw-lid jar acrost the table. That jar was full of belt buckles and metal buttons and cheap one-blader pocketknives, part steel, part brass, except the steel was all et out by rust. And a few—a very few—spent bullets. Accordin to Henry, he found this stuff in an unfarmed piece up in the north-west corner of the Bend. All that box had picked up near the building, Henry said, was metal scrap and a few busted tools.

"Lee Harden grew very very quiet. He said, 'You find anythin else?' And Henry said, 'Bones.' 'Well hell,' Pa said, 'he had cows on there and pigs, even a old horse at one time, so bones ain't nothing!' 'Skulls,' said Henry. 'And three or four had holes that might been made by bullets.' Said them bones was laying in these shaller graves along with the knives and buckles. About half the graves had a single bullet layin in amongst the bones, and one grave had three.

"Pa was still resistin Henry's story. He went and mentioned that old horse again, and bones of old-time Injuns that used to live there, and this time some color come to Henry's face. Says 'Darn it, Lee, there ain't no mistakin a human skull, not for no horse or hog! And anyways, domestical animals don't generally wear belts and buttons, and only a very few will tote a pock-etknife!'

"Lee Harden lit up his cob pipe, took a few puffs to settle down his nerves. He was very surprised to hear Henry Short snap out at him that way, and Henry looked startled, too, but he didn't quit or nothin. He said, 'And they ain't no old-time Injuns, neither! You know who them poor souls were just as good as I do!' My pa put them pathetical things back in that big jar while he got a bridle on his temper. Then he said, 'All right. How many skulls?' And Henry tells him nine or ten and probably some more where them ten came from.

"Pa went back with him to Chatham that same day. He seen for himself them molderin green bones in the dirt and leaves. Straightened up to get his breath and looked south through the trees at the back of the Watson Place out on the river, and the sight of that old walleyed house give him the shivers." Here Whidden paused. "He told Henry that Colonel Watson might not care to have them graves dug up nor even spoke about. He said, 'Let's you'n me fill in them graves and cover 'em up and never speak of 'em again.' I reckon Pa and Henry never spoke of it again. Pa never told nobody except only me, and this was some years later."

"How did Speck Daniels hear about it, then?"

"He didn't. The rumor Speck heard—Andy mentioned it day before yesterday—come from that one body that showed up on the bar down from the Bend. That's where that whole story got started, back in your dad's lifetime."

Whidden checked his line, picking off weed. "I sure am sorry, Mister Colonel."

Lucius remembered that torn sodden body, and how it was shown to him by a black man who came south with Papa from north Florida. Over the years, as he now recognized, he had sealed away the entire episode, and "Black Frank" with it, so resolutely that he might have gone to his grave without recalling it—well, no, not quite. Reese's name had resurfaced in those court documents in Columbia County. And even before Andy's mention, that dead man on the bar would rise to the surface of his dreams from the farthest reaches of unknowing, as petroleum rises in strange rainbow traces in black marshland pools.

"So Henry found his buried treasure after all," Lucius felt poisoned by his own bitterness. "I mean, dammit, Whidden, where's that boy with the black box? Where's that damn button jar? There has to be evidence for this kind of story!"

"That young feller went adrift, I reckon—we ain't never heard about him. Charlie Green, he's acrost on the east coast someplace."

"You never saw those graves and bones yourself."

Whidden shook his head. "Dig out all that hard shell ground back in that thorn? With all them rattlers that's back in there?"

"It's a colorful story," Lucius decided. "But without evidence it's only hearsay, like all the rest."

"Think it's hearsay?" Whidden looked up. "Who you aimin to call a liar, Mister Colonel? Me? Lee Harden? Maybe Henry Short?"

"Oh no. I don't mean that, Whidden. No, no. Somebody killed *some*body, all right." A terrible despair choked off his voice. "Yes, that's quite a story," he repeated stupidly.

Chapter 11

The Fire

From far off, faintly, came strange heavy thumping. The sound agitated Lucius, but moments passed before he awoke to what it was. "Damn," he said. A moment later, Whidden, who had dozed a little, sat up straight to stare off toward the north. The sound was muffled in high white haze and clouds. Then the air shifted and the thumping changed to the hard chatter of a helicopter. The sky to the northeastward opened in a broad slow flare of light, and in moments a plume of dark smoke rose and broadened swiftly, shrouding the huge thunderheads over the Glades.

Whidden grabbed his knife and cut the fish lines and scrambled to yank the pull rope on the outboard. Boring downriver, the skiff threw plumes of brown tannin water and a seething wake. Whidden was shouting—*sonsabitches . . . come in a day early!*—but the voice was whipped away across the wind.

Hearing the howl of the outboard, Sally had guided the blind man aboard the *Belle*, dumped the bedding and loose cooking ware into the cockpit, even cranked the engine. Whidden eased the *Belle* into reverse as Lucius hauled on her stern anchor line. Then she was clear, and the current carried her on a turning drift downriver past the bars. Towing the skiff, she crossed the delta and the sandy emerald flats to deeper water, where she picked up speed, heading north along the island coasts.

The skiff yawed wildly back and forth across the wake. "Bridle her!" Whidden yelled, tossing Lucius a line. Lucius's hands remembered how to rig a tow line to a bridle, and for a moment he took comfort from the feel of the old rope, the hot hard chafe and pull of coarse tarred hemp, and the good smell of it, so familiar from his long days on the water. But the dread lay and curled up in his lungs like a hard black worm at the stem of an apple.

*

The *Belle* was north of Plover Key when the helicopter came in view, looming out of the glinting pall of fire smoke inland. A sharp tacketing like gunfire came and went as it turned and hovered, probed with a loud *snap-whacking* of the rotors, then rose away like a great maddened dragonfly.

In the delta, the odor of the burning was heavy on the heavy air. Whidden drove his boat recklessly upriver, scattering dark water birds before the bow, churning brown waves from the shallow channel that crashed among the red mangrove stilts along the banks.

The explosion of hard pine in the Watson Place had blasted black pitch high into the clouds, but already the smoke plume was thinning, drifting back inland, casting its sepia pall on the Glades thunderheads. On Chatham Bend was a shadow presence where the house had stood, and the forest all around was gray with ash. Gaunt, blackened trees formed an amphitheater around the dying flames, behind thick oily shimmerings of melted air.

Near the charred uprights, in the pulse and glowering of fallen timbers, a spectral figure raised a slow uncertain hand. Even at a distance, that hand appeared to twitch, like a chronometer calibrating old slow seconds.

The man did not move when Lucius jumped ashore and ran toward him. The face, the hair and clothes and heavy shoes, were ashy, and the ash was wet, caked and runny with green algae, as if this figure had arisen from the swamp. All around on the blackened ground lay rotted gator hides. Closer to the fire, the hides lay twisted and curled into black crusts, and a stench of charred flesh infiltrated the rank smell of the dead house in the hellish air.

Addison Burdett appeared slow and passive, like a retarded person left to await the bus. Next to Ad's big work shoe was Rob's satchel. Lucius reached out to him, pushing gently at his shoulder when he did not respond. "Ad," he murmured. "Ad? Where's Rob?" At his touch, his brother commenced weeping. The red shine of the mouth and eyes were wounds in the caked ash, and his tears, descending, made smooth tracks on his ash skin, and the spent teeth in the gray mask were chattering.

"I stink," Ad said.

Lucius could not reach out to his brother. It was less the outlandish appearance, the wet reek of him, than because—in his own need to hold himself together—he feared that touching him might shatter some fragile surface tension, causing Burdett to come apart entirely.

"Ad? Where's Rob?" His brother turned slowly and pointed at the fire bed of the old house. It was so *hot,* Ad whispered. Then his yelps came, slurred by tears and mucus, and the gray face twisted out of shape as if his head had been run over. Shocked by that dark macabre image, Lucius Watson took his brother in his arms.

*

Late into the night before, the gunrunners had roared upriver with their cargoes. With no help from the one-armed man, only rough orders, Mud and Dummy heaved the heavy crates, and by midnight Mud was stumbling with exhaustion.

The men had provided moonshine for their old friend Chicken (Ad stated proudly that he had refused it), assuring him that his death seemed unavoidable. "We're all tore up about it," Mud Braman told him. "Gonna hurt us worse than it does you." Mud's teasing seemed very cruel to Ad, who could not believe these men were serious.

When he warned his brother that at his age, hard drink would be the death of him, Rob only smiled. Though Rob was frightened by the act of dying, the prospect of being dead upset him not at all. Holding forth over his cup of shine, he told Ad what he'd told Speck Daniels, that he was sick and tired of the ordeal of his life, he'd had enough. His one ambition was to stay drunk until the end.

Much of the night, they had lain listening to the gunrunners, who were drinking on the porch. Old Man Chicken, they agreed, would be better off dead than returned to prison "for the rest of his natural life," as Mud Braman put it, raising his voice to make sure that the old fugitive inside the house could enjoy the discussion. "Yessir, they'd just throw away the key on that mean old feller!"

Rob told Ad he meant to thwart any attempt to establish this house as a monument to a damn killer. Though he sympathized with his young brother about the waste of his fine paint job, he hoped to see the "House of Watson" burned down to the ground, obliterating the bloodstain on the floor of the front room and the remains of a thousand wasted alligators—"the desecration of Creation," the old man yelled toward the porch, while admitting to Ad that he could take gators or leave them. Purification by fire, he believed, was their family's last hope of exorcism and redemption. So long as this house of evil stood, he had declaimed—as the gunrunners shouted at him

to shut up, and threatened gagging—their family name would be synony-
mous with murder!

When Ad quoted Lucius, who had said that most of the old Watson stories were just rumors, Rob just shook his head. "Luke has to believe that," he
told Ad finally. "It's his whole life."

*

Early this morning, the last munitions crates had been dragged out of the
house and slung onto the airboat platform with loud metallic bangs and
booming thuds. The men set the brothers free outside the house on the condition that they salvage the best gator flats and stack them by the water's
edge and throw the rest into the river to destroy the evidence. If they did a
good job, Ad's skiff would be fetched from the far bank when the airboat returned, and the prisoners would be free to head downriver.

Rob told the men that Speck had promised that his old revolver would be
returned to him, since it had come down from his dear departed daddy. Retrieving it from Dummy's toolbox, Mud inspected it, saying, "If this damn
thing belonged to Bloody Watson, it's worth money!" Crockett snatched it
away from him, cursing Dummy's fecklessness when he saw that the old
weapon was still loaded. He shook its cartridges onto the deck before lobbing
it toward the old man on the bank, then bellowed at Dummy to let go the
line. The airboat backed off the bank and turned up current.

"Things always come out right in the end," Ad told Rob, watching them
go. "That's what they say, all right," Rob said. Eyes squinted in the glare and
smiling oddly—smiling and frowning *both*, it seemed to Ad—he seemed deaf
to his half brother's plea that he help with the sorting and stacking of the
hides so that they could leave as soon as the airboat returned.

"They might not be back," Rob told him, indicating his satchel, which
Mud had flung off the airboat onto the bank. He pointed toward the helicopter, thumping the heavy clouds in the eastern distance.

*

Whidden and Sally had brought Andy from the boat, and they, too, were
listening to Ad, from a discreet distance. "I know where they off-load
them weapons," Whidden said. "In a airboat, it ain't ten minutes up this
river. If they was coming back, they would of been here." Gazing at Ad's
pathetic stack of alligator hides, he looked disgusted. "Them hides ain't
no use no more to nobody. They knew that. They was finished with this
place!"

When the airboat had gone, Rob had gone down to the water's edge and hefted a five-gallon can of fuel. A cigarette was hanging from his mouth, and seeing the red can, Ad yelled a warning. Oblivious, Rob gazed a moment at the river, then lugged the red can to the house and up onto the porch. There he set it down and took off one high sneaker and shook out what looked like a small cartridge, which he held up to the sun like an elixir. His grin looked strange. "Take care of yourself, Ad." Leaving that lone sneaker behind, he limped into the house.

Faced with the empty doorway, Ad called his brother's name and heard no answer. Recounting this, he broke out in a sweat, starting to shudder. " 'Take care of yourself, Ad!' That's all he said! And he went in there and set that house afire!" Ad stared at them in disbelief. "I mean, seein him lug that gasoline in there, I thought, What in the heck can that old feller be up to? He sure is pretty strong for an old-timer!

"Then it hit me! I ran toward the porch, hollering *Stop!* I yelled with all my might! That door stayed black and empty. And right about then there came this big soft *boom*—"

"—darned cigarette!" cried Andy.

"—and the heat exploded through the door, it burned my face!" Like a child witness, frantic to exorcise what had frightened it, Ad waved away their voices, raising his own. "And that's when he shrieked how he'd dropped the gun, how he couldn't see!"

In moments, the front room filled with fire, driving him back out onto the porch as the first flames licked through the smoke behind the window. Fire rushed upward through the house in a deep thunder. But over that thunder Ad imagined he heard screaming, and he screamed back, though what he might have screamed he did not know.

Andy House said, "Addison? I knew this house. That screechin you heard might of been the workin of that iron-hard old pine in so much heat. Them uprights and old beams—"

"It was my brother! Burning alive! I couldn't get to him!" He sank down, face sunk in his hands as he coughed and blithered.

"Never heard no shot? Think that old gun misfired? Jesus!"

"Oh, Lord, Mister Colonel! We're so sorry!"

Sally Brown had stood there with closed eyes, pressing her fingers to her temples, but now she came weeping to hug Lucius.

*

Addison had run around the house to the kitchen door and poked his head in, calling. But there was no outcry anymore, only that thunder and loud crackling of pine, and the beams creaking, the black choking smell of burning pitch. By the time he retreated (he couldn't help but notice), the fire leaping upward from the windows was charring and curling his new paint. Through the old shingles, the roof seemed to glow, as if the house were swelling with trapped heat, holding its fiery breath. Then flames licked out in devil's tongues along the peak. Through a thickening pall, the hollowed house loomed and vanished like an apparition.

As if drawn to the boom and thunder of the firestorm, the helicopter came whacketing in over the treetops like a tornado. A wild light blinded him, and whips of fire flayed his skin "like the terrible swift sword in the old hymn!" He screamed for mercy, certain this machine had come to hunt him down. Cringing from the heat and noise, too frightened to run out into the open, he was driven by terror to hide himself in the old cistern, clinging like a frog to the slimy wall. He screeched with all his might for the Lord's mercy, not only for himself but for that agonized old man whose mortal cries had died but whose coil lay charring in hellfire.

Here Ad broke down again. They retreated a little, giving him time. Lucius said softly, "Nothing you could do, Ad. Don't torment yourself."

Ad did not believe that the helicopter had caused the fire, for it had materialized after that huge soft explosion. Yet he was convinced that as it passed, he had glimpsed something falling in a long swift arc, for the house had shuddered in a deep rumbling *boom*, followed by a rush of fire and black smoke, then a rain of burning bits and shingles. A minute later, when he dared to lift the cistern cover, the burning house was gone as if evaporated. There was only that devouring heat and the low rushing of the burning timbers. Where the house had been, through the oily emptiness and cindered air, he could see a swimming bird, far our on the broad bend of the river.

"Firebomb," Whidden pronounced. "I had that idea the minute I seen that first quick flare at Lost Man's. Maybe the old man blew up that gas can, but it looks to me like they firebombed just to make sure. Or maybe," he continued, trying to make sense of it, "the gas can touched off some explosives. Speck told me they was concentratin on the automatic weapons, cause there weren't no time to transfer all them cargos."

"That's right!" Ad cried. "Those crates inside were stacked right to the ceiling!"

"Made a dawn run a whole day early to catch 'em inside," Whidden decided. "And when they seen the smoke, they bombed her anyway, cause that was their damn orders. Very childish men. Enjoy all them big shiny toys, enjoy destruction, but they want it all wrote down on a paper, want it all official. Who or what might be inside, that ain't their business."

Lucius, sick and dizzy, mumbled dully that the firebomb might have been a mercy to the man burning. His brother's agonies were talons in his heart. The *uselessness* of Rob's self-immolation! The Watson house would have been destroyed without him!

Only last night, under the stars at Lost Man's Key, the death of that fore-doomed old man—in the light of the alternative—had seemed an endurable idea. This was because it was just that—an idea, an abstraction, with none of the furious pain and terror of a death by fire, none of the stunning immediacy of Ad's "hellfire," or even of that dog-eared satchel, huddled there like a reproach on the blackened ground. To perish screaming, mouth stretched wide as a black hole, twisting like the human damned in some Black Ages painting, the descent of sinners into Hell—

His lungs brought up an ugly sound like the hard cough of a choked dog. In the blackening air he lost his sight and sank onto his knees, pressing his hands to the scorched earth to keep from sinking further into darkness. Around him dim voices came and went, hoarse incantations from the netherworlds—

Rob—one word, sepulchral, formed and vanished

Rob

Who was calling?

God have mercy

. . . all right?

Old pine subsumed, crack and shudder of the burning, spiral goings and returnings, the blood, the suffering of sentient things purified to the last atom by blue mineral flame, primordial ash and ancient gases, gathered in by air and water and returned at last to ocean and to earth, world without end

Amen

Rob Watson

the whispering as he came clear again, the dim shifting of specters, the black tree silhouettes on the bend of silent river

still on his knees, staring down at the blood conduits and sinews of the two gnarled hands, affixed like dragon claws to the black earth

You all right, Mister Colonel?

What's the matter with him? What's the matter!

Faces. Whidden Thomas Harden. Andrew Wiggins House. Sally Daniels Brown Harden. Addison Watson Burdett.

What's the matter?

Lucius struggled to stand up. When the Hardens sought to support him under the arms, he shook them off, only to relapse onto hands and knees. Kneeled on all fours, letting the blackness fade, he watched a drop fall from his eyes to strike a tiny crater in the ash.

Ad whimpered. He had burned his leg. All stared at the red burn on the pale and hairy slab as he pulled aside his poor charred shreds of pant leg.

Brother, we cannot kiss your wound. We cannot make it well.

Lucius straightened slowly and sat back upon his heels, trying to clear his head, as Addison, in fits and starts, finished his story—how the helicopter had returned, how it came in low and hovered as he sank into the green water, fingers clinging to rough places in the cistern wall.

"Taking official pictures for their official damn report." Whidden was still piecing it together. By now, he guessed, the helicopter crew must have noticed that the only boat at Chatham Bend was that empty skiff on the far bank.

"Seeing no boats, they probably assumed that nobody was in the house," Lucius suggested, wondering why he needed to excuse them.

The helicopter had swung off toward the north and descended slowly until it disappeared behind the trees. Certain it had landed, Ad was terrified he had been seen, that these unknown enemies would come in on foot to hunt him down. Even when the thing rose again over the trees and headed back toward the east, and he crawled out into the hot sun, stinking with slime, he remained crouched beside the tarn until he heard the *Cracker Belle*, coming upriver.

*

Lucius wanted to stay long enough to retrieve his brother's body from the embers. Although they had no more food and little water, Whidden nodded. He did not have to say that as boat captain, he was responsible for their safety, and that the sooner they got away from here, the better. As the humid afternoon wore on, he became more and more restless, certain that the helicopter would return.

*

The housepainter, in choked fits and muffled starts, emptied out his fifty years of throttled feelings.

A week earlier in Neamathla, when he'd learned from Lucius that this house might be burned, Ad had rushed away from his sister's place feeling hugely angry and upset, though why or against whom he did not know. For the first time in years, he returned to heavy drinking, raging away at strangers and bar mirrors that E. J. Watson and the Watson Place had nothing to do with Addison Burdett. Sobered by a rude arrest for disorderly conduct, he took his savings from the bank and left next day for the Ten Thousand Islands, telling nobody, not even Ruth Ellen. "Why? Who knows why?" Ad grumbled. "Because I'm some kind of a misfit and a crank, and always have been!" He struggled to pretend this was a joke, and Lucius chuckled as best he could to help him out, but the fraternal moment failed, and they plodded onward.

"All my vacation time and all my savings! For a beautiful paint job that didn't last two days! It was hardly dry!"

"Time, paint, food, and fuel," Lucius commiserated. "And the boat rental—"

"Smallwood never charged me. Said I was crazy to waste all that good paint, but refused my money. Wouldn't explain why and went off grumpy."

Contemplating the steaming embers, Ad regretted what he saw as his own foolishness and sentimentality—he regretted this worse than the waste of time and money. Recalling Lucius's offer at Neamathla to help pay his way if he would attend the Park meeting at the Bend, he said that after Lucius left, Ruth Ellen had offered the same thing. "I refused her, too!" He yanked up his big palm in angry warning lest any man imagine he sought help. "I wanted to pay for all of it out of my own pocket. Coming here to paint the house was what *I* could do, it was *my* idea, not *your* idea, not *her* idea. I wanted to settle Ad Burdett's account with Watsons." He looked confused, not certain what he meant by this, and in confusion gave an odd, inchoate roar.

*

Without the revolver and the Tucker packet, Rob's old satchel weighed no more than a sun-dried bird skeleton high on the tide line. His estate was reduced to a change of sad grayed shorts and threadbare socks, a splayed toothbrush and plastic razor, loose among the ancient lint and crumbs. Otherwise, all it contained was a "last will and testament," a letter to his younger brother which he had begun back in Lake City after fleeing his mother's grave at Bethel Churchyard, with emendations added here and there along the way. In fact, he had scratched down his last words this very morning.

To Whom It May Concern, namely Luke Watson:

My birth date and her day of death being the same, I wish to return and be buried near that girl who was my mother. You may recall the place and name: Ann Mary Collins, New Bethel Cemetery, Columbia County, Florida. (Our fine times traveling to old family places meant a lot to me. I don't suppose I ever told you that and it's too late now but thank you anyway.)

I leave you a heirloom revolver that belonged to your father. It still works, as my remains can testify. You can probably sell it to some gun nut for enough to pay to have my carcass burned down to the bones and shook down small, so the deacon at New Bethel Church can slot me in beside my poor young mama. (I wound up kind of an old stillbirth anyway.) A man has got to come to rest someplace.

> *We are traveling far, we are traveling home*
> *One by one, we are traveling home.*
> *Across death's river, our friends have gone,*
> *And we are following, one by one.*

That is the old Baptist hymn that your own kind mother loved. Say that for me at the graveside, Luke. Under your breath will do just fine. (If that old heathen Billie Jimmie wants to mumble some Injun ode back in the swamp someplace, that is all right, too.)

Well, two days have passed, and here I am, too drunk to organize my own demise. I will, I will. The above was written in Lake City, where I found your note. (Sure took you long enough to learn my rightful name!) Today I am on the bus south to Fort Myers.

I have carried this revolver all my life, same as my pecker, but never found much use for either one. The first and last woman I ever had was a big brown gal in that old cathouse on Black Betsy Key where E.J. took the first chip (off his old block) on his 19th birthday, September 13, 1898. (Carrie's marriage was just two months earlier, remember?) But after that morning at Lost Man's River, a woman could give me loving till the cows came home, and some of them did, bless their sweet hearts, but it never did me or them one bit of good. Wrath of God, do you suppose? Sins of the fathers? I'll have to discuss this with the higher-ups when I get to Heaven.

I have hung on to this "shootin iron," I'm not sure why. Because it is my souvenir of "Papa"? I hate to think I might be sentimental, but who can know the curlicues of the human heart? This is the weapon which took the life of an innocent young woman and her unborn babe at Lost Man's Key. This humble paw that writes these words—my mortal hand—pulled this simple trigger—how incredible it seems!—which is why it is fitting that I perish by this weapon—and this finger and this hand—on this day I have known was coming all my life.

I stole this weapon when I left the Bend, to shoot my father down if he caught up with me (or blow out my own brains, if I so chose!). That day in early 1901, my life lay in a thousand pieces, like a precious heirloom which had come into my keeping and—because I did not pay attention—was smashed to shards of rubble in an instant. This gun muzzle touched E. J. Watson's temple while he lay sprawled across his table, snorting like a hog. But nothing came of it—the story of my life! I was too broken, too hysterical, to muster up the resolve required to take another life on that same day, yet I think sometimes of the harm which might have been averted with one small forthright twitch of this forefinger! Would saving those lives atone for that life I took?

And yet I keep this weapon. I touch it now and then, as a reminder. This cold cold metal, this burnished hickory, fashioned somewhere in 19th century America, the simple precision of its parts—its very simplicity puts me in touch with sanity, it seems, or at least reality. For in some strange irony, that long ago day at Lost Man's River is the only real episode in a long and ghostly life. Does that make sense?

I have never learned much about life. Maybe you know something.

Another delay. I am a prisoner and no longer have the gun, though my keepers have promised to return it. I should have gotten out of this damned life while the getting was good, because now I'm in trouble and have brought you trouble, too—"a peck of trouble" as Mama used to say, do you remember, Luke? Your mama, not mine, of course (though she did her gentle best to love me, too). It's years since I thought about dear Mama's "peck of trouble"—eight whole quarts of trouble! That's enough!

Here I am on Chatham Bend, which I prayed I would never see again! How God rebukes us! What I can't get over is this shining house, which looks almost exactly as it did when we first arrived at Chatham back in '96 except for the screened porch and covered cistern, which came later. You were seven then so you might not remember—that big new house, fresh-painted white, way out in a vast wilderness all by itself, as if it had just dropped out of the sky! The boat sheds and the little cottage (which I only know from old photos sent me about 1909 by Julian Collins)—none of those outbuildings were built when I first knew this place, and now they are all lost to flood and hurricane.

By now you have read the true story of the Tuckers. Can you forgive me for my part in that fatal deed even though I cannot forgive myself? (being quite unable to accept, therefore atone for the eternal fact that the man I see in the mirror is a killer). To this day, I howl to the highest heaven: I am not a killer! I was never a killer! But I don't suppose it is Heaven where I'm headed, so I'm ranting instead at my poor dear brother Lucius Watson, because he is all I have left.

Luke? Do you hear me? Do you believe me? Do you forgive me?

If not you, then who?

Tonight Speck's kind clean-cut young fellows gave us moonshine and white ibis and fried gator tail. Life is grand! It's just that I never got the hang of it, I'm "tuckered out."

If I don't stop talking, you will decide I am not serious about "taking my life." I *am* serious, Luke, although not gloomy and downhearted. I am still in lively spirits! *Here Lies Rob Watson: Nothing Daunted*—that's how I count on you to remember R. B. Watson, a.k.a. "Arbie Collins," a.k.a. "Chicken."

I have one last duty to perform—the house. I will not ask forgiveness, knowing you won't give it. As for my own oblivion, the prospect heals me. I have put it off for fifty years but now I'm ready. So long, ol' Luke! I miss you!

With warmest good wishes from your old pal Arbie, alias (signed) your loving brother,

Rob

Reading these hard-earned pages as Lucius passed them along, Ad Burdett wept. "Rob must have been drunk and crazy, to write stuff like this!" Lucius shook his head, attempting to explain. Their brother had suffered unspeakable loss, then the unjust penance of a long and hollow life without hope of redemption. The only crazy thing about him was the crazed endurance it required to survive such an ordeal so long on nerve alone.

Mercifully, Rob had been spared Ol' Luke's innate melancholy and self-doubt, as well as the self-pity which plagued Addison. And how very different he had been from Eddie, who had aged so early and whose mask was cracking with fatigue. Poor Eddie, worn out by propping up appearances, would end his days the craziest of all. Lucius would have to notify him of Rob's death—not that Eddie would care, having always disliked Rob, in his fear of Rob's unvarnished insights and outspoken ways.

No, he was too tired to explain this to the housepainter, who was mopping his leaky nostrils with his knuckles. Without much heart, he tried teasing Ad a little. "If you think Rob was crazy, how about us? Runs in the family— 'the crazy Watson brothers'! Wait till you meet Eddie!"

"My name's not Watson and I am not crazy!"

"No, of course not." He patted Lucius Ad's shoulder. "Carrie and your sisters are fine, too."

"I don't *know* Carrie." Ad complained, his voice starting to rise, with tears behind it. "I was *never* crazy."

"I guess I was talking about 'crazy' *gestures*, like spending all your savings to come here from north Florida to paint an abandoned house, even though you were told it might be destroyed. I mean, that is a *great* gesture, Ad! I really admire it!" But Addison would not be consoled, he would not smile, nor even take pleasure in the compliment. Bowing his neck, he stared at his own paint-spotted shoes, moved to grief once more over his losses.

Oh Lord, thought Lucius, how much he missed Rob!

Under the ancient poincianas, he reread Rob's jaunty and heartbroken letter, which brought on an upwelling of pity for this man beside him. He had no business finding fault with Ad and Eddie. In the view of his entire family—all but Rob, perhaps—the greatest fool, the brother who was given the best chance of all and threw his life away, had been none other than Lucius Hampton Watson. "It's hard to put your finger on the fool"—wasn't that dear Mama's saying, too?

Ad Burdett was not a fool, merely a casualty. Wasn't that true of all the Watson brothers? Even Dyer?

*

Clouds came from the Gulf, dragging shrouds of ocean rain across the mangrove islands and raising acrid steam from the brooding embers. The brothers took shelter with the Hardens and Andy House in the boat cabin, where in dense wet heat, they sat too close and knee to knee. Finding room for Ad, trying to make him feel welcome and comfortable, Sally actually permitted herself a few sips of the moonshine which Whidden had miraculously discovered tucked away beneath the *Belle's* rust-rotted life jackets and moldy slickers. He winked at Lucius, holding up one of Speck's unlabeled bottles. "Astoundin, ain't it?"

*

The rain had stopped, leaving black puddles on the ground. The dull thumping of the helicopter, still circling in the eastern distance, had come and gone in the close silent air, but now the sound came again, and grew much louder. There was no time to move the *Belle*, or even hide. Ad Burdett relapsed into his moans, his big hands twitching, and Lucius called to him, "It's all right, Ad! It's all right!" But Harden whispered, "It ain't all right. Not if they decided—" But he left this thought unfinished, since it was too late.

In ricocheting wind and racket, the glinting thing roared low over the river, and the mad leaves danced as it cleared the trees and rocked to a stop in midair over their heads. Shattering the sun and light, the blades spun fire sparks and smoke into sudden dust devils and small tornadoes. An emblem on the fuselage behind the portholes resembled an American flag, yet the covert machine was not identifiable with the armed forces. Perhaps it was assigned to anonymous agencies. Perhaps the vast federal apparatus and its armed might, and all the war-oriented industries behind them must be invested in this shining thing.

Binoculars peered at them out of the portholes like submariners goggling at abyssal life. Was one of these lens-eyed creatures Watson Dyer?

In a shift of wind came a metallic squawk and static, and a moment later, the machine shot skyward. Soon it was far out to the west, rising high over the Gulf where the sky was clearing. Higher and higher the great dragonfly rose, black on the sun. Then it whirled downwind, returning toward the east in its silver gleaming, magnificent in its indifference to the small figures below.

Peering after it, Lucius was dismayed when his eyes misted, and he felt an impulse to salute the power of that swift and shining thing—God Bless America!

*

Whidden crossed the river to fetch Ad's skiff while Lucius waited with his brother on the bank. Ad had relapsed into a brooding silence, and the two stood together in discomfort, pretending to watch the *Cracker Belle* while struggling to make sense of what had happened. Ad burst out, "This house, and Rob, all this bad old-time stuff—it's none of my damned business! I only came to paint the house!"

The fire steamed. An iron sun loomed through the mist and was soon gone. On the gnarled roots of the scorched poincianas beside the river, the rough bark was blackened on the side nearest the fire, and there was no shade because the leaves had burned away. "I'm sorry, Ad," Lucius said finally.

"I think Rob told the truth!" Ad cried. "And I don't care!"

"All right." Lucius kicked an old scrap of gator hide into the water.

"You knew all these things? All your life?"

"Well, yes and no. I knew it and I didn't. There were dreams . . ."

"And you're putting that bad stuff into your book? About those bodies? Weren't you the one who made excuses for him? In Neamathla?"

Across the river, the *Belle* had the blue skiff in tow and was starting back.

"There won't be any book."

Lucius had not realized he had decided this until he said it. How could he celebrate his father's real accomplishment while pretending ignorance of what he knew. And after all, he had been warned, long, long ago that Papa was an unfit subject for biography.

How bitter it seemed that the "truths" he'd learned in long hard years of research had turned out to be only marginally more dependable than the Watson myth. The only "truths" of E. J. Watson were the intuitions rising at each moment—for example, that during his long years on the Bend, his driven father, whether or not he had ever paused to listen, had heard the song of an ancestral white-eyed vireo, all but identical to the dry wheezy trill which even at this moment came and went over the thump and pop of the rain-banked fire. The Calusa Indians had heard it, and the Harden clan and the old Frenchman, and a pretty little girl named Lucy Dyer, and even the lean and hungry Cox, alone on this storm-battered river, awaiting the return of Mr. Watson. In the stark wake of hurricanes and fire, the delicate bird went on and on about its seasons, oblivious of the mortal toil of man.

Addison was sneaking looks at him, in hope of something. But the long silences which had started to occur between them would only become chronic, Lucius knew, should they try to graft kinship onto loss, for there had been no twining of their vines since those fallow days here on the Bend fifty years before. In those days, Edna's Little Ad was solid as a meteor, rushing to Lucius in his churning run, falling forward all the way from the place he started to the point of impact on his chest. His joyful voice had accompanied every activity, even maniacal banging on pots and pans. That headlong rush for life would always be his fondest memory of Ad, who seemed to have sprouted with insufficient sap and was already browning and awaiting death. He would part with him sadly, yet without sorrow. They were not true brothers. Their roots were too long separated, dug up, dried out. Their only tie had been this house at Chatham Bend.

*

Ad hurried down the embankment to his boat. At a loss as to how to comfort him, Lucius trailed him to the water's edge, where Ad stared uncomprehending at his proffered hand. Lucius seized Ad's hand and shook the lifeless thing and let it drop.

"You don't want to wait a little longer, Ad? For the burial, I mean?"

"I have to go!"

Having fumbled their parting, the brothers tried to mend things in a rough embrace, and Lucius was relieved that Andy House, who stood nearby, had been spared such a disconcerting spectacle. Uncomfortable and abrupt, they had banged foreheads painfully. In that disjointed moment, hugging the stiff bulk of his unbathed brother, Lucius sensed his fundamental hollowness, as if long ago, due to deprivation or disease of spirit, a strong skeleton had failed to form inside him.

In his last years, their father had grown rather heavy, but not in the way of this youngest of his sons, who was already in his mid-fifties, or about Papa's age on the day that Papa died. Aunt Josie Jenkins had once remarked that when she hugged her Jack—and it turned out she had hugged him almost to the end—he was firm as ever, not merely well-muscled but as hard inside as the huge pit of a mango, scarcely contained within the sheath of flesh. Only in those final months, realizing that for all his hard work and the risks taken he could no longer outstrip his lifelong failure, had the furious furnace of Jack Watson's spirit started to die. That steel inside him turned to lead as he drank more and became sodden. By the end of it, all he spoke about with love was the lost plantation at Clouds Creek, his boyhood home in Edgefield County, South Carolina.

Duly the two brothers vowed that one day they would meet again, to get to know each other. Lucius even agreed to a return visit to Neamathla. Knowing the meeting would never take place, these honest men toed and kicked the ground in great discomfort. Then Ad broke away, lurched down the bank, and sprawled into the skiff, shoving her off without first starting the motor. He was out in the current yanking at the pull cord when the motor, which he'd left in gear, took hold with a roar and drove the boat out from beneath him. While he sprawled and thrashed to regain his balance, the skiff carved a tight half circle on the current before straightening on a downriver course. Lucius waved but Ad did not look back. He sat hunched in the stern like some strange outgrowth of the motor, rusted solid.

*

A man came in out of the fire mist, crossing the shadow land of the killed woods. He drifted, disappeared, and came again through smoke and blackened thorn, moving from willow clump to bush like a panther traveling across open savanna.

Coming downriver from the inland passage, Crockett Senior Daniels had slipped ashore above the Bend and made his wary way in through the thickets. Now he straightened and came forward, and still he peered about him, trusting nothing. He said sharply, "Where the hell is Chicken?" They told him what had happened. Daniels cursed. When he turned slowly to contemplate the ruin, Lucius saw the stiffness in him, the old man. "Ol' Chicken," Speck said. "Christ Almighty!" He did not seem very much relieved that Addison Burdett had escaped death. He looked around him, arms folded on his chest, trying to take it in. "Ol' Chicken," he repeated quietly. "I give him that name years ago when he first showed up at Gator Hook. Hopeless damn drunk, was all he was. Threw him out, then come across him a week later, holed up in a little chicken coop under the buildin!"

Speck groaned and muttered as his daughter watched him with something like concern. "Purty good old man," Speck mourned. "Purty good friend of mine." He raised his arms high and his hands wide, dropped them again.

He considered Lucius, not entirely without sympathy. "Poor ol' Colonel," he said finally. "Stuck in the same ol' mud." He jerked his grizzled chin toward the embers. "Even that old man layin in there understood the way things work better'n you." After a while, he said, "Won't do no good to report 'em, case you're thinkin about it. Them people will only pump out more lies about the accidental death of a dangerous killer that throwed in with the Daniels gang."

Speck listened for the helicopter, raising a hand every little while to still their voices. "I finally figured out what Dyer wants with Chatham Bend. Look at your charts! These forty acres we are standin on right here are the only good piece of high ground in the sixty miles of wild coast country between Chokoloskee and Cape Sable. All cleared off since Injun times for villages and fields. It ain't some swamp-and-overflowed that has to be drained and filled or even leveled. What's more, it ain't but a few miles crost the sloughs from the southwest corner of the old Chevelier Road. Pave that dirt road, build a couple of causeways crost them little shaller bays like they done at Chokoloskee, and there you are—the one place and the only place where a company could start right out with a land base for development that ain't goin to be wiped out by a hurricane. All they got to do is get the Park back! They do that, and right here where we are standin on could be the heart of the biggest damn development in Florida history. Regular West Coast Miami! Dig out the river mouths for harbors, dredge and fill—see what I'm gettin at? Today the Bend belongs to Parks and Watson Dyer can't do nothin with it, but tomorrow might be very, very different. That's what he's countin on. That is his big gamble. And his gamble is the best damn kind, cause it don't cost him nothin. His partners might not realize it yet, but the man who controls the Watson Place stands to make a fortune, and if it helps to be named Watson, he's nailed that down, too."

They thought this over and they could not fault it.

"What if the Watsons contest him? I mean, real Watsons?"

"You think this Dyer ain't 'real Watson,' Colonel? That was borned here on the Bend, and you not even born in the state of Florida? Think them slick lawyers over to Miami won't cook up some bullshit argument out of that? Anyway, he's got the judges in his pocket. He don't need no 'real Watsons' no more! You ain't goin to have one thing to say about this property!

"If I was you, I would walk away from it, drop the whole business. Just forget about it. You try involvin Watson Dyer in the death of that old man layin in them embers, know what he'll do? He'll put that killin on our Daniels bunch, get us charged with kidnappin and murder, maybe drag you into it for harborin known criminals—any ol' lie it takes to do the job. And they got the Sheriff and they got the judges and they will make it stick, cause with all the big money that's behind 'em, they ain't goin to tolerate no piss-ants such as us gettin in the way.

"Nosir, you ain't goin to stop a man like that. Have to shoot him if you aim to stop him." Daniels licked his teeth. "If we was to take and shoot one of them big boys once in a while, when they push down too hard—that's about all fellers like us know how to do to make us feel better. They's plenty of good men out in the backcountry that holds to my way of thinkin, and we got us a few weapons put away. Get some fightin spirit goin in this country, we might get back the real America, y'know."

But he lost heart in this. Asked why his men had not come back, Speck glanced upriver toward the east. "Cause they ain't as stupid as they look," he snapped. "Least Junior ain't. Likely ducked into some hidey-hole in some li'l brushy creek until he's sure that fuckin helio-copter has gone for good. Only thing, the way that thing is circlin, it sounds to me like they got somethin pinned down. And they ain't but the one thing out there to pin down, and that's the airboat."

He turned to Whidden. "You think that thing might of decoyed 'em out of hidin? Pretend to head home to the east coast, then circle wide and come in low behind 'em? Cause the noise of that chopper comin in could get drowned out by their own racket till it swooped down on top of 'em from behind."

Harden nodded. "I been thinkin the same thing."

"Lord," Speck prayed, "don't let them morons get excited and start shootin."

*

Circling restlessly, Daniels picked up a charred gator flat from the black earth and stood there slapping the hard scrap against his leg. "Damn stupid waste," he said, tossing the scrap into the embers. Whidden said coldly, "Shootin so many when there weren't no market—that the waste you mean?"

His head slightly askance, Speck Daniels squinted at him. "You wasn't with us, boy? I could of swore you was in on all that gator huntin, right alongside of us."

"I got regrets about it—that's the difference."

"That's *one* difference." Speck gazed at all of them, contemptuous. "I ain't ashamed of huntin in this Park and never will be. I'd shoot the whole damn mess of 'em again tomorrow if it weren't such a damn waste of ammunition."

Speck yanked old leather gloves from the hip pocket of his jeans and set to work, heaving the last charred scraps of gator hide into the embers. He worked in silence, stopping every little while to listen. At one point he crouched a little, head cocked sideways, hand behind his ear, then stared bleakly at Harden. "You hear that? They called in reinforcements."

"Them boys might be okay. They might be hid. Ain't nothing over that way but mangrove and water, there ain't no place to set them damn things down." But Whidden's voice died as the distance broke apart in the popping roll of automatic weapons.

"*Shee*-it!" Speck yelled with all his might, slamming his parrot hat onto the ground, raising black dust. "If Junior is waitin on his old man to go over there and mix it up with two damn helio-copters, he better think again!" Already on his way upriver toward his boat, he turned and, walking backwards, howled at Whidden. "Don't you try follerin me, boy, cause I ain't goin! It won't do no good!"

Stiffly his daughter walked toward him, as if sleepwalking. He glared at her, furious, anticipating protest, and when she was silent, his thick brows shot up in surprise. She actually appeared to nod in acquiescence, although her face was so deathly calm as to seem utterly without expression. Uneasy, he dusted his parrot-feather hat. He paused another moment as they gazed at each other, holding the hat over his head like a poised lid. Then he ran his fingers through his hair and set the painted hat back on his head. "All right," he muttered vaguely. Under his daughter's gaze, he looked spent and haggard, and perceiving the man's solitude and life fatigue, Lucius felt an unexpected start of pity.

Speak beckoned to him. They met halfway.

"Don't let him bring her, Colonel. She don't need to see nothin like that." He sucked his teeth and spat, in greatest bitterness. "Unless them boys was very, very lucky, there ain't nothin left there but a bloody mess. Not only that, but them choppers will be back, so you people ain't goin to be no help, and you might get hurt." Speck watched his daughter as he spoke. "Sally knows as good as I do where Junior was headed, ever since the first day he come home. If it weren't today, it would of been tomorrow. Kind of like your daddy that way," he added carelessly, peering bleakly at Lucius for the first time. "Speaking of which—"

From beneath his shirt, he dragged his string of thirty-three spent slugs, which he gathered up and tossed at the other's chest. "I reckon that belongs to 'the real Watsons,' " Daniels said, and turned, and kept on going.

Northward

By late afternoon, there was little left of the old Watson house except small cement pillars which had held the floor above the flood in time of hurricane. Levering away black timbers, burning the leather of their shoes, they uncovered the charred and twisted form, the crusted skull with the teeth stretched wide around the dying scream. They tugged it onto a soiled blanket from the boat. Soon Harden found the blackened revolver with the lone empty cartridge in the chamber. The fire had discharged the weapon, which lay yards from the body. It could not have killed him.

Getting his breath, Lucius leaned on the syrup vat, now a rusting vessel of dead rain and green algae and mosquito larvae. He thought about that scary day in the year after their arrival when Rob, in a fit of rebellious rage, had shot the family dog in a foolish accident, then fled from his own act, running round and round the house until Papa came out suddenly and intercepted him.

And he thought about Rob sailing away with Papa on the eve of Carrie's wedding to Walt Langford, loyal to the banished father whom he adored and hated even then, Rob's slim quick figure waving wildly from high on the schooner's mast, in silhouette on the Gulf sky. And dear kind Mama on her deathbed three years later, in the grip of cancer, in and out of coma, eyes dark with pain in her graying face, worried about the stepson who had fled. "Lucius honey," she whispered, "Rob is wandering somewhere in the world, he is all alone. Oh, Rob has so much good in him! When you are older, you must find him, let him know we love him!" But he had not found Rob. Rob had found him.

As a sort of offering, Lucius brought the manuscript of the biography. Laying it in the embers, he watched the page corners turn brown and darken as his life's labor curled up into nothingness. He had not told the others. He supposed they understood what he was doing.

In a small grave spaded out between the two old poincianas by the river, they buried the scant remains in the stained blanket. Until he could return here with a casket, he would defer his brother's wish to be buried in Columbia County, but he murmured the old hymn as Rob had wished.

> Across death's river our friends have gone,
> And we are following, one by one . . .

They adorned the grave with crimson coral bean and scarlet poinciana, which reminded Sally of Rob's flagrant red bandanna. "What's the matter with me?" Sally sniffled, dabbing her eyes. "I hardly even knew that poor old man!" But of course she was mourning the lost brother, the long-lost lover, and refused to be comforted even—or especially—by Whidden. Nor had she cried out when shortly after her father's departure, the shooting stopped and the helicopters departed. "I could feel it coming," she whispered intensely. "I could *feel* it." After that, she would not speak and could not stop weeping. Even so, in a subdued way, she seemed at peace, and gentle and affectionate with everyone, even the blind man.

*

Smoke plumes rose from the darkening embers, wandering like companies of ghosts. Dark herons crossed the mangrove and the river. With his friends already in the boat, he paid a last visit to the grave. Off the bank, the snag of a drowned tree dipped and beckoned in the heavy current. The channel was shifting and the bend eroding as slabs of old alluvial earth were borne away into the Gulf of Mexico. He promised Rob he would come fetch him before his grave was taken by the river.

In the boat, the blind man murmured quietly, "Well, how *you* doin, Colonel? Goin to be okay?"

The *Cracker Belle* drifted down current before her propeller, gathering her weight, took hold of the muddy flow and churned her back upstream past the burned clearing. "Jungle will take this ol' place back before you know it," Whidden said, with a last look around him. "Won't be nothing left of the old days for our kids to look at."

Gazing downriver as the Bend turned and disappeared, Lucius saw how this wild river had looked before the first crafts of the aborigines rounded the point, in those ageless days innocent of human cry, only the puff of manatee and suck of tarpon, harsh heron squawk and shriek of tern on the gray sky, the mournful calling of the white-pated black pigeons. And he wondered if life would ever bring him back.

*

Following the inside route, the old boat headed east and north into the diadem of amber waters between the outer Islands and the coast, crossing the oyster bottoms and broad tannin reaches of the inner bays. Feeling the shift in her vibrations and the rise of water in her wake, Andy nodded in contentment. "Chokoloskee to House Hammock, we traveled these back bays, but as my granddad used to say, the water could be pretty skinny in through here."

Lifting free from the green walls, white egrets crossed the bow, and hearing their guttural hoarse squawks, the blind man said, "Them white birds scare a whole lot easier than the blue ones, ever notice? Many years have come and gone since the last plume hunting, but them egrets has learned all they need to know, because they're still scared of anything two-legged."

"Me, too!" cried Sally. She gave the blind man an impulsive hug. "Well, now, Mister Andy House, you happy you came with us? Cause we sure are!" On her way below to rest, she stuck out her tongue at the other two, and Harden smiled at Lucius. "You seen the way she took it? About Junior? I believe she has let go of something, don't ask me why. I believe she might be past the worst of it." He grinned. *"Your ex-ex-wife*—that's what she called herself just now! I believe my ex-ex-wife is really back!" And Lucius smiled, too, in profound loneliness.

Whidden would drop his passengers at Everglade, then head back south to help Speck if he could. "Them boys was my partners," Whidden said, dispensing with any further explanation. When Lucius asked him if Sally would mind the risk he might be taking, Whidden shook his head. "She knows I have to go," he said, "and she knows that I won't stay."

*

Crossing Alligator Bay, the *Belle* passed the mouth of the grown-over canal dredged originally by the Chevelier Corporation. "Follow that canal maybe six miles, you'll hit a good high hammock," Andy told them. "As a young boy, Charlie Green was in there deer huntin with his daddy and the Robertses. They'd shot four or five curlew for their supper, so Charlie's dad said, 'Well, we got enough to eat, so you boys go hunt us a good place to camp on that high hammock yonder.' Charlie and the Roberts boy found a good place, all right, but somebody was on there a good while ahead of 'em, cause his skull lay grinnin at 'em from the brush. Alongside the skeleton, fallin apart, was a flat-bottomed scull boat, hauled up and hid a little ways back in the hammock, and also an old rifle and old coffeepot and fry pan. Well, that was enough, they made camp someplace else!

"At Chokoloskee, Charlie told Ted Smallwood all about it, and some old feller in the store claimed he recalled that hunting pram from Chatham

Bend, and another chimed in, 'Well, Old Man Waller that got killed by Cox was supposed to had a muzzle loader of that same description.' So they put their heads together and come up with the idea that what those boys had come across were the remains of Leslie Cox, laid low by snakebite! Uncle Ted was so excited, he called the whole island over to the store to hear tell about it! None of 'em could think who else that skeleton might be and by nightfall it was all decided: Leslie Cox hid that boat back in the bushes before makin camp, probably stepped on some big ol' rattler that swum on there to escape high water. The good Lord had His serpent layin there just a-waitin for that evil-hearted feller!"

"Wouldn't hogs and gators pull that body all apart?" Lucius protested.

"Well, you'd sure think so. But they argued that Cox might been back there through the twenties, livin with Injuns, tradin plumes and hides. And maybe them wild things was so scarce and hunted out that they never come across the body. Buzzards'd never find him in that jungle, and bobcats nor panthers wouldn't never touch him, and anything smaller that might chew on him would leave him mostly in one piece. One or two has been found like that, across the years."

"Well, I suppose so," Lucius said doubtfully. Death by rattlesnake back in the Glades seemed too fortuitous to suit him. He preferred his own instinct that somewhere along the back roads of America, Cox was still living under a false name.

*

Coming down out of Lopez River in the twilight, they could see the weak small lights of Chokoloskee. A minute earlier, Andy House had called out from the stern, "Any lights yet, Whidden? Feels to me like we must be in the Bay." He was pointing toward where Chokoloskee had to be even before the others saw the high dark shape of it.

"Course all they had back then was kerosene lamps," Andy said, when Lucius went aft and sat beside him, "but that big dark mound rising up out of the dusk was what your daddy seen on his last evening."

*

That evening, in bittersweet mood, Lucius placed a telephone call to Lucy Summerlin. He confessed to "Miss L" his lifelong shame about the way he'd acted years before, and his regret about "the happiness I threw away." When Lucy was silent, he asked shyly if he might pay a call on her some time soon. After a moment, composing herself, Lucy asked her former lover if he had been drinking, and when he protested untruthfully that he had not, another pause made it clear that she knew better. Later he feared she had been weeping and was struggling to compose herself, for he heard a discreet sniffling into a handkerchief.

Lucy murmured that their encounter in the Fort Meyers cemetery had been "just lovely" and had "done her old heart a world of good." However, she did not think she should meet with him again any time soon. She would love him always, and wished him a long and happy life. When he pressed harder, she reproved him gently, saying that she might take him a bit more seriously if he were to ring her up again when he was sober.

"Are you doubting my word, Miss L?"

"I'm afraid so, sweetheart."

"Well, I can't say I blame you." He tried to laugh.

Making light of his drinking—surely that had been a bad mistake, worse than the whiskeys, worse than the dissembling. He would call back in the morning and apologize. But when morning came, he felt stunned and un-ravelled, sitting on the bed edge by the telephone for a long while before de-ciding it might be best to wait a decent interval before soliciting his beloved "Miss L" again. He must be patient, he must draw near with the greatest sen-sitivity and care. One day soon there was bound to come that limpid moment when they would melt into each other's eyes, in rediscovery of those illumi-nations of those fond lost days long, long ago.

Lucius had not told her of Rob's death, not wishing to win her favor by seeking sympathy. And although saddened by her refusal, he was also in-admissibly relieved, though he would not admit this to himself until days later.

Inexplicably Lucius thought about his father's urn. It seemed urgent now to restore those bones to the Fort Myers cemetery. Yet in his twisted state of mind, the brass urn spooked him—not the bones, the ancestral bones, but the raging spirit trapped in that container. Though he knew he was being su-perstitious or plain childish, he had no wish to lay eyes on the man or find himself alone with it at home.

*

The night before, over the telephone, Whidden Harden had learned that Henry Short was in the hospital at Okeechobee. Torching fields before the cane harvest, he had been caught in a back burn when the wind shifted. Lee Harden had visited him in the hospital, where he was told that the patient's burns were fatal.

Whidden delivered this news early in the morning when he and Sally came to say good-bye, and hearing it, Andy House went red, very upset. "Henry is too old for work like that—that's dangerous work! And Big Sugar don't care nothing at all about their workers! He is very experienced and he ain't a drinker, but he's too old for hard and heavy work around big burns!"

Those empty plantations were miles and miles to the horizon and Henry had been way out there, beyond help. Running hard for an irrigation ditch, he had fallen and was overtaken by the flames. Burned over most of his body, he was not recuperating. He was lucid at times, yet seemed too weak to breathe and was not expected to survive the week, Lee Harden said.

In a tumult of feelings, Lucius took leave of the Hardens and headed north at once. He did not feel he had a choice about it. Andy House, who felt the same, talked unhappily about Henry most of the way to the hospital at Okeechobee.

"Henry told Lee Harden he wanted to leave me his gold-digging equipment, all his treasure maps, cause he wouldn't have no use for 'em no more. Said he knew about some buried gold that was well off from the house on private property, where a man could go and dig at night, not get the dogs on him. He had made him a good map, wanted me to have it! Never heard that I went blind, I guess. Not that I would use it anyways. I don't care for the idea of sneakin onto private property!

"That side of Henry always did surprise me, because he was the most honest man I ever met, and the most religious, too. Come the Holy Day, he would never do no labor, that was his rest day and he read his Bible. But when it come to gold, he didn't see straight, it was gettin so he would break his own commandments and go dig on Sunday. I doubt he ever give much thought to what he'd do with all his gold if he ever found any, but after so many long years alone, I reckon he dreamed that striking gold might make up some way for the life that passed him by."

At Okeechobee Hospital

At the hospital, they had to hunt for the old Negro ward, a long room with creaking fans and narrow shafts of dusty sun and decrepit cabinets which seemed to stand at odds with the streaked walls, in a sepia light and weary atmosphere which reminded Lucius of soldiers' wards in old prints or daguerreotypes of the Civil War. Torn screens in high narrow windows let pass myriad small things which crawled and flew, and distant crow caws, and the airlessness of the hot woods.

The discreet figures wandering the ward were mostly black people. Seated humbly on small hard chairs by the door were two white men in dark

Sunday serge with weathered, steadfast faces. Recognizing Andy House, they smiled and stood, but the blind man brushed right past their hands before Lucius could mend the situation.

Henry Short lay flat and still as if extinguished by the humid heat. Pinned to the coarse sheets like a specimen, the old man twitched and shifted in his purgatory. His blue cotton nightshirt was open down the front, and his chest was patched with cracked and crusted scabs, like a side of charred beef leaking thin red fluid. From his bed on its small roller wheels rose a peculiar odor of disinfectant, broiled flesh, and sharp urine. Yet the reddened eyes that peered out from the bandages seemed calm, observing Lucius as he guided Andy House around the cot. They stood beside him, one man on each side.

Through broken lips, the burned man murmured, "Well now. Mist' Lucius! And Mist' Andy." Henry Short had first encountered Lucius as a boy of eight, down in the rivers. Even so, it astonished Lucius that this dying man had recognized a visitor he had not seen in two decades and could not have supposed he would ever see again.

Finding an unburned place on the inert forearm, Lucius pressed the cool skin with two fingertips. "How are you, Henry?" He spoke in a soft low voice in keeping with the hush over the ward. "How do, Henry," Andy said, wide-eyed and smiling. Unable to see Henry's dire condition, anxious lest he molest his awful burns, he extended his arm over the bed like a crude feeler as the black man, in great pain, slowly lifted a white mitt toward the blind hand. Lucius reached to draw their hands together just as both men lost faith and gave up.

Though Henry did his best to smile, his awful travail turned his eyes murky and twisted his parched mouth. "*Fiery furnace!*" Still working at that death's-head smile he gasped out that phrase from the old spiritual. Teeth chattering, he closed his eyes and rested a little until he got his breath.

An old black woman two beds away called to the white men that Deacon Short was a true man of God, and if he had ever sinned, none could recall it. "Praise the Lord!" the old woman cried, and there came a shy chorus of assent rose from the hushed room. Like mourners in a slow procession, the ward visitors did not gather around Henry but continued walking, and now they began a crooning in warm harmonies. And the burned man muttered, "Hear them angels? Hope they come for *me*!" Though he struggled with it, he could not work his smile.

Lucius returned to the two men by the door, who stood again, eager to know if that man at Henry's bed could be Andy House. They had come here from Arcadia, they said. Their name was Graham. Years ago, Henry had spoken of Lucius Watson's kindness, and they thanked him warmly for this visit to their brother. They were concerned that nobody was on duty to give him something for his pain, but they also said that Henry had been refusing medication. As best as they could fathom his strict code, uncomplaining acceptance of his agony signified some sort of purification to the dying man. They left the bedside frequently because they themselves could not endure the sight of such hard pain.

When Lucius told Andy that Henry's brothers were there and wished to greet him, he was overjoyed. "Grahams? Them two fellers knowed me when they seen me?" Tears came to his eyes as Lucius led him back across the room and the Grahams rose and sat him down between them.

*

When Lucius took the rickety chair beside the bed, Henry Short's mouth fixed itself in that grim semblance of a smile, but the broken eyes, discolored red and yellow, had gone glassy. "You're a tough old gator, Henry, you are going to make it," Lucius told him.

The patient dissented with a small twitch of the chin. A moment later, he gritted out, "I had enough. . . ." Tears escaped onto his caved cheeks. Again Lucius pressed two fingers to that one unburned place on the ropy forearm, and Henry pressed his forearm upward against Lucius's hand. "You come to ask about your daddy," he whispered urgently, as if he might die before their business could be finished. He nodded when the other did not deny it.

"I lied, Mist' Lucius. Lied to Houses, lied to Hardens, lied to you. Been lyin and lyin all of my whole life." He was not repentant, only bitter. "White folks ever stop to think how they make us *lie?* How honest Christian nigras got to *lie?* Lie and lie, then lie some more, *just to get by?*"

Lucius found a towel to wipe his brow. "Don't tire yourself, Henry. No need to talk—"

"Yes! A *need!* I got to *finish* it!" Henry rasped this with asperity. He gasped out the truth in fits and starts after making Lucius promise that what he had to say would never be repeated to the Hardens. "I'm scared my friends might disrespect me when I'm gone."

Henry closed his eyes and kept them closed, as if reading a history burned into his eyelids. "Yessuh, they is a need. A cryin need." He emitted a sharp cough of pain, and the churchwomen knit their brows, afraid this white stranger was draining the Deacon's strength.

"Mis Ida House, she told me grab my rifle and go foller Old Mist' Dan. Told me look out for him, cause he was agitatin about gettin old and had got himself all fired up to do some foolishness. And I stared at that old lady. I couldn't believe what she was askin me to do! I started in to actin the scared

534

nigger, only this time it was true, I was scared to death. I rolled my eyes up, prayin to Heaven, and I cried out, 'Please, Mis Ida, ma'am, that ain't no place for no nigger with no rifle! Not today!'

"So that old lady got upset, and she told me I owed it to her husband! Harked back to how Old Mist' Dan done saved the life of a pickaninny child on the road south out of Georgia. Time she got done, I didn't see no choice about it. I said, 'Yes, ma'am,' and I fetched my rifle and trailed after 'em toward the landin, so heavy in my heart I couldn't hardly walk."

As if white people had leased Henry his life, thought Lucius, and now he was obliged to give it back.

Henry said, "What I aim to tell is the God's truth." He pointed at a shelf above the bed. Though his visitor said that Henry's word was good enough, the patient closed his eyes and shook his head. Lucius took the Bible from the shelf and slid it beneath the mitt of bandages on the right hand.

"Mist' Lucius, your daddy always *seen* me." He opened his red eyes and searched the other's face, wondering if the white man understood. "Seen I were a *somebody*—some kind of a man, with my own look to me and my own way of workin. Seen I counted. Seen I weren't just nothin-but-a-nigger. By *seein* me, he give me some respect, and I was grateful, all them years I knew him." He rested a little. "But that don't mean he was aimin to put up with no gun-totin nigger, not in no line of men come there to judge him. When I went down to the Smallwood landin, I was deathly afeared of Mist' Edgar Watson, and afeared of them men waitin on him, too. All I wanted was to run and hide. Cause whether I fired or I didn't, them white men, they was honor bound to kill me.

"Mist' Edgar looked red-eyed, all wore out, like he'd laid awake most of that week. Spoke in a low and scrapy voice, said, 'Henry, you got no business here. You get on home.' And I seen he would not tolerate me. I seen the murder shinin in his eye."

"Would not tolerate your color?"

Henry closed his eyes. He was running out of time. "Nosir. What I told you. *Nigger-actin-to-be-a-man.* Somethin like that." His dry mouth twitched in that gaunt shadow of a smile. When Lucius fed him water in thin sips, he nodded minute thanks, shifting and settling his pain before resuming. In a hurry to expel his truth, he talked too fast, exhausting himself. Lucius touched his arm to slow him down.

"Knowin this here black feller could shoot, your daddy didn't take no chances. He hefted up that double-barrel nice and easy, like he was fixin to hand it over to Mist' Dan. But by the little shiftin of his feet, I knowed he was gettin set to swing that gun, shoot from the hip. I was standin apart, out in the shallers, so it weren't no trick to blow me off that line." Henry nodded. "Show them others he meant business. Show 'em that the next one he shot might be a white man."

In a bout of agony, Henry gasped. He raised a hand and lowered it again onto the Bible. "Lord is my witness, I believe that Mist' Edgar was dead soon as his gun come up. What Henry Short done or did not do never made no difference."

Henry was not looking at him now but past him. "Mist' Edgar's gun come up in a snap swing, and mine did, too," he murmured after a while. "He had me beat cause I held my fire, still prayin I would not have to shoot." Henry spoke in sorrow, as if truly regretful that Mr. Watson had not killed him. "His gun misfired, Mist' Lucius. I seen his eyes go wide—out of his surprise, y'know—but it was too late." He sighed. "I had pulled that trigger, not knowin there was no need of it, not knowin the good Lord had already went and saved me."

Henry closed his eyes. "It was all over so fast! Mist' Edgar was fallin. *Somebody has shot Mist' Edgar Watson!* Took me a minute to understand who might of done it. I was starin at him layin there while them men shot and shot, and all I could think was, Henry Short, you will die here, too."

"Is it possible you miscalculated, Henry? Maybe figuring he *might* shoot you, you fired first—"

Henry Short grimaced, raising his hand a little, then lowering it again onto the Bible. "Nosir. Weren't no time to figure nothin."

"Bill House—?"

Henry shook his head. "I heard his shot. Mist' Bill shot just behind. Young Mist' Dan, Old Mist' Dan—all them Houses was good shots, and very likely hit him, but Mist' Watson was already fallin by the time they fired."

"You *know* you hit him."

The wrapped hands jerked on the coarse coverlet.

"And you *know* you killed him."

Hollowed out like little leather dishes, the burned man's temples pulsed. When Lucius put a rag of water to his lips, he could muster up no thanks. His eyes had closed. "Hell is waitin, Henry Short," the burned man whispered.

For a long while he lay quiet, yet he seemed intent, as if trying to hear a distant birdsong in the late spring woods. When Lucius shifted and cleared his throat, the burned man lifted the stiff club of his mitt as if to hush him. When it seemed that he might sleep and not awaken, Lucius leaned and whispered at his ear.

In the stillness, it seemed that this last question had been asked too late.

Henry Short had gone and he would not return. But the lids opened and for a long moment those inflamed eyes met Lucius's gaze.

In a cardboard suitcase underneath the cot, Lucius found a large heavy cigar box bound in tarred fish line. Henry nodded, and he opened it, knowing already that the box contained old belt buckles and metal buttons, small rusted pocketknives, a few spent bullets.

Bones and skulls? Henry Short nodded. Had he ever told anyone about this? Just Lee Harden. Nobody else? He shook his head. Why not?

Henry closed his eyes without a word. Yet Lucius imagined that he understood. Perhaps Henry Short had kept his secret out of loyalty to Ed Watson, who had "seen" him. Or perhaps he had done it because of his unnameable friendship with Ed Watson's son.

The sojourners in the brown room rushed to the cot, for Henry's heart had faltered. Spasms yanked his body as one hand flew up and his eyes went wide. When he fell back, he lay as if transfixed, red eyes rolled back in his skeletal brown head in a stare of wonder, mouth stretched in a famished yawn of mortal yearning.

Then, in a twitch, the failing heart in the mortal husk of Henry Short restored faint blood to the grayed skin, and the mouth eased, and the eyes softened and dampened and came back to the room with a dim shine of bewilderment and wonder. Once again, the white mitt wandered weakly on the rough coverlet, seeking Lucius's hand. He whispered, "No more secrets, Mist' Lucius. No more lyin."

Henry Short would lie in torment in that silent ward for another seven days. On the eighth night, his Redeemer set him free.

On the way south, Andy House said, "You get the truth from Henry?" And when Lucius nodded, he said sharply, "Well? Feel any better?"

ANDY HOUSE

Hearing his boat, them island men had formed a line along the shore. Ed Watson seen that crowd waitin in the dusk before he come into gun range, but he never learned how to back up, that's what my dad said. He had his shotgun out where they could see it, and knowing them men the way he did, he probably figured he could bully 'em, same way he always done.

Some say he never left his boat. Well, the House boys was right up in the front, and they said Watson took 'em by surprise, runnin his boat hard aground and jumpin ashore in the same moment as she struck. Had his feet set and his shotgun up across his chest. When they asked him what he done with Cox, he pulled Cox's hat out of his coat, pointed at the blood splatter in the stern, claimed he had shot him in the boat but the body fell overboard and was lost in the river.

Well, there was mutterin over that, so a man who was drunk leaned in over the gunwales and put a finger to that blood and sniffed it. Said, "That sure smells like fresh fish blood to me." And Watson scowled. "You calling me a liar?" And there come a moan of fear out of that crowd. "No, Ed, we ain't calling you a liar," says my granddad, "but we will have to go to Chatham, hunt up that dead body for ourselves. Meantime, you best hand over that gun."

Well, that done it. Watson lost his temper. He hollered out, "You boys want this gun so bad, you are goin to get it!" And them were the last words that he ever spoke.

Course he might been bluffing—didn't make no difference. When he swung that shotgun up, he was a dead man. Them men was scared and their trigger fingers twitchin, and they didn't need no excuse at all to gun him down.

My dad weren't ten foot away, longside my granddad, and Henry Short was next to Dad. Henry stood half-leg deep in water, carryin his old 30-30 Winchester. You couldn't say he was in the crowd exactly, cause bein a nigra, he did not belong. But *not* countin him—that was your daddy's worst mistake, probably his last one. He let Henry distract him, that is what my dad said. He seen that nigra and he seen his gun, and he couldn't believe his eyes. Bill House thought he heard him growl something at Henry, and maybe Henry mumbled something back. Next thing he knew, Watson's gun muzzles come up like a boar's snout, they was lookin down them twin holes straight into hell. And right about then come that whipcrack shot that Granddad recognized as his old Winnie.

No two guns shoots just alike, not to a man who has hunted years and years with just the one of 'em. You don't mistake it. But knowin what might come down on Henry, Granddad never let on what he heard till he lay on his deathbed seven years later. He summoned his three older boys that was with him that day at the landin, made 'em take a swear that what he aimed to tell 'em wouldn't never go outside that room. Even then, he did not say that Henry Short fired his rifle at a white man. He only said he'd heard the *crack* of his old Winnie *if he weren't mistaken*—said that last part twice. That was Granddad's way of sayin, "Henry shot but don't you boys say *nothing,* about it, not to *nobody.*"

Dad was standin there longside of Henry. He seen his gun go up, and them other men did, too. I myself have never heard no different, not from any man who was in that line. Henry and another man fired together, and that other feller was my dad, and their two shots was so darn close that most folks never heard but just the one. There was four or five shots in the next second but they wasn't needed.

Bill House was an expert shot, but he knew Henry was better and shot faster. Henry fired. And Henry Short was not a man well-knowed to miss.

*

Because his wife was away at church, Andy tarried on his doorstep, reluctant to enter the small empty house on Panther Crescent. They sat a little while out in the sun. The blind man mourned, unable to put Henry Short out of his mind. "While you was speaking with his brothers, Henry told me he was through with life even if life was not quite through with him. He had never knew God struck me blind, that's how many years has passed since a House found time to go visit that poor feller! After all them years he lived with us, I knew no words to say to him when he was dying!

"When it comes to Henry Short, you know, you're looking at a sinner. I should of hunted him up years ago, if only just to let him know he weren't forgotten by our family just because he broke off with my dad—let him know we always wondered how he might be getting on, after all the years out of his life that good man give us. But I never done that, no I didn't, it was too much trouble!

"Funny, ain't it? My cousin-in-law over to Marco, the one who helped to lynch that nigra in the thirties? Well, that man never missed a meal until his last morning, when he overslept his breakfast. Died peaceful in his sleep and after a long, healthy life. How do you figure that one?

"I never did commit a crime against a black man, and I'm darn glad of it. But I never done a darn thing *for* 'em neither, even when I had the chance. You reckon that's why the Good Lord up there struck this sinner blind? Because I knew better? Because I *knew* better?"

Andy House held both hands high as if warding off the molten fire of the sinking sun. "Kind of late now, ain't it, Colonel? I have missed my chance. Sins of omission, they will call it, where I'm headed for."

In a long silence, the blind man gazed away, his blue eyes wide, as if to behold everything on earth. From the scarred prospect of the Golden Years Estates came the harsh grind and bang of earthmoving machines and the snort of air brakes. "Panther Crescent!" he exclaimed at last with a great rueful sigh, and slapped his big hands down upon his knees, turning to Watson. "Where you headed for, Colonel, this late in the day?"

The question startled Lucius, who had fallen silent, in the dread of home. He had nobody to meet, no place he had to be.

Sensing something, Andy House groped for his hand and gripped it with emotion. "You best stay and eat supper with us." Forgetting that Andy could not see him, Lucius shook his head, and Andy shrugged. "Well, heck!" he said. "It ain't none of my business. But I sure been happy to make your acquaintance. You ain't a bad feller, Colonel, and you never was." He grunted in his struggle to stand up. "You don't have to wait here, Colonel. I will be just fine."

Finding his voice, Lucius assured him he was in no hurry. He would be glad, he said, to stay a little longer, in case Andy needed any help fighting off those panthers.